JAMES BOND
CHOICE OF WEAPONS

JAMES BOND TITLES BY RAYMOND BENSON

NOVELS

Zero Minus Ten (1997)
The Facts of Death (1998)
High Time to Kill (1999)
DoubleShot (2000)
Never Dream of Dying (2001)
The Man With the Red Tattoo (2002)

FILM NOVELIZATIONS

(based on the respective screenplays)

Tomorrow Never Dies (1997)
The World is Not Enough (1999)
Die Another Day (2002)

SHORT STORIES

Blast From the Past (1997)
Midsummer Night's Doom (1999)
Live at Five (1999)

ANTHOLOGIES

The Union Trilogy (2008)
Choice of Weapons (2010)

JAMES BOND

CHOICE

OF

WEAPONS

THREE 007 NOVELS

RAYMOND BENSON

PEGASUS BOOKS
NEW YORK

JAMES BOND: CHOICE OF WEAPONS

Pegasus Books Ltd
148 West 37th Street, 13th Floor
New York, NY 10018

ISBN: 978-1-60598-099-7

10 9 8 7 8 6 5 4

Printed in the United States of America
Distributed by W. W. Norton & Company, Inc.

CONTENTS

INTRODUCTION

WELCOME, READERS, TO *CHOICE OF WEAPONS*, THE SECOND COLLECTION OF my continuation James Bond fiction that was originally published between 1997 and 2002. Bond fans have been clamoring for reprints, so I am extremely pleased that Pegasus Books is re-issuing these three novels and two short stories. (The first volume was published in 2008. Entitled *The Union Trilogy*, the anthology contained three novels—*High Time to Kill, DoubleShot, and Never Dream of Dying*, as well as the short story *Blast from the Past*.)

While the first collection contained three novels that were loosely connected by a villainous organization called The Union, the novels presented here are stand-alone stories.

It was late 1995 when I was asked by Peter Janson-Smith, Ian Fleming's former literary agent and then the Chairman of Ian Fleming (Glidrose) Publications Ltd. (now called Ian Fleming Publications Ltd.), if I'd be interested in taking over writing the Bond novels from John Gardner, who had announced his retirement from the job. We discussed possible directions in which the continuation novels could go, but it was finally decided that the stories should stay contemporary. I had two directives—make the character of M a woman (to stay in synchronization with the current Pierce Brosnan/Judi Dench films), and to somehow blend more contemporary elements (more action, gadgetry, humor) with the Bond character of the original books (i.e., a tough, serious, and not necessarily politically correct 007). Emphasizing Bond's vices may have made him anachronistic in today's world, but that's what also allowed him to stand out as an individual distinct from my predecessors' interpretations of Fleming's hero.

Zero Minus Ten was not only my first 007 novel, it was my *first novel.* It was originally published in 1997, the year in which Britain handed Hong Kong back to China. When I began constructing a plot, I thought the situation might be a fine backdrop for the story. I studied Hong Kong's history, explored the various reasons why it had become a British Crown Colony, and why in 1997 it was being returned to a communist country. I figured there had to be a lot of people, especially those in business with money tied up in the colony, who weren't too happy about the handover. So my villain became an Englishman who was violently opposed to the transition. For research, I traveled to Hong Kong, Kowloon, Macau, and to southern China to walk in James Bond's footsteps, so to speak. Ian Fleming's wonderful original adventures were informed by his own travels, and I felt it was important to experience first-hand the sights, smells, and tastes of the locations. I also took the time to learn how to play mahjong using Hong Kong rules (very different from Western rules) so that I could include a Bondian-style gambling game reminiscent of the bridge sequence in Fleming's *Moonraker.*

I can honestly say that my life changed with the publication of *Zero Minus Ten.* I left my day-job and concentrated on writing full-time. I haven't looked back.

Zero Minus Ten was followed in 1998 by *The Facts of Death.* Conversations with a Greek friend led my choosing his country for a locale. I created a group of adversaries called the Decada, which in hindsight may have been a trial run at generating a villainous organization (perfected with The Union in the subsequent three books). Much of the story takes place in Greece and, more importantly, in Cyprus, where Britain controls two important military complexes. Cyprus was and still is the world's only divided country—half is populated by Greek Cypriots and the other by Turkish Cypriots. Again, I felt that the volatile nature of this geo-political situation (in which Britain has a stake) would make for a good setting and plot. I also wanted to take Bond to my home State of Texas. There was a precedent for this. In one of his books, John Gardner had placed 007 in Amarillo, Texas. In addition, Fleming had created Bond's friend and ally Felix Leiter as a Texan; thus it made sense that the former CIA agent might be living there. I set the early sections of the story in Austin, the city I consider to be the "oasis" of the State. *The Facts of Death* also introduced Bond's new car, the Jaguar XK8. I worked with one of the original designers of the automobile to come up with the various weapons and gadgets. Adhering to Fleming's philosophy that it was okay for the Bond books to be "improbable" but not "impossible," the items in the car were things that could be built and actually work, even if a bit far-fetched.

The third book in this collection was actually my sixth and final Bond novel, originally published in 2002. *The Man with the Red Tattoo*, although not really a part of the "Union Trilogy," did tie up some loose ends from the previous tale, *Never Dream of Dying*. In that book, a Japanese villain named Goro Yoshida hired The Union to execute his scheme. Yoshida appeared only on a few pages. With the demise of The Union, in *Red Tattoo* Yoshida becomes the primary enemy, acting on his own. Obviously, Bond returns to Japan in this story (for the first time in the novels since Fleming's *You Only Live Twice*), a country that holds haunting memories for 007. I took the character all over Japan again, but one particular location was especially unique and important. The island of Naoshima, in the Inland Sea, is the home of Benesse House, a beautiful modern art museum designed by architect Tadao Ando. The building resembles a 007 film set that might have been created by Ken Adam, the man behind the look of the early Bond movies. I had to use it. As a result, the government of Kagawa Prefecture was so proud and pleased that Naoshima was included in a Bond novel that they not only awarded me with the title of Ambassador, but in 2005 they erected a permanent museum there called the "007 Man with the Red Tattoo Museum," dedicated to the novel! In many ways, this was the ultimate honor I received during my seven-year tenure as Bond continuation author.

ABOUT THE AUTHOR

Besides writing official James Bond fiction between 1996–2002, **RAYMOND BENSON** is also known for *The James Bond Bedside Companion*, which was published in 1984 and was nominated for an Edgar. As "David Michaels" Raymond is the author of the NY Times best-sellers *Tom Clancy's Splinter Cell* and *Tom Clancy's Splinter Cell—Operation Barracuda*. He recently penned the best-selling novelization of *Metal Gear Solid* and its sequel *Metal Gear Solid 2—Sons of Liberty*. Raymond's original thrillers are *Face Blind, Evil Hours, Sweetie's Diamonds, A Hard Day's Death* and *Dark Side of the Morgue*. Visit him at his website, www.raymondbenson.com.

JAMES BOND
CHOICE OF WEAPONS

ZERO MINUS TEN

*This novel is dedicated to
Randi and Max,
and to the people of Hong Kong*

AUTHOR'S NOTE

The architecture and layout of the Hongkong and Shanghai Bank is as described in Chapter Eleven. The events and action contained therein, however, are totally imaginary, as the corporation's highly effective security system would realistically prevent such a scenario. Furthermore, the company EurAsia Enterprises Ltd. is entirely fictional and is not intended to represent any existing trading and shipping firm. Lastly, the actual location for the handover ceremony has not been decided upon at the time of writing. (In fact, China has not yet even agreed to a joint ceremony!) My choice of Statue Square as the site is based on its historical significance and geographical importance to the city, as well as speculation by Hong Kong associates.

CONTENTS

ONE

SHAMELADY

20 JUNE 1997, 9:55 P.M., JAMAICA

Someone long ago had called it the "Undertaker's Wind" but hardly anyone in Jamaica referred to it by that name anymore. The Undertaker's Wind was supposed to blow the bad air out of the island at night. In the morning, the "Doctor's Wind" would come and blow the sweet air in from the sea. The Undertaker's Wind was certainly at work that night, whipping the long red strands of the English-woman's hair around her head like the flames of a torch.

The woman was dressed in a skin-tight black diving suit and stood on the cliff above the grotto looking out to sea. Forty stone steps cut into the cliff led down to the grotto, in front of which was a small, sandy beach. It was very dark in the grotto, for the cliffs blocked the moonlight. Up above it was just bright enough for every tree, plant, and stone to emit an eerie glow.

The woman glanced at her watch and tapped the button to illuminate the time. He would not be late. He never was.

The grotto and its private beach faced the Caribbean, not far from Port Maria on the North Shore of the island. The small community of Oracabessa was just along the coast to the west, and Cuba was a hundred miles to the north. The area was considered Jamaica's most lovely coastal country. The woman had never been here prior to this

evening, but she knew the layout of the place inside out. It was her
job to know. The land was private property and a modest, three-bed-
roomed house had been built above the grotto near the top of the
stone steps. If her plans were successful, the house would later be the
location for an evening of unbridled passion and pleasure. The man
with whom she hoped to share the pleasure had a reputation which
preceded him. Other women who had known him had indiscreetly
prepared her for the man's intense sexual allure. Although accomplishing the Primary Objective was her main goal tonight, one of her
motives for participating in the evening's escapade was a rather
selfish Secondary Objective—the physical rewards she would give
and receive after the job was done. She couldn't help it. Danger stimulated her sexually. It was why she had sought a career as a mercenary, a contemporary Boadicea. It was why she liked to play with fire.

"I'm here," a male voice whispered behind her.

"You're on time," she said.

"Of course I am," the blond man said in a thick Cockney accent,
moving closer to stand beside her, looking out to sea. He, too, was
dressed in a black diving suit. "You know what to do?" He gazed at
her, taking in the shapely body.

The woman knew she was beautiful and that men found her
attractive. She enjoyed being able to manipulate them. As she looked
at the man, she wondered again if the night would end as she desired.

He had blond curly hair, a muscular build, and classical Roman features. Most women, she thought, would gladly follow him anywhere.

"When he arrives, I get him to come up to the house. You'll 'surprise' us and kill him."

The man smiled. "Too right."

They were both in their mid-twenties and had trained for weeks to
get this far, but already possessed the skill and expertise required by
any assassin to perform a simple execution. The job in hand tonight
was anything but simple, their target a formidable one.

"Leave the first part to me, Mr. Michaels," she said, smiling and
rubbing her hand across the man's chin. "Give us a little time, and I'll
have him thoroughly distracted."

"Well, don't get carried away. I don't want to have to take you out with him."

"You sound pretty sure of yourself. Remember who he is."

"He's history."

As if on cue, a Royal Navy jet suddenly appeared, passing about half a mile from them, heading north out to sea at about 200 knots. They could just see the figure jumping from it.

"There he is," the blond man said. "Right on time." They clasped hands and he kissed her roughly on the mouth. "See you later, love . . . when we're done." And then he was off as she began to walk down the steps into the darkness of the grotto.

The man who made the low-altitude jump from the plane had opened his SAS Modified XL Cloud Type Special Forces rectangular parachute before exiting the aircraft and the jump master threw it out of the plane behind him. It served as not much more than a brake in the short fall, an extremely dangerous manoeuvre over water; but the jumper was a pro who knew what he was doing. He was one of the Double-Os.

The woman reached the bottom of the steps and peered out to sea. The man hit the water hard, and for a few moments only his dark parachute could be seen floating on the surface. Then he emerged and divested himself of the parachute. She walked to the edge of the water so that he could see her. The tall well-built man swam steadily until he was able to stand and walk towards her. He tore off the face mask and snorkel and tossed them aside, and then he stepped out of his fins.

Like the blond man, he had a sexual presence that was so overpowering she had to catch her breath before she spoke.

"The bad air is blowing out tonight," she said.

"But the sweet air will surely come in the morning," he replied as agreed.

"Right on time, Double-O Seven. I'm 05, but you can call me Stephanie. You okay?" She pronounced the number "oh-five."

"I'm fine, thanks, and my name's Bond. James Bond."

"It's pretty dangerous, isn't it, jumping at such a low altitude?" she asked, taking his outstretched hand.

"So long as the parachute is already open when you leave the plane, it's okay. Did you bring the transmitter?"

In the dim light, his features looked harsher than Stephanie had remembered them. The first time she had seen him was two weeks ago, at the funeral, when she had been struck by his air of casual self-confidence. Dark and handsome, he had piercing blue-grey eyes. His short black hair had just a hint of grey at the temples, was parted on the left, and carelessly brushed so that a thick black comma fell down over the right eyebrow. There was a faint three-inch scar on his right cheek. The longish straight nose ran down to a short upper lip, below which was a wide and finely drawn but cruel mouth.

"It's up in the house, Mr. Bond. Come, I'll show you." She took his hand and gently pulled him towards the stone steps, then dropped it and walked on ahead. Bond followed her, eyes and ears alert.

She had been told to observe him at the funeral, at which he had remained stubbornly stoical. Commander Bond, like the other pall-bearers, was dressed in Royal Navy uniform with three rows of ribbons. Everyone who was anyone had been there, including Sir Miles Messervy, the recently retired "M," head of SIS; the new "M," a woman only just beginning to take command of the Secret Service; Sir Miles's faithful secretary, Moneypenny; Major Boothroyd, the Armourer; and even the Prime Minister. When a country loses someone of the stature of Admiral Derek Plasket, all the important people are sure to be there to pay their last respects.

Admiral Plasket was something of a legend. A war hero, he had organized a commando assault team that specialized in raiding Nazi bunkers, collecting intelligence to be passed on to the Allied forces. After the war he had been Special Advisor to the Secret Service, and a personal friend of the old M.

As she had been instructed, Stephanie Lane had kept her eye on Bond throughout the ceremony. He had performed his duties with military precision, standing to attention and displaying no emotion whatsoever. Only afterwards, when she saw him embrace Moneypenny, did she detect some semblance of warmth.

Stephanie had continued her surveillance of 007 for two more weeks, taking note of his daily habits. She had followed him to his flat off the King's Road in Chelsea, where he lived alone. She tailed him to Blades, that exclusive gentleman's club which had only recently begun to admit women. She observed him enter the gaudy building across the Thames from the Tate Gallery, which was the SIS headquarters. Finally, after fifteen days, the operation had been arranged and the time had now come. Stephanie had a lot riding on the outcome of this mission, for James Bond was the target in tonight's Objective and she and her partner must anticipate his every move.

When the attack came, it surprised her—she had thought Michaels would wait until she and Bond were in the house, but he appeared at the top of the stone steps from out of darkness. With a perfectly executed manoeuvre, the man spun and jump-kicked Bond full in the face. The assault surprised Bond as well, for he fell backwards down the steps. Stephanie stood aside while the blond assassin, who was armed with an ASP 9mm semi-automatic handgun, ran down the steps after him.

Bond had rolled halfway down the steps and then stopped. He didn't move. He lay on his back at a grotesque angle, his head lower than his legs, his shoulders twisted unnaturally.

Michaels raised his gun and pointed it at the still body. "Wait," Stephanie whispered. "I think he's broken his neck!"

Cautiously, the man moved down to Bond's body and crouched to examine him more closely.

It was then that Bond made his move. He jackknifed out of his frozen position, thrusting both forearms into the blond man's face. In a split second, he formed a spear-hand and slammed it down on the man's right wrist, knocking the ASP on to the steps.

Recovering quickly, Michaels butted Bond in the stomach. Both figures tumbled down to the bottom of the steps and rolled out on to the sand, ending up with the younger man on top with his hands around Bond's throat.

This boy's strong, Bond thought.

Stephanie ran down the steps and stood waiting, feeling the adrenalin surge through her body as the two men fought. It gave her a thrill to imagine they were fighting over her. Her breathing became shallow and she felt weak at the knees.

With a superhuman effort, Bond thrust his arms between the other man's elbows and delivered dual lightning sword-hand chops, which made Michaels loosen his grip. Then, with split-second timing, Bond jerked his head forward against the man's nose, breaking it and causing him to cry out in pain.

Then they were both on their feet, each waiting for the other to make the next move.

Bond's Walther PPK was in a waterproof holster attached to the belt round his diving suit. Unfortunately, that was tightly buttoned and it would take more than two seconds to retrieve the weapon. Bond knew he didn't have two seconds. The young man was good—a bit inexperienced, perhaps, but not someone to underestimate. Bond was ready to concede that the other man was the stronger since, although he was in excellent physical shape, Bond was no youngster anymore.

The blond man made a move. With a shout, he leaped in the air and delivered a *Yobi-geri* kick to Bond's chest, knocking him back. The blow was meant to cause serious damage, but it landed too far to the left of the sternal vital-point target. Michaels was momentarily surprised that Bond didn't fall, but he immediately drove his fist into Bond's abdomen. That was the assassin's first mistake—mixing his fighting styles. He was using a mixture of karate, kung fu, and traditional western boxing. Bond believed in using whatever worked, but he practised hand-to-hand combat in the same way as he gambled: he picked a system and stuck with it.

By lunging at Bond's stomach, the man had left himself wide open, enabling Bond to backhand him to the ground. Giving him no time to think, Bond sprang on top of him and punched him hard in the face, but Michaels used his strength to roll Bond over on to his back, and, thrusting his forearm into Bond's neck, exerted tremendous pressure on 007's larynx once again. With his other hand, the young man fumbled with Bond's waterproof holster, attempting to get at the gun. Bond managed to elbow his assailant in the ribs, but this only served to increase his aggression. Bond got his hands round the man's neck but it was too late; Michaels deftly retrieved the Walther PPK 7.65mm from the holster and jumped to his feet.

"All right, freeze!" he shouted at Bond, standing over him, the gun aimed at his forehead. "I hit you in a vital point earlier but you didn't go down," he said with incredulity, looking at Bond as if he were a ghost.

007 caught his breath and said, "That was your first mistake. You were a half-inch too far to the left."

The man straightened his arm, ready to shoot.

"And now you're making your second mistake," Bond said.

"Oh, yeah?" Michaels whispered. "Not from where I'm standing."

Bond snapped his legs up and kicked him hard in the groin. Michaels screamed, doubled over, dropped the gun, and fell to the ground.

"You were exposing a vital point, my friend," Bond said, getting to his feet and retrieving his Walther PPK. "And I do mean vital."

He leaned over the writhing man. "Who are you?" The man only groaned. "Are you going to talk?" Then he remembered the girl.

Stephanie stood behind them, by the steps. She was uncertain whether to run or drop to her knees.

"Come here," Bond commanded. She stepped forward, looking at the man groaning on the ground. "Do you know him?" Bond snapped.

She shook her head convincingly. "No."

Bond handed her the Walther. "Then retire him."

She looked surprised.

"He's an assassin. He came here to kill me," Bond said. "He knows I live here. I don't care who he is, just get rid of him."

She took the pistol and aimed it at her partner. The blond man's eyes widened. Bond watched her closely. She hesitated, staring at the man on the ground intently.

"05, I gave you an order," Bond said firmly.

The wind howled as the woman stood there frozen.

After ten tense seconds, Bond said, "All right. Relax."

Stephanie dropped her arm and looked dismayed.

"I couldn't do it," she said. "I just couldn't pull the trigger."

Bond walked over to her and took the gun. "If it's a matter of not blowing one's cover, a good agent may have to kill an ally or a friend. Don't ever forget that. You gave yourself away, 05. In the old days, if I had been KGB, or worse, I would have immediately perceived that you not only recognized 03 here, but knew him well."

"Yes," she sighed. "You're right. You really get the unexpected thrown at you in these training missions. I'm sorry. I didn't think you'd win the fight—it confused me."

"Double-Os must expect nothing *but* the unexpected," Bond said. He crouched down to the man he now called 03.

"How are you, 03? You put up a bloody good fight, lad. You almost had me at one point," Bond said with good humour. "You blew the mission, Michaels, but you'll get good marks, don't worry."

The man groaned and then vomited.

"Yes, well, sorry about that, 03," Bond said. "You'll feel all right in a few hours. Sometimes Double-Os have to learn their lessons the hard way. Remember what you learned about vital-point targets. God knows I did! Better luck next time."

Bond stood, turned, and walked up the stone steps, and Stephanie ran after him.

"So did you *know* he was going to be here?" she asked.

Bond shook his head. "No, but I suspected something, especially when you didn't try to help me. These Double-O training sessions you two are taking are also exercises for me. I'm unaware of your objectives and you are unaware of mine. Someone in London orchestrated the entire scenario. Apparently my challenge was dealing with someone who has penetrated the privacy of my home. And I take it you two had a mission to assassinate me?"

She laughed. "Yes, real kamikaze stuff, isn't it? A Single-O agent assassinating a Double-O!" Bond smiled too.

"Is Agent Michaels going to be okay? Not that he was one of my favourite people. He was always chatting me up."

"He'll be fine. I don't fight dirty unless I have to, but he left me no choice. Besides, he was careless. I didn't hurt him badly—he'll be up and on his way back to Kingston in no time. In any other situation he would have been killed. My kick was nothing compared to a carpet beater."

"A what?" she asked.

"Never mind," he said as he led her on to the top of the cliff. In contrast to the darkness below, up here the moon was very bright, flooding the grounds of the estate in a chalky white light.

Bond had purchased the property a year ago. Even though the heyday of a British Jamaica was long gone, Bond had always loved the island. For years, the memories and dreams he'd had of Jamaica haunted him. He had a compelling desire to be there. When a well-known British journalist and author died, the property became available and Bond bought it. Thus, in addition to his flat in London, he now owned a secluded holiday home on his favourite island. Since buying it, Bond had spent all his available time between missions at the sparsely furnished house. He called it Shamelady, after a plant that grows wild along Jamaica's North Shore, a sensitive plant that curls up if touched.

Stephanie Lane followed Bond inside. He immediately began removing his wet suit, stripping down to briefs. He seemed oblivious to the fact that a beautiful woman was watching him undress. "You know, you should be dead, too," Bond said. "If you can't hide convincingly behind a cover, then the cover's no good."

"I'll remember that," she promised. She watched him with increasing interest as she fingered the Walther PPK that he had placed on a coffee table. "Isn't this gun a little old-fashioned?" she asked. "It's not standard issue, is it?"

"No, it was once, though," Bond said. "I was using an ASP for a few years, and I just recently got an urge to use the old one again. I don't know, it feels very . . . familiar, and I've decided to use the Walther again from now on. Old habits die hard."

Stephanie picked up the gun and pointed it at him.

"So if I shoot you now, I will achieve my Primary Objective after all," she said with no trace of humour.

Bond squinted at her. There was silence. His cold stare dared her to fire.

She pulled the trigger. It clicked empty. Her mouth dropped open.

Bond held out the clip in his hand. "You don't think I'd put a loaded pistol down with a stranger in the room, do you? Sorry, 05. You flunked this one." Bond walked into the bedroom. "I'm going to take a shower. Make yourself comfortable. But before you get too relaxed, turn on the transmitter and see if there's anything from London."

Did Stephanie detect a hint of flirtation in his voice? She smiled. When she heard the shower running, she opened an attache case she had left in the house earlier. Inside was a small black device that looked like an ordinary beeper. She flicked a switch and the code "33" appeared on an illuminated display. Bond would want to know this.

She stepped into the bedroom and called to him: "It says 33!"

Bond shouted back from the shower, "Damn! That means I have to go back to London as soon as possible. Some kind of emergency . . ."

Stephanie was disappointed. Well, she thought, she had to take what she could get. She unzipped her wet suit, peeled it off, and stepped into the bathroom.

She had failed in accomplishing her Primary Objective that evening . . . but if she acted now she would have a little time. It was a shame that the night of pleasure she had anticipated earlier would not last until dawn. If she was lucky, though, she still had an hour or two.

At least she had got the right man. Secondary Objective accomplished! Naked, she pushed back the shower curtain, and got in with him.

THREE EVENTS

17 JUNE 1997, 11:45 P.M., ENGLAND

Approximately seventy-two hours earlier, a large cargo vessel called the *Melbourne* sailed into the bay between the Isle of Wight and West Sussex, facing Portsmouth. She had travelled thousands of miles in the last few weeks. From Hong Kong, her point of departure, she went to Perth in Western Australia, unloaded cargo, picked up containers, and refuelled. From there, she sailed west through the Indian Ocean and around the southern tip of Africa into the Atlantic and on to New York. She stayed in New York Harbour for three days, then finally began the last leg of the voyage to the United Kingdom.

When word of the *Melbourne's* arrival reached the desk of the Hampshire Constabulary Tactical Firearms Unit, Sergeant David Marsh picked up the telephone and called his Detective Chief Inspector. The TFUs, along with Firearms Support Teams, are tactical special weapons groups within UK police forces, available twenty-four hours a day. Many of the members of these elite police units are ex-British Forces personnel.

"She's here, sir," Marsh said when the DCI answered. Marsh listened closely to his instructions and nodded. "Consider it done, sir." He rang off and dialled a new number. If the tip they had received was correct, there could be trouble.

A lighter had already begun to deliver cargo from the *Melbourne* to shore. A group of four Chinese men unloaded the large wooden crates from the lighter as soon as it docked and used a forklift to transfer them on to a waiting lorry.

The two token Hampshire Police officers on duty that night, Charles Thorn and Gary Mitchell, walked along the dock area, noting that the weather was unusually pleasant for a June night. Unfortunately, due to a breakdown in communications, they were not apprised of the message that was received by TFU Police Sergeant David Marsh. Even more calamitous was the fact that neither of them was armed.

Thorn suddenly stopped in mid-stride and asked his partner, "Do you hear anything?" In the distance was the whirr of a hydraulic crane used to unload cargo.

Mitchell nodded. "Sounds like someone's unloading. I wasn't aware of a scheduled docking tonight, were you?"

Thorn shook his head. "Customs and Excise didn't tell me about it. Let's have a look, shall we?"

The two men hurried around a corner past a warehouse where they could get an unobstructed view of the harbour. Sure enough, four men were loading crates on to a lorry.

"Where are Customs and Excise? They should be supervising the unloading, shouldn't they?" Mitchell asked.

"Unless this is an unscheduled unloading," Thorn said. He quickly radioed his office to request additional officers. The Communication Centre Dispatcher informed them that the Hampshire Constabulary TFU was on the way and to stay put.

The Chinese were finished with the lighter and it was already pulling away. The lorry was nearly full—only two crates remained on the ground. They would be gone in minutes.

"We have to stop them," Thorn said. "Come on."

The two men stepped into view of the Chinese men. "Good evening," Thorn called out to them. "Like to tell us what you're doing?"

One of the Chinese stepped out of the truck and produced some papers. Thorn glanced at them. "You know this is highly irregular, sir. Customs and Excise are supposed to clear your unloading. What have you got in those crates?" The Chinese man, who apparently spoke little English, pointed to the papers.

"Right," said Sergeant Thorn, looking closely at the shipping numbers and comparing them to the crates. One was still on the ground, the other on the forklift. "That one has half a ton of tea, and the other one is what?"

The Chinese man smiled. "Toys. Made in Hong Kong."

Mitchell whispered to Thorn, "Imports from the Far East generally come into Southampton."

Thorn nodded and said aloud, "Let's open 'em up now, all right?"

Mitchell took a crowbar from the side of the hydraulic crane and prised the lid off the wooden crate. It was filled with straw, styrofoam, and large bags labelled with Chinese characters. Mitchell opened one of the bags and found dozens of smaller bags inside marked with similar characters. He tossed one of the small bags to Thorn, who promptly used a pocket knife to open it. It was full of tea.

"Fine," Thorn said. "Let's open the other one."

As the forklift was pulled in front of the officers, a fully marked TFU jeep containing four men, including Sergeant Marsh, sped quickly into the cargo area of the dock and stopped.

"Sergeant Marsh," Thorn said. "Good to see you. It seems these chaps aren't aware of Customs and Excise standard operating procedures."

"A word with you, Sergeant?" Marsh said, gesturing towards the jeep. Mitchell watched Marsh whisper to Thorn, then glanced over to the four Chinese men who had gathered near the fork-lift. They were all young, probably in their late teens or early-twenties.

The conference was over. Marsh took the crowbar from Thorn and slammed it into the side of the crate containing the tea, cracking one of the side panels. He then worked the panel off, exposing a mess of straw packing. Marsh dug into the packing with the crowbar, pulling it out.

"We have reason to believe you've got something hidden in here,"

Marsh said to one of the Chinese. The sharp end of the crowbar struck a large canvas bag, bursting it. A white, crystalline powder oozed out of the tear. Having just completed a two-year tour of duty in the Hampshire Constabulary's Drug Squad, Marsh hadn't shaken the habit of carrying a drug test kit with him. He quickly retrieved a plastic vial from the kit, opened it, and scooped a bit of the white powder into the vial with his finger. He replaced the cap and shook the vial vigorously, mixing the white powder with a reagent. The clear liquid changed colour.

Marsh turned to the Chinese men. "I have reason to believe this is heroin. Now I'm going to have to place you under . . ."

Fully automatic machine-gun blasts interrupted him. Taken by surprise, Mitchell and Thorn were the first to fall. Fortunately for Marsh, his team had come prepared.

Marsh hit the ground and quickly rolled behind the crate, shielding himself from the barrage of bullets. The three other officers also leaped for cover. Using MP5 Standard Operating Rifles, the TFU returned fire on the Chinese. Even though the weapons were single-shot only, the TFU were sharpshooters. One Chinese went down.

Marsh was armed with a Smith and Wesson 15 Mag Self Loading pistol. He peered around the container and got off a couple of shots before a hail of bullets tore into the side of the crate, forcing him back.

The Chinese were formidable opponents who knew how to use their guns, which to Marsh looked like MACH 10s. He knew that they were really COBRAYs, a 9mm machine gun modelled after the MACHs. Even though they were not well-made, criminal gangs favoured COBRAYs because they were sold and traded in pieces and were therefore easily concealed.

After a minute it was almost over. All but one of the Chinese were dead. There were no casualties on Marsh's team. The lone Chinese gunman realized the predicament he was in and attempted a kamikaze stunt. He yelled something in Cantonese and ran towards Marsh, his gun blasting wildly. Marsh threw caution to the wind. He stood up, used both hands to steady his pistol, aimed at the running man, and squeezed the trigger. The man jerked back and fell to the ground.

Marsh breathed a sigh of relief, then ran to where Thorn and Mitchell lay. The TFU member everyone called "Doc" was attending to the two constables, but he turned to Marsh and shook his head.

Marsh frowned, then barked an order to one of his men. "Get Doc some help for these officers and get in touch with the DCI. Tell him the tip was good. Tell him the villains would have got away if they hadn't been detained by two brave Hampshire Police officers."

18 JUNE 1997, 8:00 P.M., HONG KONG

Of Hong Kong's many attractions, elegant restaurants on boats provide visitors not only with a superb dinner, but with one of the best tourist attractions of Aberdeen's Shum Wan Harbour on the South Shore of the island. Most of them are linked together by walkways, and their ornate gilded and painted façades look particularly glorious lit up at night. One such "floating restaurant," the *Emerald Palace,* had been booked for a special event on 18 June and was closed to the public.

EurAsia Enterprises, an old-established shipping and trading corporation owned privately by a British family since the mid-nineteenth century, was holding a dinner for its chairman who was retiring after thirty years of service. A swing band, made up entirely of Chinese musicians, was playing surprisingly faithful renditions of Glenn Miller and Benny Goodman hits as the dance floor filled with formally dressed British men and women.

Guy Thackeray, the corporation's forty-eight-year-old CEO, had lived in Hong Kong all his life. His great-great-grandfather had founded EurAsia Enterprises in 1850, not long after Hong Kong was ceded to Britain. The family had steadfastly refused to allow the corporation to go public, and Guy Thackeray presently found himself the sole owner of 59 per cent of the company's stock. The remaining stock was held by other members of the Board of Directors, including John Desmond, the retiring chairman. All of them were present, sitting with their spouses at the top table.

Guy Thackeray felt out of place at his own company's events. The past month had been hell. As the first of July deadline approached, he was becoming more desperate and anxious. The secret burden he held on his shoulders regarding EurAsia Enterprises' future was taking its toll. He knew that very soon he would have to make public a fateful bit of knowledge, but it would not be tonight.

Thackeray surveyed the dance floor, catching the eye of a friendly face here and there and nodding his head in acknowledgement. He glanced at his watch. It was almost time for his speech. He took a last swig of his gin and tonic and approached the podium.

Back in the kitchen, the sixty-one-year-old Chinese cook, Chan Wo, grumbled to himself. He enjoyed cooking and considered himself one of the best chefs in Hong Kong. In fact, the *Emerald Palace's* reputation had been built on Chan's ability to create magnificent concoctions in the Szechuan, Cantonese, and Mandarin styles of Chinese cuisine.

Glancing at the new order brought to him by a waiter, he shrugged and walked over to the large metal refrigerator to fetch more previously prepared uncooked dumplings. Much to his dismay, they weren't inside. Had he used them all already? Chan Wo silently cursed his assistant. Bobby Ling must have forgotten to make more that afternoon.

"Bobby!" he called. The kid was probably in the storeroom. "Bobby!" he shouted again. Chan slammed the refrigerator shut and left the kitchen.

The storeroom was adjacent to the kitchen, conveniently soundproofed from the noise in the dining areas. Chan thought he wouldn't mind hiding in the storeroom for a while, too; he couldn't blame Bobby for taking a break. Chan entered the container-filled room. It was dark, which was odd. He could have sworn Bobby was here. Chan flicked on the light switch. Nothing but boxes piled on other boxes, cans and containers. "Bobby, where the hell are you?" Chan Wo asked in Cantonese. Then he saw the tennis shoes.

Bobby Ling was out cold, lying between two stacks of cardboard boxes. Chan bent down to examine the motionless body. "Bobby?"

Chan never knew what hit him. All he felt was a lightning bolt in the back of his neck, and then there was blackness.

The instrument that broke Chan Wo's neck was a heavily callused hand belonging to a man whose appearance was undoubtedly unusual, even in a densely populated area like Hong Kong. He was Chinese, but his hair was white as snow, his skin very pale—almost pink—and behind the dark sunglasses were pinkish-blue eyes. He was about thirty years old, and he had the build of a weight-lifter.

The albino Chinese grunted at the two dead figures on the floor, then moved to the only porthole in the room. He opened it, leaned out, and looked down at the water where a rowing boat containing two other men was rocking steadily next to the larger floating restaurant. The albino loosened a coil of rope he had over his shoulder and threw one end out of the window. Next, he braced himself by placing one foot on the wall beneath the window, and clutched the rope tightly. One of the men from the boat took hold of the rope and swiftly climbed up to the window. The albino was strong enough to hold the rope and the other man's weight.

The other figure appeared in the porthole and snaked through, dropping to the floor. He also had a full head of white hair, pinkish skin, and sunglasses, and was about thirty years old. While the first albino secured the rope to a post, the second opened a backpack, removed some instruments, and set to work.

Meanwhile, in the dining room, Guy Thackeray stopped the music and began his speech.

"My friends," he said, "I'm afraid I don't always give credit where credit is due. On such a special occasion as tonight, I must apologize for that oversight. Everyone who works for me and for EurAsia Enterprises is always deserving of praise. I want you to know that I am very proud of each and every one of you. It is because of you that EurAsia Enterprises is one of the leading shipping and trading establishments in the Far East. But it also took someone with superior management skills, leadership, and fortitude to guide this great ship of ours through sometimes troubled waters. For thirty years he has been an inspiration and mentor to us all." He looked straight at John

Desmond and said, "And you've been something of an uncle, or perhaps a second father, to me personally, John."

Desmond smiled and shifted in his seat, embarrassed. He was nearly eighteen years older than Thackeray and unlike the CEO, Desmond had been born and raised in Britain, having moved to Hong Kong in the early fifties.

Thackeray continued, "If ever there was a person deserving of a distinguished service award, it is John Desmond. I, for one, shall miss him. He will be leaving us as of the end of June. What's the matter, John, afraid the Communists will take away your health benefits come the first of July?"

There was laughter and applause.

"Anyway," Thackeray continued, "without further ado, allow me to present you with this plaque. It reads 'To John Desmond, in recognition of his thirty years' distinguished service at EurAsia Enterprises.' "

There was more applause as Desmond left his seat and approached the podium. The two men shook hands. Desmond then turned to the room and spoke into the microphone.

"Thank you, everyone. It's been a wonderful thirty years," he began. "EurAsia Enterprises has been good to me. Hong Kong has been good to me. I don't know what the future will bring after the first of July but I'm sure . . ." Desmond hesitated. He seemed to be searching for the appropriate words. ". . . it will be business as usual."

Everyone in the room knew that on 1 July Britain would no longer be in possession of Hong Kong. The entire colony would be handed over to the People's Republic of China at 12:01 a.m. Despite China's assurances that Hong Kong would remain a capitalist and free-enterprise zone for at least fifty years, no one could be sure.

"I wish you all the best of luck," Desmond continued. "Thank you again. And to my good friend Guy Thackeray, the man who really guides EurAsia Enterprises, a very special thank you."

During the applause, the two men shook hands again. Then Thackeray signalled the band leader and the room filled with the swinging rhythm of Glenn Miller's "Pennsylvania Six Five Thousand."

Thackeray accompanied Desmond back to the table. "John, I have to get back to Central," he said. "I suppose I'll see you at the office tomorrow?"

"Leaving so soon, Guy?" Desmond asked. "Whatever for?"

"I left some unfinished business at the office which must be taken care of. Listen . . . enjoy your party. I'll speak to you soon."

"Guy, wait," Desmond said. "We need to talk about things. You know we do."

"Not now, John. We'll go over it tomorrow at the office, all right?"

Guy walked away without another word. With concern, John Desmond watched his friend leave the room. He knew that the roof was going to cave in when the rest of the Board discovered what he had learned only two days ago. He wondered how Guy Thackeray was going to emerge unscathed.

Guy Thackeray stepped out of the dining room, on to the deck, and into a small shuttle motorboat. The boat whisked him to shore, where his personal limousine was waiting. In a flash it was off to the north part of the island and the panorama of buildings and lights.

By then, the two strange albino Chinese had finished their work. The first man slithered through the storeroom porthole, slid down the rope, and dropped into the waiting rowing boat. His brother followed suit, and moments later the boat was heading east towards a yacht waiting some two hundred metres away. The third man, the one rowing, also had a full head of white hair, pinkish skin, and sunglasses. Not only were the albino brothers the most bizarre trio in the Far East, they were also the most dangerous.

Exactly fifteen minutes later, the *Emerald Palace* exploded into flames. The brunt of the detonation enveloped the dining room, and the dance floor caved inward. It didn't happen fast enough for the terrified people caught inside the death-trap. Those not burned alive were drowned trying to escape. In twelve minutes, the structure had completely submerged. Everyone was killed, including John Desmond and the entire Board of Directors of EurAsia Enterprises.

21 JUNE 1997, 11:55 A.M., WESTERN AUSTRALIA

At approximately the same moment that James Bond fell asleep on a red-eye flight from Kingston, Jamaica to London, the sun was beating down on the Australian outback. A young Aboriginal boy who frequented this area of the desert in search of kurrajong, an edible plant, was still frightened of the white men he had seen earlier. The men had driven to this isolated location in four-wheel drives, which the boy knew only as "cars."

The boy's family lived at a campsite about a mile away and had done so for as long as he could remember. He knew that further south, more than a day's walking distance, were towns populated by the white men. To the east, closer to Uluru, the mystical rock-like formation in the desert which the white men called "Ayers Rock," there were even more encroachments on the Aboriginal home territory.

The white men had arrived early that morning in two "cars." They had spent an hour at the site, digging in the ground and burying something. Then they left, heading south towards the white man's civilization. They had been gone three hours before the boy decided to inspect the ground.

The dig occupied an area about six feet in diameter. The dirt was fresh but had already begun to bake and harden in the sun. The boy was curious. He wanted to know what the white men had hidden there, but he was afraid. He knew that he might get into trouble if he was seen by the white men, but now there was no one else around. He thought he should go and find a lizard for that evening's meal, but his desire to inspect the burial mound was too great.

If he had been wearing a watch, it would have read exactly 12 noon when the sun exploded in his face.

The nuclear explosion that occurred that day two hundred miles north of Leonora in Western Australia sent shock waves throughout the world. It was later determined that the device had roughly three-quarters the power of the weapon that destroyed Hiroshima: the equivalent of approximately 300 tons of TNT. The blast covered an area of three square miles. It was deadly, indeed, but crude by today's standards. Nevertheless, had there been a city where the bomb was buried, there would surely have been nothing left of it.

Within hours, an emergency session of the United Nations degenerated into nothing but a shouting match between the superpowers. No one knew what had happened. Australian officials were completely baffled. Inspectors at the site came up with nothing aside from the fact that a "home-made" nuclear device had been detonated. Everyone was grateful that it had been in the middle of the outback, where they assumed there had been no casualties.

What was truly frightening, though, was the implication of the location. It was, in all probability, a test. Someone—a terrorist group or a foreign power operating in Australia—was in possession of rudimentary nuclear weapons.

As Australia, the United States, Russia, and Britain combined forces to investigate the explosion and search for answers, they also waited for the imminent claim of responsibility and possible blackmail. It never came. When James Bond arrived in London in the early hours of the same day, London time, the nuclear explosion was still a total mystery.

THREE

CALL TO DUTY

ZERO MINUS TEN: 21 JUNE 1997, 10:15 A.M., ENGLAND

James Bond never had trouble sleeping on a plane, and the flight from Jamaica to England was no exception. He felt refreshed and alert when the office car pulled into the high-security SIS parking garage by the Thames. Things were so open now: Bond was one of the few veterans still around who could remember a time when SIS hid behind the front of Universal Export Ltd.

The British Secret Service had a relatively new leader. Her name was no longer a secret, but Bond would never dare address her by name, just as he had never addressed his irascible former chief, Sir Miles Messervy, that way. Since his retirement, Sir Miles had mellowed considerably. He often invited Bond to Quarterdeck, his home on the edge of Windsor Great Park, for a dinner party or a game of bridge. They still met from time to time at Blades. Once they were strictly a superior officer and a civil servant with mutual respect for each other; but now, after all the years, they were close friends. Even so, Bond had consciously to refrain from addressing the man as "sir."

Bond couldn't say he was friends with the new M. He wasn't even sure he liked her, but he respected her. In her short tenure, she had already shown she was capable of being an effective leader. She wasn't afraid of proactive operations, something Bond had feared might be discontinued. If some dirty work needed to be performed, she had no problem with ordering Bond, or one of the other Double-Os, to carry it out. She wasn't squeamish, and she wasn't gullible. Bond felt he could say whatever he wanted to her, and he would receive an honest response. He also knew what the woman thought of him personally. Bond was a chauvinist and, in her words, "a cold-hearted bastard." She had said it one evening over a working dinner. Bond understood why the woman had called him that, and he didn't hold it against her because, for one thing, she was right.

He stopped in at his private office on the fourth floor before going up to see M. His Personal Assistant (Bond couldn't help still thinking of her as a "secretary"), Ms. (not Miss) Helena Marksbury, was busy holding the fort. Helena worked for all of the Double-Os, having been with SIS for about a year. Since the days of Loelia Ponsonby and Mary Goodnight, there had been a steady succession of lissome blondes, brunettes, and redheads occupying the front desk. As for Helena Marksbury, she was a brunette with large green eyes. She was bright, quick-witted, and damnably attractive. Bond thought that had she not been his Personal Assistant, the lovely Helena would have made an enjoyable dinner date . . . with an option for breakfast the next morning.

"Good morning, James," she said. She had a lilting Welsh accent, something Bond found extremely attractive.

"How are things, Helena?"

"I was called in the middle of the night. Again," she said with a sigh.

Bond had been briefed about the Australian incident. By now every department was digging into the matter.

"It happens to the best of us," Bond replied.

"I imagine you have no problem rising in the middle of the night," Helena said with a twinkle in her eye.

Bond smiled and said, "Don't believe everything you hear, Ms. Marksbury."

"Well, if you ever find that you *are* up and can't sleep, Mr. Bond, I have a very nice herbal tea that is very relaxing."

"I avoid tea at all costs," Bond said. "You should know that by now."

"As a matter of fact, I have noticed. You don't drink tea at all, James? How un-English of you!"

"I'd as soon drink a cup of mud." He shrugged. "And besides, I'm half Scots, half Swiss." He smiled warmly at her, then stepped into his office.

Bond had never been keen on office decoration. The one piece of artwork on display was an obscure artist's watercolour of the club-house at the Royal St. George's Golf Course. The one framed photo-graph on the desk featured Bond and his closest American friend, former CIA agent Felix Leiter, sitting in a bar in New York City. It was an old photo, and the two men looked surprised and slightly drunk. It never failed to make Bond smile.

He had no urgent messages, so he picked up the phone and dialled Miss Moneypenny's line (one of the few women at SIS who still didn't mind being called "Miss"). She answered after the first ring.

"Hello, James, welcome back."

"Penny, you have a wonderful phone voice, did you know that?" he said. "You could start a second career entertaining lonely men with sweet nothings."

"Hmmm, and I dare say you'd be a regular client. But I'd have to go the Chinese route and entertain you with sweet and *sour* nothings."

"Now that's an appetizing idea for a takeaway, Penny," he said, chuckling.

She laughed too. "Listen, you'd better get up here right away. She asked for you just five minutes ago."

"I'm on my way. Bill there?"

"He's here too."

"Right." Bond hung up, left the sanctity of the one quiet place in the building, and took the elevator to the eighth floor.

Miss Moneypenny's manner was no-nonsense, but her blue eyes betrayed how pleased she was to see Bond. Throughout the years, their relationship had been a mutually flirtatious one, and it had set-tled into a comfortable friendship. Like most of Sir Miles's staff, she had been reticent about working for someone new after such a long time, but for her the new M was a pleasure. They got along splendidly, and Miss Moneypenny had decided not to transfer out but to stay on. It was a good thing, for many believed that SIS wouldn't function properly without Miss Moneypenny's vast knowledge of the entire organization and its history.

Bill Tanner, the Chief of Staff, was also a Service veteran who had been around even longer than Bond. He remained 007's closest friend inside SIS and one of the few with whom Bond regularly socialized. They enjoyed the occasional game of golf, but the Chief of Staff's forte was tennis. Tanner had originally resigned when Sir Miles retired, but he was asked by the new M to stay on during what was called the "transition period" of six months. Those six months became a full year, and now Tanner had no intention of leaving.

"Hello, James, welcome back," Bill said.

"Bill . . . Penny . . ." Bond nodded with a smile.

"Sorry you couldn't spend more time in Jamaica, James," Moneypenny said. "I received a report on the exercise. It went well, I heard."

"I have no complaints," Bond said, vividly recalling the sight of Stephanie Lane stepping into his shower. "This is about Australia, I suppose?"

"Isn't that appalling?" Tanner exclaimed, shaking his head. "No one knows what the bloody hell is going on. Unfortunately, it's not officially in our laps yet. Australia wants it handled her way for the moment and the PM has agreed to stay away for the time being. God knows, America and Russia are sticking *their* noses into it. Anyway, that isn't what she called you in for."

Bond was surprised. The atomic blast, even in the few hours since it had happened, had become international news.

Moneypenny picked up the phone and buzzed M. "007's here, ma'am." The green light above the door flashed, indicating that Bond should go in. Some things never changed.

On the other hand, M's office had changed drastically with the new regime. Sir Miles's domain had been the "captain's quarters" of a naval vessel, while the new look was more akin to a posh psychiatrist's office. Sparse, ultra-modern furnishings filled the place with a stark black-and-white scheme that was surprisingly pleasing to the eye. There was a lot of shiny metal, glass, and black leather, as well as an array of artwork of all types, including an original Kandinsky on the wall behind the desk.

M sat at her glass-topped desk, looking down at an open folder. Bond stood in the doorway until she motioned to the black leather chair in front of the desk. Her eyes never left the page until Bond was sitting and facing her. Then she looked up at him. M's striking blue eyes were much like Bond's—very cool, with thin streaks of white in the irises. She was in her late fifties, had short greyish hair, and a rather severe face. Not a slender woman nor a tall one, M nevertheless possessed a charisma that commanded attention, due mostly to the obvious intelligence within her ice-cold blue eyes. Their shape hinted at some distant Asian blood, but that was only speculation on Bond's part.

"Good morning, ma'am," Bond said.

"Hello, 007, how was your flight?" Her voice was calm, even, and soft.

"Fine, thank you."

"I understand the training exercise went well."

Bond nodded.

"Your report can wait," M said. "I'm sure 03 will fill us in. Or do you think 05 will have a more favourable view of events?"

M looked hard at Bond. He shifted uncomfortably. Sir Miles had never approved of Bond's womanizing, and it was one of the bones of contention between the new M and 007. Bond swallowed and managed to say, "I'm sure either agent will give you an accurate reconstruction of the exercise."

M frowned but nodded briskly.

Bond quickly changed the subject. "What do we know about this explosion in Australia?"

"Never mind about that, 007," M said. "We've been told to stay out of it for the moment. Regardless of those orders, I have Section A doing reconnaissance. There's hardly any information at the moment. Until we hear from the party or parties responsible, I've got something else for you to look into."

"Yes, ma'am."

"Bond, do you know what's happening to Hong Kong on the first of July?" M asked.

"Well, yes ma'am," Bond said. Didn't everyone? "It reverts back to the People's Republic of China after a century and a half of British rule."

"That's less than two weeks away, 007."

Bond nodded, his brow creased. What was all this about? He vaguely remembered a report he'd read before leaving for Jamaica. Could it involve that solicitor who was killed in a bomb blast earlier in the month?

"Do you know what's happened there in the past few days?" M asked.

"There was a car bomb in the business district—what, a week ago?"

"On the eleventh of June, just over a week, yes. What else do you know about it?"

"It was a solicitor visiting from England, wasn't it? Someone in a large firm here."

"Gregory Donaldson, of Fitch, Donaldson and Patrick. A partner in one of our most prestigious law practices."

"Do we know who was behind the bombing, and why he was targeted?" Bond asked.

"An anonymous caller phoned Government House and claimed that the People's Republic was behind it. Why Donaldson was targeted is still a mystery."

"Why was Donaldson in Hong Kong?"

"I'll get to that in a moment. You know about the two Red Chinese officials who were assassinated?" she asked.

Bond remembered. "Oh, yes. That was a few days later, wasn't it?"

"The 13th."

"Yes, ma'am, two officials from Beijing were killed in a shopping mall by a man dressed in a military uniform."

"A British army uniform, to be exact. The two men were working with the local government on last-minute preparations for the changeover. They had taken some time off and were buying souvenirs or something to take back to China. Some loose cannon in uniform calmly walked up to the men, pulled out an automatic pistol, and shot them dead. Witnesses said the "officer" ran out of the store and disappeared into the crowd. All we know is that the man was certainly Caucasian."

"There's been a lot of tension over the past year. People have been waking up to what's happening to them," Bond said. "It had to come to a head eventually."

" 'Waking up' is only the half of it," M said. "People are starting to panic. Something else happened in Hong Kong two nights ago that has escalated the problem."

"What's that?"

"A bomb exploded on a floating restaurant off Aberdeen, killing thirty-three people. All of them were important members of the British business community in Hong Kong."

This was news to Bond.

"The report is probably on your desk. The first incident was disturbing, the second one was bewildering, but this third one has caused the PM to sit up and take notice. Something's going on, 007, and it isn't pretty. Fingers are pointing. There was another anonymous call to Government House the morning after the bombing."

"China."

"Right."

"That's it? Just 'the People's Republic of China?' Nothing more specific?"

"There were allusions to some general in Guangzhou, north of the Hong Kong colony. His name is Wong. It was enough to get the rumour mill churning. The press got hold of it, and needless to say there is a lot of tension in the air. Anti-Communist groups are making themselves heard, and the democracy foes are just as loud. The PM has been talking with Beijing . . ."

"But the official party line denies all knowledge of the actions?"

"Correct, 007. And they are just as quick to accuse us of killing their two officials in the shopping mall."

"Sounds like someone is stirring up trouble just before the takeover."

"Well, there's going to *be* trouble. Chinese troops are massing along the border, just above the New Territories. The Hong Kong people are afraid that they're going to invade and do away with the idea of a peaceful transition. It didn't help when a group of Hong Kong teenagers threw rocks at the soldiers. There was gunfire but no one was hurt. There was also some kind of panic-induced incident in one of the tourist areas in Kowloon just yesterday. The memory of Tienanmen Square is still very vivid."

"Isn't this a job for the politicians?"

"Normally it would be," M said. "But something else has come up that interests me."

She waited until Bond asked, "And what is that, ma'am?" The new M tended to have a flair for the dramatic.

"The three incidents—the car bomb that killed Donaldson, the assassination of the two Chinese men, and the bombing of the floating restaurant—are all connected to a multi-billion dollar international shipping and trading corporation that is privately owned and operated by a long-established British family in Hong Kong."

A BRITISH LEGACY

M PRESSED SOME BUTTONS ON A CONTROL PANEL TO HER RIGHT. THE ROOM darkened slightly and the Kandinsky painting slid up into the ceiling. A television monitor built into the wall flashed on, revealing the logo: EurAsia Enterprises Ltd.

"EurAsia Enterprises is one of the biggest shipping corporations operating out of Hong Kong," M said. "You'll find all the background you need in this file." She gestured to a manilla folder on the edge of her desk. "Briefly, I'll give you some of the details."

Bond took the folder but didn't open it. He gave his full attention to M.

"The company was founded in 1850, just a few years after Hong Kong was ceded to Britain at the close of the so-called First Opium War. How much do you remember about British colonial history, 007?"

Bond cleared his throat. "In a nutshell, the war resulted from China's refusal to open ports to the West. I believe the catalyst was an incident in which the Chinese government in Canton seized a tremendous amount of opium from British traders and destroyed it."

"Twenty thousand pounds, to be precise," M added. "At the time, it was worth three million sterling. Opium trading was a ghastly business, but in the early nineteenth century opium was the world's most valuable commodity. Be that as it may, the crux of the problem was as you said—China didn't want to trade with the West. They had reluctantly allowed Canton—they call it Guangzhou now, as you know—and Macau to become the only ports open to the West. Our East India Company had a monopoly in Guangzhou until the 1830s, but the demand for Chinese tea, as well as silk and porcelain, was overwhelming."

"It wasn't easy for the traders," Bond said. "I seem to remember that they were restricted to the fringes of the city, not allowed inside . . ."

"That's right," M said. "And all business had to go through the Co-hong, a guild of Chinese merchants. Corruption flourished, and these constraints encouraged dreams of a base on the southeast coast of China where traders could operate freely. There was a trade imbalance and it greatly favoured China. The balance of trade in tea alone ran six to one in China's favour. They didn't particularly care for anything we had to offer, except silver, perhaps. China was under the impression that she didn't need us."

"And that's where the opium trade came in . . ."

"Precisely. The traders discovered that there was a certain faction in China that desired Indian opium, and we were in the dubious position of being able to offer it. That was how several of our largest companies came into existence over there. In retrospect, I suppose, it was a nasty business; but it suited the mercantile ethic of the time. Opium traders shrugged off these scruples and maintained that trade, and the missionaries that followed, would ultimately benefit China. Well, the Chinese government became increasingly concerned about opium. Justifiably—it was an extravagant habit that ruined minds and morals—and it caused the trade imbalance to tip in our favour. Finally, in 1839, the emperor ordered the governor of Hunan Province to go to Guangzhou and end the opium trade. The British Chief Superintendent of Trade, a man named Charles Elliot, was ordered to surrender all of the merchants' opium."

"And he did."

"That's right, and the traders watched helplessly as the Chinese destroyed the opium that was the basis of their livelihood. One thing led to another, and skirmishes began. By 1840, an expeditionary fleet had arrived in Hong Kong with a mission to obtain compensation and an apology from China for the destroyed opium, and to secure a British foothold on the China coast."

"It was rather a one-sided war, wasn't it?" Bond asked rhetorically.

"Yes, China was ill-prepared to deal with Britain's warships. It all came to a temporary end in 1841 with a treaty that was never signed. The treaty promised compensation for the confiscated opium, permission for British merchants to return to Guangzhou, and the cession of Hong Kong Island to Britain. Neither side was happy with this outcome and the war continued into 1842, when the Treaty of Nanjing was finally signed and reluctantly accepted by China. The result was a hefty compensation in millions of pounds, as well as the opening of several ports to British trade."

"And Hong Kong was officially ceded to Britain."

" 'In perpetuity' the treaty said," M added. "Hong Kong became a British Crown Colony in 1843, and trade resumed. We don't have to cover all of the history, but I suppose you know how we acquired Kowloon and the New Territories?"

"That was a result of the *Second* Opium War," Bond replied, feeling like a schoolboy.

"Well, we prefer to call it the Second Anglo-Chinese War now," M said with a shrug. "It was a result of a ridiculous mistake made in 1856 by Chinese officials. They boarded one of our ships, the *Arrow,* believing it to be a pirate vessel. A battle ensued, and another war broke out. It finally ended in 1860 with the treaty signed at the Convention of Peking. We got Kowloon with that one."

"In perpetuity, once again," Bond chipped in.

"Of course. Opium was officially legalized in China from then on until the start of the Second World War. China ended up making a tidy profit from the filthy substance, using it as an excuse for levying taxes. The big blunder on our part came some forty years later, when the Second Convention of Peking was held and a new treaty was signed. A larger chunk of land north of Kowloon, along with 233 surrounding islands, was leased to Britain for a ninety-nine-year term. As you know, this area became known as the New Territories."

"Why was it not ceded in perpetuity?" asked Bond.

"Carelessness on the part of the British Foreign Secretary. He had hoped for an open-ended lease to be terminated by mutual agreement, but he ultimately agreed to the ninety-nine-year lease. I suppose that seemed like forever in 1898, when the treaty was signed."

"And now that time has run out," Bond mused. He recalled the historic agreement made between Great Britain and China in 1984. "Why did we agree to hand over Hong Kong and Kowloon in 1997? Why didn't we just give up the New Territories and keep what was still legally ours?"

"Because Hong Kong and Kowloon depend on the natural resources that are derived from the New Territories. Without the New Territories' abundance of fresh water and other utilities, Hong Kong Island would be extremely difficult to support. And, I think, there was a certain amount of guilt involved as well. Looking back, both sides felt that Hong Kong rightfully belonged to China. It was ceded under circumstances which weren't entirely ethical. It's a shame that everyone had to wait a hundred years to come to terms with that realization. The poor people of Hong Kong are now feeling the brunt of that mistake. After over a century of western and democratic rule, they are now faced with the prospect of life controlled by the People's Republic of China. But enough of the history lesson—let's get back to the topic at hand."

M pushed a button on her desk and the picture on the monitor changed. The image of a Caucasian man appeared. He had black hair with streaks of grey, dark brown eyes, and looked to be in his late forties. His face was severe and cold.

"EurAsia Enterprises was one of the trading corporations that flourished in southeast Asia after the First Opium War. It was founded by an Englishman named James Thackeray. This is Thackeray's great-great-grandson, the current CEO of EurAsia Enterprises. His name is Guy Thackeray."

Bond knew very little about EurAsia Enterprises. "The company has branches all over the world?"

"Yes," said M. "Toronto, London, New York, Tokyo, Sydney—they have a significant gold-mining operation in Western Australia—but they're based in Hong Kong. That's where Thackeray has lived all his life."

"Funny," said Bond. "I've never heard of him."

"Thackeray's not a very public person," M said. "You can count on one hand the number of times he's been to England. He rarely leaves Hong Kong, and if he does he only goes as far as Australia. There's really nothing particularly sinister about the man. By all accounts he's a perfectly respectable businessman. He's forty-eight, never married, and lives quietly and comfortably on Victoria Peak. He was the only child and sole heir of his great-great-grandfather's legacy, which was passed down from James Thackeray to his son, then to his grandson, and so on. Guy Thackeray became CEO of the company when he was twenty-eight."

"What did he do before that?" Bond asked.

M chuckled. "He was a magician."

"What?"

"He had an act that he started when he was a child," M said. "A magic act. He performed it on floating restaurants, in nightclubs, wherever . . . He even had a short-lived television show in Hong Kong in the early sixties. Sleight-of-hand stuff, optical illusions, sawing women in half . . . you know what I mean. He gave it up once he reached his twenties and entered the family business in pursuit of a 'real' career. Although he was independently wealthy, I suppose he felt he must live up to the family name and all that. So he learned the business and was very good at it. After his father died, he became CEO. Never bothered with show business again. And up until now, the only black mark we had against the man is that he apparently enjoys playing high stakes *mahjong* in illegal betting parlours."

"So why are we interested in him?"

"Gregory Donaldson, the lawyer who was killed in the car bomb blast, was Guy Thackeray's solicitor," M said with raised eyebrows.

Bond nodded thoughtfully. The picture changed, revealing a photo of Guy Thackeray with Gregory Donaldson.

"On June the 10th, Donaldson arrived in Hong Kong on an urgent mission to meet Guy Thackeray. Donaldson's partners here in London were not privy to what it was about, only that it had something to do with the privately owned EurAsia stock. Thackeray owns 59 per cent and the rest is owned by other Board members. On June the 11th, Donaldson was killed."

"Interesting," Bond said.

"That's not all," M continued. "The two visiting Chinese officials from Beijing who were shot by the alleged British army officer were shopping at a mall owned by EurAsia Enterprises. In fact, the mall is part of the huge complex that houses the company on Hong Kong Island."

"So they were killed at EurAsia's corporate headquarters?"

"That's right," M said.

"And the floating restaurant business . . ."

"That bomb killed the entire Board of Directors, the chairman, and all the other executive officers of EurAsia Enterprises—everyone but Guy Thackeray. It was a company party of some kind. The chairman, a fellow named Desmond, was retiring. Guy Thackeray was there, made a speech, presented Desmond with one of those distinguished service awards, then disappeared. At first, everyone thought he had been killed in the blast as well, but he was found at EurAsia headquarters working in his office two hours later, completely oblivious to what had happened. He's been cooperating with the local authorities in their investigation into the blast, but it's still very early. No one has any reason to suspect he might be involved. From what I can gather, most people believe the bomb might very well have been meant for him, and to hell with the other people who were killed."

M paused a moment then continued, "There's one more piece of the puzzle you haven't heard about. Three nights ago, the Hampshire Constabulary Tactical Firearms Unit busted a drug-smuggling operation in Portsmouth. Some Chinese were caught unloading a ton of heroin off a cargo ship. That ship just happened to be owned by none other than EurAsia Enterprises."

Bond nodded. "The Chinese were Triad, I would wager."

"You're absolutely correct, 007," M said. "They were all killed in the raid, but a quick investigation revealed they were part of a Triad known as the Dragon Wing Society. It's an offshoot of the San Yee On Triad."

Bond frowned. The San Yee On was one of the largest Triads in the world. Triads had existed in China for centuries and were the most misunderstood, most complex, and most dangerous criminal organizations to infect the modern world. Chinese Triads made the Sicilian Mafia look amateurish. They usually originated in Hong Kong, but their tentacles reached into nearly every Chinese community in the world. More formidable than the Tongs, the Triads had in the last fifty years become responsible for most of the worldwide drug trade. They also had a hand in illegal arms distribution, prostitution, gambling, illegal immigration, and other activities associated with organized crime. A Triad's oath of loyalty was absolute, and a member would rather die than reveal any of his organization's secrets.

"So you think that EurAsia Enterprises is involved with this Triad?" Bond asked.

"That's what I want you to find out," M said. "A lot of British subjects were killed the other night. At first I thought it could very well be coincidence that all the events in Hong Kong were connected with this otherwise very respectable company. But when the raid in Portsmouth occurred and we learned that the company's ship was smuggling heroin to Triad members, that's when we became alarmed.

"If you can, 007, I want you to find out who is behind these terrorist acts and stop them. All Britain needs is a war with China on the eve of giving back Hong Kong! And that's what we're going to get if the pattern keeps up. You're to fly to Hong Kong this afternoon—there's a flight leaving at 2:30 and it arrives tomorrow morning. They're eight hours ahead of us, as you know. Our man in Station H will meet you at the airport, a fellow by the name of Woo. I understand he's been with the service for years."

"I know of him, ma'am," said Bond. "Never met him, though."

"He'll be your guide and contact. How's your Chinese?"

"I speak Cantonese pretty well, ma'am, but I'm not so fluent in Mandarin."

"Well, I hope you won't need it. Although I dare say that we'll be hearing more Mandarin in Hong Kong next year."

"Will Guy Thackeray be accessible?"

"I have no idea," M said. "You'll have to find a way to meet him. Size him up. You are to determine if we have any reason to be suspicious of the man. I trust you won't fail. You have got ten days. The countdown to July the first is already in progress."

"Zero minus ten," Bond said. "Plenty of time. No pressure at all."

She ignored his flippancy. "That's all, 007. Be sure to stop by at Q Branch on your way out. I believe the Armourer has something for you."

Bond stood as M shut off the monitor and returned the lighting to normal. He cleared his throat and said, "Ma'am, I'm very concerned about the Australian thing . . ."

"We all are, 007. I'll keep you informed, but for the moment it's not our brief. You've got your assignment, and that's where I want you to concentrate."

With that, M looked down at the document she had been reading when Bond first entered. It was a signal that the meeting was over.

"Very well, ma'am," Bond said and started out of the room.

"James." Bond stopped, surprised that she had called him by his Christian name.

"Yes, ma'am?"

"Those Triads can be vicious. They'll cut off your hand with a butcher's knife as soon as look at you. Be careful."

Bond nodded. "Yes, ma'am. Thank you," he said, and walked out of the inner sanctum.

Seven minutes later, Bond punched in the keypad code and entered the unmarked grey metal door in the basement. He was immediately assaulted by the smell of chemicals and the noise of machinery. Q Branch was a virtual Santa's Workshop for grownups, and not very nice grownups at that.

In one corner, behind a wall of glass, technicians were spray-painting a BMW. Against a far wall was a line of cardboard human cutouts with bull's eyes painted on various portions of their anatomy.

Two technicians stood twenty-five feet away from the wall and fired propellants at the targets from what appeared to be crude prototypes of 35mm cameras.

"Oh, please, can I get just one shot of you, 007?"

Bond turned to see a tall, thin man with grey hair. He was holding one of the cameras.

"Major," said Bond, "I wouldn't have taken you for a *paparazzo*."

Major Boothroyd, the Armourer and head of Q Branch, replied, "It's for the wife and kids, actually. Come on, say cheese. *Please*."

"Major, I never photograph well," Bond said, chuckling. "I'm a bit camera-shy."

Boothroyd placed the camera on a table. "I shutter to think what this camera would do for you!"

Bond winced at the pun.

"Follow me, 007. What size shoe do you wear?"

He followed Boothroyd into a room containing a bench and a shoe salesman's stool with an inclined side. On a rack against the wall were a number of pairs of leather shoes in brown and black. Boothroyd gestured to the bench and sat on the stool. Bond sat, shaking his head. "Major, why do I feel like I'm in Harrod's? I wear a nine and a half."

Boothroyd turned to the shoes on the wall. "Nine and a half . . . nine and a half . . . do you prefer black or brown?"

"Black, please. Is this a joke?"

Boothroyd placed a pair of black shoes in front of Bond. "You know better than to ask that. Well, take off your shoes and try them on!"

Feeling ridiculous, Bond did as he was told. "Now I suppose you want me to walk around the room and see if they feel all right?"

"I want to make sure they're comfortable, 007," said Boothroyd. "There's nothing worse than sore feet."

Bond walked back and forth twice. "They're fine. Now, what's the point?"

"Take a look at the bottom of the tongue on the left shoe. You'll find a small prying tool. Remove it."

Bond did so. "Right," the Armourer continued. "Now use the tool to pry open the heel." The heel snapped off, revealing several items fitted neatly within. "As you've probably guessed by now, these are upgrades of our standard issue field shoes, model F, which all Double-O operatives are required to wear when on assignment."

"Then you've made quite an improvement. I never could get the old ones open."

Boothroyd ignored him. "As usual, they contain a variety of helpful items. In the left heel you'll find not only the plastic, X-ray-proof wire cutter and file, but also our new plastic dagger. It's very sharp, so be careful."

Bond picked out a round object with a lens on either side.

"Ah, that's a microfilm reader. Press the little button on top to acti-vate the light. Look through it as you would a child's kaleidoscope. There's a small compartment there in the heel to store strips of micro-film maps. We have an extensive library of microfilm maps detailing every square mile on the face of the planet. Before you go abroad, simply put in a request for microfilm covering the areas you may be visiting. With that handy contraption, you'll never get lost, 007."

"Thank God for that," Bond commented.

"Right. Now pay attention, 007. These shoes could save your life."

"Major, I do believe you've found your second calling."

Boothroyd went on: "The shoelaces are now easily inflammable, generating enough heat to melt a half-inch iron bar. There's a spare shoelace in the heel."

"Good thing, too," Bond said. "Shoelaces break at the damnedest times."

"There are pieces of flint and steel in there as well to start fires. Now take a look at the other shoe. You'll find the same prying tool under the tongue. Open up the heel on that one, if you would."

Bond did as he was told and found yet another cache of objects.

"As you know, this one's geared more towards first aid. In the heel you'll find some vital medicines and supplies. There's a bottle of antiseptic, a pair of tweezers, acetaminophen tablets, generic amoxicyllin, and some bandages that are folded neatly in the sole of the shoe. We've added small tubes of sunblock and petroleum jelly."

"That's great," said Bond. "I can dispense with my sponge bag altogether and travel light for a change. What about an electric razor and toothbrush?"

"Why is it you never appreciate the things I do for you, 007? I work my fingers to the bone, put in extra hours at weekends, and what do I get for it? You think my salary is anything to write home about? Why can't you ever say 'thank you' for once?"

Bond stood and patted Boothroyd on the shoulder. "Thank you, Major, but you're beginning to sound like my dear old Aunt Charmian did back when I was in my teens."

"Hmph. I imagine you were just as disrespectful to her."

"Never. She had a temper worthy of SMERSH."

Boothroyd stood. "Do you have any questions about the shoes, 007?"

"Only one," Bond said.

"What's that?"

"Do you have any socks to go with them?"

FIVE

THE PEARL IN
THE CROWN

ZERO MINUS NINE: 22 JUNE 1997, 10:30 A.M., HONG KONG

There was once a pilot who described the flight to Hong Kong as "hours of ennui, followed by a few minutes of sheer terror!" Kai Tak, or Hong Kong International Airport, consists of a single runway yet there are an average of 360 movements a day, scheduled at two-minute intervals in peak periods. Pilots consider it among the more challenging landings on the globe; for passengers, it's one of the most nerve-wracking.

Though no stranger to daredevil aerial manoeuvres, James Bond nevertheless felt a surge of excitement as he looked out of the window of the British Airways 747 on its approach to the fabled city. Down below was a harbour littered with boats and surrounded by layered levels of skyscrapers. It seemed that the plane would fly straight into the buildings; but it quickly descended to make a steep, forty-seven-degree turn and touched down on the narrow strip of land on the Kowloon peninsula.

If India was once known as the "Jewel in the Crown," then Hong Kong was perhaps the "Pearl in the Crown." Its mere existence was one of the wonders of the modern world. It began as a barren island with very little population, and now ranked among the world's fifteen largest trading entities and was Asia's busiest tourist destination. The mix of British management and Chinese entrepreneurial enthusiasm made Hong Kong a cosmopolitan mixture of East and West. It was a commercial, manufacturing, and financial dynamo; and it was the communication and transportation intersection for all Asia.

In nine days, Hong Kong would no longer be Britain's Pearl in the Crown. People had speculated for years what would happen when the colony was handed back to China. One school of thought was that Hong Kong was finally being returned to the China it had economically and culturally always belonged to. Britain had only borrowed it long enough to allow it to blossom. Bond had heard people ask, "What will China do to Hong Kong?" He thought the more intriguing question might be, "What will Hong Kong do to China?"

The airport terminal was noisy, crowded, and chaotic. Bond moved with the crowd into the Buffer Hall. The office had provided him with plenty of Hong Kong currency, so he didn't have to bother with foreign exchange queues. Immigration went smoothly and quickly. Bond's cover was that of a *Daily Gleaner* journalist covering the handover to China.

Bond took the third exit out of Buffer Hall into the Greeting Area, which was packed with the families and friends of incoming passengers. He spotted the yellow baseball cap, and beneath it the friendly smile of a Chinese man.

"No charge for ride to hotel," the man said to Bond.

"But I have the correct change," Bond replied.

"No problem," the man said, turning his r's into l's the way Chinese often do. "I even take you on scenic route, uh huh?" His English was slightly broken but his vocabulary was very good.

"That would be lovely then," Bond said and smiled. These code exchanges, though necessary, were sometimes ridiculous.

The man held out his hand. "T.Y. Woo at your service. How was flight?"

"Too long." Bond shook his hand. "I'm Bond. Call me James."

"You call me T.Y. You are hungry, uh huh?" He had an endearing habit of adding "uh huh?" to his sentences.

"Famished."

"Your hotel has excellent restaurant. I take you, okay?" Woo reached for Bond's carry-on bag, which Bond gladly allowed him to take. Bond held on to the attache case which contained documentation of his cover identity and other assorted personal items. His Walther PPK was stored in an X-ray-proof compartment in the case.

When the men reached the street, a red Toyota Crown Motors taxi cab with a silver roof screeched to a halt on the double yellow line edging the road.

"Quick, get in," Woo said. He opened the back door and gestured for Bond to jump inside.

A policeman on the street blew his whistle and shouted something in Chinese. The driver, a young teenage boy, shouted something back. By then, both men were inside and the cab sped away.

"That was restricted zone. Cabs not supposed to stop," Woo explained, smiling.

Bond noticed the meter wasn't running. "Is this a company car?"

"Yes, James," Woo said. Bond noticed that his new friend rarely relaxed his broad smile. "Meet my son Woo Chen—you call him Chen Chen, uh huh?" The boy grinned at Bond in the rear-view mirror. Bond nodded at him and smiled.

"Relax, we go for ride!" Chen Chen exclaimed enthusiastically.

The cab pulled in front of a Rolls-Royce, making room for itself in the congested traffic. Although the flow moved slowly, Chen Chen managed to swerve in and around vehicles to maintain a significantly faster speed. Bond held his breath a couple of times during the first few minutes of the journey until he assured himself that the boy knew what he was doing.

"Chen Chen too young to drive," T.Y. said, still grinning. "I pull strings to get him licence!"

Bond cleared his throat and said, "He drives very well. How old are you, Chen Chen?"

"Fifteen," the boy said, grinning just like his father. "Sixteen next month!"

The cab moved through the traffic and finally entered the Cross-Harbour Tunnel. It was a congested two-lane thoroughfare two kilometres long.

"Your hotel on Hong Kong side. Airport is on Kowloon side," T.Y. explained. Bond knew that, but nodded as if he was learning something. "Very nice hotel," T.Y. continued. "Expensive. They have good restaurant at top. Private. We can talk, uh huh?"

The cab pushed its way through the tunnel and emerged into the light of Hong Kong Island. Throngs of people cluttered the pavements. At intersections, there were queues eight people deep waiting to cross the street. Bond had studied the latest intelligence and census reports on the city-state during the flight. Between five and six million people now resided in the relatively small area that comprised the territory. It was essentially a Cantonese city, most of the population being ethnic Chinese. The other small percentage were known as "expats," or foreigners, who had taken residence in the colony. These expats were of many nationalities—Filipinos, Americans, Canadians, British, Thai, Japanese and Indians being the most prominent. Bond thought it was a cultural melting pot like no other.

"If you get tired of hotel, you come to safe house," T.Y. said. "Near Hollywood Road, east end of Western District."

The cab zigzagged through Connaught Road in the Central District of the island, and screeched to a halt beside a white block building over twenty storeys tall. The Mandarin Oriental's unimpressive exterior did a fine job of hiding one of the world's most sophisticated hotels. While most English businessmen might have stayed at the more Colonial-style Peninsula Hotel in Kowloon, Bond always preferred the Mandarin Oriental whenever he was in Hong Kong. Hotel rooms were hard to come by this week, as many had been booked as much as a year in advance of the first of July transition. Luckily, SIS had made a reservation long ago in anticipation of sending someone just to be present on the fateful night.

Woo said, "You check in. I meet you in Chinnery Bar at noon, uh huh?"

"Fine," Bond said, taking his bag and opening the door. "Thank you, Chen Chen."

"No problem," said the grinning youth.

The hotel lobby was discreetly elegant and surprisingly subdued. Bond checked in and was ushered to his room on the twenty-first floor by a cheerful bellhop. It was the "Lotus Suite," consisting of two large rooms and a terrace overlooking the harbour. The hotel even provided a pair of binoculars for sight-seeing. The sitting room included a writing desk, bar, television/stereo system, and a bathroom for guests. The bedroom contained a king-sized bed, and there was a large private bathroom. Once he was alone, Bond immediately opened the refrigerator and pulled out a bottle of vodka. He put two ice cubes into a glass and poured a large measure. It was early, but the flight had been long and he needed to unwind.

Bond stood and watched a small section of the harbour as *kaidos,* sampans, junks, and *walla-wallas* scurried back and forth. There were people in Hong Kong who lived and worked on their little boats and rarely set foot on land. As Westernized as it was, Hong Kong was still a very different world.

Bond changed from his business suit into a light blue cotton short-sleeved polo shirt and navy blue cotton twill trousers. He put on a light, grey silk basketweave jacket, under which he kept his Walther PPK in a chamois shoulder holster.

At noon, he went down to The Chinnery, a bar decorated much like an English gentlemen's club with masculine brown and red deep leather-upholstered armchairs; in fact, Bond remembered that it used to be exclusively all-male. It was only in 1990 that the bar began to admit women. It was adorned with original paintings by British artist George Chinnery, whose drawings and paintings of the landscapes and people of Macau, Canton, and Hong Kong made him the undisputed doyen of foreign artists of the China coast in the mid-1800s. The room was already filling with smoke from businessmen's pipes, cigars, and cigarettes. Bond noted that the collection of seemingly countless bottles of Scotch whisky was still behind the bar.

T.Y. Woo was already there and Bond joined him.

"Welcome to Hong Kong, *Ling Ling Chat*," Woo said. Bond knew that *Ling Ling Chat* was "007" in Cantonese. "Let us drink. Then we will go upstairs and have lunch, uh huh?"

Bond ordered a vodka martini, but he had to explain twice to the waiter that he wanted the drink shaken and not stirred. Woo shrugged and had the same. "We drink mostly cognac here," he said.

"Hmm," Bond said. "That's more of a nightcap for me."

Over their cocktails the two men began to get to know each other. T.Y. Woo had been with the Secret Service for twenty-five years. His family had come from southern China several decades ago and had made a fortune in the antiques and curios business. Woo and his brother ran a shop on Upper Lascar Row, otherwise known as "Cat Street," and this provided a perfect front for the Hong Kong head-quarters of the British Secret Service. SIS, then called MI6, had recruited him in the sixties. A British agent on self-imposed R & R had wandered into the Woos' shop during the Vietnam War. He was an elite Double-O operative who had been assigned to assist American GIs deep in the jungle. Impressed with Woo's cheerful disposition and willingness to "do something exciting," the agent brought him to London. After several months of training, he could get by with what he had learned of the English language and make succinct intelligence reports. Woo's double life as a shop keeper and an intelligence officer took its toll on his wife, who left him ten years ago. He had raised Chen Chen on his own.

At 12:30 the men took the lift to the twenty-fifth floor and entered the Man Wah Restaurant, one of the finest in the colony. A lovely Chinese woman wearing a slinky *cheongsam*, a traditional tight-fitting dress with a seductive slit revealing a bit of leg, led them to a table. Unlike most restaurants in Hong Kong, which were usually noisy and full of cheerful clamour, this one was an intimate, quiet place. The blue carpet, wood-framed maroon pan-elling, and oriental paintings all contributed to a luxurious ambience. A bonsai tree covered with tiny white blooms sat on their table, which was next to a large picture window overlooking the harbour.

The menu specialized in Cantonese-style cooking, the distinctive cuisine of Guangdong Province. It was considered the most varied and interesting in all China. This was due partly to south China's subtropical climate, which produced a huge range of fruits and vegetables and all kinds of seafood. The style of cooking used steaming and quick stir-frying to enhance the qualities of food. An experienced cook knew when a dish was done by the sizzling sound that emanated from the wok. It was the lightest and least oily of all the regional cooking styles, seasoned by a wide variety of sauces rather than spices. Vegetables, seafood, pork, and chicken were the main ingredients.

"Mr. Bond! Welcome to Hong Kong!"

He knew the voice at once. It belonged to Henry Ho, General Manager of the Man Wah, whom Bond had known for years. Ho was a most pleasant gentleman, and an expert in the culinary delights. The soft-spoken man had dark hair and smiling eyes. Never hesitating to join a party at their table, Ho always had a story to tell about the food he served. Today was no exception.

"Hello, Henry," Bond said, shaking his hand. "It's good to see you again."

"Yes, yes, it is very good to see you, too," Ho said. "Mr. Woo called yesterday to say an important guest was coming. He didn't say it was you! I have prepared some special dishes!"

The meal began with an appetizer of cucumber and what Ho called "black fungus"—ginger covered in a dark red crust. The first course was Chili Prawns, a Szechuan-style dish. Bond liked Szechuan cuisine, which was infinitely spicier than Cantonese. It was said that China's leader, Deng Xiaopeng, preferred Szechuan food. Ho explained that the food from Szechuan Province was hotter because of the humid climate—the people ate spicy food to help release moisture from their bodies. The large prawns were cooked in garlic, chili, and sesame oil, and were simply delicious.

A rich plum wine called "yellow wine," served warm, was brought to the table between courses. Bond thought it tasted like sake.

A second course was an elaborate serving of sauteed filet of sole with green vegetables in a black bean sauce. The presentation was spectacular—several large carrots had been carved to resemble a dragon boat, the kind used in the famous Dragon Boat Festival that occurs every summer, and the food was placed inside the boat. The sole was quite tender and flavourful because in Hong Kong the sole can swim in both fresh and salt water.

The main course was called Beggar's Chicken, which was Chef Lao's creation of chicken baked in clay with black mushrooms, barbecued pork, ginger, and Chinese spices. This dish had to be ordered at least a day in advance, as it was cooked many hours before serving. The chicken was cleaned and stuffed with the various ingredients, then wrapped in lotus leaves. Then the package is packed in clay and baked until the clay was hard.

When the dish was brought to Bond and Woo, all the waiters and staff stood around and applauded as the diners took turns whacking and breaking the clay with a mallet. A waiter then picked out the large bones from the extremely tender chicken, mixed in a special sauce, and served it in shreds on small plates. Bond thought it was one of the tastiest meals he had ever had in his life.

Ho brought them tea after Bond and Woo had stuffed themselves and, joining them at the table, said, "There is a region in southeast China called Fook Tien Province, and there the largest variety of tea is produced. There is one leaf that is very intriguing. Its name is Monkey-Pick-Tea.

"According to legend," Ho continued, "the tea leaves were collected by monkeys because they were positioned on high cliff-tops. But the monkeys were not very obedient, and needed to be disciplined. Whenever a monkey disobeyed, a part of his tail was cut off— a half-inch or so! This would continue until the monkey learned to do as he was instructed. Monkey-Pick-Tea is very highly regarded because it is difficult to come by, and also because it is rich in both aroma and taste. Therefore its qualities are compared to those of a fine wine. We drink it after a meal, not only because it is enjoyable, but because it also helps one to digest."

After the meal, Bond and Woo were left alone to discuss business.

"So, T.Y., what's going on? What do you know?" Bond asked.

"The solicitor who was killed—that bomb was not act of China, uh huh?" Woo said.

"That's what M thinks, too," Bond replied. "Who do you think is behind it?"

"There is a general in Guangzhou. His name is Wong. Very militant. He is violently opposed to any kind of democratic rule in Hong Kong after takeover. He has been in favour of taking over colony by force for years. He is biting his nails on other side of border, just waiting for chance to move in his troops and take control. Beijing keeps him on short leash. Someone trying to put blame on him. Not sure he is responsible."

"Why do you say that?" Bond asked.

"It is stupid! Why would he do such a thing weeks before Hong Kong goes back to China? What would he gain by starting war between China and Britain? On second thought, he just might be that stupid. Not a rational man, uh huh?"

"Those are his troops lining the border?"

"Yes. Mostly his. He would march into New Territories tomorrow if Beijing gave him okay." Woo shrugged. "It is possible that he is trying to provoke confrontation between Britain and China. He wants excuse to move in. And from looks of things, he is succeeding."

"But surely he wouldn't dare bring his troops across the border before the first of July. The whole world is watching."

"General Wong does not care. He is madman. He considers himself national hero in China. He is hard, cruel man. I tell you something else about him. Wong spent most of 1980s in Beijing. He was one of high commanders responsible for Tienanmen Square tragedy. He enjoyed giving orders to shoot those people. After that, he was promoted and moved back to Guangzhou, where he was from."

"All right, he's a suspect. Who else is on your short list?"

"My personal opinion? I think it is someone local. Could be Triad. On other hand, it is not their method. Not many criminals have guns or bombs in Hong Kong. You would be surprised—Hong Kong is quite gun-free."

"What about the two Chinese officials who were killed by a British officer?"

"That is big mystery," Woo said. "Again, I do not think it was real British officer. Whole thing was staged. He was imposter."

"I was thinking the same thing."

"Again—why would this officer want to cause trouble? Unless he has a personal grudge. And who is he to take on the government of China?"

"And the floating restaurant bomb?" Bond asked.

"Same thing. It was not China. It was not General Wong in Guangzhou, although that is rumour."

"What do you know about EurAsia Enterprises?"

"Big company. Very respectable. The *taipan*, he is well-liked but very private man, uh huh?"

"Thackeray."

"Yes. I have met him. I see him sometimes at casino in Macau. One of my few vices, I admit. I have played *mahjong* with him once or twice. Always lost a lot of money to him. EurAsia not as big as other major companies, like Jardine Matheson. But it does okay. Involved in shipping and trading. Their docks are at Kwai Chung."

"Do you know what happened in England a few nights ago?"

"Yes, I got briefing. Heroin. That surprised me. I have no records that EurAsia is involved in anything illegal. My contacts with police have assured me that nothing out of ordinary is on record."

"Yet that heroin came from one of their ships."

"I think Triad is involved. They have their fingers in everything. It is quite possible that someone in EurAsia is being squeezed by Triad and Thackeray does not know anything about it."

Bond ordered a brandy. "Are you familiar with the Dragon Wing Society?"

"Yes, I am. They are splinter group of San Yee On. Very powerful. Dragon Wing Society has interests in many nightclubs in Hong Kong.

Most of their known activities involve prostitution and gambling. The police believe they are involved in heroin trade but have not acquired evidence. They put squeeze on entertainment industry, too. Movie sets are prime targets, uh huh?"

"Do you know anyone in the Triad?"

"A Triad leader is called the Cho Kun, or Dragon Head. Cho Kun of Dragon Wing is Li Xu Nan. Very powerful businessman. Owns several nightclubs and girlie bars. The identity of Cho Kun is supposed to be secret—no one outside of Triad knows." Woo grinned. "But I know."

"All Triads work that way?"

"Usually, yes. Only top men in Triad know. Their lodge is secret, too."

"Lodge?"

"That is Triad's headquarters, where they hold meetings."

"Do you know where their Lodge is?"

Woo shook his head. "No, that *is* secret. I am working on it. They change locations often, so it is difficult."

"How can I find this Li Xu Nan?"

"Hard to say." Woo said. "He frequents a couple of his nightclubs. We maybe try later tonight or tomorrow."

"Okay, tell me more about Thackeray?"

"He is in late-forties. Bachelor. Does not go out in public much. Lives on the Peak with all the rich *gweilo*." *Gweilo*—a term meaning "ghost people"—was often used by ethnic Chinese with reference to westerners.

"Has there been any investigation since the drug bust in England?"

"Yes. My contact in police said they searched EurAsia's warehouse at Kwai Chung. They found nothing. Official company line is that they are shocked and dismayed that something like that could have happened on one of their ships. EurAsia spokesman denied all responsibility and blamed act on criminal enterprise."

"I'm going to want to take a look at that warehouse myself."

"We can do that."

"And I want to meet Guy Thackeray. Can you arrange it?"

"How's your game of *mahjong*?"

Bond had little experience with the game that was so popular in Hong Kong. "Not very good, I'm afraid. I've played one of the western versions a bit." The game's rules and play varied from country to country.

"No problem. I give you quick lessons. Hong Kong version easier than western version or Japanese version, uh huh?"

"When does he play?" Bond asked.

"He plays tonight! You have money? Big stakes. Thackeray is big winner. I do not know how he does it. Always wins. If we get there before he does, we have better chance at getting in game with him. Let us go, okay?"

"Sure. Just how much capital will I stand to lose?"

"Thackeray plays 100 Hong Kong dollars per point," Woo said with eyes wide. "With a two-point minumum, ten-point maximum! Maximum Hand is worth 38,400 Hong Kong dollars!"

Bond frowned. That meant that Thackeray played a very challenging and risky game. A winning hand must be worth at least two points or a stiff monetary penalty would be imposed. SIS might lose thousands of pounds. Nevertheless, closely observing Thackeray for a couple of hours over an intense game of chance just might be the best way for Bond to evaluate him. He believed that a man revealed every side of his personality during the course of any gaming contest in which a great deal of money was at stake.

"Fine," said Bond. "Let's do it."

Woo caught the waiter's attention and said, *"Mai dan,"* miming the international scribble gesture. "I get this, James. You are now indoctrinated into our concept of *maijiang.*"

Bond said, "I know all about *maijiang.* Face. Reciprocity. In other words, I'll get the next one. *Sikdjo.*"

Woo grinned. "Ah, you been to Hong Kong before?"

"Yes, a few times. Japan, too."

Bond knew the Eastern philosophy of *maijiang* was very important to Asian people. It meant, quite literally, the selling of credit. *Maijiang* was used when a person gave or was given face and when reciprocity was implicitly understood and expected. If a person did a favour for a man, then he was expected to do something in return. Saying *sikdjo* meant Bond agreed.

Woo paid the bill and the two men left the relatively tranquil ambience of the restaurant. They did not notice the strange albino Chinese man who sat reading a newspaper at the Harlequin Bar, just outside the entrance to the Man Wah. As soon as they left, he went to make a phone call.

THE PREVAILING WIND

4:00 P.M.

The Viking 66 Sports Cruiser skipped along the water away from the Causeway Bay docks and into Victoria Harbour. T.Y. Woo introduced the captain as his elder brother, J.J. The elder Woo, when not assisting at the antiques store on Cat Street, was a yachting enthusiast. T.Y. often used his brother's boat for official Secret Service business. Like T.Y., J.J. was very agreeable. He said little; when Bond addressed him, J.J. would just nod his head and smile. Bond assumed the man's English wasn't as good as his brother's.

The boat was built in the UK primarily for the American market with US components, but J.J. managed to have a model shipped over to Hong Kong. Apparently the Woo family had been very wealthy, and J.J. and T.Y. had each inherited a private fortune. The 66 had a solid glass hull, twin 820-hp MANs, and the capability of topping out at 30 knots. The deep-V design gave the boat true offshore capabilities— and a smooth ride. T.Y. proudly told Bond that J.J. had bought the boat for a song—only 1.5 million Hong Kong dollars.

It was still broad daylight. The harbour was extremely busy and full of all types of vessels. T.Y. told Bond that they had nothing to fear from the Marine Police—his boat was registered with them and would not be stopped. Even so, it was apparently not at all difficult to slip away from Hong Kong and over to Macau without Immigration finding out. The only trick was finding a discreet place to dock in Macau.

After twenty minutes, the boat was speeding through the strait north of Lantau Island and below the New Territories. Soon, they were out in the open South China Sea. J.J. opened up the MANs, and the Viking reached maximum speed.

"We will be in Macau in another three-quarters hour, uh huh?" T.Y. said, grinning. The wind was blowing through his short dark hair, and Woo seemed to take great pleasure in the sensation. Bond was feeling the effects of jet lag. He hoped some strong coffee would sharpen his wits enough for him to play a fast-paced game of *mahjong*, especially since he was not very familiar with it.

"Where are we going exactly?" Bond asked.

"Lisboa Hotel and Casino," Woo said. "Not one of my favourite establishments."

Bond knew the Lisboa. It was a prime tourist attraction in the legendary territory. Macau's history was almost as colourful as Hong Kong's. It predated the British colony by several centuries, its story part of the seaborne Age of Exploration that brought fifteenth century Portugal to prominence. Trade was the underlying catalyst for its development, specifically the immense wealth to be gained from the spices and silks of the Orient. The port of Macau was set up by the mid-1500s as a stop between Malacca and Japan. The territory flourished, especially during the early seventeenth century. By the twentieth, however, it had declined and had developed a reputation as a hotbed of spies, vice, and intrigue. In 1987, the anti-colonial Portuguese government signed an official agreement with China to hand over Macau on 20 December 1999. Unlike Hong Kong, Macau residents who gave up residency had the right to live in any EC country, including, ironically, Great Britain.

"You need quick *mahjong* reminder?" Woo asked Bond.

"That would be most helpful."

Woo gestured that they should get out of the wind and into the boat's cabin. They left the teak-covered deck, went below, and sat at a small table. Woo made some strong coffee and said, "Okay, tell me what you know."

"The game is a mixture of gin rummy, dominoes, and poker, you might say. There are four players who play against each other. There isn't much skill involved, mostly luck, and the trick is to play defensively and try to out-guess what your opponents need. There are three suits—Bamboo Sticks, Circles, and Characters. There are four sets of tiles numbered one to nine in each of the three suits. There are also four Red Dragon tiles, four Green Dragon, four White Dragon, and four tiles of each "wind"—the East Wind, West Wind, and so on."

"Yes, that is all true," Woo said. "There *is* skill, James. You must play fast and be creative in building your hand for most possible points. Every point worth a lot of money, uh huh?" Woo grinned. "We brought 80,000 Hong Kong dollars of company's cash to lose. I already cleared it with M. She just said we better not lose it!" Woo laughed at that. "If Thackeray on a roll like he always is, M is in for big surprise!"

"Why is he so good?" Bond asked. "The game really does depend on the luck of the draw, doesn't it?"

Woo shrugged. "I do not know. If he cheats, I do not know how he does it. It is very hard to cheat at *mahjong,* uh huh? He wins thousands of dollars a night playing."

The Viking sailed around the southern tip of Macau and made its way up the western side of the peninsula. Woo explained that it was easier to dock unseen over there, and they could take a taxi to the casino. They found a decrepit wooden dock hidden in some overgrowth.

"We use this dock before," Woo said. "Be careful when you step on it. It not very safe. Oh, I almost forget. We cannot take guns in casino. They have high security. Metal detectors. We must leave them here."

Bond remembered that from previous visits, and it made him very uncomfortable. Reluctantly, he handed J.J. his Walther PPK. "I hope I'm not going to need that later," he said.

J.J. told T.Y. in Chinese that he would stay with the boat, then proceeded to stretch out on the bunk in the cabin. Bond and Woo carefully stepped on to the dock. It was a short walking distance to an urban area, and they found a taxi within minutes. The Hotel Lisboa was a barrel-shaped concrete building painted mustard and white, with walls corrugated like a waffle and roofs fashioned to resemble roulette wheels. As they entered the lobby, Bond noticed a collection of oddities on display: a small dinosaur skeleton, giant junks of carved ivory and jade, and a tapestry of the Great Wall. After passing through an unusually stringent security check, Bond followed Woo into the noisy, gaudy casino, where he had gambled a few times before. He was always amazed by the joylessness of the Macau casinos. Gambling there was taken very seriously and the participants did not look like happy people.

Woo stopped at a slot machine. "I must feed Hungry Tiger first," he said. He slipped a two-dollar coin into the contraption and pulled the handle. He got a cherry, a bar, and an orange. He shrugged. "Come on, let's go find *mahjong* game."

The Lisboa was built on several levels, with different games of baccarat, blackjack, roulette, fan tan, and slot machines played on different floors. The main, rotunda room of the first floor was full of smoke and sweat. Playing *mahjong* at a casino was highly unusual. Thackeray's game was a private affair, and was played in a secluded, rented room.

Bond and Woo took the stairs to the third floor, past the VIP baccarat room and into a less crowded area. Woo spoke to a guard, who gestured to his right. Bond followed Woo to an archway covered by red curtains. "We are in luck," Woo said. "Thackeray not here yet." He moved through the curtains and was greeted by an Englishman in his late thirties with wavy blond hair.

"Mr. Woo!" the man said. "I thought you had lost all your money the last time you were here! Don't tell me you've come back for more punishment?"

"Ah, Mr. Sinclair, you know that I must save face and try again," Woo said good-humouredly. "This is my friend and business acquaintance Mr. Bond. He would like to play tonight, too. Is that all right?"

Sinclair scrutinized Bond and recognized a fellow Englishman. He held out his hand. "Simon Sinclair."

"James Bond." The man had a firm handshake, he noticed.

"What brings you to Macau, Mr. Bond?" Sinclair asked.

"I'm a reporter for a Jamaican paper, the *Daily Gleaner*," he said. "Covering the handover of Hong Kong next week."

Sinclair rolled his eyes. "You and how many other thousand journalists? Well, come in, come in."

It was a small room with a square table in the centre. Chairs stood at each of the four sides, and a set of *mahjong* tiles was spread out, face down, on the table. A Chinese stood behind a fully stocked bar on one side of the room, preparing a concoction in a blender. An archway on the opposite wall led into a small foyer, presumably to a private washroom.

"Do you know Mr. Thackeray, Mr. Bond?" Sinclair asked.

"No, I'm looking forward to meeting him," Bond said. "Mr. Woo here tells me that he's quite a player."

Sinclair laughed. "He takes me to the cleaners twice a week. I don't know why I continue to play with him—some sort of masochistic streak in me, I suppose."

"What do you do, Mr. Sinclair?" Bond asked.

"I work for EurAsia Enterprises. I was . . . uhm . . . recently promoted to General Manager."

As if on cue, the curtains parted and Guy Thackeray walked in, followed by two bulky men who looked like bodyguards. He stopped to survey the room, but for some reason became unsteady for just a moment. He regained his composure quickly.

"Hello, Guy," Sinclair said. "You remember Mr. Woo?"

Woo held out his hand. "Hello, Mr. Thackeray, I have come to lose my money again, uh huh?"

Thackeray shook his hand but didn't smile. "A pleasure to take it, Mr. Woo." There was a slight slur to his speech.

Woo turned to Bond. "And this is my friend from Jamaica, Mr. James Bond. He is a journalist covering the Hong Kong handover."

Thackeray looked at Bond, sizing him up. Bond held out his hand and said, "How do you do?"

There was a slight pause before Thackeray took his hand, almost as if he wasn't sure whether or not he wanted to do so. But his grip was firm and dry.

"Welcome to the Far East, Mr. Bond," Thackeray said. "I hope you're a better *mahjong* player than your friend Mr. Woo." Bond smelled alcohol. The man was very drunk.

"I'm afraid I'm mostly accustomed to western rules, but I shall do my best," Bond said.

The man looked like his photograph. He was very handsome, even if his face was severe. Bond did note that Thackeray appeared tired, with the look of a man under a great deal of stress. After what happened to EurAsia's Board of Directors, he must be dealing with a massive amount of red tape.

"What can I get you to drink?" he asked.

"Vodka martini, shaken, please. Not stirred."

For the first time since he'd entered the room, Thackeray displayed the hint of a smile. "I like a man who's particular," he said, then walked over to the bartender.

Over the next few minutes, the two bodyguards turned away other prospective *mahjong* players who had enquired about the game. Although the room was private, the bodyguards didn't prevent spectators from coming and going. By the time the men were ready to play, six or seven other Chinese men were standing around the edges, chattering quietly among themselves.

"Don't let my sycophants disturb your concentration, Mr. Bond," Thackeray said. "They like to bet on the various hands during the game."

"The more the merrier," Bond said.

Thackeray had brought Bond his martini and placed an entire bottle of vodka on the table for himself. He sat down, poured a glass, then took a gulp.

"Shall we begin?" Thackeray said, standing next to the table. "Do you know the rules for our game?" Without waiting for an answer, he continued. "Two-point minimum, ten-point maximum, 100 Hong Kong dollars a point, standard doubling, Maximum Hand is 38,400 dollars. No chicken hands allowed. Agreed?"

"Chicken hand?" Bond asked.

T.Y. explained. "Ah, in Hong Kong version of game, that is what we call a winning hand that has both types of sets—Chows *and* Pongs or Kongs. It is easiest type of winning hand to get. But remember, a chicken hand is okay if you have points from other things, like Flowers or Winds."

Bond knew what Woo meant. A winning hand in *mahjong* consisted of fourteen tiles in a combination of "sets." A Chow was a set of three consecutively numbered tiles from any suit, such as a 1–2–3 or a 6–7–8. A Pong was a set of three of the same numbered tiles from any given suit, such as three 6s in the Circles suit. A Kong was a set of four of the same numbered tiles from any given suit. To "go out," a player's hand must contain three or four Chows, Pongs, and/or Kongs, plus one Pair of the same tiles in any suit. Special hands consisting of a combination of specific tiles were worth more points.

"So, are we agreed?" Thackeray asked again.

"Certainly," Bond said, feeling as if he was signing a pact with the devil.

Each player was required to hand over 50,000 Hong Kong dollars for a cache of chips. A Chinese man working for the casino acted as moderator and banker. He stacked up four tiles face down in the centre of the table.

Thackeray handed Bond the dice. "I'll let you have the honour of rolling for the pick of Winds."

Bond quickly went over in his mind the game's procedure. *Mahjong* was divided into four Rounds, each named after the four Winds. The Round's name was known as the "Prevailing Wind" for all the hands played within the Round. Each player's seating position was also named after one of the four Winds. Players picked Wind tiles in turn to determine which seat, or Wind, they were to play at the beginning. Whoever chose the East Wind was the dealer for the first hand in the East Round. A Round consisted of a minimum of four hands with the deal being passed around the table. The game would end once each of the four Winds had been the "Prevailing Wind." There was a minimum of sixteen hands, usually more, in a complete game of *mahjong*. Fast players could complete a game in less than an hour.

Bond rolled the dice and counted the players around the table counter-clockwise, ending on Woo. He drew one of the tiles on the table. It was the South Wind. Thackeray was next, drawing the East Wind. Sinclair drew the West, and Bond was left with North. Thackeray pulled up a chair. Bond sat to Thackeray's left. Sinclair sat facing Thackeray, and T.Y. was across from Bond. Thus, for the East Wind Round, Thackeray was the number 1 seat, East, and dealer for the first hand. T.Y. was number 2, South; Sinclair was number 3, West; and Bond was number 4, North.

All four men began mixing the 144 tiles face down on the table. This was done with a tremendous clatter. Then, each player proceeded to build their side of the "the wall," consisting of 36 tiles stacked two-deep.

Bond decided this was a good time to try and get his target to open up. "Mr. Thackeray," he said, "I would welcome the opportunity to interview you regarding the Hong Kong handover. I understand your company is successful and well-regarded. You're an important man in the colony and I'd like to know what you think about living under Chinese rule."

"You're lucky, Mr. Bond," Thackeray said, building the second layer of his wall. "I'm giving a press conference the day after tomorrow at 4:00 p.m. It'll be at the corporate headquarters in Central. You're welcome to attend. I'll make sure your name gets on the list."

"Thank you, I appreciate the invitation," Bond said. He thought he would try to get some kind of reaction out of the man. "Terrible thing that happened at that restaurant. I imagine it left you and your company devastated?"

Thackeray's wall was finished. He looked up at Bond and stared at him. "Yes," was all he said.

Bond pushed the man further. "I've always thought luck comes in waves, both good and bad. Didn't something happen to your solicitor, too? I heard something . . . ?"

"Mr. Bond, did you come here to discuss my personal affairs or to play *mahjong?*" Thackeray growled. What little humour the man possessed was now totally gone. Bond was convinced he was a perpetually cantankerous alcoholic.

"Oh, I came to play *mahjong,*" Bond said. "Forgive me."

When the four completed walls formed a perfect square on the table, Thackeray took three small dice and rolled them in the centre. He got a 10. Starting with himself, he counted the sides of the wall counter-clockwise, ending up on the South Wall, in front of Woo. Then, after counting ten tiles from the right end of the South wall, Thackeray "broke" the wall by separating the tiles at that point. He took the four tiles to the left of the break. Woo picked up the next four tiles, followed by Sinclair, and then Bond. This was repeated until each player had twelve tiles. Then, Thackeray took two more tiles to make fourteen, and the other players each took one tile. East always began a hand by discarding his fourteenth tile.

Bond arranged his tiles in front of him. It was a terrible hand. He had two useless blue Flowers. The blue and red Flower tiles gave points to a player if the Flower's number matched his seat or the name of the Round. Flowers were immediately exposed for all to see, and the vacant spots in the hand were replaced by new tiles. Thackeray had one Flower—a Red 1, which luckily matched his seat. This automatically gave him one point. He drew a tile from the dead wall and kept it. The other two players had no Flowers, which was worth a point if either of them won the hand and could avoid drawing any Flowers during its play. Bond drew two new tiles—they were both North Winds, which were helpful. His hand contained a 1 of Sticks (designated by the picture of a sparrow holding a stick), a 5 of Sticks, a 6 of Sticks, another 6 of Sticks, a 2 of Circles, a 3 of Circles, a 9 of Circles, a 3 of Characters, an 8 of Characters, a White Dragon, a South Wind, two North Winds, and the useless blue 2 and 3 Flowers.

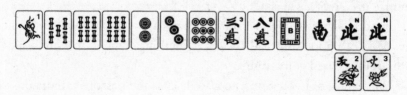

The most difficult thing about *mahjong* was deciding what kind of hand to go for and sticking with the objective. Good hands usually consisted entirely of Pongs and/or Kongs and the one Pair, or entirely of Chows and a Pair. Bond's hand was almost impossible to predict. He had a Pair of 6 of Sticks, and a possibility for a Chow of Circles. If he got another North Wind tile, he would have a Pong that matched his seat. This would automatically give him one point. Unless the draw was extremely favourable, he would have to go out with a chicken hand, so he needed to find a way to gain another point. Drawing the winning tile from the wall rather than from a discard would be worth a point as well as more money. Maybe he would get lucky.

Thackeray discarded a North Wind tile. Bond immediately said, "Pong," and picked up the tile. It was unbelievable luck on the very first discard! Bond displayed the three North Wind tiles face up on the table.

"Well, you're off to a good start, Mr. Bond," Thackeray said.

It was Bond's turn to discard. He got rid of the 1 of Sticks. It was then Thackeray's turn again, because turns resume to the right of any player that Chows, Pongs, or Kongs. Thackeray drew from the wall and discarded an 8 of Circles. Woo drew from the wall and discarded a North Wind tile, now useless because of Bond's Pong. Sinclair drew from the wall and discarded a 3 of Sticks. Bond drew a 2 of Sticks. Damn! If he hadn't discarded the 1 of Sticks earlier, he would have had a chance at making a Chow with another 3 of Sticks.

Play continued uneventfully around the table one more time until Sinclair discarded an East Wind. Thackeray said, "Kong," and picked it up. He displayed four East Wind tiles, which automatically gave him two points—one point for possessing a Pong or Kong of Winds matching his seat, and one point for matching the Prevailing Wind. Along with his 1 Red Flower, he already had a total of three points. All he had to do now was win the hand in any possible manner.

Thackeray drew a tile, then discarded a 6 of Circles. Play continued around the table. Sinclair made a Pong from Woo's discard of a White Dragon. This made Bond's White Dragon useless, so he got rid of it with his next discard.

After a while, the discards were strewn haphazardly face up in the middle of the table. When it was his turn, Thackeray reached across the table to draw a tile from the wall. He discarded a 4 of Circles. Bond could have used it to make a Chow, but a player can only Chow with the discard from the player on his immediate left. Besides, his Pong of North Winds had committed the hand to go for all Pongs or Kongs. If he had any Chows in his hand now, he would have a worthless chicken hand.

On Woo's discard of a 2 of Characters, Thackeray said "Kong" again and took it. The man certainly had extraordinary luck.

After each player had drawn and discarded two more times, Bond was no better off than he had been before. He discarded an 8 of Circles he had drawn, and Thackeray immediately said, "Out!" and picked up the tile.

All the players displayed their hands. Thackeray had a Full House, a term given to any hand worth four, five, or six points. Thackeray had six. He got three points for having all Kongs or Pongs in his hand (plus the required Pair), two points for the East Winds matching his seat and the Prevailing Wind, and one point for the Flower. He won a total of $6400—Sinclair and Woo each paid $1600; Bond had to pay $3200 because Thackeray won with Bond's discard. Thackeray would have received a seventh point if he had picked the winning tile from the wall.

After each hand, the players' Wind assignment and the deal rotated counter-clockwise, unless the East Wind player won the hand or the hand was a "dead hand," or draw. Once all four players had had a turn at being the East Wind, then a new Round, the South Wind Round, would begin. Thackeray had the privilege of dealing again. During the deal, Thackeray asked, "Mr. Woo, what was it you said you do? I can't for the life of me remember what business you are in."

"I run antiques shop on Cat Street," Woo said, smiling.

"And how do you two know each other?" Thackeray asked, gesturing to both Bond and Woo.

"T.Y. and I knew each other in London before I moved to Jamaica," Bond said casually.

Bond's new hand started off promisingly. He had three pairs. It was possible to build a hand of Pongs or Kongs, or he could try for seven Pairs—a special hand worth four points.

It was about five minutes before Sinclair declared "Out" on a self-picked tile from the wall. He revealed a hand worth three points—one point for the self-pick, one point for a Pong of Red Dragons, and one point for a 3 Flower, which matched his seat. Everyone had to pay him $1600.

This time the seat/Wind assignments rotated. Woo was now East and Bond was West. Woo rolled the dice and started the deal. During this hand, Bond lit one of the cigarettes he kept in a wide gunmetal case. There was a time when Bond smoked sixty to seventy cigarettes a day. Around the time of the Thunderball case, he reduced his intake to twenty or twenty-five. Morlands of Grosvenor Street had been the recipient of Bond's custom for many years. They had made a special blend of Balkan and Turkish tobacco for Bond and decorated each cigarette with three gold bands. Recently, Bond had switched to another tobacconist and commissioned H. Simmons of Burlington Arcade to create a low-tar cigarette for him. These still retained the distinctive gold bands, along with Simmons's trademark. With this switch, he had managed to reduce his intake of tobacco even further, down to five or six cigarettes a day. He'd onced joked to Bill Tanner that it was easy to give up—he had done it at least twelve times.

The play of the third hand went very quickly. Once, when Thackeray reached across the table to draw a tile from the wall, Bond thought he saw something strange. Was there the flash of the back of a tile in the man's hand? He couldn't be sure. He would watch the table a little more closely and pay less attention to his own hand from now on.

Thackeray won the third hand with a total of three points—one point for a self-picked winning tile, one point for having no Flowers, and one point for having a hand of all Chows and a Pair. Everyone paid him $1600.

Seat/Wind assignments rotated again. Sinclair was East and dealer, and Bond was South. He was dealt what amounted to very close to a winning hand, even though it was a chicken hand containing a mixture of possible Chows and Pongs. Luckily, he drew no Flowers, which was worth one point. He had a chance of winning small. Play progressed five times around the table when Bond drew a tile from the wall that completed his hand. He declared "Out" and displayed his miserable hand. The self-picked tile saved him, as that was worth one point. His two points garnered him a measly $800 from each player.

While the men played, several people came and went through the red curtains. Some of the Chinese spectators were apparently winning a great deal of money. At one point, Bond was struck by a bizarre sight. Two Chinese men with pinkish-white skin and white hair came into the room, stood together against a wall, and watched. They were both wearing sunglasses and looked alike. Not only were they obviously siblings, but they were both albino! That was very unusual in this part of the world, Bond thought. In the past, Asian families would have considered such children to be "unnatural" and would have found a way to get rid of them.

The seat/Wind assignments rotated for the last time of this Round. Bond was now East and the dealer. He got a promising hand containing a complete Pong of the 6 of Circles, and two Pairs. As they played, Bond thought he noticed something unusual again when Thackeray reached across the discarded tiles to draw one from the wall. Thackeray had Ponged with the 4 of Characters early in the hand. Bond decided to throw down Characters to see if Thackeray might be collecting them for a big hand. When it was his turn, Bond discarded a 6 of Characters near his side of the table. Sure enough, he noticed that the tile had mysteriously disappeared a few minutes later!

Thackeray went out for three points. He had a Semi-Pure hand, which meant that it was made up entirely of one suit with the exception of a Pong of Winds or Dragons—in this case a Pong of West Winds. Woo had thrown the winning discard, so he owed Thackeray

$1800, and the others paid him $900. Bond saw that Thackeray's revealed hand contained a Pong of the 6 of Characters.

It was agreed that they should stand, stretch, and refill their drinks in-between the Rounds. Thackeray had polished off a third of the bottle of vodka. Bond and Woo stepped up to the bar and ordered doubles. Bond took a moment to look around the room. The albino brothers were gone.

"I told you he wins a lot," Woo whispered. "I think I will lose more money than usual, uh huh?"

"T.Y., there are two things I don't like about that man," whispered Bond.

"What?"

"He's a lousy drunk, and I believe the bastard's cheating."

SEVEN

JADE DRAGON

THE GAME RESUMED WITH THE SOUTH WIND ROUND. THACKERAY, AS THE East Wind seat, was dealer. Bond was determined to verify his suspicion that the man was a cheat. He recalled what he knew about Thackeray. The man had been a stage magician when he was younger. He might very well be adept at sleight-of-hand and parlour tricks. He was probably palming discarded tiles from the table as he reached over them to draw a tile from the wall. The big question was, why would he cheat? He was very wealthy. He didn't need the money. Or did he? Could the obliteration of his Board of Directors have left his company in a bad state? Did the impending mainland takeover of Hong Kong have something to do with it? The alcohol, the cheating, and his belligerent manner all added up to something inherently reckless about him.

Bond drew a very good hand. His first discard was a lone East Wind tile. He had two Pongs and the possibility of one more. He was determined to find a way to beat Thackeray at his own game. To come out and accuse him of cheating would be unacceptable. Bond needed to gain Thackeray's confidence, not alienate him! If Bond caused a scene here in the casino, he might blow his cover and permanently botch the mission. He would have to find a way to cheat, too. As play progressed, he examined every angle. He didn't have the sleight-of-hand ability that Thackeray had, so that was out of the question. Perhaps at the next break he could enlist Woo's help.

Thackeray went out with a lucrative five points: three points for four Pongs, one point for holding no Flowers, and one point for a Pong of East Winds, matching his seat. Bond scanned the discarded tiles, looking for the East Wind tile he had discarded at the beginning of the game and didn't see it. Thackeray had to have palmed it somehow. Poor Woo threw the winning discard, so had to pay $3200. The others counted out chips worth $1600. Woo was no longer smiling.

The seat/Wind assignments did not change for the next hand. Now that the enormity of the dollar value for each hand was sinking in, a certain tension enveloped the entire room. Spectators were less animated and chatty. Whereas *mahjong* was usually a noisy, social game, this one had become deadly serious.

Sinclair won the hand on a self-pick with two points. The other players had to pay him $800 each.

Woo became the dealer for the next hand, which ended dead. The hand was played again, and this time Thackeray won small with two points on Sinclair's discard. Sinclair had to pay $800, the others $400 each.

Sinclair dealt the next hand. Woo got lucky and went out with three points on a self-pick. Everyone paid him $1600, which brought the smile back to his face.

Bond got the deal next and was determined to get through the rest of the South Round quickly so he could discuss his strategy with Woo. Thackeray won again, this time with three points on a self-pick. He was paid $1600 by each player.

They were halfway through the game. Bond had lost an enormous amount of money. He and Woo ordered doubles at the bar.

"What have we got into, James?" Woo said, shaking his head. "I did not expect to lose this badly."

"I have a plan," Bond said. "Let's go outside and get some fresh air." The two men excused themselves.

Thackeray said, "Don't be long." He was sitting alone, sipping his vodka on the rocks. Despite his winnings, he wasn't smiling. In fact, he looked downright miserable.

Outside, Bond said, "I don't get it. Why is he so morose? He's just won a few thousand dollars and he's acting as if it's his last day on earth."

"Thackeray very private man," Woo said. "He has no friends or family from what I can tell. I wonder if someone close to him was killed by bomb at restaurant?"

"Well, we've got to beat him. He's definitely cheating. He was a stage magician when he was young, and obviously knows sleight-of-hand. He's palming tiles he wants from the dead pile. I'm going to need your help."

"Sure, James. What you want me to do?"

"Listen very carefully. You're going to have to throw me some tiles that I need, and I'm going to give you some signals to indicate what they are. You have to watch me closely."

"All right."

"I'm going to scratch areas on the left side of my face to indicate that I need tiles with numbers 1 to 4. If I scratch the left side of my nose, I need a 1. If I scratch my cheekbone just under my eye, I need a 2. I'll scratch my ear lobe for a 3. And I'll scratch my neck for a 4. If I need a 5, I'll scratch the bridge of my nose. The same areas apply to the right side of my face for the numbers 6 to 9. The right side of my nose is a 6, the cheekbone is a 7, the ear lobe is an 8, and the neck is a 9. Got it?"

"Okay. What about suits?"

"Immediately after I give you one of my scratching signals, I'll take a drink. If I take one sip, I need Circles. If I take two sips, I need Sticks. If I take three sips, I need Characters."

Woo repeated all of this to make sure he had it.

"For the special tiles, I'll rub my eyes as if I have a headache if I need a Red Dragon. If I cough twice, I need a Green Dragon. If I sigh heavily, I need a White Dragon. If I need Winds, I'll light a cigarette. I'll place the cigarette on the ashtray with the butt pointing to the player corresponding to the Wind I need. For instance, if I need an

East Wind tile, I'll point the butt towards the player who is currently the East seat. Got it?"

"That is brilliant, James! We will win good, uh huh?"

"Well, we'll see. It still depends on the luck of the draw and if you even have the tiles I need, but this might give us an advantage. I may be winning on your discards, so you'll have to pay out a little more to me. I'll make sure you get it back."

"No problem, James."

"Come on, let's get back in there."

The West Round began with Thackeray as the East seat and dealer for the third time. Bond got a good hand. He had a Pong of the 3 of Circles, a Pair of the 2 of Sticks, a Pair of East Wind tiles, and a Pair of South Wind tiles. During play, Bond nonchalantly scratched his left cheekbone, then took two sips from his martini. Amazingly, Woo had the 2 of Sticks, and he threw it. Bond said "Pong" and took it. He luckily drew another East Wind tile later, and managed to form another Pong on his own. He just needed a Pair to complete his hand. He had a single White Dragon and an 8 of Characters. Bond let out a sigh, but apparently Woo didn't have a White Dragon tile. Bond went for the other one and scratched his right ear lobe, then took three sips from his drink. Woo discarded an 8 of Characters. Bond went out with three points for his all-Pong hand. Woo had to pay $1600, the others $800.

Thackeray won the second hand with another Full House. He had three points for a Semi-Pure hand, one point from a self-picked winning tile, and one point for holding a Flower tile matching his seat. Everyone had to pay him $3200!

Woo looked quite pale after that one. Sinclair took up the deal, but the result was a dead hand. It was dealt again, and this time Woo got lucky with another small win. He went out with two points. It was a chicken hand, but he self-picked the winning tile and had a Flower matching his seat. Everyone paid him $800.

Bond became the dealer for the last hand in the West Round. His hand was so bad that his signal system was useless. Thackeray managed to win with three points. He self-picked from the wall (one point), had four Chows (one point), and no Flowers (one point). Everyone paid him $1600.

During the break before the last Round of the game, Woo whispered to Bond, "Is your plan going to work?"

Bond replied, "It has to this time. It's the damnedest game—even cheating depends on luck! In a situation that involves gambling, I never trust luck. I try to get by without it. But this is one time we need all the luck we can get. Just stick to what we agreed. I'm going for broke this time."

The North Round began with Thackeray as East and dealer. Bond drew a 4 Red Flower, which matched his seat. That was one point straight away! The rest of his hand was very promising. He had a complete Pong of Green Dragons, a Red Dragon, and a White Dragon. If he could get two more of either of the Red or White Dragons and one of the other, he could go out with what was called a "Semi-Big Dragon" hand (two Dragon Pongs and a pair of the other Dragon), worth three points. If he could make the third Dragon a complete Pong, the hand would be worth six points. He also needed to complete another Pong or Kong out of some Circles or Sticks he held.

Play progressed uneventfully until Bond drew a Red Dragon from the wall. Now all he needed was a third Red Dragon and at least one White Dragon.

At the first opportunity, Bond rubbed his eyes. Woo acknowledged the signal with a slight nod of his head. A moment later, Bond sighed heavily. Thackeray looked up at Bond and said, "What's the matter, Mr. Bond? Are we boring you?"

"Oh, no, I'm starting to feel the jet lag," he explained. "I just arrived today."

When Thackeray reached across the table to draw from the wall, Bond noticed that the man palmed another tile. It was now just a matter of time before one of them went out. Bond gave Woo the signals for a 6 of Sticks and the 3 of Circles, which might complete his third Pong.

Woo did a great job of pretending to agonize over what tile to discard. He threw a Red Dragon and Bond called "Pong!" Now if he could get the White one . . ."

Play continued around the table until Sinclair discarded a White Dragon. Thackeray immediately said, "Pong!" Damn! Thackeray had the other three White Dragons and now there was no way to make a Pair with his single tile. Bond threw the useless tile when it was his turn to discard. There was still hope—he had two Dragon Pongs, worth a point each.

Thackeray Ponged again, this time with a 2 of Characters. Come on, Woo, Bond willed. Throw something good! It didn't happen. From the look on Woo's face, he was troubled by the lack of help he could give Bond.

Bond drew the 4 Blue Flower from the wall, adding another point to his possible score. On his next turn, he drew the badly needed 3 of Circles. Now all he lacked was to make a Pair out of the two single tiles he had—the 4 of Characters or the 6 of Sticks. Bond gave the signals for the two tiles and Woo took a sip from his drink. On Bond's discard, though, Thackeray called "Pong!" again. He was ready to go out as well.

Woo drew from the wall and discarded the 4 of Characters. Bond called "Out!" and displayed his hand of four points—two Dragon Pongs (one point each) and two Flowers matching his seat. Woo had to pay $3200, the others $1600.

Woo became the dealer and Bond got a terrible hand. Amazingly, Woo went out very quickly for two points on Thackeray's discard. He had a chicken hand, but he also had no Flower tiles, and a Pong of East Winds (matching his seat). Thackeray paid the $800 as if it was charity, and the others paid $400.

Sinclair got the deal next and the hand ended in a draw. It was re-dealt and Bond got another terrible hand. If he was going to beat Thackeray, he had only three more hands in which to do so. It wasn't to be this time, for Sinclair went out with Woo's discard. He got three points for holding four Pongs. Woo paid $1600, the others $800.

Bond got the deal. Bond couldn't believe the hand he drew. Of the thirteen tiles, ten of them were Circles which could easily be turned into sets. He signalled to Woo that he needed Circles. The problem was that he was only allowed to Chow from the player on his left, and that was Sinclair. Nevertheless, a chicken hand would be all right if the entire hand was made up of Circles. That would be a Pure Hand, which was worth six points.

Thackeray discarded one of the needed Circles. "Pong!" said Bond. A little later, Sinclair threw a tile Bond needed. "Chow!" he called. Thackeray looked at him. Now everyone knew Bond had a chicken hand. Thackeray's eyes were burning with curiosity. Bond was holding no Flowers, so he had at least one point. What else could he be holding?

Thackeray eventually discarded a Circle tile that Bond needed and he triumphantly called, "Out!" Thackeray raised his eyebrows when he saw Bond's Pure Hand.

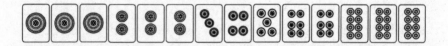

Including the point for no Flowers, Bond had a total of seven points—a Double Full House. It was biggest win of the game so far. This time, Thackeray wasn't so pleased about turning over $6400 to Bond. The others had to pay $3200 each.

Since he'd won the hand, Bond kept the deal for the last hand of the game. It started off poorly, for he had a mixture of Sticks and Circles, and one Green Dragon. He wasn't sure what to go for. When he drew another Green Dragon from the wall, he wondered how possible it would be to get a special winning hand known as a "Jade Dragon." To do this he would need a Pong of the Green Dragons, with the remainder of his hand made up entirely of Pongs of Sticks.

Bond gave Woo the signal for Sticks and coughed twice for the Green Dragon. Woo smiled when he threw the tile and Bond called "Pong!" Now all he needed was three Pongs of Sticks. He already had Pairs of 2s and 7s. He slowly got rid of the Circles, and eventually drew another Pair of the 8 of Sticks. Woo discarded a 2 of Sticks and Bond Ponged.

Thackeray clumsily knocked over some tiles from the wall when he reached across the table. Bond knew the man had dropped a tile he had palmed, but Thackeray quickly covered it and rebuilt the wall without anyone seeing the tiles. He was getting careless. The alcohol was finally getting to him. What made him so desperate to win? Was it the feeling of power he desired? Bond had certainly seen it before in men like Hugo Drax, who had cheated at cards for no reason except to satisfy his own need to prove to himself he could do it.

Sinclair discarded an 8 of Sticks and Bond Ponged again. He needed a 7 and either a 9 or 1 of Sticks to complete the hand.

Woo discarded the 7 of Sticks and Bond Ponged. He had four Pongs revealed. Everyone knew all he needed was a Pair to go out. It was Thackeray's turn, and for the first time he hesitated. Spectators around the room looked on in anticipation. Bond could very well have a Maximum Hand. Thackeray drew from the wall and looked at the tile. He considered it, unsure whether to keep or discard it. He finally threw it down on the table. It was a 1 of Sticks.

Bond picked it up and coolly said, "Out." He revealed his hand and said, "Jade Dragon. Maximum Hand."

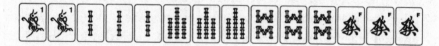

Thackeray's own hand trembled when he handed Bond chips totalling $19,200. Sinclair's face had gone white as well—he had to pay $9600. Woo gladly handed over his $9600. Bond thought the man's smile would split his face.

Thackeray stood up slowly. He turned to Bond and said with a thicker slur to his voice than usual, "You have luck on your side, Mr. Bond." He glanced at Woo. "Or . . . something." He then turned and walked towards the archway leading to the washroom. Bond collected his chips and turned them in to the cashier who was standing eagerly near the table. He and Woo combined their cash and put it in a brown bag, which Woo stuffed into his jacket. They were ready to leave, but Bond wanted to speak with Thackeray one more time and confirm that he would see him at the EurAsia press conference on the 24th. The man was taking an awfully long time.

Three young Chinese men in business suits stepped into the room through the red curtains. They had a look in their eyes that Bond recognized only from years of experience. He thought later that a younger, greener agent would have been killed immediately.

Bond leaped at Woo, pulling him down behind the bar as the men revealed large butcher-knives and meat cleavers they had concealed in their jackets. With lightning speed, they began to attack everyone in the room. They swung their blades like swords, slashing and chopping whatever piece of flesh got in their way. The room filled with the screams of their victims, and there was blood everywhere. Sinclair went down, as did the spectators and bartender. It was over as quickly as it had begun. The men turned and ran from the room.

"Are you all right?" Bond shouted to Woo.

"Yes!" Woo sounded stunned.

Bond jumped up. "Find Thackeray!" he ordered, then ran from the room. The crowded casino had become a scene of frenzied panic. People were screaming and running for the doors. Bond scanned the crowd, looking for the three thugs in suits. They had slipped out. What was that all about? Were they after Thackeray? Was it an assassination attempt? Whatever it was, they had succeeded in killing or maiming at least a dozen people.

Bond returned to the gambling room. Woo was standing in the archway leading to the washroom. It was a gruesome mess. Bodies were strewn about, drenched in blood. Sinclair had been killed. Not everyone was dead—two or three men were crawling about crying for help. There were a few fingers and hands lying in puddles of blood. The killers had dropped the weapons in the room before fleeing.

"Thackeray gone," Woo said, bewildered.

"What?"

"No one in washroom!"

Bond went into it. The two cubicles were empty, and there was no window. How the hell did he get out? Bond examined the back wall of one of the cubicles. He knocked on it and determined that it was hollow.

"It's a trap door," he said to Woo. He carefully felt the seams of the wall and finally found a minute depression. There was a tiny toggle switch there which, when flipped, activated a sliding door in the wall.

"Come on!" Bond commanded. He and Woo entered the dark corridor and ran twenty metres to another door. It opened easily—to the outside. They were behind the hotel, looking at a dark alleyway. Thackeray was nowhere in sight.

"What the hell . . . ?" Bond muttered.

They ran to the front of the casino. It was night now, and the neon from the building lit up the street. A black sedan tore out of the car park. Bond recognized the three killers in the front seat of the car. He started to draw his Walther PPK, but realized he had left it at the boat. The car sped away into the night.

The sound of approaching police sirens told them they should leave. "Come on, James," Woo said. "There is nothing we can do. Let's go back to boat."

Bond nodded.

They hailed a taxi, went to the outskirts of town, walked quickly to the old pier, hopped on the Viking 66, and woke up J.J. On the journey back to Hong Kong, they discussed what had happened.

"Were they Triad?" Bond asked.

Woo said, "Possibly. Probably. It was their method. I spoke to guard before we left. The men picked up their weapons from kitchen before entering room. That is how they do it, so they do not have to bring weapons to scene of crime. They take whatever is available nearby."

"Were they after Thackeray?"

"It seem like it."

"He must have known they were coming. Why else would he run like that? How did he know there was a secret escape route from that room? What the hell is going on?"

"You tell me, James. I am tired."

Bond also felt fatigued. It was nearly 10:00 p.m. He felt the jet-lag. He would go to his hotel and sleep until late morning.

"You saved my life, James," Woo said. "Now I owe you big time."

Bond shook his head. "Forget that *maijiang* business, T.Y. I wasn't doing you a favour, I was doing my job."

"Still, I am very grateful and indebted," Woo said with great sincerity.

Bond smiled. "Don't worry about it. Be thankful we're returning to Hong Kong with all of our body parts."

Woo grinned widely and held up the brown bag. "Not only that, we return with helluva lot of money, uh huh?"

EIGHT

PRIVATE DANCER

ZERO MINUS EIGHT: 23 JUNE 1997, 2:00 P.M.

James Bond slept until just before noon. He exercised, then ate a hearty brunch in one of the hotel's several restaurants, the Mandarin Grill. The Grill sported green decor on the walls, mirrors on rectangular columns, and a couple of large aquariums. Bond knew that the concept of *feng shui*, the art and science of positioning man-made structures in harmony with the vital cosmic energy coursing through the earth, was taken seriously in the East. Sometimes entire buildings had to be adjusted slightly in accordance with instructions from professional *feng shui* masters. Fish tanks were in abundance in restaurants, as these improved the *feng shui*. It was obvious that the Mandarin Grill was one of Hong Kong's most carefully planned restaurants. Like the Man Wah, it was pleasantly subdued and quiet—the perfect place to collect his thoughts. Bond had ordered scrambled eggs and toast, with freshly squeezed orange juice and now felt refreshed and alert.

Standing outside the Man Mo Temple in the Sheung Wan, or Western District, of the island, Bond marvelled at the city around him. The people, mostly Chinese, seemed oblivious to the historic event that would occur in eight days. Everyone went about their business completely ignoring the huge dragon to the north that was breathing down their necks. But Bond wondered what would happen to some of Hong Kong's famous landmarks, such as the temple in front of him. Following the tourists, Bond stepped inside. The rich interior altar contained polished brass and pewter ritual vessels and a pair of shining brass deer symbolizing longevity and wealth. Brass statues of the Eight Immortals stood in front of the altar, each representing the different conditions of life: male, female, lord, peasant, age, youth, poverty, and wealth. A smaller room to the right contained images of Buddhist deities like Kwan Yum, Wong Tai Sin, and Kwan Ti, the god Mo himself. The temple was dedicated to two deities, Man and Mo, the first being the god of literature who controlled the destinies of mandarins and civil servants; the latter being the god of martial arts and war, who was the guardian deity of the Hong Kong Police but was favoured just as much by the underworld. All day long, worshippers dropped in for a fast communication with the gods. Bond stood fascinated watching people use the *chim*. These numbered bamboo sticks were used to answer important questions concerning business, family or fortune. The narrow canister was shaken until a stick fell out; its number then used to predict the outcome. Of course, one could always try again if the answer wasn't favourable!

"You have question to ask gods, *Ling Ling Chat*? "

Bond turned toward the whisper and saw T.Y. Woo's smiling face. He was right on time.

Bond whispered in reply, "T.Y., I'm not sure the gods would appreciate the questions I have. And I probably wouldn't like the answers, either. Come on."

Bond and Woo left the temple and walked down Ladder Street from Hollywood Road. It was typical of the steep lanes paved with stone slabs for the convenience of sedan-chair bearers. They stepped down to Upper Lascar Row, which had once housed foreign seamen known as lascars. The lane was lined with renowned bric-a-brac and antiques dealers. Also called "Cat Street," it got the nickname from the accompanying brothels.

Woo led him to a four-storey building with a red façade surrounding picture windows. The legend "Woo Antiques and Curios

Shop" was set into the façade, and the windows revealed a clutter of expensive antiques and *objets d'art*. Two angry Chinese dragon-lions stood on either side of the single door, symbolically guarding the shop from evil.

"This is where J.J. and I live," Woo said. "This is safe house." Bond followed him inside and found J.J. polishing an antique bronze opium pipe. He looked up and nodded with a grin, then went back to work. The place was crammed with everything from inexpensive knick-knacks to fine jade figurines and ivory *objets d'art*. He led Bond to the back of the store and showed him the code to be punched into a numbered button pad on the wall. This unlocked a door, which revealed a set of stairs leading up to a large four-bedroomed flat. Bond would never have guessed such a large space could exist within the narrow building he had seen from the outside.

Woo poured two glasses of cold Tsingtao beer, and they sat down at a table near the kitchen.

"I want to meet the Triad Dragon Head today, T.Y.," Bond said.

He rubbed his chin thoughtfully. "Will not be easy. Li Xu Nan very private man. Sometimes he can be found at one of his clubs, like I told you. He goes to Zipper a lot."

"What are my chances of finding him there today?"

"Fifty-fifty," Woo said. "Either he is there or he is not, uh huh?"

"T.Y., do you think the Triad is really involved in all this? What do you think about Thackeray's behaviour last night?"

Woo shrugged. "Thackeray is hiding something. Maybe this press conference tomorrow will tell all. As for Triad, we know they somehow got into EurAsia's shipping business."

"Tell me more about them?"

"Triad members believe they are on the right side of law and honour. You know, the original Triad was founded after seventeenth-century overthrow of Ming dynasty by Manchus? Their motto was 'Restore Ming, Overthrow Ch'ing.' The name came from primal triad of Heaven, Earth, and Man. Members were like your Robin Hoods, taking wealth from rich and giving to poor. Triads originally were symbols of nationalism. Sun Yat-sen was Triad." Woo sighed. "Today they have degenerated into criminal underground. They put squeeze on many businesses. They control prostitution and illegal immigration. One of their big enterprises is emigrating young girls to West with promise of freedom and prosperity. In reality, girls become prisoners in brothels and are forced to work their way out of enslavement for several years before they are finally set free. Their largest business is drugs. They control maybe 80 per cent of world's drug traffic. You think Central America is bad? They are peanuts compared to Triads."

"Where do the drugs come from?"

"From China, Thailand, Laos, Burma. Many places. Golden Triangle in Yunnan Province is major source."

Bond nodded. "What will happen to Triads once China takes over Hong Kong?"

Woo grinned. "There are some in Hong Kong who believe Triads will become more powerful after takeover, not only because they are so ingrained in our culture, but because they will find reason to reach back to their beginnings as political activists."

"They're anti-Communist, then?"

"Most definitely. If China decides to change Hong Kong completely and destroy democratic freedoms we have here, Triads will be first to oppose them. And they will be formidable foes. Other possibility is that they will corrupt China and continue as they are."

"Triads are outlawed in China, aren't they?"

"Yes, but they exist. Hong Kong, though, is centre of all Triad activity in entire world."

"The analogy would be as Sicily is to the Mafia?"

"I suppose so, yes. You know, Triads are illegal in Hong Kong, too. Just being a member is illegal. If you possess any Triad materials you can go to jail, uh huh? That is why they are so secret."

"I think I'd better see some Triads first hand, T.Y. Where is this nightclub?"

"In Tsim Sha Tsui East. Kowloon. The Zipper. Big fancy nightclub, very popular. Very expensive. Japanese businessmen especially like it. They have very beautiful girls working there."

"Are they prisoners of the Triads as well?"

"Some might be," Woo said.

Bond stood up. "Enough talk. Let's go. When we get there, T.Y., I want to go in alone. I'm curious to see how a *gweilo* is treated there."

During the Vietnam War, Lockhart Road in the Wanchai District of Hong Kong was immortalized as the haven for servicemen on R & R. This nightlife had diversified into other areas and was no longer completely isolated in Wanchai. Tsim Sha Tsui, one of the premier tourist areas of Kowloon, provided some of the flavour of the rowdy old days. It was virtually the Times Square of Hong Kong. There was a mixture of British-style pubs, hostess clubs, karaoke bars, and noisy disco bars. There was the famous Bottoms Up club, a tame topless bar featuring waitresses who looked as if they'd been there since the place opened in the early seventies. There was the Adam's Apple, where half-naked hostesses pretended to make scintillating conversation while one drank. Hong Kong had something that appealed to the best and the worst in everyone. In theory, strip clubs as such were illegal in Hong Kong—if girls removed their clothes, they did it privately out of public view.

Bond found the Zipper easily. It was a huge place, spanning an entire block of Tsim Sha Tsui East, an area of Kowloon that had more recently developed into an expensive tourist trap. Other high-class nightclubs, such as the Club B Boss and the China City Club, were also in the vicinity. By 6:00 p.m., even before the sun had set, the brightly coloured neon of the area rivalled anything in Las Vegas. There was a buzz of excitement in the air, and he could understand how the area had achieved such a glamorous reputation.

Bond casually approached the front door of the Zipper. Two Indian men wearing turbans stood outside the door. He heard loud American soft rock. The Zipper was a hostess club, which meant that patrons could "buy" time with a hostess. She could sit and have a drink with him, dance with him, talk with him . . . whatever they happened to arrange. What went on in private rooms was negotiated. Uninitiated visitors were often taken advantage of and overcharged. Simply having a drink with a hostess could be very expensive. Prostitution itself was not illegal in Hong Kong. Brothels and streetwalking were against the law, but straightforward solicitations and private arrangements between adults were legal.

He stepped inside and paid a cover charge of 500 Hong Kong dollars, which included the first two drinks. Four lovely Chinese women in *cheongsams* sang out in English, "Welcome!" Then he entered a dark red room. It was large enough to feature a dance floor in the centre, and had at least fifty tables and/or divan-coffee table combinations scattered around its perimeter. The music was loud and a little irritating. A Chinese man flanked by three gorgeous women was on the dance floor, lip-synching an American rock tune in the karaoke style. The place was not crowded, but it was very early in the evening. From what he could see, the hostesses were of various nationalities, and were all young and attractive. There were a few Japanese businessmen snuggling with hostesses on divans. Two or three Caucasian men were sitting at tables with female companions. The place was devoid of any other clientele, but according to Woo, the club would be jam-packed by 9:00 p.m.

Bond walked to the far side of the room and sat down at a table. He could see the entire club from this vantage point, including the archway leading to the front lobby. T.Y. had said that if Li Xu Nan showed up at all, it would be in the early evening. Bond would just have to spend some money and wait and see. Within seconds, a lovely Chinese hostess approached his table. She, too, was wearing a *cheongsam,* high heels, and a smile. She sat down next to Bond and pulled her chair very close to his. Before she said a word, her bare leg emerged from the slit in the dress and pressed against his.

"Hello," she said. "What's your name?"

"James," Bond said, returning her smile. He couldn't help feeling a bit ridiculous in this situation. He played along, pretending to be the British tourist looking for a good time.

"Well, James," she said, "would you like a companion this evening?"

Surprisingly, her accent sounded American.

"Perhaps," Bond said. "Where are you from?"

"If you want to continue talking, it's 240 Hong Kong dollars for a drink and a quarter of an hour," she said with a straight face. Then she smiled again. "You're very handsome."

Bond said, "All right, I'd like a vodka martini. Please shake it—don't stir it. And get whatever you'd like." He paid her the cash.

The girl squeezed his arm. "I'll be right back, sweetheart."

He watched her walk towards the bar. She was probably in her late twenties, Bond thought; perhaps a bit older than some of the other girls he saw soliciting business in the place. She had straight black shoulder-length hair, was unusually tall, and had long, wonderful legs. She returned, set down the drinks, and then sat beside him in extremely close proximity once again.

"I'm back," she said dreamily.

"I see that," Bond said. "What's your name?"

"Veronica. What's yours?"

"I said it was James."

"Oh, yeah, you told me that," she said, then laughed. "Sorry, I'm a little out of it."

"Veronica" was either a little drunk or high on something else.

"Where are you from?" Bond asked again.

"Oh, you're wondering about the way I talk," she said. "I spent twelve years in California, living with my aunt and uncle. I went to grade school, middle school, and high school there. But I was born here in Hong Kong, and I'll probably die here in Hong Kong."

"Why do you say that?"

She shrugged. "I can't get out. I'm a Hong Kong citizen. You're English, aren't you? Why won't your country let us go there?"

Bond nodded and said, "It is pretty shameful, isn't it? England has watched over you for a hundred and fifty years and now she's turning her back on you. I know . . . I know."

"What are you doing in Hong Kong?" she asked, taking a sip from some kind of frozen daiquiri.

"I'm a journalist. I'm here to cover the handover next week."

"I see. You live in England?"

"Jamaica, actually, though I'm originally from England."

"Wow, Jamaica. I've never been there."

"Most people think it's not what it used to be. It's fairly dangerous in some areas. I happen to love it, though."

She ran her fingers along his chin and looked at him seductively. Her brown almond eyes were lovely. There was intelligence behind them, and Bond felt sorry for her. He wondered if she knew Li Xu Nan, and if she was a member of the Triad. It was highly likely. Woo had told him that most of the girls who worked as hostesses were prostitutes involved with these organizations. The Triads "protected" them, even though they blatantly exploited them.

"Veronica," Bond said. "That's not your real name, is it?"

She smirked. "What do you think?"

"I thought so. Listen, can I interview you about the changeover? I'd love to have the perspective of a woman like you."

She laughed. "What, your paper will print the views of a nightclub hostess?"

"Why not? You're as much a Hong Kong citizen as a wealthy banker."

"Don't count on that," she replied. "Wealthy bankers can buy their way out of the colony. Many already have. Thousands of people have managed to leave over the past few years. With what's happened in the last couple of weeks, people who had decided to stay are now considering getting out. There is a lot of fear in the air."

"Fear of China?"

"Yes," she said. "You know that troops are lining up across the border from the New Territories?"

Bond nodded.

"Everyone is afraid that on July the first, the troops will pour in and take command of the city. There is going to be some violence."

"China has promised that Hong Kong will remain as it is for at least fifty years," Bond reminded her.

She scoffed. "Do you really believe that? Does the world believe that? They've already demanded changes in our governmental structure. The Legislative Council will be disbanded, you wait and see. They won't have any power. There will be a crackdown on places like this. Anything that appeals to the vices of westerners will be banned—I know it will happen."

"But Hong Kong is Asia's cash cow," Bond said. "China cannot ignore that. They need Hong Kong. I honestly believe that they would lose face if they changed Hong Kong drastically."

Bond was a little surprised to find himself having an intelligent conversation about politics with a nightclub hostess. She was not only articulate, but had eyes that could melt him if he allowed them to.

"Hey, listen," she said, "would you like a private dance? We can go back to one of those rooms. We'd have complete privacy."

"Maybe later," he said. "I'm enjoying our conversation."

She looked at him out of the corner of her eye. "You're not like most men who come in here. Usually by now their hands are all over me."

Bond gave her a slight bow and said dryly, "I'm an English gentleman."

She laughed. "I can see that. You're also very handsome . . . James." She leaned closer and whispered in his ear "And I'd like to see what's in your pants, James."

It was a typical crude solicitation from this type of woman. For some reason, though, when she said it to Bond he became aroused. The girl was extremely sexy. He chalked it up to her genuine intelligence, usually conspicuously lacking in bar girls.

"Aren't I one of those *gweilo* who are treated with such disdain?" he asked.

"I lived in America for a few years, remember? I like *gweilo*."

"How much drinking have you done today?" he asked her.

"This is my third drink, James," she said. "Why, do I seem drunk?"

"You seem a little high on something."

She shrugged and sniffed, unwittingly revealing what her vice might be. "A girl's gotta do what she's gotta do to get through the working day, you know?" For a moment, she stared into her empty glass. Bond said nothing.

"I tell you what," she said, "I'm going to re-fill our drinks, all right?"

Bond said, "Fine." He gave her some more cash. She ran her fingers through his hair as she stood up, then sauntered back to the bar.

He needed to ask her about Triads. Would she talk? She might open up to him if he played his cards right.

When she came back with new drinks, Bond asked her, "Would you leave Hong Kong if you could?"

"Are you kidding? I don't want to live in a Communist country!"

"Can't you go back to your relatives in California? Take up residence with them?"

She shook her head. "They aren't there anymore. They were killed in an automobile accident. Besides, my mother is here. She's sick. I have to take care of her."

"If you had the right papers for the two of you, you would get out?"

"Of course!"

"Is that why you're with a Triad?"

She blinked. "What did you say?"

"You *are* with a Triad, right?" he said. "Aren't most women who work in places like this members of Triads?"

"You've been watching too many Chow Yun-Fat movies," she said, obviously attempting to gloss over the truth.

"Come on, Veronica," he said. "The Triads are acting as lifeboats for people opposed to living in a Communist country. I know they are illegally helping people to emigrate to other countries. You believe they will get you out, or at the very least protect you from . . . whatever. Am I right?"

"I don't know what you're talking about."

"Veronica, you can trust me. I know you're vowed to secrecy, but you have nothing to worry about. I already know everything about it, you see. I know that Mr. Li Xu Nan is the Cho Kun of the Dragon Wing Society."

Her eyes widened. She couldn't believe what Bond had just said. She was stunned and afraid.

"Veronica, it's all right," Bond said earnestly. "Really."

"Sunni," she said.

"What?"

"That's my real name. I shouldn't be telling you this. I could get in a lot of trouble."

"Sunni?"

She nodded. "Sunni Pei."

"That's a pretty name."

She leaned closer again. "How about that private dance now?" She was attempting to change the subject and get back to business.

"Not yet, Sunni. I promise I'll pay you for a dance in a few minutes. But first I need a favour."

"I don't know . . ."

"I want to meet Mr. Li."

She shook her head almost violently. "That's impossible. No one meets the Cho Kun."

Bond was right. She *did* know him.

"Doesn't he come here every now and then? Will he come in here today?"

"I don't know . . . look, I don't know who you're talking about, anyway." She suddenly seemed very frightened. She looked around, hoping no one was near enough to hear what they were saying.

"Why not?" Bond asked. "Li Xu Nan is just another businessman."

Her jaw dropped. "Stop it! Be quiet!" she exclaimed in a whisper.

"You know him, don't you?"

"No," she said. "I know who he is, that's all. He comes in most afternoons. How do you know he's a Dragon Head?"

"I'm in the media," Bond said. "I have my sources."

She was shaking with fear now. Bond was afraid he might have gone too far, too soon.

"Look, Sunni," he said. "It's all right. You won't get into trouble. I want to interview him for my newspaper. I want to get his views on the handover and how it will affect his businesses. He can remain anonymous—it doesn't matter to me—all my headline has to read is: *Triad Leader Speaks Out.* It'll make a great story!"

"He will never admit being Cho Kun. Any association with a Triad is illegal in Hong Kong."

"I know that. I don't expect him to admit a thing."

"I don't know how I can help . . ."

"Just point him out to me when he comes in."

"He might not come in today."

"Well, I shall be here every day until he does. Now . . . how about that dance?"

When he said that, she smiled again. "You want to go to a private room?"

Bond nodded.

"It will cost you 1400 Hong Kong dollars."

"I'm sure it will be worth every penny," he said.

Sunni seemed to forget the subject of their earlier conversation. She stood up, took hold of his hand, and led him to one side of the club and into a small room. She shut the door and gestured for him to sit on a chair against the wall. She took his money and tucked it into a small purse she placed on the floor.

"Just relax and enjoy the show," she said. She punched a button on a tape deck set into the wall. Music with a beat filled the room.

Sunni Pei then began a slow, sensuous dance in front of Bond. She stared into his eyes the entire time, smiling every now and then. She moved well. She might have had professional dance training, but didn't need it for what she was doing. All she needed was sex appeal and attitude, and Sunni Pei had plenty of both.

Bond watched her, captivated. Never having gone in much for strippers, he admitted to himself that she was something special. Her beauty was extraordinary, though once again it was the intellect behind her seduction that made her so appealing. He found that he wasn't playing the British tourist in search of a good time anymore. He was really enjoying this.

Sunni deftly undid her *cheongsam* and removed it. Underneath she had on nothing but a black satin bra and matching bikini panties. Her navel was pierced with a small, thin gold ring. She slipped the straps of her bra off her shoulders, unsnapped it and tossed it into Bond's lap. She laughed. Her breasts were the size of apples, firm and natural. Her nipples were erect; she frankly enjoyed playing the exhibitionist. A few beats later, she pulled her black panties down and lifted one long leg out of them. She stepped gracefully out of them, then stood over Bond. Her legs spread wide, she straddled his lap and moved her breasts within inches of his face. He could smell her sweet skin, which was lightly damp with sweat, and Bond felt an urge to touch her.

She brought her face up close to Bond's, and blew lightly around his left ear. Her lips touched his, giving him a light kiss. "You're not supposed to touch me," she whispered, "but I'll let you anyway."

Not refusing the invitation, Bond reached up with both hands and softly ran his palms and fingertips over her back. He felt goosepimples rise on her shoulders. Her skin was unbelievably soft and smooth. He pulled her to a sitting position on his lap. She began to run her fingers through his hair and along the back of his neck; he did the same with his own hands on her body. Her eyes never left his.

When his hands found her breasts, she gave a slight purr, then she pressed her mouth on his. They kissed, their tongues exploring each other's mouths with curiosity and delight. She pushed her pelvis forward into his and felt his hardness there. He wanted her, but this was not the time or place. For the time being, though, he allowed the "dance" to work its wonders on him and take him along the river of fantasy that was her primary intention. She seemed to be displaying sincere affection for him. Sometimes these girls were so good at what they did that it was difficult to tell if they were acting or not. Bond's instincts told him that she was honestly interested in him. She was having a good time, too.

When the music ended, Sunni gave him one last quick kiss on the lips, then stood up. She found her underclothes and put them back on. Bond sat there, a little dazed. This woman would be a powerhouse in bed, he thought.

"Did you like that?" she finally asked.

"Quite," Bond said. "Thank you."

She held out her hand. He took it and stood up. "Come on, let's go back out . . . unless you want another dance?"

Bond smiled. "Another time, Sunni."

"Better call me Veronica," she warned.

"All right."

She put the *cheongsam* back on, then they went back into the club and resumed sitting at their table.

"Can I refill your drink?" she asked. Bond told her yes. As she got up, she whispered, "Don't look now, but your man is sitting over there near the bar."

Sunni walked towards the bar and Bond glanced over. Three or four tables were set inside a small section surrounded by a rail, apparently a "reserved" VIP area. At one of these tables sat a Chinese man in a business suit. On either side of him were two larger men in suits—the bodyguards.

From this distance, it was difficult to tell how old Li Xu Nan was. He appeared to be fairly young, perhaps in his early- to mid-thirties. He was sipping a drink and conversing with one of the hostesses.

Sunni brought back another martini and sat down.

"So that's Mr. Li," Bond said. "He seems young."

Sunni shrugged. "What did you expect? An ageing don like in the Mafia?"

The door to the nightclub opened and three men entered. It wasn't until they entered the private section, removed their hats, and sat down at Li's table that Bond recognized them. Or rather, he recognized two of them.

All three men had white hair and pinkish-white skin. They all wore sunglasses. They were the albino Chinese he had seen in Macau! Now *that* was interesting!

"Do you know those three men?" Bond asked.

Sunni glanced over at them. "No. They're strange, aren't they? Albino brothers, it looks like."

"That's unusual in this part of the world, isn't it?"

"I should say so." She turned back to him. "Sure you don't want another dance?"

"Later, Sunn—Veronica." Bond's attention was focused on Li and his visitors. He appeared to be giving them instructions of some kind. Who were these three men? Members of the Dragon Wing Society? Musclemen? Even though their backs were to him, Bond was able to discern some visual differences. They were each of different builds and weights. He thought of them as Tom, Dick, and Harry. Tom was the heaviest, probably about 240 pounds. Dick was Bond's size—tall and slim. Harry was smaller in stature and the most animated.

After a few minutes, the three albinos nodded, stood, and left the nightclub. Li remained sitting at the table with his two bodyguards.

Bond removed a business card and pen from his pocket. He wrote a message on the back.

"Sunni," he said, "please deliver this to Mr. Li." He handed her 1000 Hong Kong dollars. "I appreciate everything you've done for me this evening." He gave her another 2000 dollars. "And this is for the dance."

She looked at the money in disbelief. "James, thank you! You don't . . ."

"Hush," he said. "You're wonderful. You're beautiful and a pleasure to talk to. I hope to see you again soon."

She nodded and said, "I do, too." She kissed him on the cheek, stood up and walked slowly to Li Xu Nan's table with Bond's card in hand.

NINE

INTERVIEW WITH A DRAGON

SUNNI APPROACHED LI XU NAN CAUTIOUSLY AND SUBMISSIVELY HANDED him the card. He looked at it and said something to her. She pointed to Bond. Li's gaze shifted over to him. It was cold and calculating. Bond could see that he could not believe that the Englishman would have the audacity to make contact with him. Li barked an order to one of his thugs. The large man nodded and walked across the dance floor towards Bond.

When he got to Bond's table, he said, "Mr. Li say you got big nose. But he also say you got big balls. He will talk to you. Come to table."

Bond followed the man to Li's table. The other bodyguard held out a chair and Bond sat across from the Cho Kun of the Dragon Wing Society. Li Xu Nan had neatly cut black hair and cold brown eyes. There was a two-inch scar above his left eyebrow, which managed to put years on his baby-faced features. With the appropriate clothing and posture, Li Xu Nan could pass either for a man of forty or a youngster of nineteen. Regardless of his age, he exuded an aura of self-confidence, charisma, and great power.

Bond spoke in Cantonese. "Mr. Li, I am grateful for this opportunity to talk to you." He imagined that Li Xu Nan probably did not like to speak English.

"Your card says you would like to interview me for a story about

Hong Kong businesses and the handover to China," replied Li in Cantonese. He had a pleasant voice. "I do not usually do this, Mr. Bond. If you were from a British paper I would have you thrown out of the club. But I have some things I would like to say. My name will be kept out of this?"

"Absolutely, if that's what you prefer," Bond said. He produced a small notepad and pen from his jacket pocket. "Let's begin with your business. I know you're a successful man here, but I'm not totally familiar with everything you do. Can you enlighten me?"

The man lit a cigarette and offered one to Bond who politely refused. Then Li began to talk. He clearly thought carefully about every phrase before he spoke.

"I am a businessman, Mr. Bond. My father, Li Chen Tam, was also a businessman. I inherited most of my enterprises from him. He came to Hong Kong in 1926 as a young boy, a refugee from the civil wars in China at that time. He worked very hard from humble beginnings. His first business was selling dumplings on the street. He fortunately joined forces with colleagues and created his own restaurant. A little later, he and his partners established a currency exchange operation. He got into the entertainment industry in the 1950s, just when Hong Kong became the holiday spot for American GIs fighting the Korean War. It was with the opening of nightclubs and more restaurants that he made his fortune. By the time he died, he was a millionaire."

"And all of it is yours, now?"

"That is correct."

"Are you the only son?"

"I am the only son," Li said.

"And I suppose your son will inherit from you?"

"I am not married."

Bond scribbled notes as the man spoke. He played the role of journalist well.

"How do you think the changeover will affect your business?" he asked.

"It is difficult to say. There are optimists who believe that things will remain the same. I hate the communists, but I have to retain a positive outlook towards my own future. We all hope that the mainland Chinese will gain a new perspective on Hong Kong once they are in power."

"What do you mean?"

"Hong Kong is very capitalist. That goes against the very nature of China's doctrines. At the same time, Hong Kong offers a tremendous opportunity for China. If they allow Hong Kong to continue in its ways, it could be the first step towards democracy in China. China has promised to keep the structure in place for fifty years. What happens after that? Who knows . . . If they are happy with the wealth that Hong Kong will undoubtedly bring them, I imagine that nothing will change. On the other hand, China may feel that having a westernized, capitalist port is hypocritical. They might think they have lost face and are selling out to the West. They may crush Hong Kong's capitalism. That would be a terrible thing."

"But *that's* what would cause China to lose face with the rest of the world, don't you think?" Bond asked.

"Yes, but they may not care. China has not cared much in the past what the rest of the world thought. As for those of us in Hong Kong . . . Mr. Bond, do you smell the fear outside? It is there if you sniff hard enough. The people of Hong Kong may be going about their business. They may have accepted the inevitable. What happens on July the first cannot be changed. But they are afraid. We all are. We can only hope that China will keep her promise and allow us to continue as we are."

"Why don't you leave?"

"My business is here, Mr. Bond. I cannot take my business with me. I must stay and adjust to whatever happens. I am resigned to do that."

"Do you believe your businesses will be affected?"

"Not at first, certainly. Whether China allows establishments like this to flourish in Hong Kong remains to be seen. If hostess clubs are banned, then I will turn it into a restaurant. But I also believe that China will find it difficult to institute too many changes within the first fifty years."

"How so?"

"China will learn that societies exist in Hong Kong that go back centuries. They go back much further than communist China. I would imagine there might be new revolutions, more resistance, and more violence. Tienanmen Square was only the first of what might be many pro-democracy demonstrations."

Bond decided to get to the heart of the matter. "You're talking about Triads, aren't you?"

Li Xu Nan smiled slightly. He spoke softly in Chinese to his bodyguard. The Cantonese went very quickly, but Bond caught the word "girl" in the sentence. Had he got Sunni in trouble? The bodyguard got up and went to the bar. "I have ordered you a fresh drink, Mr. Bond, and one for myself."

"Thank you."

"Chiang Kai-shek was a Triad member, did you know that?" he asked.

"Yes."

"I do not know much about Triads, Mr. Bond. I do know that the government of Taiwan was built on the backs of Triads resisting communist rule. Triads came into existence resisting an oppressive regime in China, many, many years ago."

"So it's your contention, then, that Triads will become more powerful after the takeover? Aren't Triads outlawed in China, just as they are in Hong Kong? Don't you think they will crack down on organized crime?"

The bodyguard came back with the drinks. Li Xu Nan looked uncomfortable. He didn't like the way the conversation was going. "Organized crime, Mr. Bond? I'm not sure I know what you mean," Li said.

"Come on, Mr. Li. You know that Triads today are not involved in patriotic activities. They're criminals."

"There are some Triads that have lost the honour of their ancestors, that is true, I suppose."

A strange answer, Bond thought. "I understand that Triads are instrumental in illegally getting people out of Hong Kong."

"That is probably true," Li said. "But is that really so bad? The British government has made it virtually impossible for a Hong Kong national to live anywhere else. Britain turned her back on the people who have lived under her rule for a hundred and fifty years. That is outright betrayal. If people want to leave, they should be able to. You speak of losing face. England has lost face with us. What was done may have been honourable towards China—handing back a territory that was rightfully theirs. But not allowing the Hong Kong people an escape route was most *dis*honourable."

"Triads are involved with prostitution, too, aren't they?"

"I wouldn't know about that." The man was becoming angry.

"Come come, Mr. Li. I know what goes on here in this very club."

Li slammed his hand down hard on the table, startling his men. The force of the blow knocked over all the drinks. Bond remained calm.

"What is this?" Li demanded. "Did you come to talk about me and my businesses or about Triads? I know nothing about Triads! Go and talk to the police if you want to know about Triads! I resent the inference that what goes on here in my club has anything to do with a Triad. You have insulted me!"

"Forgive me, Mr. Li," Bond said. "Please accept my apologies. I merely thought you would have some insight into how these organizations have infiltrated the entertainment industry. I shan't take up any more of your time." Bond stood and bowed slightly, with respect. "Mr. Li, I would like to ask you one more question, if I may."

The Cho Kun of the Dragon Wing Society stared hard at Bond in disbelief. The *gweilo* had the audacity to continue speaking!

Through his pretence of humility, Bond stared back at Li. Both men knew that their façades had been torn away. The bodyguards were unsure what to do.

Bond finally spoke. "Mr. Li, recently there has been some violence in Hong Kong. Terrorist acts have been committed against British citizens, and one on some visiting officials from Beijing. What is your opinion of the nature of these attacks?"

Li stood slowly, his face flushed with anger. "I know nothing about

those attacks. They were unfortunate and tragic. I hesitate to speculate on who might be involved with those incidents. This interview
is over. You are lucky that I do not take away that notebook. Mr.
Bond, my name had better not appear anywhere in your story."

"Are you threatening me, Mr. Li?"

Li leaned forward and whispered in English, his voice laced with
menace. "Mr. Bond, I allow you to leave with your life. You are now
in my debt. You have your story. Now leave!"

Bond gave a slight bow of his head. "Thank you, Mr. Li." He stood
up and walked away from the table. He walked around the dance
floor to the club's exit. Sunni Pei was walking towards him, carrying
a small tray of drinks to a trio of Chinese businessmen. She held out
her hand and said a little too loudly, "Thank you for coming. We
hope to see you again soon!"

Bond shook her hand and felt a small piece of paper. He palmed
it and said, "Thank you, Veronica. I'll be back." She smiled nervously, then went on to serve the drinks as Bond left the Zipper. The
neon lights from the street were blinding at first after the darkness
of the club.

He unfolded the note and read: "Help me! Meet me on the street
behind the club in five minutes! Please!"

Bond looked around to see if anyone was watching. He ripped the
note into bits and let them scatter on the street, then walked round to
the back of the large building. He waited in a small nook in the wall
near an employee entrance. In precisely five minutes, Sunni came out
of the door. She saw him and rushed to him, her eyes full of fear.

"James!" she said. "They think I told you that Li Xu Nan is Cho
Kun of a Triad. This is considered a betrayal."

"So you *are* a member of the Triad?"

She nodded. "They will kill me. You don't understand."

"No, Sunni, I do understand."

"Please, can you hide me in your hotel until I can figure out what
to do? I beg you!" She was truly frightened.

"Come on," he said, taking her hand. They rushed out of the
alleyway and into the street.

TEN

MARKED FOR DEATH

When they were clear of the club, Sunni said, "We need to go to Kwun Tong."

"I know a safer place," Bond said. He wanted to call Woo at the antiques shop. They could get a car just by speaking a code word and an address into the phone.

"My mother," Sunni said. "They'll come to hurt my mother. We have to get her out of there."

"Can you phone her?" Bond asked.

"She never answers. She's not well."

Bond wanted to wash his hands of the woman right then and there. She was going to drag him into a situation with the Triad that he couldn't afford to be in. The mission could be compromised.

"Look," Bond said, "I'll help you. I'll get you to a place of safety. But we do it now, and we go where I say."

Sunni suddenly looked at him with a mixture of fear and anger. She swore at him. "Fine, I'll go alone. I should have known. You just want to get into bed with me." She started to run up the street. Bond let her go. She would only complicate things. He'd turned around and begun to walk the other way when a black sedan tore up the street and screeched to a halt in front of the girl. Two young Chinese men jumped out of the car and grabbed her. Sunni screamed.

Bond immediately ran back to her. She was putting up a great struggle as they attempted to push her into the back seat of the car. "Leave her alone!" Bond shouted at them. The men looked at him.

"James, help!" Sunni cried.

One man reached inside his jacket. Bond was a second ahead of him, drawing the Walther and drawing a bead on the man's head.

"Let her go!" he shouted. "Keep your hands where I can see them!"

The other man must have had a pistol behind Sunni's back, for he rolled away from her and shot at Bond, just missing him.

Bond swung his aim to the shooter and fired. The bullet caught the gunman in the chest, knocking him to the pavement. The other man suddenly let Sunni go and got in the car. Sunni fell to the ground, terrified. The sedan's wheels squealed as it sped away, leaving the dead man for all to see.

Bond ran to Sunni and helped her up. "Are you all right?" he asked.

She nodded, visibly shaken.

"Come on," he said. "I'll take you to your mother. Is it close?"

"It's northeast, near the airport."

"Right, let's go."

They heard sirens in the distance and Bond knew they needed to disappear before the police arrived. He grabbed her hand and ran into a side street, thinking they might be safer for the moment mixing with the crowds. After they had sprinted a couple of blocks, he pushed her into a shop selling a variety of handmade bamboo birdcages. The screeches and whistles of the parakeets and budgerigars were completely disorienting.

"We'll rest here. Catch your breath," he said.

"Thank you," she said.

"It's all right," Bond said, but he was angry with himself. He shouldn't have got involved. Now he was in it up to his neck.

"Who are you really?" she asked.

He didn't answer.

"Are you a policeman? A detective?" she asked.

"Something like that," Bond said. "I work for the British government."

"Drug enforcement?"

He shook his head. "Just a troubleshooter, you might say."

"Right," she said. "Your shooting is certainly going to get us into trouble!"

"It was either him or me. Now, where's your flat?"

"Kwun Tong. We can take the MTR, that might be safe." The Mass Transit Railway was Hong Kong's efficient underground system.

Bond knew it was a risk taking her home, but he had already promised. "All right, show me."

She led him outside and down an MTR stairway.

The underground was impeccably clean. Bond was surprised by the shiny, unmarked surfaces of the trains and the lack of litter anywhere in the station. Unlike London, Hong Kong had no problems with graffiti and vandalism.

Sunni bought two tickets from a machine and led Bond through the turnstiles to the Tsuen Wan line. They had to wait only a few minutes for a train heading north. The rush hour was practically over, so it wasn't as crowded as it could have been. They left the train at Yaumatei station and changed to the Kwun Tong line, which would take them east.

Finally reaching their destination, Sunni and Bond got off at the Kwun Tong station. The area was a little different here, Bond thought. Kwun Tong was near the airport, so there was a mixture of industrial and residential streets. They walked to Hong Ning Road and into a housing complex called Connie Towers. It was a twenty-one-storey structure that was modern, clean, and secure. The windows were "decorated" with laundry hanging on flagpoles, as is so often the case in Hong Kong tenement buildings.

"If you don't mind my asking, how much does a flat in a building like this cost in Hong Kong?"

"About 3 million Hong Kong dollars," she replied. Apparently she made good money working as a hostess.

They walked through an underground parking area to a lift.

Chinese characters were painted above the doors, which Bond translated as: "Come and go in peace." They got into the lift and they stood there silently as they travelled to the eighteenth floor. Bond noted that she was apprehensive, a bit short of breath. The girl was truly beautiful, though, and if his better judgement told him he should mind his own business, that damnable chivalrous trait that had got him into trouble many times in the past prevailed.

Once they were on the eighteenth floor, Sunni moved to a door protected by a large, locked, metal sliding gate. She stood staring at it in fear. The lock mechanism had been scratched and obviously tampered with. She looked up at Bond and his eyes told her to be quiet. He nodded to go ahead, so she used her key and opened the door. Bond drew his Walther PPK and preceded her into the flat.

It was a modest place, but tastefully decorated. The living room contained a sectional sofa, coffee table, a stereo, and a few other pieces of furniture. A framed plaque on the table displayed a Chinese character meaning "Tolerance." There was a crucifix on the wall, indicating that Sunni was not Buddhist, but one of the minority Chinese Catholics. A tiny kitchen was adjacent to the living room.

It was far too quiet. "Mother?" Sunni called out in Cantonese. She moved along a small hallway which led to the two little bedrooms and a bathroom.

An elderly woman was lying on the bed in one of the bedrooms, seemingly asleep. Sunni approached and called to her again. The woman didn't move. Sunni touched her and gasped. She recoiled and turned away. Bond knew immediately what was wrong. He felt the woman's forehead and grasped her wrist in search of a pulse. She was cold and lifeless.

"I'm sorry, Sunni," he said.

Sunni was sobbing, her back to Bond. "She . . . she had a bad heart," she managed to say.

Bond wondered if something had happened that might have frightened the woman. There was also the possibility that she had simply died in her sleep. As he examined her further, he realized that rigor mortis had set in, indicating that she had been dead for some hours.

It was an awkward moment and he wasn't sure how to comfort her. Bond put away his gun and reached out to her shoulders. She shrugged him off and said, "Please don't touch me." She turned to him, her eyes full of tears. "It's all your fault! They came here and scared her to death!" She pushed away from him and went into her bedroom, slamming the door behind her.

Bond spoke to her through the door. "Sunni, we don't know that for sure," he said gently. "She's been dead several hours. Her body is already stiff. When did you leave the flat today?"

"Around noon," she sniffed.

He nodded and said, "She's been dead more than two or three hours. Trust me." He opened the door slowly. She stood looking out of her window. Her bedroom was as small as her mother's. Space was at a premium in Hong Kong.

Though tiny, the room was decidedly feminine. Bond noticed a small round charcoal burner plugged into the wall next to her bed. A red light was burning brightly on top of it. Sunni turned, wiping away her tears and saw him looking at the contraption.

She managed a short laugh. "That's a little stove my mother gave me. It's a Chinese tradition . . . the red light means 'fire,' and it's supposed to bring me marriage . . . a husband. My mother was quite concerned that I'm nearly thirty and wasn't married." She started to cry again.

Bond held his arms out to her, and this time she allowed him to hold her. She sobbed quietly against his shoulder.

Then he heard a creaking noise. Damn! He hadn't closed and locked the front door! How could he have been so careless? He drew his gun. "Stay here," he commanded, then moved back into the living room.

As he entered the room, the front door slid open, revealing two young Chinese thugs in dark clothes. They were brandishing long, crude machetes. It all happened very quickly. The men rushed Bond and he shot them. They were both hit in the chest, but one of the men struck 007 hard on the left arm with his chopper. Bond yelped in pain but managed to fire at the man a second time at point blank range.

He became aware that Sunni was screaming. He rushed to her and held his hand over her mouth. "Shhhhh, it's all right now," he said, as calmly as he could. A few seconds passed and she started to calm down, but then she noticed Bond's shoulder. He was bleeding profusely through his jacket. He had a huge gash across his upper arm. He needed medical attention immediately.

"Lock the door, Sunni, quickly," he said sternly to jolt her out of her panic. She snapped out of it and ran to the door. Bond went into the bathroom and removed his jacket, shoulder holster, and shirt.

The cut was three inches long and half an inch deep. Luckily, the muscle had not been severed, but blood was pouring from the wound. He quickly removed his right shoe and pulled the prying tool from under the tongue. He snapped off the heel and tipped the contents into the sink.

"Sunni, I need your help," Bond called. She hesitated at the door to the bathroom, not wanting to look. "Please," he said, "I need you to apply this antiseptic to the cut." He took the bottle and held it out in the palm of his right hand.

She looked at him. The same thought passed through both of their heads.

"Sunni," Bond said, "you're right. I suppose this is all my fault. I'm sorry."

"I should let you die, you know," she said. "I should grab a knife and cut you myself. I would regain face with them. It would cancel the death warrant on me."

"You don't really believe they can help you, Sunni? They're using you. You're a commodity."

"I am a Blue Lantern."

"What is that?"

"I've been accepted as a member but have not been formally initiated yet."

"Then you're not a member."

Sunni finally reached for the bottle of antiseptic and opened it. "You have to wash the wound first." Bond nodded. He moved to the shower and turned on the hot water. As he leaned into it, the blood swirled with the water down the drain. Sunni took a large white towel from a rack, wrapped it around Bond's arm, and held it tightly.

"According to the law, I am a member," she continued. "I could be arrested and jailed for simply being a Blue Lantern."

"I wouldn't have thought they would allow women in Triads?"

"It was once all-male, but in the last few years they've begun to admit women. Most of them stay Blue Lanterns and are never initiated."

"Then that should tell you what they think of you," Bond said. "Leave them."

She removed the towel and poured antiseptic on to the wound, which was still bleeding badly. Bond winced at the sting.

"Don't you see? I can't do anything! If I run, they'll eventually find me and kill me, or I'll be arrested and go to jail. My only way out of this is to kill you. Believe me, there are some other girls you could have met tonight who would have cut your hands off if you'd spoken to them about Triads."

"You're not going to try and kill me, are you, Sunni?"

She didn't answer. "You need stitches."

"Look," he said, "you need help, and I can help you. Come with me to a safe house. I can get medical treatment, and they won't find you there. I need to make a phone call then we could be on our way in minutes."

She wrapped some gauze around his arm very tightly, then covered it with the towel again. "There, that should hold you for a while. It's a good thing you had all that stuff in your shoe."

Bond stood up and put on his shirt. He slipped the shoulder holster back on. Extending or raising his left arm hurt like hell. He took two of the acetaminophen tablets and one antibiotic, swallowing them with water from the sink in his cupped right hand. He replaced the contents of the shoe and put it back on. Finally, he managed to put the bloody jacket back on, then walked into the living room and reached for the phone near the kitchen.

"I'm making that call. You can come with me or you can stay behind," he said. "If you're coming, you'd better pack a bag. You probably won't be coming back here."

"I can't leave my mother!"

He was dialling the number. "There's nothing you can do for her now, Sunni. You have to think of yourself. Do you want to come or not?"

He got a recording at the other end. He spoke into the phone: "*Ling Ling Chat,* need taxi immediately, repeat immediately, at . . ." He turned to her. "What's the address?"

"One forty-seven Hong Ning Road, Kwun Tong."

Bond repeated it into the phone, then hung up. "You have five minutes to pack," he said. He understood what the poor girl was going through. In the space of one hour, she had suddenly been confronted with a life-or-death decision and the frightening prospect of abandoning the life she had been living.

Finally she asked, "Can you get me out of Hong Kong?"

He said truthfully, "I can try."

"Legally?"

"I can try."

She hesitated another moment, then pulled out a flight bag, began to rummage through her bedroom, and threw clothing into the bag. She spent some time in the bathroom, dumping in supplies. Finally, she went to a bulletin board in the kitchen removed some snapshots that captured moments in her life. The last thing she did was to take a child's toy from the kitchen window. It was one of those petal-shaped pinwheels on a stick. She shoved it into the bag.

"It's for good luck," she said. She zipped up the bag and threw it on her shoulder. "I'm ready."

"Good girl," he said, then drew his gun. He moved to the front door and listened. He motioned her to follow him as he unlatched the bolt and slid the door open. The hallway was empty. They walked to the lift, and Bond noticed that it was moving up towards their floor.

"Let's take the stairs," he said.

With gun in hand, Bond led the way down, a flight at a time. At the twelfth floor, he heard footsteps hurrying up below them. He pressed Sunni back against the wall and waited. Sure enough, two more Chinese youths brandishing choppers appeared. Bond shouted "Freeze!" in Cantonese, but the thugs ignored him and charged. It left him no choice but to shoot. The gunfire reverberated loudly in the stairwell. The two Triads slammed back against the wall, then rolled down a flight of steps.

It wouldn't be long before the police arrived, he thought. They needed to get to the street and find Woo before that happened. His wounded arm felt as if it was on fire. Sunni was frozen in fear in a corner of the stairwell. He gestured for her to keep following him, and continued down the stairs.

At the seventh floor they encountered four men. They rushed at Bond, attempting to overpower him. Bond got off one shot at point blank range, but had to duck to avoid the swings of the choppers. He rolled forward, through the three standing men, but couldn't avoid losing his balance and falling down the steps. The Walther flew out of his hand and fell to the landing below. One of the men charged at Sunni, his chopper raised. Instead of screaming and cowering, however, Sunni surprised Bond by performing an expert martial arts manoeuvre. She bent forward as the man swung, blocked his arm and threw him over her back—a perfect *Yaridama*. The man crashed into the wall behind her. She immediately turned and delivered a crescent moon kick to the man's chest and fast one-two spear-handed chops to his neck, breaking it.

By now, Bond was on his feet, jumping towards the other two. They tried to swing the choppers at him, but he ducked, put his hands on the landing, and shot his legs straight out at them. The kick hit one man in the abdomen, knocking him into his partner. Sunni was behind them, and she grabbed one in a head lock, then brutally rammed him into the wall. In less than a second she was lashing out with a roundhouse kick to the other man's kidneys, sending him flying back towards Bond who simply grabbed his shoulders as the man fell into him, then sent him sailing down the stairs. All four men were now down.

Bond looked up at her with respect and smiled. "Nice work, Sunni."

She shrugged. "I grew up on the streets of Hong Kong before going to the States. I'm not totally helpless."

He retrieved the Walther as they continued down the stairs. Eventually they reached the ground floor and Bond stopped. "They probably have a car down here somewhere. There'll be at least a couple more of them."

He peered out into the covered parking area and saw the black sedan idling near the exit. There was only a driver, and he was peering over his shoulder at the lift door, waiting for the men to return. Bond realized that he would certainly see them when they came out of the stairwell.

"Stay here," Bond said. He took a breath, then bolted out of the stairwell. He performed an agile body roll and ended up behind a stone column. The driver of the car shouted something in Chinese. A shot rang out and a bullet broke away a chunk of the column.

Bond heard the car back up and turn towards him. Another shot demolished a chunk of the concrete dangerously close to his head. His left arm was throbbing with pain now, especially after the fight on the stairwell. He was thankful it wasn't his gun-arm.

He carefully leaned out and shot towards the car, shattering the windscreen, but the driver had opened the door and was squatting behind it for cover. It was going to be a standoff unless Bond could gain a better vantage point from which to fire.

He could hear police sirens in the distance. They'd arrive any minute. He was about to run back to the stairwell when he heard the screeching of tyres from the parking area entrance. A red taxi zoomed in and slammed into the driver's side of the black sedan. The driver was sandwiched between the vehicles, his body mangled like a broken doll. Chen Chen was driving the taxi, and his father was sitting beside him.

Bond called to Sunni, and they ran to the cab and got into the back seat. The taxi's only damage was a bent front bumper, so it manoeuvred around the smashed car and out of the parking area just as a police car entered from the other side.

"You call for cab, mister?" said Woo, displaying his trademark grin.

"Sunni, meet my friend T.Y. and his son Chen Chen," Bond said. "Fellows, this is Sunni."

"Welcome and hello," T.Y. said to her. "We take you somewhere nice, uh huh?"

Sunni managed a smile, but she was still too shaken to speak. She was silent throughout the entire ride as Bond apprised Woo of the evening's events.

"There goes your cover," Woo said. "I do not know many journalists who carry guns and shoot Triads in residential housing, uh huh?"

"I'm just going to have to steer clear of the Dragon Wing boys while I'm here. I hope I haven't compromised anything with Thackeray. I'll just need to watch my back on the street." He turned to Sunni. "Do you know a man named Guy Thackeray?"

She shook her head. He believed her.

"Any news from London?" he asked.

"Nothing," said Woo.

"What about Australia?"

"No one claim responsibility yet. Authorities are clueless. I got report from M. Section A's early findings indicate device was definitely home-made, probably created in crude laboratory. Sounds like someone independent. No affiliation with particular country. It could also be some stupid research lab, illegally experimenting with nuclear power."

Bond thought Woo's theories were sound. There were a lot of companies in the world that had the capability of harnessing nuclear power. The fact that no threats or extortion messages had been received by anyone now seemed to be a positive sign. Perhaps it was merely an act of careless experimentation by an irresponsible energy company, with no intent to harm.

It was 10:00 p.m. by the time the cab arrived at Upper Lascar Row on the island. They all entered the antiques shop and went up the stairs to the safe haven. Woo showed Sunni a room where she could be alone if she wanted. Bond poured himself a glass of straight vodka on ice and drank it quickly. "T.Y., I need to do something about this arm. And quickly."

"I already made call. I know good doctor, he is on his way now. Works for safe house."

Sure enough, a few minutes later a little Chinese man named Dr Lo arrived. After half an hour, Bond's wound had been sterilized and stitched up. It still hurt, but he could live with it.

"I'm going to need some clothes from my hotel," he told Woo.

"No problem. All taken care of. Chen Chen will collect your things in morning, uh huh? Right now I fix some noodles for you and girl."

"T.Y., she's going to need a foreign passport. She's in danger and I want to get her out."

Woo frowned. "M will not like that."

"Bad luck," Bond said. "Sunni provided some valuable information and now we need to protect her. She damned near saved my life at that building. She's one hell of a fighter."

"I see what I can do," Woo said.

Bond finished his vodka. Shirtless, Bond knocked on Sunni's door. She said, "Come in."

She was lying in a foetal position on a double bed in the sparsely furnished room. "Are you hungry, Sunni? T.Y. is making us some dinner." She shook her head. Bond sat down on the bed beside her. "You're going to be okay. We're going to get you a foreign passport. You'll be able to stay here safely until you leave."

"Where am I going?" she asked quietly.

"Where would you like to go?"

"I don't know. I don't really care."

"Well, we'll try England for starters, all right?"

She shrugged. The poor girl had been through a lot—the realization that she was marked for death by the Triad, the discovery of her dead mother, and the traumatic escape from her building—it was enough to make anyone a complete wreck. Sunni had a great deal of fortitude. Bond leaned over and kissed her cheek, then stood up and left her alone.

It was later, after they had eaten a delicious meal of noodles and chicken (Sunni decided to join them but ate very little), and had all retired to their respective beds, that Sunni slipped into Bond's room.

He woke up when he felt her presence in the room. She was wearing a t-shirt and panties and stood barefoot by the bed, looking at him.

Without a word, he pulled the sheet down, offering her a place beside him. She slipped into the bed and snuggled next to him. Her body was warm and soft, and her legs felt smooth against his. They kissed, slowly at first, then with more passion as their desire increased. After a few minutes, she pulled off her t-shirt and pressed her breasts against his chest. She enjoyed the feel of the hair there, as she wasn't used to it. Most Asian men lacked hair on their chests.

She opened up to him that night, over and over again. He filled her with strength and security, helping her achieve a release from the demons that had tormented her since the evening began. She needed the climaxes, for they allowed her to forget her troubles and lose herself in a floating world of ecstasy and passion. It was three or four hours later when, totally spent, they finally fell asleep in each other's arms.

ELEVEN

ASSASSINATION

SHOOTOUT IN KOWLOON

Royal Hong Kong Police say that two incidents of gunfire in public yesterday may be related. The first occurred in Tsim Sha Tsui East near the nightclub Zipper, where a twenty-two-year-old man was shot by an unknown assassin. A little over an hour later, at a residential building in Kwun Tong, seven men were found dead and two seriously injured. Two of the men were found shot in a flat owned by Sunni Pei, who is reported missing. Her mother, Pui-Leng Pei, was also found dead in the flat, but it is believed she died of natural causes. Police suspect Triad activity is behind the two incidents . . ."

ZERO MINUS SEVEN: 24 JUNE 1997, 3:55 P.M.

The papers were full of yesterday's news, for shootouts on the streets of Hong Kong were surprisingly uncommon. James Bond had made a point of examining SIS reports on the colony's crime status before leaving England. According to these, Hong Kong was perhaps the most crime-free city in Asia. Gun control was very tight, and obtaining arms was difficult even for criminal organizations. The Royal Hong Kong Police was one of the most efficient forces in the world.

It was unfortunate that Sunni's name and picture were prominently displayed in the paper. Now she would definitely be a target. It would be even more problematic getting her out of Hong Kong. At least Bond hadn't been identified. Otherwise he would have had to listen to M blame it on him getting involved with "a tart."

Bond put the news behind him and concentrated on the new task at hand. It was time for Guy Thackeray's mysterious press conference.

EurAsia Enterprises' corporate headquarters was located in a thirty-four-storey building in the heart of Hong Kong's busy Central district. Nearby were such landmarks as the Bank of China Building, the Hongkong and Shanghai Bank Building, Jardine House, Government House, and Statue Square.

James Bond arrived for the press conference early, just in time to learn that the event had been moved to nearby Statue Square for reasons unknown. It was a beautiful day, if a bit hot and humid. Perhaps Thackeray thought an outdoor setting would be more pleasant. The square was nondescript for the most part, save for the statue of Sir Thomas Jackson, a former manager of the Hongkong Bank. There was a time when it had held several statues of British monarchs, but these had been removed long ago. A neoclassical domed building next to it housed the Legislative Council Chambers, the future of which would become uncertain in six days' time. Folding chairs had been set up in a roped-off area, and security guards were checking the identification of reporters desiring a seat.

Bond showed his journalistic credentials to the security guard who found his name on a list and let him through. He sat in the second row, near the outside end. There was a microphone stand on a small platform in front of the seats. A table had been set up along the side and complimentary glasses of wine were available. Looking around him, Bond remembered that the transition ceremony between the British and the Chinese was to take place here at midnight on 30 June, in a little less than a week's time.

About forty journalists were there, mostly from Hong Kong. There were a few Westerners present. One section of the audience was made up of EurAsia employees. From the look of them, they were the executives in charge of the company since the tragedy on the floating restaurant. They all looked apprehensive, not knowing what their CEO was about to announce to the world.

While waiting, Bond glanced up and admired the adjacent Hongkong and Shanghai Bank Building, popularly known simply as Hongkong Bank. It was one of the most striking pieces of architecture Bond had ever seen. Designed by the British architect Sir Norman Foster, its structure was based on the principles of bridge technology. Huge steel trusses were slung between two core towers, and the internal floors were suspended from these. Conventional support columns and concrete coverings had been avoided by using a special cladding of super-quality aluminum. The see-through walls thus revealed all the inner workings of the lifts, escalators, and offices. The entrance to the bank was from a large open plaza underneath the first floor of the building. Standing guard in the plaza were two bronze Imperial Chinese lions similar to those flanking most important Hong Kong doorways. Dubbed Stephen and Stitt after two former chief managers, the lions served as mascots for all Hong Kong.

At precisely 4:00 p.m., Guy Thackeray entered the square followed by two other men, who were obviously bodyguards. They stood to either side of him as he approached the microphone.

Thackeray looked even more haggard than he had in Macau. There were dark circles under his eyes, and he looked as if he hadn't slept for days. He was dressed in a sharp Armani business suit, though, and managed to exude an air of authority.

"Hello and welcome," he began. Bond again noted the lack of humour. There was no trace of a smile. "I have called this press conference to make an important announcement about EurAsia Enterprises. As you know, our entire Board of Directors was killed recently. There have been a couple of recent attempts on my life as well. I have no idea why we became targets. Unfortunately, it's all had an effect on the company. Our privately held stock is at an all-time low. The future is uncertain, and I have no reason to believe that things will improve. Therefore, I am selling my family's 59 per cent holding to the People's Republic of China, effective July the first, 1997."

There was a gasp from the crowd. Bond was surprised as well. The EurAsia executives had turned white and seemed dumbstruck.

"The remaining 41 per cent is owned by the families of the deceased members of the Board. Those shares will remain with the families who will be joint owners of Eurasia Enterprises with China. If they choose to sell their interests, that is up to them. I highly recommend that they do so. I plan to retire. I will leave Hong Kong and find a nice quiet place to live out the rest of my life.

"EurAsia Enterprises was begun a century and a half ago by my great-great-grandfather. It started out modestly, but grew into an international trade organization. I have been proud to lead the company since I took it over from my own father twenty years ago. But, like Hong Kong itself, all good things must come to an end. That is all. Thank you."

He started to leave the platform, but the mass of reporters raised their arms. "Mr. Thackeray! One question!" they called. Thackeray hesitated and said, "All right, I'll take a couple of questions. You, in the front row."

A woman stood up and asked, "What made you decide to sell your company to the Chinese? Despite the troubles EurAsia has experienced recently, it's still a multi-billion dollar company!"

Murmurs from the crowd indicated that they all had the same question.

"Yes, you're right, it *is* still a multi-billion dollar company. The only comment I can make at this time is that I have no choice but to sell. One more question. The gentleman in the green jacket."

A man asked, "Where are you planning to go?"

"I haven't decided. Certainly not England. I've never lived there nor do I wish to. That's all. Thank you for coming."

He left the platform abruptly, and pandemonium broke out. The EurAsia people jumped up and ran towards Thackeray. The two bodyguards protected him but Bond could feel their anger and dismay. This was all news to them. Very bad news.

"Mr. Thackeray! What is the meaning of this? How long have you known?"

Thackeray turned to them and said, "I'm sorry. You must make other arrangements with your lives. Most of you hold foreign passports. I suggest you use them. It's been a pleasure working with you all. Now I must leave."

It was a cold and cruel response. Despite the terseness of the announcement, Bond perceived that it had been very painful for Thackeray to make it. He was doing his best to remain stoic, though. Even the Englishman who hated Britain was keeping a stiff upper lip. He turned and walked out of Statue Square and got into the back seat of a black Mercedes waiting on Des Voeux Road. His window remained down as he looked out at the crowd and gave a little wave. He wasn't smiling.

Bond watched as the Mercedes pulled away and stopped at a red light. A lorry moved into the lane between the car and the spectators, blocking their view for a moment. The light turned green, and the lorry moved forward. The car moved into the intersection slowly. Thackeray's window was still down but he had retreated into the darkness of the vehicle and couldn't be seen.

Suddenly, a young Chinese man dressed in black ran out into the intersection from the other side of the street. He passed by the open window of the Mercedes and threw something into it. Then he started running north across the square for all he was worth.

The car exploded into flames with such force that many of the people closest to it were injured. Bond felt the heat from the blast, and he was a hundred metres away. He quickly surveyed the scene— at least three pedestrians were lying on the ground, clutching their eyes. Everyone was screaming and running around in a panic. The Mercedes was totally destroyed. Only the smoking, charred chassis remained. Pieces of debris, possibly mixed with human body parts, lay in black, burning heaps on the street. Along with everyone else, Bond was shocked. The CEO of EurAsia Enterprises had been assassinated while the whole world watched.

Bond turned to locate the running man and saw him leave the square and run into the plaza underneath the Hongkong and Shanghai Bank building. Bond took off after him; no one else had been alert enough to follow him. Thackeray's bodyguards must have been blown to bits as well.

Access to the bank from the plaza was by way of what were claimed to be the longest free-standing escalators in the world. The entrance was set into a double glass ceiling above the plaza, and let visitors out on level three, the public banking business area. The assassin had disappeared up the escalator and was now inside the bank, probably hoping he could lose himself in the crowd and eventually sneak out. Determined to find him, Bond scrambled up the escalator.

Bond stepped out on to the third level and was struck by the spectacular atrium rising 170 feet through eleven levels of the building. The tellers' area was situated on the north and south sides of the atrium. Other escalators went up to a fifth level, where more public banking services were available. Bond quickly scanned the place from the east end of the building.

Black was not an easy colour to spot in a crowd. The bank was fairly busy, as it was near closing time. There was no sign of the assassin. Bond looked up to the fifth level and thought he saw a man in black moving along the right side of the atrium towards the west side of the building. He quickly ran up the next escalator to the fifth level.

Attempting to look inconspicuous, Bond stepped up to a long counter where bank customers filled out forms and deposit slips. He surveyed the large room and found his prey. The assassin was moving towards a bank of lifts on the west side of the building. He was looking around, trying to determine if he was being followed. Bond kept moving towards him, picking up his pace.

By now, police cars and a fire engine had arrived outside. Many of the bank's employees were looking out of the south-side windows at the chaos in the street below. A security guard who usually blocked access to the lifts was also curious and had wandered over to the windows. The assassin reached the lift lobby and pressed a button. Then he saw Bond moving towards him, and a look of panic crossed his face.

Bond started to run. There was a good eighty metres between them. The lift door opened and the assassin stepped inside quickly. Damn! Now Bond didn't care who saw him. He ran full speed to the bank of lifts and pressed the "UP" button. He watched the numbers on the assassin's lift, noting that it stopped on twelve. Bond's lift came and he got inside, just as he heard the security guard shout at him to stop.

Level twelve was the top of the atrium. One could look out and survey all the public areas from this impressive vantage point. Access to the higher floors was restricted to bank personnel only. A security guard stood by the lifts to prevent people from wandering up. Bond's lift door opened just in time for him to see the assassin club the guard on the back of his head. The guard fell and the assassin ran to the left towards a stairwell enclosed in glass.

"Stop!" Bond shouted. He hesitated to draw his Walther PPK—he didn't want to start a panic inside the bank. But then the assassin opened the door to the stairwell and an alarm sounded, alerting everyone in the building to their presence.

The assassin began to run up the zigzagging flights of stairs. Bond followed him into the stairwell, and took the steps two at a time. Three guards had joined the chase, and the police were most likely on their way. They entered the stairwell after Bond had climbed two flights and shouted "Stop!" in Cantonese. One of the men then shouted the word in English.

Bond called down to them. "The man who blew up the car outside is running up the stairs! He's dressed in black!" Then he continued the chase.

Who could the assassin be? Was he Triad? Was he part of the Dragon Wing? Why was Guy Thackeray killed? Had he been the target of the floating restaurant disaster after all, and was this a second attempt on his life? Was this some kind of vendetta? Perhaps someone in the organization knew of his intention to sell the company's stock to China and wanted to stop him. It was possible that the Triad wasn't involved at all. The puzzle was certainly becoming more convoluted. Bond wondered how he would get to the bottom of any of this now that Thackeray was dead.

He heard a door slam above him. The assassin had left the stair-well. Thanks to Bond's acute sense of hearing, he estimated that the sound couldn't have been more than fifty metres above him. Bond stepped on to the next landing and was met by the rattle of gunfire. The assassin had shot a security guard in the doorway of the twen-tieth floor. Normally there was no exit from the stairwell without a card key. The guard must have opened the door from the inside, hoping to intercept the killer. Now his body was lying in the doorway, jamming it open. Bond leaped over the body and bolted through the door in pursuit.

He saw the killer running towards an open-plan area full of desks and office staff. The employees were cowering against the windows. The assassin leaped on to a desk, turned, and fired an automatic pistol at Bond, who dived for the floor just in time. Then, throwing caution to the wind, he drew his Walther, but the man had already leaped to another desk and was no longer a good target.

"Everyone get down!" Bond shouted. People did as they were told, some of them translating Bond's orders into Cantonese for those who needed it.

The assassin jumped from desk to desk, flinging files and papers into the air, until he reached the other end of the floor. He ran through a door and into another office space leading back in the direction of the lifts and stairwell. Bond decided not to follow him through there, but instead to go back the way he had come in the hope of meeting him in the stairwell. The three security guards in pursuit burst into the room with their guns drawn. They shouted at Bond to halt.

"I'm a British policeman!" he shouted. "I'm not the man you're after, he's coming round through the room next-door!" The guards looked confused, unsure whether to believe him or not. Suddenly, the assassin ran into the lift area. He had a frightened Chinese woman with him, a bank employee, and his gun was to her head.

He shouted in Cantonese. Bond didn't have to translate his words. The guards froze, as did Bond. Bond said in his best Cantonese, "You won't get away with this."

An empty lift opened behind the assassin, and he took the opportunity to step inside, taking the woman with him. The door closed and the lift started moving up towards the top of the building. Bond immediately pressed the "UP" button and waited for another lift. One guard was speaking in Cantonese into a walkie-talkie, informing other men where the assassin was headed. They had obviously decided to believe that Bond was on their side.

Just as another lift arrived, Bond noted that the assassin's lift had stopped on level forty-two. Bond and the guards took the lift up to the same level and stepped out. It was a large executive conference room with a bar along one side.

"Oh, no," a guard muttered. He pointed towards an exit leading outside.

They could see the assassin on a catwalk on the other side of the window. He was inching his way along with the woman in tow. He looked as frightened as she did.

"What the hell does he think he's doing?" Bond asked. "He can't escape now!"

A guard said, "He could get on one of our hydraulic lifts on the extension. There is a ladder there he can use to climb down to another floor."

Bond could see what the guard meant. Extended on an aluminium-clad structure was a box-like "cherry picker" which apparently could move up and down the building and was used to clean the windows. Sure enough, the assassin began to force the woman towards the box. She was too terrified to move. The man pointed his gun at her, shouting at her, but this only made her terror worse.

"I'm going out there," Bond said, and moved towards the emergency exit. The killer, meanwhile, had abandoned the woman and was making his way towards the box alone. Bond stepped on to the catwalk and was surprised by the force of the wind. He didn't want to look down, for he would surely have difficulty maintaining his balance. All of Hong Kong lay before him. If it had not been from such a precarious perch, it would have been a spectacular view.

The woman was clutching a round beam that formed part of the extension, holding on for dear life. Bond reached out to her. "Give me your hand!" he shouted. The woman cried, but wouldn't move. "Please! He's gone!" Bond said. "The man is gone! Give me your hand and I'll help you get back inside!"

The woman looked at him through her tears. She was about forty, and very, very frightened. She said something in Cantonese that Bond didn't understand, but he kept his hand outstretched. He smiled at her and nodded encouragingly. Finally, she nervously extended her arm and clutched Bond's hand. She was trembling furiously.

"All right, I'm going to count to three, then you let go of the beam! Do you understand?"

She nodded.

"One . . . two . . . three!" She let go of the beam and Bond tugged on her arm. Luckily, she was very lightweight. She flew at Bond and he grabbed her around the waist with his other arm. She clutched him, hugging him in a vice-like grip. He held her, stroking her head, muttering soothing words in her ear. She looked up at him and kissed him several times on the cheek. He laughed, and she managed to smile, too.

Bond got her back inside, but by then the assassin had made his way down the ladder to another floor. There was no telling where he was now. He was probably already back in the building, trying to find a way out.

"Ever seen that man before?" he asked one of the guards as they ran back to the lifts. The guard shook his head.

They heard the sound of distant gunfire. "We should take the stairs," said the guard. Bond nodded. That way they could evaluate the situation on every floor as they went down. They entered the stairwell and flew down the steps, taking them two at a time. The guard's intercom chirped when they reached the thirty-fourth floor. The assassin had been spotted near the twelfth floor again.

"The lift!" Bond said. One of the guards used his card key to leave the stairwell, and punched the "DOWN" button by the lifts. It came quickly, and the four men piled in.

Back on the twelfth floor, Bond found utter chaos. Civilians were lying on the floor, and one security guard was dead on the carpet. Two more guards were crouched against a low railed wall and aiming off into the distance. The killer had another hostage, a man, and was moving around the perimeter of the atrium on the east side. Bond looked down the atrium and saw that several Royal Hong Kong Police officers had arrived and were making their way into the building and towards the lifts. He thought that perhaps he should let them handle this. He had got himself too involved already. He wasn't sure what the status of his mission was anymore, now that Thackeray was dead. He needed to get back to the safe house and report to London. Yet somehow he felt a responsibility to the hostage and to the people of the bank. If he hadn't chased the man inside, there might not have been any casualties. There might be even more before this was finished. On the other hand, if he hadn't chased the assassin into the bank, he would have got away.

Bond decided that he wouldn't let that happen. The man was going down. Now. He quickly calculated the distance to the assassin. He needed to be no further away than 180 feet away for the Walther to be effective.

"Talk to him. Distract him," Bond said to the guard who was now his ally. The man shouted towards the assassin in Cantonese. Bond crouched down below the rail and moved around the side of the atrium, closer to the killer and his hostage. He used a desk for cover and was ultimately able to take a position behind them. The killer was oblivious to Bond's approach for the guard was successfully distracting him. Bond wouldn't need the gun after all. He tackled the man hard, causing him to release the hostage. Bond leaned him back over the railing, holding on to his gun-arm. A shot went off into the air and people screamed.

The two men struggled for the pistol as 007 attempted to keep the assassin's arm high so that no one would be endangered. Face to face, they glared venomously at each other. Bond had never seen the other man before. As a fighter, he wasn't much of a match, obviously exhausted from all the running and the stress of the chase. Bond used his right fist to hit him in the face. The assassin dropped the gun, and it fell the nine levels to the double-glass floor of the atrium. The man attempted to fight back but quickly realized it was no use. Bond hit him again. This time the man shoved Bond away from him, then performed a daredevil leap over the railing. Bond tried to grab his legs to stop him, but it was too late. He fell 170 feet to his death, slamming into the double-glass floor below. Surprisingly, the glass didn't break.

The man had killed himself rather than let himself be caught. Who had hired him? Where did he come from?

The guards all started down, and Bond followed them. They seemed to have forgotten all about him as the employees got up and began milling about. Bond couldn't afford to be questioned by the police. He needed to get away quickly and quietly. On his way towards the lift, he took a tan sports jacket and dark sunglasses from someone's desk and put them on. It wasn't much of a disguise, but it might work if he hurried. He rode the crowded lift down to the third level, where everyone was watching the police climb on to the glass floor to retrieve the killer's body. Bond surreptitiously moved through the crowd towards the escalator down to the plaza, and managed to get out without being seen.

Once on the street, he saw that the police were still at the scene of the explosion, talking to witnesses. He walked west, away from the area, and finally flagged down a taxi.

The cab took him to Upper Lascar Row. He paid the driver and walked up the street towards the Woos' antiques shop. There, he got another shock.

The front door of the shop was smashed, the lock broken. No one was inside minding the store. He made his way to the keypad at the back, punched in the numbers, and went upstairs. The place had been ransacked. Files were overturned, papers were scattered all over the floor, and the furniture had been ripped up. Bond recognized a thoroughly professional job.

"T.Y.?" Bond shouted. "Sunni?" He searched all the rooms and floors, but no one was there. The British Intelligence station in Hong Kong had been completely destroyed.

TWELVE

ONE OF THE LINKS

6:30 P.M.

What had happened to the safe house? How was their security breached? Where were T.Y. Woo, his brother, and his son? Where was Sunni? Maybe they were all safe somewhere. Bond hadn't seen the company taxi cab parked near the building.

Then he noticed his briefcase sitting undisturbed on the coffee table. It was still locked. Had someone tried to open it and left it there, or had T.Y. placed it on the table as some kind of message to Bond? Bond opened it, making sure it still contained the new transmitter and other important documents. The number "22" was displayed on the transmitter, which worked much like a telephone beeper with unlimited range. It was a command to call London. He didn't dare do it from the safe house. He quickly changed into a nondescript black polo shirt and black trousers, then left the safe house.

Bond wandered the streets, turning over the events of the past few days in his mind. He needed to clear his head. The bright neon of Hong Kong was beginning to shine around him. Sticking to the narrow side streets, he walked past street vendors packing up their stalls for the evening. He strolled through the beautifully landscaped Hong Kong Park, which was only a few years old. A spectacular walk-in aviary within the park contained 150 species of Asian birds, and this is where Bond chose to collect his thoughts.

How did the pieces of the puzzle fit together? What about himself? Were the police looking for him? Had his actions at the Hongkong Bank been documented by photographers or hidden video cameras? Was his face known? Would the Dragon Wing Society be looking for him too, even though Sunni was the real object of their hunt? Would they recognize him if they saw him? The unfortunate stereotypical racist comment "All Chinese look alike" was also often made by the Chinese in reference to *gweilo*.

What about Guy Thackeray and his corporation? What the hell happened at that press conference? One minute the man was alive, delivering a bombshell to the world, and the next minute a bombshell was delivered to him. Who was responsible? Was it the Triad? Was it China? Thackeray had referred to other attempts on his life. Was he referring to the incident in Macau? If so, how did he know about the secret exit and when to leave by it? Bond wanted to know if the police had identified Thackeray's killer yet. If only Woo was around—he could talk to his contact with the Royal Hong Kong Police.

Bond decided to take a risk by going back to the Mandarin Oriental. A room there would provide some privacy for a phone call to London. When he left the aviary, he noticed nearly a hundred people, most of them Chinese, walking through the park carrying signs. Written in Chinese and English, they were pro-democracy slogans. One read "Stay out of our hair, China." Another read, "One country, two systems—remember your promise, China." Yet another read, "No troops at the border." It reminded Bond that Chinese troops had massed north of the New Territories. That alone would make any citizen of Hong Kong nervous.

Bond walked to the hotel, stopping only to eat a quick dinner in a fast-food Chinese restaurant. Woo had checked him out of the hotel as promised, and Bond quickly learned that there were no other rooms available. Bond asked the attractive girl at the reception desk to locate the manager. There really were no rooms available, but the manager allowed 007 to use a private office for a phone call since he knew Bond personally.

He dialled the access number to get a secure line. When the duty officer answered, Bond said, "Predator," the code name which had been his for the last several years. The duty officer asked him to hold the line. After a few clicks, he heard the voice of Bill Tanner.

"James? Where the hell are you? M's beside herself!"

"I'm fine, Bill. I'm at the hotel at the moment, but I've really no place to stay. The safe house . . ."

"We know all about the safe house, James. Woo contacted us."

"Where is he?"

"He's all right, and so is his son. They are in hiding. I'm afraid the brother was killed."

"Christ. What about the girl?"

"Girl?"

"There was a girl at the safe house who helped me. We were going to try and get her to England."

"Oh, yes, we got that request. You should have heard M's comments on that one! I won't repeat them here. I don't know about the girl. Maybe she's with Woo. As far as a passport is concerned, M is thinking about it."

Bond hoped so. "What happened? Do we know who was responsible?"

"Woo was out of the shop when it happened. He returned with his son to find his brother slashed to bits and the place in a shambles. He called a clean-up crew to dispose of the body and he and his son got out fast. We're not sure where he is at the moment, but I imagine we will hear from him soon. Woo thought it was Triad."

Then it was possible Sunni wasn't with him after all.

"Do you know what happened to Thackeray?" Bond asked.

"Yes, it's all over the news already. Our morning television news programmes have covered it. EurAsia Enterprises is the hot topic. There's a lot of speculation, and the PM is trying to contact China regarding the so-called sale of the company. It's all extremely bizarre."

"It doesn't make any sense to me, either. I've been unable to find out a thing, I'm afraid. Do we know who the killer was?"

"It's still too early. According to the Royal Hong Kong Police, the man had no identification on him. No one knows who the hell he was. Anyway, M still wants you on the case. Just because Thackeray's no longer with us doesn't mean you can't still get to the bottom of it. Keep digging. If you can establish and prove the link between EurAsia and that Triad, you'll have done your job."

"All right, I know where to go next. What's happening in Australia?"

"Nothing new there," Tanner said with a sigh. "It's as if it never happened. If anyone knows anything about it, they're not talking. No one has come forward claiming responsibility. It's a big mystery."

"Great."

"The worry now is the transition. The number of Chinese troops at the border is increasing. Beijing is complaining about all the pro-democracy demonstrations that are taking place. They've asked the Hong Kong Governor to put a stop to them, but he's refused. He's standing up for their rights. We all want the transition to be peaceful and dignified. Right now the air is full of distrust and near panic. I should probably tell you that we've sent a couple of warships your way."

"The Royal Navy?" Bond groaned. This was serious.

"Let's hope their presence will act as a deterrent."

"Right. Anything else?"

"No. How's your arm? I heard you got cut."

"Hurts like hell, but I'll live."

"You always do. Keep in touch. We'll get you and Woo back together."

Tanner signed off and Bond suddenly felt very much alone, sitting in the middle of a powder keg just waiting to explode.

The Container Port at Kwai Chung was Bond's next stop. Woo had given him directions to EurAsia Enterprises' warehouse located within the huge complex. The only problem was that he would have to get over a barbed-wire fence, but he had encountered worse obstacles in his life . . .

Bond took a taxi to Kowloon and then further north into the western New Territories. He told the driver to let him off in front of the fenced Container Terminal on Kwai Chung Road. It was night now, and Bond's dark clothing should disappear into the shadows.

Hong Kong is one of the busiest shipping ports in the world. The Kwai Chung Container Port is one of many such terminals in the colony, but it is the largest and serves as a transhipment centre for Chinese export goods because China's own transport infrastructure is inadequate. It is as important to China as it is to Hong Kong.

From where he stood, Bond could see hundreds of containers stacked high like coloured building blocks. They all had labels and logos painted on the sides—EVERGREEN, UNIGLORY, HYUNDAI, K LINE, WAN HAI, CHO YANG, HANJIN, and others. Tall orange cranes loomed over the containers at strategic points around the port, along with equally tall blue barges. White warehouse buildings were scattered throughout the extended terminal. One could easily get lost, but luckily Bond was equipped with the map that Woo had prepared for him.

He removed his left shoe, pried open the heel, took out the small wire cutter and replaced the shoe. He climbed the fence and easily snapped the barbed-wire, slipped through and over the fence, and jumped down to the pavement on the other side. He took a moment to replace the wire cutter, then pulled the map from his pocket. The EurAsia Enterprises warehouse was at the southern end of the terminal.

Apparently the port never closed, for there were men working here and there, even after hours. The place was well illuminated by tall floodlights. So much for dressing in dark clothes . . . Bond darted from one pile of containers to another, hoping no one would see him. After ten minutes, he found the warehouse. It was fully lit and its loading doors were open.

The warehouse was near the shoreline, and Bond could see a large white cargo ship in Rambler Channel, the body of water adjoining the port. It was too far away for him to read the name on the side, but he assumed it was one of EurAsia's ships. A smaller lighter was travelling from the ship to the shoreline, where cranes were ready to unload cargo. It appeared that the lighter had already made a trip or two, for men were busy moving crates into the warehouse on forklifts. Bond moved closer to the building, looking for an entry somewhere at the back.

There was a door behind the warehouse, probably an emergency exit of some kind. Bond was sure it would be locked, but he tried it anyway. He was right. Twenty feet above him was an open window, but he had no way to scale the wall. Without a second thought, Bond snapped open the clasp on his belt buckle. Q Branch had devised this standard field issue piece of equipment many years ago. A set of fibreglass picklocks was hidden inside, undetectable by X-ray. Bond squatted so that he was at eye level with the door knob, and slowly tried each pick until he found one that worked. In three minutes, the door was unlocked. He replaced the picklocks and slowly inched open the door.

He was at the back of the dimly lit warehouse. There was a token crew working, perhaps three or four men. Bond slipped in and shut the door, then moved quickly to an area containing stacks of cardboard boxes. By peering around the boxes, he got a view of the entire warehouse.

It was full of crates, boxes, forklifts, and other machinery. A prefabricated building serving as an office was built on scaffolding. Metal steps led up to the office. Its door was open, light pouring out of it. Through the single window, Bond could see that someone was in there.

The most curious thing about the warehouse was the object that sat upon a wheeled platform. It was a wooden sampan, a simple boat with a hood covering. The word "sampan" means "three planks," and that was practically all it was. What was it doing here? Unlike the sampans one could see in Aberdeen Harbour, this one looked brand new, as if it had just been built. Bond doubted that it had ever been in the water. It was painted dark brown and had a bright red hood. Red was the Chinese colour of good luck.

A figure emerged from the office and descended the steps. Bond's jaw dropped when he saw who it was. The man was the albino Chinese he had dubbed "Tom"—the heaviest of the three men he had seen with Li Xu Nan at the Zipper. Tom spoke to the workers and pointed outside. Immediately, the men moved to the sampan and began to wheel it out of the warehouse. Tom followed them.

Now was Bond's chance to get into the office. He ran up the steps, knowing that he had a minute or two before Tom came back. In addition to the window which faced the warehouse, there was also one looking out over the harbour. On a desk beneath that window was a stack of papers. Bond recognized a shipping itinerary on top, printed on EurAsia Enterprises letterhead. Even though it was written mostly in Chinese, Bond could translate the name of the ship as the *Taitai*. A pair of binoculars lay on the desk. Bond used them to look at the ship in the harbour. There was very little light, but he could just make out the name of the vessel. Sure enough, the word *Taitai* was painted on the bow. Bond put down the binoculars and ran his finger down the itinerary, noting dates and routes for the boat. Its next stop was Singapore, scheduled for 26 June, with a planned return on 30 June.

A metal briefcase also lay on the desk. Bond found that it was unlocked and looked inside. It was full of cash, all Hong Kong currency, and a lot of it—thousands of dollars.

A map of Southeast Asia was tacked on to a cork bulletin board on the other side of the room. Bond studied it closely; it was marked with yellow highlights. Several lines apparently charted different routes, over land and sea, from Hong Kong to a circled area in the Yunnan Province in China. Bond immediately recognized it as the "Golden Triangle," the infamous no-man's land, the source of most of the world's heroin.

Bond glanced out of the window. Tom was still giving orders to the men. The sampan had been positioned under a crane. The lighter he had seen earlier was nearing the shoreline and was about to dock. Were they going to load the sampan on to the *Taitai*? Whatever for?

He knew he only had a few more minutes. He opened a filing cabinet next to the desk and saw numerous manilla folders. They were all marked with innocuous headings, certainly all pertaining to the shipping business. One, however, caught Bond's eye. It was marked "Australia."

He pulled out the folder and opened it, remembering that EurAsia Enterprises owned a gold-mining operation in Western Australia. The material in the folder pertained to that. There was an official letterhead reading "EurAsia Enterprises Australia," and an address in Kalgoorlie. Thumbing through the pages, Bond found nothing of interest until he came to a large sheet of paper folded three times. He opened it up and saw that it was a map of the Kalgoorlie facility. The gold mine was clearly drawn, showing the winding passages, entrances, and locations of the lodes. One amorphous shape in the mine was marked "Off Limits Area."

That was enough for Bond. He folded up the map and pocketed it. He then replaced the folder, shut the filing cabinet and took another look out of the window. Tom wasn't there! Bond moved to the doorway and peered out. The albino was standing in the entrance of the warehouse loading doors, looking out at the harbour. If Bond moved slowly and silently, the man wouldn't see him. Bond stepped out of the door, swung his leg over the rail, heaved his body over, and carefully climbed down the scaffolding to the floor. He moved into the shadows against the wall just as Tom turned and began to walk back towards the office. When the albino reached the room above him, Bond sprinted to the back of the warehouse, where he had been earlier.

A few moments later, Tom turned out the lights in the office, locked the door and descended the stairs. He was carrying the metal briefcase. At that moment, a forklift entered the warehouse with one of the newly unloaded crates. Bond watched as Tom opened the crate with a crowbar, inspected the contents, and pulled out a hessian bag. Another man wearing a suit entered and stood beside the forklift. Bond had never seen him before. Both he and Tom bent down to inspect the contents of the bag. They seemed to be in agreement about what they saw. Tom handed the metal briefcase to the new man. He opened the case for verification, then closed and locked the case and shook hands with Tom. They walked out of the warehouse together and the place was empty again.

Bond sprinted to the opened crate and took a quick look at the hessian bag. His suspicions were confirmed when he saw what was there. He didn't have to taste it to be certain that it was refined heroin. Without hesitating any longer, Bond hastened back to his position just as Tom and the other workmen returned to the warehouse. Bond slipped out of the back door, then moved around the side of the building so he could get a better view of the unloading.

Sure enough, the sampan was in the process of being lifted by crane on to the lighter. Why the hell were they shipping a sampan to Singapore?

A grey Rolls-Royce was parked near the entrance to the warehouse. The new man with the briefcase full of money was closer and plainly visible. He was Chinese and had a long scar that went across his nose and down his left cheek. Scarface opened the back door of the Rolls and got inside, joining another man sitting in the back seat.

It was Li Xu Nan.

At last, he had found one of the links in the puzzle! He had made the connection between EurAsia Enterprises and the Triad. Some kind of smuggling operation was being managed from this very warehouse. Guy Thackeray's assassination was now making more sense. He must have learned of the smuggling and tried to stop it. The Triad must have killed him to get him out of the way. That still didn't explain why he wanted to sell his company, though.

Bond had to follow that Rolls. He made his way back through the Container Port to the fence, through the barbed-wire, as before, and jumped to the ground below. Sooner or later, the Rolls would leave the Port and drive down this road, but how could he follow it?

The answer came rolling down Kwai Chung Road in the form of a red and silver taxi cab. Bond flagged it down and got in the back seat. He told the driver in Cantonese to wait: they were going to follow another car in a moment. He handed the driver 50 Hong Kong dollars, so he was happy to do what he was asked.

Sure enough, the Rolls-Royce soon appeared and headed for Kowloon. Bond made sure the taxi kept a safe distance.

THIRTEEN

TRIAD CEREMONY

10:00 P.M.

The Rolls-Royce drove south to Boundary Street and then east across the peninsula. The road soon merged with West Prince Edward Road and the Rolls turned off into the area known as Kowloon City, not far from Kai Tak Airport. It pulled into a narrow, dingy alley, and stopped. Bond told the taxi driver to let him out at the corner and managed to get out without being seen.

It was not a well-lit or inviting neighbourhood. In fact, if Bond's memory served him correctly, he was near where the infamous "Walled City" used to be. This notorious pocket of vice and squalor was always an embarrassment. Long ago, before British rule, the enclave was a Chinese military outpost. After the British took over, a granite-walled fortress was constructed. The New Territories lease of 1898 left the area under Chinese jurisdiction due to an administrative error, and it remained unregulated by the Hong Kong government. By the mid-sixties, the Walled City was a cesspool of crime, the haven of drug smugglers, prostitutes, thieves, and murderers. Britain and China finally reached an agreement in 1987 to rid themselves of this sewer, and in 1993 the Walled City was demolished. A park was now being developed on the site. Nevertheless, Bond thought the absence of the Walled City didn't make the neighbourhood much friendlier. The side streets south of the proposed park were just as sinister. It was just the place for Triads to operate, and it was precisely where James Bond now found himself.

Bond watched the men get out of the Rolls. They entered a shabby building, and then the Rolls drove away. He waited a minute, then stealthily crept towards the middle of the alley. Li Xu Nan and Scarface had entered what appeared to be an abandoned condemned building. The door was loose on its hinges and the windows were broken or in some cases, completely missing.

Bond decided to climb up another level and perhaps slip into one of the second-floor windows. It wasn't difficult to get a foothold but once inside, he found himself in a dark room with a wooden floor. The slats in the floor were loose, allowing some light from the level below to seep through. If he wasn't careful, the floor would creak. Bond got down on his stomach and snaked along the floor, distributing his weight so that the noise would be minimized. Through the slats, he could see several men milling around, preparing for some kind of meeting. They were dressed in black robes resembling those worn by Buddhist monks, with white sashes serving as belts. They also wore strange headbands made of red cloth, with the free ends hanging down over the front of the body. There were a number of large loops, or knots, in the bands around their head.

Bond searched his memory for what he knew about Triads and their sacred initiation ceremonies. If they were about to perform one, then he could very possibly be the only Westerner ever to witness one. He had to make sure he was completely silent, as they would surely kill him if they found him.

An altar was constructed at the west end of the room, illuminated entirely by candlelight. A large wooden tub painted red and filled with rice stood in front of the altar. Four Chinese characters adorned the outer circumference which Bond translated as "pine," "cedar" (both of which signified "longevity" to the Chinese), "peach" and "plum" (both of which denoted "loyalty").

He remembered that the tub was called the "Tau," and contained various precious objects belonging to the society, including five sets of four triangular flags, or pennants, which represented the names of legendary "ancestors" of the five "Lodges" of Triad societies.

More important were the "Warrant Flags," which were used by Triad officials during the ceremony. The name "Dragon Wing" was written in Chinese down the side of the Warrant Flag of the Society Leader, and the main character "Ling" ("warrant") was in the centre. An upright, oblong-shaped flag bore the characters meaning "Order of the Commander of Three Armies," another reference to the complex legendary history of the Triads. Most of the flags had two red pennants attached to the top bearing the characters meaning "Act According to the Will of Heaven: Overthrow Ch'ing, Restore Ming."

The main altar had a number of peculiar items on and around it. Above the Tau and its contents, which stood in front of the altar, hung a sheet of red paper. It bore characters exhorting the society to flourish throughout the country. Among the other items present were brass lamps, a pot of wine and five wine bowls, an incense pot for holding joss sticks, dishes of fresh fruit and flowers, and a large mixing bowl. Finally, there was a sheet of yellow paper bearing the names of the Triad's recruits hanging above the altar, and five small triangular flags. Characters meaning "wood," "fire," "metal," "earth," and "water" were written on the five flags.

Bond heard a drum beat a few times and the room became silent. Li Xu Nan, dressed in a red robe, entered the room and sat to the left of the altar. As he was Cho Kun, the Dragon Head, his was the only robe decorated with characters. On his left arm was a white circle containing the Chinese character meaning "Heaven." On his right arm was the character meaning "Earth." On his back were two characters, meaning "Sun" and "Moon" respectively, which when combined meant "Ming." On the front of the robe was the octagonal symbol of the Pat Kwa, or "Eight Diagrams." In the centre of the octagon was the Yin and Yang symbol of opposing yet complementary forces upon which the main tenets of Chinese philosophical thought were based. Magical powers were ascribed to this venerated emblem, and for this reason it was frequently employed by priests, necromancers, geomancers, and ordinary people as a good luck or protective charm.

The man Bond referred to as Scarface entered the room and sat to the right of the altar. He was wearing a white robe, and was the only man with a string of prayer beads around his neck. Bond didn't know much about Triad ceremonies, but he did know that they were usually led by an official known as the Heung Chu, or "Incense Master," who acted as a spiritual leader and sometimes second-in-command of the society. Scarface was obviously the Incense Master.

Two men in black robes stood at the extreme east end of the room, holding swords to block the entrance to the lodge. Another official in a black robe, the recruiting officer, moved from the altar down to the east end and began the ceremony. Bond noted that four Chinese teenagers stood outside the swords. They were not dressed in black robes, but rather in simple white shirts and trousers. These were the recruits.

The recruiting officer turned his right shoulder to the "guards" and called out in Cantonese, "Lower the net!" He made a sign with his left hand, denoting his rank within the organization. The two men in black robes then performed the secret handshake of the society out of view of the recruits. After performing this ritual, the recruiting officer was allowed through the swords.

The first official then addressed the recruits in Cantonese: "Why do you come here?"

The recruits replied in unison, "We come to enlist and obtain rations."

"There are no rations for our army."

"We bring our own."

"The red rice of our army contains sand and stones. Can you eat it?"

"If our brothers can eat it, so can we."

"When you see the beauty of our sworn sisters and sisters-in-law, will you have adulterous ideas?"

"No," the recruits replied in unison. "We would not dare to."

"If offered a reward by the Government, even as much as ten thousand taels of gold, to arrest your brothers, would you do so?"

"No. We would not dare to."

"If you have spoken truly, you are loyal and righteous and may enter the city to swear allegiance and protect the country with your concerted efforts."

The recruits each handed the official some money, and in return received a joss stick which they held in both hands. The recruits then got on their hands and knees and crawled under the raised swords, symbolizing that they were "passing through a mountain of knives."

Scarface, the Incense Master, stood and picked up the Warrant Flag of the Leader from the Tau and displayed it to everyone in the room.

"The Five Founders bestow on me the banner of authority," he said. "With it I will bring fresh troops into the city. We will pledge fraternity according to the will of Heaven. None must reveal the secrets that may be disclosed to him. The brethren have elected me to take charge of the Lodge, and have entrusted the seal of authority to my care. I am determined to exercise my authority."

The Incense Master then turned to three minor officials present near the altar. Bond recognized them as the three officials who were next in the chain of command of the organization. They were known respectively as the White Paper Fan, who acted as an adviser or counsellor; The Red Pole, who was a fighter and trainer; and the Straw Sandal, who acted as messenger and communications officer.

The Incense Master said to the Straw Sandal, "An order has been issued from the Five Ancestors Altar. Investigations must be made around the Lodge. If police are present to spy on us, they must be relentlessly washed." With that, he handed the Straw Sandal a warrant flag and a sword.

Bond knew that "washed" meant "killed." The Straw Sandal went around the room, checking the identities and hand signs of everyone present. When he was finished, he returned and handed back the flag and sword saying, "I now return the order flag in front of the Five Ancestors Altar. Thorough search has been made of the Lodge. Everyone was searched. All are surnamed Hung."

This confused Bond until he remembered that "Hung Mun" was a universal surname meaning "Triad Society," and was used by all Triads. The ceremony was clearly going to be a difficult test of Bond's knowledge of Cantonese!

The Incense Master then lit two tall single-stemmed brass lamps on the altar, saying, "Two old trees, one on either side, will bring stability to the nation. Heroes are recruited from all parts of the country. Tonight we pledge fraternity in the Red Flower Pavilion." Next, he lit five joss sticks, and then held them in both hands. He began to recite a lengthy poem.

"We worship Heaven and Earth by the three lights. Our Ancestors arose to support the Ming. The Hung door is opened wide and our brothers are many. Hung children are taught to remember the oaths and rules. Politeness, Righteousness, Wisdom, Faithfulness, and Virtue are our fundamental rules. The three talents—Heaven, Earth, and Man—combine to establish the nation. We dedicate ourselves by the drawing of blood. Our Ancestors showed their loyalty by sacrificing themselves for the Emperor."

Bond watched and listened in fascination as the Incense Master continued his recitation. After several minutes, Scarface placed the five joss sticks in the main incense pot on the altar at the five cardinal points—north, east, south, west, and centre. As he did this, he said, "The smoke of the incense sticks reaches the Heavenly Court, penetrates the earth, rises to the centre, rises to the Flower Pavilion, and reaches the city of Willows. We pledge fraternity in a union to overthrow Ch'ing—to bring an end to the decadent Ch'ing dynasty, and restore the rivers and mountains to Ming."

Next, the Incense Master took the dishes of fruit and flowers and a cup of wine and placed them in front of the memorial tablet on the wall. He recited a similar poem, then poured the cup of wine onto the floor.

The recruits knelt before the Incense Master and rolled up their trouser legs. The left trouser leg was rolled three times outwards to signify the resurgence of Ming, and the right was rolled three times inward to signify the disappearance of Ch'ing. Then they removed their shoes and put one straw sandal on their left feet. The Incense Master said, "Straw sandals were originally of five strands. In a battle at Wu Lung river they were lost. Only one was saved and retrieved at Chung Chau."

Next, he poured the wine into cups and emptied them on to the floor. "Wine is offered to the souls of our Ancestors and to those who died for our cause. Our fraternal spirit will last forever. The heroes in heaven will protect us. We swear we will kill all the traitors, so that Hung brothers can enjoy happiness and peace."

At this point, two officials in black robes brought in three life-sized paper figures in a kneeling position. They were placed on the floor, and a label was attached to each figure bearing one of the names of three historical Triad traitors. An official known as the Sin Fung, or Vanguard, took a long sword from the Tau and approached the figures. He placed the five elemental flags around them and said, "A big flag is erected in the Lodge. All heroes come here to worship. When our troops move out on to the plain, this sword will first stab Ma Ning Yee." With that, he swiftly cut off the paper head of the first figure.

"When the sword is turned back, it is used to stab Chan Man Yiu." He then cut off the head of the second paper figure.

"On the third occasion, it stabs the bad Emperor of Ch'ing." He then cut off the head of the third paper figure and called out, "Brothers assembled here, will you give help when the need arises?"

Everyone in the room shouted, "We will!" so loudly that it startled Bond.

At this point, the Incense Master took each of the items in the Tau, one by one, and recited a short poem about each. Following this was a long, drawn-out question-and-answer session between the Incense Master and the Vanguard, "proving" the identity and validity of the Vanguard and his role in the ceremony.

Then it was time for the actual initiation of the recruits. Each potential Triad member was given a joss stick, which was lit and held pointed down with both hands. The Vanguard asked them, "Which is the harder, the sword or your neck?"

The recruits all answered, "My neck." Bond deduced that this was an indication that even the threat of death would not cause them to reveal the society secrets. Then the Vanguard began to read the Thirty-Six Oaths of the Society. As each oath was proclaimed, a new joss stick was lit and handed to each recruit. The recruits repeated the oath and then extinguished the joss stick on the ground in front of them, symbolizing that they, too, would be similarly extinguished if they broke the oath.

"After having entered the Hung gates I must treat the parents and relatives of my sworn brothers as my own kin. I shall suffer death by five thunderbolts if I do not keep this oath.

"When Hung brothers visit my house, I shall provide them with board and lodging. I shall be killed by myriads of swords if I treat them as strangers.

"I will always acknowledge my Hung brothers when they identify themselves. If I ignore them I will be killed by myriads of swords.

"I shall never betray my sworn brothers. If, through a misunderstanding, I have caused the arrest of one of my brothers I must release him immediately. If I break this oath I will be killed by five thunderbolts."

The oaths continued in this fashion, mostly dealing with subjects regarding honour, betrayal, loyalty, and defending other members of the society. Several of the oaths were promises not to commit adultery or harm the other brothers' family members. Finally, the Vanguard reached the last two oaths.

"I must never reveal Hung secrets or signs when speaking to outsiders. If I do so I will be killed by myriads of swords.

"After entering the Hung gates I shall be loyal and faithful and shall endeavour to overthrow Ch'ing and restore Ming by coordinating my efforts with those of my sworn brethren even though my brethren and I may not be in the same profession. Our common aim is to avenge our Five Ancestors."

The Vanguard called out, "Will you swear to obey the oaths?"

"We swear to obey!" the recruits replied.

"Those who obey will be prosperous to the end. Those who do not will die as laid down in the oaths."

During this recitation, the large yellow paper at the front of the altar was held up high, and then set on fire. The ashes were placed in the large bowl, to which was added rice wine, sugar, and cinnabar.

An official entered the room carrying a live chicken and a china bowl. He passed in front of each recruit, allowing them to touch the chicken's head and the bowl. The Vanguard, who was holding the long sword, said, "The lotus flower signifies wealth and nobility. Loyally and faithfully we perpetuate the Hung family. The wicked and treacherous will be broken into pieces, in the same manner as this particular lotus flower." That said, the Vanguard took the china bowl, tossed it in the air, and deftly smashed it to pieces with the sword. The official then handed over the chicken to the Vanguard, and helped him tie its legs together. They placed the chicken's head on a chopping block, with the bowl of ashes, wine, sugar, and cinnabar on the floor next to the block.

"The chicken's head sheds fresh blood. Here there is loyalty and righteousness. We will all live long lives."

The Vanguard stood and, with great ceremony, cut off the chicken's head with one swift blow of the sword. There was an immense amount of blood, and the headless body jerked grotesquely as if it was still struggling to get away. The Vanguard took the head and dipped it into the bowl, mixing the blood with the other ingredients. The carcass was then taken away, and the recruits all held up their left hands, palm upward. The Incense Master approached them, holding a needle and red thread.

He said, "The silver needle brings blood from the finger. Do not reveal our secrets to others. If any secrets are disclosed, blood will be shed from the five holes of your body."

The Incense Master then pricked the middle finger of each recruit's left hand, and added their blood to the bowl's mixture. Each recruit touched the mixture with the pricked finger, then placed the finger in their mouth to taste the substance. "It is sweet," they all said, one by one. Next, the Incense Master poured a little of the mixture into cups and handed one to each recruit.

"After drinking the Red Flower wine, you will live for ninety-nine years. When nine is added to this number, you will live for one hundred and eight years."

Bond's stomach turned as each recruit drank from their respective cup.

The Incense Master then formed a signal with his left hand, designating the recruits' ranks in the society. The recruits stood and bowed to the Incense Master, the Dragon Head, the Vanguard, and to each other.

The entire assembly stood and recited, "Old and new brothers gather here tonight. Loyalty and faithfulness will ensure us longevity. Wicked and treacherous will perish like the incense sticks."

Officials began to dismantle the altar as the chant continued: "The city is being dismantled from East to West, from the South gate to Peking city. No firecrackers are fired in celebration, the metropolis is reduced to ashes."

The ceremony was over. The entire rite had taken a little over two hours. The recruits joined the ranks of the other members as Li Xu Nan, the Cho Kun, the Dragon Head, stood and addressed the society.

"We will gather again in three days to perform the final phase of the initiation ceremony—in which your faces shall be cleansed. We welcome our new brothers to the Dragon Wing. We have one more piece of business to conduct tonight. One of our Blue Lanterns has broken her oaths. We must decide her fate." He turned to the Vanguard. "Bring out the traitor."

The Vanguard motioned towards a door. Two officials brought in a girl. She was blindfolded, and her hands were tied behind her back.

Bond's heart jumped into his throat. It was Sunni!

"Our sister here has betrayed the society, not only to a stranger, but to a *gweilo*. She has sought refuge with the enemy. She has sought to leave the fraternity. What must we do with her?"

The group shouted, "She must die!"

Li stood for a moment in silence. He walked around Sunni, who was now on her knees on the floor. He inspected her as if he was evaluating prized livestock.

"I agree with my younger brothers," he said, "but we shall wait. The traitor may be useful in an enterprise valuable to the society. For the time being, she will be kept in isolation." He nodded to the two guards, who pulled Sunni up and led her out of the room. It took every ounce of Bond's strength not to burst through the dilapidated ceiling and attempt to rescue her.

Li Xu Nan and Scarface stood side by side in front of the Triad and gave the hand signs for their ranks. Scarface said a final prayer and dismissed the group. The meeting was over. The members left silently and, after a few minutes, Li, Scarface, and the official who was the Vanguard were alone. They took off their robes.

Scarface took the metal briefcase from behind the altar. He handed it to the Vanguard, who apparently was the Chan So, or Treasurer, of the organization.

Li said, "This month's earnings. Make sure it is properly distributed. The families of our brothers who were killed at the girl's residence must receive special consideration."

The Vanguard bowed. "Yes, Cho Kun." He took the case and left. Bond watched as Scarface extinguished the rest of the lighting, and he and Li walked out of the Lodge.

Bond waited a full ten minutes before moving. He had to find Sunni. He crawled forward, so that he was directly above where the altar had been. There was a loose board there through which he could drop. He pulled it up, then jumped down to the floor below. He waited a few seconds to allow his eyes to adjust to the darkness. Then he moved towards the door where they had taken Sunni and stepped through it.

He was met by myriads of swords, all pointing at his chest.

FOURTEEN

BEDTIME STORY

ZERO MINUS SIX: 25 JUNE 1997, 1:00 A.M.

The speed with which Bond was disarmed was startling. He felt as if he was moving in slow-motion and that everything else was happening too fast. The Triads with the choppers marched him to the adjacent building, one that was obviously still in use. One of them unlocked the door and roughly shoved Bond inside. He was led down a hallway to a locked, steel door. Behind it was a dark staircase leading to a basement. Bond was pushed inside, and the door slammed and locked behind him.

Bond crept down the stairs in the dim light to a small, bare room containing a narrow bed and a toilet. It was, to all intents and purposes, a jail cell.

Sunni Pei was sitting on the bed. When she saw him, she jumped up and ran to him. "James! My God, James!" she cried, then fell into his arms and held him tightly.

Bond stroked her hair and embraced her. "It's all right, Sunni. We'll get you out of this."

"They're going to kill me, James, I know it!" She said this with anger and spite, not with the tears he had expected. "And after all I've done for them!"

She released him and led him to the bed.

"I told you before that they've merely used you," he said. "They never made you a full member."

"The oaths still apply to me, though," she said. "And I was taking just as much of a risk with regard to the law in Hong Kong."

She stood up and started pacing the cell. "I can't tell you how I hate myself, James! I was their goddamned *whore*! I sold my body to put money in *their* pockets!"

"Sunni," he said, "you did it because you believed in them. I understand. You believed they would get you out of Hong Kong. You believed they were your brothers and sisters. You believed they would take care of you."

She sat down again. "Well, in many ways they did take care of me. I couldn't have afforded that flat otherwise. They paid for most of it. They gave me a social life, such as it was."

"Sunni, you know that if you hadn't received an American education, that if you had grown up entirely as a Hong Kong Chinese, then you would be thinking quite differently. You *would* have killed me the other day. You would have been loyal to the Triad. Your cultural background would have prevented you from even considering associating with a *gweilo*."

"Oh, I still have a strong Chinese cultural heritage," she said. "I just happen to speak like an American." She used an exaggerated accent on the last word, then pouted. "You're right, though. It's surprising that they even allowed me into the Triad with my westernized habits."

"You had other assets that they deemed valuable."

"And what might those be?"

"You're beautiful and you're intelligent."

She smirked. "Oh, right, I'm the perfect hostess. I can go with Chinese, American, Japanese, German, *English* . . . you name it."

"I didn't mean it that way," he said.

The sound of keys in the door interrupted them. It opened and two Triads stepped in. They gestured for Bond to come with them. Sunni stood up, too, but one of the men roughly pushed her back on to the bed.

Bond shoved the thug against the wall. The other man brutally delivered a spear-handed chop between Bond's shoulder blades, sending him to his knees. The blow had hit the nerve centre below his neck, and for a moment Bond saw nothing but stars. The man shouted at Bond in Chinese, then kicked him. 007 got weakly to his feet and followed the men out of the room.

He was brought upstairs, down a hall, and up another flight of stairs. He was finally able to take in more of his surroundings as he walked. The building was a modern business office. It might have been the corporate headquarters of a small real-estate or insurance company. They passed open offices containing new, expensive-looking black and white leather furniture. In many ways, the place reminded him of the way the new M had refurnished SIS headquarters.

He was finally led into a large, plush office and left alone. It was decorated in the same fashion as the other rooms he had seen, but with a distinctive Chinese flavour. Along with the high-tech, modern furniture, there was a bamboo screen against the wall, brightly painted with a scene of Chinese fishermen snaring a dragon. A small Buddhist altar stood in a corner, with an idol of the god Kwan Ti, or Mo, on it. Bond remembered that not only was Mo the god of policemen, he was also the favoured deity of the underworld. There was nothing else in the room that would suggest that the office belonged to the Dragon Head of a Triad. It was clearly Li Xu Nan's legitimate office.

Before Bond could sit down, Li entered the room and shut the door behind him. They were alone.

"We meet again, Mr. Bond," Li said in Cantonese. "I am sorry that it is under unfortunate circumstances."

"You can't hold me, Mr. Li," Bond said. "I'm a British citizen. My newspaper will be trying to find me when they've realized I've gone missing." His Cantonese had improved since arriving in Hong Kong.

"Oh, dispense with your crap, Mr. Bond," he said. "You are no journalist. I know who you are."

"I work for the *Daily Gleaner* . . ."

"*Please,* Mr. Bond! I am no fool!" Li walked to his large oak desk and took a cigarette out of a gun metal case not unlike Bond's own. He lit it without offering one to his captive. "You are James Bond, an agent with the British Secret Service. It was not difficult to ascertain this. You see, I know Mr. T.Y. Woo and what he does. I have known for years that his shop on Cat Street is a front for your station here in Hong Kong. You were followed from Miss Pei's flat the other day. When we saw Mr. Woo's private taxi pick you up, it all fell into place."

"Then it was you who killed J.J. Woo? It was you who ransacked the place?"

Li shrugged. "We wanted the girl. She is a traitor. We deal with traitors most severely. We only messed up the place to leave a message. The elder Woo attempted to stop us. He was an obstacle that we had to overcome. It was not personal."

"Where are T.Y. and his son?"

Li said, "I honestly do not know. They were not there when we raided the building."

"Don't you see that he knows who you are and what you do? He can have the Hong Kong Police down on you at any minute."

"He cannot prove a thing. You're the only one who has witnessed anything," Li said. "Let me make this perfectly clear, Mr. Bond. You are a *gweilo*. We don't like you. You are not welcome here. Our ceremonies are sacred and secret. You have seen something no other *gweilo* has ever seen. You are a dead man, Mr. Bond. If I had not stopped them, my brothers would have already killed you."

"Why did you stop them, then?"

Li paused a moment, walked to the drinks cupboard, and removed a couple of glasses. "Drink, Mr. Bond?"

He wanted to refuse, but a drink would actually do him a lot of good. "All right. Bourbon, straight."

Li filled the glasses and handed one to Bond. "Do you remember the other day when you 'interviewed' me? I told you that you were in my debt."

"I remember."

"The time has come for you to repay the debt."

"Why should I?"

"Hear me out, Mr. Bond. You have no other choice."

Bond settled on the sofa. "All right, Li, I'll listen."

"I'll have to tell you a story," he said, sitting opposite Bond in a leather armchair. "A little bedtime story. It involves someone else you know . . . Mr. Guy Thackeray."

Bond interrupted Li. "Did you kill him?"

Li paused a moment and shook his head. "No. We had nothing to do with that. Let me tell you something: I hated Guy Thackeray. He and I were mortal enemies. But I wanted him alive. I needed him alive. And the story I'm about to tell you will explain why. No, he was killed by General Wong, a lunatic up in Guangzhou. You have heard of him?"

Bond nodded. "Are you sure? Why would he do that?"

Li held out his hands tolerantly. "Patience, Mr. Bond. Hear me out. And then you will understand."

The Dragon Head paused a moment, then spoke evenly and calmly. "The year was 1836. A twenty-six-year-old man named James Thackeray had sailed from his home in Britain two years earlier to the Pearl River Delta in southern China. He had heard a fortune could be made trading goods to the Chinese, but it was a difficult time and place to make a living. *Gweilo* were not welcome in southern China. You see, Mr. Bond, China needed nothing from the West, but was quick to perceive that the West needed China's tea, among other commodities. Therefore, the government grudgingly allowed the "white devils" to trade on the outer fringes of her empire."

Bond interjected, "It seems to me that each side treated the other as inferior."

"Yes," Li said. "Anyway . . . James Thackeray had originally attempted to trade manufactured goods and had made a meagre living from silver, but it wasn't enough to feed his wife and young son, neither of whom was allowed into Guangzhou, or Canton, as it was called then. Other British traders were in the same predicament, and it appeared for a while that trade with China would be a failure.

"No one was quite sure when it happened, but eventually some ingenious trader discovered that the English did possess a commodity that the Chinese wanted. It was opium. The merchants had no qualms about peddling opium to wealthy Chinese, and it soon became the most valuable resource in that part of the world at the time. China was quick to ban the substance, but the British managed to find a way to smuggle it in anyway."

"And the opium trade became big business," Bond said.

"Correct. In 1836, James Thackeray began trading opium and quickly developed a small clientele which provided him with more money than he had ever dreamed of. Thackeray's best customer was an extremely wealthy Chinese warlord and government official residing in Guangzhou. His name was Li Wei Tam." Li paused again, then added, "He was my great-great-grandfather."

Bond sat up straighter. This story was getting interesting.

"My honourable ancestor was a warlord who was ten years older than Thackeray. He had tremendous influence in Guangzhou and the area around the Pearl River Delta. Although the Ch'ing Dynasty was in power, Li's loyalties were with the Mings, who had been overthrown in the seventeenth century. Of course, he would never have admitted this publicly. If he had done so, he would have been arrested and most likely put to death. Li Wei Tam was part of a secret society that had pledged to overthrow the Ch'ing Dynasty.

"It was pure luck, really, that James Thackeray had an audience with the warlord and was able to establish a relationship with him. In fact, the two men grew to respect each other. Although they probably wouldn't have admitted it to other members of their respective races, they became friends. This was due in part, no doubt, to Li Wei Tam's physical dependence on the drug that James Thackeray so happily supplied." This last was said with a certain amount of venom.

Li went on: "In 1839, things started to change. The emperor decided to end the opium trade once and for all. The governor of Hunan Province was ordered to confiscate all of Guangzhou's foreign traders' opium, thus igniting the First Opium War. For the next three years, James Thackeray found it extremely difficult to get his opium into China and to his favoured customer. Likewise, Li Wei Tam had to go through unpleasant stretches of withdrawal from the drug. Finally, my great-great-grandfather used his influence in his secret society to establish an illegal pipeline from Thackeray to Guangzhou. In one of the first, albeit unethical, cooperative efforts between a British citizen and a Chinese warlord, James Thackeray was allowed to continue his lucrative opium trade and Li Wei Tam was able to perpetuate his comfortable, horizontal life on an opium bed. I suppose you know what happened in 1842?"

Bond answered, "The war had ended, and Hong Kong Island was ceded to the British."

"Yes. The ban on opium still existed, however. The Chinese government, as a result of what they viewed as an unfair and unequal Treaty, made trade an even more challenging endeavour despite the fact that the Treaty had guaranteed Britain's right to trade openly and freely."

Bond added, "In China's view, the ceding of Hong Kong Island was a humiliating experience and was never wholly forgotten nor forgiven."

"You are an intelligent man, Mr. Bond," Li said. "I can almost forget you are a *gweilo*. Shall I continue?"

"Please do."

"While companies like Jardine Matheson were allowed to build headquarters on Hong Kong Island, James Thackeray still found himself dealing independently and without any established, legal structure from which to conduct business. He, too, needed a legitimate enterprise that he could call his own. Even though he had made what some men might call a fortune over the last few years, Thackeray needed more capital. It was Li Wei Tam who came to his rescue. One night in 1850, over an exquisite meal, a tremendous amount of rice wine, and quite a bit of opium smoke, a deal was struck that would have repercussions for both men's descendants. My honourable ancestor offered to "loan" Thackeray the much-needed capital to start his own trading company. Thackeray, who was basically an honest man, was flabbergasted. He said he would accept the money only on condition that they made a provision by which Li could be repaid.

"My great-great-grandfather was drunk and high from the amount of wine and drugs consumed that night, and thought whimsically about Thackeray's request. For the sake of *xinyong,* a term that means 'trust' in our language, Li Wei Tam attempted to think of a ridiculous demand, which Thackeray could never fulfil, as a gesture of his own generosity. After all, his primary motivation was the continuing supply of opium. James Thackeray was his friend, and Li Wei Tam hadn't many friends—Chinese or otherwise.

"The ceding of Hong Kong happened to be a much-discussed and extremely controversial topic in southern China at the time. The Treaty signed at Nanking had provided that Hong Kong be handed over to the British in 'perpetuity.' "

Bond added, "There were even British citizens who thought the Treaty was absurd."

"Yes. At that time, no one could predict that it would one day be the Manhattan of the Far East. Therefore, with a sly grin, my great-great-grandfather told his friend, "Mr. Thackeray, you may have the money for your company on one condition. You must sign an agreement with me. Should Hong Kong ever come under Chinese rule again, then your assets in the company shall be handed over to me. It would then become *my* company.'"

"Thackeray, who believed that Hong Kong would *never* leave British rule, laughed and agreed. The two men drew up official legal documents. James Thackeray signed them, and Li Wei Tam applied his *chop,* our official family seal, alongside the signature. It was *maijiang* of the highest order. Thus, EurAsia Enterprises was born."

My God, Bond thought, the roots of this whole mess went back a century and a half!

Li continued. "Opium was legalized in 1856 as the Second Opium War began, and during the following years James Thackeray became one of Hong Kong's wealthiest men. EurAsia Enterprises flourished, and even London recognized his and the company's importance. The Kowloon peninsula was ceded to Britain in 1860, and finally, in 1898, the New Territories was leased to Britain for ninety-nine years. Little did anyone know at the time that this last Treaty, signed at the

Second Convention of Peking, would have a direct effect on Hong Kong Island and Kowloon as well."

"What happened to Thackeray and your great-great-grandfather?" Bond asked.

"James Thackeray died in 1871. His son Richard took over EurAsia Enterprises and continued to trade opium to Li Wei Tam, who had reached a ripe old age. The company expanded, opening branches all over the world. My great-great-grandfather finally succumbed to the gods in 1877, and the partnership between the Thackeray family and the Li family ended. My great-grandfather, Li's only son, never approved of his father's addiction to opium, nor of the *gweilo* who sold it to him. He did, however, make sure that the agreement signed by the elder Thackeray and his father remained intact and safe. Perhaps someday it would come in useful."

Li stood and refilled Bond's glass, then resumed his place in the leather armchair to continue the story. "Now the tale gets a little complicated," he said with a smile. "To cut a long story short, in 1911 civil war broke out in China. You may know that an ambitious, Western-educated revolutionary named Dr. Sun Yat-sen initiated a rebellion dedicated to establishing a republican government in China. He succeeded; by 1912, the Ch'ing Dynasty was no more."

Bond was quite familiar with China's tortured twentieth-century history, but he allowed Li to tell it in his own words.

"It was a period of great turmoil. During a skirmish in Guangzhou, my great-grandfather was killed, leaving *his* son Li Pei Wu, my grandfather, to look after the family fortune. Unfortunately, the republican government was extremely unstable; between 1912 and 1949 there were times when it didn't exist at all and the country was a . . ." again he searched for the right word, and finally said in English ". . . a free-for-all!" Li smiled at his choice of phrase.

Bond continued the history lesson. "As for Sun Yat-sen, he formed the Kuomintang party in an attempt to limit the republicans' power. The government outlawed the Kuomintang and Sun Yat-sen was forced into exile."

"You are well informed, Mr. Bond," Li said. "Ambitious warlords vied for leadership for more than a decade. In 1921, the Communists organized in Shanghai, with Mao Zedong among their original members. They made bids for power in the turbulent country, and in 1923, Sun Yat-sen agreed to admit them to Kuomintang membership. But after Sun's death in 1925, the young general Chiang Kai-shek took over the leadership of the Kuomintang and set about reunifying China under its rule, ridding the country of imperialists and warlords, and exercising a bloody purge of the party's Communist membership."

Bond wondered what all this had to do with Li's family. In answer to his thought, Li said, "My grandfather's family got caught up in the maelstrom that ravaged China during this period of unrest. The family fortune was lost to the Communists in 1926, and my grandfather was murdered for having "secret society" connections. My grandmother and her two young children became refugees and fled across the border into Kowloon. The eldest of the children was a boy of seven, named Li Chen Tam."

"Your father?"

Li nodded. "The Communists had seized all of my family's property, amongst which was the ancient document signed by James Thackeray and my great-great-grandfather, Li Wei Tam. The document was considered lost for all time. I've already told you a little about my father. Li Chen Tam fell into the hard life in which many Hong Kong Chinese refugees found themselves during the years between the two World Wars. He supported his mother and baby sister by selling food on the street. When he became a teenager, he made the acquaintance of several other young Chinese boys who belonged to a fraternal organization. They offered to help him financially and protect his family. In exchange, he had to pledge allegiance, as well as secrecy, to their organization. This organization was the San Yee On, which you know as one of the largest and most powerful Triads in Southeast Asia.

"My father rose rapidly through the ranks, especially after entering the lucrative entertainment business in the 1950s. Along the way, like so many of the Triad leaders at the time, he made a few enemies even within his own organization. In the early 1960s, when he was approaching fifty, my father broke off from the San Yee On and formed his own Triad, the Dragon Wing Society.

"He was quite aware of his great-grandfather's agreement with EurAsia Enterprises but was unable to do anything about it. So, my father concocted an underhanded scheme to get his own back. By putting the squeeze on EurAsia's shipping department heads, the Dragon Wing Society infiltrated the company's inner workings. Nothing was shipped out of Hong Kong without the Triad's intervention. Things came to a head, and eventually news of the squeeze went all the way to the top of the company."

"Who must have been, let's see . . . James Thackeray's great-grandson?" Bond asked.

"Correct. Thomas Thackeray, then the current *taipan* of EurAsia Enterprises, and Guy Thackeray's father. While being a shrewd businessman, Thomas Thackeray had inherited his great-grandfather's trait of greediness. If there was an opportunity to add to his fortune, then he would brush ethics aside and encourage the money-making to continue. It was with this attitude that Thomas Thackeray justified entering into a business alliance with my father. The two men met in person only once, and secretly, at one of my father's nightclubs. It was agreed that EurAsia Enterprises would provide the means, the Dragon Wing Society would provide the goods and muscle, and together they would share in the profits. Thus, EurAsia Enterprises began distributing heroin all over the world as couriers for the Dragon Wing Society."

Bond noted, "It seems the story has come full circle, practically a reversal of the partnership that existed in the mid-nineteenth century."

"Ironically, that is true," Li said. "There was, however, another piece of the alliance. The smuggled heroin had to come from somewhere, and that was the Golden Triangle. A certain young Chinese official in Guangzhou had influence over the operations of the poppy fields there. His name was Wong Tsu Kam. Extremely militaristic and a staunch Communist, Colonel Wong also happened to be even greedier than Thomas Thackeray! He was the unseen, silent partner of Thackeray and my father. He maintained the poppy fields. He refined the opium into heroin in his own laboratories located on site in the Golden Triangle. He cleared the way for the heroin to be safely smuggled into Hong Kong so that the Dragon Wing Society could get it onto EurAsia's ships. For his efforts, Wong received a tremendous kickback. A man with those kinds of assets in China wielded great power, and he used it to advance within the Communist party until he became a fully fledged general in 1978.

"A year before Wong Tsu Kam became a general, Guy Thackeray took over EurAsia Enterprises. I had succeeded my father as Cho Ku of the Dragon Wing Society. Our uneasy partnership continued through the eighties and into the nineties. All along, my father knew of the ancient agreement that would have given us control of EurAsia Enterprises should the Hong Kong colony ever be handed back to China. In 1984, the speculation came to an end when the treaty was signed to do that very thing in 1997. The rage that my father felt at the Thackeray family, and at the Communists who had stolen *his* father's assets, eventually killed him. He died of heart failure shortly after the news was made public. I carried on, but now a bitter rift existed between me and Guy Thackeray. Our partnership continued, but it was purely a business transaction. It had ceased being personal long ago.

"It was in 1985 that General Wong made his move. One afternoon, his people made an appointment to see Guy Thackeray at EurAsia Enterprises' corporate headquarters in Central. With a Chinese lawyer in tow, General Wong met Thackeray in the company's luxurious boardroom and pulled out a tattered document written in both English and Chinese. General Wong was in possession of the original agreement made between James Thackeray and my great-great-grandfather! According to Chinese law, the state now owned the document and what it represented. Li Wei Tam's heirs had fled China and their assets were seized by the Communist government. Therefore, as the representative of that Chinese government, General Wong informed Guy Thackeray that the 59 per cent of stock owned by Thackeray would automatically transfer to China at midnight on 30 June, 1997, just as the colony itself would be handed over after a hundred and fifty years of British rule. General Wong had been given full authority to execute the transition and implement whatever new management system he desired. Whatever he decided to do, Guy Thackeray was out. In essence, not only would General Wong gain control of a multi-billion dollar corporation, but he would also increase his profit margin in the drug smuggling operation by one-third. He would have the upper hand over me and the Society, too! General Wong would be able to call all the shots. As for Thackeray, he would be left high and dry. It made no difference that 41 per cent of the stock was owned by other British citizens. Wong implicitly made it clear that they would be persuaded to sell their shares and leave Hong Kong forever."

"What happened?" Bond asked.

"Guy Thackeray never told a soul about this meeting apart from his own English solicitor, Gregory Donaldson. He spent the following five years consulting Donaldson about the matter. Donaldson was sworn to secrecy, and they searched for a way out. But it was hopeless. Once China took over the colony, their law would reign supreme and the original agreement would be deemed legal. For the next seven years, Guy Thackeray lived with the knowledge that he would have to give up his family's company and there wasn't a damn thing he could do about it. He became a bitter, unhappy man—a friendless recluse prone to gambling for high stakes in Macau."

Bond realized that this explained the man's eccentric behaviour and his alcoholism.

"Thackeray arranged a meeting with me one rainy night in 1995 and told me the news. At first, I was ecstatic that my great-great-grandfather's agreement still existed. Then, as the truth of the matter sank in, I was filled with hatred and the desire for revenge. I hated the Thackeray family for their role in the history of the mess, and I detested General Wong for stealing what was rightfully mine."

Li smiled wryly as he ended the extraordinary story. "Since then, the drug-smuggling partnership has kept operating—it was business as usual. After all, a profit could still be made until things changed in 1997."

James Bond had listened to Li Xu Nan's story, fascinated and repelled at the same time. It was a classic case of injustice and irony. A vicious criminal was being cheated out of something of great value that was rightfully his, and Bond found himself feeling the man's outrage, too.

"So you see, Mr. Bond," Li said, "Mr. Thackeray and I had a mutual interest in keeping Wong from taking over the company. Thackeray and I were not friends. We were enemies, but we had a common goal. I did not kill him."

"But why would General Wong kill him?" Bond asked. "If he was going to gain control of the company on July the first anyway, why murder Thackeray?"

Li shrugged. "I do not know. You will have to ask him."

"And why was the solicitor, Donaldson, also killed? And the other Directors?"

"Perhaps they were going to get in the way legally," Li suggested. "Maybe there was a loophole, and that was the only way Wong could close it. General Wong may be a Communist, but he is one of the most corrupt capitalist pigs I know."

It made sense. It was Thackeray's murder that was the big question mark.

"The other night we were in Macau. Some Triads chopped up a *mahjong* game at the Lisboa Casino. Were they your men?"

"No. I give you my word," Li said.

Bond sat in thought. A big piece of the puzzle was still missing.

"Now we come to the task I must ask you to do, Mr. Bond," Li said. "As I mentioned earlier, you are in my debt. If you perform this task for me and succeed, I will release you from my debt and also spare your life."

"I don't know what it is you want me to do, Li," Bond said, "but I can tell you right now I don't work for criminals. You can kill me now. I've lived my entire life with the prospect of death coming at any moment."

Li nodded. "Brave words, Mr. Bond. Why don't you hear me out first?"

Bond sighed. "All right. What is it you want?"

"I want you to go to Guangzhou and pay a little visit to General Wong."

"And then what?"

"Steal my great-great-grandfather's agreement. Wong keeps it in a safe in his office. Bring it back to me. If you have to eliminate the good general in the process . . ." Li shrugged his shoulders.

Bond laughed. "You must be joking, Li! How the hell do you think a *gweilo* like me could get anywhere near this general, much less break into his bloody safe? Don't you think I would stick out like a sore thumb in China?"

"Hear me out, Mr. Bond. I have a plan." Bond raised his hand, gesturing for Li to continue, but he knew the very thought was absurd. "You are sceptical, Mr. Bond, I see that, but listen to me. We have learned that a new lawyer from London will be arriving in Hong Kong later this morning after the sun rises. He is Gregory Donaldson's replacement as EurAsia Enterprises' solicitor. Since Mr. Thackeray's untimely demise, this new lawyer will be handling things. He has an appointment in Guangzhou the next day with General Wong himself. I propose that you go to Guangzhou in his place. My organization has contacts at the airport. We can do a switch before the man even enters Immigration. You will be hand-delivered to General Wong by EurAsia executives. You will meet Wong privately. He will most certainly show you the original document. You will have the perfect, and probably the only, chance to get it. Then my brothers will help you get out of Guangzhou and back to Hong Kong."

"Not on your life, Li."

"I'm afraid you'll have to die, then."

"I've heard worse threats."

Li said, "Very well, I will offer you another incentive—the life of that girl, the traitor. She can leave with you, and I will cancel the death warrant on her head."

Bond closed his eyes. The man had played the trump card.

FIFTEEN

DAY TRIP TO CHINA

10:30 A.M.

The British Airways flight that carried James Pickard, Esquire, of Fitch, Donaldson and Patrick, arrived on time at Kai Tak Airport. "Representatives" from EurAsia Enterprises were waiting, not in the gate area or in the Greeting Hall beyond Immigration, but right in the movable airbridge that attached to the door of the aircraft.

Two Chinese men in business suits stopped Pickard as he stepped off the aircraft.

"Mr. Pickard?"

"Yes?"

"Come with us, please. We take you to hotel."

The men opened a service door in the airbridge and gestured towards a set of metal steps leading down to the tarmac. Pickard was confused.

"Don't I have to go through Immigration?" he asked.

"That already taken care of," one of the men said in broken English.

Pickard shrugged, chalked it up to Chinese efficiency, and was pleased he was getting the VIP treatment. He happily walked down the steps and into a waiting limousine. As soon as the car was away, James Bond ascended the same set of steps and entered the jetbridge. He walked through it and into the terminal. As he had not got much sleep the night before anyway, he looked and felt as if he really had just flown the long haul from London. He was dressed in an Armani suit borrowed from Li Xu Nan, and carried a briefcase full of law books. He was unarmed, having reluctantly left his Walther PPK with Li.

The passport and travel documents with which Li's people provided him were top-notch forgeries. As James Pickard, British citizen, he sailed through Immigration and Customs, and was met in the Greeting Hall by an attractive blonde woman and a Chinese man, both in their thirties.

"Mr. Pickard?" the woman said. She was English.

"Yes?"

"I'm Corinne Bates from the Public Relations office at EurAsia Enterprises." She held out her hand.

Bond shook it. "Hello. James Pickard."

"How was your flight?"

"Long."

"Isn't it though? I find it dreadful. This is Johnny Leung, assistant to the interim General Manager."

"How do you do?" Bond said, and shook the man's hand.

"Fine, thank you," Leung said. "We have a car waiting."

Bond allowed himself to be guided outside and into a Rolls-Royce. So far, the operation was going smoothly.

"All the hotels were booked because of the July the first transition," Corinne Bates said. "We're putting you up for the night in a corporate flat in the Mid-Levels. Is that all right?"

"Sounds fine," Bond said.

The car drove through the Cross-Harbour Tunnel to the island, made its way through Central and up into the Mid-Levels, an area of some social prominence but just a step down from the elite Victoria Peak. It finally entered a complex on Po Shan Road, just off Conduit Road.

They let him into the flat, a lovely two-bedroomed affair with a parquet floor and a view of Central.

"We'll pick you up at 6:30 in the morning, Mr. Pickard. The train leaves from Kowloon at 7:50," Ms. Bates said.

"We're taking the train?" Bond asked.

"It's the easiest way," she said. "And that way you can see a bit of the Chinese countryside. It's about a two-and-a-half hour ride to Guangzhou."

Bond nodded. After the couple had made sure he had everything he needed, they left him alone. He picked up the phone and dialled a number that Li had given him. Li himself answered.

"How is the view from Po Shan Road?" Li asked.

His men must have followed them from the airport. They were very efficient. Bond thought that for a criminal outfit they were as well-organized and effective as any major intelligence outfit in the world.

"It's fine, Li. Just make sure your men watch my back, all right?"

"Don't you worry, Mr. Bond. Just bring back my document in one piece."

"Mr. Li?"

"Yes, Mr. Bond?"

"I'd like to know what happened to T.Y. Woo and his son. Can you find them?"

"As a matter of fact, we found the boy safe and sound at one of Mr. Woo's private flats. We did not bother him. Mr. Woo is probably attempting to find you, so we left word with the boy that you are safe. I would hate for Mr. Woo to blow the whistle to your government before your job for me is completed. Do not worry about him, Mr. Bond. Have a nice trip tomorrow. Enjoy southern China."

Li hung up before Bond could say anything else. Bond stood in the centre of the living room and stared out of the window at the postcard view. He could easily get away from this place, but it would jeopardize Sunni. At times, Bond wanted to kick himself. Why did he have such a soft spot for women? Sunni meant nothing to him, really. She was just another in a long line of affairs which provided a few fireworks for a while and eventually fizzled out. His pattern with women was so predictable that he could chart the liaison's progress on a blackboard. He intentionally stayed as far away as possible from any kind of commitment to a woman. It seemed that whenever he allowed himself to get seriously involved, something terrible happened. He would never forget Vesper Lynd, the first woman he had ever really loved. She had tried to accept his love for her, but that affair ended in guilt and tragedy. There were others he had lost in recent years because of their association with him, including fellow agents and companions Fredericka von Grüsse, Harriet Horner, and Easy St. John. By far the worst disaster was when his lovely wife of fifteen minutes, Tracy di Vicenzo, was gunned down by bullets meant for him. Now here was Sunni Pei, a condemned Triad member looking for a way out of her wretched life. Bond could easily walk away from this job and from her.

"Bloody hell," he said aloud. He knew he wouldn't do that. He had already put himself on the line for Sunni. Bond stubbornly justified his actions by telling himself that this little visit to General Wong in Guangzhou was an essential part of his mission. After all, he had learned that Wong was involved with Thackeray and Li. Wong was the number one suspect in Thackeray's murder. Wong was now calling the shots with regard to the EurAsia/Triad connection. It *was* an essential step in his mission. He wasn't veering off on some wild goose chase just to save a female. This was business, and the journey just might provide him with the means to complete his job in Hong Kong.

Bond searched the kitchen and found a bottle of vodka. Pouring a double helped him accept the fact that he was *really* doing this for that lovely girl with the almond eyes.

ZERO MINUS FIVE: 26 JUNE 1997, 8:00 A.M.

The Kowloon-Guangzhou Express left precisely on time. Corinne Bates and Johnny Leung saw "James Pickard" to the station and made sure Bond got through Immigration and aboard the right train. Apparently General Wong had insisted that the new solicitor from Fitch, Donaldson and Patrick come to China alone. The train was surprisingly comfortable, with plenty of room in the aisles. Bond sat by the window and watched as the several stops within the New Territories came and went, and they finally crossed the border into southern China.

Shenzhen was the first major city just beyond the border, and at first glance appeared to be just another part of Hong Kong. Something was different, though, and Bond couldn't put his finger on it until the train had travelled a few minutes into the country: there was a lack of English signs. Throughout most of Hong Kong, public signs were written in both Chinese and English. Here, the world was strictly Chinese.

A large portion of southern China had become a "Special Economic Zone." This meant that the Chinese government was allowing free enterprise to exist to a certain extent. If a family was able to make a living selling their own goods, then they were welcome to do so. Only eligible people were permitted to live in the Special Economic Zone. For example, in the city of Shekou, women outnumbered men eight to one. This was because it was primarily a manufacturing community in which intricate work could only be performed by small hands. When Hong Kong became part of China on 1 July it, too, would be a part of the Special Economic Zone. Whether or not it would retain any semblance of autonomy remained to be seen.

Shenzhen looked extremely commercial and urbanized. Bond expected to see an obligatory McDonald's or two along the way, but when he saw the famous *Playboy* rabbit logo on a building, he was quite surprised.

The train stopped briefly to let passengers on and off, then continued northwest towards Guangzhou. The scenery flashing by the train window alternated curiously every few seconds—one moment it was rural farmland that looked archaic, then in a flash there was a sudden patch of built-up suburbia. It was not uncommon to see a wooden shanty alongside a newly built tenement high rise. Bond's impression of the farmlands was that time stood still. The rich, green rice paddy fields were still being irrigated by hand-held water poles or crude machines pulled by water buffalo. Yet, a hundred metres away from a farm would be fifteen- or twenty-storey brick buildings, many with an uninteresting mosaic tile pattern decorating the exteriors. Bond had read that the government was making room for more high rises. China's one billion people needed homes.

Bond couldn't help feeling that it was a world of incongruous contrasts. The urban areas were stark, white, and depressingly drab. He was sometimes unsure if many of the buildings he saw were empty or abandoned, or if they were simply not yet completed. They were either soulless ghost towns or they were isolated pieces of a soon-to-be booming metropolis that was not yet occupied. It was quite strange. Just when Bond thought that many of the homes reminded him of what he had seen in poor Latin American countries, or Mexico, a large, modern warehouse or factory would suddenly dominate a circle of shacks made of plywood and grass.

The train sped through smaller cities like Pinghu and Shilong, and finally pulled into Guangzhou Station, a sprawling monstrosity built in the 1960s. As Bond stepped off the train, he was met by a soldier wearing a light blue tunic, navy trousers, a red armband on his left arm, and a navy cap with a gold star on a red circle. He held a sign on which was poorly scribbled: "James Pickard, EurAsia Enterprises." The man didn't speak English, and Bond's Mandarin was terrible, so they compromised with Cantonese—which the soldier blatantly regarded as an inferior language. The soldier saw Bond through Immigration and into a government minibus. As he walked through the railway station, Bond was struck by the hundreds of rural migrants camped in the station's vast courtyard, surrounded by bundles of clothing and bedding. Some of them looked as if they had lived there for months or even years, eating, sleeping, and carving out a life for themselves right there on the pavement. Some were peddling goods and services to tourists. It was a stark contrast to the clean, metropolitan station in Kowloon.

Guangzhou itself is the sixth largest city in China, with an estimated population of three and a half million. It is the transportation, industrial, and trade centre of southern China. It has shipyards, a steel complex, and factories that produce many heavy and light industrial products. It had been the seat of Sun Yat-sen's revolutionary movement and was a Nationalist centre in the 1920s until its fall in 1950 to the Communist armies. Hong Kong was crowded, but it was nothing compared to Guangzhou. The streets were packed with vehicles and there was a traffic jam at every intersection. However, most of the people got around on bicycles, and there were hundreds zipping along the major roads in specially marked bike lanes. Open-air markets were in abundance. Also prominent were huge billboards displaying images of united workers, looking off into the distance towards a bright, bold future.

Bond found himself thinking that it was a world terribly behind the times, and that its people had absolutely no idea that the rest of civilization had passed them by. Over the years he had attempted to become more tolerant of governments such as China's, but the imperialist blood of long-forgotten generations welled up inside him when he saw the squalor and misguided complacency of the humanity around him. He had spent most of his career battling communism. These days he had to concentrate on suppressing his own personal prejudices against it.

The minibus drove along Jeifang Beilu down to Dongfeng Zhonglu and passed a large octagonal building designed like a traditional Chinese palace. It was the Dr. Sun Yat-sen Memorial Hall, an auditorium built between 1929 and 1931. The building was in a graceful park with a magnificent garden in front of it. A bronze statue of Sun Yat-sen overlooked the garden and faced conspicuous government buildings across the busy main road. The hall itself had a solemn outer appearance with red walls and panels and a roof made of blue Shiwan tiles, with four tiers of rolled, protruding eaves. It was simultaneously ornate and gaudy.

The minibus turned into the intimidating gate of the main and largest government building, a tan seven-storey structure with a red roof. The gate was set within a brick façade with a blue roof, and was connected to a high fence which surrounded the building. The driver spoke to a guard, the gate opened, and the minibus pulled into a parking area full of military vehicles—jeeps, a couple of troop transports, and one tank.

When they got out of the minibus, the guard pointed across the road. "Dr. Sun Yat-sen Memorial Hall," he said. "Nice tourist attraction." He gestured to the building in front of them. "This is our local government building. General Wong will see you here."

The guard escorted Bond into the building, where he had to sign a visitors' book under the watchful eyes of other soldiers. The next thing they did was curious—Bond was frisked from head to toe. Why would they do that to a visiting solicitor? He attributed it to the rigours of Communist China. He was then led to a lift and taken to the third floor, where the guard let Bond into a small office.

"Wait here," the guard said, then left him alone.

Bond sat down in a straight-backed chair. The room was bare except for a conference table and a few chairs. A water cooler sat in the corner. It was very hot. Either the air conditioning was off, broken, or they didn't have it at all. The weather outside had finally hit the humid summer temperature for which southern China was known. Bond had to wipe his forehead with a handkerchief.

After a moment, a man entered and stood in the doorway. He was dressed in full Chinese military regalia and appeared to be about sixty years old. He was short, probably no more than five and a half feet, but broad-shouldered and muscular. He had white hair cut short to the scalp, a snub nose, and wore spectacles with round lenses.

"Mr. Pickard?" he asked in English. "I am General Wong."

Bond stood up and shook his hand. "How do you do?"

The man didn't smile. "I trust you had pleasant journey."

"It was fine, thank you."

General Wong's expression remained sour. "We get down to business. You know about my takeover of EurAsia Enterprises."

"Yes, of course. I must admit, though, this document of yours took us all by surprise at Fitch, Donaldson and Patrick."

"Guy Thackeray was fool," Wong said. "He kept it secret. He should have told you in 1985 when I first saw him. He was idiot. He should not have held press conference to tell world he was selling company. He was not selling at all! What happened to him?"

"He was killed by a car bomb."

Wong's eyes narrowed. "I know that. Why? Who did it?"

The general did not have a pleasant disposition. It was as if he was doing Pickard a favour by stepping down from his pedestal to speak to him.

"No one knows, General," Bond said politely. He smiled in an attempt to bring some levity to their conversation. "There are quite a few people who believe you had something to do with it."

"Me?" the general shouted. "You accuse me?"

"I didn't accuse you, General. I merely said that there is speculation in Hong Kong that the People's Republic was behind the act. But that's not why I'm here, is it? Aren't we going to talk about your claim to Thackeray's company?"

"Why would I kill Thackeray? His death spoiled everything! Market value of EurAsia Enterprises went down! Company is losing money! He deliberately made announcement to bring value of company down! Why would I want him dead? You tell your friends I did not do it."

"General, I assure you, they are not my friends. I just got here from England."

The general took a deep breath and tried to control his temper. The insinuation had ruffled his feathers. Bond's instinct that Wong had no motive for killing Thackeray seemed to be sound, but he still could have been behind the murder of Donaldson and the tragedy at the floating restaurant.

"General, my colleagues at Fitch, Donaldson and Patrick have yet to see the document which gives you the right to take over EurAsia Enterprises. My first task is to see that document and make photocopies of it to take back to England."

"Document very fragile. I keep it in plastic inside safe."

"I understand that. Still, I must see the original. I must ascertain that it is genuine."

"Very well. Come." He stood up. "You want water? Very hot today."

Bond would have loved to drink some water, but he was wary of its purity. "No, thank you, I'm fine."

He followed the general into what was presumably his private office. In contrast to the rest of the building, it was full of expensive furniture, antiques, and fine art. A tiger's head was mounted on the wall, and there were *objets d'art* scattered around the room. What appeared to be a gold-plated bust of Mao Zedong sat on a bookshelf.

The most impressive artifact in the room was a life-size terracotta horse and soldier. Bond imagined that it had been part of the fantastic, archaeological dig around the tomb of Ch'ing Dynasty Emperor Qin Shi Huang near the city of Xian, where over six thousand clay soldiers and horses had been unearthed and found arrayed in oblong battle formation as an artistic reflection of the emperor's great army. Most of the terracotta figures were left in place, but a few made it to museums around China. General Wong must have spent a fortune in order to obtain one. Anyone who saw this opulent office would not have believed its inhabitant was a Communist.

General Wong pushed back a curtain behind his desk and revealed a safe. He twisted the knob a few times, unlocked it, and carefully removed a large piece of parchment enclosed in a transparent plastic cover.

The document was brown with age, but the lettering was still intact. One side was written in English and the other in Chinese. To Bond's untrained eye the wording and legality of the agreement seemed to be in order.

"This is quite an artifact," Bond said. "I'll need a photocopy to take back to England."

At that moment, the phone buzzed. Wong answered it and listened. He looked at Bond suspiciously, then barked an order in Mandarin. He hung up the phone and said, "Forgive me. There is matter I must take care of."

Bond heard footsteps in the hallway approaching the office, followed by a loud knock on the door. Wong snarled an order to come in.

Two guards entered carrying a man who had been recently beaten. His clothes were tattered and torn, and his face was bruised and bloody. They threw him on the floor, where he curled into a foetal position and groaned. Wong walked over to the man and roughly turned him on to his back.

Bond was horrified to see that it was T.Y. Woo!

"Mr. Pickard," Wong said, "this man was caught spying. Do you know him?"

Bond had to lie. If he gave the slightest indication that he knew

Woo then his cover would be blown and they would both die. The lesson he had taught Stephanie Lane in Jamaica just days ago hit home with a vengeance.

"I've never seen him before in my life," Bond said. "Who is he? What happened to him?" He played the shocked British civilian unaccustomed to such violence.

"Never mind what happened to him," Wong said. He gave an order to the guards, who pulled Woo up by the shoulders and started to haul him out of the room. For a brief moment Woo's eyes met Bond's. There was sadness there, but also a sign that he understood what Bond did and why. Bond turned away, feigning revulsion. He really felt rage and despair. He might as well have aimed the gun at Woo's head and fired it himself.

After they were gone, Bond said, "I'm sorry, I'm not used to seeing things like that."

Wong just stared at him. There was an awkward moment of silence.

"Maybe I will have that glass of water now," Bond said.

Wong didn't say a word. He took the ancient document off the table and replaced it in his safe. Then he picked up his phone and pushed a button. He spoke into the receiver and hung up. Once again, Bond heard the footsteps in the hall. This time the guards didn't knock. They came straight into the room and stood on either side of Bond.

Wong said, "You are imposter. You are not lawyer. You are spy."

"Now wait just a minute . . ." Bond began, but one of the guards punched him hard in the stomach. Bond doubled over and fell to his knees.

"Who are you? Who do you work for?" Wong demanded.

Bond didn't say anything. What had happened? Had Woo talked? No, that was impossible. He was as professional as they come. Where had something gone wrong?

"I got phone call before you arrive," Wong said. "Mr. James Pickard never step into Hong Kong airport. My people were there." He held up a photo of the real James Pickard. "You are not this man."

Bond didn't move.

"Are you going to tell me who you are? Talk! I give you one more chance. Who do you work for?"

Bond stood silent and to attention, like a soldier.

"Very well," the general said. "We move on to next step."

SIXTEEN

AGONY AND ANGER

"REMOVE YOUR CLOTHES," WONG COMMANDED IN CANTONESE.

My God, Bond thought. What were they going to do? He felt cold fear. He suddenly had total recall of another time long ago when he had been tortured naked. It had been hours of excruciating agony, and had damn nearly killed him.

"You heard me!" Wong shouted.

Bond did as he was told. As he undressed, Wong opened a cabinet behind the desk and removed a white sheet. He walked to the middle of the room and spread it out. The sheet floated down and settled neatly on the carpet. It wasn't completely white. There were several suspicious stains on it.

When Bond was naked, Wong gestured for him to stand in the middle of the sheet. Bond stood to attention in front of him. Wong slowly walked around him, inspecting him, admiring the man's body.

"You think you are fit, Mr. Englishman," Wong said. "We shall see how fit you really are."

A guard trained an AK-47 on Bond while General Wong returned to the cabinet and removed a long white stick with ridges on it. He held it in front of the vulnerable man. For the first time since Bond arrived, Wong smiled. In fact, he had become a completely different person. The sour face and unpleasant demeanour were completely gone.

"This is rattan cane, Mr. Pickard or whoever you are," he said. "I have friends in Singapore who not only employ it for punishment, but swear that it is also effective persuader. Now, I ask again. Who do you work for?"

Bond said nothing. He knew he was in for a great deal of pain. In Singapore, the maximum number of strokes with the cane was usually five; ten for extreme cases. What kind of damage could it do? He knew that the lashes would leave welts on his skin, possibly permanent scars. What if he was caned many, many times? Could he force himself to pass out, as he had trained himself to do? It was one of the most difficult tests of willpower that he knew of.

"Bend over and grab ankles," Wong said.

Bond did so. He felt humiliated and dangerously exposed.

Wong took a position on Bond's left side, and held the cane to OO7's buttocks. He rubbed the rough stick against the skin there, indicating to Bond how the cane might feel if it struck him hard.

"Who are you and who do you work for?" Wong asked again, his voice trembling with excitement.

Bond kept his mouth shut. He closed his eyes tightly and gritted his teeth. Concentrate! Focus on something! He opened his eyes and saw a dark stain on the bedsheet a few inches from his face. It was probably dried blood. Bond stared at it, willing himself to fall deep within the confines of that dark, shapeless haven.

The cane struck him with such force that he nearly lost his balance and fell forward. There was an intense, burning pain across the middle of his buttocks. They felt as if they were on fire.

Bond gritted his teeth harder and continued to stare at the spot. He had begun to sweat profusely; a drop slid down his forehead, on to his nose, then fell on to the sheet.

"You see what it can do now?" Wong asked pleasantly. "Now will you talk?"

Bond concentrated on the spot in front of him, attempting to conjure up whatever peaceful thoughts he could manage. My God, give me something of beauty to look at. Give me something pure. Give me . . .

The cane struck again, slightly lower than the first blow. Christ, it hurt! He kept up his internal litany, forming a mental picture in his mind of the image he invoked. Give me my house in Jamaica . . . Give me my flat in Chelsea . . .

The third blow slashed Bond across the tops of his thighs. It was dangerously close to more vulnerable parts of his body. God, not that again! He might not be able to take that . . . Give me . . . give me . . . Sunni . . .

The fourth blow landed on the buttocks again, overlapping the first red mark.

Sunni . . . Bond thought of the girl with the almond eyes. The spot on the sheet became her lovely face . . . Those lips . . . those eyes . . .

A fifth stroke tore his skin an inch below the last one.

Sweat was now rolling off his face in a constant flow. His heart was pounding. He wanted to scream, but he dared not. He knew that the general took pleasure in the torture. The more the victim suffered, the more the sadist enjoyed it. Bond was determined to be the most disappointing whipping boy General Wong had ever had.

The sixth stroke nearly knocked Bond over again. The madman was putting his weight into it now. He was breathing heavily. "Well?" he asked. "Have you had enough?"

Bond sensed that the general was surprised and perturbed that Bond's reaction to the torture was not what he was expecting.

Bond turned his head to the left and spat, "Please . . . sir. May . . . I have . . . another, you . . . bloody . . . bastard . . . ?"

The seventh blow knocked Bond forward and on to the sheet. He curled up in a ball on his right side and felt the blood seeping down the back of his thighs.

"Get up!" Wong shouted.

He brutally whacked Bond across his left arm, directly over the stitches of his previous wound. Oh, bloody hell! Bond screamed to himself. He didn't want to be hit there again. Getting lashed on the backside was immeasurably preferable, mainly because he was beginning to grow numb there. He weakly pulled himself up and assumed the position again.

The ninth blow seared his thighs once more. Again, Bond wanted to yell, simply to release the anger, humiliation, and tension that enveloped his body. He remained stubbornly silent.

The tenth stroke sent Bond to the sheet again. It was the hardest, most savage yet. He didn't know if he could manage to pull himself up off the floor.

At that moment, there was a loud knock on the door. Wong shouted something in Mandarin. The guard with the gun opened the door slightly and listened to a hurried whisper from another man in the hallway. He closed the door and whispered something to Wong.

Suddenly, Wong threw down the cane. "Bah!" he shouted. He said something in Mandarin that implied that Bond was nothing but excrement. He said something else to the guard, retrieved the cane, and put it back in the cabinet.

"I have appointment," Wong said. "We will continue in little while." With that, he left the room.

The guard lifted Bond from the bloodied sheet. He stood weakly, his legs shaking like mad. The guard threw Bond's clothes at his feet and said something in Mandarin. Bond picked up the sheet and wrapped it around himself, soaking up the blood and pressing his wounds. It was going to be a while before he could sit comfortably.

The guard shouted at him, indicating with the machine gun that he should get moving. Bond swore at the man in English, dropped the sheet, and pulled on his clothes. Contact with his trousers was excruciating. Unable to sit to put on his shoes, Bond went down on the left knee. He got the right shoe on, then painfully changed positions and rested on his right knee. The guard was looking out of the door into the hallway, the gun half trained on Bond.

Bond quickly removed the pry tool from his left shoe. He snapped open the heel and removed the plastic dagger. He slipped on the shoe, snapping the heel back in place as he did so. He tucked the dagger under the Rolex flexible watchband on his left wrist, then slowly raised himself up off the floor.

The guard gestured with the AK-47 for Bond to leave the room. Another guard stood in the hall and moved towards the lift.

The lift descended to the basement level. They came out into a stark white hallway, at the end of which was a locked steel door. The lead man unlocked it and held it open for Bond and the other man to go through, into another long hallway lined with five or six other steel doors. Each of these contained a small barred window at eye level, obviously opening into cells. He wondered how many individuals entered this building and never came out.

If he was going to make a move, Bond knew it had to be now or never.

The guards turned right and led him to the end of the hall. The first man unlocked the door there and held it open. Bond reached for his left wrist and firmly grasped the small handle of the plastic dagger. He knew that his timing had to be perfect or he would be a dead man.

Bond turned to the man holding the AK-47 behind him and said in Cantonese, "Would you mind not pushing that thing into my back?" The guard relaxed, giving 007 the space he needed. He pushed the AK-47 away from his body with his left hand and simultaneously swung the dagger straight up with his right. The three-inch blade pierced the soft skin of the man's jaw just under the chin, thrusting up and into the mouth. In the next half-second, Bond grasped the machine gun and chopped the man's arm with a right spear-hand, causing the guard to release his grip on the weapon. By now, the other guard had begun to react by pulling a pistol out of a holster on his belt. Bond swung the AK-47 around and fired one quick burst at the second man, throwing him back into the open cell. The first guard was now clutching at the dagger in his jaw, an expression of surprise, pain, and horror on his face. Bond used the butt of the machine gun to smash the man's nose, knocking him unconscious. He moved quickly into the cell to inspect the guard he had shot. The four bullets had caught him in the chest. He was quite dead. Bond retrieved his plastic dagger, wiped it clean on the man's shirt, then replaced it under his wristwatch band. He prayed that there were no other guards in the basement. The burst of gunfire had been quick. He hoped that the noise had not penetrated the upper levels of the building.

Bond had to get out and find Li Xu Nan's men, who must be watching the building. It was not going to be an easy escape. First, however, he had to accomplish the task he came to perform. He had to go back to the third floor and get that bloody document.

He was still bleeding, and the pain was nearly unbearable. He stepped into the cell and removed his trousers again. He slipped off the right shoe and once again pried open the heel. He used a sheet from a bed to wipe himself, then did his best to apply antiseptic to the wounds. He ripped the sheet into strips and layered them around his thighs and buttocks. It would have to do until he could get medical attention. Bond then swallowed a couple of pain-killers, replaced the items, and put his shoe back on.

He stepped over the bodies of the guards and went into the hallway. He looked through the barred windows of each door on his way out. A body, covered by a sheet, lay on top of a stretcher in one of the cells. Could it be . . . ?

Bond tried the door, but it was locked. He went back and searched the pockets of the dead guard who had held the keys. He found them and went back to the locked door, unlocked it and stepped inside. He approached the body quietly, all too sure of what he would find underneath the sheet.

It was T.Y. Woo. He was lying on his stomach with his head turned to the side. He had been shot in the back of the skull. The entire front of his face was blown away.

Bond was overcome by an immense feeling of guilt and rage. He slammed his fist down on the stretcher. The bastards actually did it. Woo had probably been tailing him, keeping an eye on him, watching his back, and Bond had betrayed him. They had executed him, and it was he who had helped to send his friend and ally to his death.

Damn it, get hold of yourself! he screamed silently. It was unavoidable. It was a matter of keeping one's cover. Any good agent would have done the same thing. Woo would have turned his back on Bond, too, if it had been the other way round. It was part of the job. It was part of the risk.

Despite these rationalizations, Bond's anger overcame him. Now he had not only to get that document and get out alive, but he had to avenge Woo's death. After suffering the degrading torture Wong had inflicted upon him, and now having discovered the extent of the general's frenzy, Bond saw red. He knew he should stay objective and keep his emotions out of it. This wasn't a vendetta, he tried to tell himself, but all he wanted to do was wring the mad general's neck.

Bond left the cell, holding the AK-47, prepared to blast the first obstacle that stood in his way. He used the guard's keys to open the main door and enter the hallway leading to the lift.

Once he was back on the third floor, Bond made his way quietly towards Wong's office. The place was unusually quiet and empty. The good general's staff was obviously not a large one.

The office door was closed. Bond put his ear to it and heard a woman moaning with pleasure. The general was having a little afternoon delight. Good, Bond thought. Now it was his turn to catch the general with his pants down.

Bond burst into the room and trained the machine gun on the couple behind the desk. General Wong was sitting in his large leather rocking chair, and a woman in her thirties was sitting on his lap, facing him. Her skirt was pulled up above her waist, and her legs were bare. Wong's trousers were around his ankles, and the look on his face was priceless.

The woman gasped and froze. She was dressed in a military uniform and the front of her blouse was unbuttoned, revealing small breasts in a white brassiere.

Bond closed the door behind him. "Get up," he said to the woman. When she didn't move, he shouted "Now!" The woman jumped up and hurriedly put herself back together. Wong sat there, exposed.

"What's the matter, General?" Bond asked in Cantonese. "Is it the humidity that's causing you to wilt?"

"What do you want?" Wong said through his teeth.

"Open the safe, and be quick."

Wong stood up. "I pull trousers up?"

"Slowly. First place your pistol on the desk with your left hand."

The general carefully took a pistol from the holster on his belt and laid it on the desk. It looked like a Russian Tokarev, but was most likely a Chinese copy. Then he bent over, pulled his trousers up and fastened them, before turning to the safe in the wall and opening it.

"The document," Bond said. "Put it on the desk." The general did as he was told.

Nearly a week ago in Jamaica, James Bond had taught Stephanie Lane always to expect the unexpected, but he was so intent on making General Wong pay for what he did to Woo that he made a near-fatal mistake and broke the rule. He didn't expect the woman to come to the general's defence.

She attacked Bond, screaming a blood-curdling warcry. The move so surprised him that he lost his balance. The woman successfully tackled him, and they fell to the carpet where only a little while ago Bond had been lying in agony. She went for the gun, obviously quite prepared not only to sleep with her general, but to die for him as well. Wong moved around the desk and kicked Bond hard in the face. The woman managed to wrestle away the AK-47 as Bond rolled away. Wong took the machine gun from her and pointed it at Bond.

In one swift, graceful manoeuvre, Bond took hold of the plastic dagger, rocked back on to his shoulders, lunged forward, and threw the knife at the general. The blade spun across the room and lodged in Wong's throat, directly below his Adam's apple. His eyes widened, and for a moment he stood as still as a statue. The AK-47 fell to the carpet as he reached for his neck with both hands. He made choking, gurgling noises as blood gushed out of his mouth.

Bond took no chances. He grabbed hold of Wong's shirt to steady him, then punched the man hard in the jaw. Wong fell back across the desk and rolled over on to the floor. Bond turned to the now-terrified woman. He was so full of violence and fury that he might have killed her, too, had he not been unarmed. Instead, he backhanded her, knocking her unconscious.

The general was still writhing on the floor. He had pulled the knife out of his throat and was struggling for air. His trachea had been severed and his lungs were filling with blood. Bond stood over him and watched him die. It took three long, excruciating minutes.

Now Bond had to act fast. He grabbed the document and stuffed it into the briefcase he had brought with him from Hong Kong, which was still sitting on the floor by an armchair where he had left it earlier. He took the AK-47, then picked up the dagger and returned it to its position in his shoe.

His trousers were wet with blood. The sheet strips had not lasted long.

How the hell was he going to leave? He looked out of a window. It overlooked the front of the building. He counted four guards outside by the gate. Across the street was the Sun Yat-sen Memorial Building. Maybe he could make it over there somehow and hope that Li's men were close by.

Bond opened the office door and looked into the hallway. It was all clear. Bond crept to the lift and pushed the button. When it opened, a guard stepped out. Bond killed him swiftly and quietly and entered the lift. At the ground floor, flattening himself against the side of the lift, he pressed the "open door" button and held it.

The ruse worked. When the lone guard got curious and decided to see why the door hadn't closed, Bond brought the man's head down hard on his right knee, then hit him on the back of the neck with the butt of the AK-47.

Two armed guards stood in the foyer. They saw Bond and immediately pulled their pistols. Bond acted with split-second timing, boosted by the adrenalin rushing through his body. He opened fire and the two guards slammed back against the wall leaving a bloody trail as they slid to the floor.

Bond stood there a moment, breathing heavily. He was still filled with rage, an emotion he usually tried to avoid because it could cause recklessness. This time, however, it served as a goad. Blasting away the guards had actually felt good. My God, he thought. This was what he lived for. It was no wonder that he inevitably became restless and bored when he was between assignments. Living so close to death was what invigorated him and gave him the edge that had managed to keep him alive for so many years.

Feeling invincible, Bond walked outside into the broad daylight of the courtyard. He didn't care that his clothes were wet and bloody. He didn't care if the entire Chinese army was waiting for him. He was quite prepared to blast his way out of Guangzhou until he had no more ammunition or he was dead, whichever came first.

There were only the four guards at the gate. They looked up and saw Bond. Their jaws dropped, so stupefied at the *gweilo's* appearance that they were unsure what to do. Bond trained the machine gun on them. They slowly raised their hands above their heads.

"Open the gate," Bond said to one of them. The guard nodded furiously, then did as he was told. Bond walked backwards out of the gate, keeping the gun trained on the soldiers.

It was mid-afternoon and traffic on Dongfeng Zhonglu was quite heavy. Bond looked in both directions and quickly calculated when he might make a mad dash across the street. When the moment came, he turned and ran. The guards immediately began to chase him. Their timing wasn't as good, as they had to dart between vehicles to get across.

Bond ran up the steps past the statue of Sun Yat-sen and into the Memorial Hall. The interior lobby was narrow and dimly lit. He went straight into the arena-style auditorium, which had two balconies and a stage at one end. It was dilapidated with a decidedly musty smell, and was empty and dark.

He ran down the centre aisle to the stage. He jumped on to the apron and ran stage right into the wings. A staircase led down to what was some sort of green room. It was probably meant to be a dressing room for performers or speakers. He heard the guards enter the auditorium above, calling out to each other in Mandarin. Sooner or later they would find him.

Bond made his way to the other side of the auditorium basement, then slowly climbed the staircase there to the other side of the stage. The guards were still searching the aisles. He slid along a counterweight system to the back of the stage behind a faded, torn cyclorama. What he was looking for was there—a loading door for bringing scenery in and out. Bond pushed back the bolt and kicked it open. He jumped down to the pavement and ran around the side of the building to a car park. Tourists were walking from their vehicles to the front of the building. Many of them stopped and stared at the bloody figure of a Caucasian running across the pavement.

It was then that a black sedan screeched into the car park and stopped in front of him. A Chinese man in a business suit jumped out and held the back door open.

"Get in, Mr. Bond!" he said in English. "Hurry!"

Bond dived into the back seat, and the car squealed out into the busy street. There were two of them—a driver and the man who had spoken. Bond thought they looked familiar. He had seen them at the initiation ceremony in Kowloon City.

The one in the passenger seat looked back at Bond. His brow was creased.

"What happened to you?"

Bond was not sitting down. He was on his knees, facing out of the rear window.

"They gave me a beating," Bond said. "Where are we going?"

"Back to Kowloon, of course. Try to relax. It's a three-hour drive."

He didn't know how he could possibly relax in this position, but had to admit he felt a hundred times better just being out of the hell-hole from which he had escaped.

Bond watched the traffic behind the sedan and saw no signs of pursuit. It was curious that there hadn't been many soldiers at Wong's building. He counted himself extremely lucky. If an entire regiment had been there, he would probably be dead by now.

The man in the passenger seat used a cellular phone and spoke Cantonese into it. Bond heard him say that they had picked up the *gweilo*. The man turned to Bond.

"Mr. Li wants to know if you got it?"

Bond said, "Tell him I've got what he wants."

The car spent the next half-hour navigating the crowded roads of Guangzhou and finally made it out onto the open highway southeast towards Dongguan and Shekou.

Bond thought of his friend T.Y. The man's death couldn't have been prevented, and Bond had merely done his duty and played by the rules.

He thought of the ironic parallel of the situation. England, by agreeing to hand over Hong Kong to China, had also acted honourably and dutifully. By doing so, however, she had turned her back on the people of Hong Kong.

SEVENTEEN

MEN OF HONOUR

9:00 P.M.

By the time the hovercraft from Shekou arrived at the China Ferry Terminal in Tsim Sha Tsui, the world's governments had learned of Bond's actions that day. The story relayed over hotlines all around the globe was that General Wong Tsu Kam had been murdered by a "mysterious" Brit. There was speculation that it was the same "Brit" who had killed the two visiting officials in Hong Kong on 13 June. China was accusing England of espionage and murder. At least four witnesses in the Chinese military force testified that they had been forced by an armed but wounded Caucasian to let him leave the governmental building located in the heart of Guangzhou. Several soldiers had been killed inside the building. For the time being, China was keeping the news from the press, but there was no telling when it might be leaked.

The Prime Minister attempted to assure China that no British "hit man" was operating on their soil. The idea was absurd—England didn't want a confrontation with China. China refused to listen.

Adding fuel to the fire was the release of James Pickard, Esquire, at 6:00 p.m. He had been blindfolded and taken from an undisclosed location in Kowloon to Kai Tak Airport to be left standing on the Departure level. He was unharmed, but immediately went to the police and reported what had happened to him. An hour later, he was surrounded by reporters and photographers. He would receive fifteen minutes of fame, and then would be shipped back to London in the morning. This bit of public spectacle only added to the series of mysteries that had plagued Hong Kong over the past month.

Government officials in Hong Kong were seriously alarmed. What if the allegations were true? The Chinese troops lining the border were under new command within the hour, and word had it that tanks were now moving up to the line. An early takeover was a frightening possibility. It was important to keep the people in the dark, but it was entirely likely that some reporter would stumble across the news at any time and splash it across the papers. A colony-wide panic had to be avoided at all costs.

The Royal Navy was due to move in to Victoria Harbour within twenty-four hours, joining the Hong Kong naval forces. Britain had sent a destroyer and two Duke Class Type 23 frigates to join the three RN Peacock Class patrol craft permanently deployed in Hong Kong. The colony's own naval force was operated by the Marine Region of the Royal Hong Kong Police, mostly a Coast Guard Force responsible for the territorial waters of Hong Kong and all of the surrounding islands. As far as the public was concerned, the Royal Navy's presence was simply to be on hand for the transition, but in reality they were on full alert. The Royal Marines had been dispatched and would be forming a line south of the Chinese border. The United States issued a private statement urging restraint, but her nearby fleets were watching and waiting. The Japanese government offered to mediate, but China refused to acknowledge the gesture.

As for James Bond, getting out of China had been relatively simple. The car had driven to Dongguan, where they stopped at a small hotel so James Bond could shower, dress his wounds, and change clothes. Li had sent yet another Armani suit for 007 to wear. After a stand-up meal at a food stall, the group continued along the superhighway to the rapidly expanding Shekou. There, they boarded a hovercraft to Kowloon. A new passport had been prepared for Bond (complete with a false exit stamp from Hong Kong Immigration), this time in the name of John Hunter. The presence of the other ethnic Chinese deflected any suspicions on the part of Chinese Immigration that Bond might be the man wanted for General Wong's murder.

A car drove Bond from the hovercraft terminal to Li's office building in Kowloon City. The Cho Kun greeted him as an old friend. He smiled broadly and clasped Bond's hand.

Bond handed over the document without saying a word. He was tired and in pain, and didn't relish the idea that he had done something to help a Triad. He was angry with himself.

"Here it is," Bond said. "I can't imagine it's worth much now."

Li inspected the document with awe and wonder. He held it gingerly, as if it was a new-born baby. Bond could swear that tears came to the man's eyes.

"Thank you, Mr. Bond," he said. He meant it.

Bond didn't wait for Li to offer to make him a drink. He went to the cabinet and poured himself a glass of vodka.

"You know, Mr. Li, the Hong Kong Police will catch up with you sooner than you think," Bond said in Cantonese.

"I have taken action to avoid that. I have not been passive while you were in China sticking your neck out for me. At approximately 8:30 this evening, the EurAsia Enterprises warehouse at Kwai Chung Container Terminal was destroyed."

"What?"

Li shrugged. "There was a fire . . . or something. It blew up. There is nothing left there. No evidence at all."

"I see."

"The police were already on to something. One of the shipping employees talked after learning he would be laid off after the handover. A story was already due to hit the papers tomorrow. EurAsia Enterprises will be accused of participating in drug-smuggling. If our friend Guy Thackeray were still alive, he would probably be under investigation. It is lucky I have friends in the press. I thought it best to obliterate any incriminating evidence."

"So your little drug-running operation is dead?"

"That one is, certainly. It is all right, I do not mind. To tell the truth, I have been searching for a way to end that vicious circle. It was very profitable, but I have other means of income. I can find another method."

"You mean, you'll just find another way to prey on the weaknesses of the human condition."

Li ignored the insult. Instead he grinned broadly. "Oh, have you heard the latest news from China? I have a source who works at Government House. Beijing has issued a demand! If the British government does not turn over the so-called murderer, there will be . . . trouble." Li looked like a Cheshire cat.

"Why does that make you so happy, Li?" snapped Bond. "Do you realize what my government will do to me when they learn I was responsible? It would be nice if we could discredit General Wong somehow."

"You are right," Li said. "After you left this morning, I received something that will help your case. It is the result of a plan I set in operation months ago. The god Kwan Ti has been good to us. It is no coincidence that this came into my hands today of all days."

Li opened a desk drawer and pulled out a brown envelope. Bond opened it and found several photographs and a cassette audio tape inside.

"Those were taken by some of my men at General Wong's facilities in the Golden Triangle. For insurance . . . in case I ever needed it. It is unfortunate that two brothers died getting me that material."

There were several black and white photos taken with a hidden camera of Wong inspecting poppies in a field, looking in a microscope in a lab, and holding bags of heroin. There was also a series of photos of Wong speaking with another Chinese man. They were standing inside the lab, near the desk of a chemist.

"Look at the photo. There is Wong, speaking to one of his lieutenants. Do you see the man sitting next to him, with the microscope? He is a brother. The conversation was recorded. It is all in Cantonese. They speak about the entire operation. Wong names not only EurAsia Enterprises as the carrier, but proudly states that he was the mastermind of the scheme. Egotistical bastard! Another brother had a camera in a packet of cigarettes and got this picture. An old trick, but it worked."

"My God, Li," Bond said. "This could save Hong Kong! We must get this to your friends in the press tonight!"

"It shall be done. In twenty-four hours, China will be eating her words and apologizing. Imagine . . . one of their top generals involved in drug-smuggling! They will need to save much face! Now, what can I do for you, Mr. Bond? What can I do to dispel this notion you have that I am some kind of evil person?"

"I'll think about it," he said. "First I need to ring London and face my boss's wrath. Then I'd like to see Sunni."

Bond was shown into a private office with a phone. He dialled the access number, and was connected to a secure line. After a moment, he heard the familiar voice of Bill Tanner.

"James! Where the hell have you been? M is about to have a stroke!"

"It's a long story, Bill."

"You're going to have to tell it to her. Hold on. She wanted to speak to you as soon as we heard from you."

"Great. All right, put her on."

There were a few pips, and then he heard the voice of the woman who would not be happy to hear what he had to say.

"Bond?" she asked.

"Yes, ma'am. I'm here."

"Where are you?"

"I'm in Kowloon."

"What the hell is going on, 007? Do you know anything about this general who was killed in Guangzhou?"

"Yes, ma'am."

There was a pause at the other end of the line. "And what do you know about it?"

"The general was involved with Guy Thackeray and the Dragon Wing Society in a drug-smuggling scheme. It was as we suspected, ma'am. EurAsia Enterprises was connected with the Triad, but it looks as though this Chinese general was as much a part of it as anyone. A story is going to break in the next couple of days, complete with photos. The man was as corrupt as they come. I have good reason to believe he was behind the terrorist acts and might have been the instigator of Guy Thackeray's murder."

"007, were you in Guangzhou today?"

"Yes, ma'am."

"I see." Bond could imagine her eyes narrowing as she sat in her office in London.

She continued, "The PM has been all over my back today. I will cover for you the best I can, 007. I hope you can tell me you were not caught on surveillance cameras?"

"I don't think so, ma'am. If it's any consolation, Wong was responsible for the death of T.Y. Woo and he damn near killed me. I couldn't have completed the mission without going to Guangzhou, ma'am."

"I don't doubt your motives, Bond. I have a problem with your temerity. You've always had a reputation of being a loose cannon, 007, and now I have the privilege of experiencing your foolhardiness first hand. I want you to stay put, Bond. Don't leave the colony. Captain Charles Plante of the Royal Navy will contact you at the safe house on June the 30th. He will get you out and back home. The front door of the safe house has been repaired and the place cleaned up. The key will be taped inside the mouth of one of the Chinese lions in front of the shop. We've got Woo's son out of the colony already. He's on his way to England where he'll live with a foster family."

"Yes, ma'am." He was under virtual house arrest! What the hell was he going to do for three days?

"Oh, and 007?"

"Yes?"

"You had requested a British passport for some tart, a Chinese girl?"

Bond tensed at the word "tart." "That's right, ma'am. She helped me. Saved my life, actually."

"Well, forget her." With that, M rang off.

Bond walked out of the room and back into Li's office. He sat down on a large leather armchair. It still hurt to sit, but he was beginning to get used to it.

"You need some medical attention, Mr. Bond," Li said. "I will have my doctor take a look at you."

"Thanks," Bond said, lost in thought. He was forgetting something and he was struggling to remember what it was.

"Where are the clothes I was wearing when I first came here?" he asked.

"They are here in the cupboard. Why?"

Bond got up and looked through them. He found what he was looking for in a trouser pocket. It was the map of EurAsia Enterprises' Kalgoorlie gold mine. "Here it is," he said. "I found this at the warehouse. Before spending the last two glorious days in your employ, Li, I had planned on leaving Hong Kong to take a look at this."

Li took a look at it. "Australia?"

"I've got a nagging feeling that there's something there that I need to see. That facility is part of this whole thing. The only problem now is how I'm going to get there."

"I can get you to Perth," Li said.

"You can?"

"I have two restaurants there. I have my own 'plane. I travel to Singapore, Tokyo, Australia, Thailand . . . wherever my businesses take me. No problem with Immigration."

"How long is the flight?"

"A good ten hours to Perth."

"Then we've got to get going. I want Sunni to come with me."

"I shall be happy to provide this service for you, Mr. Bond. What you have done and endured for my sake has gone beyond the call of duty. You have acted most honourably. For this, I am in your debt. You and the girl are free to go, of course, and I shall cancel the death warrant. We can provide you with false passports, as before."

"What are you going to do with that document? EurAsia Enterprises is finished anyway."

"I will probably go public and tell the true story of the company's history. It will further discredit General Wong. He was attempting to acquire the company on his own, you know. Beijing was unaware of what he was doing. It will appear to them that he was straying even further towards capitalism. I will take over EurAsia Enterprises. There is still a powerful shipping organization in place there. I will rebuild it and make sure it stays legitimate. The important thing is that I have restored face with my ancestors. I have got back what belongs to my family. If nothing else comes of it, that alone is enough. Now, let us hurry if we are going to get you to Australia. I am anxious to repay you for your honourable act of courage today,"

"Let's get one thing straight, Mr. Li," Bond said. "You don't owe me a bloody thing. You can talk all you like about honour, but let's call a spade a spade. You're nothing but a gangster, and I despise you and everything you stand for."

"I feel the same way about you, Mr. Bond," Li said with a wry smile. "Any business I have done with *gweilo* in the past was out of necessity. If I had ever been given a choice in the matter, I would not have done it. Your people came to our land and assumed control. It is now time for you to leave. I cannot say that I am sorry. But I must ask you to think about something. You must surely realize that if Hong Kong is to remain the capitalist money-maker in fifty years' time that it is now, it will be up to the Triads to keep a check on the communists' regulation of the territory's economy. We will be the underground defence against human rights violations and any attempts to undermine the autonomy of Hong Kong."

"You're concerned with human rights? A man who peddles drugs and women? Spare me, please. I believe the Hong Kong people will do quite well on their own, Mr. Li. They are honest and hard-working. They will stand up to oppression."

"You are correct, Mr. Bond. The Hong Kong people are among the world's strongest. Yes, I have made money illegally. You and I believe in opposing creeds. We are from different cultures. Yet we are dedicated to our respective tenets, the doctrines that are our articles of faith, you might say. I would never betray mine, as you would never betray yours. I have killed men. So have you, Mr. Bond. Are we not a little alike? Are we not both men of honour? I may not like you, Mr. Bond, but I trust you. It may be foolish to say this, but I would trust you with my life. I want you to know that, from this point forward, you can trust me with yours."

Bond shook the man's hand. The grip was firm and strong. He said, "I appreciate what you've said. I can't forget that you and I are enemies in principle, Li. That doesn't mean, however, that you don't have my . . . respect." It was the strongest compliment Bond could manage.

Zero Minus Four: 27 June 1997, 12:01 A.M.

Avoiding the immigration authorities once again, James Bond and Sunni Pei boarded Li Xu Nan's private British Aerospace 125 Corporate 800B jet at Kai Tak Airport. As soon as it was in the air, a bomb exploded on one of the Star Ferries in Victoria Harbour. It had been placed in the machine room, and a hole was subsequently blown in the hull. The boat sank rapidly. Luckily, the ferry wasn't crowded and most people made it on to life rafts or were able to grab lifebelts. Marine Police were magnificently efficient in responding to the incident in record time and saved the lives of everyone aboard. The only casualty was the boat itself. The Royal Hong Kong Police received three claims of responsibility within the hour, two of which were discounted as hoaxes. The third reportedly came from an anonymous caller in China. The message simply stated that the bombing was in retaliation for the murder of General Wong. However, the caller went on to say, since no lives were lost on the ferry, another attack somewhere in the colony was imminent.

EIGHTEEN

THE GOLDEN MILE

27 JUNE 1997, 10:30 A.M., WESTERN AUSTRALIA

Perth is the fastest-growing city in Australia, the capital of the largest and wealthiest state in the country. Western Australia, covering a third of the continent, is comprised of harsh, desolate expanses of the Great Sandy, Gibson, and Great Victoria deserts, caught between the Kimberley Plateau and the Nullarbor Plain—2 1\2 million square kilometres in total. Yet within all this space are a mere 1 1\2 million inhabitants, most of them in or around the relatively youthful city of Perth, located in the southwest coastal region.

Li Xu Wan's private jet flew into Perth International Airport at mid-morning. It was a pleasant, sunny day. James Bond, with Sunni Pei at his side, had no problem with their counterfeit visas and passports. They passed through Immigration as John Hunter and Mary Ling, then went straight to the Hertz Rent-a-car counter. Bond asked for their best four-wheel drive. Li had even provided Bond with an American Express credit card in the name of John Hunter.

"It's about a seven-hour drive to Kalgoorlie," he said to Sunni. His backside was still sore, especially after the long flight, but the herbal treatment Li's doctor had given him had worked wonders. Besides, Bond wanted the feel of driving on the open highway—it would do him more good than another plane flight.

"Oh, James," she said. "This is going to be fun. I haven't taken a road trip since I lived in California!"

"I imagine we'll find a decent motel in Kalgoorlie, have a good dinner, and rest until early tomorrow. Then I'll take a look at the EurAsia mining facility."

"I'm going with you," she said. "I'm not letting you out of my sight anymore."

Bond wasn't sure he wanted her along while he was working. Instead of replying, he leaned over and kissed her forehead. She looked fresh, rested, and very pretty. She was wearing a white blouse with the lower buttons undone and the bottom tied in a knot, exposing her pierced navel. Her blue-jean cutoffs were short, exposing the full length of her splendid legs. As they walked through the airport, Bond noticed other men turning their heads to look at her. He had known many beautiful women in his lifetime, but Sunni was surely one of the most striking.

As for Bond, he had dressed for the warmer climate in a short-sleeved, light blue polo shirt, and navy blue trousers. Although sitting for long periods of time was still uncomfortable, Bond felt 100 per cent better. The mysterious concoction of herbs and ointments which Li's Chinese doctor had used had been remarkably effective, although he had been extremely sceptical at first. He thought that when he returned to London he might seek out a doctor who practised Chinese herbal medicine.

Hertz provided Bond with a 1995 Suzuki Vitara wagon. It wouldn't have been his first choice, but it would do. It was a red hard-top, two-door, short wheel base affair with a part-time four-wheel drive and a 5m/4a transmission. Bond didn't plan on going "off-road," as they called it in Australia, as there was a paved highway all the way to Kalgoorlie.

It was lovely country for the first half of the trip, as the land around the vicinity of Perth was rich and fertile. Once they were past Northam, things began to dry out. Even in June, a winter month in Australia, it was quite warm. The scenery turned to golden brown, and Bond felt they had entered an entirely different country. This was the desert, and it wouldn't do to be stranded on the highway. They had bought a supply of drinking water, and he personally checked out the tyres and running condition of the Vitara before starting out.

As the land grew flat and expansive, traffic thinned out. They felt totally alone.

"This is beautiful," Sunni said. "I remember going to Las Vegas when I was a child. It was a lot like this."

Bond nodded. "I've been to Vegas myself a few times. I've never been here, though."

A large rabbit scampered across the road.

"There's something about the desert that is so mysterious," she said. "It looks as if nothing could live here, yet it is full of life. I wonder if we'll see any kangaroos?"

They drove in silence for a while. Finally, Sunni asked, "All right. You haven't said a word about all of this, and we were on that damn' airplane for ten hours. When are you going to let me in on what's going on? I know you're some kind of cop for the British government. What are you doing in Hong Kong? Why are we in Australia now?"

Bond had wondered when she would start asking questions. He didn't see any reason to keep her in the dark. "You know about the terrorist acts that have been committed in Hong Kong over the last month?"

"Who doesn't?"

"I'm investigating them. At first I thought your Triad was involved, but it wasn't true. There was a rather impetuous Chinese general up in Guangzhou who is no longer with us—he may have been responsible. I'm checking out one more lead in Kalgoorlie. A major British company has a gold mine there. I have a hunch I'm going to find some things there that will shed more light on the whole situation."

"Will we be back for the handover?"

"Yes. We have to be. I have an appointment with the Royal Navy on the 30th."

"And when will we leave Hong Kong? On the 1st of July?"

Bond hesitated. He remembered what M had said.

"I'm not sure yet, Sunni," he said. "I'm working on that."

"I can't wait to get out. England sounds nice, but I will probably go back to America. I'd like to go back to school and study medicine. I think I know enough about the human anatomy to have a head start, what do you think?" She laughed, rubbing her hand along Bond's leg.

"You'd make a wonderful doctor," Bond said, smiling. "Your bed-side manner is particularly inviting."

She laughed, then became silent. After a moment, she said, "I'm not ashamed of what I've been doing. I had to do it. There are many girls who find themselves in the same situation. It supported me and my mother. I had a nice home. I had money . . ." Her voice choked as she attempted to hold back tears. Bond put his arm around her, keeping one hand on the wheel.

"Sunni, you're right," he said. "You don't have to justify anything to me. Or to yourself. You did what you had to do."

"I was exploited," she said. "I'm damaged goods."

"No, you're not," he said. "You have a strong heart and a good head on your shoulders. You can leave all that behind you."

"I *am* anxious to go," she said. "I have no family ties in Hong Kong anymore." She was quiet for a few minutes, then wiped away a tear. Bond knew the poor girl hadn't been able to grieve properly since her mother's death. Finally, she said, "You're right. I can start over. Will you help me, James?"

"I'll do my best, Sunni," he said truthfully.

By late afternoon, they had entered Australia's gold fields and driven through the ghost town of Coolgardie, at one time the gold rush capital of Australia. Half an hour later they finally entered the frontier town of Kalgoorlie and its sister suburb Boulder. Kalgoorlie was a semi-thriving place dubbed the "Queen of the Golden Mile," reputedly the world's richest square mile of gold-bearing earth. The surrounding land was hot, flat, and terribly arid. If it hadn't been for the gold rush of the 1890s, the town wouldn't exist. At one time, there were more than one hundred working mines in the Golden Mile. Kalgoorlie's gold fields continued to produce during the 1920s but faltered after the war. A big nickel boom in the 1960s brought renewed prosperity and tourism to the town.

The streets were very wide. If it were not for the modern street lights and the cars, the place might have been mistaken for the set of a Hollywood western. The historic main street, Hannan Street, was lined with antiques shops, pubs, hotels, and large buildings that displayed the long-gone wealth and opulence associated with gold frenzy. The side streets were home to all manner of industrial service facilities such as gas and electric providers, bitumen and bobcat services, machinery repair shops, and drilling equipment sales. It was clearly a roughneck, hard-hatted man's world. Bond now understood why the local law enforcement agencies quietly allowed brothels to prosper along notorious Hay Street, which ran parallel to Hannan Street.

They stopped at the Star and Garter, a motel on Hannan and Nethercott Streets. Bond got a room which was overpriced considering the rustic "quaintness" of the place. Sunni appeared to be extremely happy with it, though.

It had been a long drive and they were hungry. They walked along Hannan Street towards the downtown area until they found a noisy pub. Bond thought he had stepped back in time when he entered the place. It was more like a Wild West saloon than any sort of English pub. The place was full of men, the hard-drinking type, and they all looked like extras from a *Crocodile Dundee* movie. All conversation halted when they got a look at Sunni and her long legs. Then there was a long, loud whistle, followed by raucous laughter. A barmaid yelled, "That's enough!"

Bond led Sunni to a table away from the bar and whispered, "Are you all right in here?"

She nodded confidently. "After what I've done for a living, nothing can faze me."

The men at the bar started talking to each other again. Bond overheard the words "Sheila," "bird," "skirt," and "beaut," all "Strine" words, or Australian slang, meaning an attractive woman or a tart, depending on the context.

The barmaid, who looked as if she had been born during the gold rush, took their order. She was smiling, but her manner was such that she might have thought they were aliens from Mars.

"She'll be right," the woman said. Bond took this to mean they needn't worry. "They've been on the piss for a while," she went on. "Where you from?"

"England," Bond said.

"You too?" the woman asked Sunni.

"I'm from America," Sunni replied.

The woman sniffed, then said, "Whadallibe?" Bond, amused, translated this as "What will it be?"

"If you're hungry, all we got is counter lunch."

A man at the bar called out a little too loudly, "It's your shout, Skip!" The man he addressed groaned and ordered a round of drinks for his mates.

"What's counter lunch?" Sunni asked.

The woman looked at her. "Steak and chips."

"That's fine," Bond said.

The woman scribbled on a notepad. "You get a salad too."

"We'll have a couple of pints of beer. I understand you brew your own here."

"Goodonyamate. Hannan's—best beer in Western Australia. Two pots, then?"

"Hold it, Mary," one of the men said. The one that had been addressed as Skip brought over two large mugs of beer. "It was my shout, so our two guests here are included." He plopped the two mugs down on the table and held out his hand to Bond. "I'm Skip Stewart. Welcome, mate."

Bond shook his hand. "Thank you. I'm James, and this is Sunni."

"Sun-*ni*! " he said, making a slight bow to her.

Skip Stewart was dressed for the bush, in sturdy boots, moleskins and a grimy cotton shirt with the sleeves rolled up. He also had on an Akubra hat high on his head. Strapped to his right calf was a large knife in a sheath. "What brings you to our fair city?"

"Just passing through," Bond said.

"Ya know, I can tell you a thing or two about this town," Stewart said. "My great-grandaddy on my mother's side was the engineer who first brought water to Kalgoorlie."

"Is that so?"

"That's right. C.Y. O'Connor was his name. It was at the turn of the century, during the gold rush . . ." Stewart took a chair at their table and proceeded to tell his story. Bond didn't mind, and Sunni was grinning at the man. He was overflowing with local colour.

"Ya see, the miners were dropping like flies what for the lack of water. Drinking water, that is. My great-grandaddy came up with an invention—a wood and pitch water pipe that stretched from Kalgoorlie all the way to Mundaring Weir, near Perth. Nobody thought he would succeed. They all called him a strop, but he kept going. Well, the pipeline was finished and turned on, and after three days—there still weren't no water yet! My poor great-grandaddy shot himself 'cause he thought he'd failed, eh? But you know what?"

"What?" Sunni asked.

"He didn't realize that the water would take *two weeks* to travel that distance, eh? He *had* solved the problem. A week and a half after he killed himself, water poured out of the pipeline and began to fill up the town's new reservoir!"

"That's quite a story," Bond said.

"It's true, mate."

The men at the bar called to Stewart and held up their empty mugs.

"Oh, uhm, it's your shout, mate," Stewart said to Bond.

That meant it was Bond's turn to buy everyone in the bar a drink. "Sure," he said, and nodded to the barmaid.

Skip Stewart stood up, obviously pleased with Bond's response to the men's request. "Goodonyamate. I can tell you're no two-pot screamer. Hey, if you need anything while you're here, you don't hesitate to call on me. I run guided tour packages into the outback. I have four by fours, utes, campers, and dirt bikes. If you need to get somewhere in a hurry, I've got a little plane at the airstrip for hire. Rent the plane, you get the pilot for free."

"Who's the pilot?" Bond asked.

"You're lookin' at him." Stewart said. He reached into his back pocket, pulled out a business card, and handed it to Bond. It was a little limp and damp from the man's sweat. "That's my card, mate.

Like I said, call if you need anything. I'll leave you two to your dinner now." He took the opportunity to get another eyeful of Sunni, then sauntered back to the bar and rejoined his friends. Bond stuck the man's card in his pocket and smiled at Sunni. She was enjoying this. The barmaid brought the counter lunch, which consisted of greasy, tough, overcooked steak, and thick, oily french fries. The salad was a couple of lettuce leaves, one piece of sliced tomato, and a slice of tinned beetroot. Bond ate it anyway. Sunni picked at hers.

"We'll go to a proper restaurant next time," he promised.

"It's all right," she said. "I'm not that hungry. When are we going back to the motel?"

When they got back to the Star and Garter, Sunni bolted the door, turned and leaned back against it. She held her arms out to Bond. Still dressed, he went to her and they embraced. He pressed her against the door with his own hard body. "Oh, darling James," she moaned as she wrapped her long legs around his waist. He held her, suspended between the door and his torso, thrusting his pelvis between her legs and grinding into her slowly with force. They kissed deeply, forgetting their surroundings and losing themselves in each other.

She unwrapped her legs and moved him towards the bed. They removed their clothes. Because the wounds on his backside and legs were still sensitive, she pulled him on top of her smooth, soft body. She undulated beneath him, rocking against his flesh with a rhythm not unlike the waves in Victoria Harbour. They continued to kiss, all the while exploring each other's skin with their hands. Eventually she grasped him firmly and guided him inside. Locked together, they moved with passion and anticipation, urging each other on toward the moment of climax that they finally experienced together.

They continued to make love for what seemed like hours. The bed squeaked and the air conditioner rumbled, but at least the room was cool.

ZERO MINUS THREE: 28 JUNE 1997, 5:00 A.M.

"I'm coming with you," Sunni said, slipping on her shorts and blouse. Bond had already showered and was dressed.

They had got a few hours of sleep after a blissful night. Bond thought he should go to the facility alone, and had hoped he could slip away without waking her.

"Sunni, I don't know what I'm going to find there. There could be trouble."

"Oh, stop treating me like a helpless bimbo. I could watch your back. You've seen me in action. I'm a Hong Kong girl, remember?"

"All right, but put on something to cover your legs. We're going down a mine."

The sun was just beginning to rise as they drove away from the motel and out of town, heading north towards more remote mining towns such as Broad Arrow, Comet Vale, and Leonora. The EurAsia Enterprises facility was about an hour's drive away.

Many of the mines in Kalgoorlie-Boulder were open pit mines. This meant that the ore was mined and hauled from what was basically a large hole in the ground. The maximum amount of payable ore was moved by the shortest route to the processing plant with the minimum amount of waste. The aptly named "Super Pit" was the largest of this kind in the area, and the city's gold-mining industry was now primarily centred around it. The Super Pit would eventually swallow the last of the traditional underground mine shafts that could be found in the Golden Mile.

EurAsia's mining operation was of the old-fashioned underground type. The ore was drilled and blasted by conventional means, leaving a cavern which was partially filled with barren rock from the same mine. The broken ore produced by the blast was carried by haul trucks or rail cars to a primary crusher underground, before being winched to the surface via a shaft. Trucks, loaders, and other vehicles and equipment used underground were dismantled on the surface and lowered in pieces down the shaft. They were then reassembled in workshops cut from the rock beneath the surface. Large head-frames, prominent features in the Kalgoorlie-Boulder skyline, were used for hauling ore to the surface or raising and lowering miners and equipment.

The entrance to the facility was just off the highway. A faded sign read "EurAsia Enterprises Australia Pty—Private Property—No Trespassing." A road led from the paved highway off into the distance. Bond turned into the drive, then moved off the dirt road and travelled along the side of it over the rough terrain.

"What are you doing?" Sunni asked.

"I don't want to leave fresh tyre treads in the dirt road. No one will notice the tracks out here."

After ten minutes, the adjacent dirt road opened up into a large gravelled area surrounded by a barbed-wire fence. A closed gate barred entrance to the compound. There was a two-storey, white wooden building just inside the fence. Several 4x4 vehicles and a couple of other standard cars were parked in front. Most notable was the private airstrip alongside the building. A Cessna Grand Caravan single turboprop sat on the runway. Bond thought it was probably used by company executives to get to and from Perth in a hurry. It was the type of plane that was commonly owned by corporations and even private individuals in an area as large as Western Australia.

Bond parked the Vitara behind a clump of eucalyptus trees that he hoped would shield it from sight. He and Sunni got out and moved closer to the fence. Some distance away, on the other side of the white building, was the entrance to the mine. A headframe fifty metres high marked the spot. Two trucks sat on the "decline," the dirt road that led into the big dark hole. Another small structure stood next to it, most likely a miners' barracks or storehouse. Two men wearing overalls were walking towards the main building. Bond wondered how many more employees would be present.

From this vantage point, he could see inside the loading bay of the building. Sitting on a flatbed lorry was the dark brown sampan with the red hood that he had last seen at the EurAsia warehouse at Kwai Chung. What the hell was it doing here? Hadn't the *Taitai* shipped it to Singapore? That ship couldn't have travelled as far as Perth in four days. It was very curious—there wasn't a body of water for miles, and these people had a Chinese boat sitting in the loading bay of a mining operation.

He held the barbed-wire open for them to slip through. They both ran for cover behind a pile of boulders near the mine entrance. When the coast was clear, Bond slipped over to the small structure and listened at the door. There was silence. He gestured for Sunni, and together they entered the small building.

He had been right. It was full of mining tools, hardhats, lockers, and a shower. Bond tossed a pair of overalls to Sunni and put some on himself. They found hardhats that fitted (Sunni tucked her long hair underneath the hat), took a couple of torches and pickaxes, then proceeded out of the door. There was no one in sight. It was probably too early for the miners. If they hurried, they could be in and out before anyone arrived for the beginning of the working day.

Bond and Sunni entered the mine and made their way down the decline into darkness. They switched on the flashlights, revealing a colourless shaft of stone not much higher than Bond's head. Props were inserted every few yards to support the ceiling. He consulted the map he had found at Kwai Chung.

"We have to travel quite a way to this point here," he said, referring to a junction some distance away. The decline curved to the left there, while the map showed another passage leading right towards the "Off Limits Area."

It was about fifteen degrees cooler in the mine, which felt wonderful, but the air was stale and smelled of minerals. They soon came to an area that had recently been excavated. A couple of pickaxes lay on the ground, and the wall to their left had been chipped away. Bond pointed his flashlight at the wall. Streaks of dull brown-yellow spread through the rock.

"See that?" Bond gestured. "That's gold."

Sunni was amazed. "Really? It doesn't look like gold."

"That's because gold is never bright and shiny when you first find it. It's actually quite dull. It's very soft and malleable, too. The stuff that sparkles is really 'fool's gold.' "

They moved on further into the mine and finally came to the junction. The passage to the right was so narrow that they had to squeeze through single file. They moved down the tunnel for several minutes until it opened up into a large cavern. Bond consulted the map.

"We're nearly beneath the main building. They've excavated back under the compound. I wonder if they have lifts or something going up to the surface."

He shone the torch around the room and saw that lights had been installed in the ceiling. Bond found the switch and turned them on. The room was furnished with tables, lockers, chairs, and a vending machine for soft drinks. A large steel door was built into the far wall, with a sign reading "Off Limits Area. Danger: Radiation." There was a small porthole in the door. Bond walked over to it and looked inside. It was some kind of airlock, for another steel door was just a few feet away.

Radiation? What was behind that steel door? Bond's heart suddenly started to race. What had he stumbled on? Had he found the source of the Australian nuclear explosion? Could this possibly be the answer?

He turned quickly and searched the lockers. They were full of radiation-resistant body suits. He took one and put it on.

"Wait here," he told Sunni. "I'm going inside."

"Be careful," was all she said. She was getting a little nervous now.

Bond found the airlock controls easily enough and opened the outer door. He stepped inside and closed it behind him. He then opened the inner door and stepped into another mine shaft. He flicked on an electric generator which powered up some lights. Bond studied the rock walls and found no traces of gold. Instead, he saw net-like veins of a dull, black, sooty material that was neither smooth nor craggy. He didn't need a Geiger counter to identify the oxide. EurAsia Enterprises was mining uranium!

He followed the passage into another large work area, this one set up more like a laboratory. A lift had been installed here, and Bond presumed it went up into the main building on the surface. There were also other large machines in the room, and Bond thought they might be the reactors that converted the non-fissionable uranium-238, or natural uranium, into uranium-235, which was the material used in atomic bombs. He knew that natural uranium contained both isotopes, but usually only 0.6 per cent of the material was the fissionable U-235.

A U-235 atom was so unstable that a blow from a single neutron was enough to split it and bring on a chain reaction. When a U-235 atom was split, it would give off energy in the form of heat and Gamma radiation, which was the most dynamic form of radioactivity and the most lethal. The split atom would also emit two or three spare neutrons that would fly out with sufficient force to split other atoms they came in contact with. In theory, it was necessary to split only one U-235 atom, and the neutrons from this one would split other atoms, which would split more . . . and so on. All of this happened within a millionth of a second. Bond knew that the minimum amount to start a chain reaction was known as Super Critical Mass.

It only took the materials, the recipe, and a certain amount of expertise to make a bomb. Bond saw that the first two of these elements were in this room, and someone obviously had the necessary skill.

The big question in Bond's mind was whether Guy Thackeray himself had been involved at all. The man was dead, but this facility was obviously still operating. Who was behind it?

In the centre of the room, on a steel table, was a metal object that resembled a large skittle. On closer examination, Bond knew it was a bomb that was almost complete. The top of the device had been removed. It was the section that held the detonator and fuse which would be used to set off the chain reaction. A hollow cylinder of U-235 was inside the device. The missing section would contain another phallic-shaped portion of U-235 which would be injected by a plunger into the cylinder, thereby causing Super Critical Mass. The detonator that fired the plunger was activated by a fuse set to a timer, not an altimeter. This bomb was going to be placed somewhere, not dropped from an aeroplane.

He had to get out of there and contact London immediately. Bond could handle M's displeasure that he had disobeyed orders and left Hong Kong. If she suspended him, so be it. At least he had found the source of the nuclear "accident." Now if he only knew who was behind it and what their motives were . . .

Bond switched off the lights, went back through the passage, and opened the door to the airlock. He closed it behind him, then opened the outer door.

He stepped into the room where he'd left Sunni and got the shock of his life.

The three albino Chinese thugs, the ones he'd dubbed Tom, Dick, and Harry, stood facing him, armed with pistols. Harry held Sunni, with his hand over her mouth.

It was the fourth man in the room who took Bond completely by surprise.

"Did you find what you were looking for, Mr. Bond?" asked Guy Thackeray, alive and well and looking very fit.

NINETEEN

FAREWELL TO HONG KONG

THE ALBINO TOM IMMEDIATELY MOVED FORWARD AND DISARMED BOND. HE tucked the Walther PPK in his belt, then moved back into position. Harry slowly released Sunni, and she moved to join Bond.

"How touching," Thackeray said. "It looks as if you two have some sort of affection for each other. Surprised to see me, Mr. Bond?"

Bond was speechless.

"No, I'm not a ghost," Thackeray said. "Still alive. I haven't felt better in years!"

"What's going on, Thackeray?" Bond ground out. "Let us go!"

"But you two are my guests," the man said with mock sincerity. "I was about to have breakfast. Won't you join me? I promise to tell all." He gestured to the albinos. Bond and Sunni were shoved roughly towards the passageway. Bond removed his radioactive-resistant suit, then the entire party made their way out of the mine. They walked across the gravel towards the main building. The temperature had risen considerably in the hour Bond and Sunni had been underground.

They were led into a comfortable private dining area on the second floor. Tom shoved Bond towards a chair. Angered, 007 turned and swung at the albino. Tom was unbelievably quick for his size—he blocked the blow effortlessly, grabbed Bond's arm and twisted it sharply. Bond winced in agony.

"Enough of that!" Thackeray commanded. Tom released Bond, who jerked his arm away from the albino and stared at him menacingly.

"Who are the three stooges, Thackeray? I should have known they worked for you when I first saw them in Macau."

"Oh, these are the Chang brothers. All three of them were born albino. Their parents were my grandfather's servants. My own father saw to it that they were raised in a safe environment and they have been loyal to my family ever since," Thackeray said.

"Sit down, Mr. Bond. Sit down, Miss . . . uhm, what shall I call your lovely companion?"

Before Sunni could answer, Bond replied, "Her name is no concern of yours. She's completely innocent. You should let her go. She won't go to the police."

"I cannot believe she is *completely* innocent, Bond," Thackeray said.

"For that matter," Bond said, "you have no right to keep me either. I promise you, my newspaper won't publish anything about you."

"Your newspaper?" Thackeray laughed loudly. "Come, come, Bond. Cut the crap, *please*. I know all about you. You're no reporter. I knew you weren't a reporter before we parted company in Macau. You work for the British Secret Service. You see, my albino friends here kept tabs on Mr. Woo after he had played *mahjong* with me a couple of times. I wanted to know more about him. It wasn't difficult to ascertain that he worked for your government. You people really are becoming careless, you know. I was about to do something about him, but General Wong in China beat me to it. Woo knew too much. It wasn't a huge leap of logic to see through you, Mr. Bond."

A Chinese servant brought in a tray of food: scrambled eggs, bacon, toast, orange juice, and coffee.

"Ah, breakfast," Thackeray said. "Eat up, please. It may be the last good breakfast you'll ever have!" He sat down and started piling food on his plate.

Bond looked at Sunni. She was terribly frightened. He took her hand. It was trembling. He wished she had stayed at the motel and was angry with himself for allowing her to come. Once again he had put a girl he cared about in jeopardy. Bond gave her hand a squeeze as if to say, "Don't worry." He then put on his best façade of nonchalance.

"I bet you say that to all your guests, Thackeray," he said, sitting down. "This looks good. We're quite hungry, aren't we, Sunni?"

She looked at him as if he was mad. Bond gestured with his head for her to sit. Sunni sat down and played with her food.

"So, tell me," Bond said, "how did you manage to survive that car bomb?"

"Oh, that," Thackeray said. "Simple stage illusion. I once made a paltry living doing magic, but you probably already know that. I used to perform the same trick on stage with a cabinet and a curtain. I'd step into the cabinet, and my assistants would hold a large drape in front of it. The top of the cabinet could be seen behind the curtain, but it shielded my escape through the bottom. The cabinet was set on fire, and then I miraculously appeared at the back of the house and walked down the aisle to the thunderous applause of the audience. It was a nice illusion. On the day of my 'disappearance,' I simply got out of the limo when the vehicle was shielded by a large lorry that pulled up beside it. I jumped on to the side of the lorry and rode with it up the street. A man I'd hired then threw the bomb into the car. It was quite spectacular, if I do say so myself. I understand you had something to do with the man's demise?"

Of course, Bond thought. He should have known it had been a magician's illusion. It just proved the old adage that the hand really was quicker than the eye.

"Very clever, Thackeray," Bond said. "But why? I know all about the contract between your great-great-grandfather and Li Xu Nan's great-great-grandfather. But why disappear? Unless it was simply to escape being arrested as a drug-smuggler?"

"Yes, well, the contract . . ." Thackeray suddenly seemed lost in thought. "It's extraordinary, isn't it? My father had told me about the agreement, and I thought it had been lost forever. Li Xu Nan hated me on principle. He thought my family had cheated his family. But *we* didn't lose the contract. The Thackerays had nothing to do with his family's exile from China. Yet he blamed me for some reason." Thackeray chuckled. "It didn't stop him from doing business with me!"

"And then General Wong came to see you . . ."

Thackeray nodded. "Yes. A black day, to be sure. General Wong came to see me in, what year was it . . . ? 1985. At first I couldn't believe he could get away with what he told me. I was determined to find a legal defence against him. At the same time, though, I had to keep silent. I couldn't put the company's market value in jeopardy. If the news that EurAsia Enterprises was going to change 'management' in 1997 had been made public then, I could not have conducted business. There are plenty of big corporations that have pulled out of Hong Kong in the last ten years. I was stuck, so I had to make it work until that fateful day."

Thackeray stood and began to walk around the room as he spoke. He took a bottle of vodka, poured some into a glass, and drank it quickly. For the next half hour, he continued to refill the glass regularly. His address slowly became a rant, as if he was justifying himself to the gods rather than talking to people in the same room as him.

"I had to live with it for ten years!" he said. "Ten . . . bloody . . . years . . . Imagine it! Imagine knowing that everything your family had built was going to vanish in one swift blow, and there wasn't a damned thing you could do about it! I alone carried that weight on my shoulders. My solicitor knew of course but he was helpless as well. So, about a year ago, I finally knew what I had to do. I would get everything I could out of the company, escape, and then wreak havoc on the society that had destroyed five generations of wealth and success."

He sat down again and faced Bond and the girl. His face was flushed and he was now beginning to lose his composure. "I *hate* the Chinese. I hate the two-faced bastards! They smile to your face, eager-to-please, but behind your back they have nothing but contempt for you. And you know something? The British are no better! I hate them as well! What idiots! They agreed to hand over the wealthiest city-state in Asia to the yellow bastards, and it was rightfully theirs!"

So, Bond thought, not only was Thackeray a raving madman, he was a racist as well. "There are many who would argue with you, Thackeray," he said. "It was the Chinese who got the unfair deal back in the nineteenth century. The land was originally theirs. Hong Kong was won only because of the greed and opportunism of opium traders. That was the reasoning behind the treaty Britain signed with China in 1984. China has lived with what they felt was shame and humiliation that England has nurtured one of her children. Hong Kong is a part of China, Thackeray. You cannot refute that."

"Balls!" Thackeray shouted. "Don't speak to me about opium traders! My great-great-grandfather was a pioneer, and if it weren't for men like him there wouldn't *be* a Hong Kong! Do you think the territory would have flourished the way it did if it had been under Chinese rule all this time? It might never have been developed at all! No, Bond, I don't buy that argument. You think Britain is selling out because she feels *guilty*? If that is the truth, then it's a stupid reason to hand over a gold mine to a country full of ignorant people who will most likely run it into the ground!"

"Mr. Thackeray," Bond said evenly, "China is full of people who have worked and sweated all their lives just to have a piece of land on which to build a home. They have a heritage of defending themselves against all manner of threats. Their country has been conquered and restructured countless times over the centuries. They have learned that not everything in life is about wealth. You know as well as anyone how important *maijiang* is in the East. If Britain decided to hand over Hong Kong, it was because she felt it was the honourable thing to do. She had to save face."

"Don't talk to me of honour, Bond. It was a business transaction. Nothing more."

"I'm afraid there are a lot of people who don't see it that way."

"And after July the first, will those people still see it as an act of honour? When six million people suddenly find themselves living under communist rule, they will come to the realization that they were the pawns in a business transaction gone wrong. They were betrayed. I think they'd rather be dead."

"What are you saying, Thackeray?" Bond was now beginning to lose his temper, too. "What is it you're planning to do? I know you have a bomb down there in your mine. It was you who tested a device in the outback a few weeks ago, wasn't it?"

"Yes, that was me. I had to make sure my little home-made toy worked before I exacted my revenge on those who have done me wrong."

"And who might they be?"

"Don't you see?" Thackeray pounded the table. "If I can't have my company, no one is going to have it! If Britain can't have Hong Kong, then no one is going to inhabit it! The world has to be taught a lesson."

The magnitude of what Thackeray was implying hit Bond with great force. "*You* were responsible for all those terrorist acts, weren't you! You've been intentionally trying to start a conflict between Britain and China!"

"Bravo, Mr. Bond, bravo!" he said with sarcasm. "Yes, I was behind it all. I decided that if my plan was going to be a success, I had to build up to it. I had to plant the seeds in everyone's minds that China and Britain were at each other's throats."

"What the hell is your plan?"

"Why, the culmination of a hundred and fifty years of lies, betrayal, and pretension," Thackeray said. "No more kowtowing on either side. No more speculation about what will happen to Hong Kong in the future. At exactly one minute after midnight on July the first, that bomb will detonate somewhere in the Hong Kong territory—successfully wiping out the entire legacy."

This time it was Sunni who cried out. "No! You're a madman! Why do you want to kill six million innocent people? You're a child having a tantrum! Someone's taken away your toy and now you want to get even! You're pathetic!"

There was silence for a moment as Thackeray stared at her. Bond finally said, "I couldn't have said it better."

Thackeray stood again and began to pace the room. He was trembling with rage. The alcohol was starting to get to him, too. He was displaying the same signs of recklessness he had shown in Macau. It was not even mid-morning, and already the man was drunk on his feet. "You don't know the half of it. Starting about a month ago, I slowly began to transfer EurAsia holdings into a private Swiss bank account, a little at a time. I had to be careful, for there were many people in the organization who could have found me out. First I had to get rid of my solicitor, Gregory Donaldson. He knew too much. At the same time, I could get at that bastard General Wong. I was going to make sure *he* wouldn't get EurAsia! I made Donaldson's death look like Wong's work. Once that was done, I thought that Britain would reciprocate. When nothing happened, I had my aide Simon Sinclair assassinate the two officials from Beijing. I later got rid of *him* for that very reason. You were present at his demise, Bond."

"The massacre in Macau? *You* staged that?"

"Of course I staged it! I wanted it to look like a Triad hit. The Chang brothers here hired some men to do the dirty work. You and your friend Woo should have been killed that night, too, but it didn't work out that way."

"What about the floating restaurant? You killed your entire Board of Directors?"

Thackeray nodded, his eyes wide. As he stared into space, he involuntarily brought his hand up and pulled on the left side of his face. Bond thought he resembled the famous detail in Michelangelo's Sistine Chapel painting in which a condemned sinner suddenly realizes that his soul is damned forever.

"Yes, I did that," he whispered, almost to himself. "They all had to go. They would have found out what I was doing." Thackeray was talking to himself like a child, as if he was defending his actions to an adult who had caught him doing something wrong.

For a moment he seemed lost, his mind in a faraway place. Then he quickly snapped out of it and turned to Bond. He became his vindictive, angry self once again.

"I blamed that on General Wong, too, of course. For a while, it was working," he said. "Britain sent a Royal Navy fleet to Southeast Asia. Chinese troops lined the border. The fuse had been lit. You, Mr.

Bond, helped it along without any prompting on my part. You assassinated General Wong, didn't you? I have my sources. I know all
about it. It *was* you, was it not? You did it for that gangster Li. Tell
me I'm right?"

Bond lied. "It wasn't me."

"I don't believe you, but it doesn't matter. Wong is dead, and I can't
tell you how happy that makes me. I suppose Li has that document
now? Well, if he thinks *he's* going to take over EurAsia Enterprises,
then he needs to throw the *chim* again. He's not going to be so lucky.
Anyway, Wong's murder only made China that much more suspicious and confrontational. My little surprise the other night was the
penultimate move."

"What was that?" Bond asked.

"Oh, you probably haven't heard. One of the Star Ferries sank.
Someone put a bomb on board."

"You bastard," Sunni whispered.

"And now the stage is set for the big transition," Thackeray said.
"Just as Hong Kong changes hands, my bomb will explode. No one
will know who to blame. China will blame Britain. Britain will blame
China. There are sure to be some . . . misunderstandings." He
laughed. "It will be *wonderful*!"

"You're going to start what might be World War III!" Bond said.
"Why? What do you get out of it? Just revenge? You think that
destroying one of the wonders of modern civilization will make you
happy? I don't think so, Thackeray. I think you're going to remain the
miserable drunken wretch you are for the rest of your life, no matter
what you do."

"Oh, I intend to be perfectly happy, Mr. Bond. As I said, I've been
slowly transferring my assets to a Swiss bank account. The company's
coffers are almost dry. I liquidated my entire stock the morning of my
press conference, the day of my 'death.' It's a good thing I died when
I did, too! I probably would be under arrest for drug smuggling,
wouldn't I? I heard about the warehouse. You were probably responsible for that, too, weren't you, Bond? Never mind. To answer your
question, I think I will be very happy to see Hong Kong go up in

flames. I plan to live anonymously here in Australia for the rest of my life. The Chang brothers will look after me. They are very loyal. I pay them well, too."

Bond knew he had to stop the man. He needed to find out more about the bomb, so that in case he got away he could alert SIS. "How did you make an atomic bomb, Thackeray? It's not something you learn out of a textbook."

Thackeray laughed. "No, not a textbook. It was the Internet, actually. I found a most peculiar website called 'How to Make an Atomic Bomb.' That gave me the idea, and I hired the right people to help me. I had discovered uranium in my gold mine several years ago, but never reported it. I hired a nuclear physicist named VanBlaricum to work on it and design the machines you saw down below to extract U-235 from the U-238. That's the difficult part. It's not a sophisticated bomb. It's really quite crude. But it's big enough. It will be the best trick I've ever performed!"

"Where will you plant it? How will it be detonated?"

"You ask too many questions, Bond. I'm certainly not going to tell you where it's going to be, even though you won't be alive to witness it. Detonating it is easy. A small digital clock will be inside the cone. You know, it runs off of one of those small round batteries you find in wristwatches. It will be set as a timer to explode at 12:01 on July the first. When the time comes, the detonator will set off some conventional explosive inside the cone, thrusting a small portion of U-235 into the main chamber, thereby achieving Super Critical Mass. In an instant . . . farewell to Hong Kong! It will destroy forever China's hopes of regaining the colony, and it will teach Queen and Country a lesson they will never forget. I have nothing for which to thank England. I have lived in Hong Kong and Australia all my life. England can go hang, for all I care."

Thackeray seemed to be in a better mood now. He was quite drunk, but he was no longer in a rage. He moved behind Sunni and put his hand on her long, soft hair. She recoiled, but he grasped her neck and held her firmly. "You're full of fight, you know that, my dear? I think you'll make a nice figurehead for my little firecracker.

I'll see to it that you make it back to Hong Kong safely, and you can witness the event from a front-row seat! My ship is docked in Singapore, and it's got a lot of nooks and crannies where we can hide you. I have a cargo seaplane in Perth waiting to take us to meet her. It's a rather long voyage, so we must get started."

He released her, then nodded to Tom and Dick. The two albinos grabbed Sunni and pulled her from the table. She screamed, "No!" and started to struggle. Bond rose to come to her aid, but Harry aimed an AK-47 at him and gestured for him to be still. Sunni attempted to use karate, but the two men held her fast and removed her from the room. The sound of her struggles became fainter as they took her to another part of the building.

Thackeray produced a pistol from thin air—another sleight-of-hand trick. It was Bond's own Walther PPK. "Now, what shall we do with you, Mr. Bond? I can't let you live, that much is certain. I should probably just shoot you here and now and get it over with. I've always wondered why the bad guys never do that to the heroes in action movies. Instead, they have to use some elaborate method of torture or execution. The hero ultimately uses the delay to his advantage and escapes. So I should just shoot you now, right?"

For a second Bond thought the sight of the madman pointing his own gun at him would be the last thing he would ever see. Thackeray only smiled.

"No," he said. "Not yet. I don't want anyone from your service coming to look for you. The Australian police and INTERPOL have already done a thorough search of our facility here a couple of weeks ago. As you can imagine, every mining company in Kalgoorlie was investigated over my little nuclear test in the outback. One of the area's many side industries is explosives. Luckily, my uranium lode was adequately hidden, and EurAsia Enterprises Australia was given an all-clear. But one can't be too careful. I don't want anyone finding your body, or any remains of it."

He gestured to Harry. "My friend Mr. Chang will take you for a ride in my private airplane. We'll take you to a part of the country you've probably never seen. For that matter, it's a part of the country you'd probably never want to see. We'll shoot you there and dump your body. If anyone other than an Aborigine ever finds it, it will have been completely eaten by predators. I think that is best." He then nodded to Harry, giving him a signal.

Harry slammed the butt of the AK-47 into the back of Bond's head. He saw a flash of light, felt a moment of extreme pain, and then plunged into total darkness.

TWENTY

WALKABOUT

28 JUNE 1997, 6:00 P.M.

The white and red Cessna Grand Caravan was the largest single-engine utility multi-use turboprop, widely used by mail carriers and cargo-delivering companies. Its overall length was 41.6 feet, with a wingspan of 52.1 feet. Its engine was a PT6A-114A with 675 SHP, and could take the plane on a cruising speed of 341 kilometres per hour. The Grand Caravan was exceptional because up to five distinctive interiors could be customized. At the moment, it was fitted out with a 10-seat commuter interior—ideal for carrying passengers in first-class comfort.

Cruising at 182 knots at an altitude of 20,000 feet, James Bond was anything but comfortable. He awoke from a deep sleep, strapped into the last seat on the right of the cabin. His head was pounding, and he felt drugged. They must have given him some kind of sedative after the head injury. The unmistakable hum told him where he was and what was happening. The plane's cabin had two rows of five seats each, the front two in the cockpit. One man he hadn't seen before was piloting the aircraft, while Harry, the smallest but wiriest of the three albinos, was sitting two seats up from Bond in the opposite row. They were the only passengers in the plane.

Bond squinted out of the window. The sun was setting, and the ground below looked golden brown. They were flying over what seemed to be an infinite desert.

He tried to move, but he was strapped in tightly with duct tape wrapped around his body and the chair. They were probably going to land somewhere very soon, kill him, dump his body, then take off back to Kalgoorlie. Guy Thackeray and his bomb were most likely already on their way back to Hong Kong . . . with Sunni in tow.

Bond groaned, indicating to his captor that he was just waking up. Harry turned around to look at him. The man got out of his seat and moved back. He was carrying an AK-47. There seemed to be an awful lot of AK-47s in this part of the world!

Harry grunted at Bond as if to say, "Oh, you're awake. Having fun?"

"Untie me, you bastard," Bond moaned. "This is uncomfortable."

Harry said something in Cantonese that Bond couldn't understand. He only caught the words "almost there."

"Come on," Bond said in Cantonese. "I have to stand up and stretch. My head is killing me."

The albino thought about it. Finally he said in English, "No tricks."

"You're the one with the gun, my friend," Bond said.

Harry produced a pocket knife with his left hand, and sliced through the duct tape. Bond pulled his hands free and ripped the tape away from his body. Harry resumed pointing the gun at his prisoner. Bond stood up and held his hands high. The cabin's ceiling was low, so he couldn't stand up perfectly straight. In fact, he had to lean over to stretch.

"I'm unarmed, see?" he said. "No need to point that at me yet." He squatted on his haunches and twisted his body backwards and forwards, working out the kinks.

"What did you shoot me up with?" he asked. "I feel as if I'm in a recovery room. Where are we, anyway?"

He started to move into the aisle and towards the cockpit, but Harry stopped him. He gestured towards the seat. "Down," was all he said.

"Oh, come on, now," Bond said. "You just let me up. Can't I move around a bit?" Harry fired a single shot from the AK-47 at the seat next to Bond, blowing a hole right through it. "All right, all right, you made your point," Bond said. "Does your boss always allow you to shoot up his plane like that? You know, it's not a smart thing to do, firing guns in a pressurized cabin. There was a Korean fellow I knew once . . ."

Then Bond used the oldest trick in the book and it actually worked. He looked towards the cockpit and feigned an expression of alarm. "Christ, what the hell is your pilot *doing?*" he said.

Harry turned toward the cockpit and Bond jumped him. It was vital to get the machine gun away from the man, so he used both hands to grab it and Harry's right arm. He threw the full weight of his body against Harry's smaller frame, knocking them both to the cabin floor in the middle of the aisle. Harry was on his back, Bond on top of him, both of them struggling for control of the gun. A blast of gunfire ripped across the ceiling of the plane and all hell broke loose inside the cabin. Every unsecured object flew towards the holes, disorienting the two fighting men. The noise of the escaping pressure was deafening. The pilot shouted something, but no one could hear him.

Harry was firing the gun wildly. Bond could barely hold on to the man's arm, for the recoil was intense and Harry was agile. He didn't want any of the windows blown, or they all might be sucked out into the sky. The pilot reached for a pistol hidden in a compartment by his side, but the plane lurched and forced the pilot to stay with the controls of the aircraft.

Bond repeatedly slammed his elbow into Harry's face, but the albino still clutched the AK-47. Finally, in an attempt to pull the gun up and away from Bond, he swung his arms above his head. Unfortunately, this action aimed the gun towards the cockpit. Another blast of gunfire riddled the control panel and the pilot, who slumped forward in his seat.

The plane immediately swerved and started to dive. Bond and Harry were slammed against a seat, and Harry dropped the gun. They continued to roll as the plane spun upside down. The cabin's ceiling was now the floor as they rolled over the seats. The little man suddenly delivered some severely painful karate blows to Bond's sides, then squirmed away from him. He was trying to find the gun again, but it had fallen out of sight.

The plane rotated again so that everything was right side up, but it was dangerously out of control. Both of them were tossed against the seats. Harry leaped towards Bond and began to pummel him. Stiff and in pain, Bond did his best to ward off the blows and protect himself. If only he could get a good punch in, but all he was able to do was to push the man's face back with his right hand. It was enough to cause the albino to fall back. Bond jackknifed up, held on to a seat, and kicked Harry hard in the head. It didn't seem to disable him. He grabbed Bond's foot and twisted it sharply, nearly spraining his ankle. Bond cried out in pain, then used his other foot to kick Harry, who let go and scrambled into the aisle. He had seen the machine gun and was going for it.

Bond jumped on to the albino's back as he crawled towards the AK-47, which was not quite within his reach, but he was so wiry that he slipped through Bond's arms and managed to get hold of the gun. He then attempted to get himself off the floor and on to his knees, but the plane lurched again, knocking both of them against the exit panel on the left side of the craft. Bond went for the gun, which Harry held across his chest. The albino's back was pressed against the door, and the men were face-to-face.

By now, all of the pressure had escaped from the cabin. It was difficult to breathe, but Bond could now use this to his advantage. Using all the strength he could muster, he kept his right hand on the gun to keep Harry from pointing it at him, and used his left hand to reach behind the albino to get at the door's emergency lock. He found it and released it.

The door swung open and Harry fell out, the gun still in hand. He screamed, a look of horror on his face as he flew away from the craft to his death. Bond managed to brace himself against the opening, then slowly climbed back through the aisle towards the cockpit.

He threw the dead pilot out of his seat and quickly buckled himself in behind the controls of the aircraft. Christ, they were only a mile from the ground! Could he land the plane without smashing it to pieces? Bond levelled the aircraft as best as he could, slowing it to a safer speed. There was a patch of flat, sandy ground below. It would have to do. Thank God there were no cliffs or canyons in the area.

Bond took her down, but it was going to be a crash landing no matter what he did. He braced himself, attempting to keep the plane straight so that the wheels would touch the ground before the nose did. Bond covered his face and hands and bent forward.

As it happened, the plane landed square on the front and left wheels. The front wheel broke away and the nose slammed into the ground. Miraculously, it wasn't crushed, but the propeller snapped off and the windscreen shattered into a hundred pieces. The entire aircraft skidded across the sand and finally came to a halt. It was broken and useless, but still in one piece. It was a testament to Cessna's reputation and the durability of the Grand Caravan.

Bond took several deep breaths and took stock of his body. He hadn't been hurt. He slowly got out of the seat. The enormity of what he had just been through paled when he suddenly realized where he was. He looked out of the broken windscreen at his surroundings. Outside the sun was setting on a vast horizon of nothingness. He was quite literally in the middle of nowhere.

The first thing he did was try the plane's radio, but it was inoperable. The burst of gunfire from the AK-47 had blown a hole through it. Next, he searched the cockpit for anything that might be useful—maps, canisters of water . . . There were some navigational maps of Western Australia and the Northern Territory, but they didn't tell Bond where the plane had actually crashed. He folded the maps and put them in his pocket. The pilot had reached for a gun in a compartment. It happened to be Bond's own Walther PPK, but there were only a few bullets left in the magazine. Unfortunately, there was not a single bottle of water. The only other possibly useful items in the plane were a couple of life jackets, a fire extinguisher, a blanket, a pillow, and a torch. He tried the torch, but the batteries were dead. Wonderful . . .

Bond climbed out of the plane and looked around. The horizon was a simple straight line circling him. The sun was setting quickly to his left, so it was fairly easy to ascertain the cardinal directions. However, knowing where north and south lay didn't answer the big questions—where in God's name was he, and how far was he from civilization?

Fear gripped Bond's heart. He could withstand many tortures, but if he was stranded many miles into the outback he would never be able to stop Guy Thackeray from destroying Hong Kong. He couldn't even send a message to someone. He was totally alone.

It was dusk, the sun casting a breathtaking orange splash across the sky. Bond noted its relation to the plane so that he could at least remember which way was west. How cold would it get at night? Bond tried to remember all the esoteric details of the Special Forces desert survival training course he'd taken many, many years ago. He had not once been called to practise any of the things he had learned when he was much younger and very green.

Bond sat down on a rocky patch of brown dirt and removed his left shoe. He used the prying tool to open it, then took out the miniature microfilm reader and a thin packet of microfiche he had checked out of the Q Branch library before departing from London. He had known he was going to Hong Kong, so picked up as many maps of the surrounding area as he could. Australia had been an afterthought, as the nuclear testing in the outback was on his mind at the time. It was a damned good thing he had done so, he thought.

Although he would have to wait until the stars were out before he could make a reliable estimate of his location, Bond could study the maps and compare them with the navigational charts he had taken from the cockpit. He started with the Kalgoorlie-Boulder area. He examined the maps and determined that the plane must have flown north over the desert. Exactly how far it had flown he didn't know.

How long had the plane been in the air before Bond woke? He had been unconscious for at least six hours, as the last thing he remembered was an unpleasant breakfast. The navigational chart showed previously marked flight paths to and from Perth, Alice Springs, and

Uluru. Alice Springs, or "Alice," was the legendary town in the heart of Australia famous for its red-baked ground and status as a popular tourist centre for exploring the outback. Uluru was also known as Ayers Rock, one of the natural wonders of the world. It was billed as the largest monolith on the globe, and some people believed it might be the crest of a mountain buried beneath the ground. The Aborigines regard it as a sacred site, and recently the Australian government had given Ayers Rock and the surrounding land back to them. They renamed it Uluru, the proper Aboriginal name for the rock, and managed the tourist business at the site, operating the attraction as a national park.

Bond guessed he was somewhere along a route either to Alice Springs or to Uluru. They weren't that dissimilar. Alice Springs was a little northeast of Ayers Rock. The plane would eventually have flown over Aboriginal reserve land.

It was starting to get chilly. The desert could become frighteningly cold at night. It was a good thing he had the blanket.

In an hour, the sun had completely disappeared. He had never seen a night sky so clear and so abundantly filled with stars. He spent half an hour studying the constellations and comparing them to southern hemisphere winter sky charts that came with the microfiche. The microfilm reader conveniently provided its own illumination. The bisecting lines of the Southern Cross was the celestial south pole. It was sharp and bright in the sky. Using simple geometry, Bond compared the south pole star to the spot on the horizon where the sun had set. The angle was less than 90 degrees, indicating that the plane had indeed flown northeast. He had two choices—walk back southwest towards Kalgoorlie, or continue northeast. The other small mining towns like Leonora were very far away.

The Aborigines are known for practising something called a "walkabout," a rite of passage for young and old people alike. They would go out into the bush and stay there for days, weeks, or even months, living off the land, becoming one with the spirits whom they believe live there, and then return. Some say that the spirits act as guides and protect the humans. Bond wasn't a religious man, but he stood there under the stars and closed his eyes. He breathed deeply several times, concentrating on the silence of the desert.

Following the instincts that had brought him luck and fortune in some of the world's elite casinos, Bond started walking northeast. He was gambling that the plane had been flying at least two hours, maybe more. He believed he was closer to Uluru than to any other inhabited place.

With the blanket wrapped around him, Bond walked across the flat land. He kept the south pole star in sight, checking his route every half hour. He tried to remember what types of plants indigenous to Australia the Aborigines used for water and food. He knew that the mulga tree had moist roots and seeds and the bottle tree contained water in its trunk, but was damned if he could remember what they looked like. There were others, he knew, but most of them grew in other parts of the continent. Central Australia and most of the Northern Territory were the most barren and arid sections of the country. Some bushes and plants held fruit, but he wasn't sure which were poisonous and which were safe to eat. There was something called a yellow bush tomato which he thought he might recognize, and another called the ruby saltbush. He might find a desert fig bush if he was lucky. It was difficult at night, so he would just have to wait until the sun came up before he could seriously examine the flora. He was already hungry, but he could wait. The important thing was to travel as far as possible while it was cool.

The minutes turned into hours and Bond kept walking on course. At one point, he heard the howls of wolves. No, they weren't wolves—they were dingos, the wild dogs of Australia. He saw them, a pack of eight, some twenty metres behind him. They were curious, following him. Were wild dingos dangerous? He couldn't remember. There was one famous case in which a woman claimed they stole her baby from a camping area, but would they attack a full-grown man? He was certainly in danger if they were rabid.

The dingos moved closer, surrounding him. They resembled small wolves in the moonlight. He didn't want to waste the few bullets he had in his pistol, but he would if he had to. Perhaps there was another way to get rid of them.

Bond sat down and removed his left shoe. He extracted one of the inflammable shoelaces and two pieces of flint. Then he broke off a three-foot branch from a dried bush nearby. The dingos growled when he did that. Bond rubbed the flint against the steel. A couple of sparks flew, then the shoelace caught fire. He quickly wrapped it around the branch, and eventually he had a torch.

007 jumped up abruptly, shouting at the dingos and waving the torch. A few of them yelped and immediately ran away, but three of the larger dogs stubbornly held their ground. They growled and bared their teeth, then barked fiercely. Bond ran at them, swinging the torch and yelling. Two dingos backed off, but the third, the leader, attacked. Bond swung the torch at the animal, hitting it on the head. It yelped and retreated, having got the message that the human was indeed too much for them to handle. Once the leader moved away, the others followed. In minutes they were gone.

Bond carried the torch until it was extinguished. Then he walked on . . .

ZERO MINUS TWO: 29 JUNE 1997, 6:00 A.M.

The sun rose over the land, bringing warmth and life to the desolation around him. He folded the blanket and tucked it into his trousers. He sat down to rest a while and removed his right shoe. He took out the tube of sunblock ointment which Major Boothroyd had thoughtfully included in the field shoe and applied some of it to his face, neck, and arms.

He was very hungry and thirsty now. If he was to keep up the same pace in the hot sun, Bond desperately needed water. He looked around him. There was some vegetation here and there, but he didn't know what it was. It all appeared to be dead. He stopped and dug up a shrub to examine its roots. They were black, dry, and totally useless.

At mid-morning, he saw three kangaroos in the distance. They were feeding off some kind of bush. When they heard him, they scampered away. Bond examined the bushes and found that there were several specimens of a yellow tomato-like fruit still attached. If the kangaroo were eating these things, then the fruit couldn't possibly be poisonous. He recalled his desert survival instructor's words: be sure to take notice of the wildlife, for animals are usually good judges of what is nutritious and what is deadly. Bond plucked one of the small yellow tomatos and bit into it. It was sour, but fresh-tasting and full of liquid. He ate two, then picked the remaining five and put them in his pockets.

By midday, Bond was sweating profusely and becoming dehydrated. The sun seemed to fill the entire sky. He wished he had a hat, but the blanket became an asset once again. The fruit provided nourishment and some liquid, but he needed water badly. He kept going, pausing to rest for five minutes every hour. Sometimes he would see an animal. There was an anteater frantically searching the ground for an antbed. A perentie lizard scampered over some rocks. Bond would have liked to catch it, for he had heard that such lizards were edible. The most incongruous sight he saw was a herd of wild camels galloping across the desert. He had no idea where they had come from or where they were going—it was just another surreal occurrence in a land where anything, or nothing, could happen.

He came upon a large graceful tree, probably a she-oak, standing alone on the barren ground. The roots were thick and hard, but probably contained some kind of moisture. Bond removed the file from his shoe and started to dig around the base of the trunk when he saw something that made his heart jump. There, in a patch of soft dirt, was a human footprint. It was probably a fresh one, for it was perfectly formed and showed no signs of erosion. It was a small bare print, probably belonging to a child. Were there Aborigines nearby? Bond knew he was on their land. Aborigines were traditionally a peaceful group—they could very well offer him assistance.

He stood up and looked around. There was nothing but the horizon. He put his hands to his mouth and called out, "Hello!" He did it three times in every direction. If there was anyone within a mile, they might have heard him.

Bond knelt back down and continued digging around the base of the tree. After a while, one of the roots was exposed. He wasn't sure what to do next. It was too large and thick to break with his bare hands, and he had no appropriate tool for cutting it. He tugged on it and squeezed it, but quickly found he was wasting energy.

Damn! There were other plants that contained water, he was sure of it. As he pondered the problem, he ate one of the yellow fruits from his pocket. It went a long way towards quenching his thirst. Perhaps he could make it through the rest of the day without water, but what about tomorrow? And the next day? Of course, by then it would be too late. In fact, if he didn't reach civilization by midnight, he doubted that he would make it back to Hong Kong before the first of July deadline. Maybe he could alert the proper authorities in time. Then the problem would be finding the bomb. They surely wouldn't have much time to search an entire territory. The situation seemed quite hopeless.

Bond sighed, then stood up. He glanced at the sun to get his bearings, then turned to continue walking. What he saw stopped him dead in his tracks.

A black girl stood twenty feet away from him. She was an Aborigine, probably in her late teens or early twenties, and was wearing a dirty white t-shirt and dusty khaki shorts. Her legs and feet were bare. The girl was thin but looked healthy. It had most likely been her footprint that Bond had seen. She was carrying a long, thin, sharpened wooden stick in one hand, and also had a netted bag slung over one shoulder. The bag was full of tubers of some kind.

She looked at Bond with a mixture of curiosity and fear. Her brow was creased, as if she was questioning the evidence of her own eyes.

Slowly, Bond raised his hand in the universal gesture. "Hello," he said pleasantly.

The girl tensed and looked as if she might run.

"Wait," Bond said. "Don't be afraid." He dropped the file he was holding and held out both hands. "Can you help me?" He gestured towards the tree. "I was trying to find water. You know . . . water?" He mimed drinking with cupped hands. Did Aborigines speak English? He thought they did; but now, out here, he wasn't sure . . .

She just stood there, staring at him. Bond tried to review what he knew about the Aboriginal people during the few seconds of silence. He knew that many were nomadic, were family-oriented, and were probably the most neglected and poorly treated races in history. He knew that the women were usually the food gatherers, while men hunted and performed spiritual rites. This woman was probably out gathering food for her family.

"Can you speak?" Bond asked. He pointed to himself. "James."

She didn't respond.

He reached into his pocket and pulled out one of the yellow fruits. "Oh, I have some of these. You want one?" He showed it to her and offered it. She eyed it, then looked back at him. Her large brown eyes were full of wonder. She did not fear him anymore, she was wondering what the hell he was doing there.

Bond tossed the fruit to her, underarm. She caught it with her free hand. Bond said, "Good catch." He smiled at her.

Her eyes never left his as she brought the fruit up to her mouth and bit into it. The juice ran down over her chin and dripped on to her shirt. The moisture spread until the erect nipples of her firm breasts clearly protruded through the fabric. Bond watched her eat the entire thing. Despite the heat, his thirst, and the awkwardness of the situation, he found the sight incredibly erotic.

When the fruit was gone, she did nothing to wipe the juice off her chin and neck. Then, suddenly, she laughed. Bond laughed with her, and nodded.

"Water?" he asked again. "Can you help me get water?" Once more he cupped his hands to his mouth.

The girl nodded. Confidently she squatted on the ground by the tree and began to dig with her hands. Her hands were tough and coarse, virtually tools with which to dig into hard dirt. In less than five minutes, she had dug deeper than Bond had done with the file. She pulled on some smaller roots, breaking them off of the larger vein Bond had found earlier. She stood up and showed them to him. She snapped one in half, then sucked on the broken end of one part. The girl made a loud slurping noise, indicating that there was indeed moisture within the root. She handed the other end to Bond. He placed the broken root in his own mouth and sucked. There was water inside! It wasn't much, only three or four small swallows. He smiled at her and nodded. The girl squatted again and broke off more roots, then handed them to him. He sucked on a couple more, then stored the remainder in his pockets.

"Thank you," he said.

She nodded and smiled, although it looked a little like a smirk.

"Uluru," he said. "I'm going to Uluru."

She nodded her head and pointed in the northeasterly direction Bond was travelling. He had been right.

They heard an animal's cry in the distance. She turned around, waved, and made a similar shrill call. It hadn't been an animal's cry at all. Off in the distance, Bond could see two other human figures, obviously part of her family or tribe.

The girl turned back to Bond and did something very strange. She reached up and placed her hand on Bond's face. She felt his features, tracing his eyebrows and the bridge of his nose. She ran a finger along the faint scar on his right cheek. Then she felt his mouth, pinching his lips slightly. She inserted her index finger into his mouth and touched his teeth, as if she was amazed he still had a full set. Bond ran his tongue lightly across the tip of her finger. It tasted salty. She didn't remove her finger; instead, she giggled.

Then she spoke! "If you keep walking, mate, you'll reach Uluru by sundown."

"Christ, you speak English!" Bond exclaimed. "Why didn't you say so?"

The girl laughed, then abruptly turned and ran towards her companions.

Bond watched her go. The girl turned and waved at him, and soon she had disappeared beyond the horizon. She had made him feel foolish, but she was one of the most sensual creatures he had ever encountered.

Bond continued his walkabout. The sun's heat became worse as the day moved into afternoon. He applied more sunblock and used some more of the water-saturated roots. Around 3:00 p.m. he came upon a dirt road. It seemed to head in the same direction as his destination, so he followed it. At 4:00 he saw signs of civilization. An old tyre had been discarded on the road. There were telephone poles in the distance.

Finally, he saw it. At the edge of the horizon was a red bump. From this distance, it was a mere pimple where the earth met the sky. As he walked closer, the bump grew in size until it was a mountain. Uluru . . . Ayers Rock, the big red heart of Australia. It was a sacred shrine to the Aborigines, and the main reason why tourists ventured to the desolation of central Australia. The 348-metre-high monolith was indeed a breathtaking sight. Its fiery glow and haunting colours were at their peak, illuminated by the setting sun.

It was 6:00 p.m. Bond had spent nearly twenty-four hours in the Australian outback, and had made it to civilization. He nearly wept with awe, joy, and relief.

TWENTY-ONE

COUNTDOWN

JAMES BOND STUMBLED INTO THE ULURU NATIONAL PARK RANGER STATION and nearly collapsed on the floor. An Aborigine dressed in a park ranger uniform stood up in surprise.

"You all right, mate?" he asked.

"Water . . . phone . . ." Bond whispered.

An hour later, Bond had showered, eaten a meal, and spent fifteen minutes with his eyes closed. He was dead tired and probably had a mild case of heat exhaustion. He would have liked to have crawled into a hole for a week, but there was just a little more than twenty-four hours left. It was precious little time, and he had to find the quickest way back to Hong Kong. The rangers had provided him with a clean uniform, as his clothes were soiled and torn. When he went through his pockets, Bond found the business card that Skip Stewart had given him in the pub in Kalgoorlie. Perhaps the man's tourguide service would come in handy after all. Bond placed a phone call to Stewart and luckily found him in. Stewart agreed to fly to the Ayers Rock airport and pick up Bond for a small fee. He would arrive in about three hours.

Now it was time to call London. He dreaded M's wrath, but it had to be done. He went through the usual security measures, was connected to Bill Tanner, and finally to M herself.

"007? Where the hell are you?"

"Australia, ma'am. I've found the source of the nuclear explosion, and it's directly related to our man Thackeray and EurAsia Enterprises," he said quickly.

There was silence at the other end. He'd expected her to say something about orders to remain in Hong Kong.

"Tell me more," was what she finally said.

Bond gave a brief version of everything that had happened in the last forty-eight hours, and how he had got to be where he was.

"You're lucky to be alive," she said. "I'll put out an all-alert to our fleet in Hong Kong. Any idea where Thackeray is going to put this bomb?"

"No idea. Could be anywhere. We haven't much time."

"Precisely. How fast can you get back to Hong Kong?"

"I expect a ride back to Perth in a little while. I'm afraid the only transportation I can get back to Hong Kong is a commercial airline. Leaves tomorrow morning and doesn't get in until the evening."

"That's cutting it much too fine," she said. "All right, do what you can. When you get back to Hong Kong, contact Captain Plante aboard the *Peacock*. She's one of our Peacock Class patrol craft, and she'll be in Victoria Harbour. Got it?"

"Yes, ma'am, but I request permission to contact Li Xu Nan again. He may be able to help with this."

"007, this department does not sanction your dealing with Triad members or any other criminal organization. We'll deal with your insubordination and leaving Hong Kong against my orders when you're back in London. Mind you, if you hadn't discovered what you did, I'd have had your hide!"

She rang off. Without a second thought, Bond dialled Li Xu Nan's private number in Kowloon.

Skip Stewart arrived at 9:30 p.m. He flew a Piper Navajo PA-310, an American-manufactured plane that had an all-weather and night capacity performance.

"Howzitgoin,' mate?" he asked when he jumped out of the cockpit to greet Bond. "When did you become a park ranger? Never mind. How do you like her? I bought her from the Royal Flying Doctors a couple of years ago when their Alice Springs headquarters upgraded."

"Just get me to Perth before morning, Skip," Bond said. "I have a Qantas flight to Hong Kong that leaves at 8:30."

"No worries, mate. My little Airy-Jane will get you there. We'll have to stop in Kalgoorlie for a refill, ya know . . ." he said. "Wish I could help you out and take you all the way to Hong Kong, but my little bird, there's only so far she can go. Say, did I tell you about my auntie who struck gold in Coolgardie when she was twelve years old . . . ?"

By 10:00 p.m., James Bond was in the air over the outback once again. The only problem this time was that he had to listen to three hours' worth of bush stories.

Zero Minus One: 30 June 1997, 9:30 p.m., Hong Kong

The news had hit the morning papers of 29 June. The *South China Morning Post* front-page headline declared CHINESE GENERAL IN DRUG-SMUGGLING SCHEME. The *Hong Kong Standard* carried the photographs Li's men had taken, accompanied by the headline: MURDERED CHINESE GENERAL IN DRUG PLOT. The story detailed how Wong had been involved with "Triad societies" in a worldwide drug-smuggling plot that also involved EurAsia Enterprises. The general was also implicated in the several terrorist acts that had occurred in the territory over the past few weeks, including the car-bomb murder of Guy Thackeray. Wong's own assassination was being attributed to a disgruntled EurAsia employee. According to the article, the assassin had been caught and killed at the border. Even the official Chinese news agency, Xinhua, issued a statement denouncing General Wong's involvement with a criminal organization. Although Beijing stopped short of an apology for accusing Britain of Wong's murder, the official word was that the general deserved what he had got.

The news literally saved Hong Kong from an early Chinese takeover. The troops had been prepared to march south across the border on the morning of 29 June. The Royal Navy fleet of three Peacock Class patrol craft had been joined by the destroyer and two frigates that had arrived on 28 June, and had combined forces with the Hong Kong naval fleet. Royal Marines had moved on to the peninsula and were now stationed in the New Territories, anticipating the crisis that ultimately never happened. The Hong Kong government breathed a sigh of relief at the news, for it meant that perhaps the handover, scheduled for midnight on the 30th, would be a peaceful one after all. Despite the averting of the immediate crisis, tensions were still very high and mistrust of China was rampant.

Festivities began early on the morning of the 30th. The Chinese New Year was of only secondary importance compared to the coming event. Shops closed and the population took to the streets. There were celebrations on every corner. Hong Kong Park was full of both pro-democracy and pro-China groups. The Royal Hong Kong Police had to provide a heavy presence to ensure that peace was maintained. Statue Square was blocked off from traffic in preparation for the night's event, and visiting officials from around the world had flown in for the occasion. Every hotel was totally booked.

Once again James Bond disobeyed his superior's orders and went straight to Li Xu Nan's office building when he got to Kowloon that evening. The Dragon Head had assembled ten men, all outfitted with miscellaneous automatic weapons. They were ready to move at a moment's notice.

Bond made contact with Captain Plante aboard the *Peacock*. Although Plante was perturbed that 007 was in Kowloon, he was willing to cooperate and do whatever he could to find Thackeray and the bomb. The Royal Hong Kong Police had been put on alert as well, and they were working double-time searching the Central District.

"Where could Thackeray place that bomb for maximum effect?" Bond asked Li.

"I have been thinking about that. I would suspect that it would be Central. That is where EurAsia's headquarters is, and where all the important bank buildings and businesses are. It is the financial centre of Hong Kong. The police are already searching the area."

"That's what I thought, too. Somehow, though, I feel it's wrong," Bond said. "It's too obvious."

"Yes, I know what you mean."

Something was nagging at Bond's memory, and he knew that it was a clue to the bomb's whereabouts.

"Think, Mr. Bond," said Li. "Did Thackeray say anything about where he might put it? Did its shape or size indicate where it might be placed?"

Bond went over everything he could recall about his fateful meeting in Australia. Mostly he remembered an alcoholic madman with a childish lust for revenge.

"He's also got Sunni," Bond said. "He said that . . ."

And then he remembered. "My god," he said. "Do you have a boat? It's going to be in the harbour on a boat."

"How do you know?"

"Thackeray said that Sunni would make a nice figurehead for the bomb. There was a sampan at the Kwai Chung warehouse, and I saw it again in Australia. They're going to put the bomb inside the sampan and casually float it out into the harbour!"

Li nodded. "I have a boat. Let's go!"

11:10 P.M.

Li's Sealine Statesman 420 was a high quality British import equipped with twin 370-hp Volvo diesels and had a cruising speed of 27.7 knots and a top end of 33.5. A large yacht, the Statesman 420 was nevertheless sleek and sporty. She had sped out into the harbour at precisely 11:00, but quickly had to reduce her speed because of the congestion in the water. Bond and Li were on the upper deck, looking through binoculars at the hundreds of vessels crowding the relatively small body of water.

The Marine Police had given up directing the traffic on this particular night. Too many seagoing individuals wanted a good view of the fireworks display scheduled for midnight. A free-for-all was finally allowed, so long as everyone kept their speed down and didn't crash into each other. Along with the numerous police and Royal

Navy vessels, there were sampans, junks, tugboats, cargo ships, ferries, sailing boats, yachts, motorboats, and rowing boats—all jamming what was at that moment the world's busiest harbour.

Bond was looking for a dark brown sampan with a red hood. Unfortunately, most sampans were dark brown. He prayed that the red hood would give it away.

There was no sign of the *Taitai*, and Bond wondered where she could possibly be. Keeping close contact with Captain Plante, Bond had made enquiries about the ship's movements. Records showed that the *Taitai* had indeed left Singapore two days ago and was headed for Hong Kong, but no one had seen her since. Bond could only speculate that Thackeray was lying low, probably lurking near one of the outlying islands. The sampan was probably flown to Singapore in the same cargo seaplane that Thackeray and Sunni took from Perth. It made sense—cargo seaplanes had long been used to rendezvous with and smuggle drugs on to ocean-going vessels. The *Taitai* had sailed to the waters near Singapore, where the sampan was loaded on to the seaplane and then flown to Australia. The trip was made in reverse to get it back to Hong Kong. The sampan would probably be sent in by itself, piloted by an unsuspecting minion.

"Can't we get this thing going any faster?" Bond snapped.

"I am sorry," Li said. "You can see the harbour is crowded. This is as fast as we can go."

"We'll never make it across to the other side at this rate," Bond said. He felt utterly helpless.

A call came in on the radio for Bond. It was Captain Plante.

"Uhm, Commander Bond?"

"Yes, Captain?"

"You say you're looking for a sampan with a red roof?"

"Yes!"

"Well, there's an odd thing over here by us. There's a cargo ship—a British one, I think. Called the *Glory*. They have a sampan fitting that description tied to the side like a lifeboat."

Captain Plante was calling from the *Peacock*, which was directly in the centre of the harbour, facing Central. Bond turned and scanned the area with his binoculars.

"Where's the *Glory* in relation to you, Captain?" he asked.

"Due north, about a mile."

Bond found the ship. The *Glory* looked exactly like the *Taitai*, except that it had red stripes painted across the hull. The *Taitai* had been entirely white.

"The bastard painted his ship," Bond said. "He's disguised the *Taitai* and renamed her. That's it there!"

Li barked an order to the man at the helm of the Statesman and they turned towards the *Glory/Taitai*. They had about forty-five minutes to find the bomb and disarm it.

TWENTY-TWO

NO TEARS FOR HONG KONG

THE STATESMAN APPROACHED THE *GLORY* AND STOPPED THIRTY METRES away. The sampan was tied and hung over the starboard side of the ship like a lifeboat, ready to be lowered into the water. Bond wasn't sure, but he thought he could see the outline of a figure inside the small boat. Was it Sunni?

The *Peacock* had pulled away from its position as well, and was heading towards the *Glory*. The Royal Navy ship's movement must have alerted the crew of the *Glory*, for Bond and Li saw men appear on its deck. A tarpaulin covered a large object amidships. The men pulled off the tarpaulin to reveal a 76mm OTO Melara Gun. They began to swing it towards the *Peacock*.

"Captain Plante," Bond said into the radio. "The *Glory* has a gun aiming at you. Take defensive action immediately. We're preparing to assault the ship."

Plante acknowledged the call and wished Bond good luck. He was going to radio the other ships for back-up. Unfortunately, they were all deployed evenly across the harbour. Due to the congestion, it might take half an hour for the ships to work their way through to the site. If Thackeray was going to be stopped before midnight, it would be up to the teams aboard the Statesman and the *Peacock*.

"Li, give the order to begin the assault," Bond said.

Li shouted in Cantonese to his small band of dedicated gangsters-turned-patriots. He then gave an order to the man at the helm. The Statesman was brought as close as possible alongside the *Glory*. Then, three men aimed M-16 .233 semi-automatic gunlines and fired grappling hooks, attached to long ropes, at the deck of the big ship. The hooks stuck, and the men, dressed in black, immediately used harness and pulley systems to pull themselves over and board the enemy vessel.

Bond followed behind the first wave of men. He heard a siren wailing on the deck of the *Glory*, alerting her entire crew that they were under attack. Then the gunfire started.

Thackeray's men were leaning over the side of the ship and firing machine guns at the Statesman. Two of the men on the ropes were hit and fell into the harbour. Bond clenched his teeth and kept climbing. He felt the hot air of a few rounds whizz past his head, but he kept moving. He reached the rail on the side of the *Glory* and hauled himself up. He was met head on by a man who attempted to push him back overboard. Bond swiftly dispatched him by punching him hard in the stomach, then slinging him over his shoulder and into the water. He moved to a metal ladder and climbed it to a higher vantage point and crouched behind a smokestack. Armed only with his Walther PPK, Bond began to pick off Thackeray's force, one by one.

Li held what looked like an M-16 and was firing from the deck of the Statesman. It was difficult to tell how many of the Triads were left to fight. The first barrage of gunfire had knocked off several of them. Bond could see at least four bodies lying on the deck, and he knew at least two had fallen into the water. The *Peacock* was still some distance away.

Suddenly, the *Glory*'s big gun went off. It scored a minor hit on the *Peacock*, setting the bow on fire. Damn! Bond moved forward from his position until he was above the Melara Gun. Bond shot the two men manning the weapon, then jumped down and ran for the sampan.

Thackeray's voice boomed out over a loudspeaker: "Get them all, damn you! Take out that yacht! I'm lowering the sampan now!"

The man was probably at the helm or somewhere nearby. Bond would deal with him later. He had to reach Sunni first. The girl's figure could be seen huddled just inside the sampan. She was tied up, unable to move. Another object was built into the sampan's deck, beneath the hood. It was the bomb.

Before he could reach the hoist, however, Bond was confronted by one of the albinos, the big one he called Tom. 007 raised his gun to fire, but the albino adeptly kicked the Walther out of his hand. The man was big, but he had amazing agility. Bond attempted to return a blow with a back kick, but Tom grabbed his leg, twisted it, and effortlessly slammed Bond hard against the side of a cabin wall. He fell to the deck, only to be on the receiving end of three vicious kicks in the ribs.

Li Xu Nan was having troubles of his own. He had climbed one of the ropes on to the *Glory* and was struggling with the other albino henchman, Dick. They were of equal height and weight, and both of them were skilled martial arts practitioners. If their fight hadn't been a life-or-death struggle, it would have been one of the most impressive displays of eastern fighting techniques imaginable. Each blow delivered by one man was calculated to kill or maim, but it was met with an equally considered counterblow from the other. They moved with great speed, forcing each other to think split seconds ahead of their actions.

Bond managed to get to his feet. He leaped for Tom and grabbed hold of the man's head. The large albino simply locked Bond in a bear hug and picked him up off the deck. Bond used his free arms to deliver sword-hand blows to his opponent's neck and shoulders, but they seemed to have little effect. Tom was squeezing him hard, and Bond began to feel the strain against his ribcage. My God, he thought, the man was strong enough to crush him with his bare arms!

If that wasn't enough for him to worry about, Bond heard the hoist rumble into life. The sampan was being lowered into the water.

The fight was interrupted by a huge, deafening explosion that rocked the *Glory*. It caused Tom to release his grip on Bond and the two men fell to the deck. At first, Bond thought the bomb had detonated, but he soon realized that the *Peacock* had returned fire with its own Melara Gun. The *Glory* had taken a critical hit broadside. At least the Royal Navy were better marksmen than Thackeray's crew!

Bond jumped up and leaned over the rail. The sampan with Sunni and the bomb was floating away from the ship. Large hands grabbed his shoulders and pulled him away, and he was thrown back against the cabin wall. Tom was on him again. Bond gave the henchman everything he had. He knew a few tricks of his own, and delivered them with skill and determination. Bond struck the man's abdomen with a *Nidan-geri* double kick, chopped him on the throat with vicious one-two spear-handed blows, then swung his body around, leaped, and kicked the man full in the face. Tom staggered back against the ship's rail, broke it, and fell overboard.

Bond caught his breath and surveyed the situation. The *Glory* was on fire. Several of Thackeray's men had given up the fight and were running to lifeboats. The *Peacock* was close. The Royal Navy forces had extinguished their own fire and Bond could see three RIBs—Rigid Inflatable Boats—with several men aboard and heading towards the *Glory.* Turning towards the Statesman, he could see that Li's yacht was on fire and was sinking. He peered through the smoke on the deck of the *Glory* to try and find Li. Then he saw them. Li and the other albino, Dick, were fighting dangerously close to the flames. Bond tried to run towards them but a burst of machine-gun fire stopped him in his tracks. He leaped to the side of the cabin wall for cover.

"I'll get you, you bloody bastard!" It was Thackeray's voice, coming from a deck above him. Bond had to snake along the wall to avoid being hit. A companionway was twenty yards away from him. If he could make it there before Thackeray did . . .

Li and Dick continued their assault upon each other. Dick executed two brutal kicks at Li. The Dragon Head retaliated by jumping up, grabbing a low-hanging pipe, and swinging out towards his opponent. Li's feet caught Dick in the head, knocking him backwards into the flames. Li jumped down to the deck and bulldozed the albino, head first. He hit the man in the stomach, successfully pushing him further into the fire. The albino fell to the burning deck. His clothes were on fire, and he was screaming. Suddenly, the wooden planks beneath him gave way and he fell into the inferno below.

Li moved away from the fire and saw Bond. 007 pointed above his head and shouted, "Look out!" Li looked up and saw Thackeray on the upper deck, aiming the machine gun at him. Bond couldn't see the Englishman—he only saw Li's expression change from shock to resignation.

The Cho Kun of the Dragon Wing Society looked death in the face and accepted it with honour. The machine-gun blast caught him in the chest. Li Xu Nan was propelled back into the flames, where five generations of secret society leadership finally ended.

Bond reached the companionway and climbed to the upper deck. He caught a glimpse of Thackeray running to the other side of the ship. The *Glory* was going down fast. There were no signs of any of Thackeray's men left aboard.

He took off after Thackeray and chased him down a ladder into the depths of the ship. At one point, Thackeray turned to fire the machine gun at Bond, but he leaped out of the way, successfully dodging the bullets. Thackeray moved on. Bond followed him through a smoky passageway that was filling with water. It was difficult to breathe, and Bond knew it was extremely dangerous to continue. He could die of smoke inhalation before he got to the man. He pressed on, though, determined to stop Thackeray from reaching wherever he might be headed.

The answer to that question became obvious when Bond saw an open hatch at the end of the passageway through which Thackeray had jumped. Bond looked out of the hatch and saw that Thackeray had dropped into a speedboat, large enough to carry four people, which had been hoisted on the port side of the *Glory*, just as the sampan had been tied on the opposite side. It was about eight feet below the hatch. Thackeray was preparing to release the cables securing it to the *Glory*. This had been Thackeray's planned escape route. He had intended to set the sampan and bomb afloat, then speed away in this boat, probably with his albino henchmen, and easily manoeuvre through the crowded harbour to a safe distance. He would have fled to one of the outlying islands, then flown to safety in a hidden 'plane.

Thackeray was fiddling with the controls of the hoist that would drop the speedboat thirty feet down to the water. His attention was not on Bond for a few precious seconds. 007 leaped out of the hatch just as the cables released the boat. As the speedboat dropped, Bond was falling just a few feet above it.

The boat hit the water hard, knocking Thackeray to its deck. A second later, Bond landed in the boat with force. He might have broken his legs if the recoil from the boat hitting the water hadn't caused it to bounce and somewhat cushion Bond's fall. Even so, his right leg was injured badly. His knee hurt like hell.

"You!" Thackeray shouted. He leaped on top of Bond, and the two men locked their hands around each other's throats. Temporarily dazed by the fall into the boat, Bond was at a disadvantage. Thackeray squeezed hard, attempting to crush Bond's windpipe. 007 almost passed out but managed to bring his knee up hard into Thackeray's side. The man's years of alcohol abuse probably saved Bond, for the blow hit Thackeray hard in the liver. Thackeray jerked in pain, then released his grip on Bond's neck. He rolled off, clutching his side.

Bond sat up to catch his breath. Thackeray was doubled up in pain.

"All right, Thackeray, let's go and disarm that bomb," Bond said.

Thackeray, with a grimace on his face, simply nodded. Bond turned the ignition and got the outboard engine started, then something hard hit him in the head. The next thing he knew, half of his body was hanging over the side of the motorboat.

Thackeray had taken an oar from the bottom of the boat. He had hit Bond with it, attempting to knock him overboard. Thackeray hit him again across the back, sending a jolt of pain up Bond's spine. 007 willed himself to turn the pain into energy. He swung around and rolled just in time to avoid another direct hit from the oar. Now it was his turn. He lunged for Thackeray's legs and tackled him. They both fell overboard into the harbour.

It was murky, smelly water, but at least it wasn't freezing. In fact, it was rather warm. They clung to each other and thrashed around.

Thackeray was struggling to get to the surface. Now Bond had the advantage, for he was an excellent swimmer. Despite his injuries and the pain in his knee, he was able to turn the water into his element.

Their heads broke the surface. Thackeray had a look of rage and terror on his face. He tried to reach for the motorboat, but Bond struck out and latched on to his adversary's waist. Thackeray clutched Bond's hair and pulled it as hard as he could. He squirmed and kicked, hoping Bond would loosen his grip. Bond swam away from the motorboat with Thackeray, lifeguard-style. Thackeray was yelling something, but Bond paid no attention. They submerged again, and this time Thackeray broke away from Bond. He reached for 007's neck and locked his fingers around it. Bond tried to pry the man's fingers away, but Thackeray's adrenalin was pumping hard. If it was going to be a test of stamina, Bond thought, then so be it. He locked his own fingers around Thackeray's neck and started to squeeze. It was now a matter of who would give out first.

The bodies rolled and twirled in the dark water, performing a grotesque underwater ballet as they tried to choke the life out of each other. For nearly a full minute, which to Bond seemed like an hour, they were locked together, somersaulting like a single jellyfish. Finally, Thackeray's face changed. His eyes bulged, and bubbles began to escape from his mouth. The eyes rolled up into his head, and his grip on Bond's neck relaxed. Because of his years of training and experience, Bond was able to hold his own breath for an uncanny amount of time. He kept his grip tight on Thackeray's neck until he was sure that the man was unconscious. The *taipan* of EurAsia Enterprises, heir to a fortune won and then lost, drowned in Victoria Harbour at the hands of James Bond.

Bond let Thackeray's body drift away, then he swam to the motor-boat and climbed aboard. He looked at his watch. It was 11:45. Bond quickly got the boat going and sped around the sinking *Glory* to the other side.

The *Peacock* was broadside of the damaged cargo ship, and the RIBs were busy overtaking the enemy lifeboats and arresting Thackeray's remaining men. Bond guessed that none of the Triads survived. With their leader dead as well, he thought that the Dragon Wing Society would most likely fade into obscurity, or be absorbed by some other secret criminal society.

The sampan had not drifted far. Bond reached it in minutes, cut the motor, and leaped aboard. Sunni was tied and gagged, her eyes wide with fear and surprise. Bond removed the gag.

"James! Oh, God, James!" she cried.

"It's all right! Hold on," he said, untying her. Once she was free, he gave her a quick hug and kiss. She didn't want to let him go, but he broke away.

"Sunni, the bomb!" he said, then turned his attention to the large metal object fastened to the deck of the sampan.

The cone was screwed to the main casing. Bond removed his left shoe and opened it up. He took out the metal file, which was just the appropriate size to use on the screws. He removed the cone, revealing a digital clock face, its mechanism, and wires connecting it to the main casing and the conventional explosives surrounding the U-235 within. The clock read 11:55.

Before Bond could progress any further, the sampan lurched hard to one side. Someone was pulling himself on to the boat! Sunni screamed. It was Tom, the largest and strongest of the albino henchmen! Bond had forgotten about him after the man had fallen off the *Glory*.

"Stay with the bomb, James, I'll take care of this creep!" Sunni shouted.

Fine, Bond thought. Do it, girl. He had to concentrate. What would be the quickest way to disarm the damned thing? Maybe he could simply stop the clock.

Sunni, who once displayed a knack for street fighting, used the frustration and pent-up energy from being tied up to attack the big man like a dynamo. She hit him hard in the face with a *Mae-geri* front kick, swung around and kicked him again, then leaned in and struck him hard in the solar plexus with a stiff spear-hand. Surprised by the girl's ability, Tom was momentarily stunned. He swung at her, but she deftly dodged the blow, ducked, then brought herself up with a leap nearly as high as his head. In mid-air, Sunni kicked out hard at the man, knocking him on his back.

Bond remembered what Thackeray had said about the clock. It was run by a small battery: "the kind used in wristwatches." Bond used the file to pry off the clock face, revealing the circuitry. A small, round lithium battery was encased in metal connectors. The file was too large a tool to pop it out. Bond tried using his fingers, but that was too awkward.

Sunni continued attacking the albino henchman as if she was making up for years of abuse, exploitation, and pain. She wouldn't let up. The big man couldn't get a manoeuvre in to save his life. With one great lurch, though, he managed to get to his feet. He was standing with his back to the side of the sampan, dazed and confused. Sunni, with one final dynamic leap in the air, double-kicked the man hard on the breastplate. It was enough to force him overboard and into the water. By that time, a Royal Navy RIB had arrived. A naval officer trained his gun on the albino and was prepared to arrest him, but it wasn't necessary. Sunni had broken the man's sternum and stopped his heart.

The digital numbers read 11:58. Once again, Bond looked at the contents of the shoe that Major Boothroyd had given him. Was there another tool . . . ? Of course! The tweezers! Bond plucked them from their position in the shoe and used them carefully to extract the lithium battery. The digital clock blinked out at 11:59. The crisis was over. Thackeray's bomb was a dud.

Bond and Sunni climbed into the RIB, which took them over to the *Peacock*. Captain Plante met them on deck.

"Commander Bond?"

Bond nodded. "The bomb's defused. Your men can salvage it off that sampan."

"Excellent, Commander. Your chief is on the line there on the bridge," he said. "Just up those steps. I've orders to deliver you back to England."

What about Sunni? Bond thought. What were they going to do with her?

Bond got on the line, and after a few pips, heard M's strained voice.

"Well, 007, I see that you persist in disobeying my orders." she said.

"I'm sorry, ma'am. I assure you it won't become a habit. It's just that . . ."

"Never mind, 007. I understand you stopped that man Thackeray from doing whatever it was he was planning."

"Yes, ma'am."

"I imagine the handover ceremony is in progress as we speak."

"It's midnight here, ma'am," Bond said. "I suppose so."

"Good. You're to accompany Captain Plante back to England. I'm putting you on three months' suspension for insubordination."

Bond closed his eyes. Fine, if that's the way she wants to play it.

Then M added, "With pay."

"Ma'am?" He wasn't sure he heard her correctly.

"As for the girl, I've arranged for a passport in her name. Just give the details to Chief of Staff. We'll need to know which country she prefers. She can choose between England, America and Canada."

Bond couldn't believe it. "Thank you, ma'am. I'll ask her. I'm sure she'll be very appreciative."

They rang off and Bond joined Sunni on the deck of the ship. It began to pull away, heading east out of the harbour.

He put his arm around her. "England, America or Canada?" he asked.

"What?"

"You have your foreign passport."

"Oh, James!" She kissed him. "Do I have to decide this second?"

"No."

They looked out at the magnificent skyline of Hong Kong Island. At that moment, its sovereignty was changing hands. The future of the fabled city-state was now in the hands of the People's Republic of China.

Bond thought about T.Y. Woo and his brother, and the lives they'd given for the colony which was now lost. He made a mental note to contact Woo's son in England and offer to provide any assistance that Chen Chen might need. As for himself, he would have to live with the guilt he felt for being forced to turn his back on T.Y. that fateful day in Guangzhou. He knew he could eventually bury it, for it was no dif-

ferent from what he'd felt when his friend Felix Leiter lost a leg at the
hands of Mr. Big's men in Florida, or when his colleague Darko Kerim
was killed by Russian agents on the Orient Express, or when his companion Quarrel was burned alive on that island in the Caribbean.
James Bond had lost many friends during his career with the Secret
Service. He had learned long ago how to deal with it and turn the pain
into an asset that contributed to his self-made shell—the hardened,
tough armour that protected him from the inevitably maddening, and
conceivably fatal, aspects of consciousness called human emotions.

He looked over at Sunni and saw that tears were streaming down
her cheeks. Bond gently used his finger to wipe them away.

"You miss your mother, don't you . . ." he said tenderly.

She nodded. "That's not why I'm crying, though," she said. "I'm
crying for Hong Kong. I fear for its people."

"No," Bond said, kissing her softly. "The people will manage.
Don't worry about them. They are strong, and they are determined.
So don't cry."

"All right." Sunni smiled and wiped her face. "No tears for Hong
Kong."

She allowed him to encircle her with his arms as they looked
towards the skyline to watch the fireworks.

ZERO: 1 JULY 1997, 12:01 A.M.

In Statue Square, the handover of the British Crown Colony known
as Hong Kong was executed peacefully and smoothly. Formal statements were read by both sides, and the representatives from China
shook hands with the representatives from Great Britain. As soon as
the transition was declared official, there were tumultuous cries from
the people standing in the congested streets. Some were cries of joy,
and others were cries of sadness. The fireworks began, filling the sky
with colours, noise, and celebration.

Over at Government House, a few blocks away, the Union Jack was
lowered for the last time, and the red and yellow Chinese flag was
raised in its place. A new chapter in the history of Asia, and mankind,
had begun.

THE FACTS
OF DEATH

FOR MY PARENTS

Morris H. "Benny" Benson
Beulah "Boots" Benson

CONTENTS

PROLOGUE

IT WAS SUPPOSED TO HAVE BEEN ROUTINE.

In early October, Carl Williams, a fifty-eight-year-old African-American, had gallbladder surgery at Veterans Hospital in Los Angeles. He needed a blood transfusion to make up for what he had lost during the procedure. He was type A, and there was plenty of that in supply. The operation was a complete success, and he spent an hour in the recovery room before being wheeled back to his bed.

Several hours later, as his wife sat by his side reading, Williams began to choke. At first, Mrs. Williams thought some juice he was sipping had gone down Carl's windpipe. She slapped his back, but it didn't seem to work. Carl's eyes started to bulge and he panicked. Mrs. Williams screamed for the nurse.

A code blue was declared. A doctor rushed in and attempted to save the patient, who went into cardiac arrest just as they were fitting an oxygen mask over his face.

Carl Williams died fifteen minutes after the onset of the symptoms. His wife was hysterical. The hospital staff were shocked and bewildered. The doctor ordered that a postmortem examination be performed.

The next morning, Mrs. Williams was sitting in her kitchen in Van Nuys, trying to make sense of what had happened to her husband. It must have been the hospital's fault. She was going to speak to a lawyer that very day.

As she stood up to pour some more coffee, she inexplicably felt her throat close. Gasping for air, she lunged for the telephone to dial 911. She managed to get through, but could barely speak into the receiver to tell them where to send the ambulance.

When the paramedics arrived, she was dead.

Halfway across the metropolis of Los Angeles, in Culver City, the nurse who had first attended to Carl Williams's emergency also died of respiratory failure and cardiac arrest as she was unloading groceries from the back of her car. Fifteen minutes later, in Pasadena, the doctor who had rushed into the room to help the nurse collapsed of the same ailment. He had been on the fourth hole of his favorite golf course.

By the end of the day, eight more people who had come into contact with Carl Williams were dead.

The next day there were several more.

By the third week of October, health officials realized they had a crisis on their hands. Although they tried to keep the mysterious epidemic a secret, news leaked out and was reported in the *Los Angeles Times*. A small story ran in the *Times*, but few people in London paid much attention to it.

By the end of October, thirty-three people had died. Health officials were stumped and scared.

Halfway around the world, in Tokyo, Hiroshi Nagawa received his October injection. It was his monthly shot of blood to help combat the leukemia that he had contracted five months ago. Doctors were hopeful that the transfusions would prolong his life at least another six months. Hiroshi was optimistic, for he felt much better every time he got a shot.

Hiroshi went from the doctor's office to his job as a computer programmer. The day went well, but he began to feel a little dizzy as he got on the underground train to go home. In the middle of the packed train, Hiroshi suddenly felt as if his esophagus had been clamped with a vise. Thankfully, the train was just pulling into a station. Choking horribly, he pushed his way through the crowd of people to the opening doors. He stumbled out onto the platform and collapsed a few feet away from the train.

Everyone in the subway car with Hiroshi that afternoon was concerned, but they went about their business and let the medics handle the situation. Little did they know that in twenty-four hours, they too would be in the morgue.

ONE

THE SMELL OF DEATH

THE TABLEAU OF PAIN AND SUFFERING MIGHT HAVE BEEN A FREEZE-FRAME from a macabre dance of death.

The twelve men—three corporals and nine privates—were sprawled about in various positions in the barracks room. They were fully dressed. One man was half on, half off a cot. Three were piled together, clutching one another in a final embrace. All of them had vomited and bled from the nose and mouth. They had clearly experienced a horrible death.

The team of four investigators dressed in protective clothing made a thorough search of the premises. Each wore a Willson AR 1700 full face gas mask with respirator and "in-cheek" filters, airtight goggles, a hood, an impermeable butyl rubber suit, eighteen-gauge rubber gloves and boots. Every inch of skin was covered. The investigators were thankful that the gas masks blocked out the stench of death. They were sweating profusely beneath the suits, for in late October, it was still hot in southern Cyprus.

James Bond peered through the eyepieces of his gas mask, taking in every detail. Twelve soldiers had been killed by an as yet unknown chemical agent, possibly administered through the air ducts. It seemed the only possible explanation. Equally disturbing was the number "3" painted in red on the wall of the room. Beneath the number, on the floor, was a six-inch-high alabaster statuette of the ancient Greek god Poseidon.

Bond watched the two British SAS investigators do their work and then followed them outside into the sun. One investigator, the sole Greek in the team, remained inside to finish making notes and to take photographs.

The men removed their gas masks and hoods. The temperature was already eighty-five degrees. It would have been a good day for a swim.

The British Sovereign Base Areas in the Republic of Cyprus cover approximately three percent of the island's land area. The Western Sovereign Base Area, which consists of the Episkopi Garrison buildings and the Akrotiri RAF airfield, and the Eastern Sovereign Base Area—the garrison at Dhekelia—remained under British jurisdiction when the Treaty of Establishment created the independent Republic of Cyprus in 1960. Prior to that time, Cyprus had been a British crown colony.

Bond had been dispatched to Cyprus shortly after midnight and had been shuttled to Akrotiri by a Royal Navy aircraft. He had been met by Captain Sean Tully and taken directly to Episkopi, the area which housed the Sovereign Base Areas Administration and the headquarters of the British Forces Cyprus. James Bond always thought the island was a lovely place, with its beautiful beaches, its rolling hills in the north, its near-perfect climate, and its quaint and colorful cities. It was unfortunate that Cyprus had such a turbulent recent history.

It was an unnamed British officer who had drawn a line with a green marker across the map in 1963, when tensions between the Greek and Turkish Cypriots culminated in violence. The United Nations moved in shortly thereafter in an attempt to keep the peace along the aptly named Green Line. Eleven years later, as a result of an attempted coup by the Greek government and the Turkish invasion of the northern part of the island in reaction to that attempt, the island was divided not just by a symbolic Green Line, but by a physical and political one. Today, Her Majesty's Government, along with the UN, recognizes only the government of the Republic of Cyprus, which administers the southern two thirds of the island. The so-called Turkish Republic of Northern Cyprus, which illegally occupies the northeast third of the island, is not recognized by any nation other than Turkey. The situation has been a source of tension, mistrust, and conflict for over thirty years.

The current disaster had struck in a barracks near the Episkopi helicopter landing site. Bond had been joined by two SAS forensic identification specialists from London and, at the last minute, by a member of the Greek Secret Service. He was a bit puzzled by the presence of the Greek agent, who was still inside the barracks taking notes. M had advised him that a Greek agent would be contacting him in Episkopi, but this was obviously a British matter, as it involved British military personnel and occurred on territory governed by neither the Republic of Cyprus nor Greece.

Winninger, one of the London investigators, wiped the sweat from his brow and asked, "Commander Bond, do you have any preliminary impressions?"

"It was some kind of aerosol agent, I would imagine," Bond said. "The number on the wall and the little statue are some kind of signature that the killer or killers left behind. I understand there was something similar at Dhekelia two days ago."

"Right," the second man, Ashcraft, said. "A small squad of men was killed by a nerve toxin called sarin. The same stuff that was used in a Japanese underground train recently by a religious fanatic."

Winninger added, "And then there was poor Whitten two days before that."

Bond nodded. He had been briefed. Christopher Whitten had been an MI6 operative in Athens. His body had been found by the Greek police sprawled on the steps of the Temple of Hephaisteion in the Ancient Agora near the Acropolis. He had died by an as yet unidentified poison, but Forensic Toxicology believed the cause of death to have been ricin, a deadly chemical derived from the simple castor bean plant.

In all three cases, the perpetrators had left a number painted near the body or bodies. The number "1" had been scrawled on a rock by Whitten's head. The number "2" had been painted on the wall of the Dhekelia barracks where the small squad of soldiers died the other day. A similarity to the Episkopi incident was that another small statuette of a Greek god was left at the Dhekelia scene.

Ashcraft said, "And now we have the third attack in four days. Looks like we've got a serial terrorist or something. . . . One complete section and half of another from the platoon were killed. That's three corporals and nine privates—three fire teams. It happened late last night after they had come in from drill. What do you make of the condition of the bodies, Ray?"

Winninger rubbed his chin. "From the amount of bleeding the victims experienced—from nearly every orifice of their bodies—it appears to be Tricotheneces. Wouldn't you agree?"

"Yes," Ashcraft said. "We'll have to get the lab to verify, of course. Terrible way to go." He turned to Bond. "Tricotheneces is a poison that causes radical bleeding from the eyes, ears, and mouth, internal bleeding, burns, convulsion and death—all within half an hour."

Bond was familiar with the various types of chemicals used in terrorist attacks and in warfare.

"Is it my imagination, or can I smell their bodies from out here?" Winninger asked.

The Greek agent emerged from the barracks, still wearing the gas mask and protective hood. Now out in the fresh air, the gas mask and coverings were quickly removed, revealing a head of long, black hair. She had Mediterranean features—tan skin, thick eyebrows, brown eyes, full lips, a large but not unattractive nose, and a long neck. She was unusually tall—nearly six feet. Bond and the other two men were surprised. They hadn't realized the agent was a woman when she walked into the barracks after them. She hadn't spoken and the protective uniform covered any hint of female shape.

"Are you from the NIS? You're Mirakos?" Winninger asked.

"That's right," she said. "Niki Mirakos of the Greek National Intelligence Service." She pronounced her first name "Nee-kee."

"What are you doing here, exactly?" Ashcraft asked. "If you don't mind my asking."

"I'm investigating these terrorist attacks, just as you are," she said with a look of disdain. "Your man Whitten was found in a public area of Athens—in a national park that was a holy place for the ancient Greeks, no less. These attacks are not random. There is a purpose behind them. My government has an interest in what has happened."

"Maybe you can fill us in on your hypothesis, then?" Ashcraft said.

"Later," she said. "I want to get out of these hot clothes and take a shower." She turned to Bond. "You're 007, aren't you?"

Bond held out his hand. "Bond," he said. "James Bond."

"We're supposed to have a little talk," she said. She glanced at the two other officers and added, "Alone."

Bond nodded. He led her away from the other two toward the building in the barracks that had been assigned to them as temporary quarters. As they walked, she unzipped her coveralls, revealing a white T-shirt soaked in sweat. Her full breasts were perfectly molded into the shirt. Bond couldn't help stealing a glance or two as they walked. She wasn't "beautiful" in the cover girl sense, but she exhibited an air of sensuality that made her extremely attractive.

"We believe this to be the work of terrorists specializing in chemical and biological weaponry," she said. "The targets thus far have been British, but we believe there is something behind the attacks which will ultimately involve Greece." She had a fairly thick accent, but her English was very good. Although most people under the age of forty in Greece have learned English, very few practice it on a daily basis.

"Do you have any idea who these people are?"

"No, and that's part of the problem. We're still investigating the death of your man Whitten, with the cooperation of your government, of course."

"Is there a significance in the site where the body was dumped?" he asked.

"Perhaps. The Ancient Agora was the Athenian marketplace. You know about the coin?"

Bond nodded. "Whitten had an ancient Greek coin in his mouth."

Niki continued, "That's right. The ancient Greeks believed that the dead should have a coin handy to give to Charon, the boatman on the River Styx, so that he could ferry them across the river to Hades. A dead person was usually buried with a coin in their mouth to use as fare."

"So the body placement, the coin, the number . . . are all symbolic," Bond said.

"Of what?" she said. "If we can find the connection between that murder and the incidents here on Cyprus, it would be a big help."

"The statuettes could be a substitute for the temple," Bond said. "Ideally, maybe the killers wanted to send some sort of message linking the deaths to ancient Greece. That's why Whitten's body was dropped where it was. Since they couldn't do that here on Cyprus, maybe the statuettes are supposed to symbolize the equivalent. Whatever that is."

"That's an interesting point, Mr. Bond," Niki said. "The statuette at Dhekelia was that of Hera, the queen of the gods. This one was Poseidon. I wonder if that means anything."

"I'm no ancient Greek scholar," Bond said, "but I do know that Hera was a vengeful, jealous god."

"What do you make of the numbers?"

Bond shrugged. "It's a definite indication that these three acts were committed by the same group . . . and that there will probably be more."

They had now reached two three-story white buildings of brick and plaster, some two hundred meters from the Helicopter Landing Site. The orange wind sock could be clearly seen blowing in the wind. The sound of an approaching Westland Wessex Mark II search-and-rescue helicopter was growing louder. They glanced up toward the sun and saw it descending from the sky, its silhouette resembling a humpback whale.

"I'm going to take a shower," Niki said. She looked at her watch. It was just after noon. "Let's meet in the mess at one? We can compare notes before we meet the base personnel at two. They will want answers."

"Fine," Bond said. "I'll take a shower too. Perhaps we can go for a swim after the debriefing? And then maybe dinner?"

"You work fast, Mr. Bond," she said with a slight smile.

He shrugged. "I leave in the morning."

"We'll see," she said as they separated. Bond went up to the second floor of one building, normally occupied by a platoon. As he passed the showers, he noticed a sign on the door proclaiming that the plumbing was out of order. Bond turned and shouted to Niki, who was entering the barracks across the road.

"I need to use one of your showers! Mine are out!"

Niki waved and gestured for him to come over.

Bond had been assigned a room that was currently vacant, although bits of the kit of three soldiers were still there. The rooms were all alike—sparsely furnished with three cots, three cupboards, a sink, a ceiling fan, two strips of fluorescent lights, and a dozen posters on the walls of various popular pinup celebrities. He grabbed his open carry-on bag and made his way across the road to Niki's barracks. Bare shouldered, she stuck her head out of her door as he passed by, and said, "You can use the next room. The showers are a few doors down. You go first, I can wait."

"Why not join me? We could do our part in conserving Cyprus's precious water supply."

The door shut in his face.

Bond entered the room, removed his clothes, and threw his bag on one of the cots. He hadn't brought much with him, as he knew that he would be on a plane back to London in the morning. As an afterthought, he had thrown in his swimming trunks and a diving utility belt that Q Branch supplied to agents normally working near water. Perhaps there really would be some time for that swim with the lovely Niki Mirakos. . . .

Bond wrapped a towel around his waist and walked out of the room to the showers.

There were five shower stalls, two bathtubs and toilets. No one else was around. Bond dropped the towel and stepped into one of the stalls. He twisted the knob and turned on the hot water. It got warm very quickly and he felt the spray begin to wash away the sweat. As he reached for the soap the water suddenly turned cold. He ducked back and held his hand under the spray. Suddenly, the water cut off. In a few seconds, warm water burst out of the spigot. Bond chalked it up to poor plumbing on a military base and moved under the spray once again. When the water turned cold a second time, he became suspicious and stepped out of the stall. Immediately the smell of ammonia enveloped the room. Smoke funneled out of the stall as some kind of abrasive chemical poured onto the tiles on the floor.

Bond ran out of the room naked. He ducked into his temporary quarters, taking a few seconds to grab his swimming trunks and slip them on. He grasped the utility belt, which also held his new Walther P99 in a waterproof holster, and ran back outside. Niki, a towel wrapped around her shapely body, stepped out of her room in time to see him leap over the railing and gracefully land on the grass below in his bare feet. A couple of perplexed privates in uniform were standing beside a jeep watching him.

Paying no attention to them, Bond ran around the building in time to see a figure dressed in camouflage fatigues running away from the barracks toward the helicopter landing site. The Wessex that had landed earlier was still there, its rotor blades spinning. Bond took off after the running figure, who was wearing a gas mask and protective hood.

The figure made it to the Wessex and climbed into the open door. The helicopter immediately began to rise just as Bond made it to the HLS. He leaped forward and just managed to grab hold of the trooping step, the metal attachment used as an extra step to assist soldiers entering or leaving the aircraft. The Wessex continued to rise, with Bond hanging on for dear life. Within moments, they were flying over the base toward the Mediterranean.

The door was still open, and Bond could see two camouflaged figures from his position. One was holding a gun to the pilot's head. The aircraft had been hijacked!

The gas-masked figure he had seen earlier leaned out of the door and saw Bond hanging on to the trooping step. He pulled a large knife from a sheath, then squatted down closer to the floor of the aircraft. Holding on to the inside of the cabin with one hand, the figure leaned out with the knife in the other. He swung the knife across Bond's knuckles, slicing the skin. Bond winced with pain but forced himself to hang on. The helicopter was a good two hundred feet above the ground. He would surely fall to his death if he let go. The assassin leaned out again, but this time Bond was ready. As the knife swung, Bond lifted one hand off the trooping step and grasped the piece of metal beneath the step mat fastened onto the helicopter. It wasn't as good a handhold as the step itself, but it was shielded from the assassin's knife. He then inched out onto the wheel axle and wrapped his legs around it. The killer would have to venture out of the aircraft to get him now.

As the helicopter flew over the RAF airfield at Akrotiri, the pilot was ordered to maneuver the vehicle wildly in an attempt to throw Bond off. The pain was almost unbearable, and the blood from the cuts dripped onto his face. But he hung on tightly. If only he could manage to keep hold until they got over the water . . .

The figure leaned out of the door again, this time holding an automatic pistol—a Daewoo, Bond thought. Bond swung his body up under the helicopter as the assassin fired at him. The bullets whizzed past him as he swung back and forth. Fortunately, the jerking movement of the helicopter spoiled the man's aim and he shouted angrily back at the pilot.

The helicopter was now over the Mediterranean, flying south. The water below was choppy and rough.

The assassin did what Bond was afraid he might do: he crawled out onto the trooping step. Now that the chopper was flying level, Bond could be shot at point-blank range. He couldn't see the assassin's face behind the gas mask, but he knew the man was smiling in triumph. The assassin raised the pistol and pointed it at Bond's head.

Bond used all of his strength to swing back underneath the trooping step and used the momentum to push himself away from the helicopter. In midair, he somersaulted so that his body ended up in the diving position. He heard the shot ring out above him as he soared down to the sea. The impact might have killed an ordinary man, but Bond's graceful Olympic-style dive smoothly cut through the surface of the water.

He swam up for air and saw the Wessex continuing its trek southward. He looked at the shore, which was at least a mile away. Could he swim back? The water was very rough. It would be a challenge for even the strongest of swimmers. It was lucky that he had thought to take the utility belt.

While treading water, Bond unzipped the belt and removed two coiled rubber items which, when shaken, opened out to their proper size. They were portable flippers. He quickly placed them on his feet. Next, Bond removed a small can the size of a shaving cream container. Two long elastic bands allowed him to strap the can onto his back. A flexible tube uncoiled from the top of the can, and he stuck the end in his mouth. The can was a ten-minute version of an aqualung, which would be helpful in swimming through the choppy water. He hoped that the current wasn't so strong that he couldn't make headway toward shore.

Bond began the slow crawl toward land, thankful that he had brushed up on his diving skills a couple of weeks ago. He was also grateful that Major Boothroyd was indeed a genius.

He fought the sea as best he could, but it was a case of two steps forward, one step back. Still, he was an expert swimmer and extremely fit. An ordinary man might have drowned by now. Five minutes later, Bond estimated that he was about half a mile from shore. The air would last him another five minutes and then he would have to depend on short, deep breaths stolen from the choppy surface.

The sound of another helicopter grew nearer and its shadow blocked out the sun. Bond stopped swimming and treaded water. A Gazelle was directly above him, and a rope ladder was being lowered to him. He took hold of it and swiftly climbed up into the small, round helicopter. To his surprise, it was piloted by none other than Niki Mirakos. An RAF airman had manned the ladder.

"What kept you?" Bond asked.

"You said you wanted to go swimming!" Niki shouted over the noise. "I wanted to make sure you had a little time to enjoy yourself."

The Gazelle pulled away toward the shore and back to Episkopi, passing two more Wessex helicopters heading out to sea in pursuit of the hijacked aircraft.

Back at the base, Bond and Niki learned that whoever it was wearing the gas mask had managed to attach a tank of cyanogen chloride to the water line. The chemical was classified as a "blood agent" because it attacked blood cells and spread quickly throughout the body. If it had made contact with Bond's skin, he would have been a dead man. Investigators believed that this same assassin was responsible for the attack on the fire teams. More disturbing was that it was a blatant attempt on Niki Mirakos's life.

That evening, the search-and-rescue personnel made their reports. The hijacked Wessex was found abandoned, floating in the sea about a hundred miles south of Cyprus. The saltwater flotation cans had been activated, allowing the helicopter to land on the water safely. The pilot's body was found on board. He had been shot in the back of the head. It was surmised that the killer and his accomplice had somehow hijacked the craft and forced the pilot to fly them in and out of the base. It must have been met by a boat or a seaplane, for there was no trace of them.

After the briefing, Bond and Niki rode in her rented Honda Civic into town. They found a loud, festive restaurant, but managed to be seated at a small table for two in the back, away from the noise.

"How do you feel?" she asked. The candle on the table cast a glow across her bronze face.

"That fight with the sea today exhausted me, but otherwise I couldn't be better," Bond said. "I'm hungry, how about you?"

"Famished."

They shared a Cypriot mixed grill—ham, sausage, and beef burgers—and *halloumi,* a chewy cheese, all grilled over charcoal. The house wine was Ambelida, a dry, light wine made from the Xynistri white grape.

"Why is it that Cypriot cuisine normally consists of an enormous amount of meat?" Bond asked.

Niki laughed. "I don't know. We eat a lot of meat in Greece too, but not this much. Maybe it's the reason for the high level of testosterone on this island."

"Why do you think someone tried to kill you in the shower, Niki? That dirty trick was meant for you," he said.

"I don't have a clue. Someone obviously knew I would come to investigate. I've been on this case since they found your man Whitten. Maybe whoever's responsible knew that. Don't worry, I can take care of myself."

"I'm sure you can. When do you go back?"

"Tomorrow morning, same as you," she said.

Bond settled the bill, even though she wanted to pay for her own meal. In the car on the way back to the base, he asked her if they would see each other again. She nodded.

"My middle name is Cassandra," she said. "Believe it or not, I think I've always had the ability to see into people's hearts, and sometimes into the future."

"Oh, really?" Bond asked, smiling. "And what does the future hold for us?"

"We'll see each other again at least once," she said as they pulled into the front gate of the base.

After saying goodnight, he returned to his barracks room and slipped under the blanket of one of the cots. He was about to drift off to sleep when a knock at the door jarred him awake. "Come in," he said.

Niki Mirakos, still wearing civilian clothes, stepped into the dark room. "I told you we'd see each other at least one more time. Besides, I wanted to make sure you were all right. You must be very sore after that fall into the sea."

She moved closer to him. He sat up in the bed, about to protest, but she gently pushed him back down. She turned him onto his stomach and began to massage his broad shoulders.

"This will work out all the . . . uhm, how do you say in English . . . kinkies?" she asked.

Bond turned over onto his back and pulled her down on top of him. "The word is 'kinks,' " he said, chuckling. "But I'll be happy to show you what 'kinky' means. . . ."

With that, his mouth met hers and she moaned aloud.

A DAY IN THE CITY

THE BEGINNING OF NOVEMBER BROUGHT A BONE-CHILLING RAIN TO LONDON, and it looked as if winter would come very early this year. Gray days always made James Bond feel a little melancholy himself. He stood at the bay window of the sitting room in his flat off the King's Road in Chelsea, looking out at the square of plane trees that occupied the center of his street. The trees had lost their leaves, which made the scene even more dreary. If he hadn't been on call, Bond would have flown to Jamaica to spend a few days at Shamelady, his recently purchased holiday home on the north shore of the island. After returning from Cyprus, however, M had given him strict orders to remain on call. The business of the terrorist attacks was far from over.

"Yer watchin' the time—sir?" came the familiar mother hen voice behind him. May, his elderly Scottish housekeeper, was his cook, maid, and alarm clock. The way she pronounced "sir" came out as "suh." Apart from Bond, she would never call anyone else "sir" except for royalty and men of the cloth.

"Yes, May," Bond said. "I won't be late. I'm not expected for another hour or so."

May gave her obligatory 'Tsk . . . tsk . . . tsk . . ." and said, "I don't like to see you this way—sir. Yer hardly touched your breakfast. 'Tisn't like you."

She was right. Bond felt the malaise that never failed to plague him when he was "on call" or between assignments. He always became restless and bored.

Bond sighed heavily and moved away from the window. He sat down at the ornate Empire desk and stared at the room around him. The white and gold Cole wallpaper was terribly out of date, but he didn't care. He hadn't changed a single thing in his converted Regency flat since he moved in many years ago. He disliked change, which was one of the main reasons he had remained a widower since the death of his only bride.

Bond managed a smile when he reflected back to an evening he'd had a few weeks ago at his favorite club, Blades. He'd been having drinks with Sir James Molony, the Service's staff neurologist, who jokingly accused Bond of being so obsessive about details and set in his ways that he walked a thin line between sanity and sociopathy.

"Look at you, James!" Molony had said. "You were *painfully* specific about how you wanted that martini made. *No one* does that except someone who's obsessed with minutiae. You don't want just any martini, you want *your* martini! A Bic lighter won't do for you! It's got to be a Ronson lighter and nothing else! You've got to have your tobacco made specially for you, because you have to smoke *your* cigarettes! I wouldn't be surprised if you're wearing the same kind of underwear you wore as a boy."

"As a matter of fact, Sir James, I am," Bond replied. "And if you get any more personal than that, I'll have to ask you to step outside."

Molony chuckled and shook his head. "It's all right, James." He finished his drink and said, "Given the life you've led and the work you do for our good government . . . it's a small wonder you're not already in the madhouse. Whatever it takes to keep you on this side of the line, then so be it."

Bond was brought back to the present when May entered the room with a cup of *his* favorite strong coffee from De Bry in New Oxford Street. "I brought you somethin' to perk you up—sir," she said.

"Thank you, May, you're a dear," he said. He took the cup and set it down in front of him. He liked *his* coffee black, with no sugar.

Bond stared at the pile of mail he needed to go through. It was one of his least favored activities. May stood at the doorway watching him with concern. Bond looked up at her. "What is it?"

"Tsk . . . tsk . . . tsk . . ." was all she said; then she turned and left the room.

Bond took a sip of the coffee and felt it warm him up a little. The piece of correspondence now on the top of the pile had somehow got buried under other papers when it arrived. It was an invitation to a dinner party at the home of Sir Miles Messervy, the former M. The party was that night, to be held at Quarterdeck, his home near Windsor Great Park. Bond supposed he would go, although it would be full of people he really didn't want to meet. There would be the usual crowd of Sir Miles's parliamentary friends, retired Royal Navy officers and their wives, and colleagues from SIS whom he saw every day anyway, but he did enjoy seeing his old boss from time to time. Since Sir Miles's retirement as M, he and Bond had developed even more of a mentor-pupil relationship than they had had when the old man was in charge. A more apt description was perhaps that of a father-son relationship, and it had lasted.

Bond picked up the phone and called Quarterdeck. He spoke to Davison, Sir Miles's butler and manservant, and said he hoped he could still RSVP. Davison replied that Sir Miles would be very happy to hear that Bond was coming.

An hour later, Bond drove his ageing but reliable Bentley Turbo R onto the Embankment, then to the gaudy building by the Thames that housed SIS headquarters. Stepping out of the lift onto the fourth floor, he was greeted by Helena Marksbury, his attractive personal assistant. Her warm smile and sparkling large green eyes never failed to cheer him up, even when he was in the darkest of moods. She had recently cut her silky brown hair in a pageboy style that some of the newer fashion models seemed to favor. Bond also found her to be highly intelligent, a hard worker, and easygoing—all of which made her that much more desirable.

"Good afternoon, James," she said.

"Helena, you're looking lovely," he said with a nod.

"James, if you smiled when you said that, I might believe you."

Bond managed to form his normally cruel mouth into a grin. "I never lie to women, Helena, you should know that by now."

"Of *course* you don't, James . . ." She quickly changed the subject. "There's a new file on your desk concerning the incidents in Cyprus, and M would like to see you in an hour."

Bond smiled, nodded, then turned and walked toward his private office.

The file on his desk contained a number of reports—the forensic findings from the murder sites in Cyprus and Athens, analyses of the chemical weapons used in the attacks, and various other documents. Bond sat down and studied each report, losing himself in the work so that he might climb out of the dark hole he was in.

For lack of a better term, the reports now referred to the perpetrators as the "Number Killer" because of the numerals left at the sites. The Number Killer was believed to be several individuals—a team of terrorists—although evidence seemed to indicate that only one person was involved in the actual attacks. Because no communication from the perpetrators had been received, the motives were still unclear. At present, there was no connection between the victims except that two were groups of military personnel on Cyprus. Since three different chemical weapons were used in the attacks, investigators speculated that the terrorists were receiving their supplies from a separate and sophisticated source. In other words, it was unlikely that a Middle Eastern or Mediterranean terrorist group would have the means to manufacture so many different types of chemical weapons. Bond doubted the reasoning behind that report. He believed that there were groups entirely capable of creating such deadly materials. Recipes were widely available in books sold in alternative bookstores and even on the Internet.

Another document listed known terrorist groups around the world and their bases of operation. Among these were the ones already in the headlines, such as the Islamic militant groups working out of the Middle East, the Aryan Nation factions in the northwestern United States, the IRA, and the Weathermen. Some of the names Bond wasn't familiar with, such as the Suppliers, an American outfit working out of the southwestern U.S. Bond made a point to study the lists of lesser-known groups, especially those working out of Europe.

The biggest question was—what were these people after?

"I assume you've read all the relevant reports, 007?" M asked, swiveling around in her chair to face him.

"Yes, ma'am. I can't say they've added to what I already knew."

M made a gesture with her eyebrows as if to say, "Right, of course not." Since she took over as the head of SIS, James Bond's relationship with his boss had not always been comfortable. The woman had respect for the man who some said was her top agent, but he always felt she saw him as a loose cannon. She was also more vocal than her predecessor had been in criticizing Bond's womanizing and sometimes unorthodox methods of working. Still, 007 had proved his worth to her more than once, and she had learned quickly that she had to put up with his lifestyle if she wanted to keep him.

"All right, then," she said. "What's your guess about the terrorists?"

"There's not a lot to go on, really," he replied. "Without knowing their motives, it's difficult to analyze what it's all about. I'll admit I'm baffled by the whole affair."

"We're having some professional profiles drawn up based on the crime scene evidence. There's something you don't know about our man Whitten. He was working on something top-secret."

"Oh?"

"As you know, he was a field agent temporarily working out of Station G. About six months ago, the Athens police confiscated two suitcases full of chemical weapons at the airport. They were unclaimed, and they were never traced to their rightful owners. You'll never guess what the toxins were smuggled in."

"Tell me."

"Sperm," she said with a straight face. "Frozen sperm. Vials of frozen sperm. They were in refrigerated cartons—very sophisticated, with timers and locks. Acting on a tip, Whitten had learned of some sort of pipeline of chemicals being shipped to Athens from London. This one, supposedly a second shipment, was confiscated, and Whitten was about to pin down exactly where it had come from. He believed the shipments did not originate in London. That was on the day before his death."

"Then Whitten's murder may have been nothing more than an act to silence him."

"Correct. Perhaps he learned more than our terrorist friends wanted him to know. His office and files have been thoroughly searched. So far nothing has turned up."

"Any more news on the Cyprus incidents?"

"Only that there was hell to pay in their security areas. How the assassin and the accomplice hijacked a helicopter is a mystery. There may have been an insider. The Greek Secret Service are very concerned, because an eyewitness described the man holding a gun to the pilot's head as 'Greek-looking.' How did you get on with their agent, by the way?"

At first Bond didn't know who M was talking about. "Ma'am?"

"Mirakos. That was her name, wasn't it?"

"Oh, right. She seemed very . . . capable, ma'am."

"Hmpf." M could see right through him.

"Other than the possibility of the hijacker being Greek, why are the Greeks so concerned? These were our people."

"Cyprus is a very touchy issue with them. You're aware of all the trouble that island has gone through. When we allowed the Cypriots to form their own country in 1960, it opened up a can of worms. There aren't many races who hate each other more than the Greeks and Turks. It's gone on forever, and it's one of those things that *will* go on forever, I'm afraid. It's as bad as Northern Ireland, or Israel and the Arab states."

"Do you think the attacks on our troops have something to do with the Cyprus problem?" Bond asked.

"Yes, I do," she said. "The Cypriots look at our presence there with disdain. In my opinion, the Greek Cypriots would like to see us out of there, although if it came down to a matter of life or death—such as a further Turkish invasion—then I'm sure they would reverse their stance and be grateful we were there to help. On the other hand, I have a feeling that Turkey doesn't mind our being there. They want to propagate the notion to the world that they are peace-loving and cooperative."

"So you think that Greek Cypriots are behind this?"

"If the terrorists aren't Cypriots or Greek nationalists, then their sympathies lie with that side. I think the attacks on our bases were meant to be warnings of some kind."

"The numbers would indicate that there will be more attacks," Bond said.

"It will be interesting to see what the next target or targets are."

"What would you like me to do, ma'am?"

"Nothing at the moment except study everything you can get your hands on about terrorist factions in Europe and the Middle East. Brush up on the history of Greece, Turkey, and Cyprus. I'm afraid we haven't much to go on until they strike again. Just be where I can find you should I need you in a hurry. Don't go running off."

"Of course not."

"Good. That's all, 007."

He stood up to leave and she asked, "Will I see you tonight at Sir Miles's dinner party?"

"I thought I might make an appearance," he said.

"There's someone I'll want you to meet," she said. "Until tonight then."

Did he detect a hint of excitement in her clear blue eyes? If he wasn't mistaken, M had just betrayed the fact that she would be accompanied by a man. Interesting . . .

Bond stepped out of the office and caught the ever faithful Miss Moneypenny at the filing cabinet.

"Penny?"

"Yes, James?"

"M's divorced, isn't she?"

"Yes. Why do you ask?"

"Just wondering."

"James, really. Now I *know* she's not your type."

Bond leaned in to kiss Moneypenny's cheek. "Of course not. You know the truth, as always." He opened the door and turned back to her. She was looking at him expectantly. "I don't have a type," he said as he closed the door.

Major Boothroyd lit the cigarette, puffed once or twice, then threw it as far as he could across the room. The cigarette landed in a pile of hay in the middle of a fireproof container. The hay burst into flames. Technicians immediately rushed in with fire extinguishers to put it out. Boothroyd coughed and gasped for air.

"I don't know how you can smoke those things, 007," he said, wheezing. "Didn't you cough the first time you inhaled tobacco smoke?"

"I'm sure I did. I really don't remember," Bond said.

"Well, it's the body's natural way of warning you to stay away! I need a glass of water . . ."

The major had been with SIS longer than Bond could remember. Boothroyd had run Q Branch with a keen eye for detail and the imagination of a science fiction author. His knowledge of weaponry and technical devices was unmatched. Bond enjoyed teasing him, but the truth was that Boothroyd would always have Bond's respect.

"How are you getting on with the P99?" Boothroyd asked.

"It's quite an improvement, I must admit," Bond said. "I like the way I can operate the magazine release, the decocker, or the trigger without changing the position of the gun in my hand."

"Yes, Walther has certainly stepped up the technology," Boothroyd added. "I like the way the magazine release is ambidextrous and can be operated with the thumb or index finger."

The Walther P99 9mm Parabellum was a new gun, advertised by Carl Walther GMBH as the gun "designed for the next century." It was a hammerless pistol with single and double action, developed in strict conformity with the technical list of requirements of the German police. With a high-quality polymer used for the frame and other parts, the weight of the gun with an empty magazine was only

700g. The steel sheet magazine had a capacity of sixteen rounds, with an additional round in the chamber. A very special advantage of the P99 was the ability to fire more rapidly than most other semiautomatic pistols. Due to the missing hammer, the barrel was positioned low over the hand, which reduced recoil. Bond loved the new gun, but he still preferred to carry the thinner PPK in his shoulder holster. He used the P99 when he didn't need to conceal the weapon under clothing.

"How's the new car coming along?" Bond asked.

"It's nearly finished. Come and have a look." Boothroyd led Bond into another area of the laboratory. The Jaguar XK8 coupe sat on a platform as technicians made last-minute modifications to it. It had a solid blue base paint with a zinc coating, giving it a sheen that was undeniably glamorous. Bond had been wary of the car's future when Ford took Jaguar under its wing, but the move proved to be a wise one. While it remained a British-made and -designed car, Jaguar adapted Ford's maintenance program. This improved its service reliability immensely in other countries, particularly the U.S.

Bond had given the XK8 a test drive when they first hit the market in 1996 and he fell in love with it, but the price tag had prevented him from purchasing one himself. When he learned that Q Branch had bought a coupe for company use, 007 took an active interest in it. For once, he made the time to collaborate with Major Boothroyd on the features it would have, something that was unprecedented.

The vital thing was the engine, a completely new four-liter V-8 of advanced specification that set it apart from Ford and maintained Jaguar's individuality. The AJ V-8 four-valve-per-cylinder engine normally had a maximum output of 290 horsepower at 6,100 rpm and 284 foot pounds of torque at 4,200 rpm. It was the first V-8 engine designed by Jaguar. Major Boothroyd, however, commissioned Jaguar's Special Vehicle Operations unit to improve the car's power to do 400 bhp. The rev limiter, which would otherwise limit top speed to a paltry 155 miles per hour, was removed. The car was equipped with a Z 5HP24 automatic transmission, which offered five forward gear ratios to optimize performance. First through fourth gears were selected for sharp response and effortless acceleration, while fifth was an overdrive ratio for fuel economy. The transmission's versatility began with two driver selectable gear modes, Sport and Normal. Switching into Sport mode timed the gear changes for peak response. Bond had never cared for automatic transmissions, but the XK8 offered something different.

"I'm sorry to say that M has decided that you are to be the lucky man to test-drive it in the field," Boothroyd said. "It was nice knowing this car. I'm sure I'll never see it again."

"Bollocks, Major," Bond said. "I'm in love with this car. I promise I'll take good care of it. When can I have it?"

"It'll be ready in a day or two. I don't know where you'll be, but I'll have it shipped to you. We want to find out how the car handles in extreme conditions."

"So you're giving it to me."

"Right."

"I'm glad to hear that everyone thinks so highly of me."

"Now pay attention, 007," Boothroyd said, stepping up to the car and tapping the hood. "We've coated the car with chobam armor, which is impenetrable. We use it with reactive skins that explode when they're hit. This deflects the bullets. It's a case of an equal and opposite force negating the energy of the bullet."

"Naturally," Bond said.

"Not only that," Boothroyd said, very proud of himself, "the metal is self-healing. On being pierced, the skin can heal itself by virtue of viscous fluid."

"Remarkable."

"We've also used certain paints that have electrically sensitive pigments which will change color. Used in conjunction with the electronically controlled standard interchangeable license plate, the car can change identity a number of times.

"Now, as you know, the Jaguar is fitted with an intelligent automatic gearbox, and gears are changed by means of a combined manual and automatic five-speed adaptive system through a 'J' gate mechanism. When you want to use the manual system, you merely select the left hand side of the J gate mechanism and change gear in the normal way, except that there is no clutch pedal. On the right side of the J gate is the switchable adaptive system, which electronically changes to suit individual styles of driving. If you want to wind the engine up and drive aggressively, electronic software will recognize that you're in a hurry and will allow the engine to reach higher revs before changing to the next gear—thus giving you better performance. Alternatively, if you choose to drive the car more gently, which is highly unlikely in your case, the adaptive system will switch and change up earlier. The gear patterns are computer-controlled, yet driver-dependent."

"I knew that," Bond said smugly.

"Well, did you know that there are sensors which recognize wheel slip? If that happens, the power will be cut until traction is established again. Sensors on the rack tell the gearbox not to change gear when cutting a corner. You can behave like a complete lunatic and floor the throttle midway through a bend—but you'll find that the electronics will take over and never permit the car to go out of control. Clearly, the combined gearbox system has advantages over manual only. Specifically, in your case, in conjunction with GPS navigation, it's a matter of hands off the driving and hands on your female passenger!"

"I resent that remark," Bond said. "What about offensive features? Did you get what I asked for?"

"If you're referring to satellite navigation . . . yes. The car will drive to a set of coordinates and can actually drive itself with you in place or not. I daresay that it runs less of a risk on the road without you."

"Thanks."

"Now, look here"—Boothroyd got into the car and pointed to various devices—"the heat-seeking rockets and cruise missiles are used in conjunction with the satellite navigation. They're deployed to a set of coordinates, or they can follow a moving target selected by the screen and joystick on the dash.

"Inside the car you have a deployable air bag on the passenger side—guaranteed to smother someone with safety. Notice the wind-screen. Optical systems magnify available light or heat at night to produce an image on this screen." Boothroyd pulled down a sun visor. "You can drive in the dark without headlamps, through smoke, fog, whatever—and because of the satellite navigation and intelligent cruise control, the vehicle will drive, steer, and avoid obstacles elec-tronically. By the way, the car's microprocessors are stored in a box in the boot."

The major released the latch of the center-console armrest storage compartment. "Under the storage tray you'll find a holster for your P99."

"Very handy," Bond said.

Boothroyd got out of the car and pointed at the headlamps. "Holo-grams can be projected from both the front and rear headlamps. Additional holograms can be projected inside the car to give the appearance of a driver when there's no one there. We have a wide range of holograms that we can project outside the car. You'll want to go through our library and select a few to store into the computer."

"I'll bet you're saving the best for last," Bond said.

"You're absolutely right, 007," Boothroyd said with a wide grin. He walked over to a table. On top of it was a device that looked like the wings of a small model airplane, the size of a boomerang.

"This is our flying scout," he said. "It stores underneath the chassis until you activate it from inside the car. It will fly out from under the car and reach an altitude of your choosing. You can man-ually steer it by a joystick, or it can follow a predetermined flight route using the satellite navigation. The scout can send back pictures and coordinates of targets to you. It can tell you what's around the bend ahead. It can tell you if you're about to get caught speeding."

"That's quite handy, Major."

"As an afterthought, I equipped the scout with the ability to drop mines. Just be sure you're not underneath it if you happen to use them."

"Is that all?"

"*Is that all?* What do you want, 007, a tank?"

Bond shrugged. "I am quite good in tanks."

"Hmmm . . . Well, we can always add accessories as we think of them. That's the beauty of the XK8—it's so adaptable."

"Well, thank you, Major, I look forward to giving her a spin around the world."

"Oh, I almost forgot." Boothroyd opened up a steel cabinet and removed a remote control device and some goggles. "These are now standard issue. This control box will fit in the heel of your standard field-issue shoe. It's an alarm-sensor nullifier. It's guaranteed to deactivate any alarms within a twenty-five-yard radius. Just push that button there and aim it at the walls, the furniture, the doors— whatever you want. And these are our latest improvement on an old reliable—the night-vision goggles. If you find yourself outside of the car at night, you can always use these."

Bond tried them on. "I can't see a thing," he said.

"Oh—you've got them on sleep mode. I installed an extra feature. You can completely black out all vision so that the goggles perform like night shades. They're perfect for taking naps on aeroplanes."

Bond was mortified but did his best not to show it.

THREE

AN EVENING IN THE COUNTRY

AFTER A THIRTY-MINUTE DRIVE OUT OF LONDON AND INTO BERKSHIRE, James Bond reached what once was one of the more beautiful areas of England. The old farmlands on his left and the forest on his right had unfortunately been overtaken by urban development in the last twenty years; yet the amount of rural scenery still provided him with the feeling that he was in the country. The Bentley sailed across the Windsor-Bagshot road, and thankfully the familiar landmarks were still there—the Squirrel public house on the left and the modest stone gateway of Quarterdeck on the right.

The former M, Sir Miles Messervy, had lived in the rectangular Regency manor house made of Bath stone as long as Bond had known him. The property was remarkably well kept. The dense growth of pine, beech, silver birch, and young oak that grew on three sides of the house had been recently trimmed. There were already a number of elegant motorcars parked in the short gravel drive, and Bond was forced to park the Bentley near the end behind a Mercedes. He would be arriving at a fashionably reasonable hour—precisely half an hour before the scheduled eight-thirty dinner and just in time for a couple of stiff drinks.

The brass bell from a long-forgotten ship still hung on the front door. Bond fondly remembered the Hammonds, who had looked after

Sir Miles for many years. They had met their untimely deaths during the Colonel Sun affair and were afterwards replaced by the Davisons. Like Hammond before him, Davison was a former chief petty officer.

The door opened and Davison stood there smiling broadly. "Good evening, Commander," he said. "Sir Miles was just asking about you."

"Good evening, Davison," Bond said. "I hope I'm not too late?"

"Not at all, sir. We're still expecting some of our guests."

Bond stepped into the hall. The smell of polish from the pine paneling was as strong as ever. The meticulously detailed 1/144 scale model of the battle cruiser *Repulse* was still the focal point on the table in the hallway. A dull roar of conversation and the soft strains of Mozart came from the main room. The smell of roast beef filled the air, and Bond suddenly felt very hungry. Davison took his overcoat, and he made his way through the open Spanish mahogany door.

The entire roomful of people couldn't help but notice James Bond, a splendid figure of a man dressed in a black three-piece single-breasted Brioni dinner suit with peaked lapels and no vents. He wore a deep bow tie, and the tucked-in white silk pocket handkerchief made the picture complete.

Bond walked inside and went straight to one of the servants and asked for a vodka martini. He then surveyed the guests. There were about twenty people in all, mostly faces he recognized. There was an MP and his wife in the corner speaking to a retired admiral and his spouse. Three women of various ages were eyeing him from the bay window. Sir James Molony and Major Boothroyd were locked in conversation near the fireplace. Miss Moneypenny waved to him and began to edge her way toward him. Some stray wives were huddled around a table covered with hors d'oeuvres. More voices came from the library through the double doors. He could see Sir Miles standing by a leather armchair, smoking a pipe. Two other retired Royal Navy officers sat across from him, speaking animatedly. Sir Miles nodded every ten seconds or so in response to whatever the men were saying.

As Bond's martini arrived, Moneypenny joined him. "You always cut a dashing figure, James," Moneypenny said. She was dressed in a gray satin gown which revealed a little more cleavage than usual.

"Moneypenny, you look marvelous. Have I missed much?"

"Not really. Only some delicious nibbles."

Bond lit one of his Simmons cigarettes and offered one to Moneypenny.

"No, thank you," she said. "I gave them up long ago. Have you forgotten?"

Bond shrugged. "I must have. Forgive me."

"You become distant when you have nothing to do, did you know that?"

Bond shrugged. "It's just the soft life slowly eating away at me. I hate being on call."

"I know. But I do like you better when you're all chirpy."

Bill Tanner, M's chief of staff and Bond's longtime friend in the Service, walked over to them. "Go easy on the vodka, James—there're at least twenty other people here tonight who'll want some."

"Hello, Bill." Bond put down his glass. "Guard this for me, will you? I'm going in to say hello to the Old Man. I'll be right back."

The smell of his old chief's distinctive blend of Turkish and Balkan tobacco filled the library. Sir Miles's damnably clear blue eyes looked up from his weather-beaten face and actually twinkled when he saw Bond. "Hello, James," he said. "Glad you could make it." Since his retirement, Sir Miles had dispensed with calling Bond 007. While Sir Miles was M, he never called Bond "James" unless something out of the ordinary was up for discussion. Now it was always "James," spoken as if Bond were the long-lost son whom he'd never had.

On the other hand, it was difficult for Bond to call Sir Miles anything but sir. "Good evening, sir. How are you feeling?"

"I'm fine, I'm fine. James, you know Admiral Hargreaves and Admiral Grey?"

"Yes, good evening," Bond said, nodding to the other men. They mumbled hello in return.

"Well, enjoy yourself. Dinner won't be for a few minutes. We'll have a chance to talk later, all right?" Sir Miles said.

"Fine. It's good to see you, sir." Bond walked back into the other room.

A mousy but not unattractive woman in her thirties nursing a gin and tonic intercepted him as he came through the double doors. "Hello, James," she said.

Bond thought she looked familiar but couldn't place her. "Hello," he said hesitantly.

"I'm Haley McElwain. My maiden name was Messervy."

"Oh, of course!" Bond said, slightly embarrassed. "I must admit I didn't recognize you at first." He hadn't seen Sir Miles's eldest daughter in years. The old man had been a widower for as long as Bond could remember, and had two grown daughters from the marriage that few people knew anything about. "How are you? You're looking well."

"Thank you," she said, gushing. "You look splendid yourself."

"Are you still living in America?" Bond asked.

"I was," Haley said with a hint of disgust. "My husband was an American. We're *divorced* now." Bond thought she accentuated the word a bit too pointedly.

"So you're back in England?"

"That's right. I'm living with Daddy for the moment. With Charles and Lynne, of course." She meant her two children.

"Oh, yes, they must be quite grown up now . . ." Bond's eyes wandered around the room looking for an escape route.

"Charles is nine and Lynne is six. I'm sure they'll find an excuse to come downstairs and join the party at some point during the evening. Daddy will have a heart attack." She giggled too much for Bond's taste. Haley McElwain was not holding her drink too well.

"Well, it's good to see you," Bond said, starting to walk away.

"It's good to see *you* too!" she said, unwittingly licking her lips. "I hope you'll come by Quarterdeck more often. I'll fix us a lunch sometime."

"That would be lovely," Bond muttered softly. He forced a smile and moved toward Bill Tanner, who was watching the entire scene with amusement.

"You know, James," he said, "it's quite all right to flirt with the boss's daughter now. He's not the boss anymore."

"Go to hell, Bill," Bond said, taking a large sip from the martini which he had left with Tanner.

"She's really quite lovely," Tanner said.

"Then *you* go and have lunch with her," Bond said. "She's a divorcee with two children, and that's enough to keep me away."

"James, you're becoming more and more misanthropic every day. Keep it up and you'll be living in a cave somewhere in the highlands of Scotland before long."

"That's not a bad idea, Bill. Someplace where M would never find me . . ."

Right on cue, the grand lady of SIS walked into the room. M was escorted by a tall, distinguished-looking gentleman in a dinner jacket. He had snow-white hair, a mustache, and dark brown eyes. He appeared to be in his sixties, but he looked fit, tanned, and he was very handsome. M was dressed in a formal black evening gown that was low-cut in a V, revealing more of their boss than anyone at the office had ever seen. Accentuating the overall effect was a spectacular diamond necklace that gracefully caught the light. She looked dazzling. Together, the couple made a striking pair, and all heads in the room turned toward them. Nearly everyone was surprised to see who the man was.

"Hello, Chief of Staff, er, Bill. Hello, James," M said, smiling broadly at the two men. She was glowing with happiness. Bond immediately confirmed his earlier suspicion. M was in love.

"Good evening, ma'am," he said.

"Oh, please, we're not at the office. Call me Barbara," M said. Unlike the way the Service operated in the old days, everyone knew what M's real name was. "How are you, James?"

"I'm fine, ma'am. You're looking great this evening."

"So are you, James. Do you know Alfred Hutchinson?" She indicated the man who was escorting her. She held on to his arm and looked at him with pride.

"We've never met." Bond held out his hand. "Bond. James Bond."

Alfred Hutchinson shook his hand. It was a firm, dry handclasp. "How do you do?"

"And this is my chief of staff, Bill Tanner," she continued.

Tanner and Hutchinson shook hands and greeted each other; then Hutchinson turned toward the hallway. "What happened to Manville? Did he have to park the car on the other side of Windsor?"

"Well, we did come a bit late," M said. "Oh, here they are."

Another couple came into the room, slipping off their overcoats and handing them to Davison. They were younger, a man and woman in their thirties.

"I had to park at the Squirrel," the man said. "You'd think there was a party or something going on here!"

"James, Bill, I'd like you to meet Manville Duncan. He's Alfred's lawyer. And this is his wife, Cynthia. These are James Bond and Bill Tanner—they work for me."

Manville Duncan and his wife shook their hands. Bond noticed that Duncan's handshake was cold and soft, like a woman's. He was probably the type of man who had spent his life in an office pushing pens and using computers. He was of medium height, with dark, curly hair and deep brown eyes. Bond thought he had Mediterranean blood in him. Cynthia Duncan was plain, pale-skinned, thin, and seemed intimidated by her surroundings.

"I'm going to see if I can get us some drinks straightaway," Hutchinson said.

"I'll come with you," M said. She nodded and smiled at Bond and Tanner. "I'm sure we'll run into each other later on."

She followed Hutchinson. Manville Duncan and his wife smiled sheepishly at Bond and Tanner, then moved past them into the room.

"Well, I'll be damned," Tanner said quietly.

"Did you know she was seeing Alfred Hutchinson?" Bond asked.

"No. It's unbelievable. She actually looks human."

"Bill, if I'm not mistaken, that's a woman in love. She's radiant."

"But . . . Alfred Hutchinson?" Tanner shook his head. "This could bring SIS some publicity that we don't really need."

Alfred Hutchinson wasn't just a dapper, distinguished English gentleman. He was already world-famous. He was Great Britain's "Goodwill Ambassador to the World." Two years ago, the British government had created the position for him in an attempt to improve worldwide public relations. Prior to that time, Hutchinson was a respected university professor, author, and historian. He had spent several years as a foreign relations adviser, although he had no real experience in politics. Hutchinson was a man who was very outspoken, and his frequent appearances on BBC news programs brought him national fame. Two of his books about the history of English politics and foreign relations were best-sellers. Hutchinson now traveled all over the globe, speaking on behalf of Britain and spreading "goodwill." Among his accomplishments, at the very least, was simply making news—"Hutchinson visits Beijing," "Britain's Ambassador to the World in Tokyo" . . . Although he had no political power whatsoever as a real ambassador, Hutchinson managed to recreate a British presence in the world where many felt that it had drastically waned.

The fact that Barbara Mawdsley, otherwise known as M, was romantically involved with him astonished everyone at the party that night. It was obvious the two had planned to make their relationship public on this very occasion. Bond quickly got over the shock of realizing M had a sex life, and found that he was amused by the situation. He wondered what the press would have to say about the Goodwill Ambassador to the World dating the head of SIS. On the other hand, why should it matter? They were human, like anyone else. They were both divorced. Bond wasn't sure, but he thought that Hutchinson had been married twice before.

Bond didn't know Manville Duncan. His first impression of the man was that he smoothly fitted the role of a sycophant to someone with a far greater intellect. Bond could imagine Duncan leaping to fill Hutchinson's coffee cup if his boss wished him to do so.

The main course at dinner was roast beef, new potatoes, fresh peas, and what Bond thought was a rather disappointing Saint-Emilion. He watched M and Hutchinson throughout the meal. They were obviously fond of one another, for Hutchinson would whisper something into her ear every now and then and she would smile broadly. At one point, Bond could have sworn that she must have squeezed the man's inner thigh, for he suddenly registered a look of surprise and then they both laughed. Bond glanced over at Sir Miles, who was also watching the couple. He had a frown on his face that could have been chiseled in stone.

After coffee, several of the men retired to the library. Sir Miles passed out A. Fuente Gran Reserva cigars, one of the few brands that Bond would put in his mouth. After a few minutes of chitchat, he was motioned into a corner by Sir Miles.

"How are you, James? Enjoy the meal?" he asked.

"Yes sir, it was splendid. I must give my compliments to Mrs. Davison."

"Oh for God's sake, stop calling me sir. I've told you a hundred times."

"Old habits die hard, Sir Miles."

"You didn't answer my first question. How are you?"

"I'm fine, I suppose. We have a curious case at the moment. We're not sure what to make of it."

"Yes, I've heard. Serial terrorists. Sounds messy. No leads at all?"

"Not yet. The Greek Secret Service is doing most of the investigation at the moment. We have some military investigators looking into matters in Cyprus. I may have to go out there again. We have to wait and see."

"How are you getting on with M?"

Bond hesitated, then smiled. "She's not you, sir."

"That doesn't answer my question."

"We get on fine, Miles. She's on top of it. We may not see eye to eye on everything, but I respect her."

"Well, if you ask me, she's making a bloody mistake in her choice of men."

This surprised Bond. "Oh?"

Sir Miles shook his head and made a face as if he'd just bitten into something bitter. "Despicable man."

"Really! I thought Alfred Hutchinson was one of the most revered men in Britain these days. He's quite popular in Parliament and with the PM." Sir Miles didn't reply. "Isn't he?"

"The man cheated on his ex-wife, he's a liar, and he has the manners of a pit bull."

"I guess that just shows you how much I know about politics. Actually, he seemed very charming to me. It's fairly obvious that M is attracted to him."

"It's just my personal opinion, of course. This is between you and me," Sir Miles said gruffly. "Goodwill Ambassador to the World, indeed. What a bloody joke."

"Why is that?"

"Let's just say I know a few things about his family. I shouldn't have said anything—forget about it."

"Do you know him well?"

"Not really. We've played bridge at Blades a few times. He gets into a terrible temper when he loses. He reminds me of that man we played against a while back . . . you know, the German with the disfigured face and the rocket."

"Drax?"

"That's right. Oh, never mind. There's just something about Hutchinson that I don't like. That's all. Forget I said anything about it."

For a moment Bond caught a hint of jealousy in Sir Miles's voice. Could it be that he was attracted to the new M himself and was merely sounding off against her choice of suitors? Bond quickly dismissed the absurdity of that idea.

They were interrupted by M herself. She stuck her head in the door and spotted Bond and Sir Miles. "Oh, there you are, James. Might I have a word with you? Excuse me, Sir Miles."

"Quite all right, my dear," Sir Miles said with charm.

Bond followed her out and over to where Hutchinson was standing, admiring a new watercolor print that Sir Miles had recently completed.

"The old man has an extraordinary gift for capturing light and shadow, doesn't he?" Hutchinson said, peering closely at the painting.

"James," M began, "Alfred has some information about the Cyprus case which might be useful."

"Is that so?"

"Be at my office at ten o'clock tomorrow morning, please? Is that good for you, Alfred?" she asked.

"Yes, my dear," he said conspiratorially. "That will be fine."

"Why not just tell us now?" Bond asked.

"My dear man," Hutchinson said, "we're here to enjoy ourselves, aren't we? Let's not discuss business now, for heaven's sake. I'm going to have another drink. Can I get you something?"

"Thank you, no," Bond said. Sir Miles was right. There was something inherently sleazy about the man. "Ten o'clock, then," he said. He nodded at M and walked away.

Bond went into the hallway to find Davison. He had had enough socializing for one night. He was surprised to find none other than Helena Marksbury sitting alone. She was just putting out a cigarette in a glass ashtray. Bond had seen her earlier conversing with other SIS personnel, and he didn't want to join them. Now that she was alone . . .

"What's the matter, Helena? The bus doesn't stop here."

She smiled. "Hello, James. I was wondering if you were ever going to talk to me this evening."

"I've been trying to, but you were always engaged. Care to take a walk outside?"

"It's a bit cold and damp, isn't it?"

"We'll put on our coats. Come on, let's find them."

A few minutes later, they had their overcoats on and they quietly stepped out of the house. The air was chilly and the night was full of dark clouds. Bond lit two cigarettes and passed one to Helena. They walked around the side of the house to a sunken patio. A large fountain with a statue of Cupid in its center stood in the middle of the patio, but the water had been turned off.

"I felt a bit lost in there," she said. "They're really not my crowd."

"Would you believe me if I told you they're not my crowd either?"

"Yes, I would," she said. "You're not like the others at the office, James." She laughed to herself. "Not at all."

"I suppose that's a compliment," he said.

She smiled but didn't elaborate.

A bit of light from windows at the back of the house shone across the patio. He gazed at her oval face, the short brown hair and big green eyes. She was very beautiful. She returned his stare and finally said, "What would you like to do now?"

"I want to kiss you," he said.

She blinked. "You're very direct," she said.

"Always," he said; then he leaned forward and kissed her. She welcomed the embrace and opened her mouth to make the kiss more intimate. After a few seconds, they separated, but Bond kept his face close to hers. He felt a raindrop on his forehead.

"It's starting to rain," she whispered.

He moved in and kissed her again, and this time she responded even more passionately. The raindrops began to increase in tempo.

Eventually, she pulled away gently. Breathlessly, she said, "I know this isn't sexual harassment, but I'd better point out that you're my boss, James."

He kept his hands on her shoulders. He nodded. "I know. We . . . I shouldn't do this."

"We'd best go back inside. We're getting wet."

A thunderclap roared and the rain started to come down in earnest. Bond held her as they ran around the house to the front door. By the time they got there, she was laughing. They stood beneath the awning for a moment. Now there was an awkward silence between them.

"I was about to leave when I saw you," he said finally.

"It's pouring now, you'll have to wait. You couldn't possibly drive home in this."

"No. I'm going now. I'll see you tomorrow."

He gave her shoulders a squeeze and said, "Forgive me." Then he walked out into the rain and onto the gravel drive. Helena Marksbury watched him go and muttered under her breath, "You're forgiven."

Bond let the rain soak him as he walked to the end of the drive where he had left the Bentley. He cursed himself for what had just happened. He knew better than to get involved with women at the office. If only she wasn't so bloody attractive! What was it in him that made him want to seduce every woman he found desirable? Temporary recreational love was satisfying and always had been, but it certainly didn't fill a greater need Bond had. Was it possible that what he craved was a woman to love—*really* love—in order to fill that hole? The bitter answer to that was that he got burned every time he allowed himself to truly love someone. The scars on his heart were many and deep.

He got into his car and set off through the torrent toward London. Bond's darker side took hold of him once again as he pondered his lonely, wretched life. He would have liked the rain to wash away the familiar melancholy, but he ultimately accepted and embraced it as an old friend.

FOUR

TOO CLOSE TO HOME

THE PHONE WOKE BOND ABRUPTLY OUT OF A DEEP SLEEP. THE ILLUMINATED digital clock read 2:37. He switched on the light and went for the white phone, but the ring continued. Bond felt a sudden rush of adrenaline when he realized that it was the red phone that was ringing. The red phone rang only in an emergency situation.

"Bond," he said into the receiver.

"James, code sixty." It was Bill Tanner.

"I'm listening."

"M's orders." Tanner gave an address and flat number. "You know where it is? Just off of Holland Park Road. It's the block of flats called Park Mansions."

Tanner rang off and Bond jumped out of bed. "Code sixty" meant that the matter had a special security classification. In other words, Bond must use utmost discretion.

It took him ten minutes to get to Holland Park, an area of affluence on the western edge of Kensington. The district grew as a result of the reputation of Holland House, a mansion built four hundred years ago primarily for the purpose of entertaining king and court. Town houses sprang up in the early to mid-nineteenth century on various streets and squares west of the park. Many MPs and governmental elite lived in the area.

Park Mansions was a long block of brown and red brick buildings three stories high. A security gate provided protection from traffic, but at the moment there seemed to be a lot of activity in front of one of the buildings. An ambulance was parked there, its lights flashing. A police car and two unmarked MI5 cars were double-parked in front as well. Bond left the Bentley outside the gate and walked through. He showed a constable his credentials and was shown through the front door of the building.

Bill Tanner met him at the open front door of the flat. Police tape had been stretched several feet away from the door, preventing any curious neighbors from peering inside.

"James, come inside," Tanner said. "M's in here."

"What's going on, Bill?"

"It's Hutchinson. He's dead."

"What?"

Tanner leaned in closer and kept his voice down. "This is his flat. M was here spending the night with him. She's quite distraught."

"Do we know what happened?"

"You'd better have a look. I phoned Manville Duncan after I called you. He's on his way."

Tanner led Bond inside the flat. MI5 Forensics were taking photographs and examining the scene. M was in the sitting room, dressed in a white and pink silk housecoat. She looked pale and frightened. She was holding a cup of coffee in her lap. When she looked up, Bond could see that she was extremely upset, not only because her lover was dead, but because she was embarrassed to be seen by her staff in this condition.

Bond knelt beside her and took her hand. "Are you all right, ma'am?" he asked gently.

M nodded and swallowed. "Thank you for coming, James. Poor Alfred. I feel so . . . exposed."

"Don't worry about that, ma'am. What happened?"

She shook her head and trembled. "I don't even know. One minute he was fine, and the next . . ." She closed her eyes, attempting to get hold of herself.

Bond stood up and said, "I'm going to have a look at him, ma'am. We'll talk in a moment."

He followed Tanner into the bedroom.

Bond had seen many cadavers and crime scenes, and this one was no different. Death brought an unnatural chill to an otherwise warm hued room with oak wall paneling, a king-sized bed and ornate headboard, and distinctly masculine furnishings. Alfred Hutchinson lay naked on his back on the bed. He might have been asleep but for the fact that his eyes were wide open, frozen in fear. There were no marks on the body. There were no signs that there had been any violence. He looked as if he might have been a victim of cardiac arrest. In this state, Alfred Hutchinson was no longer the distinguished Goodwill Ambassador to the World Bond had met a few hours earlier. Now he was simply a chalk-skinned common corpse.

"Heart attack?" Bond asked the MI5 medical examiner, who was sitting by the bed, writing in a notebook. A member of the MI5 forensic team was taking photographs of the body with a multi/fixed-focal length Polaroid Macro 5 SLR instant camera, one of several special-purpose cameras that the team was using at the crime scene.

"That's what it looks like," the doctor said. "We'll have to conduct a postmortem examination, of course, but I don't think that's the whole story."

"What do you mean?"

"Hutchinson died of cardiac and respiratory failure, but he was in perfect health. After hearing Ms. Mawdsley's statement and examining the body, it's my preliminary opinion that he was murdered."

"How?"

"Some kind of poison. A neurotoxin, most likely, a substance that stops your heart and the automatic function of breathing. It's something that is irreversible once it's been introduced into the bloodstream. It acts fast, but not fast enough, I'm afraid. The man suffered terribly for several minutes."

"Any marks on the body?"

"One suspicious contusion on the anterior of his right thigh. See the little red mark?" The doctor pointed to a small, swollen puncture wound on Hutchinson's upper leg. "At first I thought it was just a pimple, but further examination revealed that he had been jabbed with a needle."

Bond looked at the body again. The man in charge walked into the bedroom.

"Commander Bond?"

"Yes."

"I'm Detective Inspector Howard. We're ready to take the body away if you are."

"Have you had a good look at all his personal effects?" Bond asked.

"We're just getting around to that now. Might I ask you to have a talk with Ms. Mawdsley? I wasn't able to get much out of her earlier."

Bond nodded and left the bedroom. He found that M had not moved, nor had she drunk her coffee. He sat down next to her in an armchair.

"Ma'am, we need to know exactly what happened tonight," he said softly.

M sighed heavily and shut her eyes.

"I'm still trying to piece it together," she said. "We left Sir Miles's house around eleven. Maybe eleven-fifteen. We were all together— the Duncans, Alfred, and me. We decided to stop at the Ritz for a nightcap."

She paused and took a sip of the coffee. She turned to Tanner. "Mr. Tanner, this is cold. Could you please get me a fresh cup?"

Tanner nodded and took the cup from her.

"What time did you get to the Ritz?" Bond asked.

"I think it was around midnight. We were there three quarters of an hour, I suppose."

"What did Mr. Hutchinson have to drink?"

"He had a brandy, as did I. We all did."

"Then what?"

"It was raining heavily. Alfred offered to drive the Duncans home, but they insisted on calling a taxi. They live out of the way, in Islington."

"So you and Alfred drove here together?"

She nodded. "He had parked near the hotel. We both had umbrellas, so I didn't mind walking in the rain. We got to the flat twenty minutes later. He seemed fine. We . . . got undressed . . ."

Bond knew this was extremely difficult for M. She was exposing a personal, intimate side of herself that no one else ever saw.

"It's all right, ma'am," Bond said. "Go on."

"We made love," she said. "Afterwards, he—"

"Excuse me, ma'am, but did he show any signs of fatigue or illness during your lovemaking?"

"No," M said. "He seemed completely normal. Alfred is . . . was . . . very energetic."

"I see. Go on."

"I got up to go to the loo. While I was in there, I heard him gasping for breath. I ran out to him and he was struggling for air, clutching at his throat. Oh, James, it was horrible. I reached for the phone to call an ambulance, but he grabbed my arm. All he could say was, 'Your hand . . . your hand . . .' So I let him hold my hand. He went into a terrible convulsion, and then he died. I called the ambulance and Mr. Tanner immediately afterwards. I thought about dressing him, but I knew that wasn't the thing to do. I . . . left him . . . like that . . ." She started to sob.

Bond put his arm around his chief and let her cry on his shoulder for a full sixty seconds until she finally pulled herself together.

Tanner brought another cup of coffee. "Manville Duncan just arrived. Here you go, ma'am."

Duncan's face was white when he hurried into the room. "What happened?"

Tanner gave him a quick rundown of what they knew so far.

"Christ, was it a heart attack?" Duncan asked.

"That's what it looks like," Bond said, "but I'm afraid that's not the case. Alfred Hutchinson was murdered."

M's eyes grew wide. "How do you know?"

"It's the medical examiner's suspicion. Mine as well. You see, ma'am, what you described is not consistent with a heart attack. Mr.

Hutchinson was alive for several minutes, apparently choking, correct?"

"Yes."

"Then he went into convulsions?"

"That's right."

"Ma'am, can you come look at the body again? I'd like to show you something."

A complete change came over M. When she heard the word "murder," she summoned all of her professional integrity. Even though she was dressed in only a housecoat, she became the head of SIS once again. She stood up and gestured toward the bedroom for Bond to lead the way.

Bond took her in and showed her the tiny wound on Hutchinson's leg. "The medical examiner believes that's where the poison entered the bloodstream."

"Oh my God," M said. "I know how it happened. I remember now."

"What?"

"It was outside the hotel. We had just said goodbye to the Duncans. We were walking toward his car. There was someone with a broken umbrella on the pavement. He was struggling with it, trying to open it."

"What did he look like?"

"I don't know," she said, angrily. "I don't even know if it was a man or a woman. They were dressed in a hooded yellow raincoat—completely covered."

"And?"

"As we walked by, the person accidentally poked Alfred with the end of the umbrella, I think. I know it struck him somehow, and he said, 'Ouch.' . . ."

"What did the person with the umbrella do?"

"Nothing! They didn't even realize what had happened, for they moved on without apologizing or saying a word. Alfred shrugged it off and we kept walking toward the car, although now that I think about it, he seemed a little shaken up by the incident. He did act a little strange until we started driving. While we were walking, he kept looking behind us. And he insisted on holding my handbag until we got into the car, for fear that it might get snatched. In two minutes we got to the car. It all happened so fast that frankly I had forgotten all about it."

"You know what this reminds me of?" Tanner asked.

"Yes," Bond said. "Markov."

"By God, you're right," M said.

"What?" Duncan asked. "Who's Markov?"

"Georgi Markov," Bond said. "He was a Bulgarian defector. He was assassinated on Waterloo Bridge in . . . 1978, I believe, in this same fashion. Someone poked him with an umbrella. The tip of the umbrella injected a tiny capsule of ricin into his bloodstream."

"Ricin?"

"It's a toxic protein-based poison derived from castor beans. Depending on the dosage, it can be effective in fifteen minutes to an hour. It's lethal, and it leaves no trace in the bloodstream. To all intents and purposes, the victim dies of respiratory and cardiac failure. It attacks the nervous system and shuts off those basic motor functions."

"But . . . who would want to kill Alfred?" Duncan asked.

"That's the big question," Bond said. "Who would?"

M sat down. "He never mentioned anything to me. It's not as if anyone were after his job. Manville, was there anything going on diplomatically that we should know about?"

"I can't think of a thing!" Duncan said. "He was . . . well, he was loved by everyone who met him!"

"You ever play bridge with him?" Bond asked Duncan.

"No. Why?"

"Never mind."

There was silence in the room and everyone pondered the situation. Detective Inspector Howard came into the room with an overcoat.

"Is this the overcoat Mr. Hutchinson was wearing tonight?" he asked M.

"Yes."

"There's something you should see. This was in the pocket."

He had a small white alabaster statuette in his gloved hand. It was the Greek god Ares.

"That's just like the statues found in Cyprus," Bond said. "Anything else in the pockets?"

"Just a coat check receipt," Howard said. He held it out. It had been carefully placed in a clear evidence bag to protect it from contamination. Bond took it and saw that the receipt was from the Ritz Hotel, and the number "173" was printed on its face. He almost dismissed it, but as he handed the receipt back he turned it over. Scrawled in a red marker was the number "4."

"It's the Number Killer," Bond said. "Alfred Hutchinson was victim number four."

"The bastards have brought this a little too close to home," Tanner said.

"Would you please explain what's going on?" Manville Duncan asked.

Bond looked at M for approval.

She nodded and said, "As his lawyer, Manville will be taking over for Alfred. I suppose it's information he should be aware of. Manville, please understand this is all strictly confidential."

"Of course," he said.

"Mr. Duncan," Bond said. "I have just returned from Cyprus. Over the past week, three separate incidents killed some British citizens. The first was one of our SIS people, in Athens. A fellow named Whitten. Did you know him?"

"No."

"His body was found in the Ancient Agora with the number '1' painted in red on a rock nearby. The second incident was on our Sovereign Base at Dhekelia in Cyprus. Several soldiers were killed—by poison. The number '2' was painted nearby, and one of these Greek god statues was left at the site. Just the other day, another group of soldiers at Episkopi were killed by another chemical weapon. The number '3' and another statue were left at the scene. This makes number '4.' "

"You're sure it's the same killers?"

"It seems obvious," Bond said. "I wonder if he was silenced to keep him from telling us what he knew about the case? Ma'am, does Mr. Hutchinson have any family? Where are his former wives?"

"His first wife is in Australia, I think," she said. "The second one lives here in London."

"Any children?"

"He has a son by his first wife. His name is Charles. He lives in America somewhere. In Texas, I think."

"That's it?"

"Charles is all I know about," M said.

"Then we'll have to get in touch with him."

"I'll do it," Tanner said.

"Oh hell," Duncan said.

"What?"

"Alfred was due to fly to the Middle East tomorrow. He had an appointment in Syria!"

"You're his lawyer, Manville," M said.

Duncan nodded, realizing the implication of that remark. "I'll have to go in his place."

"You'll have to fill his shoes until the powers that be decide what to do about his position," she said. "Are you up to it?"

"I'll have to be," Duncan said. He looked at his watch. "I'd better go home and get some rest, if I can, then get up early and go to the office and get ready. He had . . .

"A five o'clock flight," M said. "I know."

"Look, uhm, Mr. Bond," Duncan said. "Please, I want to help all I can. If you have any more questions for me or simply want to pick my brains, call me at the office. They can get a message to me and I'll call you back."

"When will you be back in England?"

"In two days, I think. I'll have to check his schedule."

"Fine. Go on. Have a good trip. Don't mention to anyone what really happened to Mr. Hutchinson. We'll make sure that the public and the rest of the world believe that he died of a heart attack. Naturally."

"We'll have to keep me out of it," M said.

"That goes without saying," Bond said. "Let's get you out of here. You had better get dressed before any reporters get wind of this."

M nodded, turning to accept Manville Duncan's condolences before he left the flat.

Just before fetching her clothes, M said to Bond, Tanner, and Inspector Howard, "MI5 will handle this investigation here in Great Britain. But as it is linked to the events in Greece and Cyprus, 007, you're going to have to handle that end. This is obviously an international incident, and that gives MI6 full authority to act. Let's meet at ten A.M. in my office and discuss strategy, shall we?" Without waiting for an answer, Barbara Mawdsley turned and went into the bedroom where her lover lay cold and stiff.

Bond was relieved that she was beginning to sound like her old self again.

FIVE

RENDEZVOUS ON CHIOS

APPROXIMATELY TWO DAYS LATER, A MEETING WAS CALLED TO ORDER IN A remote and secret fortress hidden away on the Greek island of Chios.

The island is only eight kilometers from the Turkish peninsula of Karaburun, one of the closest of all Greek territories to the country with which Greece has had such a precarious relationship for centuries. Not one of the major tourist islands, Chios has several Greek Army bases and camouflaged enclaves of weaponry.

Crescent-shaped, Chios is hilly and cultivated with olives, fruit, vines, and most important, gum trees. The capital, locally known as Chios Town, sits on the edge of a plain facing the Turkish coast on the site of its ancient ruins. Approximately twenty-six kilometers west of the capital, at the end of a winding, mountainous road that leads to nowhere, is a quiet, forsaken ancient village called Anavatos. It is built on a precipitous cliff, with narrow stepped pathways twisting between the houses to the summit—an empty, dilapidated medieval castle. Virtually a ghost town, Anavatos's abandoned gray stone buildings stand as memorials to one of the island's great tragedies. Nearly all of the inhabitants were killed in the atrocities committed by the Ottoman Empire in 1822, and today the village is inhabited only by a few elderly people at the base of the cliff. The villagers chose to throw themselves off the cliff rather than submit to capture and torture.

At noon on this early-November weekday, there wasn't a single tourist in sight. Anavatos never lured many sightseers, and those who did venture there to make the climb to the top never stayed long. Once visitors have seen the deserted ruins, there is nothing else to do. There are no shops, tavernas, or hotels. One restaurant at the base of the cliff serves its small population, every now and then enjoying the business of a tourist or two. Neither sightseers nor the current residents of Anavatos could ever have guessed that within the bowels of the decrepit medieval castle at the top of the lonely village were the sophisticated, modern headquarters of a peculiar group of people.

Since many notable legendary figures such as Jason and Homer reportedly visited the island, it was entirely conceivable that the noted sixth-century-B.C. mathematician Pythagoras set foot on Chios. He came from neighboring Samos, where he founded a brotherhood called the Order of the Pythagoreans, or the Pythagorean Society. Pythagoras was a respected scholar of mathematics and philosophy, and his lecture rooms were often packed. Even women broke the law that prohibited them from attending public meetings, just to hear him speak. It wasn't long before the Pythagoreans began to revere their leader as a demigod. They believed in, among other things, transmigration of souls, and followed moral and dietary practices in order to purify the soul for its next embodiment. According to the Pythagoreans, all relationships—even abstract concepts like justice—could be expressed numerically.

Deep within the silent and desolate medieval castle at the top of Anavatos, Pythagoras was about to address his followers once again.

The man who professed to be him was dressed in a white robe. He had dark, curly hair with traces of gray, cut short and neat. His large, round, dark brown eyes were set deeply into a handsome, chiseled face, with dark eyebrows and a hawk nose. He had a tanned Mediterranean complexion and ruddy lips that seemed to be permanently formed into a frown. The fifty-five-year-old man was clean-shaven, tall and broad-shouldered. He could have been a film star, a priest, or a politician. The man had an indefinable charisma that captivated those who knew him. When he spoke, everyone listened. When he explained, they all understood. When he commanded, no one dared to ignore his instructions.

After the several minutes of silence that traditionally began their meetings, he would begin. During this time, the man who believed that he was Pythagoras reincarnated gazed at the nine people reclining on cushions on the floor in front of him. They were also wearing robes. Nine men and women looked at their leader with anticipation. There was an American and an Englishman. Three of them were Greek, two Greek Cypriots. One was Italian and one was Russian. Number Ten was a brilliant physician and chemist; Number Nine was an expert in transportation—he could fly anything anywhere. There was Number Eight, the prestigious president of a Greek pharmaceutical company and a distinguished biologist and chemist; Number Seven, a man extremely close to the leader in that they were related by blood; and Number Six, a banker, someone who knew the ins and outs of stock markets, investments, and foreign exchange. Number Five was a loyal friend who normally wore a Greek officer's military uniform; Number Four was a woman in charge of buying and selling on the black market. Number Three had been in charge of the first four strikes and normally handled overseas business, and the lovely Number Two was one of the most highly skilled assassins and terrorist soldiers on earth. The leader fondly gazed upon Number Two, whose work clothes included a gas mask and a protective suit.

They were in a room designed to replicate an ancient Greek interior. The large square area was made entirely of stone. Benches lined the perimeters, but the middle of the floor was devoid of furniture. An archway with curtains the colors of the blue-and-white Greek flag led to a completely different room. It contained modern office equipment—workstations, computers, monitors, and machinery. Beyond that again were living quarters as elegant as those of a luxury hotel. Here group members slept if they needed to stay overnight in Anavatos. At a lower level lived the various personnel employed by the ten people in the Greek meeting room. These included personal bodyguards and trained, armed "soldiers" who were so well paid that their loyalty was without question.

A cache of military weapons was stored in an armory. This consisted mainly of guns and ammunition stolen from Greek military bases. Some of the more sophisticated equipment had been stolen from NATO, or purchased from underground organizations operating in the Middle East and southern Europe. The most impressive device in the complex was an empty missile silo and launching pad. Its cover, which could be opened at the touch of a button, was cleverly disguised as a flat, dirt roof of the medieval castle that housed these unusual secret headquarters. The roof could easily be used as a helicopter pad. It had all been built under the noses of the villagers. They had been paid to turn their backs.

The period of silence was over. The leader picked up a lyre and strummed a perfect fifth. The Pythagoreans knew that vibrating strings produced harmonious tones when the ratios of the lengths of the strings were whole numbers, and that these ratios could be extended to other instruments if desired.

The meeting had begun. Pythagoras set down the lyre and smiled wryly at the nine people before him. They were ready. They leaned forward slightly, waiting for the soothing voice of reason. They were impatient to hear him speak, for he was the Monad, the One. And they were called the Decada.

"Welcome," he said. "I am happy to report that Mission Number Four was successful in preventing sensitive information concerning the Decada from reaching British intelligence. Unfortunately, the information the targeted man possessed is missing. Retrieval of it is essential. We cannot complete the *Tetraktys* without it. I have given Number Ten full responsibility for recovering it."

Number Ten nodded in acknowledgment.

"In the meantime, the Decada will continue its goal of achieving worldwide recognition. The first four strikes were simply samples of what the Decada can do. We were testing the waters, getting our feet wet, so to speak. And thus we have successfully warned the British not to interfere in our future plans."

The Monad turned and moved toward the stone wall behind him. He slipped his index and middle fingers in between the edges of some stones and released a catch. The panel of fake stones slid across, revealing a metal square embedded with red light bulbs. The bulbs were positioned to form points in an equilateral triangle:

```
        •
      •   •
    •   •   •
  •   •   •   •
```

The bottom four bulbs were lit.

"The foundation of the holy *Tetraktys* is complete. Four base digits have been completed. Note the perfection of the triangle—how it can be rotated and it will remain the same. A base of four always leads to a line of three, then to a line of two, and finally to a single point. Ten points in all. Ten—the holy *Tetraktys*. The basis of the Decada. The creative connection between the Divine Mind and the manifest universe."

The Monad indicated the line with three unlit bulbs.

"Our next three strikes will build upon the first four. Two will follow these, and they will be the pivotal actions that will set up the Decada for its ultimate assault. After that, we will simply start again with a new *Tetraktys* of ten points. I can assure you that the world will be paying attention to us after the first *Tetraktys* is complete."

He turned to one of the followers sitting before him. "What is the Principle of Oneness, Number Four?" he asked.

Number Four, a woman, replied by rote, "The Principle of Oneness is Unity, and that is represented by the Monad. Completeness, perfection, eternity, the unchanging and the permanent are all qualities of the Monad, the number One."

"And how can One become the Many?"

"One can become the Many only through the manifestation of the *Tetraktys*, the Ten."

"And when One becomes the Many, what happens?" the Monad asked the entire group.

As if in a trance, they all replied together, "The Limited will become Unlimited. Limit is a definite boundary. The Unlimited is indefinite and is therefore in need of Limit. We will meld with the Monad. We will all have the power."

The Monad nodded with pleasure. "Let us recite the Decada of Contraries. I'll begin with Number One: Limited and Unlimited."

Number Two said, "Odd and Even."

Number Three said, "One and Many."

The remaining members of the Decada spoke in turn, repeating what they had learned from the Monad.

The Monad continued, "The Ten points of the *Tetraktys*. They are the perfection of Number and the elements which comprise it. In one sense, we could say that the *Tetraktys* symbolizes, like a musical scale, an image of Unity starting at One, proceeding through four levels of manifestation, and returning to Unity. Ten. Everything comes to Ten. And who are the Ten?"

"The Decada!" the group shouted.

The Monad was pleased. His followers were totally under his control. He paused and looked at each of the other nine members. He stared into their eyes for a full minute, person by person. They could feel the man's strength and power filling them as he looked into their souls. They felt invigorated and whole.

"The gods are pleased," he said. "Our first tribute was to the ancient Greeks, who built the Agora in Athens at the base of the holy Acropolis. We owe our allegiance to these ancestors of all mankind. It was in Greece where true Western thought materialized. They built the Temple of Hephaisteion, where Zeus and the other gods of Mount Olympus were worshipped, and it was there that we left our little . . . sacrifice. Our second tribute was to Hera, queen of the gods. The third was to Poseidon, god of the sea and brother of Zeus. Our fourth was to Ares, the god of war."

The Monad smiled. "How fitting that Ares be associated with the final point of the first four strikes, for he was a bloodthirsty god. Yes, with Ares we have declared war on our enemies. The British have been marked. It is a pity that our attempt to eliminate the Greek Secret Service investigator in her shower failed. But now we turn our attention to the Turks and the Turkish Cypriots. Once we have completed our first set of goals, the ones that will make us a force to be reckoned with, the Turks will be run out of northern Cyprus forever. My friends, we will move through the holy *Tetraktys* like lightning! I am happy to report that Number Eight is progressing with her work in the laboratory and we are now ready to break all ties with our American soon-to-be-former partners. It will not be long before we strike with our own swords, and the world will remember us forever!"

After the meeting, Number Two, Number Eight, and Number Ten huddled together in a private room in the complex. The three women spoke quietly.

"Deaths have already been reported in Los Angeles," Number Ten said.

"How quickly does the virus gestate?" Number Two asked.

"The quickest way is direct injection into the bloodstream," Number Eight explained. "A person will get sick in about eight hours. It's during these hours that the virus is most contagious. Otherwise, it takes ten to twenty-four hours for an onset of symptoms after exposure to someone who is already infected."

"Then it's working," Number Two said.

"More or less."

Number Ten replied, "By the time we've completed the tenth mission of the *Tetraktys*, all the deliveries will have been made. It will be too late to stop the process."

"Good," said Number Two. "Number Eight, keep perfecting the virus and the vaccine. Number Ten, you have your assignment. I have my own work for the Monad ahead of me. Ladies, by the time we're through with this, we shall be wealthy beyond our wildest dreams."

They hugged each other. Number Eight left the room. Number Two gazed into Number Ten's eyes.

"I must leave," Number Ten said. "There's a plane waiting for me."

"I know. Take care. I'll see you soon," Number Two said. They kissed each other intimately, on the mouth, then parted.

Number Two watched her lover leave, then made her way to her room. As she expected, the Monad was there, waiting in her bed.

TEQUILA AND LIMES

LONDON'S COLD, RAINY WEATHER CONTINUED, GIVING WAY TO A BITTER high wind that chilled one to the bone. It was unseasonably cold for the first week of November. Walking outside for more than a few minutes was an ordeal, and people had to make sure every inch of skin was covered to avoid being miserable.

James Bond looked out the window of M's office on the eighth floor of SIS headquarters and yearned for Jamaica. The weather wouldn't be perfect there either; it would most likely be raining too, but at least the temperature would be tolerable. He imagined hearing the warm laugh of Ramsey, the young Jamaican he had hired to look after Shamelady during his absence. Ramsey would have cheered him up with his broad smile, white teeth, and good humor.

Bond breathed deeply, attempting to motivate himself to go over the paperwork on his desk once again. The lack of progress on the case was certainly part of the problem, but he knew that the only way he would feel like he was accomplishing something was to get out of London. He was restless and irritable. The previous evening he had put away half a bottle of The Macallan and had woken up in the middle of the night in the armchair of his sitting room. He had crawled into bed, and didn't wake up until Helena Marksbury phoned him to inquire if he was coming to the office. Now he not only had a pounding headache, but he felt he was coming down with a cold.

"You look terrible, 007," M said behind him. "What the devil is the matter with you?"

"Nothing, ma'am," Bond said, turning away from the window. "This weather is dreadful."

"You're not catching flu, are you? It's going around."

"I never catch the flu," Bond said, sniffing.

"Nevertheless, I want you to see the doctor. I need you in top form if we get a break in the case," she said.

Bond sat down in the black leather chair across from her desk. M didn't look so great either. The stress and heartache she felt at the loss of her lover were all too apparent. To her credit, she had shown up for work every day since Hutchinson's murder.

"Have you located Charles Hutchinson yet?" she asked.

"No, ma'am, he's nowhere to be found," Bond said, suppressing a cough. "I'm thinking it might be a good idea if I took a trip to Texas. There may be some clues at Mr. Hutchinson's house there."

Bill Tanner had quickly gathered some useful information on Alfred Hutchinson. He owned a house in Austin, Texas, where he had spent time as a guest professor at the University of Texas. His twenty three-year-old son, Charles, lived and worked there and Hutchinson had continued to make frequent trips there. Hutchinson's ex-wife was insisting that funeral arrangements be postponed until Charles Hutchinson could be reached. All attempts to contact the young man had failed. Either he was out of the country or something had happened to him.

"I suppose it couldn't hurt," M said. "Yes, I think that's a good idea. Should I get in touch with the CIA and let them know you're coming?"

"That won't be necessary, ma'am," Bond said. "I know someone in Austin who will be much more helpful than they would be."

Bond flew to Dallas on American Airlines and changed planes for the short hop down to Austin. It was late afternoon when he arrived, and the weather was better there than in London. The sky was overcast but it was pleasantly warm.

Bond hadn't spent much time in Texas. He had been to the area known as the Panhandle during the case a few years back that involved the last heir of Ernst Stavro Blofeld, but he had never been to Austin or any of the other more scenic areas in central Texas. He was surprised by the lush greenery, the hills, and the stretches of water that could be seen from the air. He had no idea that any part of Texas could be so beautiful. It was no wonder that his friend and longtime associate Felix Leiter, who actually hailed from Texas, had gone back to settle in Austin.

At the airport, an exotic Hispanic woman dressed in tight-fitting blue jeans and a western shirt with the bottom ends tied together above her bare midriff approached Bond as he came out into the terminal. She appeared to be in her early thirties, had long black hair and small brown eyes that sparkled.

"Mr. Bond?" she asked with a Spanish accent.

"Yes?"

"I'm Manuela Montemayor. I've come to pick you up." The way she said "peek you up" was tantalizing. "Felix is waiting at the house. He's very excited to see you again."

"Lovely. I'm all yours," Bond said with a smile.

Bond collected his luggage and followed Manuela outside into the fresh warm air. She led him to a 1997 red Mitsubishi Diamante LS in the parking lot.

"Felix said you would hate the car, but I like it," she said.

"Looks fine to me." It felt good to get into the passenger seat after the long flight from England.

Manuela drove out of the parking lot to Interstate 35, then headed south. Bond looked to his right and saw the expanse of the University of Texas at Austin, an enormous campus well known for its American football team, fine arts department, and beautiful girls. The main building, or UT Tower, stood twenty-seven stories tall, overlooking the campus and city with the grandeur of an all-seeing sentinel.

"You been to Austin before?" she asked.

"Never. I've always wanted to come, especially since Felix moved here."

"We love it. The people are friendly, the music is great, and the climate is perfect."

"How's Felix doing?"

"He's fine. You know he's not so good on his legs anymore. The one leg with the prosthesis has deteriorated, so he stays in his wheelchair most of the time."

Christ, Bond thought. He hadn't known that Felix was in a wheelchair. He wondered how he would feel when he saw his friend in that condition. Bond never forgot that fateful day in Florida when Leiter lost the leg and an arm to a shark owned by Mr. Big and company. At the time, Leiter worked for the CIA. After the mishap, the Texan had been with Pinkerton's Detective Agency for a number of years. He had then spent a few years with the DEA, before going into private practice as a freelance consultant on intelligence and law enforcement matters.

Eventually, the car crossed the Colorado River, locally known as Town Lake. Manuela turned off of the interstate and headed west, entering the section of Barton Springs Road populated by trendy restaurants and nightspots, and on through Zilker Metropolitan Park.

"Now we are in West Lake Hills," Manuela said. "It's where we live."

This suburb of Austin seemed more fashionable than what Bond had seen along the way. The area was very hilly, and the houses were elegant and impressive. The car turned into a long, narrow drive surrounded by large oak trees that disclosed a wood-and-stone ranch house at the end.

"Here we are," she said.

As they walked toward the house, the cicadas were making a tremendous racket in the trees. Bond felt he was really out in the wilderness.

"You should hear them in the summer," Manuela said. "They're actually pretty quiet now. We have a lot of critters here in Texas."

A wheelchair ramp had been set up on the steps leading to the front porch. Manuela unlocked the door and held it open for Bond. "Hello!" she called. "Where are you, sweetheart?"

"In here!" It was a familiar voice, and Bond smiled.

"Put your luggage down," she said. "Felix is in the den."

A full-grown dalmatian jumped out from around the corner of the hallway. She immediately growled and barked at Bond.

"Esmerelda!" Manuela commanded. "Stop that. This is our friend, James."

Bond held out his hand, palm upward, then stooped down to the dog's level. The dalmatian sniffed his hand, then gave it a solid lick.

"Oh, she likes you already," Manuela said.

Bond scratched the animal's head and behind her ears. The tail started wagging; he had made a friend.

Bond and the dog followed Manuela through the long hallway, past a dining room and kitchen area, and into a large wood-paneled room full of furniture and high-tech equipment. There were large windows on two sides of the room, facing out into the woods behind the house. They were open, but the mesh screens kept the bugs out. It was an extremely pleasant atmosphere.

Felix Leiter turned away from the computer terminals and faced Bond with a big grin. He was sitting in an Action Arrow power chair, which silently turned on its wheels, steered by hand controls. Felix was still thin, and the way his knees stuck out from the chair reminded Bond how tall the man was. His straw-colored hair had gone a little gray, and his chin and cheekbones seemed sharper. What hadn't changed at all were the gray eyes, which had a feline slant that increased when he smiled broadly. The right hook had been replaced by a prosthesis that looked more like a hand, and it seemed to operate quite well. He held out his left hand.

"James Bond, you old horse thief!" he said. The slow drawl was warm and friendly. "Welcome to Texas, you goddamned limey!"

Bond clasped the hand. It was a firm, dry handshake. "Isn't the word 'limey' a bit old-fashioned, Felix?"

"What the hell, *we're* old-fashioned," Leiter said. "You can call me a bloody Yank for old times' sake, if you want."

"It's good to see you, Felix."

"Likewise, my friend. Sit, sit! Manuela will rustle us up some drinks. You met my lovely Manuela?"

"I did indeed."

"Hands off, James. She's mine, and she's loyal as hell."

"That's what *he* thinks!" Manuela called from the other room.

Bond laughed. "Don't worry, she couldn't do better than you. How long have you been together?"

"Two years. She's great, I tell you. Smarter than me too. She's a hell of an investigator. She's a field agent for the FBI. We hooked up when I did some freelance work on one of her cases. We've been on it ever since. We make a good team. She does all the dirty work while I stay at home and play with all these toys you see around the room."

"Glad to hear it. I take it you got my faxes?"

"Yes indeed, and I've already got some information for you. But drinks first!"

Bond smiled. It seemed that the most enduring element of their friendship throughout the years was their rather adolescent penchant to try to outdrink each other. He would never forget the barhopping they used to do in New York City, or Las Vegas, or in the Bahamas. Despite the fact that they came from two countries separated by a common language, Bond and Leiter understood each other. They were made of the same material. Both were men who had lived on the edge and survived to tell the tale. Leiter was also a man who, despite his handicap, could never be satisfied with retirement or inactivity.

Esmerelda settled down at Bond's feet, claiming him as her territory. Manuela brought in a tray with three shot glasses, a bottle of Jose Cuervo Gold tequila, some sliced limes, and a saltshaker. She set the tray on the small coffee table.

"What the hell?" Bond asked.

"You're in Texas now, James," Leiter said. "You're gonna do shots like the Texans do!"

"Oh for God's sake," Bond muttered, shaking his head.

"You know how, don't you?" Leiter asked, laughing. "Manuela, show him how we do it." Leiter poured tequila into one of the little glasses.

Manuela held her left hand to her face and licked the back of her hand just below where the thumb and index finger meet. She then took the saltshaker and sprinkled a little on the wet spot, so that the salt stuck to her skin. With a sly grin and her eyes glued to Bond's, she sensuously licked her hand again, this time lapping up the salt. Quickly, she took the shot glass and swallowed the entire measure of tequila in one gulp. She then grabbed a slice of lime and bit hard into it, sucking the juice and savoring it. She closed her eyes and her body shivered for a second.

"Now you try it," she said, holding out the saltshaker and pouring tequila into a glass.

"Are you serious?" Bond asked.

"You bet we are," Leiter said. "And later we'll go out for some real Tex-Mex cooking and have frozen margaritas!"

"Margaritas! You must be joking!"

Leiter laughed. "Come on, James, you'll love 'em. You know me. I was a hard liquor man like yourself . . . wouldn't touch anything but bourbon, whiskey, or vodka . . . but my Texas blood just took over once I moved back here. We all drink margaritas in Texas."

"And frozen ones are the best," Manuela added.

"Fine," Bond said with sarcasm. He went through the ritual of putting the salt on his hand, drinking the tequila, and biting the lime. It certainly wasn't the first time he had done it, but he felt a little silly. He had to admit that the tequila was good and strong, and the shock of lime added a burst of flavor which he had forgotten.

"Hell, you did that like an old pro," Leiter said, taking the bottle and pouring one for himself.

"I wasn't born yesterday," Bond said.

"Neither was I, my friend, neither was I," he said, licking the salt and going through the ritual himself.

The threesome polished off a couple more shots as they continued to talk. Bond and Leiter reminisced about past adventures together, and eventually the conversation got around to the Texan's condition.

"I got the chair a year ago, James," Leiter said. "It's been a big help. Not as much as Manuela, though."

Manuela blushed and looked down. She was feeling the effects of the alcohol and her face was glowing.

"Invacare is the company that distributes it—and this Arrow model is the top of the line in power chairs," Leiter said. "The sensitivity of the controls is amazing. Watch this."

Leiter's chair suddenly bolted forward and smashed into the coffee table, knocking over the tequila and glasses. Esmerelda yelped and jumped out of the way.

"Felix!" Manuela shouted. Luckily, she caught the bottle of tequila in midair.

Leiter, laughing hysterically, maneuvered the chair to the center of the room and spun it around three times very fast, then stopped on a dime. He popped a wheelie and landed hard, showing off the durability of the shocks, then backed up, spun around three times again, and started chasing the dog around the room. By then, everyone in the room was laughing.

Leiter stopped the chair and drove back to its earlier position. "I can go seven and a quarter miles an hour. That's fast, man. And I've also installed a few features of my own."

He popped open the right arm to reveal a cellular phone. Then he opened the left arm and had an ASP 9mm handgun in his left hand before Bond could blink.

"Very nice, Felix," Bond said. "That's the weapon I was using for a while."

"It's a great piece. You're not using it anymore?"

"No, I went back to the Walther."

"That old thing? Not much stopping power compared to some of today's stuff," Leiter said, replacing the pistol.

"I also use the new P99. It's a fine weapon."

"Yeah, I've seen that, it's a beauty. I've also got a baton under the seat." Leiter reached under the chair quickly and produced an ASP expandable police-style baton. 'They get too close, I'll just whack 'em on the head."

Bond chuckled. "As long as you're happy, Felix," he said. "That's all that matters."

"What about you? How many women in your life these days?"

"None," Bond said, lighting a cigarette. He offered one to Leiter, who took it. Manuela refused.

"You're still smoking this shit?" Leiter asked. "You always liked them gourmet cigarettes. Give me a pack of Chesterfields or Marlboros any day. I want to *feel* that tar and nicotine poisoning my body!"

"Felix, you haven't changed a bit," Bond said. "I can't tell you how happy I am to see you."

"The pleasure's all mine, James. Oh . . . while I'm thinking about it . . ." He wheeled over to a desk and grabbed a cell phone.

"Take this," he said, handing it to Bond. It was an Ericsson, light and compact. "You might need it while you're here. My number is programmed into the speed dial. Just punch it and I'll come running . . . well, rolling, I suppose. Now . . . how can we help you?"

"Have you found out anything about Charles Hutchinson?"

"Yeah. Manuela did some digging after we got your fax. Seems like the boy's gone missing for a few days. He might be on a business trip. He works for a big-deal infertility clinic in Austin, one of those sperm bank things, and we've gathered that he travels around the world on their behalf. They're called ReproCare, and apparently they do business all over Europe and the Far East. It's owned by a European pharmaceutical company called BioLinks Limited."

"What a coincidence. One of our people was killed in Athens. He had confiscated a cache of chemical weapons smuggled into the country in frozen sperm."

Leiter and Manuela looked at each other. "We didn't know that," Leiter said. "That just confirms what we've been thinking all along. There's something between that infertility clinic and an underground militant outfit that operates around here called the Suppliers. This is the case we've been working on for two years."

"The Suppliers?" Bond asked. The name rang a bell. Of course! They were one of the terrorist organizations he had spent some time reading about recently.

"They've been under investigation by the FBI for some time now," Manuela said. "They reportedly deal in arms and military weapons. Lately they've been pushing chemical weapons and maybe even biological stuff. We do know that they're not picky about who they sell to. They've been known to supply some Middle Eastern terrorist factions with stuff. They've sold to the IRA. I've come to the conclusion that their main headquarters is right here in Austin or in a neighboring town."

"Where do they get their goods?"

"This is America, my friend," Leiter said with a sigh, as if that explained everything.

"Where did Alfred Hutchinson live?" Bond asked.

"It's actually not far from here. It's in West Lake Hills too. We've taken a look at it a couple of times, and it seems deserted. Charles has an apartment in the city, over in the Hyde Park area. It's an older section of town, but a lot of college students live there. The young man apparently has a thing for the young coeds. Can't say I blame him."

Manuela slapped Leiter on the shoulder. "Just kidding, dear," he said.

"We need to locate Charles," Bond said. "We're not sure if he knows his father is dead."

"We haven't made contact with ReproCare yet. We've been observing them, but I think it's about time we did make contact. How would you like to handle that, James? The doctor in charge is a woman who frequents the restaurant where we're going later. You've always been good at bringing out the best in women. Charles Hutchinson hangs out there too, because it's one of those college nightspots that are so popular."

Manuela spoke up. "He is some kind of playboy, this Charles. He drives a fancy sports car and always has a lot of girlfriends. He came to Austin a few years ago to attend the university, but he dropped out when he discovered he could get by on his good looks, English accent, and his father's notoriety."

"What's interesting is that once his father became a roving ambassador in England, Charles would accompany him on trips around the world. He's a real jet-setter. I imagine he's got a lot of money too. A spoiled rich kid," Leiter said.

"But that's not all," Manuela added, with an inflection that hinted that the best was yet to come.

"We suspect Charles Hutchinson may be involved with the Suppliers," Leiter said as he poured another shot of tequila.

"How do you know?"

"We have a list of people who we think are members of the Suppliers. We haven't got any hard evidence yet. We're on a wait-and-observe status, but we certainly have our suspects. Charles has been seen in their company . . . at the restaurant and in other public places. And these people aren't normally who you would expect an ambassador's rich kid to associate with. They're the type of people who still flaunt Confederate flags and look like Marine recruits."

"What evidence do you have that links this sperm bank with the Suppliers?"

Leiter shook his head. "None. We haven't found it yet. We're working on hunches. The connection just might be our little friend Charles. You coming here looking for him just might be the break we've been waiting for."

"Then we've got to find him."

"Agreed. Are you hungry?"

"Starving."

"Good. Prepare to feast at one of Austin's most popular and best restaurants. It's nothing fancy, but you can't get better Mexican food."

"It's Tex-Mex, not Mexican," Manuela said huffily.

"Manuela's a purist when it comes to Mexican food," Leiter explained. "Let's go."

With that, Leiter stood up and got out of the wheelchair. Bond was surprised at the ease with which the lanky Texan did so.

"What are you staring at, limey?" Leiter asked. "I can still walk!" He limped over to a corner of the room and grabbed a mahogany walking stick. "I just use the chair around the house 'cause I'm lazy and enjoy the ride. And it's got a great built-in vibrating lower lumbar massager in it. That's the best part! Let's hit the road, Jack."

SEVEN

THE SUPPLIERS

MANUELA DROVE BOND AND LEITER BACK TO THE AREA OF BARTON SPRINGS
Road just east of Zilker Park. The sun had set and the college kids
were out in force. "Restaurant Row" was lined with several establishments specializing in trendy Texas-style foods and other cuisines,
plus a sports shop featuring Rollerblade and surfboard products. She
pulled into the crowded parking lot of Chuy's Restaurant, a gaudy
establishment that resembled the drive-ins of the late fifties and early
sixties.

Bond had changed into casual wear—navy trousers, a light blue
Sea Island cotton shirt, and a light navy jacket. He wore his Walther
PPK in a shoulder holster underneath the jacket. Manuela had
assured him that he was "casual" enough.

When they walked in the door, they were assaulted by loud pop
music and the cacophony of a large crowd. Bond felt like a fish out
of water, for many of the patrons around him were twenty years
younger or more. Here was the youth of America in all their glory,
and in all shapes, sizes, and colors. There were clean-cut yuppies
dressed in designer clothes, and shabby pseudohippies with long hair
and tie-dyed T-shirts. Some of the men were dressed like cowboys;
others wore jackets and ties. The women wore anything from business suits to T-shirts and cutoffs.

This onslaught on Bond's senses was nothing compared to the shock he got when he focused on the interior design. "Overly festive" and "much too colorful" were the descriptions that came to mind. In the front entry way was an Elvis Presley shrine behind glass. It was decorated with a bust of "the King," a toy guitar, colored wooden fish, and other odd items. The *mil pescado* bar was decorated with a thousand colored fishes hanging from the ceiling. It was all designed to evoke a hip, pop-art style with a slightly off-center sensibility. Bond realized that some people would find it amusing, but he was put off by the atmosphere. It wasn't his kind of place.

"So you really recommend this spot?" he asked.

"You'll love it," Leiter said.

"I'm not loving it so far."

"I know, it's crowded and noisy, and it looks like your worst nightmare, but the food is incredible. Look at those women. Christ. You know, Texas girls are the most beautiful in America."

"I thought that's what they said about California girls."

"No way, José. Just look around."

"He's right, James, the women are beautiful in Texas," said Manuela. "Too bad the men are all jerks."

Leiter had some pull with the manager, so they didn't have to wait the usual forty-five minutes before being shown to a table at a booth. A waiter placed a basket of hand-fried tortilla chips with fresh homemade salsa in front of them. The utensils were inside a wax-paper packet which read, "This silverware has been SANITIZED for your protection!" Leiter ordered two rounds of frozen margaritas, much to Bond's dismay. Made from silver tequila, squeezed lime juice, and triple sec, margaritas were a staple in Texas, and the frozen variety made a slushy beverage that Bond liked to call "a musical comedy drink." It was served in a salted wineglass with a lime wedge. When he tasted it, however, he was surprised by its satisfying flavor. It certainly went well with the hot salsa. Leiter and Bond were soon laughing and reminiscing about old times.

The menu featured a variety of Tex-Mex specialties. Leiter and Manuela ordered fajitas for two. They recommended that Bond try either the fajitas or the enchiladas. He chose the latter. As an appetizer, they shared a bowl of chile con queso—a hot cheese dip made from cheddar and American cheeses, red peppers, and roasted tomatoes. When the food arrived, Bond could hardly believe his eyes. It is said that everything is big in Texas, and that certainly applied to the food portions. The enormous enchiladas were hand-rolled corn tortillas stuffed with ground sirloin and topped with the restaurant's special Tex-Mex sauce—a red chile sauce with chili meat—and then with melted cheese. On the side were refried pinto beans cooked with garlic and onions. The Mexican rice was mildly flavored with onions and tomatoes.

"All right, Felix, you win," Bond said after tasting the food. "This is good."

"What'd I tell you?" Leiter said, his mouth full of chicken. He and Manuela were sharing chicken fajitas which were marinated in beer, oil, and spices, then grilled with onions, cilantro, and bell peppers.

"Do you see any of our targets?" Bond asked, once he had finished with the rich food.

"As a matter of fact, Dr. Ashley Anderson just sat down at the table over by the aquarium," Leiter said.

"She's the boss at ReproCare," explained Manuela. "She was brought into the company when it was sold to BioLinks. ReproCare was about to go bankrupt when BioLinks stepped in and took it over."

Bond glanced across the room. A tall blonde woman who looked like a model a bit past her prime was just sitting down opposite a large cowboy. She was still quite striking, probably in her late thirties, and was dressed conservatively in a business suit. The skirt was short, revealing long shapely legs in high heels. Dr. Anderson exhibited an aura of self confidence and authority. Bond might not have guessed that she was a physician, but he certainly would have placed her at the top of a large corporation.

The cowboy, on the other hand, was in his forties and looked like redneck white trash. He was bulky and overweight, but most of the mass was muscle. He was dressed in a sleeveless blue shirt, revealing large biceps. Tattoos were prominent on both arms. Sewn across the back of the shirt was a Confederate flag. He wore a large Stetson, blue jeans, and brown cowboy boots. His round baby face was distinctively marked by a scar that ran down the length of his left cheek. He was the complete antithesis of Dr. Ashley Anderson.

"Well, well," Leiter said. "This could be our first big break."

"How is that?"

"The fellow she's with is Jack Herman. He's a lowlife who's been on our list for a long time. If he's not a member of the Suppliers, then they're missing out on an excellent employment opportunity."

"What do you know about him?"

"He's been convicted of a couple of crimes, served some time, got out. He's probably on parole as we speak, but ten to one says he's breaking it. He was busted for selling drugs about fifteen years ago and spent three years in the penitentiary. His next biggie was armed robbery. He got ten years for that but only served six. I can guarantee you that he's not sitting with Dr. Anderson discussing how he can become a donor to the sperm bank."

"You thought that the clinic might have connections to the Suppliers . . ."

"I never would have thought Dr. Anderson would be involved," Manuela said. "She always seemed so respectable. But then again, she tends to enjoy the nightlife quite a bit. She's been seen with all kinds of men—and women—when you think about it, Felix. I actually wouldn't be surprised if she swings both ways."

"Yeah, and don't forget our friend Charles Hutchinson. They were an item for a little while."

"I don't know if it was sexual," Manuela said. "But yes, they were often seen in public together for a couple of months."

"If they were an item, it was sexual. She is, after all, a woman who collects sperm," Bond said in mock seriousness. Leiter burst out laughing. Manuela rolled her eyes.

"How can they sell sperm outside the U.S.? I find that very odd. Can they do that legally?" Bond asked.

"Apparently so," Leiter said. "You're right, it *is* unusual. Other sperm banks just deal their stuff domestically. ReproCare, however, is touted as having 'the finest sperm' in America. They sell it to other infertility clinics all over the world. I guess people think they're getting a good deal if it came from America."

"Tell me more about the Suppliers," Bond continued.

"They've been around about six years," Manuela said. "The FBI caught one of their leaders three years ago, before I was on the case. Fellow by the name of Bob Gibson. He was suspected of organized crime, selling illegal weapons and smuggling arms overseas, but the only thing we could convict him on was possession of illegal arms. He's still in prison. We're not sure who's in charge now, but as we told you, they operate out of Austin or somewhere nearby. They have tentacles that reach all over the country, though. There was a fellow who was driving a truck from Alaska to Canada, en route to Arkansas, who was implicated in carrying a deadly material called ricin."

"I know about ricin," Bond said.

Leiter continued the story. "When the Canadian customs agents searched the truck, they found four guns, twenty thousand rounds of ammunition, thirteen pounds of black powder, neo-Nazi literature, and three books that you can't buy at most bookstores, but that can be purchased by mail order or over the Internet. They were all about subversive warfare. A couple of the books detailed how to extract ricin from castor beans. Also in the truck was a plastic bag filled with white powder, and about eighty thousand in cash."

"What happened?"

"The man actually warned the inspectors not to open the bag of white powder. He told them it was deadly. The computer check on the guy was clear, so they let him go—without the powder. It turns out that it was enough ricin to wipe out a large suburb—it's one of the deadliest nerve poisons, and there's no antidote."

"I'm familiar with it," Bond said.

"Well, what was he doing with it? Even though it's not against the law to possess the stuff, the FBI became interested in him and he was arrested later in Arkansas on a minor traffic charge. He hung himself in his cell before any answers could be found. It turned out he lived in Austin."

Manuela picked up the story from there. "We searched his house and found a tin can filled with a pound and a half of castor beans and more recipe books for making ricin. His lawyer said his client had planned to use the ricin for peaceful purposes, such as killing coyotes that threatened his chickens or something like that. He claimed people had the right to have rat poison or coyote poison, just like they had the right to carry a handgun. The federal prosecutor in Arkansas replied to that one by saying it was tantamount to insisting you could use an atomic bomb to protect your property from a burglar. The most important thing we found in the house was literature about the Suppliers. That's what really clued everyone in on the organization. He was one of their couriers."

"It's believed that he was supplying ricin to the Minnesota Patriots, another nasty group of right-wing freaks," Leiter said.

The cowboy, Jack Herman, stood up and shook Dr. Anderson's hand. He left the restaurant without looking back. Dr. Ashley Anderson sat at her table alone.

"Well, it's now or never," Bond said. He got up and strolled over to where she was sitting.

"Hello, Dr. Anderson?" he said. She looked up at him, prepared to brush him off. Before she could say, "Get lost," the words caught in her mouth. Who was this dark handsome stranger standing before her?

"The name is Bond. James Bond. I saw that you were sitting alone," he said. "I'm visiting Austin from England for the first time, and I'd like to talk to you. May I buy you a drink?"

"Well, I don't normally accept drinks from strangers," she said in a broad Texas accent, "but since you're here all the way from England you can't be all bad. Have a seat. How did you know my name?"

Bond extended his hand. She shook it briefly; then he sat down.

Before answering her question, Bond caught the waiter and ordered two frozen margaritas.

"I'm a friend of Alfred Hutchinson. I'm looking for his son, Charles. I understand you know him."

Ashley Anderson blinked. Bond was sure that he had caught her completely off guard, but she rebounded quickly and said, "Yes, he works at my clinic."

"Do you have any idea where he is? It's imperative that I find him."

"Why?"

"Well, his father died three days ago."

The woman blinked again. Bond searched her face for signs that she might be surprised at hearing this news, but his instincts told him that she already knew.

"Oh dear," she said. "I'm sorry to hear that."

"I've been dispatched over here to find Charles, as Mr. Hutchinson's lawyers have been unable to contact him. He's wanted for funeral arrangements and other matters."

"I see," she said. "I haven't seen him in over a week. I've been in Europe for several days. In fact, I just got back today. Charles is one of our couriers. He carries sperm for our clinic—I run an infertility clinic—"

"I know," Bond said.

"Unfortunately, I really don't deal with our couriers' schedules. I think he left for Europe while I was gone. I'm not exactly certain when he's due to be back, but he's never gone more than a few days."

"Where did he go?"

"France? Or Italy. I'm not sure. I could check tomorrow at the clinic. I can find out when he'll be back too. Maybe we can get hold of him. Why don't you give us a call tomorrow? I'll give you my card."

"Could I come by the clinic instead of phoning? Maybe we can have lunch and you can tell me what all I'd have to do if I wanted to become a donor."

Ashley Anderson smiled. The English stranger worked fast.

"If you'd like to do that, come on by. I can't do lunch, though." She handed him her card. "I'm tied up until the afternoon. Can you come about two o'clock?"

"Fine, I'll be there." The drinks arrived and there was a short silence. Bond studied Ashley Anderson's face now that he was close to her. She had a wide mouth and large blue eyes. Her blond hair was shoulder-length, thin and straight. She was looking at him as if she were evaluating prize livestock. He finally broke the silence by saying, "Tell me a little about the clinic. I've always been curious about how those things work."

"Sperm banks? Well, we basically serve two functions. The first is we supply sperm to patients with infertility problems. The second is we provide the means for cancer patients to freeze and store their sperm before undergoing radiation therapy."

"So how *does* one become a donor?"

"There is a rigorous screening process," Dr. Anderson said. "We only take the best." She said that with a seductive smile. "You look like you have good genes. Are you serious about applying?"

Bond laughed. "Oh, I don't think so. I doubt that I'd meet your requirements."

After a moment's pause, she said, "I don't know if you'd meet the clinic's requirements, but you definitely meet mine."

Bond had hoped that she might be attracted to him. Throughout his long career as a secret agent, he had often gained the most ground with the enemy by sleeping with them. Seduction was a method used by spies dating all the way back to the time of Cleopatra. James Bond happened to be very good at it.

"Two o'clock, then."

The waiter brought Dr. Anderson her meal, breaking a moment of sexual tension that seemed to have generated from nowhere. She had ordered cheese enchiladas, refried beans, and guacamole.

"That looks good," Bond said.

"I love Tex-Mex," she said. "As long as there isn't any meat. I'm strictly a vegetarian."

"I'm not sure I could live that way," Bond said. "I do eat animals."

"I'm sure you do," she said suggestively.

"Well, look, I think I'll let you enjoy your meal. I'm going to rejoin my friends over there. I'll see you tomorrow afternoon, all right?"

"I look forward to it, Mr. Bond, but don't rush off on my account," she said.

"Believe me, I'd stay if I could, but I must get back. Have a lovely evening." He got up and went back to Leiter and Manuela.

"She swallowed it, hook, line, and sinker," Bond said. "Charles is in Europe on a business trip for the clinic. So she claims. We'll find out tomorrow where he is."

"Great," Leiter said. "I thought we'd go take a look at Hutchinson's house on the way back home. Or are you too tired?"

"No, no," Bond said. "I'm getting my second wind. Let's do it."

Alfred Hutchinson's American home was in a secluded wooded area off the beaten track on the western outskirts of West Lake Hills. The house wasn't visible from the road, so Manuela had to park out by the mailbox at the entrance to the drive. Bond got out of the car.

"Give me an hour," he said.

"We'll pick you up back at the top of the road," Leiter said. "Use the mobile phone if you need us before then." The car quietly sped away and left Bond standing in the dark. There were no streetlights, and the dense woods blocked all available moonlight. The cicadas were out in force, so he doubted that anyone could hear his footsteps on the dead leaves.

He slipped on the Q Branch night-vision goggles, which brought the surroundings to life. He could now make out everything clearly.

Bond crept down the path about a hundred meters and came to the broad ranch house that had a rustic, log cabin feel to it. It was dark and quiet. He paused long enough to open the heel of his right shoe and extract the alarm-sensor nullifier which Major Boothroyd had given him. He turned it on and pointed it at the house. A red light indicated that alarms were indeed set to go off if someone tried to break in. Bond pushed the green button and the red light stopped blinking.

He moved around to the side of the house, looking for a window that he might open without having to cause any damage. He found a back door. It had a standard lock—no dead bolt—so he thought he could pick it easily. He deactivated the alarms at the back of the house, then removed a wire lockpick from his belt buckle. He worked for two minutes on the lock, and the door swung open.

The house smelled damp and felt cold, as if it hadn't been occupied for a while. Bond moved through what was apparently a laundry and utility room into a kitchen. Beyond the kitchen was a dining room and a hallway to the rest of the house. He made a quick survey of the living room, then moved down the hall, past two bedrooms, and finally found what he was looking for. He took a deep breath when he saw what had happened.

Hutchinson's office had been ransacked. The room was covered in papers and opened manila filing folders. The filing cabinet drawers were left open. A large rolltop desk dominated the room, and it had been broken into as well. Its drawers were out and on the floor, the contents scattered over the gray carpet. A Gateway 2000 IBM-compatible computer sat on the desk.

Bond carefully stepped through the rubbish, looking for anything of interest. Most of the papers were teaching materials or nonsensitive diplomatic information. Nothing was left in the filing cabinets. Whether or not whoever did this had found what they were looking for was unclear. What could Alfred Hutchinson have been hiding? Was he involved with the Suppliers? Could they be behind the attacks in Greece and Cyprus? Did they kill Alfred Hutchinson?

Bond went to the computer and booted it up. After a minute, the familiar Windows 95 desktop glowed on the monitor. Bond clicked on the "My Computer" icon and perused the names of file folders on the hard drive. A personal folder called "My Data" was the only thing that wasn't a part of any normal system. Inside that folder were a couple of internal folders, one labeled "Teaching," and one labeled "Ambassador." Bond clicked on the "Ambassador" folder and found about four dozen files of various subjects. They all seemed innocuous and useless. The "Teaching" folder also contained nothing of interest.

Bond was about to perform a search for the word "Suppliers" on all the files when he heard a car door slam outside. He froze. Another door slammed. Someone was out in front.

He quickly shut down the computer. The front door of the house opened and he heard a man's voice say, "Hey, the alarm's turned off."

A woman said, "That's weird. I could have sworn I turned it back on when I left."

"You've left it off before."

"I know. Come on, let's hurry. It's in the office."

Whoever it was, they were walking down the hallway straight for Bond!

EIGHT

MANSION ON THE HILL

THERE WAS NO TIME TO LEAVE THE ROOM. BOND LEAPED ACROSS THE FLOOR to the empty filing cabinets. He gently pushed one away from the wall and squeezed in behind it. From here, he had a narrow view of the desk and the computer terminal. He held his breath and waited.

The man and woman entered the office and flicked on the lights. The shock of illumination nearly blinded Bond. He switched off the night-vision goggles but kept them on.

"Place is still a mess," the man said.

"What did you expect? The maid to clean up after us?" the woman said sarcastically. Bond thought he knew the voice. He noted that the couple knew about the condition of the room before entering.

She stepped over the debris and went to the computer on the desk. Bond could see her back now, and he wasn't surprised to see the business suit and long blond hair. Dr. Ashley Anderson booted up the computer and then sat down in the office chair on wheels. The man came into view and stood at her side, looking at the monitor. It was the cowboy, Jack Herman.

"How do you know how to find it on that thing?" Herman asked.

"Haven't you ever used a computer, Jack?" she asked. "You can ask it to find any file that's on the hard drive."

"Is it there?"

"Hold your horses. I'm looking."

The cowboy shrugged and moved away from the desk. He started kicking some of the debris. Bond was afraid he might wander over to his side of the room. If he looked too closely, he would see Bond hiding behind the filing cabinet. Bond leaned back against the wall, now unable to see anything in the office. He listened and waited. The cowboy's boots were shuffling the papers on the floor. The sound was coming closer. He was just feet away from Bond.

"Would you stop that noise?" Dr. Anderson commanded. "It's annoying."

"Sorry," the cowboy said, and sauntered back to the desk. "I just don't understand why we're doing this. Who is this guy, anyway? What does he have to do with the Suppliers?"

"Don't worry about it and just do what you're told, Jack."

The cowboy grunted. "Found it yet?"

"Hell, no," she said. "It's not here. The file must have been deleted. Listen, I've got to get to the clinic. Remember the man I introduced you to the other day?"

"You mean that guy from Greece?"

"Yes. He's out at the mansion. I need you to go there and let him know we couldn't find the file. Would you do that?"

"I was going over there anyway. Shut that thing down and let's go," Herman said.

She turned off the computer; then they switched off the lights and left the room.

"Reactivate that alarm, would you?" Dr. Anderson said.

Bond waited a moment, until he heard their footsteps at the front door. He slipped out from behind the cabinet and reactivated his goggles. He quickly moved to the back of the house, used the sensor nullifier on the alarm once again, and went out of the door he had come in by. As quietly as possible, he moved over the crackling dead leaves to the front of the house.

Dr. Ashley Anderson was getting into a pink Porsche. The cowboy was inside a beat-up Ford F-150 pickup truck. Tied down in the back of the truck was a Kawasaki Enduro motorcycle. Dr. Anderson drove off down the path out of the property. The cowboy started the pickup.

It was now or never. Keeping low, Bond ran and climbed onto the back of the pickup truck just as it was leaving. He slipped over the tailgate and flattened himself on the bed of the truck. The cowboy drove out onto the street and followed the Porsche. Bond was unable to watch where the track was going because he had to stay down. He removed the goggles and tightened the strap so that they clung to his neck. Luckily the cowboy was alone in the cab. Bond could see a shotgun propped up on a rack behind him.

The two vehicles separated when they reached Bee Caves Road. The Porsche turned left and headed toward Austin. The pickup turned right and went west out toward the hills. It eventually reached Loop 360, also known as the Capital of Texas Highway, and turned right.

While officially still in Travis County, this was the country. A half moon shone through a dark cloudy sky, casting a soft glow on the rolling hills. Most of the autumn leaves had fallen, giving the trees a skeletal, ghostly appearance. The wide road curved up and around the cliffs, every now and then passing side roads leading into the darkness. After nearly twelve minutes, the track turned off the highway and headed west again on Farm Road 2222, a somewhat treacherous highway that led to Lake Travis. The cowboy drove recklessly, taking the curves too sharply. All Bond could see, though, was the sheer cliff towering above him on one side of the truck, and the night sky on the other.

Soon the track turned left onto City Park Road, an uphill winding two-lane road. Raising himself slightly, he could see the vast city lights spread out to the east of the truck. He would have liked to be able to remember the route they had taken, but he was a stranger and totally lost.

The truck finally stopped on a gravel road that sliced through some dense trees. Bond pressed himself against the side of the truck bed, hoping that the cowboy wouldn't look in the back when he got out of the vehicle. The door opened and Bond heard the boots stomp down onto the gravel. The door slammed shut, and the footsteps moved away from the truck.

Bond peered over the edge of the truck bed and saw a mansion designed to look like an ancient Greek temple. The cowboy was walking toward an archway at the front of the house. Old-fashioned gas pole lamps were positioned around the mansion, and there were even caryatids sculpted along the perimeter of the roof, matching those that still remained on the Erechtheion of the Acropolis in Athens. Full-size statues of Greek gods and heroes were scattered around the front lawn. The place was decidedly sinister, and it was obvious that this was its owner's intention.

As soon as Jack Herman was out of sight, Bond leaped over the tailgate and hugged the back end of the truck. After making sure no one was outside the house, he ran to the side of the building. The front of the house was well lit, but luckily the sides were not. He crept up to a large window and looked inside.

The cowboy was greeting a large, swarthy man dressed in a black turtleneck cotton shirt and black trousers. He had black curly hair, a black beard and mustache, and black eyebrows. The size of the man was extraordinary. Jack Herman was a big guy with plenty of muscle, but the swarthy man was even larger—obviously a bodybuilder with the biceps to prove it. He probably weighed 250 pounds or more, but there wasn't an ounce of fat on his body. He had no neck, just a large block of a head sitting on a wall of shoulders.

Another man dressed as a cowboy appeared next to the body-builder and shook hands with Jack Herman. He was tall and blond, another roughneck type who seemed to be part of the same team as Herman. The bodybuilder, in contrast, looked out of place with his swarthy Mediterranean features. Bond recalled Jack Herman saying that the man was Greek.

The three figures moved from the entry hall into a living room which matched the ancient Greek design theme of the house. The floor was made of marble. The furniture was a chic wooden fake antique, and a collection of swords, shields, and maces adorned the stone walls. Bond moved along the side of the house to the next window and looked in. The three men joined another man sitting in an armchair. He was much younger, probably in his twenties. He was a good-looking fellow with brown hair and blue eyes, dressed sharply in a tweed jacket and dark trousers. Bond recognized him from the file photos. He was Charles Hutchinson.

Bond couldn't hear what the men were saying, but inside the room Jack Herman was shaking his head at the European. Bond figured that the cowboy was breaking the bad news that they didn't find whatever it was Ashley Anderson was looking for on Alfred Hutchinson's computer. Charles Hutchinson stood up, an expression of uncertainty and fear on his face. The swarthy bodybuilder turned and gave Charles a glare that Greeks would have called "the evil eye." Charles was distressed, and he attempted to say something. The Greek backhanded Charles, who fell to the floor. The two cowboys just stood there and grinned. The bodybuilder dismissed them and they left the room.

After a moment, Charles pulled himself up off the floor and rubbed his chin in humiliation. He sat on the wooden armchair he had been in before and stared straight ahead. The bodybuilder said something to him, then walked out of the room.

Bond could hear the two cowboys leave by the front door. He crouched down into the shadows and watched as the two men proceeded to open the tailgate and remove the Kawasaki from its cradle. After five agonizing minutes, the men got the cycle out of the truck and wheeled it onto the gravel driveway in front of the house, out of Bond's line of sight. He stood up again and looked in the window. Charles was still sitting there, looking glum.

Bond moved down to the next window in line. The bodybuilder was sitting at a desk, typing on a computer terminal with one finger. His hands were so large that his fingers were easily the size of cigars.

The room was a small office with some modern furnishings. Bond was particularly struck by the strange flag on the wall above the desk. It was roughly four feet square and it pictured an equilateral triangle made of ten red dots on a black background. There were four dots along the bottom, then three, with two on top of those, then one— much like the setup of bowling pins seen from above. A large mirror was on the opposite wall, and Bond was fortunately at just the right angle so that he could see the bodybuilder's back and the computer monitor in the mirror. It was too far away to read what was on the screen, but Bond could glean that the man was on-line, talking "live" with someone over the Internet. He knew this because lines of text appeared at the bottom of the screen, and then the bodybuilder would type with one finger and hit the return key. New lines of text would appear, followed by another set of lines.

The sound of one of the cowboys kick-starting the motorcycle came from the front of the house. One of them yelled, "Yee-ha!" The machine sat there idling, and every now and then the engine would rev up. It was quite loud.

It wasn't half as loud as the sudden dog bark that Bond heard a few yards away from him. The noise had attracted the attention of a Doberman that had been at the back of the house. She was full-grown, black as coal, and had fierce eyes that practically glowed in the dark. She growled and barked again at Bond, ready to pounce if he so much as twitched.

He knew he couldn't wait for her barking to bring out the men, so he braced himself for the attack and faced the dog. She leaped at him, teeth bared. Bond deftly rolled onto his back as the dog made contact and at the same time he grabbed her neck. In a maneuver that could only be equaled by circus acrobats and other Double-O agents, Bond used the dog's forward momentum to pull her over his body and into the glass window. The Doberman shattered the pane, howling. That set off the alarms.

Without hesitation, Bond got to his feet and ran to the front of the house. The dog would certainly jump back through the window in pursuit. The two cowboys were frozen in stunned amazement at the sudden flurry of activity. Jack Herman was standing by the motorcycle, and the blond fellow was sitting on it. Bond made a running jump and kicked Jack Herman in the face, knocking him to the ground. He then swung his leg around and caught the other man on the chest, knocking him off the Kawasaki. Bond caught the cycle before it fell on its side, and jumped on. He revved it up and took off down the gravel path.

"Hey!" he heard one of the cowboys shout, followed by the barking of the Doberman, hot in pursuit.

The Kawasaki KDX200 is a bike specifically made for heavy-duty off-road riding. Its single-cylinder two-stroke motor is fast and tractable. Ideal for heading into rough country, its dogleg control levers are covered with plastic handguards. Bond was extremely lucky that it had been made "available" to him!

He sped out of the gravel drive and onto City Park Road. In no time he was doing seventy miles per hour, which was particularly precarious on the winding, two-lane road. He had left the dog in the dust, but the Ford pickup was not far behind. With one hand, Bond slipped on the night-vision goggles again and cut off the lights on the bike. He then increased his speed to eighty and leaned into the motorcycle. Becoming one with the machine, he cut through the air and concentrated on curves in the road. There were very few oncoming vehicles.

The truck was gaining. A shotgun blast rang out behind him, but from too far back for the shot to be effective.

Bond felt his heart stop as he rounded a blind curve to see two oncoming cars—one in his lane! Its driver had been foolishly attempting to pass the other car and was two seconds away from colliding with the motorcycle!

Bond swerved to the right and the Kawasaki shot off the road into the woods. The terrain went into a dangerous incline, and 007 held on for dear life as the cycle plummeted down—remarkably, staying upright on its wheels. He dodged trees the best he could, but a branch hit him in the face and shoulder, nearly knocking him off the vehicle. The incline got worse and Bond realized that at any moment the cycle would lose its traction and they would begin to fall down what was to become a sheer cliff. He attempted to brake, but that only caused the Kawasaki to skid. Gravity took over, and the motorcycle fell sideways down the side of the mountain. Bond jumped and tried to grab hold of a tree, but he missed. He started rolling down the side of the cliff behind the cycle, unable to stop. He fell hard against a large rock, getting the breath knocked out of him, but he continued to plummet downward.

The incline ended abruptly at a sharp cliff edge. The Kawasaki sailed over the cliff into the air. Bond rolled and exerted a super-human effort to grasp a tree branch that extended out over the cliff. He hung there, gasping for air.

Twenty-five feet below him was Farm Road 2222. He was hanging over the highway. The cycle had crashed onto the road and lay there beneath him. He could probably drop down and roll without injuring himself any more than he already had. For the moment, he held on to the tree branch and caught his breath. His face and shoulder were in great pain, and his right side was injured. He was afraid he might have broken a rib.

Then the pickup truck came barreling down the road below him. The driver didn't see the wreckage of the Kawasaki in time. He plowed into it, causing the pickup to swerve into the lane directly beneath Bond; 007 let go of the branch and dropped into the bed of the truck. The Ford kept going and got back into its lane. The pas-senger, the blond cowboy, had a pistol of some kind. He leaned out of the window and shot back at Bond, but he was in an awkward position and couldn't hold the gun steady. Bond removed his Walther PPK from its holster and blasted a hole in the back windshield of the truck. The blond cowboy caught the slug in the face.

Bond moved up to the driver's side of the truck, stuck his arm through the broken windshield, and put the Walther to Jack Herman's head.

"Stop the bloody truck," he commanded.

Herman nodded, but kept driving.

"I said stop it, or I'll make you stop it," Bond said.

There was traffic behind the truck, and more was beginning to appear in the oncoming lane.

"I can't stop it here! Let me pull over up ahead where there's an extra lane," the cowboy pleaded.

"Just make sure you do."

Instead of slowing down, though, Jack Herman floored the pedal and swerved the truck into the slow-traffic lane. To the right of the truck was a serious cliff—it made the one Bond tumbled down seem like a sand dune. Christ! Bond thought. The bastard intended to kill them both rather than be arrested!

Bond pulled his arm out of the broken windshield and jumped over the side of the truck just as the Ford careened over the guardrail. He hit the pavement hard and rolled with the impact. The pickup seemed to sail through the air in slow motion. He heard Jack Herman scream, and then the truck disappeared from view. Bond heard the impact a second later as the truck smashed into the side of the cliff and exploded.

He pulled himself off the road and limped to the side. The truck was aflame and was continuing to roll down the cliff into the darkness below.

Bond examined his body. His forehead and the left side of his face were scraped badly and bleeding. His shoulder hurt like hell, but nothing seemed out of joint. His right side was the worst. He had experienced broken ribs before, and this sensation was aggravatingly similar. It was a miracle he could walk away from what had just happened.

Bond found his Walther lying nearby and holstered it. He reached into his pocket and found that Leiter's cell phone was smashed. Cars were zooming past him, unaware of the fireball at the base of the cliff to their right. Bond limped along the road, heading east back toward town. No one stopped to see if he needed help, and he wasn't about to hitchhike.

Two hours later, Bond saw a small bar called the Watering Hole off the road to the right. A sign on the door warned, "Don't Mess with Texas." He stumbled inside and surveyed the place. A saloon would have been a more appropriate description, as it was full of an odd mixture of cowboys and long-haired biker types. The jukebox was blaring one of George Jones's more famous beer-drinking songs at an extraordinary volume. Everyone stopped what they were doing and looked at Bond. A pool player in the middle of a shot scratched the table as he looked up and saw the battered figure in the doorway.

Bond ignored them all and went straight to the bar.

"Whiskey," he ordered. "A double."

The bartender didn't say a word and poured him two glasses of Johnny Walker. "Have a double double, mister. What the hell happened to you?"

"Nothing much," he replied. "Just fell off a cliff."

Bond drank one glass quickly and felt the warmth invigorate him. He closed his eyes tightly, then coughed. Considering that he was still suffering from jet lag and fighting a cold, it was a wonder that the ordeal he had just been through didn't kill him. He was exhausted.

He drank the other glass of whiskey, then asked to use a phone. The bartender pointed him to the pay phone, then said, "Nah, forget it. Here, use mine." He placed a phone on the bar and let Bond call Felix Leiter for free.

The old adage that Texans were genuinely friendly people was apparently true. Most of them, anyway.

NINE

THE SPERM BANK

THE MYSTERIOUS MALADY THAT STRUCK LOS ANGELES HAD ATTRACTED THE attention of the Centers for Disease Control in Atlanta. A special investigative team arrived to find that fifty-two people had died from what was being called "Williams's disease," named after the man who had the first known case. Health officials in the city were opposed to making a public announcement for fear of creating a panic. The team from Atlanta began the tedious task of locating anyone who may have been in contact with the victims in the last twenty-four hours of their lives. At this point, no one could discern where the disease came from or how it worked. Preliminary tests revealed that the virus died shortly after its host did, leaving biochemists without a sample to study.

In Tokyo, things were worse. The death toll had risen to seventy. In twenty-four hours, the disease would surface in New York City and London, leaving in its wake a total of twelve people dead in one day.

Bond slept late to allow his body to recover from the previous evening's exertions. Manuela had examined him thoroughly—she turned out to be a qualified registered nurse as well as a damned good investigator—and had determined there were no broken ribs. Bond had one hell of a bruise, though, and his side was quite tender.

His forehead and cheek had been scraped, but that would heal quickly. The left shoulder had been knocked out of joint, but wasn't completely dislocated. Manuela performed a bit of chiropractic therapy and got it back in place.

Since he was unable to say exactly where he had been the night before, after lunch Manuela and Leiter took Bond back over Farm Road 2222, past the bar where they had picked him up. He recognized the City Park Road turnoff, so it was only a small matter of time before they found the mansion in the hills. Leiter said he'd work on finding out who lived there, while 007 kept his two o'clock appointment at ReproCare. Bond's revelation of seeing Charles Hutchinson in the house was most interesting. Manuela had gone to Hutchinson's apartment in the Hyde Park area and learned from the manager that the young man had vacated it. The manager was very angry, because Hutchinson had broken a lease and taken off without a month's notice. Movers had taken away his things yesterday. The manager had not seen Charles Hutchinson personally, but received word of his departure from a lawyer. Manuela impressed the manager with her FBI credentials and gained access to the empty apartment, and also saw the letter from the lawyer. An hour later, she had confirmed that the lawyer didn't exist.

Either Charles Hutchinson was in with the bad guys or he was a prisoner being held at the mansion against his will.

Before they took Bond into town, Leiter gave him another cell phone. "Let's not break this one, it's the last spare I've got," he said.

"You're beginning to sound like an armorer I know in London," Bond replied.

ReproCare was located on Thirty-eighth Street in an office park near the large medical center that serviced much of north central Austin. A glass door carried the inscription "ReproCare—Infertility Therapy, CryoCenter."

Manuela and Leiter dropped Bond off and he went inside. The waiting room was small but typical of a doctor's office. An attractive young nurse with a Dictaphone headset in her ears was typing inside the reception office. She looked up at Bond and smiled broadly.

"May I help you?" she asked in a thick Texas accent.

"Uhm, yes, I have a two o'clock appointment with Dr. Anderson? The name is Bond. James Bond."

The nurse consulted her book. "Oh yeah, I have a note here. She's been detained for a while. But she wanted you to fill out all these forms, and when you're done someone'll take you back to a room for your first specimen."

"My first specimen?"

"You're here as a donor applicant, aren't you?" She smiled knowingly, quite used to having to deal with men who were embarrassed by what they had come to do.

It wasn't exactly what Bond had in mind, but he went along with it. "Right."

"Read the instructions on the forms and that'll explain what'll happen today. The doctor will talk to you beforehand, so don't worry."

Bond took the clipboard from the nurse and sat down in the waiting room. The forms numbered about ten pages, front and back. The cover sheet explained that donors needed to be over the age of eighteen and must go through an intensive screening procedure that included completion of a medical and genetic history questionnaire, a personal interview by the laboratory supervisor and complete semen analysis, a physical examination by a physician and testing for major infectious diseases. The first step to being accepted as a donor was to complete the questionnaire. If the applicant met the requirement of sexual abstinence for at least forty-eight hours prior to visiting the clinic, a first semen specimen would be taken after a brief interview. All information about the donors was kept completely confidential.

The questionnaire was very thorough. It asked about the applicant's medical and ethnic history. There were questions about personal interests and hobbies. Lifestyle and behavioral questions took up a large portion of the document. There were queries on nearly every disease known to man, sexual preferences, current and past medications and surgeries. Bond figured that the clinic had extremely high standards and that nearly everything in the questionnaire must be answered satisfactorily. He chuckled as he pondered that it was probably more difficult to be accepted as a semen donor than it was to become an agent with SIS.

It took him nearly an hour to fill out the forms. He falsified much of the information, but for his own amusement he attempted to remember all of the various injuries and hospitalizations he had sustained during his illustrious career. He handed the forms back to the nurse, who told him to have a seat and that someone would be with him in a moment. Ten minutes later, a man wearing a white lab coat opened the door to the back and said, "Mr. Bond?"

Bond stood up. The man held out his hand. "Hi, I'm Dr. Tom Zielinski." They shook hands. "Come on back," he said.

They went into a small office. "Have a seat," Dr. Zielinski said.

"Where's Dr. Anderson?" Bond asked. "I think I was supposed to see her."

"She had an emergency or something, I'm not quite sure. Don't worry, we'll take good care of you." Dr. Zielinski was of medium build and looked to be in his late thirties.

Bond really didn't want to go through with this. He wanted to talk to Ashley Anderson and see what he could get out of her, but perhaps if he played along with these people he could find a way to have a look around.

"I've gone over your questionnaire briefly, Mr. Bond," the doctor said. "We'll have to look at it more thoroughly, of course, but on first glance it looks very good. It says here your father was Scottish and your mother was Swiss?"

"That's right."

"You wrote that their deaths were accidental. Can you be more specific?"

"It was a mountain-climbing accident. They died together."

"I see. I'm sorry," the doctor said with no emotion. He scribbled on the form. "How old were you at the time?"

"Eleven. I went to live with an aunt. She was very doting."

"I see. I'm sorry." He turned the pages and landed on the hospitalizations section. His eyes grew wide. "Well, you've sure been hospitalized a lot! This is pretty remarkable. What kind of work did you say you were in?" He looked back on the front page. "Oh, here it is. Civil servant?"

"That's right."

"What's a civil servant?"

"I worked for the British government."

"I see." He added, "I'm sorry," out of habit, then cleared his throat, embarrassed. "And you'll be in this country for a while?"

"I'm now a permanent resident," Bond lied.

Zielinski nodded, still staring at the form. "This *is* quite a medical history. Broken finger . . . second-degree burns . . . barracuda bite? . . . hospitalization for nerve poisoning . . . bullet wounds . . . you have a pin in your ankle . . . and severe depression?"

"That was due to my wife dying."

"I see. I'm sorry." He continued scanning the document. "Knife wounds . . . concussion . . . electric burns . . . What's this here about trauma to your testicles?"

"That happened a long time ago."

"What was it?"

Bond shifted uncomfortably. "I was kicked in a fight," he lied again. The memory of Le Chiffre's carpet beater was all too vivid.

"I see. I'm sorry," the doctor said. "But you've never had any problems with ejaculation since then?"

Bond smiled wryly. "None."

The doctor scribbled something on the form and then explained that the specimen taken today would be analyzed for the number and motility of sperm cells and other qualities. If Bond passed the first test he would come in for a complete physical, blood work, and another specimen. He then asked Bond why he wanted to become a semen donor. Bond sincerely told the doctor that he would gain satisfaction if he could provide help to a couple who couldn't have a child on their own.

Satisfied with his patient, Dr. Zielinski led Bond down a hall and through a door to another section of the building. There were four closed doors in the hallway, each with a sliding sign that could be set to "Occupied" or "Vacant." Dr. Zielinski opened one and led Bond into a small room that looked more like a bedroom than an examination room. There was a vinyl couch, a table, a sink, a television, and a VCR. On top of the table were empty specimen containers, a box of tissues, and a towel. There were some X-rated videotapes on the VCR and a few men's magazines in a rack by the table. There were no windows, and the door locked from the inside. A phone was attached to the wall.

The doctor said, "You'll need to wash your hands with soap and water before beginning. Please collect a specimen without using lubricants or condoms. They're toxic to sperm. Label the specimen with your name, the time, and hours of abstinence since your last ejaculation. Take your time. You can lock the door for privacy. When you're done, just put the specimen in this incubator." He pointed to a small white machine on the table. "It'll keep the temperature of the sperm stable until it's ready to process. If you need anything, just dial 'O' on the phone. Okay?"

"Fine," Bond said.

The doctor shook his hand and said, "I probably won't see you again today. I have to go freeze some sperm."

"I see," said Bond. As soon as the doctor shut the door and left him alone, Bond added, "I'm sorry."

He waited five minutes, then opened the door. There was no one in the hall. Bond slipped out of the room and went farther down the hallway to a door marked "Personnel Only." He opened it quietly and glanced inside. It was another hallway with offices, and it was empty. He carefully closed the door behind him and walked purposefully down the hall. Some of the office doors were open. Unnoticed, he saw doctors and technicians busy with paperwork or microscopes. At the end of the hall was a large metal door. A keycard was needed to gain access. Bond presumed it was where they kept the tanks that stored the frozen sperm. He wanted to know if ReproCare kept anything else in there as well.

The outer door opened and he heard voices. Bond ducked into the nearest office and flattened himself against the wall. He closed the door slowly but kept it ajar. As the voices approached his end of the hall, he recognized Ashley Anderson's Texas accent.

"Your plane gets into Heathrow at eight forty-five tomorrow

morning," she was saying. "Your connection leaves at noon, so you've got a bit of time."

Dr. Anderson and her male companion stopped just outside the office. Through the crack of the open door, Bond could see her use a keycard to open the unmarked metal door. She replaced the keycard in her lab coat pocket, and then held the door open for her companion, Charles Hutchinson. She followed him inside the inner sanctum and closed the door.

Bond emerged from the office and listened at the metal door. It was too thick for him to hear anything. He had to find a keycard and break into the clinic later after hours.

He made his way out of the "Personnel Only" area and back to the examination room where Dr. Zielinski had left him. Ashley Anderson and Charles Hutchinson would have to come back this way, unless there was another exit from the lab. He kept the door slightly ajar and waited.

Sure enough, in ten minutes Dr. Anderson and Hutchinson came down the hall. Through the ajar door, Bond saw that Hutchinson was carrying a metal briefcase.

Dr. Anderson was saying, ". . . and under no circumstances should you open the vials. I'll see you later. Have a good flight."

Bond heard Hutchinson go out into the waiting room; then he made his move. He quickly removed his jacket, shoulder holster, and gun, and hid them in a drawer. Next he grabbed an empty specimen container and held the door to his room wide open. He stood in the doorway and waited for Ashley Anderson to come back down the hall.

When she saw him, she smiled and said, "Well, hello there. How are you? Jesus, what happened to your face?"

Bond said, "I had an accident last night. It's nothing, really."

"I hope so. Sorry I wasn't available earlier—I had to tend to something. Did you fill out all your forms?"

"Yes, and now I'm ready to deliver a specimen." Bond held up the empty container.

"I see that. Well, don't let me stop you," she said with a grin.

Ashley Anderson was one of those women James Bond was very

familiar with. He instinctively knew that certain members of the opposite sex immediately found him desirable. Bond was quite aware of the sexual impact he had on them, and he had always been able to use that gift to his advantage.

"As a matter of fact, I was, uhm, having a little difficulty getting in the mood. I mean, it's all so . . . clinical here, isn't it?" he said, flirting with her.

Her eyebrow went up.

"I thought perhaps you could join me and tell me a little more about your company . . . or something." He gestured with his hand for her to enter.

Ashley Anderson was certainly tempted. She looked up and down the hall, then came into the room with Bond. She closed the door and locked it.

"All right, Mr. Bond, what is it you need help with?"

Bond moved closer to her, backing the woman up against the door.

"I lied to you and to that doctor who interviewed me," he said softly, looking into her blue eyes and examining her mouth. He gently ran his fingers through her blond hair.

"Oh yeah?" she whispered.

"Yeah," Bond said, mimicking her accent. "I'm not interested in being a semen donor. At least not this way." He held up the empty container and smoothly tossed it across the room into the sink.

"I could get into a lot of trouble doing this. What's your game, Mr. Bond?" she asked, breathlessly.

"You're my game," he said as he moved in for the kiss. Their mouths met, and she wrapped her arms around his neck. They kissed passionately, and he felt her tongue explore the inside of his mouth. She started breathing very heavily and running her hands over his strong shoulders and back.

"Well, I'm sorry," she said in between kisses, "you committed yourself . . . to the program . . . I'm obligated to make sure that you're a . . . desirable donor."

Bond removed her lab coat and slowly unzipped her dress at the back. Underneath she wore a black lace bra and panties, and a black garter belt. He picked her up and carried her to the couch as she wrapped her legs around his waist. Ashley became enthusiastic very quickly, even breaking off one of the buttons on his shirt in her attempt to remove it. Her feline qualities extended to the love-making, for she spent most of the time clawing Bond's back with her fingernails and moaning with delight.

Afterwards, as they lay naked on the vinyl couch, their clothes scattered around the room, Dr. Ashley Anderson was satisfied that James Bond was indeed a desirable donor.

"How did you get into this business?" he asked her.

"I was always interested in reproductive issues. I thought I would be a gynecologist, but then I became more interested in infertility. That led to a job with a European pharmaceutical company called BioLinks Limited. When they bought out ReproCare a year ago, BioLinks put me in charge. So it's all mine now."

"Where is BioLinks based?"

"Athens. The president is a brilliant physicist by the name of Melina Papas."

"And you sell the sperm all over the country?"

"All over the world, actually," she said, sitting up. "We're one of the leading distributors, especially in Europe and the Middle East."

"How do you keep it alive?"

"In liquid nitrogen. We have some freezing machines in our lab. They're computerized, and they use liquid nitrogen vapor to do the work. It takes about two hours to freeze the sperm. We lower its temperature to minus eighty degrees centigrade, then store it in tanks at minus a hundred and ninety-six degrees centigrade. The samples are stored in vials in separate boxes, and then kept in our special fifty-five-gallon drum tanks. When we transport them, we have special metal briefcases that keep them frozen for several days."

"Fascinating."

"Sure," she said, laughing. "I find you fascinating too, Mr. Bond. How did you get that horrible bruise on your side? What happened to you last night?"

"I fell off one of those spectacular hills you've got here in central Texas," he said.

"I'll bet you did," she said, standing up. Bond admired her long legs and muscular physique. For a doctor who spent her time indoors, she was remarkably well built. She had firm, tight buttocks and a thin waist. "I've got to get back to work."

Bond stood up and helped her gather her things. He picked up her white lab coat and discreetly reached into the pocket and palmed the keycard. When her back was to him, he dropped the card on his own pile of clothes and used his foot to move his shirt over it. He then helped the doctor get dressed. He was still naked when she turned and kissed him again.

"I hope that you'll consider making some more specimen donations," she said.

"I might," he said. "How about dinner tonight first?"

"All right."

"Want to meet at that restaurant?"

"Chuy's? Sure, why not. I can eat Tex-Mex twice in a row. What time?"

"When do you leave here?"

"I think I can get out at five today. The clinic normally closes at five-thirty. I could meet you there at six."

"Six o'clock then. Oh, one other thing. The primary reason I came here today was for Charles Hutchinson. Did you manage to find out where he was and when he'll return?"

Ashley Anderson nonchalantly said, "Yeah, he's been in Italy. He's not scheduled to be back until next week, but we got a message to him. He's going to London today, I believe. I hope that doesn't mean you'll be leaving Austin?"

"We'll have that date first," Bond said.

She kissed him again and left the room. Now the only trick was to find a way to get back in the building after everyone left at five-thirty.

He got dressed quickly, retrieved his gun, and stuck the keycard in his pocket. He left the room and went out into the reception area. The nurse there smiled at him knowingly, quietly acknowledging the little secret she shared with all the men who visited the clinic.

Bond went outside. It was nearly four-thirty. He walked a block to get out of sight of the clinic, then called Leiter on the mobile.

"Felix, you need to get on to Charles Hutchinson right away. He's probably at the airport as we speak. He's headed for Heathrow with a metal briefcase. Probably somewhere in Europe after a layover. I have reason to believe there's something quite deadly in the briefcase, and it's not just someone's sperm."

"I'll get right on it. So I take it your visit to the clinic was profitable?"

"It was one of the more pleasant doctor's appointments I've ever had. I'm going to try and sneak back in when they close. There are some things I think I need to see. I need you to do one more thing. Can you or Manuela phone ReproCare at exactly five twenty-five? Here's what I want you to do." Bond took a minute explaining his scheme.

"Okay," Leiter said. "You have my number. We'll alert the authorities at the airport now."

After they hung up, Bond went into a small coffee shop to wait.

TEN

OFFENSIVE ACTION

FIVE O'CLOCK CAME, AND ASHLEY ANDERSON LEFT REPROCARE, CROSSED Thirty-eighth Street to a parking lot, got into her pink Porsche, and drove away. Bond waited awhile longer, until five twenty-five. He had watched many of the employees already leave the building.

He sprinted across the street to the clinic and went inside. The nurse behind the partition was packing her purse and putting on a light jacket.

"Hello," he said. "I think I left something in the room I was in earlier today. May I look?"

The phone rang and the nurse answered it. She listened to Leiter's voice and frowned. Bond mimed his question once again and the nurse nodded and waved him through. He went inside and quietly made his way to the examination rooms. Instead of going into the room he had been in earlier, he stepped into a different one, left the door open, and stood behind it.

Leiter's distraction had provided the right amount of confusion to the end of a busy day. The Texan had asked about a nonexistent account and the nurse had to look it up on the computer. By the time she had confirmed to the caller that no such account existed, it was five thirty-one. She hung up the phone, gathered her things, and looked in the hallway. She wandered down to the examination rooms and saw that they were all open and empty. The nurse shrugged, assuming that Bond had got what he had left behind and slipped out the front door while she was looking in the files. She turned and left the building, locking the front door behind her.

Bond waited a couple more minutes before emerging from his hiding place. The building was completely quiet. He was fairly sure that no one was around. He stuck his head through the "Personnel Only" door to verify he was alone, then went into the hallway and down to the unmarked metal door. He slipped Ashley Anderson's key-card in the slot and heard a click. He opened the door and went inside.

It was a large laboratory with several workstations. Sixteen Taylor Wharton 17K-Series Cryostorage tanks sat along two walls. They resembled top-loading washing machines. Complete with solid-state automatic controls, each refrigerator was equipped with an adjustable low-level alarm with visual and audible signals, as well as a delayed remote alarm signal. If Bond tried to open any of the tanks, someone's pager would go off.

What was most curious were the shielded workstations. Two glass enclosed booths contained mechanical arms and hands, which a technician would normally operate to handle volatile or dangerous chemicals. Why would there be a need for such protection in a sperm bank?

To Bond's amazement, another door led into a small greenhouse. The ceiling allowed the sun to shine directly into the place. Several plants were growing in trays on two tables. He took a close look at the plants and he was sure that they had nothing to do with infertility or the storage of sperm. The three plants he recognized were the castor bean plant, a jequirity bean vine, and hemlock. All three of them could produce toxic substances.

Bond went back into the lab and found a PC displaying a colorful screen saver. He moved the mouse, and the desktop appeared on the monitor. It was an in-house system, but the menu was quite clear. Bond selected a folder marked "Shipping" and opened it. There were hundreds of files; Bond opened the most recent one. A list appeared that detailed sperm shipments since the beginning of the month.

DATE	CLIENT	QUANTITY	COURIER
11/2	Family Planning Inc. New York, NY	1 s/1 b	C.H.
11/4	Reproductive Systems Los Angeles, CA	1 s/1 b	C.H.
11/6	The Family Group London, UK	1 s/1 b	C.H.
11/7	Rt. 3, Box 2 Bastrop, TX	1 b	C.H.
11/8	BioLinks Ltd. Athens, Greece	1 case	C.H.

Bond scanned the log for other shipments with those initials. Other couriers' initials had made deliveries in other parts of the world. The Bastrop, Texas, address was odd. It didn't sound like a medical clinic. Bond memorized the Bastrop address and shut down the program.

He restored the computer to the way he found it, then studied the controls on one of the refrigerated storage tanks. He wondered if the handy alarm-nullifier that Major Boothroyd gave him would be effective on the tanks. It was worth a try. He opened the heel of his right shoe and extracted the device. He aimed it at one of the tanks, and the red indicator light switched from "Alarm Set" to "Alarm Off." Bond made a mental note to offer to take Major Boothroyd to lunch when he was back in London.

He opened the tank and was hit by a blast of cold air. Bond looked around the lab quickly and found some heavy insulated gloves. After his hands were protected, he took a look at the racks inside the tanks. There were several boxes filled with vials on the racks. Bond made a rough guess that there were anywhere from five to seven thousand vials of substance in one tank. He picked up a couple of vials and examined them. They were labeled with the donor number, date of specimen, and other pertinent information. It looked like sperm.

Bond tried three more tanks before he found one that didn't contain sperm. He knew he had hit the jackpot when he opened the tank and saw that the boxes on the racks were labeled "Danger! Use caution when handling!"

He took out one box and examined the vials inside. Some were marked "cyanogen chloride" and others were labeled "hydrocyanic acid." Powerful stuff. Another box contained vials marked as "soman" and "abrin," both deadly materials. A third box contained "ricin," "rabun," and "sarin." Finally, a fourth box was filled with vials of "botulin." Not only were they dealing with toxic chemicals, but the bastards were playing with biological warfare materials.

"Don't drop that," an all-too-familiar voice behind him said.

"Dr. Anderson," Bond said without turning to her. "Since when do couples experiencing infertility need botulin to have a baby?"

"Put the box down very carefully and turn around. Slowly."

He did. Ashley Anderson was holding a briefcase in one hand and a Colt .38, pointed at Bond, in the other. "I'll use this. Don't think I won't," she said. Her flirtatious, snappy personality was gone. She stared at him with cold eyes and a sneer. "Take those gloves off and drop them."

"My dear Ashley," Bond said as he removed the gloves. "If you shoot me at this range, the bullet will go right through me and into this tank. I'd hate to think what would happen to you if the materials in those vials were exposed to the air. I might be dead, but you'd never make it out of here without being contaminated."

She knew he was right. "Lie down on the floor. Do it!"

"What, you want another semen specimen so soon?" he quipped.

"Shut up and get down. I mean it!"

"It's a stalemate, Ashley. You won't shoot me."

She fired a round at the floor near his feet. The gunshot was deafening inside the laboratory.

"The next one will be your foot," she said. "Get on the goddamned floor!"

Bond complied. He did his best to conceal the fact that he had managed to grasp her stolen keycard in his right hand.

"So, am I correct in assuming that ReproCare is the front for the Suppliers?" he asked.

Ashley Anderson set the briefcase on a worktable and opened it with one hand, the gun in the other still trained at Bond. "Since you're going to die in a few minutes, I suppose it won't hurt to tell you. Yes, this is the laboratory for the Suppliers. It has been for a year, when I made a very lucrative deal with them."

She removed from the briefcase four cylindrical objects the size of coffee mugs, which appeared to be blocks of plastic explosive. She began to distribute them slowly on tables around the room, keeping the gun aimed at Bond. "But now my job with the Suppliers is finished. My orders come from a higher authority. Your people—I assume you're a cop of some kind—your people won't have to worry about the Suppliers anymore."

"Where's Charles Hutchinson going? What's he got with him?" Bond asked.

"You ask a lot of questions for a dead man, Mr. Bond, if that's your real name. Hutchinson's a little worm. He's the courier for the Suppliers. He delivers chemical and biological weapons that the Suppliers create to the various clients around the world. They're hidden inside vials of sperm. It's the perfect method for smuggling. There are not a lot of customs officers who want to start digging around in frozen sperm."

"Ingenious," Bond said. "Who's the higher authority you're working for?"

"That's knowledge you won't even take to your grave," she said. She punched some buttons on a device inside the briefcase. All four explosives beeped. "There. This building will be on another plane of existence in five minutes." She stood about six feet away from where he was lying. "So, this is goodbye, Mr. Bond. Too bad. You really were an excellent donor candidate."

"Aren't you worried that the explosion will release the deadly toxins?"

"The fire will consume them. They won't be dangerous. Not the ones we keep *here*, anyway." She grinned. "You know, the last few shipments Charles made had something totally original in them. I don't mind telling you that it was state-of-the-art shit. But it's all gone. Now shut up."

She assumed a firing stance and pointed the gun with both hands at Bond's head.

Using the skills he had trained for and practiced all of his professional life, Bond rolled to his left and onto his back. Dr. Anderson fired a shot and barely missed him. Bond threw the keycard at her with a jerk of the wrist. It was a technique he had developed and taught in his own class at SIS, "How to Turn Everyday Items into Deadly Weapons."

The corner of the card struck Ashley Anderson hard in the face, piercing the skin about three centimeters. The pain and surprise threw her backward. The card was stuck directly into the bridge of her nose, between the eyes. Bond leaped to his feet, ran to her, knocked the revolver out of her hand, and slugged her on the chin. She fell to the floor, unconscious. Bond pulled the card out of her forehead. She would live, but she might have a nice little scar to remember him by.

He picked her up and carried her out of the laboratory. He didn't have the time or the inclination to attempt to disarm the explosives. If the Suppliers' headquarters and laboratory were destroyed, it would be fine with him.

He carried her body out of an emergency exit and onto Thirty-eighth Street, and ran across the road. Cars screeched to a stop when the drivers saw a man rushing across the street carrying a woman with blood on her face. They assumed he was rushing her to the hospital just down the block.

ReproCare exploded with a boom that could be heard for a mile around. The blast had a direct effect on the electric and utility lines underneath the building, immediately cutting off power and water to the surrounding streets. Two cars collided in the road, and pedestrians screamed. The entire block turned into chaos.

Bond laid Ashley Anderson down on the pavement and grabbed his mobile phone. The first call he made was to the local fire department and police. The second call was to Felix Leiter.

—•—

Bastrop, Texas, is a quiet farming and ranching community about thirty miles southeast of Austin. It is known for its lush greenery and fields of cattle and is on a well-traveled route between Austin and Houston.

At sunrise on the morning after the ReproCare clinic was destroyed, an FBI SWAT team assembled on the perimeter of a ranch property that was a mile away from Highway 71. Manuela Montemayor had requested a raid after James Bond supplied the address he had found in the computer at the clinic. Bond and Leiter went along as "observers" and were told to stay back and let the FBI do their job.

"That's easier said than done," Felix told Manuela. "If we start shooting, James here is going to go absolutely nuts. He'll want a piece of the action, and so will I! Isn't that right, James?" He looked at his old friend for approval.

Bond shook his head. "Don't look at me, Felix. I'm just an observer."

"Quiet," Manuela said.

They were crouched in the trees just beyond a barbed-wire fence surrounding the property, which consisted of a ranch house, a barn, a silo, and thirty acres of grazing land. About thirty cows were lazily chewing their cud on the field. Leiter was in his Action Arrow power chair, but Bond could tell he was itching to jump out and join in the fun. They were both dressed in borrowed FBI team jackets and bulletproof vests, just in case.

Manuela introduced Bond to the man in charge of the raid, Agent James Goodner. He was a tall man with a cruel jowl but sparkling, pleasant eyes.

"Any friend of Felix Leiter's a friend of mine," Goodner said, shaking Bond's hand. "Just keep yourselves back and out of trouble. Hopefully this will be over quickly."

"What do you know about this place?" Bond asked.

"The property is owned by a rancher named Bill Johnson. He legitimately raises cattle and wasn't on any of our lists. If he works for the Suppliers, then he's done a good job hiding it. We're going to send some men to the front door of the ranch house there and present him with a warrant. If a team is allowed in to search the place peacefully, we may not be needed. Somehow, though, I don't think that's going to happen."

"We don't want to end up with another Waco," Leiter said. Bond remembered the disastrous raid the FBI made on a militant cult group in that Texas town a few years ago.

Manuela approached Goodner and said, "Your men are ready. I'm going to the door with them."

"What for?" Leiter asked.

"Sweetheart, it's my case. This is my territory. It's my job!"

"Well then, be careful, honey," Leiter said. She leaned over and kissed him on the cheek.

"Don't worry. Just think about what tonight will be like," she said. She winked at Bond, then left with two other agents.

"Tonight?" Bond asked.

Leiter shrugged and had a mischievous grin on his face. "There's something about gunfights that really turns her on. Must be that spicy Hispanic blood in her, I don't know. She turns into a hot tamale. One night—"

"Quiet," Goodner whispered. They could see Manuela and two agents approaching the front of the house, fifty yards away. From their vantage point, they could see the house, the barn, and part of the silo. Another group of men had assembled on the opposite side of the property. The place was surrounded.

Goodner was watching through binoculars. "They just knocked on the door. They're waiting. . . . All right, the door's opening. Manuela's presenting her credentials and warrant. A woman answered the door. Must be Mrs. Johnson. She's letting them inside."

He spoke into his wireless headset. "All right, keep cool, everyone. They're inside the house. Hopefully this will all end peacefully."

Three minutes went by, and the house was still quiet. Suddenly, the back door flung open and a large man dressed as a cowboy ran outside. He was headed for the barn and was carrying a shotgun.

Goodner held up a loudspeaker and said, "Stop where you are! This is the FBI! Halt or we'll shoot!"

Bill Johnson swung the gun up and fired in the direction of the voice. At the same time, three other men emerged from the house with what looked like AK-47s. They began to sweep the trees with bullets.

"Go! Go! Go!" shouted Goodner into the headset.

The FBI team shot a tear gas shell at the cowboys, then fired their own guns.

The barn door opened and more men with automatic weapons poured out. There were at least ten of them. They ran to various objects in the yard for cover.

"Where's Manuela?" Leiter shouted. "Is she okay?"

"Quiet, Felix," Bond said, watching intently. He felt like joining the action too. "I'm sure she's fine."

The volley of bullets continued for several minutes. Two FBI agents were hit, but their bulletproof vests saved their lives. Three of the Suppliers went down.

Bill Johnson made a run back to the house while his men covered him with a barrage of gunfire. He got inside, then returned holding Manuela in front of him. He had a pistol to her head.

"Put down your guns, or the bitch gets it!" he yelled. Manuela was struggling against him, but he was just too big.

"He's got Manuela!" Felix cried.

"Easy, Felix," Bond said. "Let the FBI handle it."

Goodner said into the headset, "Hold your fire, men."

After the tremendous cacophony, the abrupt silence was unnerving.

"All right, we're gonna get in a truck and leave," Johnson yelled. "You're gonna let us out of here or the bitch gets a hole in her head!"

Goodner held up the loudspeaker. "You'll never get away with this, Johnson. The place is surrounded. Let her go and tell your men to put down their weapons. None of you will leave here alive if you don't!"

"Bullshit!" Johnson yelled back. He moved, clutching Manuela, toward the barn.

Bond glanced at the supply of weapons the FBI had at their disposal. There was an American M21, a modified version of the old

M14. It was a perfect sniper rifle. He picked it up and whispered to Goodner, "I'm pretty good with this. Let me move over there and see if I can get a bead on him."

"This is highly irregular, Mr. Bond," Goodner said. "We have our own sharpshooters."

"But we're in the perfect spot. If he moves into the barn with her, our chances will be slimmer."

"All right, but I know nothing about it."

"Keep him talking," Bond said, then moved a few yards away, next to a large oak tree. He quietly climbed up to a large branch. From there he could see the entire area.

Goodner said into the speaker, "Johnson, just what is it you want? Talk to me!"

"Fuck you!" Johnson yelled.

"Let me at that bastard," Leiter said. He opened the secret compartment in the wheelchair and pulled out the ASP.

Johnson moved Manuela closer to the barn. There were several of his men around him, crouched behind food troughs and barrels.

"We need to distract the asshole so James can get a better aim," Leiter said.

"Don't do anything stupid," Goodner said.

Johnson got to a large door on the barn and gestured for one of the men to open it. Inside was a Ford pickup truck. The man got in and started it.

"Damn it, they're going to get away!" Leiter mumbled. He looked up at Bond and said, "Can you get that son of a bitch, James?"

Bond aimed the rifle. Johnson was not in a good position: Manuela's face was in the way. "Not yet," he whispered.

"Fuck it," Leiter said. He suddenly burst out of the cover of the trees and drove the wheelchair at full speed onto the field toward the house.

"Leiter! What the hell . . . !" Goodner shouted.

"Yeeeee-haaaaa!" Leiter hollered.

It was such an incongruous sight that both sides stared in disbelief. There, in the middle of a gunfight standoff, a man in an electric wheelchair was barreling out into the wide open and yelling like a madman.

"Felix!" Manuela shouted.

The surprise proved to be enough for Johnson to involuntarily loosen his grip on her. She felt the release, then elbowed the man hard in the stomach.

At that moment, James Bond got a clear aim at Johnson's forehead. He squeezed the trigger. Bill Johnson's face burst into a red mess, and his body flew back against the barn door. Manuela ran away from him and toward Leiter.

The other Suppliers started firing into the trees again. The FBI resumed shooting as well. James Bond watched in horror as Leiter and Manuela met each other in the middle of the field, yet somehow the flying bullets avoided them. Manuela jumped into Leiter's lap, and together they sped in the chair back toward the trees.

Before they were safely out of there, Leiter let out another "Yeeee-haaaa," popped a wheelie with the chair, turned, and soared over the field into the midst of the cattle. The cows, totally unnerved by the gunfire and the sight of the strange wheeled vehicle, began to panic. Backed up against the barbed wire, they had no choice but to run forward, toward the barn. Rushing past the wheelchair, the cattle began to stampede, driving the Suppliers out from behind their cover. The cattle also supplied adequate cover for Leiter and Manuela, who rolled back into the trees and safety.

Bond couldn't help but shake his head and laugh.

In five minutes, it was all over. Once the Suppliers were running in the open, they were easy targets. Two more of them were killed, and the rest surrendered. The cattle were rounded up and penned with the help of one of the arrested men, who gladly cooperated with the FBI.

The barn was full of containers of chemical weapons and crates of illegal arms. Goodner said there was enough material there to start a small war. Bond was especially interested in the chemical and biological weapons.

"We have a special team for that stuff," Goodner said. "We ain't touching it."

Bond found Leiter and Manuela at the side of the barn. She was still in his lap.

"James! Great shot!" Leiter said.

"Thank you," Manuela said. "You saved my life. Well, you both did."

"Felix, you damned fool, you could have been killed!" Bond said.

"Hey, the risk was worth it," Leiter said, nuzzling Manuela's neck. "We've been in worse situations than that, my friend." He held up his prosthetic hand. "I've got nine lives, remember? I've only used up a couple of 'em."

Bond glanced over at the team and noticed that one man was carrying a metal briefcase similar to the one Charles Hutchinson had been carrying.

"Wait!" he called. The man stopped. Bond took a look at the case. He called Goodner over to see it.

"Your chemical and biological weapons team should open this one. I have a feeling there's something nasty inside."

"Will do," Goodner said. "After hearing about what's going on in L.A., you couldn't pay me a million bucks to handle that thing."

"Oh? What's going on in L.A.?"

"Haven't you heard? There's some kind of weird epidemic. One of those Legionnaires' disease things. Only in L.A.—wouldn't you know it? Well, thanks for all your help, Mr. Bond."

"Don't mention it."

Bond paid little attention to the irrelevant news about Los Angeles and forgot about it completely when he turned back to his friends and saw that they were fixed in a passionate embrace. He quietly withdrew, allowing them a little more breathing room. He walked round the barn, lit a cigarette, and thanked his lucky stars that they were alive.

ELEVEN

THE NEXT THREE STRIKES

NICOSIA, THE CAPITAL OF CYPRUS, IS A FORTIFIED, TIGHT-WALLED CITY WITH a circumference of just three miles. The Turks and Turkish Cypriots call their side of the city Lefkosia, Nicosia's official name prior to the twelfth century, when the country was under Byzantine rule. The Turks reverted the city's name to its former one after the invasion of 1974. They refer to the occupied northern area of Cyprus as the Turkish Republic of Northern Cyprus, founded in 1983 by Rauf Denktash, once a friend and colleague of Archbishop Makarios, the first president of the Republic of Cyprus.

Largely supported by the West, the Greek Cypriot side of the city and country has managed to become a tourist attraction and formidable political voice in the Mediterranean during the last several years. In contrast, the Turkish Republic of Northern Cyprus must work at getting tourists to visit. Travelers wishing to travel from Greece or southern Cyprus into the north can only do so for a day trip, and only if they are not Greek Cypriots or Greeks. Travelers who enter the TRNC from Turkey or other countries cannot enter the southern side. As a result, the prosperity of the TRNC has not been equal to that of its southern neighbors. Where the Republic of Cyprus expanded its half of the city to include modern shopping malls and business centers, the TRNC's side remains underdeveloped, underpopulated, and in a state of poverty.

The Greek and Turkish Cypriots have always been passionate in backing their respective sides of their history. The two viewpoints conflict in their interpretations of the facts, and there is often outright denial of them. Objective parties such as Britain or the United States have been working with the Cypriots in an effort to help settle their problems, but both sides seem to have dug in their heels. A stalemate has been in existence for years. When incidents of violence erupt sporadically in what is now called "the last divided city," as they often do, further escalation of the tensions between the two factions is an unavoidable outcome.

A so-called buffer zone along the Green Line ranges from one hundred meters in one spot to up to five hundred in another. It is an eerie no-man's-land in which time has stopped since the Turkish "intervention" of 1974. Patrolled by the United Nations, the strip cutting through Nicosia and the rest of the country is lined with barbed wire, high fences, and signs forbidding photography. The buildings that remain in the buffer zone are abandoned, bombed out, and achingly quiet. Propaganda of both sides is displayed on the respective borders so that any visitors who choose to cross the line will get both points of view. A banner hangs over the northern gate so that people traveling to the south can read it. "The Clock Cannot Be Turned Back" is what it proclaims in English.

The buffer zone gateway between southern and northern Nicosia is known as the Ledra Palace Checkpoint. The Ledra Palace was once the most luxurious hotel in Nicosia. Now it is the headquarters for the UN and lies in the middle of the buffer zone between two military gates. Visitors are allowed to walk across the no-man's-land during the day, but at night access is denied. During the five-minute walk between gates, visitors will see numerous soldiers. On the southern side are the dark brown camouflage uniforms of the Greek Cypriots and Greek Army. On the northern side are the Turks' green camouflage outfits, and in the middle are the light brown uniforms of the United Nations.

At five o'clock on the day after the Suppliers' headquarters was blown to bits in Austin, Texas, things were relatively peaceful along the Green Line in Nicosia. The four Turkish soldiers who manned the gate on the northern side officially closed down for the day, and if there were any tourists still in the TRNC then, they would be forced to spend the night at one of northern Lefkosia's run-down hotels. A small parking lot behind the two-story white guard post was just emptying itself of taxicabs and vehicles belonging to the administrative staff that worked in the building.

Not far from the guardhouse, a dark green 1987 Plymouth moved slowly along Kemal Zeytinoglu Street. The word "Taksi" was printed in English on the bubble on top of the car, as on all cabs in Lefkosia. The driver waited a minute, watching the empty street leading south. At precisely five-ten, the car tore into the silence of the dusk with squealing tires, bursting out onto the street and speeding down to the avenue. It cut the curve to the right without stopping and was now headed south, straight for the checkpoint gate.

The Turkish soldiers saw the car coming and thought at first that a taxi driver had had too much to drink. As it approached, however, it increased its speed so that it would smash through the gate and enter the buffer zone illegally. The four men simultaneously jumped up and ran out to the street, ready to draw their weapons. The driver of the Plymouth slammed on the brakes and spun the wheel so that the car made a screeching 180-degree turn in front of the checkpoint building. A figure dressed in a gas mask, hood, and camouflage protective gear jumped out of the back seat of the taxi. The soldiers, who were spread out in a semicircle facing the cab, shouted at the figure and prepared to open fire. Before they could, the figure tossed a grenade onto the ground in front of the men. It took them completely by surprise, and they had no time to react before it exploded in their faces.

The chemical grenade produced an immense white cloud. The four soldiers were not hurt by the blast, but they were blinded by the smoke. There was something in it that irritated their eyes and made breathing extremely difficult. They fell to the ground and groped their way toward what they believed would be safety. One man heard the taxi's engine roar into life as it sped away a half-minute after the explosion. When the smoke finally cleared three minutes after that, the men were still coughing and gasping for air. They didn't notice that the number "5" had been spray-painted on the wall of the checkpoint building. Sitting on the ground below the number was a small alabaster statue of Athena, the Greek goddess of wisdom.

The soldiers made it to their feet, and one crawled into the guard post to call the authorities. He was able to dial the number and tell his superior officer what had just happened. He then became violently sick and was stricken with cramps.

When the police and more soldiers arrived at the checkpoint, two of the soldiers were dead and the other two were nearly so. In the half hour since the grenade exploded in front of them, the men experienced a number of symptoms that came on suddenly and escalated from one to the other without warning. The difficulty in breathing led to excessive nausea and vomiting, cramps, involuntary defecation, spasms, and finally reduction of the heart rate. They had been killed by the nerve agent sarin, a particularly nasty chemical that acted quickly and aggressively.

As for the Plymouth and the mysterious masked figure that made the attack, the car had been abandoned three blocks north of the checkpoint. The assassin had jumped into a 1988 Volkswagen and was now heading innocently toward the port city of Famagusta.

The Turkish Republic of Northern Cyprus uses two major ports on the northeastern part of the island. Kyrenia, directly north of Lefkosia, is mostly a passenger harbor, the point of entry for mainly Turkish tourists or immigrants. Famagusta, on the east coast of Cyprus, is the harbor for shipping and trade. Like Nicosia/Lefkosia, it is a walled city, and it has certainly seen better days. Probably the city with the longest and most colorful history on Cyprus, Famagusta has changed hands a number of times. Now the TRNC's flag, which is similar to the Turkish red and white flag except that the colors are reversed, blew in the wind at the dock along Shakespeare Street.

Dominating the northeast shoreline are the docks themselves, an entrance into the city called the Sea Gate, and an impressive ancient citadel known as Othello's Castle. Shakespeare supposedly based his famous play on the citadel and a legendary dark-complexioned Italian mercenary who fought for the Venetians and was called *il Moro*, "the Moor."

The lone man standing in the dark on the roof of the castle could just see the long boardwalk projecting southeast. He could also see the small white Turkish guard post, the one crane in operation, and two ships that were docked at the port. One of the ships was loaded with food and supplies from Turkey. Looking through binoculars, he panned the edge of the dock and finally saw the camouflaged figure emerge from the shadows. Right on time.

The figure turned toward the castle and flashed a penlight three times. It was the signal for the man to get the escape route ready. He made an acknowledgment of one flash with his own penlight, then made his way down the dark stone steps to the first floor of the castle. He had paid admission to get inside the citadel during business hours and had found a place to hide until dark. Now all he had to do was use the long wooden ladder he knew would be in the maintenance shed, and climb over the wall of the castle to the street.

Meanwhile, on the dock, the figure in camouflage protective gear, gas mask, and hood slithered up to the lonely white guard post. Only two Turkish soldiers manned the booth at this time of night. The unloading of the supply ship would take place in the morning. Security was normally reliable and there wouldn't have been a need to post extra guards around the ship. The soldiers had no reason to believe that the Famagusta dock was about to become the latest target of the most skillful trained assassin in the Mediterranean. The Number Killer was probably right to think there was no one in the world better at this job.

The murderer boldly walked up to the guard post and stood in the doorway. The two Turkish guards looked up in surprise at the frightening shape before them. For the brief moment the men were able to gaze upon their killer, all they could see was the gas mask and its likeness to an insect's head.

The Number Killer shot both men with a Daewoo DH380, a double action semiautomatic pistol made in South Korea. The silencer muffled the sound of the .380 caliber bullets that slammed into the soldiers and knocked them back against the wall. They slumped into a heap on the floor, bleeding profusely.

The camouflaged figure moved quickly to the ship docked a few meters away. One lone sailor was on deck, smoking a cigarette. The assassin calmly walked to the end of the ramp and proceeded to climb aboard the ship. The Turkish sailor saw the bizarre creature appear in front of him and was too frightened to scream. The Daewoo let off another round, kicking the sailor over the rail and into the water.

Another sailor called from below in Turkish. "What's going on?" he yelled. The Number Killer confidently opened the hatch and descended the steps into the bowels of the ship. It took two more bullets to make sure that no one was alive to witness the assassin's next act.

He opened the cargo hold and stepped inside. The ship was full of much-needed food from the mainland. There were crates of vegetables, cartons of eggs, bags of potatoes and other types of produce. There was enough food to stock all the grocery markets in northern Cyprus for at least three days. If all went as planned, when the goods were unloaded and shipped to diverse parts of the TRNC they would be covered with an invisible and deadly germ.

The figure in the protective suit removed a backpack and set it on the floor. He opened it up quickly and removed a metal canister. He unscrewed the top to reveal four glass vials full of liquid attached to the inside of the canister. The Number Killer then removed a spray gun from the backpack. It was a type of everyday garden tool used for pesticides. The canister with the vials fitted perfectly onto the back of the spray gun.

The assassin stood up and began to spray the crates of vegetables. The heads of lettuce and potatoes were covered with the fine mist. The breads and eggs were blanketed by the tasteless, odorless chemical. After ten minutes, the Number Killer had efficiently emptied the spray gun, and the entire cargo room was covered with the already drying liquid. There was still one more task left to do. Reaching into the bag of tricks, the assassin pulled out the spray paint can and drew the number "6" on the wall of the cargo hold. He then carefully set a small alabaster statue of Hermes, the ancient Greek god of trade, commerce, and wealth, on the floor. He quickly packed up his equipment and left the ship the same way he had come in.

There was still no activity on the dock. No one had discovered the bodies of the two guards yet. The Number Killer walked calmly across the boardwalk to the Sea Gate. The rope he had left earlier was still there. He climbed up the wall and over the barbed wire. This time he pulled up the rope as he perched on top of the wall, straddling the barbed wire. Down below, on the other side of the wall, was a public utility truck. It was the kind used for highway building and maintenance, and the back was full of sand. The killer calmly jumped into it.

The man who had been on top of Othello's castle was sitting in the driver's seat of the truck. He heard the thump of the assassin landing in the sand. That was his cue, and he started the truck and headed northwest out of Famagusta on the main road, Cengiz Topel.

If it hadn't been for the anonymous phone call to the Famagusta police one hour later, the food aboard the ship would have been sent out to feed over eighty thousand Turkish Cypriots. The voice on the other end of the line spoke English and sounded neither Greek nor Turkish. The message was that the food in the cargo ship at the dock must be burned. Under no circumstances should the hold be entered without protective clothing and gas masks, for a deadly biological agent had been distributed inside. The call was dismissed at first as a hoax, but one Turkish Cypriot policeman decided it wouldn't hurt to go take a look. When he found the dead soldiers in the guard post, he sounded the alarm.

By noon the next day, the authorities had determined that if the food had been shipped to its final destinations, within a week northern Cyprus would have been hit by a devastating anthrax plague.

The sun shone on Anavatos and produced an unseasonably warm day for November on Chios. There had been a couple of tourists from

Italy early in the day, but they were gone by midafternoon. The Italians had no idea that the medieval fortress at the top of the cliff masked the modern headquarters complex of the Decada. They walked right over a trapdoor made of stone, completely unaware of the meeting going on below in the square meeting room.

The Monad was not pleased. Eight members of his elite group were present. The cushion usually occupied by Number Ten was vacant. The Monad had dispensed with many of the formalities of the meetings, and began after only five minutes of silence. He strummed the lyre and spoke.

"Welcome," he said in the quiet voice that mesmerized his followers. "I am happy to report that Mission Number Five was entirely successful. Four Turkish soldiers in illegally occupied northern Cyprus were eliminated. Mission Number Six was also implemented quite successfully, and I must commend Number Two, the Duad, for bravery and two jobs well done. However, I am distressed to inform you all that Mission Number Six was not a total success. While Number Two completed the mission, it was not carried through to our ultimate goal of spreading anthrax over northern Cyprus. The deed was discovered by the authorities before the cargo ship was unloaded."

The other members of the Decada looked concerned. Number Two was especially angry.

The Monad raised his hands to reassure them. "Do not trouble yourselves, my friends. I have the answer. I know what happened. The gods have been good to me and have revealed to me the source of betrayal in our organization. But before I have the traitor brought in for trial, I have other grave news. Number Ten will no longer be joining us. Dr. Anderson was arrested in the United States two days ago. I have not received official confirmation yet, but I believe that she is probably dead by now. I am sure that she would have followed our strictest policy and taken her own life rather than subject herself to interrogation. It is a shame."

Number Two did her best to control her emotions. She looked over at Number Eight, who acknowledged her pain.

The Monad continued, "The Decada has cut its business ties with the militants in Texas. We don't need them anymore. The One will become the Many through the actions of our own efforts from now on. Unfortunately, we have to revise our plans somewhat. Mission Number Seven must now be used to deal with a traitor to the organization."

The Monad clapped his hands twice. A soldier in a dark green camouflage uniform entered, dragging a young man by the arm. The rest of the Decada didn't know him by sight, but they knew who he was.

"Loyal members," the Monad said, "I present to you Charles Hutchinson, an Englishman. He is, as his father was, an enemy of the Decada. He alerted the Cypriot authorities that the cargo ship at Famagusta had been infected. Do you deny this charge, Mr. Hutchinson?"

"You killed my father, you bastard," Hutchinson spat out.

"Your father failed to provide us with some valuable information that we needed. Instead of supplying it to us, he attempted to go to British authorities and expose us before we had accomplished our first set of goals. He had to die."

Charles Hutchinson suddenly realized what his fate was. He began to tremble with fear.

"Look," he stammered, "I'm sorry . . . I was just upset about my father . . ."

"Spare us your pleading," the Monad commanded. "Are you aware of what has happened to the Suppliers in Texas? And to our loyal Number Ten, Dr. Ashley Anderson?"

Hutchinson, now speechless with fear, shook his head quickly.

"They are no more. The laboratory was destroyed by Number Ten, as instructed. The names of the major personnel in the Suppliers' organization were supplied to the FBI in America, along with incriminating evidence. They are being rounded up as we speak. The headquarters was discovered and raided. We will have to find a replacement for Number Ten. I will recruit one of our more loyal employees."

The Monad stood and stepped over to Charles Hutchinson. He

placed his hand at the base of the young man's head and gripped him tightly.

"Decada!" the Monad said with force. "I present to you Charles Hutchinson, traitor and enemy to our principles. What say you, guilty or not guilty?"

"Guilty!" the eight followers cried.

The Monad turned to Hutchinson and said, "I do so love a brief trial. It is decided. You have become Limited. Now you must join the One. Perhaps when the One becomes the Many, you will be forgiven."

The Monad nodded slightly to the guard, who pulled Hutchinson out of the room.

The medieval castle at the top of Anavatos was at the edge of a cliff wall that dropped virtually straight down a quarter-mile to a wooded, hilly landscape. It was a breathtaking sight when one stood at the small stone wall which served as some protection to visitors to the ruins.

The stone trapdoor opened and three guards forced Charles Hutchinson out. He was screaming and crying, but there was no one around to hear him. Even the elderly residents who lived at the base of the ruined city wouldn't hear him. Only the few birds circling the foreboding precipice in front of him could hear his cries.

The guards led him to the edge of the cliff and offered him a blindfold. He was too shaken to realize what they were asking. The guards shrugged and put the blindfold away. Hutchinson knew he was going to die, but he didn't know how. He figured they were about to take him off Anavatos and drive him somewhere remote.

When the push came, he was surprised.

Watching on a video monitor from inside the complex, the Monad nodded his head and said a prayer to the gods. He was pleased. They told him that he had been adequately avenged.

Number Two stood behind him, struggling to keep her feelings to herself. At least Number Ten had set their plan in motion before she died. It was now up to her and Number Eight to see it through to the end.

TWELVE

HIDDEN AGENDA?

BOND SPENT ANOTHER TWO AND A HALF DAYS IN TEXAS, THEN RETURNED TO London in time to receive the news of the Number Killer attacks in Cyprus. He stopped by the flat and quickly examined the neatly stacked pile of post and newspapers from the past several days. Bond took a couple of hours to freshen up, then drove the Bentley to the office in time for a debriefing. It was still rainy and cold.

The green light flickered above the door just as Bond walked into Moneypenny's outer office.

"Looks like there's no time for chitchat, James," she said. The green light was a signal for Bond to come inside. He raised his eyebrows at Moneypenny and went on through.

M stood with her back to Bond, gazing out the large picture window that overlooked the Thames. He waited a moment before saying, "Good afternoon, ma'am."

She turned around and gestured to the black chair in front of her desk. "Sit down, 007," she said, then moved back to her desk and sat across from him. The lines on her face seemed to be more prominent. Bond thought she looked tired and pale.

"Are you all right, ma'am?" he asked.

"Yes, yes," she sighed. "It's been a difficult few days."

"I can imagine."

"I was called on to help Alfred's solicitors with his estate. His former wives wanted nothing to do with him, although I daresay he's probably left something tidy to them in his will. Now I know how celebrities feel when their personal lives are displayed in public. It hasn't reached tabloid stage, but my name was mentioned in the *Times* obituary. I would like to go away to the country for a month or so."

"Perhaps you should," Bond said.

"That would be cowardly. Forget it. I was just speaking with Manville Duncan. He returned from the Middle East quite distraught. Manville is almost as upset about Alfred's death as I am. He's not cut out for Alfred's job, but he'll do fine as a temporary replacement, I suppose. You've heard about what happened in Cyprus?"

"Yes, I've read the briefing."

"Two more attacks. One in Nicosia and one in Famagusta. Both directed against the Turkish side. More numbers. More Greek god statuettes. It was a blessing that someone called the Turkish Cypriot authorities and warned them of the poisoned food. Someone is on our side, at least."

"It makes no sense," Bond said. "Why attack our British bases, then go and strike against the Turks? It's not as if we're on Cyprus to protect the Turkish presence. If anything, we disapprove of their occupation as much as the rest of the Western world."

"Quite so," M said. 'Turkey is the only country to sanction their government in northern Cyprus. We do not recognize the TRNC as a true republic, it's just easier to say than 'illegally occupied northern Cyprus.' I'm afraid the world has tolerated the occupation far too long, mainly because, in many ways, the Turks were right to intervene. According to them, the Greek Cypriots did unspeakable things to the Turkish Cypriots in the 1960s before the Greek military coup. Turkey was supposedly protecting her people. Mind you, I'm not defending the Turks. They've committed horrible atrocities on Cyprus. But never mind that. Tell me about the Suppliers."

"We won't have to worry about the Suppliers anymore," he said. "Their organization has been completely dismantled. I stayed around for two days assisting with the investigation. They raided the homes of all suspected Suppliers members and made a number of arrests. The main headquarters and storehouse for weapons was a barn in Bastrop, a small town near Austin. The amount of chemical weaponry they found was simply staggering. It is now believed that the Suppliers were one of the largest and most powerful distribution organizations in the world. The FBI found evidence that sales were made to over fifty clients worldwide."

"Who was the mastermind behind it all?"

"They're still trying to find out. That's the only glitch. The original boss is in prison. We don't know who the interim chief was, but apparently he got away. None of the arrested members will talk. There was nothing more I could do for the FBI, so I came back. It's their show now."

"What happened with the woman from the clinic?"

Bond frowned. "She died."

"Suicide?"

He nodded. "She didn't give them a chance to interrogate her. Swallowed a tablet of concentrated potassium cyanide."

M tapped the desk with her fingers. "Why would she do that? What did she know?"

"She was working for someone other than the Suppliers. She mentioned that her orders came from a 'higher authority.' I definitely got the impression that she had no loyalty to the Suppliers."

"Was she connected to our Number Killer?"

"I believe so, yes. The Number Killer's arsenal came from the Suppliers. I don't have proof, but I'm sure of it."

"And what about Alfred's son?"

Bond shook his head. "The FBI tracked him after he left Austin. He took a flight to London and apparently spent a day here taking care of the arrangements for his father. Did you speak to him?"

"No. I tried to reach him but he was tied up with solicitors all day. The next thing I knew, he was out of the country."

"That's right. He flew to Athens. He had already arrived by the time we all learned where he was. It was too late for customs to stop him."

"So he's somewhere in Greece?"

"That's what we presume. ReproCare was owned by BioLinks Limited, a large pharmaceutical firm in Athens. We'll have to look into that."

M got up and poured two glasses of bourbon. She handed one to Bond without asking if he wanted it.

"Now that he's delivered his package of chemicals to whomever the Suppliers sold them to, don't you think he'd come home?" she asked. "Surely he knows that the Suppliers are no more."

"He's either on the run, or he's hiding somewhere."

"Or he's dead."

"There is that possibility too." Bond took a sip of the bourbon. "The men in that house in Austin did not treat him as an equal. My first thought was that he was being held captive. The Suppliers were after a file on Mr. Hutchinson's computer. They didn't find it. If we knew what the file contained, it would be a big help."

"Do you remember that Alfred was going to show us something concerning the Cyprus case?"

"Yes. What was it?"

"I don't know. He didn't tell me. We've had a good look through his flat too. I wonder if Charles was connected to this information?"

"The FBI raided that mansion on the hill in Austin and it was completely empty. The occupants had made a hasty departure. Even the furniture was gone. Leiter found out who owns the house, though: a Greek fellow by the name of Konstantine Romanos."

"I've heard of him," M said. "He's some kind of teacher/tycoon?" She began to punch up his name on her computer.

"That's right," Bond said. "Independently wealthy, he's a respected mathematician at Athens University. He's also a writer and a philosopher. I don't know a lot about him yet, I just looked him up on the computer myself."

He tapped a file folder in his lap and opened it. "The man in this photo, though, is not the man I saw in the house." Bond took out a black-and-white publicity shot of Konstantine Romanos. The man he had seen in the house was a bodybuilder with huge hands, dark hair, and a thick mustache. The man in the photo was in his fifties and was tall and thin. His curly hair was dark, but it had hints of gray. Strikingly handsome, he had the looks of a screen idol now in the autumn years of his career.

"There's not a lot here. I've already put in a request to Station G and to the Greek Secret Service for more information on him. According to Records, Romanos is clean, but I found something interesting. He has one living family member, a second cousin, Vassilis, who was a champion bodybuilder in his hometown in Greece. There's no photo of him, but the man in charge of the Romanos mansion the night I was there looked a bit like Romanos. It could have been his cousin."

"Why would Romanos have a house in Texas?"

"One of Konstantine Romanos's several accomplishments was serving as a guest professor for five years in the University of Texas philosophy department. This was around the same time that Alfred Hutchinson was also a guest professor at the college."

It was a frightening coincidence. M said nothing, so Bond continued, "We know that Charles Hutchinson carried a supply of chemical weapons to Athens for the Suppliers. Where he's gone from there is a mystery. We need to find him."

She nodded. "I agree. You're to go on to Athens. Find out what happened to Charles Hutchinson and see if you can meet this Romanos fellow. Observe him. I'll make sure you get complete cooperation from the Greeks, and we'll try to get more information on that pharmaceutical company."

M stood up and slowly walked toward the window. It was raining again. "You know, Alfred might have been killed because he found out what his son was up to. He never spoke of Charles. The only time he did was to say that his son had been an 'embarrassment' to him."

Bond didn't want to say that he suspected Alfred Hutchinson of much more than simply not nurturing a positive father-son relationship. The coincidence of Hutchinson and Romanos being in the same Texas city for five years was too compelling. They had to have known each other. What if Hutchinson himself was involved with the Suppliers? He could have used the diplomatic bag as a means to deliver weapons to other countries.

"I'm concerned about the pattern in the attacks," M said. "Our people are trying to determine what the significance of the Greek god statuettes might be. The numbers, I'm afraid, are just there to add up. There will be more, but when and where? You have to find out. The severity of the attacks is also escalating. That anthrax could have caused a terrible epidemic. Many people would have died. My own personal stake in this matter aside, this could turn into a predicament that might threaten national security."

Bond waited for her to go on.

"The Cyprus situation is a tinderbox waiting to explode. Greece and Turkey are both members of NATO. If they were to go to war against each other, all of Europe would suffer. The government of Turkey has been unstable for some time now. The fundamentalist Muslims would welcome an opportunity to take control away from the seculars. If they did, it wouldn't be long before they formed dangerous alliances with countries like Iran or Iraq. A war with Greece would put quite a strain on a country that already has twenty percent unemployed. The fundamentalists could take advantage of the situation."

M handed the file folder back to Bond. "I'll have Chief of Staff contact the Greek Secret Service and let them know you're coming in the morning. One of their people will meet you at the airport. I want to know what happened to Charles Hutchinson. Follow his trail. If it happens to cross one made by Konstantine Romanos, you'll know what to do."

"Yes, ma'am."

"You've always had a knack for uncovering the mountain after first finding the molehill. I'm counting on you to do it again. That's all, 007."

Bond stood up to leave, then hesitated.

"What is it?" she asked.

He shook his head. "Nothing."

"No, I know." She paused a moment, then said, "You want to say that you suspect Alfred had something to do with all of this. The thought has crossed my mind as well. I'm trying not to let my personal feelings cloud my reasoning, but I refuse to believe it until I see some strong evidence."

"Of course," Bond said.

She looked at him intensely. After a moment, her eyes dropped. "I'm sorry about the other night, James. People that work for you should never have to see you in such an exposed condition. I feel so . . . humiliated."

"Don't give it another thought, ma'am," Bond said. "We all go through traumas in our lives. Just take comfort in knowing you were among friends."

She raised her eyes and said, "Thank you. I also want to thank you for how you're handling all of this. Tanner almost called 004 that night, but I asked him to call you. I knew that you would . . . understand."

Bond didn't know what to say, so he nodded reassuringly and left the room.

He would always remember that moment in the months to come. From then on, the level of mutual respect they had for each other was significantly strengthened.

Bond looked into his office and found a message to call Felix Leiter. When he got through to him, Leiter said, "James! Glad you reached me!"

"What is it, Felix?"

"Listen, you know that metal briefcase you spotted in Bastrop?"

"Yes?"

"It had some kind of weird shit in it, my friend. It was opened in quarantined conditions, but everyone who was exposed to it is *dead*. I'm telling you this bug is unlike anything we've ever seen. It produces symptoms similar to ricin poisoning, but it's a germ—it's contagious! The stuff has been sealed off and sent to the Centers for Disease Control in Atlanta."

"Christ. What exactly was inside the case?"

"Sperm samples. There were tiny vials of liquid hidden in the sperm. One of them was broken. We think the bug was in the vial. And that's not all."

"What?"

"Apparently there's a strange epidemic happening in L.A. and over in Tokyo too. Mysterious diseases, killing off people right and left."

"I remember your FBI man mentioning it."

"I'm just now learning what details there are, but this has been going on for days. Anyway, they're in a panic there. They've sealed off buildings to keep the sick people in, and health officials are working like mad to figure out what's going on. We're just now hearing about it because the authorities in the respective cities wanted to keep it quiet at first. I'm wondering if the germ you found is identical to the bugs in L.A. and Japan."

"My God, Felix, I think Charles Hutchinson may have delivered a lot of those cases recently. Not just Los Angeles or Tokyo!"

"That's what I'm thinking too, James. And all of ReproCare's records are destroyed. The FBI is suddenly very worried. We need to track down those cases and quarantine them. They've already begun to check every medical clinic in the cities you saw on the computer at ReproCare. Damn, New York and London. Do you realize how long that's going to take?"

"I understand. I'll alert M immediately and we can help out over here."

"That's my man. Thanks. Don't panic yet. There's no proof that the bug you found is the same one as in L.A. and Tokyo."

"Fax me any other information as you get it, all right?"

They wished each other luck and said goodbye.

Bond hung up the phone and went back up to see M.

Little did he know that a sixty-two-year-old woman had already contracted the first London case of Williams's disease after receiving a blood transfusion at a hospital in Twickenham.

Alfred Hutchinson had kept an office near Buckingham Palace in Castle Lane. James Bond got out of the taxi, stepped over a large puddle of dirty rainwater to the pavement, and entered the building. He gave his name to the security man and was told to come on up.

Manville Duncan was holding the door open and waiting for Bond when he stepped off the elevator.

"Mr. Bond, this is a surprise," he said. "I just got back from the Middle East. I'm off to France tomorrow."

"I'll just take a minute of your time," Bond said. They shook hands and Bond noted once again that Duncan's handshake was clammy.

"Come in, come in."

The office was elegantly decorated in a grand Edwardian style. Bond felt he had entered the library of a stately mansion.

"This is where Alfred worked," Duncan said. "I've barely had time to move things in from my old office. I find that it's easier just to stay where I was!" He led Bond to an outer office where Bond spotted a portrait of Manville Duncan's wife on a desk. Papers and file folders were scattered about, indicating that the temporary ambassador was a bit disorganized.

"Sit down, please—oh, just move those books out of the way. Now, what can I do for you?" Duncan sat behind the desk and faced Bond.

"On the night of Sir Miles's party, Mr. Hutchinson told us that he had some information about the Cyprus case. He was planning to turn it over to M and me the next day. Do you have any idea what that was?"

"M mentioned that to me. I'm afraid I haven't a clue."

"There was a file on his computer in Austin. Something important. He might have had a copy here. Any thoughts as to what it might have contained?"

Duncan thought a minute and shook his head. "No, and MI5 went though his hard drive here. I can't imagine what it was."

"What do you know about Charles Hutchinson?"

"I know he's a bad lot. He's done a few things which were never made public, thank God."

"Oh?"

"Shortly after his father became Ambassador to the World, Charles was arrested in Germany for being drunk and disorderly. A few months later, he was almost brought up on rape charges in the Philippines. His father got the charges dismissed. I don't know if it was true or not, but Charles got away with it."

"How often did they see each other?"

"More frequently than Alfred let on. He took frequent trips to Texas, because he loved it there. I'm sure he saw his son when he was in Austin."

"M says that Hutchinson was disappointed with Charles."

"You wouldn't know it. The boy often accompanied Alfred on diplomatic trips. Charles went along for free under a diplomatic umbrella. He got to see the world. He got to perpetuate his playboy image and get himself into trouble without really getting into trouble. Diplomatic immunity has its advantages."

"Do you know anything about the clinic in Austin where Charles worked?"

"No. Alfred rarely spoke about what Charles was doing in Austin. I do know that he wasn't happy that Charles had dropped out of university. He thought the boy wasn't measuring up to his potential. But as far as his occupation or activities, I don't think Alfred really cared. If you ask me, I think Alfred *knew* that Charles was up to something illegal."

"How do you know?"

"I can't really put my finger on it. It was the way he often spoke about his son. It was as if he were protecting him from something. That reminds me—I just remembered that he had an argument on the phone with Charles about a week before he died. I couldn't make it out, but I did hear Alfred tell Charles that something was 'too dangerous.' When I walked into the office, he was just ringing off. His last words to his son were, 'I have no other choice.' "

"What do you think that meant?"

"I'm afraid to speculate, but do you really want to know what I think?"

"Yes."

"I think Alfred himself was up to something," Duncan said gravely. "I think his fingers were in places they shouldn't have been. He was using his position to achieve something. He had some kind of ambition, a goal. I can't explain it, because I don't know what it was. It's just that I always got the impression that Alfred had a hidden agenda. While he was working for England, he was also working for himself. He had some kind of grand scheme."

"Something criminal?"

Duncan shrugged. "It's just speculation. The fact that his son has a dark cloud over him makes me more suspicious."

"Did Hutchinson ever talk about Cyprus?"

"Only within the context of work. He was very concerned about the situation there. He felt that Cyprus was one of his priorities."

"Do you think he favored any particular side?"

"If he did, he didn't mention it. I think he was fairly neutral on the subject. He always said that both sides were wrong and that they knew it. Neither side wants to admit they're wrong, so it's a contest of stubbornness. Alfred hoped to be a part of the peace process there. Maybe he wanted a Nobel Prize."

"Ever hear of a man named Konstantine Romanos?"

Duncan frowned, then shook his head. "Who's that?"

"A philosopher and mathematician. He's a teacher in Athens who once had a guest stint in Texas at the same time as Hutchinson. You don't recall our late ambassador mentioning him?"

"No."

Bond was grasping at straws. It looked as if Manville Duncan didn't know anything. Even his speculations were dubious. Still, Bond's instincts told him that Duncan was right about one thing: Alfred Hutchinson *did* have a hidden agenda. He was up to something that didn't fall under his duties as an ambassador. Bond didn't know what it was either, but he was determined to find out.

"Thank you, Mr. Duncan," Bond said, standing. "That's all I need for now. Have a good trip tomorrow. When will you be back?"

Duncan sorted through some papers and found his diary. "I'm in France for two days."

"If you think of anything, please get in touch with us. A message can be sent to me."

"Where are you going?"

"I'm trying to find Charles Hutchinson."

"I see. Any clue to where he might be?"

Bond didn't want to say. "He's in Europe somewhere. Probably hiding."

Duncan nodded. "Probably. Well, good luck."

As Bond left the office and walked out into the rain, he couldn't help feeling that the ghost of Alfred Hutchinson was laughing.

THIRTEEN

THE GREEK AGENT

SERGEANT MAJOR PANOS SAMBRAKOS OF THE GREEK MILITARY POLICE WAS usually up at the crack of dawn, ready for his routine monthly inspection of the camouflaged military storehouses on the island of Chios. This time, though, the sun was setting over the horizon, casting a hazy orange glow over the Aegean. He looked over at the coast of Turkey, plainly visible to the east, and still found it amazing that they could be so close to their enemies and shots were never fired.

Sambrakos, a tall young man of twenty-five, enjoyed his role as an MP. It gave him an elite status that allowed him and his fellow policemen access to any area on the island. The opportunity for meeting women was also a perk that he didn't ignore. Most of the time, though, he used his position to exert authority over common soldiers. It gave him a feeling of power to put on the uniform and assume a different, authoritative persona. He enjoyed strutting down the streets and writing citations as the servicemen cowered in front of him. He had originally dreaded his compulsory military service, but after landing a position with the Military Police, Sambrakos had come to the conclusion that he was having the time of his life.

He also felt important because he was working on top-secret projects for one of the commanding officers on Chios, Brigadier General Dimitris Georgiou.

The general had approached him two months ago, requesting someone to replace a recently deceased officer, a man who had been the general's personal assistant for twelve years. The officer had died tragically in an automobile accident. The general asked Sambrakos if he would like to be considered for the job. The duties would involve highly classified material, and everything they discussed would be privileged information. Sambrakos was surprised, flattered, and intrigued by what General Georgiou had said. He readily agreed to perform clandestine duties for the general as some kind of test.

One of these duties turned out to be a simple, mundane chore. Sambrakos had to inspect the several weapons bunkers scattered over the island which the general had personally shown to him. Large caches of weapons and equipment were hidden in these bunkers, all camouflaged so that they couldn't be seen from above. The areas were blocked from the public by barbed-wire fences and intimidating signs forbidding the use of cameras. Sergeant Major Sambrakos's job was merely to drive a jeep alone to each storehouse and make sure everything was safe and secure. The monthly inspection took him an entire morning, since he had to travel all over the island.

Tonight was different. The general had asked him to perform an inspection beginning at sundown. This was Sambrakos's third inspection and he was eager to do well. Unfortunately, he also had a terrible headache. On the previous day, he had drunk a little too much ouzo in the afternoon, then attended a dinner party that lasted until three o'clock in the morning. With no sleep, the sergeant major had reported for regular M.P. duty at four o'clock in the morning.

Sambrakos climbed into the 240GD Mercedes military jeep, still half asleep, and drove away from his encampment. He would begin with a base located at the northern end of the island and work his way down. The storehouse there, near the small village of Viki, was different from the others for two reasons. For one thing, it was not marked like the other supply posts. From the outside it appeared to be an abandoned barn. Secondly, it contained an old Pershing 1a missile that was missing a warhead. General Georgiou had told Sambrakos personally that the Greek military had acquired the missile

from NATO in the early eighties. It was delivered with the understanding that if there was ever a need to arm it, NATO would supply
the warhead. General Georgiou convinced Sambrakos that because of
Greece's vulnerable geographic position with enemies on three
fronts, he had managed to get the missile "on loan" from NATO. The
Pershing even came with its own Ford M656 transport truck, from
which it could be launched. One day Sambrakos had to familiarize
himself with the truck so that he could drive it if necessary. Georgiou
told Sambrakos that he was one of the handful of men who knew of
its existence. Sambrakos was sworn to secrecy, for it was essential
that Turkey never learn that Greece had a Pershing on an island so
close to its shores.

That was the story the general told Sambrakos, and the sergeant
major naively believed him.

The jeep moved over the rolling hills of the island toward the
north shore. At one point, he drove along the coast. He admired the
silhouettes of the hollow stones that had been placed at intervals
along the shore by the ancient Greeks. They looked like rooks on a
chessboard and had been used to warn villagers of approaching
pirate ships. Firewood was permanently kept inside the stones so
that a blaze could be lit when an enemy ship was sighted. The smoke
signal could be seen by others along the line, and the people were
thus ready to repel the pirates.

The sky was black when Sambrakos eventually stopped the jeep
on the road a hundred meters from the dilapidated old barn. He
jumped out and unlocked the two padlocks that secured the gate.

Sambrakos approached the barn and noted that the padlocks on
the double doors were unlocked. Feeling a rush of adrenaline, the
sergeant major swung the doors open.

When he stepped inside, his heart nearly stopped.

General Georgiou was standing there, waiting for him. He held a
flashlight and a briefcase.

The missile and its truck sat in the barn behind the general,
gleaming in the work lights. The American-made Pershing 1a, or
MGM-31A, is nearly thirty-five feet long with a three-and-a-half-foot

diameter. It has a range of 100 to 460 miles, and is one of the most successful mobile nuclear missiles ever created. Its support equipment includes an automatic azimuth reference system which allows the Pershing to be launched from unsurveyed locations, and a sequential launch adapter which reduces the response time in a quick-reaction role.

"Ah, you're here," the general said. "Get in the truck. We're taking the missile somewhere. We're on a classified mission."

Sambrakos was surprised. "Sir?"

"You heard me, let's go," Georgiou said, pulling the sergeant major inside.

Sambrakos didn't feel right about it. There was something about the general's behavior that bothered him.

Two other men dressed in Greek MP uniforms stepped out from behind the truck. Sambrakos didn't recognize them, and he thought he knew all of the other MPs on the island.

"Oh, this is Sergeant Kandarakis and Sergeant Grammos. They'll be coming along," the general said, turning to walk toward the truck.

Sambrakos stood his ground. It wasn't right, whatever was happening. He didn't know exactly why he felt that way, but he instinctively rebelled against the order.

"Sir, I need to have a little more information about this," Sambrakos said. "Who are these men? I've never seen them before."

The general turned to his aide and said, "I gave you an order, Sergeant Major. Do not question it. Let's go."

Now Sambrakos knew something was terribly wrong. The general sounded scared himself. It was obvious that *he* was doing something wrong and he didn't want to be challenged.

The general turned back to him again and said, "Sambrakos? Are you coming?"

"No, sir," Sambrakos said.

The general narrowed his eyes at the young man. He shook his head and said, "I knew I shouldn't have brought you in on such short notice. I had no time to see if you would really work out. Well, it looks like this *isn't* going to work out."

The general turned and walked away, nodding to the two other men.

Sambrakos was too stunned to react when one of them raised a handgun and shot him in the chest. The MP crashed backward to the floor as blackness overtook him.

The assassin looked outside to make sure no one had heard the shot; then he pulled the body over to the side.

"You'll have to drive instead," the general told the other man. "I hope you can do it. Let's go."

The three of them boarded the M656 and drove out of the barn. Brigadier General Dimitris Georgiou, Number Five of the Decada, was angry about his choice for a new recruit. The sergeant major had been useful for a while as a buffer between him and the rest of the Chios military administration, but the test of loyalty came too soon. At least the boy wouldn't talk. Now the general was the only one in the Greek military left alive who knew about the Pershing missile he had stolen from a NATO base in France twelve years ago.

James Bond arrived in Athens mid-morning. There was a time when Ellinikon International Airport's security record was considered poor. Its reputation had improved after the terrorist-plagued eighties, but Bond never felt completely comfortable there. It was a place where he felt compelled to keep looking over his shoulder.

He entered the country under the name "John Bryce," an alias he had not used for many years. He carried the two Walthers—the PPK and the P99—in a specially lined security briefcase that prevented X-ray penetration. The gruff customs agent sent him through quickly, and Bond stepped into the arrivals terminal. His eyes scanned the faces for the agent from the Greek National Intelligence Service who was supposedly meeting him. Even though he didn't know who it would be, Bond was trained to recognize fellow agents simply by their posture, clothing, or accessories. There was no one who caught his eye.

He was walking through the crowd toward the exit when Niki Mirakos stepped up to him from nowhere and said, "The guided tour of Greece begins in five minutes. Do you have your ticket?"

Bond smiled broadly and responded, "Yes, and it's been punched twice."

"Then hold on to it and follow me," she said with a smile.

"How are you, Niki?" he asked.

Her brown eyes sparkled. "I'm fine. It's good to see you, James . . . er, John."

"I must say this is a surprise and a pleasure."

She led him outside to the parking lot. "They came to me and said that you would be in Athens. Since we had worked together briefly in Cyprus, I got the job."

"Lucky you."

Niki looked at him warmly. "You're the lucky one—you just don't know it yet."

They eventually found a white 1995 Toyota Camry. Niki opened the passenger door for Bond, then went around and sat behind the wheel. As they drove away, she said, "Sorry I have to use this old thing. You're probably used to something better."

"You're the second person in a week that has apologized to me about their car," Bond said. "If it gets you where you need to go on time, then it will do."

"I just wondered, because your company car arrived late last night from London. It's parked in your hotel lot."

So the XK8 had arrived ahead of him. That was something.

"Yes, well, the Service was a bit extravagant with the Jaguar, mostly due to my insistence."

The sun was shining brightly. Compared to London's dreadful weather, Bond thought, Athens was a tropical paradise.

"It's still very pretty," Niki said, reading his thoughts. "You know, Hellas has the best three hundred and sixty-five days a year of any country on the face of the earth. I think the climate had a lot to do with the evolution of society. People migrated to ancient Athens because the sun was always shining." She had used *Hellas*, the Greek word for "Greece." Bond was not fluent in Greek. He could read it, but he couldn't speak it, except for a few common words and expressions.

Bond had been to Greece on a number of occasions. He always

found it to be a warm, friendly country. The people are hard workers, but they play even harder. The afternoon ritual of drinking ouzo, eating *mezedes,* and discussing the meaning of life is standard procedure in Greece. He particularly liked the fact that nearly everyone smoked and he had no problem lighting a cigarette in a public place. Greece has the dubious distinction of having the highest number of smokers per capita in Europe.

"I'm glad you flew to Greece on Thursday, and not Tuesday," she said.

"Oh, why?"

"Don't you know Tuesdays are bad luck in Greece?"

"How come?"

"It was a Tuesday when the Byzantine Empire fell to the Ottomans. Many Greeks won't do anything important on a Tuesday, like have a wedding, or start a journey, or sign a contract."

"I'm afraid I'm not very superstitious."

"That's all right. We Greeks tend to be overly so." She fondled the chain around her neck. It contained a blue glass stone resembling an eye. Bond knew that it was a charm to ward off the evil eye.

Niki drove Bond to the Plateia Syntagmatos, the heart of the modern city of Athens. A large, paved square is at its center, just across from the old royal palace. It was from the palace balcony that the *syntagma,* or constitution, was declared in 1843. The building now houses the Greek parliament. Bond's hotel was directly across from the palace, to the northwest. The Hotel Grande Bretagne at Constitution Square is arguably Athens's grandest hotel, built in 1862 as a mansion to accommodate visiting dignitaries. It was converted into a hotel in 1872 and became the preferred destination for royalty. The Nazis occupied it as their headquarters during World War II, and it was the scene of an attempted assassination of Winston Churchill on Christmas Eve in 1944. The hotel is still aptly referred to as "the Royal Box of Athens."

"Are you hungry?" Niki asked.

"Famished," Bond said. It was time for lunch.

"Why don't you check in and I'll meet you at the hotel restaurant in half an hour? I'll go park the car."

"Fine."

Bond hadn't stayed at the Grande Bretagne since the Colonel Sun affair, many years ago. Memories of the hotel came back to him as he walked into the lobby. It has a large and lofty foyer with stained glass, green marble pillars, and a good copy of a Gobelin tapestry featuring Alexander the Great entering Babylon. Bond was given a corner suite on the eighth floor. It had a sitting room with a window overlooking the parliament building. The bedroom contained a king-sized bed and a terrace with a magnificent view of the Acropolis.

He dressed quickly in a sharp Nassau Silk Noile outfit of tan trousers, a white mesh crew knit shirt, and a tan waistcoat. The Walther PPK fitted snugly in the chamois shoulder holster underneath a white, fully lined silk jacket. Normally the Walther wouldn't have fitted into the Berns-Martin holster, but Q Branch had commissioned the company to make one specially for Bond.

The two-story GB Corner Restaurant was decorated just as elegantly as the hotel it served. The booths, benches, and chairs were covered in maroon leather, and frosted glass lamps at each table cast cool light around the room.

Niki was waiting for him in a booth. She had already ordered a bottle of Chatzimichali red wine.

"Welcome to Athens, Mr. Bryce," she said conspiratorially. "Everything on the menu is quite good."

"I was here several years ago. I remember the food. I take it you live in Athens?"

"Yes, I live west of the tourist areas. I've been here most of my life. I spent some time in the country when I was a girl."

"How long have you been with the service?"

"Would you believe ten years?"

"You've kept your youth remarkably well," Bond said. He guessed that she was in her mid-thirties. Her tan skin glowed in the soft light. Bond found Mediterranean women exotic. She was a delight to look at and talk to. Besides being extremely attractive, Niki was also very professional. He normally preferred working alone or with other men, but this time he looked upon the prospect with a positive attitude. He had a sudden recall of how soft the inside of her thighs had been, and forced the memory out of his head for the moment.

"Thank you. As I said before, it's probably the climate here. Let's order, then we'll talk."

They both started with traditional dishes of moussaka, which was similar to lasagne but made with ground beef, fried eggplant, onions, and béchamel cream and baked. For a main course, they each had souvlaki with rice. Bond knew he was really in Greece when he tasted the succulent beef grilled on a skewer with peppers and onions.

They ordered coffee and she said, "Since we're officially working together, I can now share information with you. I can, how do you say in English, 'feel you in'?"

Bond smiled. "That expression, 'fill you in,' is more American than English, I believe. Yes, it's good to be working with your service. Station G, I'm afraid, was a casualty of one of SIS's administrative changes made during the last several years. Budget cuts eliminated the entire operation, save for a token agent. Old Stuart Thomas is still the head, but he only works twenty hours a week and uses a temporary secretary. Needless to say, the London office was disappointed with what little intelligence Station G had provided on the case. The late Christopher Whitten was a field agent working in Athens temporarily. But never mind that. Feel me in."

She laughed and lit a cigarette.

"As you know, the Greeks are very concerned about the Cyprus situation. The people do not tolerate the Turkish presence in the north. Many feel very passionate about it. Greece is in a constant state of readiness in case a war ever broke out with Turkey. Naturally, no one wants that to happen. Except for the joy of kicking some Turkish butts, a war would be very foolish."

"I understand."

"We believe the Number Killer is attempting to provoke a conflict between Greece and Turkey over Cyprus."

"How do you know?"

"Before it all started, the secret service received a letter from someone who called himself the Monad. It was untraceable. The letter said that a group called the Decada would commit ten acts of violence over the next two months. When the tenth act was completed, war would break out between Turkey and Greece. The southern Cypriots would be reunited with the north under a Greek flag. It was written in a flowery, poetic style, much like ancient Greek verse. It ended by saying that the gods would be watching and waiting, for this was their wish."

"That's it?"

"Yes. It went into the prank pile until the two incidents in Cyprus occurred. I mean, we get a lot of stuff like that. There are so many 'groups' out there and a lot of them claim to be militant ones with violent intentions but they turn out to be harmless. It's not the first time someone has threatened to start a conflict at the Green Line in Cyprus just to break the stalemate. There are a lot of people who might do something crazy. It isn't something to take lightly. Anyway, someone remembered the letter and pulled it out. We now believe the letter was not a hoax. The Decada, whatever it is, exists. We don't know a thing about them. We don't know who they are or where they're based."

"What can you tell me about Charles Hutchinson?"

"He's disappeared. We put a tail on him when he arrived in Athens two days ago. He rented a car and drove south to Cape Sounion. He successfully lost our man there. I suspect he got on a boat or aircraft and went to one of the islands. The rental car was found yesterday in a parking lot near the pier."

"What can you tell me about a man named Konstantine Romanos?"

She laughed. "Great minds think alike. We've had our eye on Mr. Romanos for a little while, actually. He has a very mysterious past."

Niki went through the details that Bond already knew—that Romanos was a lecturer at Athens University, was a noted author, and was considered one of the most brilliant mathematicians in the Western world.

"Where does he get his money?"

"He's extremely wealthy. That's one reason why he's been under suspicion for a few years. He spends a lot of time at the casino on Mount Parnitha. Wins big, loses big, wins it back. He's also the leader of a spiritual and philosophical organization called the New Pythagorean Society. They're a collection of mathematicians who follow the teachings of Pythagoras. It's all legitimate. There is one funny thing, though."

"What's that?"

"They're based in Cape Sounion. And Romanos lives there in a big house when he's not in Athens."

"Well well. Mr. Romanos has suddenly become more interesting to me. What do you know about his background?"

"We know he's a, how do you say, a 'self-made' man. He was a refugee from northern Cyprus in 1974, one of the many Greek Cypriots who fled the Turkish invasion. In Cyprus he had been a noted lecturer and mathematician as well. He had a good life in Nicosia. When he came to Athens he had very little money and was homeless. He had lost his wife and children in a fire caused by the Turks. He was given government housing and a job. Then there was a period of his life that is unaccounted for in our records. Between 1977 and 1982, no one knows where he went or what he did. In late 1982, he reappeared on the scene, with more money than a dozen people make in a lifetime. The tax boys investigated him and he claimed he got the money in the Middle East during those years by investing in and selling real estate. Since that time, he formed the New Pythagorean Society, secured his various teaching and lecturing affairs, bought and sold companies, and he now owns a big yacht called the *Persephone* that sails all over the Aegean."

"A real success story," Bond said.

"A year ago he acquired a pharmaceutical company in Athens called BioLinks Limited. The president is a fairly well-respected scientist named Melina Papas."

Bond smiled. "Great minds *do* think alike. BioLinks owned the clinic in the United States where Charles Hutchinson worked. It's also where he delivered some rather tainted sperm samples."

She nodded and said, "I just read the report. That is amazing. Our joint investigation is paying off, isn't it? We've already gone in with a court order to seize their entire sperm and blood supply until this is sorted out. No one's got sick yet, thank God. We can go over there whenever you'd like and take a look around. I can't imagine that our case is related to those epidemics in America and Japan, though. Do you think it is?"

"If the Americans match the bug I found in Texas with the one in L.A., then I would say it is. Unfortunately, that takes time. Why would Romanos want to own a pharmaceutical company?"

"Who knows. The company was in the red before he got hold of it. This year it looks as if it may turn a profit. They are in the research-and-development area of prescription drugs. We've looked into the company and it's all quite legitimate, but we have a good surveillance team watching them closely."

Bond shook his head, pondering the details. "What does maths have to do with pharmaceuticals?"

"If you ask me, the guy is nuts," she said. "I've seen him on television. I don't understand a thing he says. Then again, maths was my worst subject."

Bond laughed again. "Mine too. What do the New Pythagoreans do?"

"I'm not entirely sure. They pretend to hold philosophy symposiums. They offer courses, both in mathematics and philosophy. It's something of a religion with those people. They're also heavily into numbers . . . numerology, and that might mean something."

"I want to meet Mr. Romanos. What about this casino you mentioned?"

"It's pretty cool, you'll like it," she said, unconsciously dropping her businesslike persona. "It's up on a mountain, and you have to take a cable car to get to it. He usually plays on Friday nights."

"Sounds like my kind of place."

"So what would you like to do first? Where do you want to begin?"

"I believe we should pick up the Jaguar and take a drive down to Cape Sounion. I'd like to take a look at this New Pythagorean Society and see where Romanos lives. Tomorrow we'll go to BioLinks."

"Fine. Are you armed?"

"Certainly."

"Then let's get going."

The blue Jaguar XK8 sped smoothly into Attica, the tip of the Greek peninsula jutting out southeast from Athens. The coast road was perfect for Bond to try out the new car. It was a winding, twisting four-lane highway that eventually narrowed to two lanes with mountains on one side and the sea on the other. They passed resorts with deluxe beaches and hotels, such as Glyfada and Voula. Traffic wasn't very heavy, so Bond took the car at a safe but slightly accelerated speed all the way. He loved the grip of the wheel and felt the engine's power in his hands. He longed for a stretch of road where he could push the Jaguar to its limit.

Niki sat silently in the passenger seat, looking out at the sea. Her reverie was interrupted by the cellular phone in her handbag. She answered it, spoke in Greek, and hung up. "We need to go straight to the Temple of Poseidon when we reach Cape Sounion. Something's happened there. Do you know the story of Aegeas and the Temple of Poseidon?"

"Please enlighten me."

"There was an ancient king named Aegeas. His son went out on a long expedition. Aegeas told his son that when he returned, he should put white sails on his ship so that the king would know that the expedition was a success. However, even though the mission was a success, the son forgot to change the sails and approached the cape with black ones. The king thought his son was dead and threw himself into the sea. The sea was thereafter called the Aegean Sea, and the Temple of Poseidon was built there in his memory."

"I've seen it," said Bond. "It's a magnificent set of ruins."

The temple was built on a craggy spur that plunged sixty-five meters to the sea. It was erected in 444 B.C., around the same time as the Parthenon, and was constructed of Doric marble columns. Only sixteen of the columns remain.

"It is widely believed that the temple was built by Ictinus, the same architect who built the Temple of Hephaestus in the Ancient Agora," Niki said.

"That's where Whitten's body was dumped?"

"Right."

They reached Cape Sounion in just under two hours. They could see the monument from the road, gleaming white in the late-afternoon sun. As they approached the site, though, they were met by police vehicles and were prevented from going farther.

Niki spoke to the officer and then showed him some identification. Reluctantly, he let the car through and radioed his superiors at the ruins that Bond and Niki were on their way up the hill.

The popular tourist attraction was closed for the day, and several official vehicles were parked in the gravel lot. A group of people were up at the base of the temple, looking at something covered by a sheet. Bond parked the car and they walked up the hill to join the police. A sergeant spoke to Niki, then led them through the crowd to the white sheet.

The first thing they saw was the number "7" scrawled in red on a sign reading "Deposit Litter Here" in English and Greek. Under the sheet was a dead body. The policeman said something else in Greek, then pulled the sheet down so that they could see the victim.

Although the body was badly battered, Bond recognized him. It was Charles Hutchinson.

FOURTEEN

THE NEW PYTHAGOREANS

BOND AND NIKI SPENT TWO HOURS AT THE CRIME SCENE SPEAKING WITH Greek police inspectors and gathering what information they could. Before leaving the Temple of Poseidon, Bond stood at the edge of the cliff and looked out to sea. A wave of melancholy hit him inexplicably. He looked out at the horizon toward the west. The sun was on its way down, casting its orange glow over the water. Although the scenery was quite different, the view reminded him of Jamaica and his beloved Shamelady. He longed to be there. Niki came up behind him and watched with him for a moment before speaking.

"I feel a great sadness in you," she said finally. "What is it?"

Bond sighed. "Nothing. Come on, there's not much more daylight. We had better go and see Romanos's house."

Niki looked at him sideways, then let it go. "Look there, to the north."

She pointed toward the hills away from the temple.

"Do you see that building there? That's the Hotel Aegaeon. Now, just beyond that, do you see the mansion with red windows and beige walls?"

"Yes."

"That's where Romanos lives. Let's go. I'll tell you in the car what the inspector told me."

They got into the Jaguar and drove away from the site.

Niki said, "They have to perform a postmortem examination, but the medical examiner at the scene thought that Charles Hutchinson had been dead about three days. He obviously wasn't killed here, but his body was moved here overnight. It was discovered by tourists this morning."

Bond said, "The number 'seven'—if Charles was killed three days ago, that's around the same time as the two incidents in northern Cyprus. They were numbers 'five' and 'six.' "

"Yes, they were all done the same day."

"The first series of attacks didn't occur on the same day. And there were four of them."

"Yes, but they were committed very close together in time," she said. "I think the significance is in the numbers, not in the time frame."

"What else did you find out?"

"We'll get the full autopsy report, but from the looks of it, Charles Hutchinson was killed in a fall of some kind. His body was badly battered—not from a beating or torture, but from an impact. He also had an old Greek coin in his mouth."

"Just like Whitten. Payment for Charon the boatman to take him across the River Styx."

"I'm trying to figure out why the body was dumped at the Temple of Poseidon."

"Poseidon was one of the statuettes found at Episkopi."

They pondered the mystery in silence as the car pulled up to the gate of the large mansion they had seen from the temple. A stone fence surrounded the property, and an intercom screened visitors before the automatic gate would open. The two-story house was built in the 1920s. Some lights were on in a few of the windows, but the only other sign of activity was that a man dressed in black was washing a black Ferrari F355 GTS on the drive. He looked up and saw them peering through the gate, but kept on washing the car.

"We've just been spotted. Where is the headquarters for the New Pythagoreans?" Bond asked.

"Just down the road. Let's see if the office is still open."

They drove away from the mansion and got on the main road. She directed him to a large white building of stone and plaster. It was a modest structure that might have been a restaurant or a shop. A sign outside the building read in both Greek and English, "The New Pythagorean Society." There were three cars parked in front, and the front door was propped open.

They got out of the Jaguar and went inside. The entry way was lit by candles. Literature was piled on a table by the door. Bond examined the pamphlets which outlined the organization's tenets and provided membership applications.

"May I help you?" came a voice, speaking Greek.

They turned to see a man of about forty wearing a white robe. He had come in through an archway that led to the rest of the building. He had dark hair and bright blue eyes.

Niki answered him in Greek, and then he spoke English. "You are welcome. If you have any questions, feel free to ask."

"I'm very interested in your organization," Bond said. "I'm from England and am writing a book about the ties between philosophy and religions. I'd be grateful if you could tell us a little about the New Pythagoreans. If I end up using the material in the book, you'll get some publicity out of it."

The man smiled broadly. "I'd be delighted to help you. I am Miltiades. I run the facility here at Cape Sounion. And you are . . . ?"

"I'm John Bryce, and this is . . ."

"Cassandra Talon," Niki said. "I'm serving as Mr. Bryce's guide in Greece."

"I see. Well, do you know much about Pythagoras?"

"Just a little," Bond said.

"He was a great mathematician who founded his own group of philosophers. It was called the Pythagorean Society, and they based everything in life on numbers. They believed that everything in the universe could be explained or defined with numerology. It's not something I can make you understand in ten minutes, mind you."

"That's all right. What does your group do?"

"We follow the teachings of Pythagoras, which often went beyond mathematics. He was one of the first philosophers to link spirituality with the challenges of everyday life. For example, he believed that one's diet was important in achieving a soul that was at peace with the body. We believe that animals and man are on the same journey, and that man is a little farther along than his animal brethren. Knowing this, we are expected to refrain from the eating of flesh. Our members are noted mathematicians and philosophers, mostly Greek, but we have members all over the world. We publish a quarterly magazine that is read in universities. Some of the greater minds in the Western world write for us. We donate a sizable amount of our income to various charities. We also provide a scholarship in mathematics at Athens University for qualified students."

"I've heard of your leader, Mr. Romanos. Is he here?"

"No, I'm afraid Mr. Romanos is away. He rarely shows his face here these days, he's such a busy man. He leaves me in charge, which was quite a leap of faith on his part, I must say!" He chuckled to himself.

"He lives nearby, doesn't he?"

"Yes, he does. You may have seen the mansion with the red roof on the way here. That's where he lives. Mr. Romanos is a man who enjoys his privacy. He has become very famous over the last few years."

"Can we see the rest of the building?"

"Certainly. Follow me."

Miltiades led them through the archway and into a large room that resembled a sanctuary. Pews covered the floor, facing a podium at the front of the room. Bond's heart skipped a beat when he saw what was printed on a tapestry hanging on the wall behind the podium.

It was an equilateral triangle of ten points, just like the one that he saw at Romanos's house in Austin, Texas.

"What is the significance of the triangle?" Bond asked.

"Ah, that is the symbol of the New Pythagorean Society. It is our logo, I suppose you can say. You see, Pythagoras and his followers believed that the number ten was sacred. This triangle consists of ten points. Notice that if you turn the triangle, it will always rest on a base of four points. The next level has three points, then two, and the tenth point is at the top of the triangle. It represents perfection."

Miltiades then led the couple out of the sanctuary and into a sitting room and library. The place was lined with full bookshelves. There were tables and chairs for studying, some occupied by young men and women.

"This is our library, where we keep over five thousand works on mathematics and philosophy. Students are allowed to use the library for a small fee. They come from all over Europe to use our resources." Miltiades had a kind of patronizing attitude that rubbed Bond the wrong way.

Niki and Bond stepped over to a wall to study some framed photographs. There was one of the board of directors, all dressed in white robes. Several photos featured Konstantine Romanos at various public functions. In one he was accepting an award from the prime minister of Greece. In another he was shaking hands with Melina Mercouri.

Still another photo featured Romanos sitting at a dinner table with several other men dressed in tuxedos. Next to Romanos was none other than Alfred Hutchinson. The photo was dated "1983."

"Do you know where this photo was taken?" Bond asked Miltiades.

Miltiades peered at it and shook his head. "Alas, no, I'm not sure. I think it might have been some kind of banquet for the university."

Bond and Niki exchanged glances. Here was proof that Alfred Hutchinson knew Konstantine Romanos. Bond feared what the news might mean to M. Had she been "sleeping with the enemy"?

The rest of the tour was unremarkable. Bond politely asked for some of the organization's literature and took Miltiades's card. They thanked him and left the building.

Back in the Jaguar, he said, "That triangle was the same as the one I saw in Texas. I think I'm beginning to understand the pattern of numbers. They're following that triangle. The first four attacks occurred around the same time: Whitten's murder, the two attacks on the Cyprus bases, and Alfred Hutchinson's assassination. There were only three in the next group—the next line up in the triangle: the two attacks in northern Cyprus and Charles Hutchinson's murder. I would wager that the next group of attacks will consist of only two, and they will be big ones. They're leading up to the coup de grâce, the tenth and biggest one yet."

"I think you're right," Niki said. "So do you think the New Pythagoreans might be a front for the Decada?"

"That's what I want to find out. I think the sooner I meet Konstantine Romanos, the better."

The sun had set and they were hungry. Niki suggested that they eat dinner at a taverna she knew before setting off back to Athens. They stopped at a quaint little place called Akroyali, which means "the edge of the beach." It was a white wooden building with blue trim and blue tables. Blue-and-white-checked tablecloths covered the tables both indoors and on a patio outside.

At first the taverna didn't appear to be open for business, until the proprietor, a woman named Maria, recognized Niki and hurtled out of the kitchen with an enthusiastic greeting. They chose an indoor table because the wind had come up outside, but they had a full view of the beach and sea.

Maria went on and on in Greek about that evening's "special," which apparently was the only dish they happened to be serving on a November weekday. Niki whispered to Bond that the taverna was normally closed for the winter season during the week, but because Maria was her friend, she would make something for them. It was another example of Greek hospitality.

Maria brought out a bottle of Villitsa, a local white wine, some water, and two small bottles of ouzo. For the ouzo, she provided two glasses with ice.

Bond poured the ouzo. The clear liquid turned milky when it touched the ice in the glass. The licorice taste was refreshing, and it reminded Bond of drinking sake.

"May the poisons go down with the ouzo," Niki said as she took a sip.

Someone in the kitchen turned on the radio. A Greek folk song was playing, and Bond and Niki listened to the energetic but plaintive music until the tune was over.

"Did you feel the pain in that song?" Niki asked. "All Greek music has pain in it. In a way, we enjoy the pain. The songs are really about sad things, but they *sound* happy."

Bond poured the wine. They raised their glasses and clinked them together.

"Do you know why we clink glasses when we drink wine?" Bond asked her.

"No, why?"

"Drinking wine satisfies all but one of the senses. We can see the wine, touch it, taste it, smell it . . . but we can't hear it. So we—" He tapped her glass again to make the clink sound. "To hear the wine."

Niki smiled. "It's good to see you chirpy again. I really saw a dark cloud come over you earlier."

"I'll always be chirpy if you're going to ply me with ouzo."

Niki laughed and Maria brought out an overflowing bowl of Greek salad and two forks. It was a true Greek salad, consisting of tomatoes, cucumbers, onions, olives, feta cheese, and olive oil, and there were also plates of fried octopus and bread. Niki showed Bond the Greek way of eating bread and salad—she took a piece of bread and dabbed up some of the olive oil on the bottom of the salad bowl, then fed it to Bond.

The main course was sargi, a saltwater fish about a foot long. Maria's husband caught the fish just outside the taverna, where they congregated around the rocks in the sea. It was grilled with a mixture of eggs and lemon shaken over the fish. It went well with the wine.

Maria beamed as she spoke at a furious pace over their table as they ate. She used her hands expressively as she talked.

Niki translated. "She says it's wonderful to see two romantic people again for a change. Usually all she gets are people doing business on cellular phones. 'How is one supposed to enjoy a meal if one is doing business at the same time?' she asks."

"Are we romantic?"

"We were once. Maybe it shows."

When they had finished, Bond paid for the meal and left a large tip. Maria happily fussed over them as they got up to leave.

The coast highway was very dark by the time they left Cape Sounion in the Jaguar. They didn't notice that a black Ferrari F355 GTS had pulled out onto the road behind them.

Bond drove at seventy-five miles per hour, feeling the car grip the two-lane road as it twisted and turned along the mountains. The darkness of the sea was on the left side of the car. The only thing preventing a vehicle from shooting off the road and down the cliff was a useless short metal rail. Traffic was light, but every now and then an oncoming car would pull around a curve and pass by the Jaguar.

He noticed the headlights after ten minutes had passed. The car behind him was keeping a good pace with the Jaguar.

"Tell me, Niki, do Greek drivers always drive as fast as I do?" Bond asked.

"No one drives in Greece like you do, James. I love your car too, but you could slow down."

Bond decreased the speed to see what the car behind him would do. Once he had slowed to nearly fifty-five, the Ferrari crossed the yellow line and illegally passed him. Bond caught sight of a dark, hulking shape looking over at him as the car went by.

"That was the black Ferrari we saw in front of Romanos's mansion," Bond said.

He immediately activated the GPS navigation controls. A screen popped up inside the windshield. An aerial view of the coast road rendered in real-time Silicon Graphics appeared on the screen. A flashing yellow blip indicated the Jaguar. The Ferrari was speeding ahead, a flashing red blip. In a moment, Bond felt the wheel turn independently, following the route transmitted by satellite navigation. If he had wanted to, he could have let go completely and used his hands for other tasks, but he preferred to control the car manually. He continued to slow down, putting some distance between the Ferrari and the Jaguar.

"He must not have been very interested in you," Niki said. "He's gone pretty far ahead." The red blip soon disappeared off the screen. It was more than three miles ahead of the Jaguar.

"You spoke too soon," Bond said as two more red blips appeared behind the Jaguar on the screen. They were traveling at a tremendous speed toward Bond.

He responded by increasing his own speed back to seventy-five. Bond flipped another switch and the outline of the flying scout appeared on the screen. The graphics revealed that it was stored neatly beneath the Jaguar. He pushed a button and the readout proclaimed: "Readying Scout." A small joystick popped out of a compartment on the dashboard. In three seconds, the display changed to read: "Scout Ready." Bond pushed a red launch button and they felt the car lunge. At the same time they heard a sudden whoosh behind the Jaguar as the scout ejected from its bay. The batlike vehicle soared out and up into the air, then turned so that it was traveling thirty feet above and parallel with the Jaguar.

Keeping one hand on the wheel, Bond used his left hand to manipulate the joystick. He guided the scout so that it changed course and flew back toward his pursuers. Once it was above the two cars, Bond pushed another button. The viewscreen on the dash displayed the makes and models—they were both black Ferraris and they were gaining fast.

Bond sped up to a hundred. He heard Niki gasp slightly as she clutched the armrest on her door. The tires screeched when he pulled around a curve, but the Jaguar's control was outstanding. Then they heard gunfire.

Three bullets hit the back of the Jaguar in rapid succession. One of the Ferraris was about thirty yards behind Bond. He could see in the rearview mirror that someone was leaning out the passenger window and was firing at the car.

More bullets hit, but the chobam armor deflected them. Major Boothroyd's reactive skins exploded as they were hit. Viscous fluid spread around the bullet holes in the metal, and within seconds a new patch of coating had covered the penetrations.

He shut off the headlights in order to take advantage of the night-vision capabilities. The optical systems intensified the available light and projected a view of the road on the secondary screen inside the windshield. The gunfire continued, but the shooter's aim was hampered now. The bullets whizzed past the Jaguar without hitting it.

An oncoming car shot around a curve, nearly hitting Bond. The horn blared. Bond punched another button so that the scout would transmit the aerial view of the road again. Now he could "see" around the curves ahead and determine if there were any oncoming cars in the opposite lane. Bond drove around slower-moving vehicles in his path, speeding past them in the dark. The Ferraris, however, kept up with him.

Bond slowed a little to let one of the pursuers catch up.

"What are you doing?" Niki asked.

"Let's see how badly these fellows want us."

The Jaguar's speed went down to seventy-five, and the Ferrari was on its tail. Confused as to why his bullets weren't piercing the car's body, the shooter let loose a volley of gunfire from the Uzi he was carrying. The driver pulled into the opposite lane, taking a chance that there were no oncoming cars.

Bond let the Ferrari pull up alongside him. The two men inside glared at Bond, attempting to peer in the dark window to see his face. Bond punched a button. Suddenly, the lights from an oncoming car zoomed around a bend in front of the Ferrari. Niki screamed. Bond could see the surprised looks on the pursuers' faces as the driver swerved to the left to avoid the car. Unfortunately, he swerved off the road, through the metal rail, and out into space. The Ferrari crashed on the cliffside below two seconds later and burst into flames.

Bond punched another button and the hologram of the oncoming car disappeared.

"What happened to the other car?" Niki asked, her eyes wide.

"It was a projection of your imagination," Bond said.

The other Ferrari sped forward, attempting to shorten the distance between the two cars. Another man leaned out of the window and fired. This time the bullets sprayed across the back of the Jaguar. Bond pushed down the accelerator and increased his speed to one hundred twenty. The GPS navigation showed that the original

Ferrari, the one that went ahead of Bond earlier, had turned around and was now coming back.

"Do you think they recognized you from Texas?" Niki asked.

"Unless there were hidden cameras at the infertility clinic, they couldn't have. No one saw me at Romanos's house except men who are dead now. I suppose the clinic is a possibility. Hang on, this fellow behind me is asking for it, and our old friend in the first Ferrari is coming back."

Bond used the joystick to maneuver the flying scout directly over the Ferrari behind them. There was about twenty feet between them now. At one point, the Ferrari inched up close enough to ram the Jaguar's rear bumper. The scout's targeting mechanism locked onto the Ferrari and maintained its speed. Now, there was nowhere the Ferrari could go without the scout flying directly over it.

The headlights of the first Ferrari appeared around a curve ahead. It was coming toward him at a high speed. The lights were on bright, but luckily the night-vision opticals prevented the beams from blinding him. The Ferrari pulled into his lane, ready to meet the Jaguar head-on.

Bond was about to swerve into the westbound lane, but the GPS navigation screen indicated that another car was there, slightly behind the Ferrari. It was probably a civilian. The Ferrari behind him was gaining and the man was shooting again. In a few seconds the Jaguar would collide with the oncoming Ferrari. If he swerved to the right, he would crash into the mountain. If he pulled into the other lane, he would hit the civilian car or go sailing off the cliff.

Bond flipped two switches, one right after the other, and felt the car lurch as a cruise missile shot out from beneath the chassis. The Ferrari in front of him exploded into a huge ball of flame and went careening into the mountainside. The civilian car went on past. The driver's eyes were wide with terror as he passed the Jaguar.

The Ferrari in back was very close now. Bond manipulated the joystick so that the flying scout inched ahead of his own car. He pressed a couple of buttons and the computer made instant calculations comparing height, speed, and distance. He moved the flying scout into position and once again locked onto the target behind him. Bond pushed a button and looked in the rearview mirror.

The flying scout released a swarm of mines on tiny parachutes. The computer had carefully calculated the time it would take for the mines to reach the ground. Then it had positioned the scout far enough ahead so that the Ferrari would be in the right spot on the road when the mines hit. When they did, the Ferrari was blown out of the lane and off the cliff.

Now that the threat had been eliminated, Bond turned on the car's headlights and proceeded toward Athens at a safe speed. He slowed down long enough for the flying scout to dock underneath the car. Once it was in its bay, Bond locked it down.

"Well, I'm impressed," Niki said. "I'm going to have to speak to our armorer. We never get any toys like these."

"Do girls use toys like these?"

"This girl does."

Bond opened a small compartment in his armrest. He pulled out a set of keys and handed them to her.

"These are spares, in the event that you might need them."

She took them, wide eyed. *"Efharisto!"*

"And just in case we meet any more Ferraris, I'm going to give the Jaguar a little face-lift. It won't change the car, but it will confuse the enemy for a few minutes." He flipped a switch, and the electrically sensitive pigments in the car's paint changed. The Jaguar went from blue to red. Another switch turned the license plate from an English registration to an Italian one. Bond then reached out to turn off the GPS satellite navigation device, but decided not to. He set the cruise control to maintain the car's speed and punched in the commands for the car to guide them along the coast road straight into Athens. With his hands free now, he turned in his seat and put his arms around Niki.

"Oh my God," she said. "The last time I ever did anything like this in a car, I was a teenager."

Bond kissed her and slowly put his hand on her breast. He could feel the nipple harden beneath her cotton shirt. She let out a tiny gasp and arched her back so that he had easier access to her erogenous zones.

"We probably have another hour and a half before we reach Athens," he said. "The back seat can barely hold one person, much less two. Unfortunately, bucket seats are not my idea of comfort for this sort of thing either."

She said, "Who says we have to be comfortable? I think we'll manage just fine—at least until we reach a little viewpoint I know up ahead where we can stop for a while."

Then she pulled off her shirt.

FIFTEEN

BIOLINKS

INEXPLICABLY, BOND AWOKE WITH A START. HE LOOKED OVER AND SAW THE curves of Niki's body beneath the sheet next to him. She was sleeping soundly.

He looked at the clock and saw that it was late morning. It had been an extremely pleasant night. They had made love on the terrace of his Grande Bretagne suite with all of Athens before them. There was something appropriate about the act of copulation in full view of the Acropolis. They had continued the lovemaking on the large bed inside. Niki's cries of passion were loud and were probably heard in other parts of the hotel, but Bond didn't care. He enjoyed lively women, and this girl was definitely a fiery Mediterranean. She seemed to be insatiable. They had finally fallen asleep in the early hours before sunrise.

As he watched her breathe quietly, Bond wallowed in the melancholy he now felt. The night had been an assault on the senses: a terrific meal, a brush with death, then hours of sex. Bond had felt completely alive when Niki's legs wrapped around his waist and she looked into his eyes with her own deep brown ones. Now that it was morning and a new day, all that had vanished. The previous night was just a shadow of a memory and now he felt empty.

Niki must have sensed him watching her, for she stirred and

stretched. She turned to him and reached out, saying, *"Kalimera,"* in a sleepy voice. He took her in his arms and kissed her. "Good morning," he replied.

"What time is it?" she asked with a yawn.

"Nearly eleven o'clock. I never sleep this late."

"You needed your rest after last night."

He ran his hand along the contour of her side, following the curve across her ribs to her waist, then up and over the hip.

"I'm going to make a phone call," he said. He kissed her again, stood and slipped on one of the hotel's terry cloth robes, and walked into the sitting room. He used a small standard-issue Q Branch device to check the phone for any bugs, then picked up the receiver.

There was a two-hour time difference between Greece and England. Sir Miles Messervy was probably up by now, pottering around his garden at Quarterdeck or sitting drinking coffee and reading *The Times*.

A gruff voice answered, but it lightened considerably when Bond said who it was.

"Hello, James, where are you?"

"I'm abroad, sir. I wanted to ask you something. I hope it's not too early."

"Not at all. I was just sitting here drinking coffee and reading *The Times*. I take it you're on the Hutchinson case?"

"Right. Do you remember the night of your party, you said that you knew something about his family. What was it?"

Bond heard the former M sigh. He said, "I think I was reacting to my own prejudices against the man. We just didn't like each other much, I suppose."

"You can tell me, Sir Miles."

"I don't know if you remember any of the brouhaha that occurred when Hutchinson was first given the post of Ambassador to the World?"

"I only remember it was greeted with an enthusiastic response."

"There was one article, buried somewhere, I don't know, in the

Daily Express or some such paper, about his father's court-martial during the war. It raised a few eyebrows but it disappeared quickly."

"I didn't see that. What was it about?"

"Hutchinson's father, Richard Hutchinson, was an officer stationed in Greece. He was court-martialed for 'mislaying' a horde of Nazi gold. That sort of thing was happening all over the place in Europe. The Swiss didn't get it all. It was a similar situation as that other officer you investigated in Jamaica, I don't recall his name. The one who died on his beach."

"Smythe."

"That's right. Anyway, Richard Hutchinson was accused of stealing a large amount of the Nazis' gold supply from a cache in Athens. He was eventually acquitted for lack of evidence and he got an honorable discharge. That's why nothing more was ever made of it. Hutchinson went on into civilian life. Needless to say, the gold was never found."

"Interesting. Do you believe the old man was guilty?"

"If he had been *Alfred* Hutchinson, I'd say yes, because I know . . . er, knew the man. I didn't know his father. But the army doesn't usually go court-martialing officers unless they have a damned good reason."

"Why did Alfred Hutchinson rub you up the wrong way, Sir Miles?"

"He had an air of superiority that was obnoxious. He thought he was a cut above everyone else. I wouldn't have bought a secondhand motorcar from him. I never trusted him. That's all. Only gut feelings, I'm afraid."

"No, that's fine, Sir Miles. You've been enormously helpful."

"Goodbye, James," the old man said. "Be careful."

They had an appointment with Melina Papas, the president of BioLinks Limited, after lunch. It would not be a pleasant meeting. The Greek police force had already confiscated the building's entire sperm and blood supply and had put a serious deadlock on the facility's business operations, but it couldn't be helped. Bond and Niki expected to get an earful from Ms. Papas about that.

Niki drove the Toyota while Bond studied a file marked "BioLinks Limited." Inside was a black-and-white photo of a woman in her forties with dark hair, a hawk nose, and a puckered mouth. The caption read, "Melina Papas, President." Her résumé was impressive, as she had worked in research and development for three major international drug companies before founding BioLinks six years ago.

BioLinks Limited was located near Athens University in a large, three-story modern complex. The lower floor held medical offices that served patients with infertility problems and acted as a family planning unit. The upper floors contained offices, laboratories, and drug manufacturing equipment.

They were taken to the elevator by a plump woman with a mustache and eventually brought into the executive office of the president. It was a large, well-lit, and comfortable room with a conference table at one end and an elegant desk at the other. Medical and biochemistry books lined the walls.

After a moment, a frumpy woman with a hawk nose walked into the office. She was short, roughly five feet tall.

"I'm Melina Papas," she said. She didn't look happy.

Niki introduced them in Greek, but before she could finish, the woman said in English, "When can we have back our sperm and blood supplies? Do you realize what this has done to our business? Our research and development has completely halted!"

"We want to make sure that there isn't anything wrong with your bodily fluids, Ms. Papas, or rather, the company's bodily fluids," Niki said. "You wouldn't want to give someone anything that might hurt them, would you?"

"It's been twenty-four hours. How long will this take?"

"Ms. Papas, I think you can count on not getting any of it back. It will probably be destroyed."

"This is outrageous! You will hear from our lawyers." Melina Papas clenched her puckered mouth even more tightly.

"That's fine," Niki said, "but we have the law on our side. Now, we'd like to ask you some questions if you don't mind."

"I do mind, but go ahead and let's get it over with."

"Do you know Charles Hutchinson?" Bond asked.

"No."

"He delivered a case of sperm from your clinic, ReproCare, in Austin, Texas."

Ms. Papas shook her head. "We haven't had any deliveries from them in weeks. I told your other inspectors that."

"Ms. Papas, we know that Charles Hutchinson delivered a case here, and we'd like to know what was in it," Niki said.

"Why do you have samples shipped here from the United States?" Bond asked. "Can't you get your own sperm here in Greece?"

"Yes, of course we can. It's just that our clients tend to think they get better quality if it comes from America."

"Being Greek, I consider that an insult," Niki said.

"Surprisingly, it's true, to an extent," the woman said. "The sperm tends to be healthier and have better motility. I'm not saying that really makes it better, but it sounds better to our clients. It's marketing, that's all. You understand that many races are represented by the sperm we market. We get people who want an Asian father, or a Caucasian, or a Hispanic . . . We have to get what sperm we can."

"What kind of research and development are you doing here?"

"We make drugs, Mr. Bryce. That is our primary business. We also have a small team working on fertility issues. There is a team working on vaccinations for various diseases. We have an AIDS researcher. We have a cancer researcher. Our facility is one of the most highly respected medical research laboratories in Greece."

"How well did you know Dr. Ashley Anderson?" Bond asked.

"I met her three times, I think. She came here on business a few times. I was certainly unaware that she was involved in criminal activity."

"ReproCare *was* owned by BioLinks, wasn't it?" Niki asked.

"Yes, but it was an independent clinic. They operated on their own."

"Then why were you getting sperm samples from them?" Bond asked.

"It was just part of our business! Really, I was terribly distraught when I learned what happened in America. I couldn't believe that she was using our laboratory and clinic there to distribute chemical weapons. She was a talented and intelligent biochemist. I think the Americans must have got the wrong person or something. It just can't be true."

"I'm afraid it is true," Niki said.

"Luckily our insurance will cover the loss of the clinic. I still don't understand how she died, though."

"She took her own life, Ms. Papas," Niki said.

"I see."

"Do you know a man named Konstantine Romanos?" Bond asked. He noticed that the woman flinched a little.

"Of course I do—he owns the company," she said. "He doesn't have anything to do with the day-to-day operation of it. That's my job. I think he's been in the building only a couple of times."

"He's put a lot of money into BioLinks, has he?"

"Well, yes. We would have gone bankrupt two years ago if he hadn't purchased us. Now we're worth millions."

It was difficult to pin anything on her or the company. The Greek police and secret service had absolutely nothing out of the ordinary on BioLinks. Melina Papas had a clean record. Bond thought it was possible that whoever was behind all of this was just using BioLinks as a tool of convenience, but his intuition told him otherwise.

"Did you know a man named Christopher Whitten?"

"No, I don't think so. Is he English?"

"Yes."

"I don't know him."

"Does the name Alfred Hutchinson mean anything to you?"

Again, Bond detected an involuntary blink. "No," she said.

Bond looked at Niki. They silently acknowledged that they weren't getting anywhere.

"Thank you, Ms. Papas," Niki said. "We're sorry to have troubled you. I'm sure arrangements will be made to reimburse you for the loss of the, uhm, bodily fluids."

"Can I have your guarantee?"

"I'm not authorized to do that, but I'll see what I can do."

They were shown out of the office and led to the elevator by one of Ms. Papas's aides. Once they were alone, Niki whispered, "So how good a liar was she, James?"

"A good one," he said. "But not good enough."

Back in her office, Melina Papas poured a glass of scotch and sat at her desk, trembling. She picked up the phone and dialed her secretary.

"Christina," she said, "I have to go away for a few days. I'm leaving now. Please handle all my correspondence and phone calls. . . . No, I can't tell you where I'm going. If you need to get hold of me, leave a message on my voice mail. I'll call you. . . . Right."

She hung up, then opened a cupboard behind the desk. She removed a travel bag and stuffed it with some of her more treasured office possessions. Melina Papas fought back tears, for she knew she would never be returning to work in this capacity again.

After she was finished, she picked up the phone again and placed a call to the island of Chios.

By the end of that day, fifteen people in London had died of Williams's disease. One of them had brought it across the English Channel to Paris. New York's casualties numbered in the thirties. In Japan, the death toll had climbed to well over a hundred. In Los Angeles, ninety-eight people had met their end from the mysterious affliction.

Inevitably, the news agencies realized what was going on. That night, it was reported on CNN that a deadly epidemic was threatening to spread worldwide.

ROMANOS

THE AU MONT PARNES CASINO SITS ATOP MOUNT PARNITHA, ONE OF THE three hills surrounding Athens. It is in the Thrakomakedones area, a suburb at the outer limits of the city. While it is possible to drive up the mountain to the casino and park a car right outside, almost everyone who visits the establishment chooses to park down below and ride the cable car. It is a pleasant five-minute ride, and at night the view of Athens is spectacular. The city lights fan away from the mountain and spread across the dark vista as far as the eye can see.

At ten P.M., James Bond parked the Jaguar in the cable-car parking lot and joined a group of twelve people in the waiting room. He was a bit overdressed in a gray Brioni tailored three-piece suit, but he wanted to make an impression on Romanos when he met him.

After their visit to BioLinks, Niki had gone back to her headquarters in Katechaki Street. Bond told her that he would call her in the morning after his night at the casino. He had wanted to do this alone. Partners were fine in most situations, but Bond didn't like distractions when he gambled, and he thought a partner like Niki would be distracting for what he had to do tonight. Besides, Niki needed to follow up on the police investigation of Charles Hutchinson's death. Frankly, he wanted a little distance. It was a familiar malaise, and unfortunately, it was a vicious circle. She had called him twice during the evening, probably in an attempt to get him to change his mind and allow her to accompany him. As usual, it seemed that women always became more interested in him when he tried to avoid them. As Felix Leiter once said to him, "Women are like stamps—the more you spit on them, the more they get attached to you."

The casino itself was a bit of a letdown after the spectacular cable car ride. Bond had to walk through nondescript hallways to the main room. Not nearly as opulent as Bond had expected, the Au Mont Parnes was small. It consisted solely of one room containing all of the various gaming tables. Although there were no slot machines and the red carpet was ornate, little else in the casino was striking. Off to the side of the room near the bar was a section for sitting and drinking that contained several tables covered in white tablecloths.

Despite its overall shabbiness, the casino attracted a crowd. The place was already full, and smoke filled the room. Several blackjack tables were in operation, the roulette table was packed with players and spectators, and the poker tables were unreachable.

Bond went over to the only baccarat table in the casino. It too was crowded, with no vacant seats. He lit one of his cigarettes from H. Simmons of Burlington Arcade and ordered a vodka martini from a waitress. When his drink came, he stood casually to one side and observed the people around the table.

Konstantine Romanos had the "shoe." There was a singular aura around the man, as if he exuded an invisible, yet tangible, charisma. He was very handsome, sat very tall in his seat, and had a dark complexion. His eyes were cold as steel. He incongruously smoked a thin cigar in a cigarette holder, the smoke circling his head in halos. Romanos was apparently doing very well. He had a large stack of chips in front of him.

Bond recognized the cousin, Vassilis, standing behind Romanos. He was the bodybuilding, swarthy man he had seen in Texas. Vassilis wasn't fooling anyone—he was there as a bodyguard for his boss. The man was simply a mountain.

Baccarat is closely related to chemin de fer and its rules vary from casino to casino. Bond observed that the game in the Au Mont Parnes was closer to chemin de fer in that the bank was held by a single player until he lost. The bank, and shoe, then rotated around the table to the players willing to put up an amount of cash. The object of the game was to obtain cards totalling as close to 9 as possible. Court cards and 10s were worthless.

A woman sitting at the table said, "Banco," and placed a large bet in the Players' field on the table. Calling "Banco" was a bet against the entire bank's worth, which in this case was around a million drachmas. No one else at the table was betting, except a Middle Eastern man wearing a fez. Bond studied the woman, who looked to be in her late twenties or early thirties. She had fiery red hair and was extremely attractive, with pale white skin and blue eyes, and a hint of freckles on her face and bare shoulders.

Romanos dealt the cards. He had a natural 8 and turned his cards over.

"Eight," he said. The redhead lost her money.

A man shook his head and stood up from the table, leaving a seat open for Bond. He casually took the chair and said, "Banco." He matched the bank's bet of two million drachmas. At the exchange rate of roughly 365 drachmas to the pound, this amounted to almost 5,500 pounds. Earlier Bond had drawn out the cash from an SIS fund specifically for "nonreimbursable" business expenses.

Konstantine Romanos looked up at Bond and nodded his head slightly in a greeting. He dealt the cards from the shoe. Bond had a 1 and a 3. Romanos examined his cards and left them facedown. Bond asked for a third card. It was dealt face up—a 4. Romanos was forced to stand, then turned his cards over. Bond's 8 beat Romanos's 7.

"Lady Luck is on your side, Mr. . . . ?" Romanos said in English.

"Bryce. John Bryce," Bond said. "It's not luck. I say a little prayer to the gods before playing. Don't you?"

Romanos blinked slightly and smiled. Bond wasn't sure if the man knew who he was. Vassilis, the cousin, was staring hard at him. Up close, Bond thought Vassilis looked like a circus freak of old. Once again he was amazed that the man had practically no neck— just a large football shaped head on top of a wall of shoulders. His biceps were so large that Bond doubted he could get both hands around one.

Romanos forfeited the shoe. It was offered around the table, but no one wanted it. It finally came to Bond, who set the bank at half a million drachmas.

Romanos called, "Banco." Bond deftly slipped the cards out of the shoe and slid them across the table. Bond had a total of 7. He had to stand. Romanos asked for a third card, which was revealed to be a 5. The two men revealed their cards.

"Eight," Romanos said. "Seems as if the gods forgot about you that time."

Bond offered the bank and shoe to the next person, but it eventually found its way back to Romanos. He set it for one million drachmas.

"Banco," Bond said. Another two cards came across the table. This time Bond had a natural 9, but so did Romanos.

"Push," said the croupier.

The cards were dealt again. Bond had a total of 7 again and had to stand. Romanos drew a 3, then revealed a court card and a 2. The spectactors gasped as Bond raked in the chips.

"It's too bad that nine is the best possible number in baccarat," said Bond. "It really should be ten, don't you think?"

Romanos flinched and the thin smile disappeared. "What do you mean?"

"You *are* Konstantine Romanos, aren't you? Head of the New Pythagorean Society?"

Romanos smiled and nodded. "You know something of our little group?"

"Just a little, but I'd love to learn more."

"Perhaps that can be arranged," Romanos said. Everyone at the table felt a sudden tension between the two men. Play continued in a back-and-forth fashion until Romanos ended up with the shoe once again. Bond glanced at the other people. The attractive redhead was watching him intently. She placed a large bet against the bank.

Romanos dealt Bond two totally useless court cards. Lucidly,

Bond's third card was a 7. Romanos had a total of 6, barely losing. Bond glanced at the redhead, who was smiling knowingly at him.

"Mr. Bryce, you're going to clean me out before I've had time to finish my drink," Romanos said. "Might I buy you one, and we can adjourn to the bar?" The man's English was very good.

"One more," said Bond. He declined to take the bank. Romanos held on to it, and it was worth nearly four million drachmas.

Romanos nodded his head as if to say, "Very well." He dealt the cards. Bond had a total of 5, the worst possible number to get in baccarat. He had to draw a third card, which could very well push him past 9. The third card came across the table and was revealed to be a 4. Romanos drew a card, then turned the hand over. He had a total of 7. Bond won again with his 9.

"My compliments," Romanos said, passing the shoe. "I shall quit while I still can." Although the man was polite, Bond could tell he was perturbed at losing so much. He had forfeited nearly five million drachmas to Bond. As Vassilis pulled back his chair, Romanos stood up. He was well over six feet tall, statuesque and authoritative. It was no wonder he had followers who would do his bidding. Did that bidding extend to murder and terrorism?

Bond politely passed the shoe, tipped the croupier, then joined Romanos at one of the tables near the bar. He asked for another vodka martini. Romanos ordered a gin and tonic.

"Tell me, Mr. Bryce," he said, "why do you want to learn more about the New Pythagoreans? Are you a mathematician?"

"Lord, no," Bond said. "I'm a writer. I'm preparing a book about philosophy and religion. I thought your group was interesting. I know that you base much of your teachings on Pythagoras."

"That's correct. Pythagoras was much more than a mathematician. Socrates and Plato owed a great deal to Pythagoras. You should come to one of our gatherings down in Cape Sounion sometime. It is a wise man who looks and listens. Pythagoras argued that there are three kinds of men, just as there were three classes of strangers who went to the Olympic Games. The lowest were those who went to buy and sell, and next above them were those who came to compete. The best of all were those who simply came to observe. We are all lovers of either gain, honor, or wisdom. Which do you love, Mr. Bryce?"

"I love a little of all three, I think," Bond said.

"The Master—that is, Pythagoras—demanded that those desiring instruction should first study mathematics. The Pythagoreans reduced everything in life to numbers because you can't argue with numbers. We usually don't get upset about mutiplying two and getting four. If emotions were involved, one might try to make it five and quarrel with another who might try and make it three, all for personal reasons. In maths, truth is clearly apparent and emotions are eliminated. A mind capable of understanding mathematics is above the average, and is capable of rising to the higher realms of the world of abstract thought. There, the pupil is functioning closest to God."

"I should have studied harder in school," Bond said.

"The Master said that we are all part of the world in an unlimited boundary. When, however, we come to the process by which things are developed out of the Unlimited, we observe a great change. The Unlimited becomes the Limited. That is the great contribution of Pythagoras to philosophy, and we must try to understand it. Life is made up of many contraries, Mr. Bryce. Hot and cold, wet and dry, one and many. The most consistent principle underlying Pythagorean philosophy and mathematics is a dialectic procedure involving the relationship, and usually the reconciliation, of polar opposites. We believe that when the One becomes the Many, a new order will take its place on earth."

"And who is the One? You?"

Romanos shook his head. "That is not for me to say. The One is perfection. I'm certainly not perfect. You saw me lose at baccarat a few minutes ago."

"No, you're not perfect, Mr. Romanos. Not yet. Only when you reach the number ten will you be perfect, am I right?"

Romanos looked hard at Bond. "What do you mean?"

Bond tried to make light of what he had said. "The ten points of the equilateral triangle. Your logo. I've seen it. You haven't reached the number ten yet, have you?"

"No. It is difficult to do in a lifetime."

"Is it something like nirvana? Getting closer to God?"

"You might say that."

"Well, seeing that you've completed number seven, you don't have too far to go."

Bond could see Romanos stiffen at that. In those few minutes, Bond perceived that Romanos might be a genius, but he was also a madman. He had taken basic and inherently positive principles of Pythagorean philosophy and twisted them into something bizarre. If he were truly the leader of the Decada, then it wasn't difficult to believe that weak-minded fools would follow him.

Sensing something was wrong, Vassilis stepped up to Romanos and whispered in his ear. Romanos never took his eyes off Bond. Romanos nodded slightly and said something to his cousin in Greek that Bond didn't understand.

"I must step out for a minute. Please enjoy yourself, Mr. Bryce. In parting, let me tell you something that was attributed to Pythagoras. In mathematics, the logical process is to first lay down postulates— that is, statements that are accepted without proof—and then go through deductive reasoning. I apply that logic to everyday life, Mr. Bryce. Proof must proceed from assumptions. Without proof, an assumption is meaningless. Remember that the next time you start making assumptions. I'll be back at the baccarat table in a little while if you'd care to try your luck again."

"Thank you. It was nice meeting you, Mr. Romanos," Bond said. Romanos got up and followed Vassilis out of the room.

Bond finished his martini and had started to get up when he noticed the redheaded woman eyeing him from an adjacent table. She was sitting alone, sipping a glass of wine.

"Whatever did you say to Mr. Romanos to upset him so?" she asked in a thick Greek accent.

"Did I upset him?" Bond asked.

"He looked upset to me," she said. "I don't think it was because you beat him at baccarat."

"Do you know Mr. Romanos?"

"I know who he is. He is something of a personality in Greece."

"And you are . . . ?"

She held out her hand. "I'm Hera Volopoulos. Please sit down . . . Mr. Bryce, was it?"

"John Bryce." Bond took a seat beside her and admired her even more than before. She was absolutely stunning. The blue eyes stood out like jewels against her white face and red hair. He removed his gunmetal cigarette case and offered her one. She took it; then he lit hers and his own with the Ronson lighter he always carried in his pocket.

"What brings you to Greece, Mr. Bryce?"

"I'm a writer," he said.

"Have I read anything you've written?"

"I doubt it. Mostly articles in obscure English journals. They're not widely distributed."

"I see."

"And what brings you here on a fine Friday night?"

"I come here because I enjoy gambling. My late husband used to come here often, and I suppose I got into the habit. I have friends whom I see here every now and then. Sometimes it's a pleasant way to meet men."

She exhaled audibly, accentuating the last thing she said with a billow of smoke. Bond interpreted that as an invitation. He briefly thought of Niki and wondered if she might turn up at the hotel unexpectedly. The possibility was remote.

"What do you know about Mr. Romanos?" Bond asked.

"Only that he's very rich, and he's supposed to have a better than average brain. I think he's very handsome."

As she said that, Bond noticed Romanos and his cousin reentering the casino. They went straight for the baccarat table without looking in their direction.

"I can see that he has a certain charm," Bond said.

"How long will you be in Greece, Mr. Bryce?" she asked.

Bond made a whimsical gesture and said, "As long as the gods will have me."

Hera smiled. "I was named after one of the gods," she said.

"The queen of the gods, if I remember correctly."

"Yes, but she wasn't a very nice queen. Very jealous. She made poor Hercules go mad and kill his wife and children. She came between Jason and Medea. She was always doing something nasty. However, she did possess the ability to renew her virginity every year by bathing in a magical pool."

"Is that really an advantage?"

"I suppose to Zeus it was. He was a lecherous old fool, chasing after virgins all the time. It was the only way she could keep him interested."

"And what do *you* do to keep someone like Zeus interested? Do you have a magic pool?"

Hera smiled seductively. "I like you, Mr. Bryce. Why don't we have dinner? I can show you around Athens."

Bond was tempted. He thought briefly of Niki again, then discarded any feelings of loyalty to her. He was on an assignment. It was his way, he couldn't help it.

"It's awfully late for dinner, isn't it?"

"In Greece we eat very late and stay up until the early hours. Come on, you can follow me to my home in Filothei. It's pretty there. I'll fix us a light snack. We can sit on my balcony and enjoy the night air."

He had to admit that she was irresistible. "All right," he said. "Are you parked down below?"

"Yes, we'll ride the cable car together."

He got up and took her hand to help her up. As he looked into her eyes, her pupils dilated slightly.

As they walked out of the casino, he looked over at the baccarat table. Romanos was glaring at the cards. His luck hadn't improved. He had relit his thin cigar and was puffing on it furiously. Vassilis, the big man, was staring in Bond's direction. Bond nodded slightly to him, but the bodyguard only scowled at him.

They walked out through the plain corridors to the cable car entrance. There were two men waiting for the car, which was on its way up. When it arrived, one of the two men gestured graciously for

Bond and Hera to step inside first. They got in and settled themselves at the back of the car so they could look at the view of the city. The two men got in, the door closed, and the car began its five-minute journey back down to the base of Mount Parnitha.

As soon as the cable car left the platform and was in the air, Bond glanced back at the two men. Each held a semiautomatic handgun, cocked and ready to fire.

SEVENTEEN

QUEEN OF THE GODS

ONE OF THE MEN BARKED SOMETHING IN GREEK AND GESTURED WITH THE gun for Bond and Hera to get down on the cable car floor. Bond figured that these goons worked for Vassilis Romanos. Perhaps they knew his identity after all. He had been so distracted by the woman that he had carelessly let down his guard.

Hera asked the man something in Greek.

"Markos says lie down on the floor," the other man said in English. "This will only take a second."

Hera looked at Bond with fear in her eyes. He whispered to her, "Don't worry, just do what they say."

The cable car was approaching the first support tower. There were three such towers between the casino and the ground terminal. Bond remembered from the earlier trip that when the car passed one of the support towers, it lurched slightly as the wheels moved over the metal housing the cable. If he timed it just right . . .

Bond held up his hands. "What is this? A robbery? I really didn't win that much, fellows."

"Move!" the second man commanded.

"Look, I'll give you my wallet." Bond slowly reached for the inside of his jacket.

"Keep your hands up," the English-speaking thug said. The one called Markos asked the second man something in Greek. Bond caught the words "Ari," "money," and "wallet." This aroused the curiosity of the second man, who Bond presumed was called Ari. He hadn't planned on robbing his victim. Perhaps the Englishman did have a bit of cash on him. Markos spat out an order in Greek.

"All right, give us your wallet first. Slowly. No tricks," Ari said. "And we'll take the lady's handbag too."

The cable car was two seconds away from the support tower. Bond reached inside his jacket and grasped the Walther PPK. The car moved over the cable housing in the tower and the entire cabin lurched. Bond jumped up and landed on the floor hard, causing the cable car to tilt. The two men lost their balance. Bond drew the gun and fired at Markos, hitting him in the shoulder. He dropped his gun. Ari began firing his pistol wildly. Hera screamed and cowered in a corner of the cable car. Three bullets smashed windows behind Bond. Shards of broken glass scattered all over the floor of the car. Bond leaped to the floor, slid forward, and tackled the thug. Both Bond and Ari dropped their weapons.

The cable car was rocking now, still descending to the ground. The guns slid to the opposite end of the car and lay out of reach. Bond rolled on top of Ari and punched him hard in the face. Markos, bleeding profusely from his bullet wound, climbed on top of Bond and attempted to pull him off. Bond brought his left elbow back hard into the man's nose. He cried out in pain.

By now, the element of surprise had worn off. Ari raised his knee into Bond's stomach. He then landed a blow on Bond's chin, knocking him over and onto the floor. Both men jumped on top of Bond and began to pummel him with their fists. Trying desperately to protect himself, Bond brought his arms up in front of his face. The two men were strong and tough. Their ugly faces were right above him, snarling.

Out of the corner of his eye, Bond saw Hera huddled on the floor at the other end. One of the guns was inches from her, but she was frozen with fear. Bond realized that he couldn't rely on her to help.

Bond reached out quickly and grabbed the men's heads in his

hands. He slammed them together hard, then thrust his fists into their noses. They fell back, giving Bond time to get to his feet. Ari leaped for his gun but Bond grabbed his legs. He couldn't reach it. This gave Markos time to make a move for his weapon. Bond stuck out his leg and tripped him, and Markos slammed into the side of the car, breaking more glass. Ari grabbed a large shard of glass and swung it at Bond. The edge cut through Bond's jacket and sliced the front of his shoulder along the collarbone. Bond released the man's legs and jumped to his feet. He immediately attacked Markos with a *Ushiro-geri* back kick, causing the thug to bend forward, out of breath. Bond took hold of his shoulders and pulled him up and over. Markos crashed through the opposite window and out of the cable car. He screamed loudly as he fell to his death.

Ari got to his feet and lunged at Bond with the glass shard. Bond grabbed his arm and struggled with him. They fell to the floor. The glass was inches away from Bond's face. The thug held it so tightly that it was cutting his own hand; blood was seeping out through his fist. Bond summoned all of his strength to twist the man's arm back toward him. They were evenly matched and it was now simply a matter of who would give out first.

The cable car went over the second support tower. In another minute or so they would be on the ground. Bond knew he had to avoid any police action or his cover would be blown and the assignment would be compromised.

The two men's arms trembled. Bond took a deep breath and strained harder to push Ari's arms backward. They slowly moved so that the shard was now pointing at the man's throat. His eyes widened as he realized he was losing the struggle. Bond kept pushing. The point of the shard was now touching the assailant's Adam's apple.

"Who are you working for?" Bond asked through clenched teeth.

Ari spat in Bond's face.

Suddenly, Hera came to life and got up from her position on the floor. She knelt behind Ari, reached for his hair, and pulled it. Ari yelled but kept his attention on Bond and the glass shard. Enraged,

Bond used his last remaining ounce of strength to shove the man's arms. The glass shard pierced the man's throat, cutting through his windpipe and severing his spinal cord. His eyes glazed and his head rolled over in a final, ghastly exhalation of bad breath and bloody spittle.

Bond stood up and retrieved his gun. Hera collapsed back against the wall of the car, breathing heavily.

"Are you all right?" he asked.

She nodded. "You're hurt."

He examined the wound on his shoulder. It was minor, but he had to get it treated. He looked out the front window of the cable car and saw the ground terminal approaching. He didn't want to be in the car when it stopped.

"It's not so bad. Look, you don't have to come with me, but I'm going to jump out of the window. I can't let the authorities question me about this."

"Of course," she said. She reached into her handbag and pulled out a card. "This is my address. Go there. I'll handle the authorities. I have some influence at the casino. They all know me. I'll be home shortly and tend to that wound. Don't worry, I'll be fine."

Bond climbed through one of the broken windows and prepared to leap out to the ground before the car entered the terminal. He counted to three as the cable car brushed the tops of the trees on the ground, then jumped, landed hard on the ground, rolled, and got to his feet. The cable car entered the terminal. Bond ran to the parking lot and got into the Jaguar before any of the authorities knew what had happened.

Hera lived in a luxurious suburb of Athens called Filothei. It was full of green parks, quiet wide roads, and many large houses and villas with big gardens. Using the Jaguar's satellite navigation and road map features, he drove onto Kiffisias Avenue, a large three-lane street with trees in the middle. Eventually he found L. Akrita Street, and the three-story building of flats where she lived. Bond parked the Jaguar and waited. Nearly an hour later, he saw her pull up in a

Mercedes-Benz, get out, and walk toward the front. He got out of his car and called to her.

"Oh, there you are, Mr. Bryce," she said. "Come on up, I live upstairs. How do you feel?"

"All right. Call me John. How did it go?"

"Not a problem, John," she said. "I just flashed a smile at the manager and said that we were almost robbed and that you jumped out the window and ran. It was the truth! The only thing I didn't tell them was your name."

They got to the third floor and entered a tastefully furnished flat that was filled with artwork and statuettes. She threw her handbag on a chair and went straight into the bedroom.

"Get yourself comfortable and come on in. We'll take a look at that shoulder of yours," she called from behind the door.

Bond took off his jacket. His shirt was very bloody. He went into the bedroom, where she was standing next to the bathroom. He removed his shirt and looked at the wound. The gash wasn't too bad—just messy. He had managed to sop up most of the blood in the car on the way to the flat.

"You poor thing," she said, leading him into the bathroom. She wet a cloth, then took her time cleaning the three-inch wound. Afterward, she led him back into the bedroom.

"Press that cloth against it," she said. "Just hold it there awhile."

He sat on the edge of the bed and watched her undress. She did it slowly, sensuously, like a professional striptease artist. When she was naked, she pulled down the sheets and slipped under them. Her long red hair spread out over the pillow.

"I was afraid you'd cancel our date," she said. "I'm glad you didn't. I wanted to see what was under that hood of yours," she said.

"I don't want to bleed on you," he said. "It's closed a bit. If you're not too rough with me, I don't think it'll open up."

She raised up, letting the sheet drop to her waist. Her naked breasts were firm and full. She had large, red nipples that complimented her hair. There was a concentration of freckles on her chest, a physical trait that Bond always found tantalizing.

"Oh, I'll be gentle," she said, reaching out to him and sliding her hands around his shoulders. She started kissing the back of his neck and nibbling on his ear. Her right hand moved across his hairy chest and down to his abdomen. He was immediately aroused. "As gentle as a little tiger," she whispered.

He turned to her and pressed his mouth on hers. She pulled him back onto the bed and then climbed on top of him, straddling his torso.

"You just lie back and let me do all the work," she whispered.

Hera leaned over him, giving him access to her breasts. She moved down a little, guiding him into her, then kissed him on the mouth.

Konstantine Romanos sat in a stretch limo, traveling from Mount Parnitha to his Athens residence. Vassilis sat across from him, his eyes closed. All in all, the evening wasn't a total loss. He had made back most of his money that was taken by the Englishman.

He opened up a laptop computer and logged on to the Internet. An E-mail with an attached JPG file was waiting for him.

"Ah, here's the information I wanted," Romanos said, but Vassilis was asleep. Romanos downloaded the JPG file and in a moment, a grainy black-and-white photo that was obviously a still frame from a roll of videotape appeared on his screen. It showed James Bond in the hallway of the ReproCare clinic in Texas, most likely shot from a hidden security camera. Typed underneath the photo were the words "Man Responsible for Suppliers' Shutdown."

Well! Romanos thought.

He kicked Vassilis awake. The big man snorted and shook his head.

"Take a look at this," Romanos said, showing him the screen. Vassilis stared at it.

"The guy at the casino," the brute said. "He killed Markos and Ari."

"Right. Now, are you sure you didn't see him in Austin?"

"I don't know who it was. I didn't see the guy. The two cowboys chased him and they both died. It could have been him, who knows? After what he did to Markos and Ari, I'd believe it was him. It took someone with balls to mess up the clinic in Austin. It took someone with balls to do what he did to Markos and Ari. If this is the same guy, then we'll just have to make sure he has his balls for dinner."

Vassilis grunted and rubbed his hands eagerly.

"Vassilis, please," Romanos said. "I have a difficult decision to make. Our plans may have to be altered. I haven't spoken to Number Two yet. This man may be the same one who was in Cyprus."

Romanos took back the computer and studied the photo. He then created an E-mail and attached the JPG file to it, and addressed the correspondence to someone named "Three."

Romanos typed: "Am sending you copy of JPG file. Find out who this man is. Currently using alias John Bryce. Was responsible for incidents in Texas. Was seen snooping around Cape Sounion HQ. Believed to be man responsible for destroying three of our security vehicles and the murder of six security men near Cape Sounion. He killed two of our security men tonight in Athens. He may have been in Cyprus when Number Two implemented Strikes Two and Three. My guess is that he's a British Secret Service agent."

He signed the E-mail "Monad" and sent it.

The limo drove into the heart of the city and ended up near Athens University. Romanos had a flat that overlooked the campus. The driver let him and Vassilis out inside a garage. They went into an elevator and made their way to Romanos's flat.

"Vassilis, I have an assignment for you," Romanos said, walking to the bar and taking a bottle of brandy. He poured two glasses and gave one to his cousin. Vassilis would do anything for Konstantine.

He continued. "This man Bryce, or whoever he is—I'm afraid he may have to replace our current target for Strike Eight in the *Tetraktys*. This will alter our plans significantly, but it must be done. The man is a menace to us. The gods have spoken to me. He must not be a menace any longer."

"Number Two made a backup plan in case Ari and Markos failed, my cousin," Vassilis said.

"Really! She has more initiative than any of us. She is a true warrior, Number Two. She will not fail."

The men finished their brandy, then Vassilis hugged his cousin and left the flat. Konstantine Romanos sat at the desk and booted his own computer. Within moments he was back on the Internet, setting up an IRC channel with which he could talk live with someone. In a moment, three users popped into the virtual room.

It only took a few minutes. Romanos typed out his instructions. The three users acknowledged and signed off. He then shut down the computer and stood up.

Looking out of his window at the university from the sixth floor, Romanos reflected on what the gods had told him. The destiny he was to fulfill was near at hand. There were just a few little obstacles in the way, and he would have to make sure they disappeared. Soon, very soon, the Decada would strike again.

The Monad began to plan his next move.

An hour had passed. Bond and Hera sat up in bed smoking cigarettes.

"Why is it such a cliché to smoke a cigarette after love-making?" Hera asked.

"I suppose for those of us who enjoy smoking, it adds punctuation to the statement," Bond said.

"Make it an exclamation mark, then," she said.

Hera snuggled against him and ran her fingers through the hair on his chest. After a moment, she got up and threw on a terry cloth robe.

"I'm going to get some snacks and something for us to drink," she said. "Stay there, handsome. I'll be right back."

Bond heard her clanging around in the kitchen for a few minutes. She came back carrying a bottle of Taittinger, two glasses, and two covered dishes.

"You open the champagne, and I'll fix our plates," she said.

He rolled out of bed and took the bottle. He expertly opened it, popping the cork out at the ceiling. He poured the champagne while Hera uncovered the plates of Greek salads, bread, and cheese.

She removed her robe, and they sat on the bed naked, eating and drinking. The champagne was cold and tasted wonderful.

"So what do you do with your life besides visit casinos and take strange men home with you?" he asked.

"I don't make a habit of the latter!" she said, laughing. "I'm in real estate. I manage some properties in north Athens and have an interest in a hotel or two."

"Must be lucrative."

"It's not bad. One of these days, though, I will be a very rich woman."

"Oh?"

She smiled. "It's in the cards. So, what are you writing about in Greece?"

"Philosophy and religion."

"Rather broad topics, aren't they?"

Bond smiled. "I don't like to talk about my work. I let it speak for itself."

"You don't strike me as the shy type, Mr. Bryce. From what I saw in that cable car tonight, it didn't look like you spend all of your time writing."

"John, please."

"Well, John, where did you learn to fight like that? That was quite impressive."

"I learned it in the army," he lied. "Luckily I rarely have to use it. I was just glad you weren't hurt."

"So you're really a writer, huh? You'll have to send me some of your work so I can read it."

"Your English is very good."

"I'm fluent in Greek, English, and French," she said. "I did have an education."

"I can see that."

"You must try to hear Konstantine Romanos speak somewhere. Just sitting in on his lectures at the university can be interesting."

"I thought you said you didn't know him?"

She blinked and said, "I don't. But I have heard him speak. At the university. So am I going to show you Athens when the sun comes up?"

"I'm afraid I have some business to attend to," he said. "Perhaps we could get together tomorrow night . . ."

"Of course. I'll take you to one of my favorite restaurants. You'll love it."

A sudden wave of nausea came over Bond. He wasn't sure what hit him, but it was like a ton of bricks. Then there was a ringing in his ears.

He barely heard her continuing to talk. "It's all healthy food, no meat at all, a lot of vegetables and fruits . . ."

Bond struggled to speak, but his speech sounded slurred. "Are you on some kind of diet . . ."

"I don't eat meat," she said. "Strict vegetarian."

The warning bells went off in Bond's head, but it was too late. The drug in the food was acting too quickly.

How could he have been so stupid? he thought. He had waltzed right into their trap. A vegetarian! Ashley Anderson had been a vegetarian. The man at the New Pythagorean Society at Cape Sounion said that the members don't eat meat. Was Hera a member of . . .

The wall of confusion rapidly enveloped Bond's mind. He looked at Hera, who was watching him intently. She didn't ask him if anything was wrong.

Then she said, "Sorry, John . . . or whoever you are. You're going to wish that Ari and Markos had got you in the cable car. The fools didn't know who I was, or they wouldn't have tried to rob us. I could have intervened and finished the job, but you impressed me. I wanted your body, and now that I've had it and have no more use for it, we have to say goodbye."

"You . . ." he began. He tried to stand up, but the room spun wildly. He fell to the floor with a thud. He opened his eyes and saw Hera standing above him.

". . . bitch," he managed to say. Then the darkness spread over him like a blanket, and he was dead to the world.

EIGHTEEN

A MURDERER'S TOMB

DARKNESS AND VIBRATION. A LOW RUMBLING NOISE. MOVEMENT. CRAMPED muscles.

These were the sensations Bond felt as he slowly inched back into consciousness. He was curled up in a small, dark space. Some kind of box? No, there was movement and vibration. He was in the boot of a car.

Sore and stiff, Bond attempted to flex his muscles as best he could and shake away the drug's cobwebs. He was dressed in a shirt and trousers, but was barefoot.

So Hera Volopoulos was on the side of the enemy. Bond cursed himself for being such a fool. Once again his libido had got him in trouble.

Bond could hear two men speaking Greek inside the car. The voices were faint and he couldn't understand them. Where were they taking him?

He couldn't see a thing. He felt along the interior of the boot, looking for anything that might be of use to him. There was a box of some kind—a compact disc changer? Eventually he found a couple of buttons. Bond pushed them and the interior boot light switched on.

He immediately recognized where he was. He was inside his own Jaguar XK8. Apparently whoever it was that was driving was planning to destroy all traces of him. They were probably taking him to some remote place where they would kill him and bury him, then get rid of the car.

Bond examined the latch and determined that he couldn't open it from the inside. If he had some tools, perhaps . . . What should he do? Wait until they stopped the car, then make his move? They would most likely be ready for him. Was there anything that Major Boothroyd told him about the car that he could deploy?

Inside the car, Vassilis Romanos was driving. Next to him in the passenger seat was another brute, named Nikos. Vassilis had never had the pleasure of driving a Jaguar and he was enjoying it immensely. Too bad they had to get rid of the vehicle after they killed the Englishman. He would have liked to keep it.

"What time is it?" Vassilis asked Nikos in Greek.

"Four-thirty." The sun would come up in a little less than two hours. "How much farther?"

"About another hour."

"Is he still out back there?" Nikos asked.

"I haven't heard anything, have you?"

The car sped west on the highway. They were already an hour out of Athens and were approaching the Peloponnese, the southernmost section of the Balkan Peninsula, which contains some of the more beautiful parts of Greece, but the two men didn't care about the area's natural beauty. They had no appreciation for such trivialities.

Bond tried his best to relax and regain his strength. It was terribly uncomfortable in his cramped position, but he practiced a technique of flexing and stretching one limb at a time. He also took the time to examine every inch of the boot. Besides the CD changer, the microprocessor box was fastened to the back. Perhaps he could hot-wire some of the internal defense systems . . .

He opened the box, revealing a mass of circuits and wires. Luckily, a wiring diagram was printed on the inside of the lid. The light wasn't adequate—he had to strain his eyes to read it—but he was able to trace an auxiliary power feed, which he could maybe connect to one of the terminals. He studied the various options. The passenger or driver air bags were possibilities. If he got rid of one of the men, his job would be that much easier when the time came to open the boot.

After another half hour, the car approached the barren foothills of Mount Agios Ilias and Mount Zara, where the ruins of ancient Mycenae lie. They were the remnants of a kingdom occupied mostly by Agamemnon, who had been murdered by his wife, Clytaemnestra, and her lover after he returned home from the Trojan War. Both Agamemnon's and Clytaemnestra's tombs are located in the ruins of Mycenae.

Bond felt the change as the car went from a paved highway to a gravel road. Perhaps they were approaching their destination.

The car had in fact turned onto the path leading to the ancient ruins. It came to the wire gate and stopped. Nikos got out of the car and used a key to unlock it. The car's headlamps provided the only illumination. The sky was pitch-black and the ruins were dark silhouettes of slabs, arches, and columns.

Bond felt the car stop and one of the doors open and close. He had managed to pull the auxiliary feed and was ready to connect it to a terminal. He figured that thirteen amps for thirteen microseconds would be enough to do the trick.

Nikos got back into the car, and Vassilis drove through the open gate and up the hill past the closed concession-and-souvenir stand.

When he was sure that the man was back in the passenger seat, Bond brushed the auxiliary feed across the "Air Bag—Passenger" terminal.

The dashboard in front of Nikos exploded in his face, releasing an oversized air bag that totally enveloped him. It surprised Vassilis too, for the car swung out of control and came to a sudden stop against an embankment. Vassilis struggled with his door and got out. He could barely hear Nikos's muffled screams. He turned, stooped to the ground, and pulled a commando knife from a sheath attached to his shin under the trouser leg. Vassilis then climbed back into the car, attempting to cut away the air bag. The material was too thick. This was no ordinary air bag, Vassilis realized. Before he could think of anything else to do, the struggling beneath the air bag ceased.

Vassilis replaced the knife, drew a Sig-Sauer P226, walked around to the boot and unlocked it. He raised the lid and stepped back, pointing the gun at the back of the car.

"Get out," he ordered. "Keep your hands up."

Bond was finally able to straighten his body and climb out of the boot. He kept his hands behind his head, but he took the opportunity to stretch his back.

"I can't tell you how good this feels, thank you," Bond said. "Oh my, did something happen to your friend? Personally, I think the automobile manufacturers are going a little overboard with all these new safety features, don't you?"

"Start walking!" Vassilis said. He gestured to a path leading up the hill to the ruins.

Bond had no choice but to do as he was told and stall for time. He turned, and Vassilis followed him away from the light of the Jaguar's headlights. The path grew very dark, and it didn't help that he was barefoot. The stones were hard and sharp. At one point, Bond tripped over a rise in elevation that he couldn't see.

"Get up!" barked Vassilis. "Keep those hands up."

Bond managed to palm a stone, then stood up and replaced his hands on the back of his head. The stone felt rough against his scalp.

They walked past the ruins of a large stone pit called the Grave Circle. An even larger one, full of grave shafts, was farther up the path. They were very near the Lion Gate, the main entrance to the citadel, with its carved lintel showing two lionesses supporting a pillar.

"This way," commanded Vassilis. They turned right onto a smaller path moving away from the Lion Gate, then went around a bend to face a wide space carved out of the hill. The space was lined with stones, forming a passage leading to the tomb of Clytaemnestra. The open doorway was framed by carved stones and was supported by modern scaffolding. The lower portion of the door was a rectangle, but the upper portion was a triangle.

"Inside," Vasslis said, shoving the barrel into Bond's back. They went inside the dark tomb. After a few seconds, Vassilis turned on a flashlight and set it on the ground. They were inside a dome made of stones, about twenty meters high. One portion of the ceiling was held up by scaffolding. Apparently some restoration work was still in progress.

Vassilis aimed the gun at Bond.

Bond took just a second to memorize the room and get his bearings. "Wait," he said. His voice echoed loudly in the tomb. "Aren't you going to ask me anything first? Don't you want to know who I work for? What my real name is?"

Vassilis shook his head. "It won't make no difference." His accent was thick.

Without warning, Bond hurled the stone at Vassilis with all his might. It hit him dead on the forehead. The echo in the dome amplified his yell tenfold. Bond took the split second of opportunity to leap in the air and deliver a *Tobi-geri* jump kick to the man's sternum. Bond's bare foot slammed into one of Vassilis's vital points, causing him to drop the gun and fall back. But whereas the kick might have killed an ordinary man, Vassilis was only stunned. Before Bond could grab the gun, the Greek rolled into him. Bond fell over Vassilis and landed hard on his wounded shoulder.

Vassilis got up and swung at Bond. The blow knocked him hard back to the ground. For a few seconds all he saw was a bright light, and the pain in his head was unbearable.

My God, Bond thought. This was possibly the strongest man he had ever encountered.

The big man was about to land another blow, but Bond responded quickly enough to roll to the side. Vassilis couldn't stop his fist, so he hit the ground hard. Instead of hurting his knuckles, he made an impressive indentation in the dirt.

Bond staggered to his feet and shook his head. He got his wits about him just as Vassilis got to his feet. Bond delivered a *Nidan-geri* double kick, in which he leaped into the air and slammed his left foot into Vassilis's stomach, and then kicked the right one, the jumping foot, into his face. It barely fazed the bodybuilder. With a deafening growl, Vassilis reached out, grabbed Bond by the shirt, and like a wrestler, swung him around and around. He let go after four rotations, sending Bond flying across the dome into the brick wall. The man had done it as if Bond were made of paper.

Before he could recover, Bond's opponent was on him again. He picked up Bond from the ground, raised him high over his head, and threw him once more across the room like a beanbag.

Bond landed hard on his back, sending painful sparks up his spinal cord and igniting every nerve in his body. In the dim light, he could see Vassilis searching for the gun. Bond could see it, three feet in front of him. He tried to roll toward it, but Vassilis jumped on his hand before he could grab it. Bond grunted in pain and pulled his hand away. Vassilis stooped down and snatched the gun.

"Okay, you had your fun for today," Vassilis said, grinning. "It is past your bedtime."

He aimed the pistol at Bond's head.

Bond kicked out with his foot and connected with the flashlight that Vassilis had left in the middle of the room. The light went out, plunging the dome into darkness. Bond rolled as the gun went off. The sound was amplified tremendously, the echo lingering for several seconds.

"You will not leave here alive," Vassilis said in the dark after the noise had died down.

The only light coming into the room was from the open entrance, but the door's silhouette was all that could be seen. It was all the way on the other side of the dome. Bond knew that Vassilis was somewhere between it and him. If he could lure the thug where he wanted him . . .

"Over here, you overgrown lump of lard," Bond said.

He ducked out of the way as he felt the big man lunge for him. He felt a brush of air as Vassilis barely missed him. The room was so dark it wouldn't have mattered if they had been wearing blindfolds.

"Nice try, you rotter," Bond said. "Now I'm over here."

He sidestepped Vassilis again, and they continued to play this bull-fighting game in the dark for the next several seconds, until the big Greek became frustrated and angry. With every lunge he shouted something that sounded like an animal in pain.

Bond maneuvered to the side of the room where the scaffolding held up the ceiling. His lack of shoes gave him an advantage now—his feet moved quietly over the ground, whereas Vassilis's boots made loud crunching sounds. Bond reached out slowly and found one of the scaffolding supports. He carefully moved inside and under the scaffolding, keeping his hand on one beam.

"Hey, fathead. Here I am," Bond said.

Vassilis roared like a beast. Bond slipped out under the beam and ran for the entrance to the tomb. Vassilis crashed wildly into the scaffolding, knocking it to pieces. There was a loud rumble, and then a crash as the stones in the ceiling fell. Vassilis screamed. Bond waited until the noise settled and it was completely quiet in the tomb. Bond groped for the flashlight and shook it. It flickered on, illuminating the now dust-filled chamber. Coughing, Bond held it close to the pile of rubble. Vassilis was completely buried by the heavy stones, but he could see part of the henchman's arm sticking out from under a large rock. His head was somewhere farther beneath the rock, completely flattened. Bond tried to find the handgun, but it was buried along with its owner.

Bond left the tomb and made his way back down the path to the Jaguar. Thankfully, the strongman had left the keys. Bond found the hidden catch beneath the dash that released the inflated air bag. He pulled it out of the passenger side of the car, then tugged on Nikos's body and threw it to the ground. Bond found some loose change and a few drachmas in the corpse's pockets, all of which would come in handy. Then he went around to the driver's side and got in the car.

He backed up the Jaguar and sat there on the gravel road for a moment, catching his breath. The first thing he did was open the secret compartment where the Walther P99 was kept. He pulled it out and made sure the magazine was full of Teflon-coated, full-metal-jacket bullets. Underneath the storage compartment was a shoulder holster made especially for the P99 by Walther. He started to slip it on, wincing at the pain in his shoulder, and decided against it. He put the gun back into the compartment, then took a look around the car. Vassilis had left a black notebook on the floor by his feet. Bond picked it up and looked inside. It was a diary. The last entry was the new day's date and he could just make out the Greek words: "Number Two, Monemvasia, 11 A.M."

He took the cellular phone from its compartment and dialed Niki's number. A sleepy voice answered.

"Wake up, darling," Bond said. "I need your help."

"James! Where are you?" she said.

"I think I'm at the ruins in Mycenae. It's so dark I can't tell. The sun's just beginning to come up here."

"Are you all right?"

"I could use some shoes, but otherwise I'm fine."

"What happened?"

He gave her a brief rundown of the events. He left out what had happened with Hera.

"Wait, I didn't get one part," she said. "How did you get drugged, again? Where did you say you were?"

"I'll tell you later. Listen. I think there's something happening this morning in a place called Monemvasia."

"I know it. It's a medieval village on the east coast of the southern end of the Peloponnese."

"Can you meet me there today?"

"I'll leave right away. It will take me, uhm, four or five hours. Meet me at the entrance to the causeway between Gefyra and Monemvasia. Gefyra is the mainland village. They're connected by a bridge."

"Right. Before you leave, see what you can dig up on a redheaded woman using the name Hera Volopoulos."

"Will do. Take care, James."

Bond backed out of the ruins and drove to the main highway, leaving the two dead bodies for the site caretakers to deal with.

Before he got very far, Bond flipped a switch and changed the color of the car again. This time it went from red to a dark green. The license plate changed to a Greek registration.

He utilized the road map feature of the GPS navigation system and made his way to the E-65, the main highway that led to his destination. He passed through Tripoli and stopped at a roadside café to buy some coffee and a roll. The proprietor, who spoke no English, noticed that Bond wasn't wearing any shoes. He jabbered in Greek and gestured for Bond to wait a minute, then went into the back room and came out with three pairs of old shoes. Bond laughed and tried on the pair that looked closest to his size. Surprisingly, they fit snugly.

"How much?" Bond asked.

The proprietor shrugged and held up five fingers, meaning he wanted five thousand drachmas. Bond handed over a bill and thanked him. The proprietor saw the nice, shiny Jaguar that Bond got into, and kicked himself for not asking for more.

Three hours later, Bond drove into Gefyra and parked near the causeway leading to what was commonly referred to as "the Gibraltar of Greece." Monemvasia is a medieval town built on a rock which emerges dramatically from the sea off the east coast. It is topped by a fortress with a few scattered buildings at sea level.

Docked off of the edge of Gefyra and just visible from Bond's vantage point was Konstantine Romanos's yacht, the *Persephone*.

NINETEEN

THE NUMBER KILLER

B OND TUCKED THE W ALTHER P99 INTO THE BACK OF HIS TROUSERS, LEFT the Jaguar parked out of sight near the causeway, and walked along the narrow streets of Gefyra so that he could get a better view of the boat. He ducked behind a wall and peered around.

The *Persephone* was a new Hatteras Elite series 100 motor yacht, an impressive, hundred-foot-long white and black vessel with walk-around side decks. There were a few men dressed in black working with a hydraulic crane and loading material onto the boat. Bond saw Hera Volopoulos on the starboard deck, speaking with one of the men. She was dressed in a dark jacket and trousers.

After a moment, she was joined on deck by Konstantine Romanos. He was "dressed for sailing," in dark navy trousers, a white sports jacket, and a nautical cap. They spoke briefly. Hera nodded her head, then walked off the boat and down the plank to the shipside area of the dock. She spoke to a man at a forklift, then walked off the dock toward the causeway. The men continued loading crates onto the *Persephone*, and Romanos disappeared below.

Bond felt cold. It had become windy, and the temperature was much cooler here than in Athens. He was also tired and hungry, but he felt that he was onto a breakthrough in the case. Should he try to sneak onto the boat or follow the woman? There was a score to settle. He moved away from the safety of the wall and followed the woman.

Hera walked onto the causeway, crossed the strait, and headed toward the lower town of Monemvasia. Bond waited until she had passed the cemetery and gone through the main portal into the populated area. He sprinted across, and ran up the road to the town.

When he stepped through the opening, Bond thought he had entered some magical place in another time. It was as if the little village had been hidden for centuries from the entire world. Facing this quaint pocket of antiquity was the rich blue sea, which spread out to the southeast. The narrow streets were walkways between the many tourist oriented souvenir shops, tavernas, and churches. There was even a former mosque from the time when the Turks occupied the town.

Bond started looking for Hera. The village was quiet except for the folk music playing on a radio in the distance. The streets were a complex maze of stairways and narrow passages, and as he moved along the stone path he spotted Hera's red hair disappearing around a corner ahead. He continued onward, moving like a prowling cat and staying close to the buildings in case he had to duck quickly into one of the shops. Along the way, small prune-faced old women sat in doorways and looked at him with curiosity.

Hera stopped at a shop and bought some bottled water. Bond waited behind a corner, then moved on when she did. She soon entered the central square of the town, where she stopped briefly to stand and drink some of her water.

What the hell was she doing? Bond wondered. Was she waiting for Vassilis to meet her here? Let's get on with it!

After finishing the bottle and tossing it into a rubbish bin, she turned and walked through a passage rising above the campanile of a large church in the square, then along the north side of another church. From there a path led uphill to the upper town. She started the climb up the zigzagging stone steps that took visitors to the upper town, which was virtually in ruins. All the way up to the summit of the rock, pieces of buildings still stood facing the sea—a wall or two here, a foundation and corner over there.

Bond waited a couple of minutes before starting up after her. He crouched down and moved from ruin to ruin, waiting until he saw her climbing higher and higher. It was not an easy ascent. Only the fittest of tourists ever made it all the way to the top.

Now that he was in the upper town, Bond felt totally alone. No one else seemed to be around except Hera. He saw her reach the top of the cliff and walk toward the twelfth-century Hagia Sophia, the church built on the ledge of the sheer cliff. It was the only building in the upper town that was complete and in use.

Bond watched her go in the front door. It must have been the designated meeting place with Vassilis. It was close to eleven o'clock. He waited several minutes, then stealthily moved to the front of the church. He drew his gun and carefully pushed the door open and stepped inside.

It was too quiet. He moved slowly around the perimeter of the nave and went into the diaconicon, the room behind the altar. Narrow, elaborately ornamented windows were set into the stone walls about six and a half feet up.

Bond heard a creaking sound in the prothesis, the area on the other side of the altar. As silently as possible, he stepped through a portal into the other room. The glass in one of the windows was broken and the frame was open. Bond waited and listened. There was no other movement around him. Was he being watched?

He tucked the gun back in his trousers, took hold of the window ledge, and pulled himself up to look out. A bit of ground was some twenty feet down below, but the church was extremely close to the edge of the cliff. He could just squeeze his shoulders out of the window to get a better view.

A muzzle of cold metal poked him in the back of the neck.

"I know you didn't come here to pray, Mr. Bryce, but you had better start," Hera said. The voice came from above his head. She was hanging upside down on a tension line above the window. The rope was attached to the roof of the church; she had simply climbed out of the window, pulled herself up, attached the rope to her belt, and waited for him to stick his head out the window. After spending a night with her, Bond knew that she was extremely agile.

"Hand me your gun, carefully," she ordered.

"We really must stop meeting like this," Bond said.

"Shut up. Do it."

He did as he was told. She took the P99 and stuck it into her utility belt.

"Now slowly move back inside the church. Keep your hands up."

Bond squeezed back through the window and jumped to the floor. Before he had time to run for it, Hera had lowered her body down on the line and was aiming her gun at him through the window. It was a Daewoo that looked vaguely familiar.

"Turn around and put your nose and palms against the wall behind you," she said. He did. In less than two seconds she performed a smooth maneuver of pocketing the gun, twisting her body upright on the rope, thrusting her legs through the window, and hopping to the floor. She retrieved the Daewoo and pointed it at Bond.

"I assume that since you're here and Vassilis isn't, Konstantine's cousin isn't with us anymore. Konstantine isn't going to like that. All right, start walking out. I'm right behind you. We're going down to the lower town. No stupid moves—I'm very good with this gun," she said.

He turned and looked at her. There was something very familiar now about her shape and her stance with the gun.

"The Number Killer . . . a woman," Bond said.

"Oh, you realize we've met before, Mr. Bryce? Or should I say Mr. Bond?" she said with a smirk. "It's too bad I didn't get you in Cyprus. Too bad for you. Now it will just make your ugly death that much more enjoyable. For me. But Konstantine would like to have a little talk with you first. You wouldn't want to miss a talk with Konstantine, would you? It's your chance to find out what all this is about, right? I know you'll cooperate. Now march."

They went back into the nave. Bond said, "So what was the other night about, Hera? Are you a praying mantis who eats the male after she mates?"

Hera found that image flattering. "I never thought about it that way," she said.

Bond turned around slowly and brought his face close to hers. "Or did you want to go to bed because you really are attracted to me."

She held the gun to his temple. "Back off and get those hands up," she said.

Bond leaned in and whispered, nuzzling her ear. "You don't mean it. You know we were good together. Now why don't you forget this nonsense and join me." He kissed her neck, but his hand was an inch from the Walther P99 in her belt.

"If you so much as touch your gun, I'll blow your brains out. I don't care if Konstantine does want to see you first." Bond froze. "Now put your hands up and step back."

Still not moving his arms from around her, Bond sighed audibly and said, "Very well. If that's the way you want it." He made an exaggerated shrug of the shoulders as he brought his arms up and away from her back. That shrug was enough to throw off Hera's concentration, for Bond snatched her wrist with a lightninglike strike with his left hand. The gun was knocked away from his head, but it discharged loudly into the ceiling. Bond grabbed her arm with his other hand and with both hands attempted to control the weapon. Hera coolly brought her knee up hard into his left kidney. Bond was momentarily frozen in pain. Hera took that second to strike him hard on the back of the head with the Daewoo. He bent over and fell to the floor.

Niki Mirakos drove her Camry at close to ninety miles per hour down the E-65 and twice had to radio policemen with her credentials. She got to Gefyra at just around eleven o'clock, and was going down a side street to find a place to park when she saw the green Jaguar. Could it be . . . She pulled over and parked near it. There couldn't be that many Jaguar XK8s in Gefyra—Bond must have changed the color again. She got out and walked toward the bridge. He was nowhere in sight, but the *Persephone* was docked in full view. Aside from two men walking on the decks, there seemed to be no one else about.

She had punched up the records on Hera Volopoulos before leaving Athens. According to the Greek Secret Service files, Volopoulos was suspected of being a trained soldier working eight years ago for the Greek Cypriot militant underground. She had been linked to an arms-smuggling racket in Cyprus before it was broken up by the Cypriot police. There was nothing else on file, except that she was last seen in Cyprus two years ago.

Niki knew that organized crime on Cyprus was big business. Because of its strategic location in the Mediterranean, the island was a convenient stopping place and temporary safe haven for smugglers, terrorists, arms dealers, thieves, prostitutes, pimps, and other forms of low life. Several factions of underground criminals developed on Cyprus during the last thirty years. Part of her training in the Greek Secret Service included extensive study of the Cyprus situation.

The file photo of Hera Volopoulos was not very good. It was a black and-white picture of a woman wearing sunglasses, looking over her shoulder and running. The motion blur made it virtually impossible to identify her. Why did Bond want this information? Was she connected to the Decada? As a precaution, Niki put out an advisory to all law enforcement agencies to be on the lookout for the woman.

Niki supposed she should wait a bit to see if Bond showed up. If he weren't around in fifteen minutes, she would start snooping.

Sometimes she felt guilty working to protect the Turks and Turkish Cypriots. Here she was, a Greek, trying to make sure that Greek or Greek Cypriot terrorists didn't do something terrible to the Turks. She shook her head at the irony. She hated the Turks as much as she might hate a Greek Cypriot terrorist. She could remember her grandfather telling horror stories about Turks when she was a little girl. The Turks were always the bad guys, and she grew to fear them. It was how bigotry was always perpetuated, she realized—through the mouths of older generations. As legends, knowledge, religion, and art were all passed down from generation to generation, unfortunately so was hatred. It was one of the unpleasant side effects of history.

Niki was shaken from her musings when she saw James Bond

emerge from the Monemvasia side of the portal and begin walking toward her across the causeway. Behind him was a redheaded woman wearing sunglasses. It was she. Hera Volopoulos. Niki knew it. Bond was walking slowly, looking a little dazed. He saw her but didn't register recognition. Niki knew something was wrong. The woman had a concealed gun on him. She was taking him to the *Persephone*.

Niki casually moved from her position and walked back toward the street where she had parked her car. She hid in the doorway of a taverna twenty feet away from the causeway entrance as Bond and Hera came across and started walking toward the dock. They would have to pass her on the way. She thought Bond glanced at her, but he kept on walking as if he had not seen her.

She could have stopped them. She could have pulled her gun and kept them from getting aboard, but something in Bond's face said not to do it. It was too dangerous. She needed backup. If they were taking him aboard the yacht, then it would be a far better plan to follow it and see where they went. Bond might be in danger, but he could handle himself.

It was gut instinct that told Niki to wait and see what happened. She would call for backup and arrange to follow the boat. They weren't going to kill Bond yet. They wanted him alive for a while.

She just hoped that she could find a way to get him off the yacht before they changed their minds.

Earlier, Hera had slapped Bond repeatedly until he regained consciousness. When his eyes fluttered open, she grabbed him by the chin. She dug her nails into his skin and said, "Don't ever try that again. I'm real good with a knife. It would be a great pleasure to remove the piece of equipment you seem to be so fond of using, James Bond. I'm sure thousands of rejected women all over the world would thank me. Now get up and walk."

His head throbbing, Bond got to his feet and staggered to the front of the church.

"Besides," she continued. "You're not supposed to fight in a house of God. This is a holy place."

"Since when do you care about what's holy?" Bond asked.

"Shut up and get going," she said.

Bond made up his mind to see it through. The woman had the upper hand now, and he should take no more unnecessary risks. Besides, she was right. He really wanted to hear what Romanos had to say to him. He had been in tight situations before. This one was no worse.

It took them twenty minutes to descend the steps to the lower town. Bond lost his balance once and fell. His head was throbbing and his vision was a bit blurred. She had struck him hard in the church.

They moved through the alleylike main path and out the portal. Bond saw Niki at the other end of the causeway, expertly playing it cool. She was as professional as they came. He hoped that she would remain so and not try to stop them; he wanted to get on the boat.

They walked past her and he looked at her briefly but intently. He thought she got the message. If she did her job right, she would get back to her people and have the yacht followed.

He stopped at the edge of the ramp leading onto the *Persephone*.

"Get aboard," she said.

Bond walked forward to the deck, wondering if he should have brought an ancient Greek coin to give to Charon the boatman.

TWENTY

GODS NEVER DIE

THE *PERSEPHONE* WAS A SUPERB YACHT. AS BOND WAS LED ABOARD AND down below, he noticed that there were several rooms. A lavish galley and dinette were located on the main deck. There was a midlevel pilothouse with a complete control console, helm, and lounge seating, as well as steps to the flying bridge above.

What was extraordinary about the setup was that the interior didn't look like a modern boat. It was decorated in the style of an ancient Greek galley: The walls were covered in wood that looked hundreds of years old. The light fixtures were made to look like flaming torches. The pilothouse was indeed equipped with the latest technology, but it was all disguised by a bizarre facade of theatricality and make-believe. The entire ship was a stage setting for a Greek tragedy by Aeschylus or Euripedes.

Obviously Konstantine Romanos didn't mind flaunting his wealth. Bond thought he was two sandwiches short of a picnic.

Hera knocked on a wooden door that was the entrance to the master cabin. They heard a bolt draw back, then the door creaked open.

Konstantine Romanos stood in the doorway, still wearing the captain's uniform which was completely incongruous with the setting around him. His room was illuminated entirely by candles.

"Ah, Mr. Bond, come in," he said. He gestured to a chair at a table. Hera followed him in and shut the door behind her. From then on, she stood in silence like a sentry.

"Your costume and set designers need to communicate better," Bond said. "Are we in the twentieth century or in ancient Greece?"

Romanos ignored him. "Sit down. What would you like to drink? Wait . . . I know. You like martinis, don't you? Vodka martinis. I know that. It's in the information we dug up on you," he said. He was playing the gracious host, but his voice was laced with menace.

"Unfortunately, we don't have any martinis this morning, but we do have some nice red wine," he said, then walked over to a bar and poured two glasses from an unmarked wine bottle. "Would you like something to eat?"

Bond was actually starving, but he shook his head. "Let's just get on with it, Romanos."

"Tsk tsk," he said. "You look famished. I insist. Have some bread and cheese." He placed a wooden plate with a fresh loaf of bread and a chunk of goat cheese on the table. A large kitchen knife was stuck in the cheese.

"I trust I don't have to worry about you trying to take that knife," Romanos said. "Hera here will make sure that you remain sensible." He began to cut the bread and cheese and placed several pieces on a plate in front of Bond. Sitting down across from him, Romanos held up his glass and said, *"Yasou."*

Bond would have preferred not to eat and drink with the man, but he needed sustenance. He slowly began to eat, but he was eyeing the knife and trying to form a plan to grab it.

"Here you are again, Mr. Bond," Romanos said, as if Bond were a naughty child and had been sent to the school headmaster.

"The name is Bryce."

"Please, dispense with the spy stuff, we know who you are. You are a civil servant working for the British government. We got your picture from a closed-circuit television camera at ReproCare in the United States. That was quite a job you did on that place."

"I didn't set the explosives."

"No, of course you didn't. The late Dr. Ashley Anderson did. We shall miss her. That facility was due to be closed down anyway. What you did do, Mr. Bond, was hasten its demise. We wanted to rid ourselves of those awful Suppliers, and you helped us do that."

"So you *are* the leader of the Decada?"

"I am the Monad, the One," he said. He gazed intently at Bond. The man's eyes seemed to glow, and Bond couldn't look away. He found himself mesmerized by Romanos; there was something in his eyes that beckoned Bond to stare into them. It was several seconds before Bond's willpower alerted him to the fact that Romanos was attempting to hypnotize him. He managed to look away, but it was an effort to do so.

Bond realized that Konstantine Romanos was one of those rare men who possess a unique power of persuasion. If he could hypnotize weak-willed people, use his flowery talk and philosophical conundrums and eventually charm subjects into trusting and believing him, then he was the sort of man who might be looked on as a prophet (or a devil). Many men throughout history had had this kind of charisma, and they were always leaders.

Bond now understood why Romanos had a large following who believed his unique brand of mumbo jumbo.

"What are you after, Romanos? I know you're dying to tell me."

"Mr. Bond, it's quite simple. I'm on a mission from the gods. They do exist, you see. I know, because they speak to me. The soul of Pythagoras lives within me, and he was a very religious man."

"What is that mission?"

Romanos sipped his wine and glared at Bond with fire in his eyes.

"I suppose I can tell you, since you will be tortured to death very soon. You will be held accountable for the death of my cousin Vassilis. He was my Number Seven, you know. Very important to the organization. He was family. You will be made to suffer for what happened to him. But before that I will tell you the story of my life."

"If it's all the same to you, I think I'd rather just get on with the torture," Bond quipped.

"You won't have many witticisms left when we're through with you, Mr. Bond. I'm a Greek Cypriot, born and raised in the northern town of Kyrenia. In 1963, I was just out of university, having studied mathematics and philosophy. I had landed an important teaching job in northern Nicosia, was married and had two beautiful children. I was apolitical. It was a good life, but I was unenlightened at the time. The gods had not spoken to me yet. It took a crisis to open the communications between me and them. My life crashed around me that year, for violence broke out all over Cyprus. Our former president and spiritual leader, Makarios, was making too many concessions to the Turkish Cypriots. Your troops and the United Nations' so-called peacekeeping forces invaded the island and tried to keep the peace, and they succeeded, for a while."

"You forget that many Greeks and Greek Cypriots on Cyprus looted and destroyed many of the Turkish Cypriot settlements. The United Nations and our troops came in to keep Greek Cypriots from killing Turkish Cypriots."

"That's what the Turkish propaganda wants you to believe."

"Romanos, these are facts. But go on, we can argue semantics later. We'll call an assembly, put on our sandals, and have a proper debate in the Parthenon."

Romanos smiled wryly at Bond's sarcasm, then went on. "Throughout the rest of the sixties, a very tentative peace existed, but there were always small outbreaks of violence. I moved my family to the outskirts of Nicosia, unfortunately to an area that became over-populated with Turks and Turkish Cypriots. The worst was yet to come. As you know, a military coup d'etat occurred in Greece in 1967. Makarios retained control of the Republic of Cyprus, but he had many enemies in Greece. Seven years later, in 1974, the Greek National Guard ousted Makarios and set up a junta on the island. Makarios fled. It was . . . chaos. The Turks used the opportunity to invade the island. They began to systematically massacre Greeks and Greek Cypriots, working their way down from the north."

"Uhm, you forgot to mention that when Makarios was ousted and the junta was set up, the same thing was happening to the Turks and Turkish Cypriots. Turkey has always claimed that they were 'intervening,' not 'invading.' They were protecting their people."

"Again, that is the Turkish propaganda speaking. The Turks are animals. They are like jackals, waiting until their prey is in a weakened state. Then they strike and are merciless."

"I'm not defending the Turks, Romanos," Bond said. "They have done some unspeakable things on Cyprus. If you ask me, both sides are equally misguided and bigoted. It's simply another example of two races disagreeing with each other over centuries of misunderstandings."

"Do you expect us to get together, hold hands, and sing 'All You Need Is Love'? You're just like all the other British mediators who have tried to dictate policy on Cyprus. You know nothing about our people. If you think our problems can be solved by talking about them, then you're out of your mind."

"I'm not the one who talks to gods who don't exist."

Romanos looked at Hera and nodded sharply. She stepped over and slapped Bond hard across the face. He jumped up and prepared to defend himself, but Romanos pulled a Walther PPK out of his jacket and pointed it at Bond.

"Sit down, Mr. Bond," he said. "Oh, is this yours? I believe we found this at Number Two's flat. Tie him to the chair, Number Two."

Hera laughed quietly and took some thick nylon cord from a cabinet. She wrapped it around Bond's chest and tied him tightly to the back of the chair.

"All right, you've got a captive audience, Romanos. You might as well continue your little story," Bond said.

"I will. There was a war. The northern third of Cyprus was occupied by the Turks, and they forced out or killed all of the Greeks and Greek Cypriots living there." Romanos paused a moment, as this part of his tale was obviously painful. "Our house was bombed. My wife and children died. I was wounded in the head and left for dead. All I remember was regaining consciousness in a hospital in southern Nicosia. My only memory is that shortly after the bombing I saw some British soldiers. I begged them to help me and they ignored me."

Bond figured that might explain the Decada's attacks on the British bases.

"I was in hospital for six months," Romanos continued. "I wasn't sure if I would lose my mind and the very faculties by which I made my living. I couldn't remember simple mathematical problems. I forgot my Latin. It was only after I was discharged and I fled to Greece that I regained what I had lost."

No wonder the man was mad, Bond thought. The serious head injury had left him unbalanced.

"I admit I was in a bad way when I got to Greece. I lived on the streets of Athens, homeless and poor. I drank. I was invisible to the people around me. Then, one day, I slept in the Ancient Agora in Athens. I had crept in and found a place among the ruins where I could sleep. It was there that the gods first spoke to me."

A change was coming over Romanos as he spoke. He seemed to be assuming the persona of an orator, preaching to a large crowd. His voice grew louder, and he stood up from the table. He walked around the room as he spoke, gesturing to the invisible masses around him.

"The Greek gods sent me messages that I, and I alone, was able to hear. One night, I experienced an epiphany of the highest order. Zeus himself spoke to me and entrusted me with the soul of Pythagoras. Konstantine Romanos died that night, and the Monad took his place. Divine assistance led me to an organization that helped homeless people get back on their feet. Once I could prove that I had teaching credentials before the war, I got a job in a university library. I read everything I could about Pythagoras and his philosophy.

"I went to lectures at the university and to student gatherings, for I met many young people through working in the library. I became involved with some students who were violently anti-Turk. They were Greek Cypriots who, like me, were forced out of their homes in northern Cyprus, and they wanted something done about it. It turned out that they were a little militia. They had smuggled guns and bombs into the country and were planning on instigating revenge against the Turks."

"Who were they?"

"It doesn't matter now," Romanos said. "They're all dead now. What's important was that I learned a great deal from them about guerrilla warfare and terrorist tactics. It was with this experience that I got my first job as a mercenary. I left Greece for Lebanon in, let's see, 1977, it was. While I was away, the group attempted an ill-conceived attack on a Turkish supply ship off the north coast of Cyprus. They were never heard from again. But the knowledge I took from them was invaluable. I applied Pythagorean philosophy to their lessons. They were seeking to make the One into the Many, which was what Pythagoras wanted to achieve."

Bond now understood that Romanos had combined the teachings of Pythagoras and the tenets of the militant group. The philosophies had blended together unnaturally and he believed them.

"But I digress," he said. "I spent the next few years working as a freelance mercenary in the Middle East. I performed jobs for various factions, for which I was paid handsomely."

"You mean acts of terrorism, don't you?" Bond interjected.

"I found that I had an extraordinary ability to organize men and lead them. The gods had given me a gift of persuasion. There was one particular excursion in 1981 in which I made a sizable amount of money. I decided to retire from the mercenary business and come back to Greece and do what I was ordained to do. I settled in Athens and made some wise real estate investments. I founded the New Pythagorean Society. Through connections I had made with the Greek government, I landed a teaching position at Athens University. I wrote and published a book. I suddenly found myself in demand, so to speak, and I became well known in Greece. People actually paid money to hear me speak. I received invitations from other countries to visit their universities and lecture. I spent five years in the United States, in Texas, in the late eighties, off and on, with frequent trips back to Greece. For the remainder of the decade, I expanded my power base and laid the groundwork for the future policymakers of Greece and Cyprus—the Decada."

Bond glanced at Hera to see what she made of all this. She was standing at attention, staring straight ahead, expressionless.

"I selected nine of my most trusted and faithful followers to occupy the other seats of leadership in the Decada. Each of them an expert in their own field, each with a sizable team of followers to perform the various tasks we needed done. Five men and five women, each representing the Pythagorean contraries of Odd and Even—odd being male, even being female. I, naturally, became the One, the Monad. I appointed Hera here to be the Duad, the Two. My late cousin Vassilis was the Seven. I regret that I must replace him. You are responsible for the deaths of two of my numbers, Mr. Bond. You will pay dearly for that."

"Why did you attack the British bases in Cyprus?" Bond asked.

"The gods commanded it. The British played no small part in what happened in Cyprus in 1974. They did nothing to stop the Turks from invading."

"And Alfred Hutchinson? Why did you kill him?" Bond turned to Hera. "It was you, wasn't it? You were the assassin with the spiked umbrella in London."

Romanos answered for her. "Yes, it was Hera. She is my sword. I met Hera in Cyprus in 1978. She was a mere youngster then, weren't you, Hera? She was the most vicious, hardened, and most dangerous twelve-year-old girl I had ever seen. We became very close, I'm not ashamed to say. She has been with me ever since."

"Lovely story," Bond said. "Sick, but lovely."

Hera reached over to slap him again, but, curiously, she hesitated. She resumed her silent stance as Romanos continued.

"But you asked about Hutchinson. As I mentioned before, I was in Texas for a while. Through my underground connections, I was put in touch with an American militant group there called the Suppliers. A go-between introduced me to Charles Hutchinson, a spoiled, rich playboy who was a courier for the Suppliers. He also happened to be the son of another distinguished guest lecturer at the University of Texas, where I was teaching. The boy and I—we did business together. The Suppliers began to transport biological and chemical weapons to the Decada via the Suppliers' front of selling frozen sperm to countries around the world. Eventually, I masterminded a plot to frame the Suppliers' leader, a redneck named Gibson. He was arrested and put in prison. From then on, I assumed leadership of the

Suppliers from afar without the rest of their organization realizing it. I controlled all of their connections worldwide. It allowed the Decada to broaden its power base and make more money, but the militant group's usefulness soon wore out.

"The boy's father, your late Ambassador to the World—what a joke—obtained some vital information regarding the so-called Turkish Republic of Northern Cyprus. The Decada tried to obtain that information by employing Charles to get it. Charles made a complete mess of it, and his father got wind of what he was up to. Alfred Hutchinson threatened to go to your secret service with the information, so he had to be eliminated. His son betrayed us. Of course, once his father was killed, he foolishly tried to get even by alerting the Turkish Cypriot authorities in Famagusta of our little anthrax scheme. The Duad here kept close tabs on Charles when he got to Greece a few days ago. He was eliminated too. I can't abide traitors."

"Then you never got Hutchinson's information?" Bond asked.

"I didn't say that. Number Ten, Dr. Anderson, knew that Hutchinson had stored the information on his computer in his Austin home. She had infiltrated the ranks of the Suppliers on my orders, before Gibson was imprisoned. I felt it would be useful to have one of our own keeping an eye on those Texas rednecks. They had become a bit careless in the past few months—several of their couriers had been caught, and it was only a matter of time before Charles would have been arrested. Your agent in Athens, Whitten, he was onto them. Had he been alive when Charles made his next delivery, Whitten would have nabbed him. The link between the Suppliers and the Decada would have been discovered. Therefore, Whitten had to die. He was the target of the first strike."

"And you destroyed the Suppliers' laboratory because the authorities were onto you?"

"That's right. The FBI was too close to shutting them down. We didn't need them anymore. Our Number Eight is a brilliant biochemist. We're coming up with a little bug of our own. It is still in the experimental stage, but it will soon be ready to test. It will make the ebola virus seem like the common cold."

"I take it that Number Eight is Melina Papas, the president of BioLinks Limited?"

"You *are* clever, Mr. Bond!"

"Is this the same bug that is causing epidemics in Los Angeles and Tokyo?"

Romanos looked at him as if he were mad. "I don't have the slightest idea of what you're talking about."

Bond wasn't sure if he believed him. "Just what do you want, Romanos? What the hell are you after?"

"The gods have ordered the Decada to disgrace and humiliate Turkey for what they did to Cyprus, and to make a statement to the world about the power of the holy *Tetraktys*, the number ten."

"And how do you plan to do that? Are you attacking mainland Turkey or just northern Cyprus?"

"I've told you too much already, Mr. Bond. That part of our plan will remain a secret. Let's just say we have a little help from the Greek military. One of their senior officers, a brigadier general, is Number Five in the Decada."

Romanos finished his wine and set down the glass. "I must leave you now, Mr. Bond. I have business to attend to in Athens. You will be sailing on the *Persephone* for a short while. Hera will watch over you and see that you're made perfectly uncomfortable."

"Wait a minute, Romanos," Bond said, stalling for time. "You didn't tell me everything about Alfred Hutchinson. You knew him before you were in Texas. I saw your picture with him at the New Pythagorean headquarters in Cape Sounion."

Romanos shrugged. "I didn't say we weren't acquainted before then. As a matter of fact, we worked together. Remember that great deal of capital I told you I received in 1981 that allowed me to quit the mercenary business? I came into possession of a large cache of seized Nazi gold that was hidden in Athens since the war. It had been secreted away by Alfred Hutchinson's father, who was stationed in Greece. During my mercenary days, I became business partners with Alfred, and together we sold off the gold all over the world. It's how he financed his political career. Then, with Alfred's diplomatic connections, we were able to completely cover our tracks. We both became very wealthy."

Christ, Bond thought. Hutchinson *was* a crook. "And was he a member of your Decada?"

"I'm not going to answer that," Romanos said. "Oh, and by the way . . . we did eventually recover Hutchinson's information that he had on his computer. There was a copy of the disk that we got our hands on. We now know everything there is to know so that we can proceed with our next three *Tetraktys* attacks. It's a shame you won't be around to see them."

"You're a raving lunatic, Romanos!" Bond shouted. He turned to the girl. "Hera, you can't possibly believe this man! He's deranged, don't you see?"

"This is the Monad," Hera said. "His will is that of the gods."

Bond closed his eyes. She was as far gone as Romanos.

"Why the numbers, the statuettes of the Greek gods? Why were bodies dumped on sacred ruins?"

"It was how the gods ordered it. They wanted the world to know that we were working for them. The gods used to walk the earth, you know. All of those places were homes to them. If a location wasn't available, we were instructed to leave a small icon representing them at the site. The numbers were simply a count-off from the holy *Tetraktys*."

"You know your plan won't accomplish what you hope, Romanos," he said. "If you attack Turkey, they'll blame Greece."

"Bravo, you're not as stupid as I thought," Romanos said.

"But a war between Greece and Turkey? What good will that do? The entire Balkan area will be in ruins. NATO will find a way to stop it swiftly."

"If that is a side effect of our strikes, then I can't help that. The Greek government is too cowardly and weak to initiate the war with Turkey. I have to lead them and show them the way. The Greeks will realize that I am the One and they will follow me to victory. We have the gods on our side, and the gods never die."

Romanos gave Bond a slight bow. "Goodbye, Mr. Bond. *Andio.* I hope you die a painful death so that my cousin's and poor Dr. Anderson's souls receive some satisfaction."

With that, he left the room. Bond had known some insane men in his time with equally mad schemes to bring destruction to the world. Romanos just moved to the top of the list. Only in a world full of fanaticism, bigotry, terrorism, and evil could such a scheme exist, much less be believed and implemented by a mass of people. What were the three remaining *Tetraktys* attacks? Could the virus that was found in the briefcase in Texas be the same homemade bug created by Melina Papas? If so, then it certainly was not still in the experimental stage—it was ready for mass murder. Could Romanos have something else up his sleeve that he wasn't revealing?

Bond was alone with Hera. She took the chair that Romanos had used and pulled it up in front of him. She sat on it with the back facing Bond, her arms draped around it. She reached over to the block of cheddar cheese and removed the kitchen knife.

"Now, let's see," she said. "What are we going to do to amuse ourselves while we're on our journey?"

Niki Mirakos waited on the causeway separating Gefyra and Monemvasia. It had been an hour since Bond was taken onto the yacht. What were they doing in there? Torturing him? Killing him? Three times during the hour, she was tempted to storm the boat alone, but she knew she was outnumbered. She had placed a call to headquarters in Athens as soon as Bond was on the boat. A team was on its way and would be there any minute by helicopter.

Suddenly there was movement on the boat and Konstantine Romanos walked down the ramp to the dock. He got into a black Mercedes and was whisked away. The men on the *Persephone* began to untie the yacht from the dock. The motors started. She was about to sail away.

Niki elected to stay with the boat rather than follow Romanos. She ran back to Bond's Jaguar and used her spare key to get inside. She then called her headquarters to see what was keeping the team.

The *Persephone* pulled away from Gefyra and out into the Mirtoön Sea.

TWENTY-ONE

BY THE SKIN OF THE TEETH

HERA BEGAN BY LIGHTLY SLIDING THE SHARP POINT OF THE KNIFE OVER Bond's face. She took her time, slowly moving it along the skin. Any more pressure and the knife would penetrate the outer layer of tissue. Bond kept perfectly still.

She didn't say a word. She seemed fascinated by Bond's face, the way a young girl might gaze upon a new doll. She traced the nose and around the nostrils with the blade. She ran it along his lips and even placed it gently in his mouth and twisted it. She moved it around his eyes and eyebrows, and repeated these various patterns of sadistic massage for what seemed like an hour. In a way, it was a pleasurable sensation. If Hera had been a woman he trusted, it might have been an extremely sensual way of tormenting someone. Bond wondered, though, how long it would take before she got a little rougher.

She ran the knife along his right cheek and finally asked, "How did you get the scar, James? Shall I add a matching one on the other side? I do like things to be symmetrical. I've been studying your face. I think I know how I'm going to reshape it."

"It's only a matter of minutes before the Greek Secret Service stops this boat. My associates know I'm here," he said. "If I don't report in, they'll come for sure."

"And if you're nowhere to be found on the boat, they will have to admit their mistake and leave. We have nothing to hide here."

"What's in all those crates?"

"Food. Supplies. For our base."

"Oh? Where's your base?"

Hera placed the edge of the knife at Bond's throat. "You ask too many questions, James. Along with rearranging your face, I just might have to cut out your vocal cords. The Greek government knows Konstantine Romanos. He's a respected citizen. His boat is known to the authorities. They wouldn't dare stop it."

"Can't you see he's mad, Hera?"

She slashed the knife lightly and swiftly across his neck. A thin stream of blood appeared.

"That was only a scratch. Next time I'll press harder."

Bond said nothing. He stared at her coldly, daring her to do her worst. The blood trickled down his chest onto his shirt.

"Did you see that film about those American bank robbers?" she asked. "You know, the one where a psycho bank robber tortures a cop? The cop is sitting there in the chair, tied up like you are. The bank robber cuts off the cop's ear. Did you see that movie?"

"No."

"It was bloody. Pretty violent. The cop gets beaten up pretty good. Then he gets his ear cut off. It was very realistic."

She circled his left ear with the knife.

"I saw another movie where a woman had an ice pick and she stabbed her lover to death in bed. She just stabbed him and stabbed him and stabbed him . . . It was very bloody. Did you see that one?"

"I don't go to the cinema much."

"There was another movie that had these two crazy killers—a man and a woman who were lovers—they went on a spree across America, killing people. They get caught and sent to prison. In the prison, they cause a riot and everybody gets cut up or shot. It was the bloodiest movie I ever saw. Did you see that one?"

"I'll bet you're loads of fun on a date, Hera," Bond said.

The nylon ropes were tied around Bond's upper arms and chest.

His forearms were free and he could bend his arms at the elbows. She took his right hand and raised it from his lap.

"You have nice hands, James," she said, tracing the veins on top with the point of the knife. Bond had a sudden recall of a night many years ago, when a SMERSH assassin cut a Russian letter into the back of his right hand. The skin had been grafted, but a faint white patch remained. "Look at this," she said. "Looks like you burned yourself or something. That's not your original skin there, is it?"

Bond didn't answer her. She turned his hand over so that the palm was facing up. She peered closely at it.

"You have a very strong head line," she said. "The heart line is interesting. There are a few breaks in it. Your heart was broken . . . one, two . . . three . . . four times? You've been married once. Your life line . . . hmmm . . . it's very strong. Your head line is strange. You are not a happy man in your life, James. It seems that nothing completely satisfies you. Am I right? Why is that? I should think you would have everything your heart desires. Well, it's too late to do anything about it now. You know we can change the destiny that our palms foretell. We just have to redesign the lines . . ."

With that, she viciously and swiftly carved a triangle into the palm of his hand with three deliberate strokes of the knife. Bond almost cried out in pain, but he gritted his teeth and held it in. He clenched his fist tightly, pressing on the wound to stop the bleeding.

Hera stood up and kicked away her chair. "I think it's time we take that ear off. Which one shall it be? The right or the left? After we do the ears, we'll do the lower lip. Then I'll carve off the upper lip. You'll never kiss anyone again, lover boy. Doing the nose will be pretty messy, but I think it should be next. You'll still be alive by the time we get to your eyes. One at a time. Pluck. Pluck. We'll save the tongue for last. I'll split it in two, then I'll cut the entire thing out and feed it to the fish. I haven't decided if I want to examine other parts of your body after all that, but I probably will. It's going to be a slow, painful death, James. It's a pity, for you're very handsome. Well, you are now. You won't be too pretty in a little while."

She took hold of his right ear and placed the blade of the knife against his scalp. Bond closed his eyes, willing himself to fight the oncoming pain.

There was a buzz on the intercom. She picked it up and spoke impatiently. "What is it?" She listened a moment, looked at Bond, frowned, and said, "All right. We'll be right up."

She hung up and began to cut the nylon cords. "It seems we have some visitors. I'm going to take you out on deck so they can see you. You're not to try anything. Do not look at them. Do not give them any signals. Keep your hands to your sides. I'll give you something to wrap around that hand."

She found a handkerchief in Romanos's desk, used it to wipe the blood from around his neck and chest, then wrapped it around Bond's right hand. She continued cutting the ropes until Bond was free.

"Let's go. Get up slowly and don't try anything foolish. Walk around like you're enjoying yourself. I'll have a gun on you the entire time."

She picked up Bond's Walther PPK that Romanos had left behind. He noted that she still had the P99 in her belt.

Bond stood up, clutching the handkerchief tightly around his hand. It was involuntarily shaking.

They went up the wooden steps to the deck above. Four men were there, dressed in wet suits, standing at attention with their arms folded.

A helicopter was hovering above the boat. It was an unmarked Gazelle, and Bond could see two people in it. He wondered if Niki might be the pilot, but it was too high to tell. He looked around the sea and saw other vessels on the water—a couple of sailing boats, a catamaran, and what looked like a cruise ship not too far away. There was an island about two miles off the bow of the ship.

"Where are we?" Bond asked.

"Near Santorini. Lie down on the deck chair," Hera said. "Act like you're enjoying the sun." Together they sat on two chairs side by side. Bond stretched out and did as he was told. Was there anything he could do to signal the helicopter? Surely they were Niki's people, keeping an eye on the boat.

Hera said something to one of the men in Greek. He acknowledged the order, then proceeded to put on a Dacor tank.

Hera turned to Bond and said, "We'll just make it look like we're having a nice time out here on the water, so relax."

Bond glanced around him. He didn't see any usable weapons. There were some doughnut-shaped life belts near the door, a coil of rope behind him. He had to get off the boat, regardless of whether or not Niki's people figured out that he needed help.

Inside the Gazelle, Niki and a National Intelligence Service agent studied the sea below them. Niki was piloting the craft, while the other agent peered through binoculars at the ship.

"Well?" she yelled over the noise of the helicopter.

"I see him. He's on the upper deck lying down. He's with the red-headed woman. He looks like he's not in any trouble to me."

"Are you sure?"

"There's three . . . four men standing on the deck, but they look like crewmen. Looks like one is serving drinks, another one is getting into diving gear."

"Then we'll wait," she said. "I'd hate to blow his cover. James is up to something, I know it. He's infiltrated them through that woman." A pang of jealousy streaked through her heart, as she suspected that James had slept with Hera Volopoulos. Niki clenched the controls of the helicopter and fought to contain her emotions.

He was doing a job, she told herself. Sometimes field agents had to do whatever was necessary to obtain information.

"We're going on to Santorini," she said. "We'll refuel and keep tabs on the boat."

"The records at Gefyra said they were headed for Cyprus."

"What a surprise."

Niki pushed away her feelings and concentrated on flying the helicopter. It hung in the air for another minute, then flew away toward the island.

———•—

Bond watched the helicopter move toward Santorini with disap-
pointment, but he had put together a risky plan which he had to try.

"All right, get back up," Hera said. "We're going below."

"But it's such a nice day. Can't we get some sun while you torture
me?" Bond asked, standing.

"Shut up." She stood and aimed the Walther at him. "This gun is
puny. Why do you use it?"

"Why do you care?"

She marched him to the stairs leading back down. He eyed the life
belts mounted on the wall by the door. Acting quickly, Bond grabbed
one and, with all his might, flung it at Hera like a discus. It took her
completely by surprise, temporarily knocking her gun hand away.
The Walther went off, then flew out of her hand and sailed across the
deck and off onto one of the lower decks. The stray bullet hit the man
with the aqualung, and he plummeted over the side of the yacht into
the water. Bond followed up the attack by ramming Hera in the chest
with his head, which sent her tumbling to the deck.

"Bastard!" she cried. She was on her feet immediately. The three
other guards made a move for Bond. He took a defensive stance,
while desperately looking for an escape route. The men rushed him,
but Bond easily warded off their attack and knocked them down.
Hera pushed past the falling bodies and delivered a hard kick into
Bond's stomach, but he managed to grab her leg and twist it. She fell
to the deck again. Bond threw himself on top of her, grabbed the P99
from her belt, leaped over her body and ran.

"Get him!" Hera cried. The guards drew guns and fired at him, but
the bullets missed as he jumped from the upper deck to one of the
walk-around side decks on the port side. He landed on his feet and
ran to the stern. As the bullets zipped past him, Bond stuck the P99
in his trouser pocket, took a breath, and dived neatly into the cold,
blue water.

"We can't let him get away!" Hera cried. She ordered the three men
to put on aqualungs and dive into the water.

Bond surfaced and gasped for air. He was about thirty meters from the boat. Getting his bearings, he saw that he was a good mile and a half from Santorini. Could he make it? The water was rougher than he had thought. It would be a challenging test of stamina.

Then he saw the cruise ship. It was approximately a hundred meters away. He began to swim toward it instead.

The three guards quickly equipped themselves with tanks, fins, masks, and harpoon guns. They jumped into the water and began swimming swiftly toward Bond.

Bond didn't look back, but he knew that the men were in pursuit. He was hoping they'd come after him. The water was indeed far too choppy, so he had to find a way to snatch one of their aqualungs. Then he remembered the man who was shot. Bond dived and swam deep, looking for the dead guard. A stream of bubbles marked the location, for he was caught on some rocks about thirty meters below the surface. Bond held his breath and fought the pressure, willing himself to swim down to the body. It took nearly two minutes to reach him. His lungs were about to burst and he felt the pain in his ears as he made the final approach—then grabbed the dead man's regulator and inserted it into his own mouth. He took a few gulps of air, then removed the aqualung and strapped it onto himself just as a harpoon shot past his head.

Diver number one caught up with Bond and attempted to stab him. Bond kicked him hard in the chest, then grabbed his arms. They struggled in the water, their bodies turning over and over like jellyfish. Bond, the far superior swimmer and fighter, easily chopped the knife out of the man's hand with a blow to the wrist. He caught the knife as it floated in front of him, then thrust it into the man's throat. Blood clouded the water as Bond struggled to get back to the dead man to remove his fins and mask. Bond had many years of experience compensating for the slow-motion delay that inevitably occurred while fighting underwater. He ripped off the dead man's face mask. Another harpoon shot toward him, but Bond swung the body into its path just in time. The spear plunged into the man's side but before Bond had time to think, divers two and three were on top of him. They were both armed with knives. Bond performed a somersault in the water, kicking the men as he turned. Still wearing the shoes he had bought in Monemvasia, Bond smashed the glass on diver two's mask with a heel. Blinded, the guard temporarily left the skirmish. That gave Bond enough time to pull the knife from diver one's throat and thrust it at diver three. His opponent was held at bay for the few seconds Bond needed to pull the fins off the first dead man's feet, kick off his shoes, and slip them on. Diver three swam toward Bond at full speed with his knife-wielding hand outstretched. Bond swung his own knife and caught the man's shoulder with it, but the attacker succeeded in nicking him in the side. Bond dodged another swing, only to discover that diver two had recovered his eyesight and was back, ready to tackle him from behind.

Bond broke away from the melee and swam to the cruise ship, which was almost on top of them. The two men chased him. He maneuvered dangerously close to the ship's rotor blades, hoping the men would follow. The force of the water was immense, and it took all of his strength to keep from being sucked into the propeller. He took hold of the metal casing around the blades, climbed up halfway out of the water and held on for dear life as the boat took him at top speed through the water.

Bond thought he had successfully escaped, when a hand grabbed his ankle. Diver three was hanging on to him as the ship pulled them along. Bond felt the man's knife slice into his calf. He kicked out and connected with something very hard, but the man refused to loosen his grip. Bond moved forward on the rotor housing by pulling himself along some metal rungs. His injured palm screamed in agony. He finally made it to a point in front of the rotors. His lower body and the diver attached to his ankle were being dragged into the current that flowed through the rotors and out the other side. The suction was extremely powerful.

The attacker attempted to pull himself up Bond's leg. Bond kicked him again and again until the man lost his grip. The force of the water immediately pulled him into the rotor blades, and the blue water turned to a dark red as bits of the body spread out into the sea.

Bond climbed back to his position above the rotors and held on to the housing again, allowing the cruise ship to take him toward Santorini. He had time to catch his breath and rest. Diver two, the one whose mask was broken, was nowhere in sight. Bond put the knife in his belt and examined his hand and calf. The wound that Hera had made in his palm was bleeding badly and hurt like hell. The cut in his leg was superficial and would not need stitches. He then checked the Walther P99 and found that the magazine was missing.

The area around Santorini is famous for its underwater volcanoes. The foam from the rotors prevented him from seeing them, but he remembered that the caldera was quite beautiful—white, black, and gray, with patches of multicolored, sparkling strata made of lava and pumice. The volcanoes were really just craggy rocks with large holes, dormant for centuries.

The ship began to slow down, signaling its approach to the island by blowing its siren. Bond rode the boat all the way in to the bay at Fira, Santorini's major port. Just as he was about to slip off the ship and swim to shore, a harpoon struck the hull by his head. He looked behind him and saw diver two swimming hard toward him. Bond let go of the rotor housing and swam down to the rocky volcanoes. Just as he had hoped, the diver followed him.

Bond swam into one of the dark holes and hid behind an outcrop of hardened lava. He watched and waited, ready to ambush the guard and slit his throat. Suddenly, two small bright lights appeared in front of him. Bond's heart skipped a beat when he realized that they weren't lights at all—they were eyes! He was face-to-face with a moray eel, what the Greek fishermen called a smerna. This one was snakelike, a meter and a half long, and it had shiny black skin which was speckled prominently with large golden-yellow spots. The eel had a huge mouth equipped with what looked like hundreds of sharp teeth. Bond knew that the bite could produce a toxicity and might take days to heal. Normally moray eels didn't bother divers unless they were disturbed, but they especially didn't like being threatened when they were sleeping on rocks or in caves.

Bond pushed back slowly from the lava as the eel watched him closely. At that point, the diver in pursuit appeared above him, knife in hand. Bond deflected a fatal blow just in time, but was nicked again in the shoulder. The two men struggled a moment until Bond managed to perform another somersault and sling the guard over him onto the rock where the moray eel was resting. The diver slammed into the eel, which reacted ferociously. The smerna swiftly clamped its huge jaws on the diver's neck and wouldn't let go. Bond watched in horror as the surprisingly powerful eel shook the man like a snake with a rat. The water turned dark red, clouding the gruesome sight. Bond turned away and shot out of the lava outcrop.

Back on the surface, Bond swam along the port side of the cruise ship to the dock. Exhausted, he climbed onto the rocks, removed his fins, and made his way onto the shore. A few tourists disembarking from the cruise ship saw him and pointed. A man wearing bloody street clothes and an aqualung had just climbed out of the water!

Bond dumped the diving gear and walked barefoot to the Fira Skala building, where he immediately contacted the local police.

TWENTY-TWO

SECRETS OF
THE DEAD

HERA VOLOPOULOS ORDERED THE MEN TO OPEN A HATCH ON THE UPPER deck of the *Persephone,* disclosing a prototype of a new Groen Brothers Hawk H2X gyrocopter that sat inside. Only about twenty-two feet in length with a height of nine and a half feet, the Hawk was powered by an Allison 250 C20 turbine and had a range of 600 miles at its cruising speed of 140 miles per hour. It could also lift off without a runway, unlike most gyrocopters of the past.

Hera put on a helmet and got inside the little white vehicle that resembled the head of an ostrich. She gave the thumbs-up sign to the two men on the deck and started the motor. The Hawk rose gently into the sky and flew away toward Cyprus.

Exactly fifteen minutes later, the *Persephone* was met by two secret service helicopters and two coast guard ships. The remaining three men on board fought to the death rather than be arrested.

"I'm sorry, James, but it looked as if you were having a good time on that yacht," Niki said. "If I had known they had guns on you, we would have taken action."

Bond was sitting up in a village police station where the Greek National Intelligence Service had temporarily set up shop on Santorini. He was drinking hot coffee and eating a plate of scrambled eggs that Niki had prepared for him. A doctor had spent the last hour sewing up his palm. Bond would have to be left-handed for a while. The wounds on his neck and leg were superficial.

"Besides," she continued, "I was convinced you were screwing that woman and was a little pissed off at you. Well, I'm glad you're okay. You're like a tomcat—you have nine lives."

Bond grinned, but didn't address Niki's concerns.

The chief of police stepped in and said something in Greek to Niki.

"I have a fax coming in, I'll be right back," she told Bond as she left the room.

Bond sighed heavily, then took a sip of coffee. He was feeling better. The lack of food or sleep for so long, and his ordeals on the boat and in the sea, had taken their toll. Niki's comment about Hera had irritated him too. He hated being paired with a partner, especially a female one.

Niki returned and sat on the desk across from him.

"Romanos has disappeared," she said. "That is, he's nowhere to be found in Greece. They're on the lookout for him in Cyprus."

"Was he followed from Gefyra?" Bond asked.

"No, the team arrived too late, and I stuck with the *Persephone* because you were on it. We sent word all the way up the line to Athens to watch out for his car, but no one ever saw it. He must have gone somewhere else and hopped on a train, a boat . . . who knows?"

"And where's the *Persephone* now?"

"Within five hundred miles of Cyprus. We've sent a force out to intercept them. Your redheaded *friend* should be under arrest by now. Let me hear what Romanos told you."

"He's planning three big strikes, most likely against northern Cyprus or Turkey, and he said he had the help of the Greek military—some general or other is on his team. Melina Papas has been creating a new virus for him, and I suspect it's already made. It could be the one I found in Texas. If it is, then he's already attacked Los Angeles and Tokyo with it. He's going to want to hit a lot of people at once. Is there an event coming up that will bring a big crowd together in northern Cyprus or in Turkey?"

"Damn, there is. November fifteenth is the day the so-called TRNC declared its independence. There are parades and celebrations in Lefkosia."

"That's tomorrow."

"That's right."

"I had better get in touch with London. Can I use your mobile?"

Niki gave it to him and left the room so that Bond could call his office in privacy. After the series of code words and forwarded connections, Bill Tanner came on the line.

"James! Good to hear from you."

"I need to speak with M, Bill."

He put Bond through and soon he heard the weary voice of his chief.

"Double-O Seven?" she asked.

"Yes, ma'am. I have some news. I'm afraid you're not going to like it."

"Go ahead."

"Alfred Hutchinson's father was court-martialed during the war over some unrecovered Nazi gold."

"I knew that."

"Alfred and Konstantine Romanos were partners in selling it off all over Europe. It's how Alfred financed his political career. I fear that Ambassador Hutchinson was more involved in this affair than we realized. He may have been a member of the Decada."

"Are you sure, 007?" M sounded more angry than upset, as if she wanted Bond to prove it before she would believe it.

"That's what Romanos himself told me. They've known each other since the early eighties."

There was silence at the other end of the line.

"Ma'am, I understand how this news makes you feel, but I must ask you something. Romanos said that the information Hutchinson was going to give us the morning after his death was about the Decada's plans. It's imperative that we get hold of that material. I think they're going to strike very soon, possibly tomorrow. Please think very hard once again. Is there anything in your memory that might lead us to this information?"

M said, "His flat was searched thoroughly, but I'll have a team go over there again right now. Let me think about it."

Bond gave her the number of Niki's mobile.

"I'll ring you in three hours or less," she said.

It was now six o'clock and the sun would be going down soon.

"Right. Take care, ma'am."

"You too, 007." She hung up.

Bond went out of the room and found Niki talking on another phone. She was agitated and speaking rapidly in Greek. She slammed down the phone and said, "She wasn't on the boat, James."

"What?"

"Hera Volopoulos. She wasn't on the *Persephone*. Only three men were found on the yacht and they were killed. She wasn't on board."

"The boat didn't make any stops after she left Monemvasia?"

"No."

"That's impossible. Unless she got away in another boat."

"That must be what happened. Now what?"

"M will call on your mobile in three hours."

Niki nodded. "We have a room where we can wait."

She made love to him as though the world would end that night. She was ravenous after having hungered for him for two days and she submitted enthusiastically to his caresses. Bond thought that Niki demonstrated a unique and earthy emotional response to sex. She made involuntary guttural sounds of pleasure that were somewhat primal, and which he found exciting.

They were at the Hotel Porto Fira, in a room made partly of volcanic rock. It was built on the caldera's edge and was one of the finer establishments in the port town. If he hadn't needed the release of tension that Niki had just provided, Bond would have been happy to light a cigarette, sit on the terrace, and gaze at the classic postcard views of colored balconies, blue-domed churches, and warm, sunny beaches that make Santorini one of Greece's most beautiful islands.

The lovemaking had eased the earlier tension that had risen between them. They each lit a cigarette, lay in bed and looked up at the white ceiling. They could hear the sound of the sea outside.

"James, you like me, don't you?" she asked.

"Of course I do. Why?"

"You seem distant, as if you were somewhere else."

"Am I?" he asked, but it was true. He was concerned about M and was thinking about the relationship she had with Alfred Hutchinson. Bond knew what it was like when a lover betrayed everything you stood for and believed in.

"James, listen. I ask nothing of you," Niki said. "You don't have to be afraid that I'm going to try and keep this relationship going after the assignment is over."

"I wasn't thinking that at all."

"I just—" Niki caught her breath, then continued. "I mean, I'm aware of your reputation, James. You have a girl in every port. It's all right. I don't mind being the girl in this one. I just thought you had only *one* girl in each port."

Bond looked at her and took hold of her chin. "Don't be a silly goose. You are the only girl in this port."

"I'm not sure I believe you, but anyway, we have an assignment together and shouldn't be doing this in the first place. Why would we want to continue it?" She sounded hurt.

"Niki . . ."

"No, really, it's all right. Just promise me one thing."

"What?"

"Before the very last time we make love . . . that is, when you know it's the last time . . . before you leave Greece . . . tell me. Don't just leave without saying a word. All right?"

"All right."

Her lips were slightly open, an inch from his. She kissed him and explored his mouth with her tongue. Then she said, "The assignment isn't over yet. Put out that cigarette and let's do it again."

"M on hold for you, James," Bill Tanner said over the phone. The ring had awakened Bond and Niki in the hotel room. Bond looked at his watch. It was 8:10.

When she got on the line, M said, "We found it, 007, I think we've got it."

"Yes?"

"I've been going over and over the events of that night," she said. "Something compelled me to look inside the handbag I was carrying then. It's one I don't usually use. You see, when he was dying, he kept saying, 'Your hand . . . your hand . . .' He was gasping, he couldn't speak well. I thought he wanted me to hold his hand. What he was trying to say was, 'Your handbag . . . your handbag.' Well, I hadn't touched that handbag since the night of the murder. I got it out and looked inside, and found an envelope. Inside were instructions and a key to a safety deposit box at a branch of Barclay's. The instructions gave the address of the bank and authorization for me to open the box if anything happened to Alfred. He must have slipped the note inside when he insisted on holding it. He knew what had happened to him on the pavement. He knew that he was going to die."

"Go on."

"I just got back from the bank. Inside the box was a note he wrote to me, a piece of paper with a triangle drawn on it, a marked-up map of Cyprus, and a floppy disk. On the disk we found details of a meeting he had set up with the Rauf Denktash, the President of the Turkish Republic of Northern Cyprus. He was going to visit the President on their independence day."

"That's tomorrow."

"Yes, the fifteenth of November. There are some plans of the Presidential Palace on Tanzimat Street on the disk as well, an invitation to a breakfast celebration tomorrow morning, and something else far more disturbing."

"What's that?"

"Aerial maps of Istanbul. There is one large map of the Aegean, with the longitude and latitude of the city highlighted. There's a series of numbers on this map, and Bill Tanner confirmed that they were the target coordinates for a missile."

"And the note?"

"It's personal, but I want you to see it. It clears up the business with the Nazi gold. I'm going to fax all of this to you. Once you've had a look, call me back."

Niki opened her Compaq laptop and plugged it in. She set it up to receive faxes, and soon the data was being transmitted and downloaded onto her hard drive. Bond read Hutchinson's letter to M:

My Dear Barbara:

If you are reading this, then I am probably dead. I hope you will find all of this material useful in stopping the Decada. I believe they are planning to assassinate the President of the Turkish Republic of Northern Cyprus on November 15. They have something else planned for Istanbul.

I took the precaution of placing a copy of this data in my safety deposit box because I recently discovered my computer had been tampered with. The files may have been copied. I have since deleted them.

You'll probably learn that I was involved with Konstantine Romanos in a scheme to sell off a large cache of Nazi gold that my father had secreted away after the war. I regret to tell you that this is true. Even though I became a wealthy man from the sale of the gold, Romanos cheated me out of 50% of my share, and I was unable to claim it. I couldn't go public, for it would have destroyed my political career. The suspicions about my father were damaging enough. The scandal would have been more than I could bear.

I attempted to extort the money from him, threatening to go to the authorities with the information that Romanos was a terrorist. When I learned that my son was involved with the Decada, I knew it was time to do something aggressive. Romanos used my son as a hold over me. He thought he could keep me from talking if Charles was under his wing. Instead, I resolved to give you all of this information.

The facts of life are such that we are all human and we all make mistakes. Alas, the facts of death do not allow us to properly correct those mistakes. By then it is too late to clear out the dark, dirty secrets from the closets of our souls.

I want you to know that I love you very much, and once this

*ghastly business is over, I hope you can forgive me and that
your memories of our time together will be pleasant.*

With all my love,
Alfred

So the man was somewhat honorable after all, Bond thought.

Bond studied the rest of the data and decided that the President of
the TRNC was definitely one of the three *Tetraktys* targets. If Istanbul
was another one, what was the third? There was no indication of
what the Decada planned to do with Instanbul, except that there
were cruise missile coordinates written on a map. Had they obtained
a cruise missile? Was this the military connection? And what about
that virus? Was there a connection to all this?

"Niki," Bond said. "Get on to your people and pull any reports
from the last few months dealing with arms trading in the area. Look
for missiles, anything relevant."

He phoned M back and told her that he had gone over the
information.

"Romanos said he had recovered all of Hutchinson's information
after all. I believe he has a missile that he's planning to use on Turkey.
They're going to try and kill the President of Northern Cyprus in the
morning. We have to put together a team and get there as soon as
possible," Bond said.

"I agree," M said.

"We have to go into the north. That will be tricky with our Greek
friends. They might refuse to cross the border."

"Damn it, convince them that their country will be blown to hell
if they don't stop these fanatics. You're also going to need the assistance of the Turks. I'll call Station T in Istanbul and alert them that
they are under attack, but *not* by Greeks or the Republic of Cyprus."

"Romanos admitted that his people were creating a virus. That
may have been the bug we found in Texas. What's the status of the
epidemics?"

"Just a minute, Chief of Staff is handing me something." She was
silent as she read for a minute. "Christ."

"What?"

"The death tolls in Los Angeles and Tokyo are rising. There have been new cases reported in New York and London during the past forty-eight hours. Do you think this is his virus?"

"According to him, it wasn't yet ready for use!"

"Well, somebody's using it. All of the infected people have been quarantined, and the clinics where they got the blood have been sealed. Hospitals are on full alert to isolate anyone who comes in with similar symptoms."

"Then we need to find him fast. If there's really going to be an assassination attempt on the Turkish Cypriot president tomorrow, that may be our only chance of tracking him down. What I don't understand is how he is going to get to the President. It was Alfred that had the invitation to meet with him tomorrow, right?"

"Yes. He was supposed to be part of the President's entourage for the day's festivities. Of course, Manville Duncan had to step in. He's in Nicosia now at the British Embassy. I'll get hold of him and see if he can handle this situation with a diplomatic approach."

"That would help a great deal," Bond said. "How is he doing being Ambassador to the World?"

"Oh, he just complains that he's not very worldly about food. He's a picky eater, I suppose. He's especially at a disadvantage in a meat-eating country like Cyprus."

"Why is that?"

"You didn't know? Duncan is a strict vegetarian."

A cold chill ran down Bond's spine. "My God. Ma'am, it's Manville Duncan who is the member of the Decada. It was never Alfred Hutchinson. Hutchinson wasn't killed because of the secrets he knew. He was murdered so that Duncan would be free to replace him for this event tomorrow! He's a traitor, and *he's* the one who will try to assassinate the President!"

TWENTY-THREE

INDEPENDENCE DAY

MANVILLE DUNCAN NERVOUSLY LOADED THE RICIN PELLET INTO THE GOLD-plated ballpoint pen that would serve as the method of execution.

"Are you sure you can handle this?" Hera asked him impatiently.

"Don't worry," he said. "You just worry about *your* job."

The sun was rising in Lefkosia, and the two of them had met in Hera's room in the Saray Hotel on Girne Caddesi, probably the best hotel in Lefkosia.

"The parade begins at nine o'clock," she said. "You'll be meeting with the President at nine-thirty. He's supposed to address the people at ten. If you're on time, he'll collapse of a heart attack in the middle of his speech. Remember to place the number and the statue where they won't be found for a while. Then get the hell out."

Duncan felt his pocket to make sure that the piece of paper with the number "8" on it and the small statuette of Apollo were still there.

"What about your equipment?" he asked. "Was it here, as arranged?"

She nodded. "It's an old American M79 grenade launcher, the kind used in Vietnam." She pulled it out from under the bed. It was a short, rifled, breech-loading weapon that fired a fixed cartridge. Its maximum range was about 350 yards.

"And four cartridges." They were in a metal briefcase, packed in foam, and looked like oversized short and fat bullets. "They're filled with sarin. I'm firing them at ten oh-five whether the President is dead or not. Make sure you don't follow him outside. If you breathe this stuff you'll die." The rest of her accoutrements—the gas mask, the protective suit and hood, the boots and gloves—already lay spread out on the bed. On the bedside table was a can of red spray paint and a small alabaster statuette of Hermes.

Duncan watched Hera prepare. He said finally, "I know what you're up to, Number Two."

"What do you mean?"

"I know what you and Number Ten and Number Eight are planning."

"And what is that, Mr. Duncan?"

"You're planning to split off from the Decada and form your own group. You're planning a mutiny."

"Why would we do that?"

"I don't know. I know that you and Number Ten were . . . well, that you were intimate with each other. Number Eight made it a ménage à trois. Am I right?"

"What if you are?"

"The Monad won't like it."

Hera suddenly seized Duncan by the throat and squeezed hard. His eyes bulged as he struggled for breath. After allowing him to feel the pain for thirty seconds, she said, "Listen, you worm. If you so much as breathe a word of that to the Monad, I'll cut out your liver and stuff it in your mouth, do you understand me? If you're smart, you'll keep quiet, and maybe we'll have a place for you when we form the *true* Decada. I've been with the Monad since I was twelve years old. I want to break free. It's my destiny. The gods have spoken to me too. Pythagoras himself experienced a mutiny among his own followers. This is meant to happen. Besides, the Monad is misguided. We all agree with his goal to teach the Turks a lesson, but after that, we have our own plans. Bigger ones. Once this *Tetraktys* is completed, we're moving on. I promise you that what we leave behind us won't be pretty, so you had better start choosing where your loyalties will lie."

She released him, then continued getting ready. Duncan gasped for breath and sat on the bed. He waited a few minutes to regain his composure. Then, as if nothing had happened, he stood up.

"I had better get going," Duncan said, clipping the gold pen in his jacket pocket. He straightened his tie and said, "Good luck, Number Two."

"You too, Number Three."

Manville Duncan left the room for his appointment with the gods.

It was nine o'clock in the morning. Hundreds of Turkish Cypriots had gathered in the streets of Lefkosia for the parades and celebration. The President of the Republic was due to speak from a stage set up near the Saray Hotel. A few blocks away, he was greeting visiting dignitaries at a special breakfast reception in the Presidential Palace. No one in the streets noticed the British helicopter that flew overhead. After all, British aircraft were seen in the sky all the time.

Niki Mirakos flew the Wessex helicopter from the RAF base in Akrotiri, carrying four Greek Secret Service commandos and James Bond. M had arranged the whole thing in secrecy with the Greeks. It was best that neither the Republic of Cyprus nor the TRNC knew what was happening for the moment. The government of Turkey, however, had been alerted to the situation.

They were all dressed in protective uniforms with gas masks hanging loosely around their necks. Armed with AK-47s, the commandos were a highly trained professional antiterrorism unit. Crossing the Green Line was something they had thought they would never have to do.

Down below, at the Presidential Palace, Manville Duncan was greeted by the President's aides and brought inside the splendid white building. He was led into a room full of diplomats and other important visitors from Turkey and abroad. Fruit juice, breads, and fruit were laid out on a table. Rauf Denktash, the President of the TRNC, was surrounded by friends and colleagues near a large bay window looking out over the street. The festive atmosphere of the place was infectious.

"Mr. President," the aide said, leading Duncan up to him, "this is the Goodwill Ambassador to the World from Great Britain."

"Mr. Hutchinson?" the President asked.

"No, Manville Duncan. I believe my office alerted yours—Mr. Hutchinson died suddenly over a week ago. I was Mr. Hutchinson's lawyer and have temporarily taken over his duties."

"I am sorry to hear about Mr. Hutchinson," the President said in English. "We had never met but had spoken on the phone. Nice man. But you are just as welcome here, Mr. Duncan."

"Thank you. I am here representing Her Majesty's Government in the interest of promoting peaceful relations between the TRNC and the Republic of Cyprus."

The President nodded his head in acknowledgment and said, "Ah, but Her Majesty's Government refuses to recognize the Turkish Republic of Northern Cyprus as a nation. What can we do about that, Mr. Duncan?"

Duncan displayed his most rehearsed, charming smile. "My dear President, now is not the time to get into *that* discussion, is it?"

They both laughed. "It is a pleasure to be here," Duncan continued. "Congratulations. Enjoy your day."

"Thank you," the President said, then rejoined his colleagues.

Manville Duncan stepped over to the table and picked up a glass of orange juice, then felt his inside jacket pocket to make sure the ballpoint pen was still there. As a precaution, he also wore a shoulder holster with a Smith & Wesson Bodyguard Airweight .38 Special.

The Wessex flew over the crowds toward the western side of the Venetian wall that surrounded Lefkosia. Looking down, Bond saw quite a different city than what was south of the Green Line. Lefkosia was not nearly as modernized as Nicosia was. The buildings below looked hundreds of years old. As a result, Lefkosia had distinctly more character than its southern counterpart. There were numerous historic monuments dating from the Middle Ages and subsequent eras, including many examples of Gothic and Ottoman architecture.

"Where do you want me to land this thing?" Niki shouted.

Bond pointed to a mosque. "There, that's it. Put it down in the courtyard."

He checked the AK-47 he was carrying, and then made sure the P99 was loaded. He had been lucky to obtain extra magazines and ammunition from the Akrotiri base.

The Wessex descended into the courtyard of the Kanli Mescit Mosque. The commandos jumped out and Bond followed them. He gave the thumbs-up sign to Niki, who then took the Wessex back up into the air.

For a few moments, nothing happened. Bond and the men waited and watched the walls surrounding the courtyard.

Suddenly the gates of the mosque opened, and twenty Turkish soldiers poured in, their rifles ready. They were wearing green camouflage uniforms. The men encircled the perimeter of the walls and within seconds had the entire courtyard covered. They knelt and aimed their rifles at the five men. A captain shouted in Turkish for the Greek commandos to lay down their weapons and surrender. For several tense moments, the Greeks and the Turks stared at each other without moving. Face-to-face with their ancient enemies, both sides were unsure how to proceed.

The four Greek commandos looked at Bond. "What happens now?" one of them asked. Bond scanned the faces of the Turkish soldiers, but he didn't see the man he was looking for.

"Steady, men," Bond said quietly. "This has to be a mistake . . ."

Then, two men in civilian clothes marched through the gate and spoke quietly to the sergeant in charge of the soldiers. The sergeant nodded and barked a command to his men. They immediately lowered their weapons and stood at ease. The two men in civilian clothes then walked toward Bond and the Greek commandos. One fellow, a large man with a thick mustache and big brown eyes, resembled someone from Bond's past.

"It's all right," Bond said to the men. "He's here."

Bond stepped forward and stood in front of the men, then held out his hand. The mustached man looked Bond up and down, then grinned broadly. He vigorously shook hands and said, "Mr. Bond, it is so good to see you again."

"You too, Tempo," Bond said. He had not seen Stefan Tempo, the son of Bond's Turkish friend Darko Kerim, in many years. Bond remembered well that fateful day aboard the Orient Express when he had found Kerim's body, murdered by the Russian assassin Red Grant. Later, Kerim's son Stefan had assisted Bond on that assignment, which seemed a lifetime ago. The mature Stefan Tempo was the spitting image of his father.

"How's Station T these days?" Bond asked.

"We do a lot of desk work now," Tempo said. "But when the British start requesting permission to perform commando raids in northern Cyprus with the help of the Greeks, we put down our pencils and take notice."

"Tempo, we don't have much time. We have to get to the Presidential Palace," Bond said.

"We'll lead the way," Tempo said. He barked an order in Turkish to the soldiers, then gestured for Bond to follow them out of the gates. The four Greek commandos looked at the Turks warily, but they went along with the group without complaint.

They all rushed through the gates and onto Tanzimat Street, which was packed with civilians. The men ran in formation, the crowd parting for them as they moved toward the elegant white building.

The TRNC guards in front of the palace were taken by surprise. Tempo and the Turkish sergeant approached the guardhouse and presented papers. They were to be allowed in quietly. Bond had planned it so that Duncan would not be forewarned of their arrival; hence, the TRNC knew nothing about it. At first the guards could not believe that they had a security breach on their hands. Tempo's credentials convinced them otherwise. Finally, the palace head of security nodded his head and let them through the gates.

The TRNC guards led the way into the building. Bond looked at his watch. It was precisely 9:30. They stepped quietly up the grand marble staircase to the second floor and were ushered to the President's greeting room, where the breakfast party was still in progress.

Manville Duncan had his gold ballpoint pen in hand. The President was standing at the food table, pouring a cup of Turkish coffee. All Duncan had to do was press the pen point into the President's arm or leg, and then push the button on the end to release the pellet. The President would feel only a slight pressure and maybe a pinprick.

"Mr. President," Duncan said, leveling the pen at his target's hip. "I am expected back at the British high commissioner's residence very shortly, and I wanted to thank—"

The door burst open. Three of the Turkish soldiers and a TRNC guard came into the room and pulled their guns. They shouted in Turkish for everyone to freeze. Bond pushed his way inside the door.

Duncan, panicking, lunged at the President and grabbed him around the chest. He held the pen at his neck and shouted, "Stay back!" He started to back up to the bay window with the frightened President in the crook of his arm, but the President tripped and fell backward. Duncan dropped the ballpoint pen and reached into his jacket for the .38 Special.

A shot rang out and caught him in the chest before the gun was out of its holster. He flew backward into the food table. Dishes crashed to the floor. Bond lowered the Walther P99 and replaced it in the holster he was wearing on his back. He approached Duncan and knelt beside him. The man was coughing up blood and clutching his chest.

Stefan Tempo rushed to the bewildered and frightened President and spoke rapidly in Turkish, taking him out of the room. Other TRNC officials began to reassure the rest of the guests that everything was under control.

"All right, Duncan," Bond said. "Now's your chance to tell me what you know. Where is Hera? What's Strike Number Nine?"

Duncan spat bloody phlegm from his mouth and gasped, "The One . . . will . . . become . . . the Many . . ."

He exhaled loudly and died. Bond searched his pockets and found a piece of paper with the number "8" scrawled in red and the alabaster statuette. In his other pocket was a map of Lefkosia and a piece of Saray Hotel stationery. A building on the map was marked in a yellow highlight. The notepaper had something scribbled in pencil—

#Numbers, 17:00

Bond wasn't sure what that meant, but he put the paper in his pocket, then looked at the map again.

"Tempo, what's this building?" Bond asked, showing him the map.

"That's the Saray Hotel."

"Get your men and let's go. We're finished here."

The Saray Hotel was eight stories tall and provided a magnificent view of Lefkosia/Nicosia from the roof. Hera Volopoulos, dressed in her Number Killer uniform, had completed setting up the M79 grenade launcher and had armed it with one of the shells containing sarin nerve gas. The shells would explode in the air and distribute the chemical, and the breeze would do the rest. Hundreds of people would be affected. All Hera had to do was fire the four shells in different directions, take her previously prepared escape route down to the first floor, run to the rental car she had parked a block away, and drive to the area north of the city where she had hidden the gyrocopter. No one would notice her amidst all the celebration going on in the streets. The Turkish Cypriots were out in force, and nothing could distract them. Hera thought that it was devilishly appropriate that the strike was being made on their independence day.

At ten o'clock, she looked over at the temporary stage that was set up in the square across from the hotel. The President hadn't shown up. Had he died from Duncan's pellet too soon? Or had Duncan failed in his mission?

She wasn't about to wait until 10:05. She examined the grenade launcher one more time, checked her gas mask, and prepared to fire the first shell.

"Hold it, Hera!" Bond's voice rang out from the roof entrance to the lift. He stood thirty feet away, the P99 pointed at her, daring her to make another move. Behind him were several Turkish soldiers with their weapons trained on her. They were all dressed in gas masks and protective gear.

"Step away from the launcher." Bond's voice sounded metallic through the mask's filter.

Her finger was on the trigger. "Just one of these shells will be enough, James," she said through her mask. "It will only take a reflex to pull the trigger. If you shoot me, I can't guarantee that I won't fire the launcher involuntarily."

Bond knew that she would fire the launcher no matter what happened. If he had only been a little closer to her, a shot from the Walther might have knocked her away from the weapon. But at this range it wouldn't do the trick.

Before anyone could move, they all heard a low rumbling sound headed in their direction. Something they couldn't see was rising from the ground. It sounded like a lawn mower at first, but it grew louder. Bond recognized the noise and knew that the stalemate would be over in a moment. It was right on time.

The Wessex helicopter suddenly pulled up and over the Saray Hotel, skimming the edge of the roof where Hera was poised. Niki expertly brought the aircraft across the building, knocking her away from the launcher before the woman had time to react. Hera fell to the roof, rolled and jumped to her feet on the ledge of the building. She reached for a submachine gun strapped on her shoulder and swung it around at Bond.

"Fire," he said, and the men let loose a volley of ammunition. But before the bullets could slam into her, the woman had calmly stepped backward off the building.

Bond ran to the ledge and looked down. She was nowhere in sight! Then he saw the rope. It had been attached to a gutter on the side of the building, and ran down to an open window. Given the rope-climbing ability she had demonstrated in Monemvasia, Bond knew she had got away.

The commandos ran down the stairs and spent a half hour

searching the hotel, but there was no trace of Hera Volopoulos except a protective suit and a gas mask, which she had dropped in the hotel room. Giving up, Bond went back up to the roof.

The Wessex hovered over the hotel. Niki waved at Bond and he gave her the "okay" sign. He then carefully retrieved the four shells and put them back in the foam case.

Stefan Tempo stepped up to Bond and said, "We must go back to Turkey. This never happened. Our government has no record of these incidents today."

"Nor does mine."

"Thank you, Mr. Bond. You have done a great service for Turkey, Greece, and Cyprus. My father was a man of tolerance. He befriended everyone—the Gypsies, the Bulgars, the Russians, even Greeks. He was made of different substance than most of us."

"Your father was a great man, Tempo," Bond said. "I'm sure that had he lived, he would be working very hard to keep the peace between your people and the Greeks."

Tempo shook hands with the Greek commandos, then watched as the Wessex came back around. A rope ladder was lowered to the roof of the hotel. Bond and the four men climbed up and into the aircraft. He looked down as the Wessex ascended, and waved to the son of his old friend. Bond then leaned over to the pilot's seat and kissed Niki on the cheek.

TWENTY-FOUR

GHOST TOWN

EVEN IN MID-NOVEMBER THE SUN WAS SHINING BRIGHTLY IN AKROTIRI, Cyprus. Bond and Niki sat in a hangar at a folding card table studying the material they had received by fax from the Greek National Intelligence Service, as well as the items found on Duncan.

"You think this might be related to the Decada?" Niki asked, reading him a translation of the report, as it was written in Greek.

TO: NIKI MIRAKOS

FROM: RECORDS

DATE: NOVEMBER 15, 1998

WITH REGARD TO YOUR QUERY ON ANY MILITARY INCIDENTS WITHIN
    PAST TWO MONTHS, WE HAVE FOUND THE FOLLOWING:

CASE 443383: *Three privates charged with possession of mari-
    juana. Athens.*

CASE 250221: *Stolen property (stereo, compact discs, computer,
    etc.) reported by colonel. Athens.*

CASE 449932: *Sergeant major found shot. Attempted murder
    under investigation. Chios.*

CASE 957732: *Four privates and two sergeants found guilty of
    disorderly conduct. Crete.*

CASE 554212: *Sergeant killed in traffic accident with civilian.
    Civilian arrested for driving while intoxicated. Crete.*

"Where's Chios?" Bond asked.

"It's the Greek island closest to Turkey. It's not much of a tourist center."

"What is there?"

"Mostly military camps. Gum trees."

"Why would this sergeant major be murdered? Does that happen often in the Greek Army?"

"Not at all. You want more details?"

"Please."

As Niki sent a message via her laptop's E-mail system, Bond looked at the map with the coordinates of Istanbul that was on Hutchinson's computer file.

"They have a missile, that's got to be the answer," he said. "Have them search your records for anything unusual involving a missile."

"That's a rather broad search request, isn't it?"

"Just do it, please," Bond said. He was weary and hot. Someone brought them soft drinks, but he chose to drink bottled water.

Niki sent the request through and waited until a list appeared on the screen.

"There's . . . two hundred and thirty-three instances involving a missile," she said. "You want to take a look?" She saved the message and logged off the Internet.

Bond studied the monitor. Greece was a country that depended on NATO for any nuclear support. If the missile was something used to deploy nuclear weapons, NATO might be a link. He looked for any matches that involved NATO. There were twenty-three.

One entry struck him as curious. In 1986, a NATO Pershing 1a missile was reported missing in France. A thorough investigation indicated that the missile might have been lost in a transport accident that occurred outside of Paris. What was especially interesting was that a Greek officer, First Lieutenant Dimitris Georgiou, was in charge of the transport. There was some question as to whether there had been a Pershing in the shipment at all or whether it had been listed by mistake.

Niki was looking at the other materials on the table. She picked up the piece of paper that Bond had found in Duncan's pocket.

"What does this mean? 'Numbers seventeen hundred'?" she asked.

"I don't know. It's a code for something."

"Wait a minute," she said. "I know what it is. This is an IRC address."

"A what?"

"On the Internet, people can set up IRC addresses and 'chat' live in what they call a private room, or channel. If you know the location of the channel, or the name the creator or operator gave it, then you can join the chat."

"I knew that, I've just never used one. I know that the benefit of using an IRC channel is that it can't be traced."

"Right. Unless you know the name of the channel, it's totally secure."

Bond looked at his watch. It was 4:40 p.m. "It's almost seventeen hundred hours. Do you know how to find that channel?"

"Sure, it's easy. Let's go on-line again and I'll show you."

Niki took control of the laptop and logged on under her own screen name of "PilotGrl." Once she was connected, she started a program that handled IRC communications. She then scanned the active list of IRC channels. Sure enough, there was one in use called "#Numbers."

"Now we can see who is in that room." She used the mouse to click on the highlighted "#Numbers" designation, then a menu popped up that listed only one screen name, which meant that only one person was in the room. It was the name "monad." She used the mouse again to click on the "Who Is" icon. The information that appeared was "monad@ppp.chios.hol.gr."

"Monad," Bond said. "That's Romanos."

"And he's on an on-line service in Chios. See?"

"He's on Chios?"

"I would bet money on it."

"So Duncan and Hera were probably supposed to contact Romanos by this IRC channel at five today. Probably to make a report?"

"That's what it looks like."

"Say hello to Romanos."

"What?"

"Say hello to him. Shake him up."

"Since he's the operator of the channel, he'll have the ability to kick me out if he wants."

"Then say something immediately to him."

Niki entered the room with a couple of mouse clicks. Her screen name "PilotGrl@spidernet.com.cy" appeared on the list of room users. She began typing and downloaded the following transcript onto the hard drive as they "talked":

> PilotGrl: Hello. Number Two sent me. Is Number Three not here yet?
>
> Monad: Who are you?
>
> PilotGrl: No one you know.
>
> Monad: This is a private IRC channel. Please leave or I will kick you out.
>
> PilotGrl: You are expecting Manville Duncan, your Number Three? . . .
>
> PilotGrl: I don't think he's coming.

There was a long pause before Romanos responded.

> Monad: Who are you?
>
> PilotGrl: Just a friend. :) I don't think Duncan is going to show.
>
> Monad: Why not?
>
> PilotGrl: I'm afraid he got shot. Pity.
>
> Monad: You must be working for Bond.
>
> PilotGrl: Bond who? I don't know what you're talking about. Do you want to . . .
>
> PilotGrl: have cybersex?

At that point, the listing for "Monad@ppp.chios.hol.gr" disappeared from the list of users.

"He's gone," she said. "We scared him off."

"We have to get to Chios. Try your people again and see what they've found out."

She sent another E-mail and immediately received an Instant Message from her superior in Athens.

"They say that the sergeant major on Chios, a young man named Sambrakos, wasn't killed. He was shot and has been in a coma since the shooting. He's in a military hospital on the island."

"Ask them who the commanding officer is there."

Niki typed the question. After a moment, the answer came back.

"Brigadier General Dimitris Georgiou," she read.

"That confirms it," Bond said. "Let's go. Get them to alert the base that we're coming, but to keep the brigadier general in the dark."

She typed in the request, and in a moment got another reply. "They say that the brigadier general is currently on leave. They'll be expecting us at Giala—that's the military headquarters on Chios. Wait a second . . . there's a message for you. From F Leiter?"

"That's my friend Felix, in Texas. Let me see." Bond looked at the screen and read:

CENTERS FOR DISEASE CONTROL CONFIRMS YOUR BUG IS IDEN-
TICAL TO BUGS IN L.A. AND TOKYO. THE CIA AND JAPANESE SECRET
SERVICE ARE NOW AFTER YOUR GUY TOO. HOPE YOU GET HIM
BEFORE THEY DO.

—FELIX

Bond jumped up to make yet another request of the British Forces Cyprus.

The RAF arranged for Bond, Niki, and the four Greek commandos to travel on an Olympic Airways flight that was leaving from Larnaca airport for Athens at six-thirty P.M. With the help of the Greek government, the flight was diverted to Chios, much to the chagrin of the thirty-six other passengers. They arrived there at approximately eight-thirty, after the sun had already set. A young Greek soldier met them at the gate and led them to a Mercedes jeep in the parking lot.

They drove to the military headquarters in Chios Town. It was a small but efficient base made up of several beige-and-white buildings of brick and plaster. Jeeps and trucks were kept under camouflaged nets. A large gate in front kept nonmilitary personnel out of the area.

The jeep was waved through and Bond and Niki were led to an office where a tall man awaited them.

He spoke English. "Hello, I'm Lieutenant Colonel Gavras. I'm in charge right now. Brigadier General Georgiou is on leave."

Niki showed the man her credentials and said, "This is James Bond of the British Secret Service. We have reason to believe that a terrorist is hiding somewhere on the island, and that General Georgiou is involved. It is imperative that we find the terrorist tonight."

"That's a tall order, Miss Mirakos, and quite an accusation."

"Where is the general?"

"He's supposed to be in Spain."

Bond interrupted. "Can we get a jeep and driver to take us around the island?"

"It's pitch-dark," Gavras said. "You'll probably want to wait until the morning."

"There isn't time," Bond said. "The man is probably planning something for tonight."

Gavras frowned and looked at Niki's papers again.

"My orders come from the head of the Secret Service, sir," she said.

"I see that. Well, I'll see what I can do."

"Another thing," Bond said. "This boy who was shot. Is he still in a coma?"

"Sergeant Major Sambrakos recovered consciousness yesterday, as a matter of fact."

"Can we see him?"

He frowned again. "Let me make a call."

Sergeant Major Panos Sambrakos lay with a dozen tubes connected to his body. He looked weak and disoriented.

"Panos?" the nurse said in Greek. "Panos, these people are from the Greek Secret Service. They'd like to ask you some questions."

Bond and Niki greeted him, and Sambrakos's eyes flickered.

"Ask him if he knows General Georgiou," Bond said.

Niki asked him and Sambrakos nodded.

"Who shot him and why?"

Again she asked the questions. Sambrakos replied and closed his eyes. Niki said, "He says it was General Georgiou who shot him and left him for dead. He doesn't know why."

"What about the missile? Ask him about the missile."

Niki spoke again, and the boy replied softly and slowly. "He says that there was a Pershing missile hidden in a barn up north. General Georgiou told him that it was a secret, and that if he wanted his military career to stay clean, he should keep it that way. On the night he was shot, the general and two strange men were planning to take it somewhere."

"Ask him if he knows if the missile was armed or not."

The boy looked at Bond and replied in English, "It wasn't armed."

Bond said, "Don't worry Panos, we'll get the bastard."

They thanked him and left the hospital room.

"My bet is that Romanos has fashioned his own warhead."

"How will we find him?"

"It's not *that* big an island, is it?"

They started by heading west toward Karyes.

"Where might a militant group set up camp?" Bond asked.

"There's nowhere they could do it without being noticed," Gavras said. He was driving the jeep himself.

"No abandoned villages, old buildings that are not in use anymore?"

He shook his head. "There are villages on the island that are small and practically invisible. But I doubt an operation like the one you're talking about could even exist on the island."

"Believe me, it does," Bond said.

Karyes wasn't promising, so the jeep moved on until it came to a crossroads. Avgonima was straight ahead, and Anavatos was to the right.

"Wait a minute," Gavras said. 'There's Anavatos. No one lives there. Well, a few old people do down at the base of the cliff."

"What is it?"

"It's an ancient village built on a mountain. It's all in ruins now, but a few businessmen have bought some land and hope to turn it into a tourist attraction someday. They're slowly moving in and renovating the ruins."

"Let's see it."

"It's a long shot."

"Romanos would want to place his missile somewhere high up. I want to see this place."

The dark road snaked up into the hills until it stopped at the base of the village. The residents had all gone to bed, for there were no lights at all in any of the houses. The moonlight cast an eerie glow on the cliff. The whitish ruins stood out sharply in contrast to the blackness of the mountain. They looked like ghostly artifacts of another world and another time.

"How do you get up there?" Bond asked.

"On foot," Gavras said. "You just have to go up the path there, see? It winds all around the ruins and eventually gets to the top. Be careful, though. In the dark it can be quite dangerous. At the top is a sheer cliff drop on the other side. It's where the residents of the village jumped and committed suicide instead of being taken prisoner by the Turks a hundred years ago or so."

Bond thought briefly of Charles Hutchinson and wondered if he might have been thrown off that cliff.

"I'm going," he said. He reached into a backpack where Niki had placed his belongings that she had brought from his hotel in Athens. He pulled out Major Boothroyd's night-vision goggles, then checked his Walther P99 to make sure the magazine was completely full. He stuck two extra magazines in his pocket.

"I'm coming with you," Niki said.

"I think I had better go alone," Bond said. "I'm just going to do a quick reconnaissance. Give me a half hour."

Before Niki could protest, Bond walked away from the jeep toward the structures at the base of the cliff. Suddenly there was a flash of bright light. A tremendous explosion blew the jeep over on its side. Both Niki and Gavras were thrown several feet.

"Niki!" Bond shouted, and ran to her. She was dazed and confused, and there was a nasty cut on her forehead.

"What happened?" she mumbled.

"Someone fired a bazooka, I think," Bond said. "From up the cliff."

She tried to get up, but her leg was bent awkwardly behind her. "Oh God," she said, gasping. "My leg. I've twisted it. What about the colonel?"

Bond moved over to Gavras. His body was still and lifeless.

"We've lost him. I'm going to call for help if the radio is still working."

The smoking jeep had a large hole in the back end but was basically in one piece. Bond unclamped a fire extinguisher from the floorboard and put out the flames, then climbed inside to try the Motorola radio. Surprisingly, he got a signal to the base and made a report.

He then ran back to Niki with a charred blanket he had found in the back of the vehicle, and wrapped it around her.

"Help is on the way," he said. "Stay here. I've got to go up and see what I can find."

She nodded. "Don't worry about me, I'll be okay. It only hurts if I think about making love to you."

He affectionately placed his left palm on her cheek. "I'll be back."

He left her there in the dark and went up past the closed taverna and onto the main stone path that ascended the cliff. She was a strong girl, she would be fine, he thought. He couldn't stop to help her— there was no telling when Romanos was planning to initiate his attack on Turkey. Now that Romanos knew they were there, he could set it off at any time.

At night, Anavatos was an eerie place. The ruins looked war-torn and skeletal in the moonlight. It was a black-and-white world of ghostly shapes and shadows. Bond kept thinking that specters were moving about, watching his every move. The spirits of the dead

Greeks who threw themselves off the mountain were haunting him, taunting him, urging him forward so that he too could take the fatal plunge into blackness.

Bond put on the night-vision goggles and things improved immensely. The infrared filters turned the little moonlight into a warm green glow that enabled him to see the path clearly. The shapes and shadows were still all around him, and they weren't any less unnerving, but at least he could find his way up the cliff without groping.

The ascent reminded him of the ruins at Monemvasia, except that these were far more desolate and lonely. The narrow passages were claustrophobic, with broken buildings on all sides gaping at him like openmouthed tombs.

At one point, he was able to look down and note his progress. He could see the path he had traversed zigzagging down through the ruins to the base of the mountain below. He could barely discern the outline of the overturned jeep, and the two figures lying on the ground nearby.

Bond kept going up. At the halfway point, he stopped to get his bearings and take a look at what was above him. A large structure was at the summit of the cliff. There was no sign of any lights coming from it, of course, but Bond guessed that the Decada was hiding there. Turning a corner, he was met head-on by a man dressed entirely in black. A fist plunged into Bond's stomach, causing him to double over. A boot rammed into his face, and he fell to the hard ground. Another kick assaulted his ribs.

He had the wind knocked out of him and was struggling to catch his breath when he heard the unmistakable click of a semiautomatic handgun being cocked. Bond swung his right arm out and across the man's shin. His spear-hand chopped the bone with enough force to break a block of ice. The man yelped and fell down.

Bond jumped up and gave him a taste of his own medicine, kicking him twice in the ribs and once in the face. The man lay motionless.

Bond continued to climb, rubbing his side to make sure nothing was broken.

When he reached the top, Bond took a look at the ledge, below which was a seemingly bottomless canyon of trees and rocks. He then carefully moved around the large building, listening for the slightest sound.

He had completely circled the building before he saw the ventilation grille partially covered by a plant. It was built into the bottom of one of the walls, and smoke was trickling out of it. If Bond had not been wearing the goggles, he never would have seen it. The goggles had picked up the faint light coming from the vent, and the smoke was silhouetted neatly over the illumination.

Bond bent down and examined the vent. It would be easy to pry off but that might make too much noise. He tried to budge one side of the grille, but it squeaked from the rust. Bond used some natural lubrication to loosen the vent—he spat on his fingers and ran them across the edges. Once they were moist, he tried again. This time, the grille pulled out of the wall with only a slight scraping sound.

The opening was big enough to squeeze through. He looked inside and saw a floor of carved stone. It was dimly lit, probably by candlelight. He listened to see if anyone was in there, then he slowly put his feet through and wormed his way into the shaft. He turned over onto his stomach, held on to the edge of the vent opening, and hung over the floor of the room. He let go and dropped to the ground.

He was in some kind of temple, he thought. There was a stone altar at the front of the room, and there were benches around the perimeter. The middle of the floor was empty. There was only one way out of the room, so Bond stepped lightly to the hanging curtains and listened.

Hearing nothing, Bond parted the curtains and looked out. It was a hallway, lit by a single burning torch mounted on the wall. If the inside of the *Persephone* looked old, it was nothing compared to the interior design of this place. Bond felt as if he were really walking through a building in ancient Greece.

Bond removed his goggles and let them hang around his neck. He drew the Walther and held it in his left hand—his right palm still hurt too much to handle the weapon effectively. He took a step at a time, watching and listening.

He came to a closed wooden door and listened. Silence.

Bond tried the handle. It clicked softly and the door opened.

It was another dim, empty stone room, except that a large equilateral triangle made of ten points was on the wall directly ahead. The points were made of little red light bulbs, all of them lit except the last three on top.

When Bond walked into the room, lights flashed on around him.

Eight men held Uzis trained on him from all sides. Konstantine Romanos stood at the top of a stone staircase to the left.

"Welcome to Anavatos, Mr. Bond," Romanos said.

TWENTY-FIVE

THE FACE OF DEATH

BOND WAS DISARMED AND THEN LED THROUGH A SERIES OF STONE CORRIDORS to a large dark space. Romanos flicked a switch and electric lamps made to look like torches illuminated the room. It was a missile launch pad. The Pershing 1a was mounted on an M656 transport truck, aimed at the ceiling. The double hatch in the ceiling was closed.

Besides Romanos, Bond counted eight armed guards, a man in a military uniform whom he surmised to be General Georgiou, and four women dressed in civilian clothes. One of the women was Hera Volopoulos. He recognized another as Melina Papas, who had a metal briefcase handcuffed to her wrist. It was identical to the case that Charles Hutchinson had brought from America.

"You have done my organization a considerable amount of damage, Mr. Bond," Romanos said. "You don't deserve to die quickly. In ancient Greece, criminals were often tortured in public. They were kept alive as long as possible so that their suffering would be prolonged. Unfortunately, I do not have the time to indulge myself with the pleasure of watching your agony. I have my orders from the gods. We must abandon our headquarters here in Anavatos. I am sure that by now the Greek military and secret service are on their way."

Another guard entered and whispered something to General Georgiou. The general then said something to Romanos in Greek.

"Ah, our transport has just arrived," Romanos said. He turned to one of the women and issued an order. She nodded and left the room.

"Mr. Bond, this is not the end of the Decada. We will regroup at another location and continue our path. We will, however, complete the task we began here so many months ago."

He gestured to the missile. "As you see, a Pershing. It's been missing from NATO for a long time. We happened to find it and we fit it with a warhead we got through our Russian friend, Number Four. The Russian mafia drove a hard bargain, but we eventually got a good deal. As you may have guessed, it will detonate over Istanbul. This is a small price for the Turks to pay for northern Cyprus."

"It's just going to cause chaos all over Europe, Asia, and the Middle East!" Bond said.

Romanos nodded to the guards. They grabbed Bond and pulled him down onto a table. The men held him in place as Romanos flipped a switch on a control panel. Metal cuffs shot out of the table and snapped over Bond's ankles and wrists. He was now horizontal, helpless and vulnerable.

"Do you like puzzles, Mr. Bond?" Romanos asked. "My maths students like puzzles. Well, some of them do. I give them fiendishly diabolical puzzles on their exams. I enjoy games of chance, crosswords, riddles . . . but I truly love mathematical puzzles. How were you as a student, Mr. Bond?"

Bond just stared at him incredulously.

"Don't tell me," Romanos said. "You were kicked out of Eton, after which you went to a military school. I would bet that mathematics was not one of your strong subjects. Am I right?"

Bond closed his eyes. The man was indeed correct. Although he was adept at many, many things, Bond was not a mathematician.

Romanos stepped over to the missile and pointed to a panel on the base of the launcher.'

"I imagine you possess the capability of stopping the launch if you had access to the controls. A man of your expertise has probably disarmed hundreds of bombs, haven't you? Surely you can stop a Pershing missile from launching? Do you see this panel? Inside are the launching controls, covered by a thin glass cover that serves as a safe-guard. You see, this entire complex is armed with explosives."

He pointed to four egg-shaped devices mounted in the ceiling.

"They will go off if that glass cover is broken without following a certain procedure. You must deactivate the alarm system to get to the controls."

He took a notepad from his pocket and scribbled on it for a few seconds. He tore off the piece of paper and opened the launching mechanism panel, then carefully placed the notepaper inside and closed the panel.

Romanos looked at his watch and twisted a timer knob on the control board. He then indicated a switch. "When I flip this switch, the timer will start. In four minutes from that instant, you will be released from the table. In four more minutes, the doors on the ceiling will open and the missile will launch automatically. *However,* I've written down a puzzle on the piece of paper that's now inside the panel. The answer to the puzzle will tell you how to disarm the alarm system. Once you've done that, you'll then have however many seconds left to stop the launch. If you can get to those controls, you have my permission and blessing to stop the launch. This was the gods' idea, not mine. They admire you for some strange reason. They have shown mercy on you and have ordered me to give you this one, slim chance, however hopeless. It also amuses the hell out of me. Think you're up to it? By the way, the puzzle I've given you has taken my students anywhere from fifteen minutes to an hour to solve. That's why I'm confident that when five minutes is up, you'll be scrambling around on the outside of this missile and scratching your head like a primate."

General Georgiou said something to Romanos.

Romanos nodded and said, "Number Nine has been good enough to fly a helicopter here to pick us up. We must go. One last thing. Alfred Hutchinson was never a member of the Decada. Manville Duncan obtained the copy of his disk and gave it to us, of course. Alfred was an old fool. He could have been my partner. We could have become rich together and perhaps ruled a country or two. Instead he chose to expose us and betray me. If he hadn't, you might have been spared all of this. Goodbye, Mr. Bond. May the gods . . . have mercy on your soul."

With that, he placed his hand on the timer switch.

"Wait!" It was Hera. She was pointing a handgun at Romanos. Bond recognized it as the Daewoo he had seen her use before. Five of the armed guards aimed their weapons at the other guards. Melina Papas stood away from General Georgiou and the others.

Romanos was confused. "Number Two?"

"The gods have given me orders too, Konstantine. The Decada has benefited greatly from your leadership. You supplied us with money, equipment, contacts, and a plan to make ourselves heard round the world. But as Pythagoras himself knew, it was possible that some followers might have other plans. Your leadership ends here, Konstantine. You are no longer the Monad. The True Decada is born here and now."

"Hera, you fool, what are you talking about?"

The gun went off, wounding him in the shoulder. Romanos fell back onto the concrete floor, clutching his bloody arm.

General Georgiou lunged at Hera, but one of the guards turned to him and fired an AK-47. Bullets riddled the general's body, knocking him lifeless next to Romanos.

The other Decada members cowered against the wall. Hera turned to them. "You others can join me if you like. If not, you die here with him."

Eyes wide, they nodded their heads furiously.

"Then go and get into the helicopter." They complied, running outside, escorted by two guards. Melina Papas remained with Hera.

Hera walked over to Romanos and stood over him. She pointed the gun at his right leg and fired again. He yelled and bent over in agony.

Bond, helpless on the table, watched in fascination and horror.

Hera squatted beside Romanos and tenderly stroked his sweating head. "I once knew a little girl," she said. "She was only twelve years old. Her parents were killed by Turks in Cyprus when she was nine. For three years she lived on the streets and fended for herself in an extremely hostile world. Then, one day, she met a man. He was two decades older than she was, but he was very handsome. He had a magical way of speaking. He became a father to her. He promised to rescue her, to take her away to his land and teach her about life. And that he did . . . while he kept her a prisoner for ten years. It's true that he taught her many things and fed her and clothed her and took care of her. But it's also true that he systematically *raped her for ten . . . long . . . years!*" Hera said it with venom.

"Hera," Romanos gasped. "I never meant it that way . . ."

She stood up and kicked Romanos hard in the face. Then, tenderly again, she said, "I thought I loved you once. You were so many things to me at so many different times . . . You were my torturer, you were my father. You were my brother, my lover, my teacher. I worshipped you!"

She kicked him again.

"We share many ideals," she continued. "I promised myself that I'd help you see the Decada's first *Tetraktys* through to the end, because I hate the Turks as much as you do. But what I hate even more is how you corrupted me. Now I'm taking back the life you took from me so many years ago in Cyprus. Hera, the queen of the gods, was always a vengeful deity. I'm taking over the Decada, for it's my destiny to do so. I see our role in the world as being far bigger and more profitable than you ever did. You taught me well. You made me what I am today, Konstantine. Remember that!"

Her voice began to tremble with rage. She aimed the pistol at his chest.

"You always pushed me to be the best—the best climber, the best fighter, the best assassin, the best *killer* . . . the best . . . lover . . . Well, it's no wonder I was a good pupil. After capturing me and breaking me, it was easy to teach me to hate and murder. Now I know no other way."

She paused and took a breath as tears rolled down her cheeks. "You taught me more about life than I ever cared to know, Konstantine. Now I'm going to teach you about death."

With that, she pointed the gun at his head and fired. Romanos's skull blew apart, spraying blood and tissue several feet, around them.

After a long, tense silence, Bond said, "My God, Hera, you're madder than he was."

She turned and looked at him curiously, as if she had completely forgotten that he was in the room. Then Hera stared past Bond blankly, traumatized by the act she had just committed. Melina reached out and touched her arm. Hera turned to Melina and the two women embraced. The metal briefcase dangled awkwardly.

"What's in the case, Hera? The BioLinks virus?" Bond asked.

After a pause, Hera moved away from Melina. She had regained her composure, but she was a time bomb of nerves just waiting to explode. She replied, "We call it the Decada Virus. It was a project that the Monad began, but that we're going to finish. Melina here extensively studied the effects that ricin has on the human body. There is no antidote for ricin poisoning. She successfully created a chemical compound from the castor bean which acts like a virus. In other words, she has made the symptoms that one experiences with ricin poisoning infectious. The germ lives and breathes like bacteria. Once a person is infected with it, everyone they come in contact with will also become infected. People will die, one after another, very quickly—unless they're given the vaccine. Yes, there is a cure, which Melina also created, and we have all been inoculated."

She pointed to Melina's briefcase. "In there are several samples of the Decada Virus in protective tubes, as well as all the information we need to create more. The only samples of the vaccine and its formula are in there as well. That's why we don't want that case to leave Melina's wrist, do we? Melina, why don't you go on out to the helicopter. I'll be there in a minute."

The hawk-nosed woman nodded and left the room. Hera was now alone with Bond and the dead bodies around them.

Bond looked at her and said, "You've sent that virus to medical clinics all over the world, haven't you? Hidden in sperm samples!"

"You never cease to amaze me, James. You are indeed a clever and resourceful man. Yes, the virus is out there waiting, swimming around and just waiting to be injected into someone. We have people on the payroll in clinics all around the world. Their instructions were simply to transfer the material from the sperm to an available blood supply. Cities like New York, London, Los Angeles, Tokyo—boom— they're hit with a deadly epidemic. It's not pretty."

"Why, Hera? Because you were abused as a child? Because Romanos twisted your mind and turned you into a killer? That's not a reason to set off a chain reaction that will destroy all human life on the planet!"

"That's not going to happen, James," she said with confidence. "Once the virus starts spreading like wildfire, I will announce to the world that BioLinks have developed a cure. The price to receive it, though, will be . . . very high. The deaths of millions of people will simply be the example of what the virus can do. In order to sell a product, you have to prove to the world that there is a need for it!"

"Don't you think there are biochemists in the world who are smart enough to study your virus and come up with their own vaccine?" Bond asked.

"Of course, but by then it will be too late," Hera said. "As we implement new *Tetraktys* strikes in different parts of the world, there will be rapidly increasing outbreaks of the virus. The nations of the world will have no choice but to quickly buy the only available vaccine—ours."

Bond shook his head. "So you're just another cheap extortionist. You're only in it for the money. I might have known."

"Goodbye, James," she said. "I think I'll leave you with Konstantine's little maths problem. He always did have a perverse sense of humor. Maybe you can at least stop a war between Greece and Turkey. But that seems so *insignificant* now, don't you think?"

With that, she flipped the switch to set the timer in motion, then turned and left the room. The door slammed shut and Bond was left alone.

A Huey UH-1 Iroquois helicopter sat on a landing pad that had been built on the summit of the cliff outside. The pad was actually the launch doors for the missile, which would open in less than eight minutes. Hera emerged from the lair into the night air and joined Melina Papas, the loyal guards, and the remaining Decada members aboard the helicopter.

Back in the launch room, sweat was pouring off Bond's face. No matter how hard he tried, he couldn't free himself from the manacles. He would just have to wait until the four minutes was up.

Where was the bloody Greek Army? How long was it going to take them to get there?

Bond's heart was pounding. It felt as if it would push right through his sternum. What was happening to him? Was this the end? Was this what happened when you knew you were going to die? They said that your life passed in front of your eyes when the moment of truth finally came. Bond had been close to death before, but somehow he felt that this time it was real. Had he been placed in a hopeless situation? Was that it? Was he subconsciously accepting the fact that no matter what he did in the next few minutes, it would all be over soon?

No! he cried to himself. Not this way! He would not let it end like this. He was not about to give up. If he died, then so be it. He had seen plenty of death in his lifetime, but he had also seen an enormous amount of life. He had beaten the grim reaper so many times before . . . why would he think that it would all end now?

The manacles suddenly sprang open. He was free.

Bond leaped to the missile and pried the control panel off with such force that he cut the ends of his fingers. A wire-cutting tool and the piece of paper fell out. Underneath he saw a glass panel covering a control panel and a single toggle switch that was obviously the abort button. On top of the glass was the booby trap—three colored wires, one red, one blue, and one white. One or more of them had to be cut before he could get to the controls. Bond grabbed the paper and read it. In English, it said:

PYTHAGORAS WAS FAMOUS FOR HIS THEOREM THAT STATES THAT IN A RIGHT TRIANGLE, THE SUM OF THE SQUARES OF THE LEGS IS EQUAL TO THE SQUARE OF THE HYPOTENUSE. THE CONVERSE IS ALSO TRUE. IF THE LENGTHS OF THE SIDES OF A TRIANGLE ARE "A," "B," AND "C," WHERE "C" IS THE HYPOTENUSE AND $A^2 + B^2 = C^2$, THEN THE TRIANGLE IS A RIGHT TRIANGLE. SO IF A TRIANGLE HAS

SIDES 3, 4, AND 5, IT IS A RIGHT TRIANGLE, SINCE $3^2 + 4^2 = 5^2$ $(9 + 16 = 25)$. FURTHERMORE, IF $A^2 + B^2$ DOES NOT EQUAL C^2, THEN THE TRIANGLE IS NOT A RIGHT TRIANGLE.

LET'S SAY YOU HAVE SIDES OF LENGTHS 17, 144, AND 163. DOES THIS FORM AN ACUTE, RIGHT, OR OBTUSE TRIANGLE?

CLIP THE RED WIRE IF YOUR ANSWER IS "ACUTE."

CLIP THE BLUE WIRE IF YOUR ANSWER IS "RIGHT."

CLIP THE WHITE WIRE IF YOUR ANSWER IS "OBTUSE."

YOU HAVE FOUR MINUTES. GOOD LUCK!

TWENTY-SIX

THE WORLD IS NOT ENOUGH

THE CLOCK HAD TICKED AWAY FORTY-FIVE SECONDS.

Bond stared at the puzzle in horror. It *was* impossible to solve in two minutes! He searched the depths of his brain to recall what he knew about the Pythagorean theorem. If it was a right angle triangle, the sum of the squares of two sides must equal the square of the hypotenuse. Bond could mentally calculate that 17 squared was 289, but there was no way that he could calculate the squares of 144 and 163 in the time available.

There had to be a trick to this. Why would Romanos simply pose a routine problem made difficult because Bond had no calculator? It must be a logic puzzle, not a math problem. Did he have the time to think it through? Or should he gamble with life and death by selecting a wire and cutting it? How could he decide which wire to cut? Had his entire life come down to a flip of the coin?

Sixty seconds had elapsed. He had three more minutes to stop the missile.

Wait! What was it Romanos had said about "assumption"? It was at the casino in Athens. He had said that a mathematician begins with assumptions and must provide the proof from there. What was the puzzle's question again?

LET'S SAY YOU HAVE SIDES OF LENGTHS 17, 144, AND 163. DOES THIS FORM AN ACUTE, RIGHT, OR OBTUSE TRIANGLE?

The problem didn't actually say that the sides were part of a triangle. The question was what kind of triangle would be formed with the sides of 17,144, and 163. Bond had been *assuming* that the lengths formed a triangle. The correct answer was that *it wouldn't be a triangle at all!* For a triangle to exist, the sum of the lengths of any two sides must exceed the length of the third side. In this case, 17 + 144 = 161, which was not greater than 163.

Bond knew then that he should not cut any of the three wires. With one minute left to go, he made a fist and plunged it into the thin glass panel. The controls were at his fingertips.

Forty-five seconds . . .

He flipped the toggle switch and the timer stopped. All of the blinking lights around the control panel shut off. The missile was lifeless. A viewscreen indicated that the detonator was disengaged from the nuclear core. The conventional explosives in the warhead could still ignite, but critical mass could never be achieved.

Bond took a deep breath and slid down to the floor. Romanos had underestimated his ability to make a decision by making no decision. He thought wryly that it had been more of a Descartes-like action than a Pythagorean one, because it was Descartes who once said, "Not to decide is to decide."

He heard a loud boom on a floor below him. It sounded like an explosive demolishing a door. Bond got up and ran to the only exit from the room. Outside he could hear running footsteps and men speaking Greek. He pulled back the bolt and opened the door. Three Greek soldiers turned and pointed M16 rifles at him.

Bond held up his hands. "Don't shoot!"

"Mr. Bond?" one of them, a sergeant, asked.

"Yes."

"Let's go. We get you out."

Bond followed them out of the door in the nick of time, for the explosives inside the launch pad room went off full force. Bond and the three men were thrown several feet by the blast, and the stone walls around them began to crumble.

"Go! Go! Go!" the sergeant shouted.

The four men jumped up and kept on running. Another explosion went off near them, but by then they had made it into the Decada's conference room.

"What's the quickest way to the surface?" Bond asked. "The whole place is going to blow."

"This way," the sergeant said. He led them out of the conference room, through the control room, and up a flight of stairs, just ahead of more explosions below them. The steps fell apart as they climbed. They navigated around a ten-foot statue of the god Ares and entered a passageway that was shaking. Before they could get through it, a huge explosion rocked the entire structure. The walls, floor, and ceiling cracked open, leaving a gap of seven feet between them and the other side of the passageway.

"What now?" a soldier asked.

Bond looked back at the statue. "Help me with this thing!" He ran to it and started to push. The other men got the idea and helped tilt it over onto the ground. Together they shoved the statue across the gap, creating a bridge. One by one they crossed to the other side.

They reached the secret hatch to the outside world just as another explosion sent flames shooting up toward them from below. The men rolled out of the complex and could feel the heat as the entire mountain trembled.

More soldiers were outside. A lieutenant approached the sergeant and spoke rapidly in Greek. Bond caught the words "helicopter" and "Decada."

The sergeant turned to Bond and said, "We can still catch them if we hurry."

"What are we waiting for?" Bond asked.

They ran to the UH-60 Blackhawk helicopter that had landed on the same launch pad Hera had taken off from. They piled into the aircraft and it rose into the air.

The Blackhawk is one of many American-made machines that the

Greek military have bought. It is equipped with an External Stores Support System, which includes the carriage and live firing of the Hellfire anti-armor missile. If they could catch up with Hera, the ensuing dogfight would be in their favor.

Once they were airborne, Bond asked the sergeant, "How is your agent, Niki Mirakos?"

"She will be fine," he said. "Her leg wasn't broken, but the knee was twisted badly. She will be on crutches for a while. She might need some surgery—it's too early to tell."

"What about the Decada? Where are they headed? They have a briefcase that must be retrieved."

"They took off toward the mainland ten minutes ago. We've alerted all bases between here and there to intercept them."

Bond took a moment to look around the cabin of the helicopter. There were three Stinger missiles with one-man portable launchers attached to the side of the craft. He immediately unfastened the harness on one and removed it. He realized that the sergeant was staring at him incredulously, so he asked, "May I?"

The sergeant shrugged and said, "Be our guest."

A radio communication came through, and the sergeant translated. "One of our Apaches has engaged the target three miles ahead."

They were there in a minute. In the dark, Bond could see only the streams of fire coming from the machine guns on the Huey and the AH-64 Apache. The Greeks' helicopter was at a slightly higher altitude, pursuing Hera's helicopter at top speed.

The Huey UH-1 was another American-made helicopter that was used extensively in the Vietnam War. Its 1,400-horsepower engine sat over the cabin instead of filling up the body, leaving plenty of room for troops or cargo. It was armed with machine guns, rockets, and grenades, and could cruise at 125 miles per hour.

Suddenly a bright streak shot from the Huey and hit the Apache, which exploded into a fireball. Hera apparently had missiles of her own.

"Now it's just us," the sergeant said. He gave an order over the radio for the backup units to hurry up.

Bond slung the Stinger launcher over his shoulder and got it ready to fire. "If you can get me in position, I'll hit them with this." He had to cripple the helicopter without completely destroying it. Hopefully, the metal briefcase would survive intact.

The Huey climbed, slowed down, and positioned itself above their Blackhawk.

"They're going to drop mines! Evasive action!" Bond shouted. The sergeant translated the order into Greek, and the pilot flung the aircraft into a dive as a volley of mines poured out of the Huey.

Then the Huey's turrets went into action, battering their vehicle with bullets. One man was hit in the face. Blood splattered in all directions as he was thrown back against the cabin wall.

The pilot managed to get the helicopter side by side with Hera. Bond thought he could see her next to the pilot, but it was too dark to tell. It looked like Melina Papas was behind her, issuing orders to men in the back.

One of the Greeks' other Apaches entered the arena from the other side, assaulting the enemy with a volley of turret fire. The Huey wavered, then lost height. Bond's pilot attempted to follow, but it was a maneuver meant to trick the Greeks. As soon as they were even with the enemy, someone in the Huey launched another missile.

"Evasive action!" the sergeant shouted.

The Blackhawk swerved awkwardly, but it wasn't enough to avoid the weapon entirely. It skimmed the bottom struts, blowing them off. The helicopter went wildly out of control.

"We're going down!" the sergeant yelled in English.

Bond stepped into the open doorway of the helicopter and aimed the Stinger at Hera's Huey. They were rapidly falling away from the target.

By God, Bond thought. He was going to hit Hera before they crashed if it was the last thing he did.

"Ask the pilot to try and keep the helicopter steady for just a moment!" Bond said to the sergeant. "Then hold on to my belt!"

The helicopter was losing height at a frightening pace. No one was sure if there was land or water below.

The pilot managed to get the Blackhawk back under some sort of control, but the aircraft was still rocking and falling.

"This is the best you're going to get," the sergeant told Bond.

Bond nodded and took a bead on the enemy Huey. He straightened his body and pivoted backward out of the opening, putting his trust in the sergeant to keep him from falling. Bond aimed directly at the Huey's cockpit and fired the missile. The Stinger shot off with a loud *whizzzzz* and a flash of bright light, just clearing the Blackhawk's rotor blades.

The missile hit the Huey dead on target. Bond winced when it exploded into a fireball brighter than the sun on a summer's day. He prayed that the fireproof briefcase could be recovered.

The Huey plummeted ten thousand feet and crashed into the sea. Another explosion completely demolished it, sending all of its occupants to a dark and watery grave.

"Welcome to Hades, Hera," Bond said to himself.

The Blackhawk's pilot was having great difficulty keeping his craft in the air. It was inevitable that they would crash into the ocean too. Their only hope was that the pilot could keep the copter level so that the impact wouldn't destroy the ship and everyone in it. One man began to distribute life jackets.

There was a tremendous noise as the Blackhawk hit the water. Everyone inside was flung in different directions, but the aircraft didn't break apart. Water began to pour into the ship, and someone shouted, "Out! Everyone out!"

Bond followed the other men out of the hatch into the cold, dark water. He surfaced and saw that they had all made it, but the Blackhawk was sinking rapidly. The other wreckage was still floating on the water in flames, which provided a surprising amount of illumination. Much of the murky water was well lit.

The life jacket kept Bond afloat, but he was able to dive and swim underneath the Blackhawk. He saw a lot of debris floating down to the bottom of the sea. There were two bodies—guards—just beginning to float back up. Bond surfaced, took a breath, then continued his search for Melina Papas's body. He saw a body in a tattered dress entangled in the struts of the sinking hulk. Bond swam to it and discovered it was one of the other Decada women. Most of her skin had been burned away.

Bond removed his life jacket and tied it to the strut, decreasing his buoyancy. He dived underneath the wreck again, pushed away the metal panels and tried to get inside. The flames were intense, but he forced himself to think of nothing but the metal briefcase. Too many lives were at stake.

He crawled into what was left of the burning hull and found three bodies, all charred and grotesquely mangled. The metal briefcase was handcuffed to the wrist of one. Bond held his breath and put his arms around the warm, wet body. He hauled her out of the wreckage and into the water, picked up his life jacket, and surfaced for air. After putting on the jacket, he draped Melina's body over his shoulder and began to swim away from the floating sepulchre.

He saw some of the Greeks swimming several yards ahead of him. One of them shot off a flare into the sky, brightly illuminating the entire area. The water was rough and choppy, and Bond had a difficult time keeping afloat. He grabbed a bobbing piece of the aircraft and hung on to it, allowing it to carry him slowly toward the others.

Bond was just beginning to catch his breath when he was startled by the sudden appearance of a revolting, black, burned face. Hera, or what was left of her, broke the surface next to Bond. She looked like a demon from hell. Her red hair was completely gone, replaced by rolls of sliced, viscous flesh. One remaining eye bulged and her mouth was frozen in a silent scream. Sickened, Bond reached out to push the corpse away, but it suddenly came alive. Hera screamed and threw her hands around Bond's neck. The fright caused him to let go of Melina's body.

Bond fought her hard, kicking the mangled creature. She was grappling with all her might to bring him down. He chopped her in the neck with as much force as he could exert, then punched her in the face. The flesh on her cheek felt crusty and wet. She screamed again, and the vise around his neck loosened. Bond broke away, then lunged for her waist. Once he had a good hold on her, he shoved her head underwater and held it there. Hera struggled like a moray eel, but her wounds had taken their toll. She slowly weakened, and finally went limp after a couple of agonizing minutes. Bond let her go, and Hera Volopoulos sank to the bottom of the sea.

He then dived to retrieve Melina Papas again. She hadn't drifted far. He grabbed the body once again and swam with it, and the briefcase, toward the other men.

They bobbed in the water for fifteen minutes before another helicopter arrived to rescue them.

The Decada's headquarters on Anavatos were destroyed. Very little trace of their organization was left. Several burned bodies were recovered from the sea the next morning—three female skeletons and at least ten males. In the final reports filed by the Greek National Intelligence Service and the Greek military and by Bond, it was assumed that all of the members of the Decada had been killed.

The briefcase had indeed remained intact. The National Intelligence Service took possession of it and successfully opened it without releasing the deadly substance inside. It was immediately sent to a biochemistry lab in Athens so that the vaccine could be reproduced in quantity. Within twenty-four hours, hundreds of vials of the vaccine were on their way to the infected cities. One hundred and fifteen people had died in New York, 212 in Tokyo, and 186 in Los Angeles. Athens, London, and Paris had the least number of casualties—less than 60 in each city. It could have been far worse. In a week, the virus would have raged out of control and hundreds would have died, possibly thousands. Although it would be some time before anyone could be sure that the disease was totally contained, the authorities felt confident that they were off to a good start. The virus itself was sent to the Centers for Disease Control in Atlanta for study and breakdown.

Two days later, James Bond and Niki Mirakos lay in the king-sized bed in his suite at the Grande Bretagne in Athens. They had just eaten a basket of fruit and drunk two bottles of ouzo. Her leg was in a cast, but otherwise she was completely naked.

Bond glanced at his watch. "I have to call M."

He slipped out of bed and walked naked into the sitting room. He dialed the number and went through the routine security checks.

"Double-O Seven?" M sounded extremely pleased to hear from him.

"Yes, ma'am."

"You're right on time. I just received your report. Well done."

"Thank you, ma'am."

"Is the Greek agent badly injured?"

"It's not too bad," Bond said. "She had a bit of knee surgery. She'll be fine in a few weeks."

"That's good to hear," she said. "By the way, we all had a little surprise this morning."

"Oh?"

"The Turkish Republic of Northern Cyprus officially thanked the Republic of Cyprus and Greece for their roles in stopping the Decada. It was an unprecedented gesture."

"Amazing."

"Perhaps this will eventually lead to a new era of peace and cooperation between the two sides."

Bond was doubtful, but he said, "Let's hope so."

Then there was a pause which said volumes to Bond. She was dying to hear anything at all about Alfred Hutchinson.

"Ma'am, you'll be happy to know that Alfred Hutchinson was never a member of the Decada," Bond said. "He did once have an illegal and clandestine operation going with Romanos, until his conscience got the better of him. He was trying to do the right thing in the end. I hope that information brings you some comfort."

"Thank you, James," she said.

She rarely called him James during what was, for all intents and purposes, a business talk. Bond thought she was beginning to act like old Sir Miles after all.

"James," she said, "I want to tell you again how much I appreciate what you've done on this case."

"Don't mention it, ma'am."

"Nevertheless, you helped me through this. Thank you."

Bond hung up and went back into the bedroom. He poured some freshly squeezed orange juice for both of them, then propped a pillow up against the wall and sat on the bed. He stretched out his legs, and stared out of the window at the Acropolis in the distance.

After a minute of silence, Niki said, "What is it, James?"

Bond shrugged and shook his head, attempting to smile.

She took his hand and said, "It's probably none of my business, but I think I know what it is."

"Oh?"

"You've become jaded. The mission is over and you're not looking forward to going back to your existence between assignments. I know how you feel, James. It's like withdrawal from a drug. The threat of death hanging over you is what really makes you tick. Without it, you're unhappy. My advice to you is to try and enjoy *life* too."

Bond pulled her close and kissed her. Then he said, "But the world is not enough."

"What?"

"That's the motto on my family crest. 'The World Is Not Enough.' "

She laughed gently. "It fits you perfectly."

"It's a curse, that's what it is."

"James, you're entitled to feel that way. You are not like other men. You are human, but you have done superhuman things. All men know the facts of life, but you know just as much about the facts of death! You have thwarted Death many times. Someone once said that no man's a god. I'm not so sure that's true. Unlike Konstantine Romanos, you *are* a god."

Bond laughed.

She laughed with him. "No, really! In ancient Greece, men would have proclaimed you to be a god. You would have been another Jason or an Agamemnon or even an Alexander the Great. There would be statues of you on display throughout the country and in museums!"

Bond pushed her face into the pillow. They wrestled playfully for a few seconds, then became still and quiet. Bond knew that even though he had thwarted Death many times, he had come to think of him as an old friend. Without Death standing behind him, scythe in hand and breathing down his neck, life was just a dreadful bore.

She pulled him to her gently. He turned and snuggled closer to her, wrapping his leg around her and pressing his loins into her thigh.

"Mmmm," she said, as she pulled his body directly on top of hers. She reached down and held him. "I must add that what you know about the facts of *life* is pretty impressive too!"

Bond became aroused for the third time since they awoke. "I never told you before, but you're one hell of a helicopter pilot, did you know that?" he said.

She grinned mischievously. "It's just a question of knowing how to get it up."

LIVE AT FIVE

IT HAD BEEN SEVERAL YEARS SINCE HE HAD SEEN HER. JAMES BOND WAS surprised and happy to hear that she was in London. They agreed to meet at the bar in the Ritz Hotel, where she was staying. As he got into the de-commissioned Aston-Martin DB5 he had purchased from Q Branch several years ago, Bond thought again of her long, muscular legs and hourglass figure. This was one case in which he sided with the media: she was among the world's most photogenic women. Bond was never one to wallow in nostalgia, but the promise of the rendezvous had awakened memories of passionate kisses and warm soft skin.

As he drove from Chelsea toward Piccadilly, yet another catalyst sparked a remembrance from the past. He noticed a billboard announcing a figure skating "extravaganza" to be held at the Wembley Arena. Natalia Lustokov, the former Russian Olympic skater, was the star attraction. Bond smiled and thought of the day when he had first met Natalia.

It was the only time that Bond had appeared on television.

It was some years back, before the collapse of the Soviet Union, when one of 007's routine assignments was to assist with defections. Usually, Bond's work with defectors was carried out quietly and without any significant incidents.

In that particular instance it had been rather different.

Bond pulled the wool cap over his dark hair and wrapped the scarf tightly around his neck. The snow was tapering off, but the wind blasting off of Lake Michigan still managed to penetrate the heavy coat. They didn't call Chicago the "windy city" for nothing.

He watched as Natalia Lustokov performed an edge jump in which a skater was suddenly airborne and one was left wondering how she got there. Wearing tight-fitting leotards and a fur-lined top, the Olympic skater spun around and skated quickly around the rink to where three men were standing behind the rail. One was a heavy-set man with bushy eyebrows who barked instructions at her with a demeaning air of superiority. Bond knew that he was Natalia's coach, and that he was just as dangerous as the two body-guards at his side.

Word had apparently got out that Natalia was practicing on the rink located at the northern end of Grant Park and built over a parking garage near the lakefront. Two hundred spectators had gathered around the plaza, which was scenically located between the lake to the east and the skyline looming overhead to the west.

The skater was on a world tour as part of a cultural exchange program with the U.S.S.R. When MI6 had learned that she wanted to defect to Britain, Sir Miles Messervy, the man known as M, coordinated the operation with the CIA and FBI after an initial attempt in London had been aborted. Her entourage had already flown to the States before MI6 could try again. Bond had been dispatched to America, as M felt that the job needed someone with his particular brand of expertise.

Bond bent down, laced his boots tightly, and ran a gloved finger along the Wilson Hans Gerschwiler blades. He glanced up and saw that the few other civilian skaters on the rink were giving Natalia plenty of room to maneuver. After all, she was a star.

He moved around the railing and stepped onto the ice, then pushed off and sailed smoothly to the center of the rink. While he had always been an expert skier, Bond was the first to admit that he was only an adequate skater. He enjoyed the sport, but he was no master of it.

The truck from WLS Channel 7 television pulled up onto the snow just off Randolph Street, right on time. The reporter, a tall blue-eyed woman with blonde hair and dressed in a bright red wool coat and beret, jumped out of the back, followed by a cameraman carrying a Sony Ikegami camera and an audioman with a recorder box. They hurried to positions at the side of the rink, where the reporter quickly composed herself. Listening to instructions from her producer with an IFB earpiece, she tested the stick mike and rolled smoothly into action.

"This is Janet Davies with Eyewitness News, 'Live at Five' from Daley Bicentennial Plaza, where Olympic skater Natalia Lustokov is practicing for her performance tonight."

Natalia, now aware of the television camera, pushed away from the men and skated around the rink, gaining enough momentum to turn herself backwards and perform a flawless Axel. She landed, still gliding backwards, as the spectators applauded and cheered.

Bond skated around the periphery, moving with the six or seven other skaters who would one day claim that they shared the rink with Natalia Lustokov. He glanced at the short administrative building overlooking the rink and spotted Max, the FBI man he had met earlier, standing behind the rail. Max nodded at him with a small gesture to his left. Three city policemen had arrived and were mingling with the spectators, near the television crew.

That was Bond's cue. He sped up, overtaking the other skaters and moving behind Natalia.

Janet Davies continued her broadcast. "The snow is leveling off now, but the wind is still strong. That didn't stop spectators from gathering here to watch Natalia Lustokov strut her stuff. I believe she just did a 'toe loop,' one of the easier multi-rotation jumps for skaters to perform."

Bond increased his stride and was soon skating beside the girl. He turned to look at her and admired her classic, glamorous features. She had shoulder-length black hair that whipped around her ivory-white face. Her clear blue eyes were large and cat-like, and she had a sensual mouth painted brightly with red lipstick. Her cheekbones were high and her neck was long, and she moved with the gracefulness of a gazelle.

She turned and looked at him, impressed that he would have the gall to attempt to share the spotlight with her in front of a television camera and an audience. Bond smiled at her, then made a sharp turn, daring her to follow him. Natalia accepted the challenge and chased him, quickly overtaking this handsome stranger who had cold blue eyes and a somewhat cruel smile.

"It appears that Miss Lustokov has some competition on the rink," the reporter said. When the camera pulled away from her, she mimed to the audioman, "Who is that guy?" Her colleague shrugged.

Bond turned to face Natalia, skating backwards. He held out his hands, inviting her to take them. She smiled, nodded, and grasped hold. Without saying a word, the couple skated around the rink, face to face. As Bond pulled her along, the three Russians stepped forward, closer to the rail. Who *was* this man? The coach grunted at one of the bodyguards, a big man wearing a gray fur cap with a red star emblazoned on the front. He quickly donned boots and skates.

Janet Davies continued her commentary. "It appears that Natalia has gained a partner on the rink. We don't know who he is, but he's holding his own with the champion."

The bodyguard finished lacing his boots, then stepped onto the ice. He shoved off and began to skate, somewhat unsteadily, around the rink behind the couple.

Bond signaled Natalia, indicating that he was willing to help her with a pair throw. Using a partner, a skater could jump higher and more effortlessly with a throw assist. She scooped with her leg and leaped. Bond swung her around so that she landed smoothly in front of him and continued skating. The audience went wild.

"A perfect Salchow!" Miss Davies called into the mike. "What a treat we're getting today at Grant Park."

The bodyguard skated closer behind Bond, who saw him out of the corner of his eye. Bond kept him just short of his blind spot for another lap, and then he made his move. Bond turned sharply and slammed directly into the large man, knocking him back on the ice. The man landed with a thud and slid comically toward the edge of the rink. The audience gasped.

Janet Davies whispered to the cameraman. "He did that on purpose, didn't he?" She listened intently to the producer in her ear.

The big man struggled to his feet as the second bodyguard rushed to put on boots and skates. The first man was now angry and he took off after Bond with more confidence and determination. Meanwhile, Natalia kept skating and spinning, oblivious to the drama unfolding around her.

The first bodyguard skated behind Bond and attempted to smash into his back, but Bond deftly swerved out of the way. The bodyguard missed Bond completely and slid into the second man who had just entered the rink. They both crumbled into a pile.

Now the spectators were laughing and applauding. It was some kind of show! This was all rehearsed!

The coach, however, was not amused. He immediately began to put on his skates.

Bond sailed past Natalia, winked at her, then skated quickly around to where the two big men were getting back on their feet. Bond skated smoothly between them, grabbing their waists as he glided through. He pulled them hard, then let go, causing them to crash into each other and fall to the ice once again.

As Bond had hoped, the television camera turned away from Natalia and was focused on him. The "show" was turning out to be much more entertaining than Natalia's practice.

The coach entered the rink and skated like a pro. He zoomed around his two men and took off after Bond. It was then that everyone noticed the glint of metal in his hand.

"Oh my God, he's got a gun!" Janet Davies announced into the mike.

Suddenly, the three policemen went into action. They were not wearing skates, but they ran out onto the ice anyway. One of them slipped and slid into the two bodyguards, knocking them over once again. The other two policemen shouted for the coach to halt.

Bond was ahead of them. He crouched, like a skier, turned and skated straight for the coach. The gun fired but the bullet whisked over Bond's head. Bond rammed hard into the coach's belly, knocking him to the ice.

At the sound of the gunshot, the spectators screamed and began to panic.

"A shot was fired!" the reporter shouted. "The rink is turning into chaos!"

Bond fell on top of the coach and wrestled the gun away from him. By then, the policemen had drawn their weapons and were pointing them at the four men lying in the rink. The three Russians raised their hands, and Bond resignedly did so as well.

Once they were on their feet, the coach looked around for the Olympic champion. He shouted frantically in Russian, his face contorted in horror.

Janet Davies was confused as well. "I don't see Natalia Lustokov . . . What happened to her . . . ?"

Indeed, she was nowhere to be seen. She had disappeared into the crowd.

As the police led Bond and the three Russians away, 007 turned back to see that Max was no longer in his position either. The diversion had worked. The FBI had spirited the skater away, down into the parking garage, where an armored vehicle had been waiting to take her to freedom.

Two hours later, Bond was released, as planned, while the three Russians were held for more paperwork than was necessary. He joined his FBI colleagues and Natalia Lustokov at a safe house located in the Chicago Loop, where Janet Davies' television broadcast was being replayed.

"You put on quite a show, Mister Bond," Max said. "The most fun I've had since 'Holiday on Ice'."

Bond allowed himself a smile as he watched the antics on the television.

The following three nights in Chicago had been intense. Even now, years later, he was still reflecting on the warmth in her blue eyes as he arrived at the Ritz Hotel for his rendezvous.

After parking the car, Bond bounded into the lobby and entered the bar. He looked around for his date and found her sitting alone in the corner, nursing a glass of wine.

"Is this seat taken?" Bond asked her, indicating the empty chair beside her.

"Hello, my darling," Janet Davies said dreamily. "It's been a long time."

THE MAN WITH THE RED TATTOO

For Judy

CONTENTS

ONE

FINAL FLIGHT

WHAT WAS THAT HIGH-PITCHED BUZZ IN HER EAR? SHE WONDERED AS A WAVE
of nausea swept over her once again.

An hour ago she had been fine. Now Kyoko McMahon felt weak
and chilled, and she had an agonising headache that pounded
through her skull.

The Japan Airlines flight had left Narita Airport two hours earlier
and wouldn't reach London for another ten hours. Would she be able
to stand it? She felt woozy and disoriented. All she wanted was to
stop the world from spinning around her.

Kyoko dismissed the idea that the food Shizuka had served at their
mother's birthday party was to blame. Her sister, like all her family,
was meticulous in everything she did and her careful preparation
could be trusted. Come to think of it her father had complained of a
stomach ache at breakfast, and her mother had barely made it out of
bed to say goodbye to her that morning. Perhaps they had drunk too
much of the excellent Ginjo sake the night before.

Feeling ill on an aeroplane was never fun. The pretty twenty-two-
year-old half-Japanese, half-Scottish woman was thankful that she
was nearly alone on the upper deck executive class cabin of the aircraft. Not many travellers were aboard today. There was only the
businessman sitting two rows in front of her, and the other two men

three rows behind her. Not that she needed more room. The business class seats on JAL's 747 were luxurious: plenty of leg room, reclining and with a personal television monitor that provided a wide choice of movies. As a member of the successful McMahon family, Kyoko took business class travel as her right whenever she made the long flight from London back home to Japan.

This trip had been for a special occasion; her mother Junko's fiftieth birthday. Her father had organised a party of the immediate family. Shizuka, the eldest sister, had ensured that the banquet was appropriately elegant and delicious. It was a shame, thought the younger and more beautiful Kyoko, that Shizuka would probably never find a husband who would benefit from her accomplishments.

Kyoko had flown to Tokyo to surprise her mother. It had been a wonderful dinner party and a loving reunion. But in the middle of the family toasts and celebration, Junko could not forget her youngest child and said quietly, "I wish Mayumi was here." Nobody could speak and they all sat silent for a moment, remembering the lovely and vivacious girl who had disappeared from their lives.

"Are you feeling all right?" the young flight attendant asked her.

Kyoko moaned, "Not really. I don't know what's wrong. I feel ill."

The flight attendant felt Kyoko's forehead and said, "You're burning up. I'm not supposed to do this, but I'll give you some aspirin. All right?"

Kyoko closed her eyes and tried to smile in acknowledgement. The woman left her side and Kyoko's mind drifted back to the previous evening's festivities.

Her father, Peter McMahon, had made a short affectionate speech declaring his love for his wife, causing Junko to blush. Kyoko had thought it was sweet. Even in manners-conscious Japan, her parents had never felt that they should hide their affection for each other. It was her father's devotion to her mother that had convinced him to move permanently to Japan, learn the language and raise a family there so many years ago. Even though he had always kept his British citizenship, Peter McMahon had wholeheartedly embraced Japanese culture and integrated himself into it. CureLab Inc., the company he ran, was hugely successful. He had rescued it from bankruptcy after Junko's father, the company's founder, had retired. With Peter McMahon at the helm, the struggling pharmaceutical company Fuji-moto Lab Inc. became the front-running CureLab in just eight years. The McMahons had become wealthy as a result. The *gaijin* who had married into a long-established Japanese family had gained respect in a world where business was made up of inner circles and closed net-works. Kyoko could appreciate the hardships her father had gone through as a foreigner. She knew what discrimination foreigners could face in Japan when they attempted to squeeze into society. There was an old adage that a foreigner in Japan was "a friend after five minutes but still an outsider after twenty years." For someone who was half-Japanese it was even worse. It was one reason why she had chosen to study business at Oxford, her father's alma mater. There she was treated as an exotic and mysterious Eurasian, not as a "half breed." She hoped that she would someday be able to take over her family's interest in CureLab and gain great face in Japan.

The flight attendant brought Kyoko some aspirin and water. "Drink plenty of water. Try to sleep, all right?"

Kyoko took the pill, drank as much of the water as she could stand, and pulled the blanket around her body. She reclined the seat and closed her eyes.

Kyoko's tired and unhappy thoughts drifted to Mayumi. *Why had she gone?* Their parents' hearts were broken. The last they had heard about Mayumi was that she was living in Hokkaido, probably the girlfriend of a gangster. Mayumi had brought shame upon the family, though if she came home, Kyoko was sure that her youngest sister would be forgiven. The furious fight Mayumi had had with their parents four years ago had ended with Mayumi walking out of the house at the age of sixteen, vowing never to return. At first their father had said that Mayumi would come home once she had "found herself." Junko had been distraught. None of them had liked Mayumi's boyfriend, who was nothing but a common street thug. Peter McMahon had chalked up Mayumi's actions to teenage rebellion and put his faith in the notion that one day Mayumi would return the prodigal daughter.

Kyoko vaguely remembered thinking that "teenage rebellion" was quite an understatement. Mayumi had been a rebellious child from the day she was born. She had been plagued with colic and proved to be a big problem for her mother. Her first word was "No," and it had continued to be a regular part of her vocabulary as she grew up. Her parents, especially her father, had fought her hard over the years. It had been a losing battle for them, for Mayumi's will was shockingly strong. What a waste, Kyoko thought. Mayumi was easily the prettiest and possibly also the most intelligent of the three girls.

Kyoko's limbs felt heavy and she was struggling to think. The drone of the plane's engines reminded her of last night too, and the annoying whine of the mosquitoes. They were usually bad in the summer months but they had shown up in greater numbers this particular June. Kyoko remembered slapping at least three on her arm.

Another wave of nausea overtook her. Kyoko reached for the airsickness bag and vomited. The passenger two rows in front of her turned around to see what had happened.

Kyoko managed to close the bag and drop it on the floor before she fell back into her seat and drifted from consciousness.

The flight attendant came by and frowned before picking the bag up from the floor. She tucked the blanket snugly around Kyoko's shoulders. Thinking that the poor girl needed some sleep, the flight attendant elected to leave her alone for the next few hours. The other passengers on the upper deck were asleep as well, so there was no reason for her to do anything but walk through the cabin every now and then.

Four hours later, Kyoko was still asleep, but the blanket had been tossed aside. The poor girl was bathed in sweat. The flight attendant thought about waking her to see if she wanted water but decided against it. Best to let her sleep.

Two hours later, the call bell alerted the flight attendant to come into the cabin. The passenger in front of Kyoko had rung it. He pointed to the girl and said, "Something's wrong."

Kyoko McMahon was convulsing in her seat. The flight attendant ran downstairs and fetched the cabin officer. After he saw the writhing girl, he used the intercom to ask if there were a doctor aboard. A Japanese man in his fifties responded. The doctor came up from the main cabin, examined Kyoko, gently talked to her and held her still. Eventually she choked and coughed, gasping for air. The doctor gave her a sip of water. After a few minutes she had settled down again and drifted back to sleep. The doctor told the cabin officer that the girl probably had the flu. "It might possibly be a form of malaria," he said, "but I suggest that we just let her sleep. It's the best thing for her right now. Keep an eye on her, though."

The pilot was informed of the situation. The plane had already flown over Siberia, Russia and Finland. They could make an emergency landing in Copenhagen if necessary, but London was only three hours away.

"As long as she's sleeping, we'll continue," the pilot said. "At this point, it would be better to get her to her destination." He radioed ahead to make sure there would be no delay at the gate.

Everyone agreed.

The flight attendant looked in on Kyoko every half-hour. At one point, the girl was struggling and mumbling as if she were having a bad dream. The flight attendant shook Kyoko gently until she calmed down and began breathing deeply again.

Two hours later, the flight attendant decided to wake Kyoko, but couldn't rouse her. This time the girl felt cold and clammy.

When the doctor examined Kyoko again, he pronounced her dead.

Since they were so close to London, the flight crew agreed to keep it quiet and continue on.

Kyoko McMahon died alone, 39,000 feet above the earth. She never knew that her mother, father and sister had also died at approximately the same time with identical symptoms in their opulent house in the Tokyo suburb of Saitama.

ASSIGNMENT: JAPAN

MAJOR BOOTHROYD CLEARED HIS THROAT AND BEGAN.

"As you know, I asked you here this morning for a routine equipment briefing for all Double-Os and other field agents." He added, with sarcasm, "I see that we have the usual splendid turnout."

They were in the soundproofed shooting range in the basement of MI6 headquarters. Shooting Instructor Reinhardt stood at the back, genuinely concerned that the good major might accidentally cause a dreadful explosion inside his beloved range. Agents 004 and 0010 were present and they sat near 007, close to the table that displayed the various items Boothroyd had brought to the meeting. Three lower level field agents and several technicians also sat or stood near the major.

There never seemed to be more than three Double-Os around headquarters at any given time. Most of them, after all, were on assignments or stationed in other parts of the world. Or they were dead.

"Right," Boothroyd continued, his voice echoing in the stone room. "We have a few new pieces of hardware for you to review and most of them involve explosives."

The major, a tall thin man with wavy white hair, was wearing a pair of workman's overalls and a hard hat. A pair of safety goggles hung loosely around his neck. Bond had learned long ago to overlook his ridiculous appearance.

"Double-O Seven?"

"Yes, Major?"

He approached Bond and handed him a tubular cigar holder. "You're one of those who still indulge in the filthy habit of smoking. Might I interest you in a nice Cuban?"

Bond took it and noticed that it was slightly heavier than it should have been. "Thank you, Major. Now, what is it *really?*"

Boothroyd took it from Bond, popped off the cap and removed the cigar. He displayed it to the group and said, "It appears to be an ordinary cigar. But if you use your thumbnail to take off the end . . ." He did so and revealed that the cigar was not filled with tobacco. Boothroyd moved further back into the room some thirty feet away, where a small iron safe sat on a laboratory table.

"Two-thirds of the cigar is filled with plastic explosive. You can dispense it by squeezing the cigar like a tube of toothpaste." He demonstrated by squirting a small amount of brown paste onto the combination knob of the safe.

"The cap from the holder is a timer. It is pre-set for ten seconds. You simply set it by pushing this tiny button and placing it in the plastic explosive." The major fiddled with the cap and displayed a tiny readout to the group, although they were too far away to see the numbers clearly. Boothroyd realised this and said, "It has already begun to count down."

Boothroyd thrust the timer into the paste-like substance and moved behind a lead shield that had been set up away from the table. The Double-Os looked at each other with concern, but the technicians seemed confident that the major knew what he was doing.

Seconds later, the explosive ignited and smoke filled the room. The noise had been much louder than anyone had expected, but no one was harmed.

The front door of the safe hung on one hinge, grossly bent out of shape.

Boothroyd emerged from behind the screen and walked back to

the group. "With practice you should soon be able to estimate near enough how much explosive is needed. Note that the cigar can get through Customs with no problem and we have even given it the odour of tobacco. Now then."

He walked over to the near table and picked up a blister pack of a well known brand of indigestion tablets.

"No business traveller should be without antacids, wouldn't you agree?" he asked. "These are now standard issue. The white tablets are real antacids. The pink ones, if you throw them, burst and produce a thick cloud of smoke." He nodded at a technician, who threw one against the far wall. There was a loud pop and a dark billow of smoke appeared.

"The red ones are a little more powerful," Boothroyd said. "One of them can blow a small hole in a wall, create a pothole in a pavement, knock a door off its hinges. It can also take your hand right off, so be very careful with them."

The major dropped the blister pack. His audience didn't have time to gasp before it hit the floor. "You need not be worried. You have to throw them with great force to explode them," he said. "The packaging is designed to withstand being dropped on the floor and even the jostling that occurs within airline baggage."

Boothroyd spent the next twenty minutes demonstrating a variety of other incendiary devices. Bond thought that thirty per cent of them were not very practical, fifty per cent were possibly useful, and twenty per cent were brilliantly conceived, if not quite perfected. Q Branch was capable of designing some ingenious stuff, but only some of the products had a life beyond the initial testing period.

The meeting broke up so that the technicians could familiarise the agents with the new equipment. Bond took a look at some of the other things on the table that Boothroyd hadn't presented.

"What's this, Major?" Bond asked, picking up a Palm Pilot V. Boothroyd beamed and said, "Ah. Our little electronic organiser. That's still in the testing stage, Double-O Seven. We haven't worked out all the bugs."

"What does it do?"

"Besides being a real Palm Pilot, a cross section is filled with a stronger plastic explosive than we've seen here today. It has the force of a stick of dynamite. You set it off simply by inputting the data into the Palm Pilot. It becomes its own detonator."

"Ingenious. How much memory does it need to do that?"

"You're being facetious, but actually that's the problem we're having with the device's other function. Not enough memory. Or rather, not enough of a power source to be truly effective."

"For what?" Bond asked.

Boothroyd turned on a small desk fan that sat on the table. As the blades spun and whirred, he held the Palm Pilot a few inches away from it and pressed something. The fan's power immediately shut off. The blades slowed to a stop.

"It's a fairly weak electro-magnetic pulse," the major said. "We'd like it to be able to knock the power out of cars at a reasonable distance, but we can't figure out how to give it a large enough energy supply."

"What can it do now?" Bond asked.

"Oh, just what you saw. Small appliances. Televisions. Perhaps some security alarms. At extremely close range, mind you."

"May I have it now? I'll test it in the field for you."

Boothroyd thought for a moment and then nodded. "All right, Commander, I'll let you do that. I'll put it on your clearing slip for M. Just make sure that—"

A loud explosion made everyone in the room flinch. Someone shouted, "Whoa!" and laughed as Instructor Reinhardt cursed aloud.

"—you know how to operate it properly," Boothroyd sighed.

"I think it might have something to do with Japan," Nigel Smith said.

Bond winced. "Doesn't she realise that I'm doing everything I can about this Yoshida business? It's all that I've *been* doing since we beat the Union."

"You and me both," agreed Nigel, Bond's relatively new personal assistant, a clear-eyed young man who had been discharged from the Royal Navy due to an injury. Bond had originally bristled at being assigned a male assistant, but Nigel had shown that he was sharp and capable. He also possessed much of the same sardonic attitude towards the job as Bond. And while Nigel made it a point not to be over impressed with Bond, it was obvious that he admired his boss. Taking a cue from the style with which Bond presented himself, it wasn't long before Nigel upgraded his own wardrobe by buying his shirts from Turnbull and Asser.

Bond appreciated Nigel's candour and honesty, especially when it came to intelligence matters. The young man had a knack for reading between the lines and interpreting oblique reports from the field. His opinions were blunt and often gelled with Bond's. In a very short time the young man had become an ally.

"It might be about the G8 summit conference," Nigel suggested.

"Lord, I hope not," Bond muttered. He had seen the memo. An emergency session had been scheduled to take place in Japan in less than two weeks. "She probably wants me to babysit the PM."

"That's because you're the PM's best friend since that business in Gibraltar a couple of years ago," Nigel said, chuckling.

Bond glanced at the digital clock set into the wall, a standard feature in all outer offices. The working day was nearly over.

"How long ago did she ring?" Bond asked.

"Miss Moneypenny phoned me about a half-hour before you arrived."

"All right," Bond said. "Surely she was aware of my appointment with Q Branch. Call Penny back and tell her I'm on my way."

"Right." Nigel picked up the phone as his boss turned around and left the office.

Bond cursed silently as he got into a lift. If it wasn't about the G8 conference, then it was certainly about Goro Yoshida. He was just as concerned about Yoshida as M was. After all, the exiled Japanese extremist had been the Union's client for the recent affair that ultimately proved the unmaking of that terrorist-for-hire organisation. It was Yoshida who had put up the money. It was Yoshida who was now at the top of the "most wanted" lists of Japan and nearly every country in the world.

Just before the lift stopped on M's floor, Bond gazed into his indistinct reflection on the silver panels of the lift doors. He ran his fingers through the coal-black hair, not bothering to push the comma that hung above his right eyebrow back in place.

He got out of the lift and strode down the hall towards Miss Moneypenny's outer office, continuing to run through the precious little new information that had been uncovered since Yoshida's last venture. All that MI6 and MI5 knew about the terrorist was that he was a wealthy businessman who had hooked up with criminal elements, probably the yakuza, the Japanese mafia, and become a prominent nationalist. At first he was harmless, confining himself to travelling the streets of Tokyo in a green van, as most of the nationalists did and still do, announcing his views through a loudspeaker. He proclaimed that Japan had lost its traditional values and was being poisoned by the West. It was the same rhetoric that dozens of nationalists have spouted since before World War II. But shortly after Yoshida publicly declared "war" on the West, he mysteriously disappeared. He handed over his company to others to run, then left Japan just as several violent terrorist acts were instigated against Western countries. An embassy was bombed here, a fast-food restaurant was obliterated there. Intelligence agencies speculated that Yoshida had been behind the incidents.

Yoshida, now wanted by the police in Japan for "treasonous views and acts" as well as terrorism, was believed to be hiding somewhere in a remote part of Russia with his own private army.

Miss Moneypenny was on the phone when Bond walked into the office but her bright eyes held a greeting for him. Before she could mime a message, the door to M's inner office opened.

"Ah, there you are, Double-O Seven. I wanted to see you. Come inside."

M handed a folder to Moneypenny and walked back into her office, leaving the door open. Bond moved forward as Moneypenny gave him a wink and a little wave.

As soon as the door had closed behind them Bond said, "Ma'am if this is about Goro Yoshida, I assure you that—"

"It's not about Goro Yoshida, Double-O Seven," M said as she moved around her desk. "Please sit down."

Bond did as he was told.

So what was the score? he wondered. Something new?

M, who was dressed in a sharply tailored charcoal grey Bella Freud suit, sat down and asked, "You've seen the memo about the emergency G8 summit conference?"

Here it comes, he thought. "Yes, I have."

"The Koan-Chosa-Cho is in charge of security but every representative brings his or her own entourage. I'd like you there with our PM. Bodyguard duty. As a matter of fact, the PM requested you. You should be flattered."

Bond smiled to himself.

"Is something funny, Double-O Seven?"

"No, ma'am."

"The Japanese are a little worried about security in this day and age, as are we all. Potential threats to representatives of Western governments are a constant concern since the events of September 2001. The Japanese secret service want intelligence operatives from all of the participating governments to accompany the G8 members. I believe you are acquainted with the head of the Koan-Chosa-Cho."

"Indeed," Bond said. He had an old and dear friend who worked for the Japanese Secret Service.

"Mr. Tanaka was the one who initially put forth your name. The PM, after discussions with the US president, has agreed and made the official request. The Japanese have received some information that suggests there could possibly be a danger to the summit conference. In light of this revelation, I suppose your earlier comment about Goro Yoshida might not be too far off the mark."

"What kinds of threats have been made?" Bond asked. "Do they involve Yoshida?"

"We don't know. Tanaka will have to brief you on that. Now." She reached across the desk, picked up a folder and handed it to him. "There is something else I want you to look into while you're in Japan. In fact, I'm sending you over ahead of the summit conference so that you can do so. We don't want your presence to arouse too many suspicions in Japan, or cause undue alarm, so you will ostensibly be in the country to investigate the suspicious deaths of a British citizen and his family."

Bond opened the folder and saw photos of a man named Peter McMahon.

M continued talking. "Two days ago, the Japanese-born daughter of that man died of a mysterious illness aboard a Japan Airlines flight from Tokyo to London. It just so happens that the girl's parents and older sister in Japan died around the same time that the plane was in flight. I'm waiting for the pathology results on the dead girl, but the examining doctor at Heathrow thought that she might have died from some fast-acting form of West Nile disease. He had never seen anything like it. From what news we can gather from an unhelpful Japan, it appears that the same thing killed the rest of the family."

"Had they been together recently?"

"Yes," M replied. "At the mother's birthday party the night before, in a suburb of Tokyo."

Bond quietly cleared his throat and asked, "What does this have to do with us?"

"Have you heard of Peter McMahon?"

"I don't think so."

"A shrewd businessman. Ran a pharmaceutical company called CureLab Inc. in Tokyo. He married the founder's daughter and pretty soon the old man gave him a job. McMahon turned the company, which was in the throes of bankruptcy, into a business worth millions of pounds. They're one of the leading firms in the Pharmaceuticals industry. And he has important friends in this country."

Bond looked straight into M's cool blue eyes.

"I see," Bond said.

"The Japanese police have yet to declare whether or not the McMahon family died of accidental or natural causes or if they were murdered."

"Murdered? You think this was an assassination?" Bond asked. "Why?"

"Apparently McMahon had a lot of enemies," M said. "His father-in-law, Hideo Fujimoto, died three years ago. Ownership of the company passed to Fujimoto's daughter, as his wife was already dead. I would imagine that in the case of the McMahons' deaths, ownership would have passed to their three daughters. One of those daughters died with her parents in Tokyo. Another one died on that aeroplane."

"Where is the third one?"

"We don't know. The Japanese bureaucracy is withholding information about the McMahons. But you'll have the full cooperation of the Koan-Chosa-Cho, which seems to be taking a more aggressive view of the situation than the Tokyo police. We have a right to look into the mysterious death of a British citizen and they know it. You can begin by going out to Uxbridge tonight to have a word with the coroner who is looking after Kyoko McMahon's body. His office has been alerted and you are expected at seven-thirty this evening."

Bond felt a flicker of fear. Even the thought of going back to Japan after all these years gave him reason to pause.

"It all sounds very interesting, but with all due respect, I'm really not qualified to be a crime-scene detective," Bond said truthfully.

M looked at him hard and said, "That may be true, but that's not the real reason you don't want to go."

Bond raised his eyebrows.

"I know you better than that, Double-O Seven," M said. "I am quite aware of your history with Japan. I understand that you might have certain reservations about returning there."

Bond sighed inwardly. The old girl was perceptive. Bond had spent a significant amount of time in Japan, the victim of amnesia, after his pursuit of Ernst Stavro Blofeld. It had happened a lifetime ago, it seemed, but Bond didn't enjoy being reminded of those dark times.

"You might think of it as a holiday," she proposed with a wry smile.

"A holiday?"

"Your friend Tanaka is eager to see you."

Bond nodded. "It would be nice to see Tiger again. But still . . ."

"James," M said, uncharacteristically referring to him by his forename. "I need you there. You have the ability to see the wider picture. I want you to investigate CureLab itself. I want you to find out if Peter McMahon had an enemy who would be willing to assassinate him and his family. Was it really murder? And if so, who was responsible? And I want you to locate that missing daughter."

Bond remained silent. He knew that she was giving him an order, but the prospect of facing the ghosts that haunted his memories was daunting.

"That's all, Double-O Seven," she said. "And just to ease your mind, I'm not taking you *off* the Yoshida case. See what you can learn about him while you're there. If these threats to the summit conference concern him, well . . ."

"I understand."

"I know you hate babysitting jobs, Double-O Seven," she added. "Every Double-O has to do it every now and then."

Bond stood and raised his hand to stop her. "I'll get the details from Miss Moneypenny. You're right. It will be a change of scenery for me. And I certainly can't let down my old friend the PM."

M couldn't help but smile as he walked out of the office.

THREE

A NIGHT AT THE MORTUARY

THE SUN WAS ON ITS WAY DOWN AS BOND DROVE WEST ON THE M4 OUT OF London in the decommissioned Aston-Martin that he had purchased from Q Branch a few years back. He had always enjoyed the DB5 and he drove it around London more often than his old much-loved Bentley.

Bond came off the motorway at the Heathrow exit, turned north, followed the signs to Uxbridge, found his way to Kingston Lane and pulled into Hillingdon Cemetery. The Hillingdon Public Mortuary was in a fifty-year-old single-storey T-shaped brick structure built on a corner of the cemetery, adjacent to a playing field. A Ford and a Range Rover were the only other two vehicles in the car park. Bond parked the Aston-Martin next to them, got out and took in his surroundings. The gravestones in the cemetery were bathed in the dull glow of dusk as the sky was caught between dark navy blue and golden orange.

Bond entered the lobby through blue front doors. The building was silent and dark, save for a few lights on in the offices. The staff had gone home and the place seemed deserted.

"Hello?" Bond called.

A man dressed in a white shirt with the sleeves rolled up came into the room from an office on the right. He had the rugged look of someone who might once have been a police officer or perhaps served in the fire brigade.

"May I help you?" the man asked.

"The name's Bond. James Bond. I'm here to see Dr. Lodge."

"Oh, right. We've been expecting you. I'm Bob Greenwell, coroner's officer. This way, please."

Bond followed him into the office, where another man was looking intently at a laptop computer. The man looked up and stood.

"Mister Bond? I'm Chris Lodge. I'm the pathologist assigned to this case." They shook hands. Lodge appeared to be in his mid-thirties, was soft-spoken and had a gentle grip.

"I hope it wasn't too inconvenient to see me tonight," Bond said. "I'm leaving for Japan tomorrow."

"I quite understand," the doctor said. Greenwell sat at another desk, picked up a paperback novel and began to read.

"The staff usually go home at night," Dr Lodge said. "I come in when I'm called. Please sit down." The doctor gestured to an armchair on the other side of his desk.

Bond got to the point. "Can you tell me about Kyoko McMahon?"

Lodge shook his head with pity as he sat down. "An ugly and lonely death. We're still waiting for the toxicology results. We've sent all of our information to the Imperial College people at Charing Cross Hospital. There will have to be an inquest, I'm afraid. The coroner has yet to sign my postmortem report."

"So it's a suspicious death?" Bond asked.

"Downright baffling. We still don't know what killed the poor girl. To tell you the truth, it's one of the more interesting cases I've ever seen."

"Why don't you take me through the chain of events that occurred after the plane landed at Heathrow. Then I'd like to see your report, if you don't mind."

The doctor frowned. "This is highly unusual, Mister Bond, but as you're with the Ministry of Defence, I suppose it's all right. Postmortem information is normally kept confidential and is released only to the family . . . and to the police if the cause of death wasn't natural."

"I assure you that I'm not a reporter for the *Daily Express*," Bond said dryly.

"Right. Anyway, the pilot radioed ahead to Heathrow; the normal procedure should a passenger die on board. Under international law, when a passenger dies in flight, the death is taken to have occurred at the destination airport. The authorities were waiting for the plane; the Port Health Authority doctor examined the girl and pronounced her dead. The body was removed from the aircraft by an Uxbridge funeral director that we use. A hearse brought her here, where she was identified and tagged. Finding next of kin was quite a performance. I understand her immediate family is in Japan, am I correct?"

"Yes."

"Anyway, after failing to reach her parents, we finally got hold of her great uncle." Lodge consulted his notes. "A Shinji Fujimoto. I must say that he was rather uncooperative. He didn't want us to touch her body at all—just wanted her sent back to Japan. He was informed that it was a matter of law that we do a post-mortem in this country. Permission was granted, reluctantly. I was called in from Tooting yesterday morning, and I performed the post-mortem yesterday afternoon."

"And what were your findings?"

"It is my opinion that the cause of death was a highly virulent form of West Nile disease. Do you know it?"

"No, but it sounds as if I'm about to become an expert."

"Pretty serious stuff. Victims normally experience fever, headache, aching muscles, sometimes rashes or swollen lymph glands. Some individuals experience more severe symptoms like neurological damage, encephalitis and coma. In extreme cases it can be fatal. When we heard about the outbreak of West Nile in New York City a couple of years ago, we were all a bit concerned. They actually think that the virus came into New York via Asian mosquitoes that had been brought into the country accidentally inside a shipment of tyres."

"I remember reading about that. Didn't someone die?"

"There were a couple of deaths, but in the majority of cases it just made people ill. West Nile doesn't do what happened to this girl. The symptoms were similar, but they were magnified ten-fold. The onset was apparently very rapid. As I understand it, she boarded the plane in good health and became ill during the flight. She was dead within twelve hours. That's very fast. Normally, West Nile would take days or weeks to go through that kind of cycle."

Bond whistled appreciatively. "Is there a cure?"

"Unfortunately not. Look here." The doctor gestured for Bond to step around the desk and look at the laptop. Lodge punched some buttons and a cross-section of brain tissue appeared on the screen. "The mechanism of death, that is, what actually killed her, was that her brain suffocated. The high fever caused the meninges, the membranes surrounding the brain, to swell from the inflammation. An abscess was formed and grew very quickly, cutting off oxygen and blood flow to the rest of the brain. See this?"

The doctor pointed to indistinct blobs as Bond said, "Mmm hmm."

"She went into a coma, which is why the flight attendant thought that she was sleeping. At some point her brain simply shut off and she began to asphyxiate. The cause of death? I suppose I would say "natural" or "accidental." Depending on what the toxicology report says."

Bond sat down again and thought for a moment. "Were there any unusual marks on her body? Needle marks?"

"No," Lodge said. "As far as I could see, there was no evidence of drug taking. No herpes simplex virus, which can be a cause of encephalitis. However, speaking of mosquitoes, she did have a fair number of insect bites and they looked to me like mosquito bites. Mostly on her arms and legs."

"Could that have been it?"

The man shrugged. "West Nile disease is normally carried by mosquitoes, and humans are infected with the disease when they are bitten by them. And while the symptoms are similar, whatever this was, it was certainly *not* West Nile. I'm not ruling anything out, but in my experience a mosquito isn't capable of transmitting a disease that has *this* kind of reaction."

The sound of a crash in the back of the building caused all three men to turn towards it.

"What the hell was that?" Lodge asked.

"I'll go and see," Greenwell said as he stood and left the room, still holding a mug of coffee.

Lodge grinned at Bond. "Our guests back there are restless, perhaps?"

Bond did not acknowledge the joke. Instinctively, he rose and went to the door. There was a shout of surprise from the back of the building.

Lodge looked alarmed. "Was that Bob?"

The Walther PPK was in Bond's hand; Lodge could have sworn that the weapon had materialised from thin air.

"Which is the way to the post-mortem room?" Bond asked.

Lodge replied, "Go through the lobby and into the other office. There's a door at the back of the room that opens into a corridor. Go right, and then left. You can't miss it."

"Stay here." Bond peered into the dark lobby and saw nothing. He darted across and into the empty office behind reception. The door to the corridor was ajar. Bond crept to it and listened.

Silence.

He went through the door and into the hallway, where he found Greenwell's broken coffee mug. He heard something—a noise, a scuffling—coming from the post-mortem room. Bond moved slowly towards the door, which was also ajar. He carefully leaned in to look and felt a significant drop in temperature.

Greenwell was unconscious on the floor next to the postmortem table. Two men were bending over a nude corpse that was lying on one of the mobile metal carts. They were attempting to wrap it in a blanket. Bond could see twenty refrigerator doors lining the wall in rows behind them. Three were open. One had obviously contained the woman's body that they were wrapping. The other two cubicles were empty and were also open at both ends. The other side of the refrigerated cubicles opened into the body reception room, which was where bodies were delivered from the outside.

The two men were wearing surgical masks and from where Bond was standing they appeared to be Asian.

One of the men must have sensed Bond's presence, for he suddenly whirled around, his pistol spraying fire at the door. Bond ducked back into the hall and crouched. He heard the men shout to each other in Japanese. Bond dared to look low around the open door and saw both men climb into the open refrigerated compartments so that they could escape through the body reception room.

Bond fired the Walther at one of the men, but the intruder pulled his legs in just in time to avoid being hit. As Bond got up to run into the room, a third man who had been hiding against the wall beside the open door kicked the Walther out of Bond's hand. Before Bond could register surprise, the attacker struck him with two lightning fast *tsuki* punches to the chest. Bond fell backwards and crashed into a metal table with a scale used for weighing dissected organs.

Then Bond was hit with a powerful blow to the solar plexus, knocking the breath out of him. He fell to his knees, gasping for air as his assailant stood back, ready to kick. The young man wore sunglasses and a surgical mask. His hairstyle was a "punch perm," short and permed into tiny skull-hugging curls.

Acting quickly, Bond reached up to the metal table and grabbed the first thing he felt, which happened to be a metal tray covered with dissecting instruments. Bond flung the tray at the attacker just as the man's right foot left the ground for the kick. The tray bashed loudly into his boot, scattering the instruments over the tiled floor.

This gave Bond the time he needed to get to his feet, but not enough of an interval to defend himself against a perfectly executed *mawashi-geri,* or roundhouse kick, to the chin. Bond fell back again, this time knocking several metal trays off the post-mortem table. He hit the floor next to Greenwell, who was moaning softly.

This boy is a professional! was the only thing Bond was capable of thinking.

When he looked up, the "boy" had slithered through a refrigerated cubicle and escaped with his friends.

Bond got up and went to Greenwell. "Are you all right?"

The man nodded and put a hand to the back of his head.

"Who's the corpse?"

"It's the McMahon girl," Greenwell answered.

Without hesitation, Bond retrieved his handgun, dived into one of the refrigerated cubicles after the men, and crawled to the other end. He unlatched the door, then jumped down into the body reception room. The door to the car park was just closing. Bond hugged the wall and looked outside.

The back of the building was adjacent to a driveway where hearses and ambulances could pull up to drop off bodies. Beyond that were bushes, hedges and trees lining the edge of the cemetery. A black Toyota was pulling out of the driveway into Kingston Lane. The man he had fought was just jumping into the back seat as the tyres squealed. The light had diminished greatly, but Bond could still see well enough to take a shot at the driver. He held the gun with both hands, assumed a modified Weaver firing stance, aimed carefully, and squeezed the trigger. The Walther recoiled with a satisfying jolt.

The Toyota swerved out into the street and crashed into a telephone pole. The horn blared.

The two remaining men jumped out of the car and fired in Bond's direction. The bullets flew around him. Bond leaped for the pavement and rolled behind a tree that would shield him from the gunfire.

"Mister Bond?" Dr. Lodge called from the body reception room.

"Call the police!" Bond shouted. "And get back inside!"

Bullets sprayed around the tree, then at the open door of the building. Lodge disappeared from view.

Bond was pinned down. He was safe but he couldn't move to either side of the tree for fear of taking a bullet. He knew that the thugs wouldn't wait forever; they would have to move eventually. He just had to be patient.

When a siren could be heard approaching, the two men decided to go for it. Bond heard their footsteps as they ran off across Kingston Lane and into the cemetery, which was growing darker by the second.

Bond swung out from behind the tree and fired. One of the men jerked, cried out, and fell to the ground. The other man leapt to the side, taking cover behind a large gravestone. Bond began to run towards him, but the man reached around and fired his handgun, forcing Bond to take cover behind another tree.

As the police cars pulled into the front car park with sirens blaring, the gunfire ceased. After a few seconds, Bond carefully looked around the tree and could faintly see the man running. Bond raised the Walther to shoot, but at this light and distance, hitting him was unlikely. He let him go.

Bond sprinted to the man who was down and examined him. It was the same man he had fought in the post-mortem room. The bullet had caught him in the upper chest, a direct hit. Bond pulled off the surgical mask. He was a young Japanese, probably in his early twenties. Bond searched his clothing and pulled out a Dutch passport and a Colt 1911 A1 semi-automatic from underneath a light jacket.

Lodge came running outside with a torch. "Mister Bond, are you all right?"

"I'm over here. There were three of them. One's in the car. The third one got away."

Lodge crept warily up to the body and directed the torch on it. "Who is he?"

"I don't know. Shine your torch on his passport here."

Lodge took it and read it. "Somebody Hito. He lives in Amsterdam. Lived. What did they want?"

"It looked to me like they were trying to take Ms. McMahon's body."

"But why?"

"That's a very good question."

Then Bond noticed something unusual on the dead man's neck. "Shine that torch over here."

The light illuminated something sinister and extraordinary. Bond carefully unbuttoned the man's shirt and opened it. The dead man's entire upper torso was decorated in an elaborate, colourful tattoo depicting dragons and waterfalls.

It was a signature of the Japanese mafia, the dreaded yakuza.

FOUR

YAMI SHOGUN

THE MBB-KAWASAKI BK 117 EUROCOPTER LEFT BEHIND THE LAND MASS OF Hokkaido, the northern-most island of the cluster that make up Japan. It flew north-east towards the Kuril Islands, the so-called "Northern Territories" that Japan and Russia have been in dispute over since 1945. The Sea of Okhotsk stretched to the horizon ahead of them, while Russia lay hundreds of kilometres to the left and the Pacific Ocean expanded endlessly to the right.

Yasutake Tsukamoto shifted uncomfortably in his seat. He was not usually a nervous man. He was one of the most feared and respected men in Japan, the reigning *oyabun*, or father, of the Ryujin-kai. As *kaicho*, or boss, he had hundreds of men under his thumb, all willing to do his bidding. They were prepared to die for him. And, as the Ryujin-kai was one of the strongest and most powerful yakuza organisations in the country, with tentacles that reached into Japanese communities worldwide, Tsukamoto had no reason to be afraid. He was superior to every man in his organization—except one.

He always felt uneasy going to see the *Yami Shogun*. Even after all these years . . .

Tsukamoto didn't enjoy the flight across the sea to Russian territory. He hated the fact that Russia had occupied the islands since the 1945 Yalta Conference because they rightfully belonged to Japan. He hated doing business with Russia at all, but circumstances with the *Yami Shogun* dictated that it must be so. After all, the master was exiled from Japan and could not set foot in the country without being arrested. The deal the master had made with the Russian Organizatsiya ensured that he would have a safe haven where he could live with his private army, train them and prepare them for the battle yet to come. The *Yami Shogun* hated the Russians as much as Tsukamoto did, but business was business. Tsukamoto thought that one day the time would come when business partners would have to change.

The Kuril Islands were an ideal spot for the *Yami Shogun* to hide. They are considered a mysterious no man's land by both Japan and Russia. While they are governed as part of Sakhalin Oblast, in many ways they are still culturally tied to Japan. The islands are heavily forested and contain many active volcanoes. Hunting, fishing and sulphur mining are the principal occupations of the inhabitants, among them the Ainu, an ancient race believed to be indigenous to the area.

Eventually the helicopter approached the island called Etorofu by the Japanese and Iturup by the Russians. The helipad was on private property hidden amongst the trees. The property owner was associated with a mining operation that worked a nearby quarry; if anyone at the firm were questioned, they would have no knowledge of who that owner might be. If someone dug deep enough, they might discover that the owner was a Japanese corporation called Yonai Enterprises. It was a legitimate diversified company, involved mostly in chemical engineering.

It was also a front for one of the biggest yakuza gangs in Japan.

It was not unusual these days for yakuza to infiltrate "Big Business" in Japan. It was an unspoken and accepted part of the way society worked. Many *kaicho* and *oyabun* were heads of or sat on the boards of directors of large, influential companies. Any formidable yakuza gang in Japan had to flaunt its wealth and management skills.

Yasutake Tsukamoto was on the board of directors of Yonai Enterprises, which was one of the many reasons that he had no reason to complain about his life. He was successful. He was very wealthy. He was powerful. Two bodyguards travelled with him wherever he went. They sat across from him there in the helicopter, two burly men with punch perms and sunglasses. He saw them more than he saw his wife.

So why did he always feel like a child in the presence of the master?

Like the *Yami Shogun,* Tsukamoto was a nationalist. The type of yakuza he headed was *Uyoku,* which roughly meant "political right." It was ironic, Tsukamoto thought, that when *Uyoku* groups first came into fashion, Big Business was one of the enemies along with communists, anything from the West and anyone who suggested a deviation from a traditional monarchy. Today, however, Big Business was big business. Yonai Enterprises was a megacorp, soon to become a major player in Japan and abroad. Today's *Uyoku* might still hate the Russians and the Americans and the British and the Chinese but they didn't have a problem with taking their money.

Just as the helicopter landed in a square patch of flat land surrounded by tall trees, Tsukamoto suddenly understood why he was nervous about seeing the *Yami Shogun.* It had nothing to do with pleasing one's master. The ideological direction in which the master wished to go was what troubled him. For he, of all people, knew that the master was deadly serious about the upcoming project.

Tsukamoto knew the *Yami Shogun* better than anyone else.

He had first met Goro Yoshida when they were both children. They had gone to the same school when Goro was nine and he was eight. It was during the Occupation, when the United States dominated everything in Japan. Tsukamoto could remember the anti-American propaganda that circulated underground, the impassioned speeches of nationalists who deplored America and what it stood for. Even then, Goro Yoshida was emotional in his beliefs. He had embraced the rhetoric profoundly and it hardened into a fundamental principle as Goro grew into his teens.

Goro's family owned a consortium of small industrial and chemical engineering firms that later consolidated into what was now

Yonai Enterprises. He had been born in 1943, just in time for the climax of the war and the Occupation. His only sibling Yukiko came along a year later. Despite his family's prosperity, Goro had had a troubled childhood. As a teenager, he had turned to street gangs for a place to fit in. Wayward teenagers were prime recruitment material for the yakuza, so by the time Goro was thirteen he was involved in various levels of a Tokyo yakuza called Ryujin-kai. So was his friend Tsukamoto.

During this early period Goro despised his family. Tsukamoto remembered the horrible things Goro would say about his father. His father represented big business, and this was a Western thing. He was doing business with Western companies, many of them American, some British.

It wasn't until Goro was sixteen that he changed his mind about his father, who had secretly joined the Red Guard, a volatile nationalist group that was often blamed for terrorist incidents. And, to the amazement of young Goro, his father's name was ultimately attached to several bombings around the globe and he became a wanted man. Japan forced Goro's father into exile, so he went to live in Europe—in the West that he detested. He travelled around, working for various militant groups and was in London when a series of explosions rocked that city. Informants talked and Goro's father was identified as being a suspect.

The official word was that Goro's father died resisting arrest.

Yasutake Tsukamoto was with Goro Yoshida when the news came. They had just celebrated Goro's twentieth birthday. The sake had been flowing and Goro was very drunk. They had been talking about the latest work by Yukio Mishima, the writer who had become the most controversial and honoured Japanese author of his time. They both admired the nationalist themes that ran through Mishima's works and hoped that they could meet him someday.

To his great surprise, Goro inherited his father's fortune. It was Goro who eventually consolidated Yonai Enterprises to focus on future technology. Yonai in the 1960s became the leader in chemical engineering and it was entirely attributable to Goro's leadership.

His friends at the Ryujin-kai were very pleased with the situation.
Goro invited the yakuza to insinuate itself into the running of the
company and it wasn't long before Yonai Enterprises had tentacles
reaching into many facets of organised crime in Japan. With the
future of the company secure, Goro began to concentrate more on his
other interests, namely the philosophies of nationalism, attending
kendo and karate classes and honing his body.

As time went on, Tsukamoto watched his friend Goro withdraw
further from society. Goro spoke of nothing but his militaristic
dreams. For a while he was a member of Yukio Mishima's private
army known as the Shield Society. But disagreements over Yoshida's
connections with the yakuza led to his discharge from the society
before that fateful day in 1970 when Yukio Mishima committed
public *seppuku.*

Even though they had had their disagreements, Yoshida was
greatly moved by Mishima's act of defiance. Partly in tribute to the
writer's act, Yoshida liquidated his private assets and hid his money
in a network of front companies, bank accounts and foundations. He
formed his own private army of nationalists, modelled after
Mishima's Shield Society. Using some of his father's Red Guard connections, he made arms deals first with the Soviets and later with the
Russian mafia and supplied *his* private army with weapons.

Eventually Goro Yoshida became the shadow *kaicho* of the Ryujin-
kai. While Tsukamoto had by that time become a rising yakuza
enforcer, first as a *wakashu,* a "child," then as a *shatei,* a "brother," and
eventually acting *kaicho* of the Ryuijin-kai itself, in reality Yoshida
always pulled the strings. And Tsukamoto was honoured to work for
him. Tsukamoto thought of Yoshida as his *sensei,* his master or mentor,
but because of their lifelong friendship, Tsukamoto never called him
that to his face. Even so, Yoshida had become something larger than
life. He had a mystique among the yakuza as a man with a persuasive
charisma and a tangible inner strength that seemed to transcend the
earthly plain of existence. In essence, he became the spiritual leader
of the Ryujin-kai, a position created specially for such a unique individual. Tsukamoto could not deny that Yoshida possessed an enlight-

ened intelligence. He had seen it in action. And it should be said that Yoshida poured money into the yakuza and that didn't hurt his stature in the organisation either. There was no question that Goro Yoshida should be *Yami Shogun,* the Dark Lord, of the Ryujin-kai.

By that time, their relationship had changed. Yoshida respected and trusted Tsukamoto as his lifelong friend and loyal colleague, but there were times when Tsukamoto was the victim of Yoshida's volatile nature. Tsukamoto would never forget the shame he had felt when he had bungled a business arrangement with a rival yakuza. Yoshida had slapped him across the face, a gesture that left no doubt about who ran the organisation.

Nevertheless, Tsukamoto continued to support and serve the *Yami Shogun,* even when Yoshida went off the deep end in the 1980s with what he called the "New Offensive." The targets were all over the world: Western companies whose businesses had a detrimental effect on Japanese traditions were bombed. The countries hit the hardest were the United States and Great Britain. The bombings started in Japan and then they spread to neighbouring countries. When the terror reached the big cities in the US and Britain the authorities knew that something had to be done.

The intelligence communities of the world gathered information and compared notes. Like his father before him, Goro Yoshida became a wanted man. He fled Japan, but since he rarely made an appearance anyway, no one really knew if he was in Japan or not. What was certain was that he and nearly one hundred followers mysteriously disappeared. He was thirty-eight years old.

Yasutake Tsukamoto was one of the few men outside of Yoshida's camp who knew where he was. Most of their dealings were conducted by telephone and the Internet, but Tsukamoto had to fly to Etorofu once a month to meet with the *Yami Shogun.* He would then come back to Sapporo with Yoshida's advice and guidance on Ryujin-kai business. In 1993, Yonai Enterprises moved its base of operations from Tokyo to Sapporo so that the headquarters of the Ryujin-kai would be closer to their spiritual leader. A cover story was created to pacify the authorities: Goro Yoshida had sold Yonai Enterprises and others were now running it. In reality, Yoshida was still the owner, operating Yonai from afar through a puppet president.

The ensuing years were exciting and profitable. Yoshida master-minded several satisfying ventures, with only one notable failure— and if it hadn't been for the incompetence of that terrorist-for-hire organisation, the Union, that would not have been the case.

Now the *Yami Shogun* was about to embark on a plan that fright-ened the hell out of Tsukamoto.

Today Goro Yoshida was fifty-nine years old but he still had the vitality of a twenty-four-year-old. Yasutake Tsukamoto was fifty-eight and felt the weight of the world on his shoulders.

After the helicopter had landed, two uniformed soldiers escorted Tsukamoto to a bunker. He had been through the routine dozens of times before. Steps led down to a dugout that had been completely furnished in the style of a traditional Japanese home. Tsukamoto removed his shoes and stepped up onto the *shikidai*. A guard opened the *fusuma,* the sliding door made by stretching thick decorative paper over both sides of a wooden frame—a distinctive component of a Japanese home or inn. The room was covered in eight *tatami* mats. *Shoji,* translucent screens of thin paper stretched over frames of crossed laths, lined one wall and allowed light to come into the room. A *tokonoma,* another traditional element, adorned a side of the room. This was a recessed alcove in the wall where a scroll was hung, and, in this case, an exquisite spray of orchids was displayed. One single unfinished vertical wooden post, the *tokobashira,* helped to support the *tokonoma.*

In the middle of the room was a low table. Tsukamoto sat on one of the *zaisu,* cushioned chairs with backs but no legs, and waited for his friend and mentor.

He could hear the hum of the power generators through the walls. It was an impressive complex: barracks for a hundred men, a mess hall, training facilities, arms storage; in fact a small army base, mostly located underground. It had taken Yoshida over a year to have it con-structed. It was a monumental achievement.

After a moment, the *fusuma* at the back of the room slid open and Goro Yoshida stepped in. Tsukamoto remained in his seat but bowed as low as he could. Yoshida bowed less deeply and then sat down across from Tsukamoto.

The *fusuma* slid open again and a woman in a kimono, on her knees, looked in. She greeted the guest, placed a tray inside the room, then stood and came inside. She knelt at the table and served green tea to both men, then left the room in the same manner.

"You are looking well," Tsukamoto said.

Yoshida shook his head. "I am looking old."

"No, you are not. I look much older than you." It was true. Yoshida appeared to be a man in his late forties or early fifties, certainly not someone who was pushing sixty. He was a small but solid, man. His bodybuilding had paid off and even at his age his muscles appeared still toned and bulky through the black and white silk kimono that he wore. His hair was short, cut in the style of his idol, Yukio Mishima. A portrait of the author sat on a low table against a wall, next to portraits of Yoshida's mother and sister.

"How proceeds our latest venture?" Yoshida asked.

"Very well. It is just a matter of time before Yonai Enterprises will completely control our rival. We will no longer have to rely on a CureLab pawn to provide us with their latest technology."

"This has taken much longer than you had anticipated."

"I know, Yoshida. I apologise."

"You sound like a woman," Yoshida spat. "Sometimes I wonder if you are competent."

Tsukamoto nearly gasped. The *Yami Shogun* had never spoken to him quite so harshly before.

"Yoshida," he said, "I am very loyal to you. Why do you insult me? Without me running things in Japan—"

Yoshida slapped the table hard, startling Tsukamoto. "Do you forget who you're talking to? Would you even be where you are without my leadership?"

Tsukamoto shuddered inside. "My mistake," he said, bowing. Even though they were childhood friends, the relationship between them could be turbulent. Tsukamoto never knew how Yoshida would react to anything. This was the main reason why Tsukamoto both respected and feared his master.

After a pause, Yoshida asked, "When do you expect the final phase of the merger to take place?"

"Very soon. Within the week. With the, uhm, unfortunate death of CureLab's CEO and chairman, the family's stock has passed to the only remaining daughter. And as you know, she is under the thumb of the Ryujin-kai, making good money for us!"

"Good. Another strike against the Western barbarians. Of course, the girl must be eliminated now."

Tsukamoto was surprised. "Eliminated?"

"We cannot keep her alive, Tsukamoto. Surely you know that."

Tsukamoto cleared his throat. "Yes, of course. Pardon me."

"And the product? Have our people been working on it?" Yoshida asked.

"Yes. The strain that killed the McMahons is being perfected. That one was too slow and took too long to take effect. The next version will be much better and will work faster. We are also almost ready with a new version of the transmitters."

Yoshida rubbed his chin. "I trust it will work. Our people have been working on them at the laboratory in Hokkaido for some time. The first version was a most impressive attempt but it wasn't perfect. At this late stage, will we have enough time? You know the target date."

"Our engineers swear that they are ready. They hope to complete the work in forty-eight hours or less. After what was already supplied to us from the CureLab traitor, it shouldn't be too difficult to make the necessary adjustments."

"I hope you're right, Tsukamoto. Have all materials moved from Hokkaido to the distribution centre in Tokyo. We have to be ready by the end of the week."

"Yes, *sensei*." As soon as he said it, Tsukamoto realised that he had made a slip.

Yoshida shook his head slightly. "Tsukamoto, you know that you do not have to call me *sensei*. We have known each other since we were children."

"I know. I apol— er, my mistake. It's just that you *are* the master. I cannot help but think of you in this way."

"I appreciate your loyalty and respect, Tsukamoto-san. Let us leave it at that. And now, my friend, let's have lunch."

Yoshida smiled and Tsukamoto felt relieved for the first time in days.

It was later the same day. Goro Yoshida took a wet cloth and laid it across his forehead. The only time he felt at peace with himself was when he put his head back against the large cypress tub and closed his eyes. The hot water stimulated his skin, reminding him of the sensations he had experienced when he had received the exquisite red tattoo that covered eighty per cent of his body. The intricate tattoo, depicting an ancient battle between samurai and dragons, decorated his skin from the base of the neck, down his back and arms, across his chest and stomach, and down his legs to his calves. Its red colour dominated the design, with only hints of black out-lining figures and creatures, a few touches of yellow for highlights, and a little orange tinting. But mostly it was various shades of red. Dark red, crimson red, fiery red, pink red, blood red . . . it was totally unique. Many yakuza adorned their bodies with tattoos, but none had quite the impact of Yoshida's. It was at once marvellous, beautiful and terrifying. He had gone through many hours of pain for the tattoo, one hundred for the back alone. The technique of traditional *irezumi* tattooing was painful. It was done slowly and manually, without the use of electric devices.

Tsukamoto was in another part of the complex. He would be leaving for the mainland in an hour, but Yoshida wanted him to see something first. In the interim, Yoshida had spent an hour in the gym practising kendo, lifting weights and participating in *kenjutsu,* Japanese swordsmanship. He had become one of the finest swordsmen in the Far East and was considered a master. Yoshida had first picked up a samurai sword when he was eight. By the time he was fourteen, it was a part of him.

Yoshida used a *shinai*, a bamboo sword used for practice, but his opponent always used a *bokken,* a wooden sword that had the potential to be deadly. So far, no opponent had ever been able to strike him. For a while Yoshida thought that his opponents might be holding back simply because he was the *Yami Shogun* and no one dared to hit him with a real weapon. He told the students that he could tell if they were trying their best or not. If they did not attempt their best, then he would have them killed. From then on, Yoshida noted a discernible difference in the attitudes of his opponents.

Yoshida removed the cloth from his face and opened his eyes. The bath had been relaxing and the ritual soaking in the *o-furo* hot tub had been invigorating, but now it was time to act. He was ready to launch the project that he had prepared himself for since the death of his father.

Dressed in a *yukata* and *tanzen,* Yoshida strode through the corridors of his compound until he came to the gymnasium. The workout equipment had been cleared, and Tsukamoto and several guards were standing at attention. They all bowed when he entered the room.

"My friend, Tsukamoto, you shall now see the real beginning of our venture. We have been preparing for it for a long time and finally we have the great pleasure of watching it commence."

"I am honoured, Yoshida," Tsukamoto said, bowing again.

Yoshida clapped his hands and a *fusuma* slid open. Twenty men dressed in civilian clothes marched in quickly and formed two lines of ten. Once they were in place, they bowed to Yoshida in unison. Yoshida walked around the group once, inspecting them. Finally, he addressed his long-time friend.

"Twenty men," he said. "Not a bad luck number for us, eh, Tsukamoto?"

Tsukamoto knew what Yoshida meant. The name "yakuza" came from the combination of three numbers—8, 9 and 3. This referred to an ancient Japanese gambling game called Oicho-Kabu, in which the number 19 was the strongest hand to possess. A 20, the sum of 8, 9, and 3, was completely useless and considered bad luck. In the old days, the yakuza were known as the "useless hands" of society. The name stuck and their lucky number became 20.

Yoshida continued, "Twenty men. Twenty messages. You men will be our carriers. Like the *kamikaze* pilots during the honourable war with the Americans, you are willing to end your lives to accomplish the mission. For that I bow to you."

With that, Yoshida bowed as low as Tsukamoto had ever seen him do. As there was a definite hierarchy of superiority that determined the degree of bowing in Japanese society, it was shocking to see the *Yami Shogun* bow so low.

Yoshida rose and said, "You will fly to Sapporo tonight for a couple of days of rest and relaxation. You will be the guests of Tsukamoto. Then you will fly to Tokyo for the final preparations. By the middle of next week, you will each be on a journey to deliver our messages to the West. Go swiftly and silently. Be diligent always, and never falter from your path. You and your families have been rewarded handsomely. If by some quirk of fate some of you do not return, then know that you will be rewarded more handsomely in heaven."

The men shouted, *"Hai!"* and bowed again.

FIVE

YES, TOKYO!

BOND HAD MIXED FEELINGS ABOUT RETURNING TO JAPAN.

Sitting in the executive class cabin of the daily JAL flight from London to Tokyo's Narita Airport, Bond had plenty of time to consider the situation. On the one hand, a reunion with his friend Tiger Tanaka, the head of the Koan-Chosa-Cho, was very appealing. Bond genuinely enjoyed Japan; he appreciated the attention to detail and cleanliness that was so important to the Japanese people. He was impressed that the population had the consideration to cover their noses and mouths with surgical masks and wear them in public when they had colds. He admired their efficiency and good manners, their dedication to tradition and their generosity. He found the scenery beautiful. He enjoyed sake and Japanese beer. He thought that a lot of the food was unique and delicious, but he avoided raw fish whenever possible.

And he considered Japanese women to be arguably the most beautiful in the world. Besides possessing classically pretty, nearly perfect facial features, Japanese women held a poise and grace not found in other societies, as well as a certain delicateness that was endearing and attractive. He had once facetiously told the Governor of the Bahamas that he would only marry a Japanese girl or an airline hostess. And, considering the JAL hostesses on today's flight, it was still a half-serious proclamation.

The other side of the coin was an unknown. He had begun his first mission to Japan as a nervous and physical wreck due to his grief over the death of his only bride. By happenstance, Bond had discovered that Ernst Stavro Blofeld was hiding on a remote island in the south of Japan. The subsequent battle between the adversaries left Blofeld dead and Bond emotionally and physically scarred. He lived for months with an Áma girl, the lovely Kissy Suzuki, on a nearby island. Bond became a fisherman and boatman, with Kissy as his wife, until he was compelled to leave his simple existence as Taro Todoroki and search for his true identity in the Soviet Union.

When he had finally regained his memory, Bond retained everything that had happened on that island with Kissy. He had learned to speak Japanese (and could still do so, although he was very rusty) and had mastered the ability to read and write the script known as *kana*. He was less successful in learning *kanji*, the Japanese written language that was based on symbolic Chinese characters, but he had adopted many Japanese customs and manners and had practised them until they were second nature. It had taken him weeks to rid himself of a compulsion to remove his shoes before entering a house.

How would all this affect him upon his return to Japan? The ghosts of those he had loved or hated might be around to haunt him: Kissy and the son Bond had never had a chance to know, Blofeld, Henderson, even the phantom of Taro Todoroki . . .

What the hell is wrong with you? Bond scolded himself. The assignment was a breeze. Compared to that first mission to Japan many years ago, a task that had been considered "impossible," this one would be a holiday.

Enjoy yourself! he commanded. Drink a lot of sake with Tiger and play that silly children's game, Scissors Paper Stone. Eat a lot of fish. Meet a Japanese girl or two. Have a traditional Japanese bath, a pleasure made in heaven. Here was a chance to delight in an assignment for a change.

"May I take that away, sir?" the pretty flight attendant asked.

"Yes, please."

She took the tray that had contained a fine Japanese meal consisting of a prawn sushi and an egg roll with crab meat appetisers, sweet-simmered whitebait in soy sauce, boiled shrimp with fish roe, a piece of fried chicken in ginger starch sauce, miso soup, Japanese pickles and steamed rice. She left another bottle of Ginjo sake, his third but not his last, and cleared away the empty. It was a slightly sweet sake that came from the Kyoto Prefecture and Bond thought it did nicely as an after dinner drink. He had to admit that the service aboard Japan Airlines was in keeping with the first-class attention to detail that all things seemed to receive in Japan. The twelve-hour flight would be a pleasant one.

Bond settled back and gradually felt less melancholic and more optimistic about his stay in Japan. Perhaps it was the nice smile the Japanese flight attendant gave him every time she walked by, but eventually Bond stopped worrying. There was now no doubt that he should throw himself into the assignment and have a good time in Japan.

Bond wondered if Tiger had changed. It had been a long time since they had communicated and it was Bond who had broken off the contact, embarrassed by what had happened to him in Japan. Tiger had always said that Bond had saved great face and would be regarded as a hero if it weren't for the classified nature of his deeds, but Bond had never bought into that rubbish.

It was time to re-establish the connection with his old friend.

Bond's contact met him at Immigration. After Bond presented his passport, the officer made a quick call and she came to greet him.

"Mister Bond?" she asked. "I'm Reiko Tamura. I'm with the Public Security Investigation Agency." She bowed.

At first Bond didn't know what to say. He hadn't expected a woman.

"*Konnichi-wa,*" Bond said, bowing slightly.

"Oh, you speak Japanese?" she asked with a look of disbelief.

"*Iie, iie. Mada heta desu.*" Bond adapted the very Japanese way of being self-effacing when presented with a compliment.

"Well I don't think so. Your pronunciation is very good."

He shrugged. "*Arigato.*"

She smiled warmly. Bond thought she was stunning. She seemed to be in her mid-twenties, but with Japanese women it was always difficult to tell because they appeared to stay young forever. She was dressed in a sharp, dark grey pinstriped Armani trouser suit. It was very modern and flattering, with a tapered waist that accentuated her curves splendidly. She had a classic, pretty Japanese face with a warm smile and terrific brown eyes. Her shoulder-length black hair was shaped around her head and tucked behind her ears. One couldn't help but notice the black pearl at her neck. It had a unique pigment, like a peacock's feather, and this suited her colouring. But what made her *sexy*, Bond thought, were her glasses. He didn't know why. She looked very corporate, trying hard to look right in a man's world, but at the same time Reiko Tamura exhibited an intelligence that put Bond at ease. This woman was a class act. Tiger would not have sent someone incompetent. The fact that he had sent a woman simply had to do with Tiger knowing Bond all too well.

She presented him with a business card. Bestowing *meishi* had become a very sacred and necessary ritual in Japanese society. A person without a business card was no one. It was customary for the receiver to take the card with both hands and make a point of actually reading it before putting it carefully in a pocket. Reiko's was a company-issued card with her name, the name and address of her organisation and phone and fax numbers. The front was written in *kanji* and the back was in English.

Bond had come prepared. The service had given him cards that read, very simply, "James Bond—Ministry of Defence" and the public mailing address and phone numbers. His were written in *katakana* on one side and in English on the other.

"*Hajime mashite,*" Bond said. She laughed and repeated the phrase. They were pleased to meet each other, and shook hands.

"You have your luggage? Let's collect your handgun over here," she said. "You do understand that you cannot use it except in a case of extreme emergency."

She led him to the Customs officer and spoke some rapid Japanese that made Bond realise how out of practice he was. He hadn't understood a word she had said. The officer bowed to Bond and said something equally fast, then went and fetched a canvas bag with the airline logo on it. Bond had to sign some official papers to be able to carry his gun in the country and then they were ready.

Reiko had brought a small Honda Life that she had left in the car park. Looking at the way the Japanese utilised space, Bond was amazed that they could design a world to live in that was like the way they made electronics—compact and neat. The cars were created specifically for a society that lived in a very small, crowded space. The Honda Life was one of those tall, cube-like cars, but it appeared highly efficient. The Japanese concept of car parks was just as unique. Their philosophy of trying to put as many things as possible into the tiniest conceivable space certainly applied in these locations.

They left Narita Airport and embarked on the one-hour journey to the sprawling city of Tokyo. At mid-day, traffic was heavy as it flowed along the major arteries. Once again, the city's immense proportions bombarded Bond. There were sounds and sights and smells that attacked the senses from every direction. Even more so than in other major cities of the world—London, New York, Paris—Tokyo was bursting with energy. Bond could feel it in the air here much more intensely than he could elsewhere. The people of Tokyo *worked*, and they worked long hours. The city was a constant hustle and bustle, it never slept and the lights were always bright. It all came back to Bond: how Tokyo was a megalopolis, in reality several smaller cities connected by Japan Rail's Yamanote commuter train loop. Each of these smaller cities had its own distinct character: the Ginza was the elite shopping area, the equivalent of New York's Fifth Avenue; Shinjuku was ultramodern, with towering skyscrapers and endless department stores; Akihabara was known for electronics, and Ueno as a hip older section of the city.

"Tanaka-san is waiting for you," Reiko said. "I will take you to meet him first."

"Thank you."

"He has invited you to his home where you can relax and talk for the rest of the day. He knows that you are probably tired after the long flight."

"I'm all right, but that's very kind of him. Thank you."

"I will take your luggage and check you in at your hotel, is that all right?"

"You don't have to do that."

"It is my pleasure, Mister Bond."

"Tiger calls me Bondo-san. Please, call me James."

"James?" She smiled, saying it a few times to herself as if to see if she liked the sound of it. "All right, I will call you James. James-san. I like it."

"Your English is very good," Bond said.

"Thank you, but no it isn't. I mix it up a lot. Especially when I write it."

"Your pronunciation sounds American."

"Could be. I studied the language in America. Although we have ten years of English in our public school system, it is impossible to learn to speak it well within Japanese education. You really have to go to America or England. My parents sent me to San Francisco to a private high school." She looked at him and smiled.

"Reiko is a nice name."

"It's very common in Japan. The way of writing 'Reiko' means 'a polite or well-mannered girl,' which my parents wished me to become when I was born. Well, I am not sure if my parents are so proud of me lately . . ." She giggled.

"How long have you been with the service? Are you in Tiger's outfit? The Koan-Chosa-Cho?"

"Yes, I am special agent. I mostly work abroad, but I am to remain in Japan for the G8 summit conference. I understand you will be attending?"

"Yes."

"That pleases me. We shall see a lot of each other in the next several days," she said brightly. She gave him a sideways glance through her glasses that possibly held more meaning. Was she flirting with him?

She drove fast and with skill, skirting off the expressway and into

Shibuya. She navigated corners and intersections with the fervour of
a race-car driver until she finally pulled over near a JR rail station.

"Do you see that statue of the dog?" Reiko asked, pointing. Bond
looked and indeed saw a brown statue of an alert, sitting Akita. It was
erected on the little square outside the station. Masses of people were
going in and out of the building.

"Yes."

"That's Hachiko. Everyone meets in front of Hachiko."

"Do they?"

"Tanaka-san will meet you there in a few minutes. I will see you
later, James-san."

"I look forward to it," Bond said. He got out of the car and stood
amongst the swarm of people. He had once heard a friend refer to the
Japanese as "designer humans." They were all so attractive: the
women, the young girls, the men, the teenagers, the children.
Everyone seemed young. School-age children were just being let out
for the day. Young "salarymen" and "office ladies" were going to and
fro. A group of tourists all wore T-shirts that proclaimed, "Yes,
Tokyo!" This was Shibuya, the young person's celebration of capitalism. It was not the superchic Ginza, nor was it the techno-pop
Shinjuku. It was simply a fashionable place where a lot of young
people came to shop, work and have a good time.

Bond approached the statue and stood beside it. "Hachiko" was
sitting on a large stone cube.

"He was a very loyal dog." It was a voice that Bond would know
anywhere. He turned and there he was, appearing out of the throngs of
people. One second earlier and he hadn't been there, the next he was.

"Tiger," Bond said warmly.

"Bondo-san."

The two men embraced like brothers. When they parted, Tiger
said, "Welcome to Japan, Mister Bond."

Bond smiled. "It's good to see you again, Tiger."

"And you as well."

He looked thinner. That was the first thing that struck Bond. And
he looked tired. But he was still the same man with the glowing

almond eyes and smiling brown face. He was dressed casually, as if he lived in the neighbourhood and had just gone out to the shops.

"How are you, Tiger?"

"I am fine. Come, let us walk, and I shall tell you," he gestured. "But first let me tell you about this faithful dog, Hachiko."

"By all means."

"In the nineteen-twenties, a university professor living in this area kept an Akita dog. Every morning and evening this dog would come to the station to see off or meet his master. Even after the master's death in 1925, Hachiko continued to come to Shibuya Station for eleven years to wait for a master who would never return. Isn't that admirable? The Japanese treasure loyalty. Come, we shall walk. Are you not too tired?"

"I feel fine," Bond said. "I slept a little on the plane."

"Good. We will go to one of my private residences. It's in Yoyogi Park. We shall spend the rest of the day there. We can brief each other and eat an early dinner. Then you will be taken to your hotel for a good sleep. Tomorrow we begin. All right?"

"You're the boss, Tiger," Bond said.

They crossed the busy intersection when the light indicated that they could do so. Bond heard the sound of a bird chirping.

"That's the audio signal to alert blind people that they can cross the street," Tiger explained.

The two men walked up a street and then turned towards the block of Parco department stores.

"I walk everywhere now, it's for my health," Tiger said. "I am about to tell you something that many people do not know. I am no longer head of the Koan-Chosa-Cho. I have given up the position to my successor, Nakayama. He is looking forward to meeting you. You see, Bondo-san, I had a heart attack not long ago."

It was not easy for Bond to see weakness in men he respected but he looked with sympathy at his old friend.

"What happened?"

"They cut me open, they operated. Triple bypass. So, you see, I had to step back a little. I still work for the service, and I retain authority.

But I suppose you could say that I enjoy the 'street beat' now because my doctor told me I should walk a lot. I still have complete access to the service's facilities and work as a special advisor on just about everything."

"It sounds to me as if you're really still in charge."

"Only in the background. I pull strings. Much like the ancient feudal lords, the *daimyo,* who when they retired would shave their heads and join the priesthood, but in fact they gave orders from the background and still had much power."

"I had no idea, Tiger."

"No one does. That's still classified information. We don't want our enemies to know that I've retired yet, for security reasons."

"I understand."

They walked along the quiet and peaceful path. The sun was bright and the day was warm. Bond enjoyed the stroll past the gnarled cherry trees, the blossoms of which had disappeared for the year. They would return the following spring, but for now, only the twisted trees remained.

A swarm of schoolgirls walked past them. Bond observed that the plaid skirts of their school uniforms were daringly high. The girls were also wearing their bulky white knee socks bunched down around their ankles. Tiger noticed Bond looking at them and said "Those are our *ko-gyaru,* or 'ko-gals.' At school they wear the skirts properly, just above the knees, and their socks all the way up their legs. As soon as they leave the school, they roll up the skirts and wear them short, and they pull down their socks. All to show off their pretty legs. You like?"

"Too young for me," Bond said, shaking his head.

Tiger laughed. "You look good, Bondo-san. Are you happy?"

"As happy as a civil servant can be, Tiger."

They approached the Meiji Jinju, the famous Shinto shrine that attracted over two million people on one New Year's Day in the 1980s. It was originally built in 1920 but it had to be reconstructed after the bombing of Tokyo during the war.

"Do you mind if we go into the shrine for a moment?" Tiger asked.

"Not at all," Bond said.

They went through the huge wooden *Torii*, the archway that is the symbol of a Shinto shrine. The gate represents the division between the everyday world and the divine world.

Bond followed Tiger to the small pavilion where visitors purified their hands before entering the main courtyard of the shrine. Tiger took the wooden ladle and poured water over one hand and then the other. He took a drink, swished it around in his mouth and spat it out. Then he allowed water from the ladle to pour down the handle, cleansing where he had touched it. Bond took a ladle and followed suit.

They went inside the courtyard. The main sanctuary was built in the Nagaré-zukuri style of architecture. The corners of its green roof sloped out and upward. Several *miko,* the young female assistants to the priests, ran stalls along the sides of the courtyard that sold souvenirs and good luck charms. Bond inspected them and saw that there were talismans for good health, for scholarship, for love and even one for traffic safety.

Bond turned and saw Tiger tossing a coin into a collection box. Tiger bowed his head twice, clapped his hands twice, and bowed once again. After a moment he returned to Bond and said, "I am finished. Do you care to pray before we leave, Bondo-san?"

"That's all right, Tiger," Bond said. "The gods don't have much use for me."

Tiger shook his head as they left the grounds. "I know that you have a spiritual side, Bondo-san. We all do. A man finds it when he is ready. You just haven't found yours yet."

"Some don't find it until the day they die, Tiger," Bond said.

They walked north through the park toward Shinjuku until Tiger went off the main path and stepped over a chain and a sign with the words "Private—Keep Out" in English and Japanese. Bond followed him down a smaller path through the tall trees until they came to what appeared to be an ordinary garden shed. Tiger pulled a key from his pocket and unlocked the door. He held it open and Bond went inside.

It *was* a tool shed. The place was stocked with park maintenance equipment. One corner of the room was empty and had a metal floor.

Tiger shut the door and locked it from the inside. He led Bond to the metal floor and pressed a button. The floor began to descend to another level.

Bond couldn't help but laugh. "Tiger, what are you doing with a residence in Yoyogi Park?"

"I have several residences around the country, Bondo-san. You knew that. This is one that the government owns. It was built inside a natural cave. There is even a stream that flows nearby. I will have to move out eventually. It is completely underground, so I do not spend too much time here. It is only, how do you say, an 'oasis?'"

They walked down a stone corridor to a metal door. Tiger pushed another button and it slid open, revealing a beautifully furnished Japanese home. Bond removed his shoes as he stepped up onto the *tatami,* admiring the *tokonoma* and the welcome sight of the short table, the legless chairs and what would probably be green tea.

Four lovely women in kimonos were waiting for them.

"*Irrashaimase!*" they greeted the men in unison, then they bowed.

SIX

BRIEFING BELOW GROUND

"Would you prefer cold sake or warm sake?" Tiger asked.

"I'll leave that decision to you," Bond said, diplomatically.

Tiger barked some quick Japanese to one of the women, who bowed and left the room.

"Please sit," he said to Bond, and they took places on either side of the low table. "It is so good to see you again, Bondo-san. It has been too long."

The woman entered the room on her knees, bowed, then stood and brought two *tokkuri*—small flasks of warm sake—to the table. She placed a small flat cup, a *choko*, in front of each man. Two other women knelt beside the men; their sole purpose was to pour sake into the *choko* when the cups were empty.

"*Kampai,*" Tiger said, lifting the drink.

"Cheers," Bond said, doing the same, and then they drank. The sake was warm and not too dry.

There was a small package on the table in front of Bond. Tiger gestured to it and said, "That is something you may find useful during your stay in Japan. Please open it."

"Gifts, Tiger?" Bond raised an eyebrow in surprise.

"Please."

Bond opened it and found a DoCoMo mobile phone.

"My personal number is programmed into it. Whenever you need to reach me, punch 'memory' and the number seven. There is also a homing device inside. We'll always know where you are as long as you carry it."

"Thank you, Tiger," Bond said, admiring the compact apparatus. "They make them so small in this country."

"It's a small country, Bondo-san."

Bond put it in his pocket. "So what's the score, Tiger? What can you tell me about the summit conference? You've had some threats?"

"Nothing we can corroborate. Some of the Japanese nationalists are using their usual rhetoric about us co-operating with the West. Some violence was threatened. We thought it best that each nation brought their best people. That means you, Bondo-san."

"I'm flattered. Now what about this McMahon business?"

Tiger sucked in air through his teeth. Bond noted that the Japanese had a way of doing that before delivering bad news or replying in a negative manner. It was a way of softening what they had to say. Other times they might inhale through their teeth and then say, "Saaaa. . . ."

Tiger reflected a moment, then said, "I am afraid that this McMahon business, as you call it, is mixed up with the business of the *sono-suji.*"

"The what?"

"The 'people in *that* world,' or the 'people in *that* business.' The *Boryoku-dan.*"

"The yakuza?"

"Yes, although in law enforcement agencies today, we do not call them that. It's too nice a name for them. We call them *Boryoku-dan,* which literally means 'crime organisation' or 'violent mob.' However, old habits die hard. I still refer to them as yakuza. Ironically, they call themselves *gokudoh,* which means a man who has mastered the way of life."

"You must tell me more."

"I will. But please, let us first enjoy the delicious *kaiseki* meal that my chef has prepared for us."

They didn't talk about business during dinner. Instead, they each talked about their lives, as old friends, catching up after a long time.

The women began to bring in the first of several courses of a traditional *kaiseki* meal, the pinnacle of Japanese cuisine. Bond knew that it was a great honour to be provided such a feast. *Kaiseki* is served in several small courses, giving one the opportunity to admire the plates and bowls which are carefully chosen to complement the food, the region and the relevant season. The ingredients, preparation, setting and presentation are the most important aspects of *kaiseki*, not the food itself.

The first course was a small bowl of clear soup. Inside was a starshaped cake of green tofu. Next was a bowl of warm soup containing a baby bamboo shoot and some kind of green jelly in the shape of a cube that Bond couldn't identify. A small square tray was placed in front of him for the third course. It held an arrangement of dainty titbits that had been arranged like a work of art. Bond didn't like eating raw food, and found some of the items in *kaiseki* difficult to cope with. He did his best, though. Sashimi was next, followed by a serving of finely minced Daikon radish and fish that was grilled on a tiny charcoal cooker sitting on the table. A dish of boiled fish, vegetables and other ingredients, cooked in soy sauce and sweet rice wine with sugar, came next. Another course contained steamed egg, vegetables, fish and meat. After three more courses of varying delights, rice, miso soup and pickles were served to round off the meal. The entire dinner took nearly two hours.

"How do you feel now, Bondo-san? Tired?" Tiger asked.

"No, just excruciatingly relaxed."

Tiger laughed and said, "It is impolite to fall asleep when someone is talking to you, Bondo-san."

"So, Tiger, you've fed me and you've got me drunk, now will you tell me what the hell this case is about?"

"Certainly. How much do you know about yakuza, Bondo-san?"

Bond shrugged. "What all of us know. They're a highly organised mafia-like group of criminals. A lot like the Chinese Triads. They have powerful right wing support and they operate vast syndicates with interests in everything from guns to property. Many of their businesses are completely legitimate. They are a widely tolerated component of Japanese society. Am I right?"

Tiger sighed. "You are very right, Bondo-san. And you are wondering why they are tolerated so. You see, many yakuza see themselves as custodians of honour and chivalry, traditional values that have all but vanished in modern day Japan. The country's ultra-nationalist right—which also looks for a return to 'traditional values'—enjoys yakuza support. In the ancient days, the yakuza began as street traders and gamblers. They eventually organised into gangs and while they developed their criminal activities, they insinuated themselves into business society. Many companies, many *successful* companies, have ties to the yakuza. It is a fact of life in Japan and there is not much that can be done to change it."

"I wasn't aware that murder and extortion had been added to the list of essential qualities for honour and chivalry," Bond said.

"I know, I am fully aware of the irony, too," Tiger said. "I have no respect for these people, the *sono-suji*. The law enforcement agencies try to arrest them when they can and when they can charge them with something that will stick. But they are very clever, some of these yakuza, Bondo-san. They are so accustomed to being an accepted part of society that the big ones now all have offices. Right in the open. The one we are concerned about in this case is the Ryujin-kai. They are based in Sapporo, up north on the island of Hokkaido. They used to be based in Tokyo, but they moved a little less than ten years ago. Sapporo is a busy yakuza centre. The town attracts Russian tourists, and it's a fairly large black market trading post. The leader of the Ryujin-kai is a man named Yasutake Tsukamoto. They call their leader the *kaicho* or *oyabun*. The members are his 'children,' or *wakashu*. Higher-ranking children are called *shatei*, or 'younger brother.' Each yakuza is broken down into smaller gangs, each with their own *kaicho*, but they all report up the chain to the main boss."

"Go on."

"Tsukamoto is in his late fifties. Wealthy. In the chemical engineering business. He is also on the board of directors of a company called Yonai Enterprises, do you know it?"

Bond nearly choked on a sip of sake. "My God, Tiger, that was Goro Yoshida's company, wasn't it?"

"Yes, it was. He sold it before he disappeared. Now it is run by others."

"What do they do?"

"It's a conglomerate, mostly in the chemical engineering field. They have wanted to acquire CureLab Inc. for a long time.

"CureLab, as you know, is known as a successful pharmaceutical firm. It was once called Fujimoto Lab Inc., and was owned by Hideo Fujimoto. When he died ownership went to his daughter Junko, who was married to Peter McMahon. McMahon was not well liked in Japan, Bondo-san. I realise that he is a fellow countryman of yours, but he did not play the business game fairly, at least by Japanese standards. We are only just beginning to learn things about him."

"What do you mean?"

"Only that some of his employees said that he was very ruthless in his business dealings."

"Interesting."

"At any rate, it is no secret that Yonai Enterprises made a very good offer to McMahon to buy CureLab. McMahon refused to sell, of course. This was a few months ago."

"What makes CureLab so attractive to them?" Bond asked.

"CureLab's main business is drug manufacturing, but recently they have made strides in the medical community with the study of diseases and the discovery of cures. They are especially interested in what you might call 'exotic' Asian diseases; malaria, yellow fever and the like."

"And you think Yonai Enterprises had the yakuza assassinate McMahon and his family? Wipe out the entire clan at once so that they could take over the company?"

"It's what I think, but I am having difficulty convincing anyone at my firm that that is what happened. If it was an assassination, I still am not sure how it was accomplished. The police do have on record a report of alleged threats made to McMahon by the Ryujin-kai. The police even advised that he should have extra protection for a while, but McMahon refused their help."

"Is it possible that Goro Yoshida is involved? Does anyone know where he is?"

Tiger looked to the ceiling as if hoping for divine intervention. "No one knows, but we suspect he's hiding in Russia, possibly the Northern Territories. It is quite possible that Yoshida keeps contact with the Ryujin-kai. He was a member for a very long time."

"Are there any other McMahon family members around? On the Fujimoto side?"

"Yes. Hideo Fujimoto had a younger brother, Shinji Fujimoto. He is currently vice president of CureLab."

"Next in line for ownership of the company?"

"Perhaps."

"What do you know about him?"

"Shinji Fujimoto has monsters in his wardrobe."

"Excuse me?" Bond asked.

"How do you say it? 'Monsters in the wardrobe?' "

"Oh, you mean 'skeletons in his closet.' He has secrets."

"Yes, that is what I meant. I apologise. I have not spoken English in some time."

"We can switch to Japanese if you like, but I'm finding that my Japanese isn't as good as I thought it would be."

"No, I would like the practice, Bondo-san," Tiger said. "Shinji Fujimoto is a puzzle. He is in his sixties now, not in very good health. He has always had income tax problems, a financial scandal or two. So far, though, he seems clean as far as the yakuza are concerned."

"Is he the sort of man who would kill his niece and her family?"

"I don't think so, no. However, as you imply, he has much to gain by their deaths. I will be interested in your opinion of him. You will meet him tomorrow. We have arranged for a car to take us to Saitama, where the McMahon family lived. He is to meet us there."

"Have you located the youngest daughter? Mayumi?"

Tiger took another sharp intake of breath. "*Saaaaa* . . . no,

Bondo-san. That is difficult, but we have a lead. You see, Mayumi apparently ran away from home at the age of sixteen. She is twenty now. She has not seen her parents or her sisters for four years."

"Do we know why she ran away?" Bond asked. He picked up the girl's photo from a spread that Tiger had displayed on the table.

"She is very beautiful, is she not?" Tiger asked.

"Yes indeed."

"Mayumi McMahon was a very rebellious child. She got in with the wrong crowd, got into trouble. When she was fourteen, she got a boyfriend in the *bosozoku*."

"What's that?"

"Teenager motorcycle gangs. Juvenile delinquents who ride around on motorbikes looking for trouble. They are a prime recruiting ground for the yakuza."

"What's the boy's name?"

"Kenji Umeki. He is, as they say, a 'piece of work.' He has been arrested for a number of petty offences, once for assault, but he never served much time. He's at the age where the yakuza had better take him soon or he will end up riding a motorcycle forever or end up dead. It is surprising that he has lasted this long, with those gangs always trying to kill each other."

"I take it that her parents didn't exactly welcome him into the home with open arms."

"No, and in fact they had huge, terrible fights with the girl. Her great uncle told us that this went on for two years, and finally, at the age of sixteen, she just left with her boyfriend. She lived with him here in Tokyo. At any rate, we happen to know Kenji Umeki's older cousin, a fellow by the name of Takuya Abo. He used to be in the *bosozoku* until he was badly injured in a gun battle with police. He served three years in prison, got out and now he's straight. Today he works at the Tsukiji Fish Market. Very few people can walk away from the gangs but Abo did it. So, after the deaths of the McMahons, the authorities went to Takuya Abo in an effort to find Umeki with the hope that he knew where the girl was. Abo has told us that he would try and get a message to his cousin but it has been four days."

"Did Abo know anything about the girl?"

"He said that according to Umeki, she had left him two years ago and went north, most probably to Sapporo. He told police that she accompanied some high-ranking yakuza and that she is now probably the girlfriend of one of them."

"I'd like to meet Abo," Bond said.

"It will be arranged."

"So it's possible that Mayumi McMahon doesn't know that her parents are dead."

"If she has not read the newspapers or seen the television, then yes, it is quite possible."

"What have your pathologists learned about the disease that killed the McMahons?"

"I will show you the post-mortem reports. It was an unknown virus, something similar to West Nile disease, only many times more powerful and fast acting."

"That's what they said about the daughter who died on the flight to England. I hope the bodies haven't been cremated yet?"

Again, Tiger inhaled through his teeth. "I am sorry, Bondo-san, but last night something happened. Very curious. And suspicious. There was a fire at the morgue where the McMahons' bodies were being kept. Everything was destroyed. Not only their bodies but many others."

"Arson?"

"That's what it looks like. Not only that, but the tissue and fluid samples that were taken from the bodies during the postmortem— they have mysteriously disappeared as well."

"Well, I have a story for you too. The night before my flight I went to see Kyoko McMahon's body at a mortuary near Heathrow. While I was there, three yakuza hoodlums were caught trying to steal her body. One was killed, one got away, and one was arrested. That one's not talking, either. All the police know was that they had ties to the London-based branches of the yakuza. There are several in England. Now why would anyone want to take her body?"

"Maybe they wanted to do the same thing as they did here? They wanted to destroy the body. Perhaps they thought it would be easier to take the body and destroy it rather than burn up your morgue. I have no idea."

"All right, so we have some corpses of people who died of a mysterious, unknown virus that they could have been deliberately infected with. Then after they are dead, the bodies are obliterated. Why?"

"To get rid of evidence, perhaps?"

"Or . . ." Bond thought for a moment. "What if whoever did this didn't want us studying that virus. They don't want us to find a cure."

"That is good thinking, Bondo-san."

"Luckily for us, we still *have* Kyoko McMahon's tissue and fluid samples in England, as far as I know."

Tiger gestured for Bond to join him on reclining chairs at one end of the room. There, two young women were waiting to wash and massage their feet.

Bond lay back and allowed the girl to work his pressure points. After a moment of bliss, he asked, "Tiger, do you have a mosquito problem in Japan?"

Tiger stared at Bond and then slowly smiled. "You are reading my mind, Bondo-san. How did you know about the mosquitoes?"

"Kyoko had bites all over her, but the pathologist didn't think she got the virus from them."

"Our bodies had mosquito bites, too. The police report mentions that a few dead mosquitoes were seen in the McMahon home the day that the bodies were found. The crime scene squad probably didn't think anything of it. We sometimes have mosquitoes pretty bad in the summer months. It's all the water in our gardens, you see. Unfortunately, the investigators didn't think to bring any of the dead mosquitoes back to the lab, and now . . . we cannot find any more."

"The yakuza couldn't be sophisticated enough to create designer viruses and find a way to distribute them, could they?" Bond asked.

"It is not impossible," Tiger said. "And CureLab has the means to do it. They do virus research. There is an interesting side story to that which may have some bearing. A young molecular biologist by the name of Fujio Aida used to work for CureLab until a few months ago.

He was touted as being a genius, a man who could manipulate the structure of viruses. CureLab had employed him to create cures for certain diseases."

"He *used* to work for CureLab?"

"Right. Six months ago, Aida was accused of industrial espionage, or rather, stealing trade secrets from CureLab. He was dismissed from the company in a messy case that actually made the newspapers. After it was announced that he had been fired, he simply disappeared. Vanished. No one knows what happened to him."

"Do you think he was killed?"

Tiger shrugged. "Possibly, but why? I have left the details and a photo of him in the packet of material I have for you. You can study it at your leisure. It also contains files on Tsukamoto and other characters who may have a bearing on this case, as well the relevant McMahon crime scene documents."

"Thanks. You say that Yonai Enterprises is located in Sapporo?"

"Yes."

"I've never been that far north in Japan," Bond hinted.

"A trip has been arranged. But first you will spend a few days with us here in Tokyo. Tomorrow you'll see the McMahon home. You can have access to anyone at CureLab Inc. We will try to locate that boy, Umeki. There are plenty of things to do here before you go to Sapporo."

After a moment of quiet contentment, Bond asked, "And the girl who picked me up at the airport . . . Reiko?"

"Miss Tamura, yes, very able bodied. Very smart girl. She is one of the rare persons who pass our National Official Exams for entering the ministries and therefore never graduated from Tokyo University."

" 'Never graduated' is a distinction?" Bond asked.

"If you are in a top university in the first place, you are a very smart person already. The National Official Exams are given before the university graduation exams. If someone passes the National Official Exams, they do not have to take the graduation exams. They are allowed to walk away from the university and go right into the Ministry of Foreign Affairs. There is great status to be able to say you passed the official exam and never graduated from a top university."

The masseuses finished and the men savoured a few more moments of quiet comfort before they finally stood.

"As much as I hate to mention it, Bondo-san," Tiger said, "it is late. You are tired and need to be refreshed. My assistant will take you to your hotel. Everything has been done for you, just pick up your key at the desk. I will see you tomorrow morning."

Tanaka gave Bond the folder full of various reports and photographs. Bond thanked him, they embraced again, and then Tanaka walked Bond up through the complex, out of the park and to the waiting car, a black Toyota Majesta. The men said good night, and Bond was spirited away.

Night had fallen, and Tokyo was ablaze with life. The neon was blinding, the billboards were bright and colourful, the traffic was still dense and the noise and clamour bombarded the senses.

It was a mesmerising spectacle, but Bond couldn't wait to fall into bed.

SCENE OF A CRIME?

"WHILE WE WERE GETTING DRUNK LAST NIGHT, BONDO-SAN, MY STAFF heard from the old boyfriend, Kenji Umeki," Tiger said as they rode north-west out of Tokyo to Saitama through a vast network of suburbs that seemed to go on forever. "His cousin found him for us. We're going to talk to him later this afternoon in Shinjuku. He says that he knows where Mayumi McMahon is. He wants 100,000 yen for the information."

"Are you going to pay him?"

"I think yes, Bondo-san. The question is whether or not we can trust him to tell us the truth."

"Is he connected with the Ryujin-kai?"

"Yes. His motorcycle gang is called Route 66. The Route 66 work for them sometimes, I believe. Miss Tamura will know more about that. We will see her this afternoon."

Bond settled back and looked out the window. The roads were jammed with traffic, the trains sped along the tracks taking passengers from one end of the isles to the other, and everywhere one looked there were people. Here in Japan, he couldn't help but stand out in a crowd.

The advantage was that the Japanese tended to be extremely tolerant of any lack of etiquette that a *gaijin* might have. If the foreigner forgot to remove shoes before stepping up from the *genkan,* or entrance hall, into a house, the Japanese simply shook their head, rolled their eyes and muttered, *"Gaijin . . ."*

After travelling for an hour, the Majesta's driver brought Tiger and Bond to a pretty street that jutted off from a small park. Bare cherry trees were in abundance, but more impressive were the three large houses that occupied the land.

The McMahons owned the middle one. It was a two-storey mansion that was a unique mix of Japanese and Western styles of architectures. The interior was mostly Japanese with *tatami, fusuma* and *shoji.* Scattered through the rooms, though, were pieces of Western furniture: a dining table, chairs, a sofa, china cabinets and bookshelves.

Two police officers, introduced as Detectives Gunji and Sugahara, were waiting inside. They greeted Tiger as if they had known him for years, then they guardedly presented their business cards to Bond, bowed and shook his hand.

Another man moved forward from the middle of the living room. He had white hair and glasses and appeared to be in his sixties. He was wearing a jacket and tie and seemed to be very nervous.

Tanaka introduced him as Shinji Fujimoto, vice president of CureLab Inc. Fujimoto bowed and presented his *meishi* to Bond, and Bond did likewise. The man knew little English, so Bond attempted to converse with him in Japanese.

"My condolences for your loss," Bond said.

Fujimoto closed his eyes and nodded. "I appreciate your words. I have been full of grief. Thank you for coming all this way to find out what happened to my niece and her family."

The man indeed looked as if he were under a lot of strain. His eyes were bloodshot and his face was puffy. He wasn't getting much sleep and was probably drinking too much.

"Why don't you have a seat, Fujimoto-san," Bond said. "I'm going to have a look around the house and then we'll talk, all right?"

Fujimoto nodded, then reached for a glass of something that he had been nursing.

The two police detectives took Bond and Tanaka on a tour of the house, pointing out exactly where each body was found and what its condition was. Peter McMahon and his wife had been in the master bedroom, lying on the futon together. They speculated that the couple had felt ill, gone to lie down and died there on the bed. The daughter Shizuka was in the bathroom, having collapsed on the floor.

As they went through the home, Bond noted the abundance of plants that populated the place. There were tall palms in the living room, while the bedrooms had smaller decorations such as *ikebana* flower arrangements.

"Every vase and pot was examined, Bondo-san," Tiger said. "Nothing out of the ordinary was found."

Bond slid open a *fusuma* that led to a respectably large garden.

"It's a *Tsukiyama*-style garden," Tiger said. "It is arranged to show nature in miniature, with hills, ponds and streams." Bond could see that the landscaping featured a pond with stones serving as a walkway to a teahouse on the other side of the garden. Plants were plentiful here, too, and there were a number of mosquitoes buzzing near the water.

"Here's your mosquito population," Bond said.

"Ordinary mosquitoes, Bondo-san," Tiger said. "We have already checked. Unfortunately, in this season and with this much standing water about, they will breed easily."

"Can they get inside the house?"

Tiger shrugged. "I suppose if you leave the *fusuma* open, as you are doing!"

Bond nodded and slid it closed. "That might explain all the mosquito bites on the bodies. We'll have to think about alternative ways the virus could have been administered."

One of the detectives spoke rapidly to Tanaka, too fast for Bond to understand. Tiger realised this and translated. "He says that they are not treating this case as homicide. They have no evidence that it was so. The family simply got sick and died."

Bond said, "Tell him that until he can convince me otherwise, I'm not ruling anything out."

They continued to go through the house. Bond examined the

screens in each room, looking for an opening. As they came back into the central hallway that led back into the living room, Bond noticed a small electric-powered bonsai waterfall-fountain on a table. It was about two and a half feet high and a foot and a half wide and it was beautifully sculpted out of porous granite. The bonsai grew out of the top and an aquarium pump kept the water recycling continuously through the fountain, providing the constant sound of running water. At the moment, the motor was turned off. Bond looked inside it and saw that there was still water in the basin. He reached behind the contraption and found the switch. He turned it on, but nothing happened.

"That was a birthday gift for my niece," Shinji Fujimoto said. He had walked into the hallway behind them. "I delivered it myself a little over a week ago. When we plugged it in and turned it on, it wouldn't work. It was faulty. It made me very angry. I had promised to replace it but never found the time. But now, of course . . ."

Bond unplugged the device and said to Tanaka, "Have it analysed. Take it apart."

Tiger nodded and barked an order to one of the detectives. He proceeded to pick up the fountain, and Bond said, "Don't spill any of the water. Whatever is in there should be looked at." The man said, *"Hai!"*

Bond turned to Fujimoto and said, "Let's go back in the other room and talk, shall we?"

Fujimoto nodded. The men went and sat down on cushions around the table.

"Fujimoto-san, my government has asked me to find out what happened to your niece and her family. I am also supposed to try to locate your great niece. I know that you have answered many questions that the police have asked you, and that my colleague Tanaka-san has asked you, but I need to ask them as well. Is there anything that you can tell me about CureLab that might have a bearing on the case? Did Peter McMahon have any enemies?"

"He had many enemies," Fujimoto said with a sigh. "McMahon-san was a very good businessman. One goes hand in hand."

"Can you give me an example of what you mean?"

Fujimoto thought a moment. "About three years ago, there was a Japanese company that sold digital microscopes. They were based in Tokyo. McMahon-san had wooed them, making them think that he was going to buy a great number of them. It would have been a hundred million yen contract. At the last minute, before the sale, McMahon-san met with some Swiss manufacturers of the same type of product. He got a better deal, cancelled the order with the Japanese company and bought the Swiss models. And while you might say it was simply a business arrangement—he had found a less expensive product—it was dishonourable to cancel the contract he had already made with the Japanese firm. He was criticised in the business community for this."

"How did the business community feel about a British citizen running a Japanese company?"

Fujimoto sucked in air through his teeth. "Difficult to say. I think he was respected because he was good at his job. But he was resented for being a *gaijin*. You see, in Japan, there are clearly defined, invisible circles of influence in the business world. If you work for one company, then that is your inner circle. Your colleagues are also your friends. You go out drinking with them every evening. You develop a second family with them. Say, for instance, you accept a job at another company. You cannot then socialise with your old friends at the old company. You are now out of that circle. It would not be appropriate. I think Tanaka-san would agree with me that in our world, these circles of influence are very important. You stay within your circle, whatever that place is in society. You might be invited to visit another circle, you might be a guest and be entertained by the members of another circle, for business purposes, but you will never be a part *of* that circle. Do you understand what I mean?"

"I think so."

"McMahon-san was a man who ignored the boundaries of these circles. He stepped over the lines many times. He played the game his way."

Bond studied the man's face. Fujimoto's eyes were sincere, but

Bond could detect a faint hint of animosity. "What is your function as vice president?" he asked.

"I am in charge of administrative duties," he said. "I also run the research division."

"Doing what?"

"We are working on new techniques of controlling the spread of various diseases and looking for cures."

"Do you work with mosquitoes?"

Again, Fujimoto inhaled through his teeth. "Not really. We study them, of course, but only for reasons of learning how diseases are transmitted."

"When was the last time you saw your niece or any members of her family?"

Fujimoto was clearly irritated at being questioned, especially by a *gaijin*. "Like I said, I brought the bonsai waterfall over last Wednesday. A little over a week ago. Only Junko and Shizuka were here. Peter was at the office."

"Do you have any idea where Mayumi is?"

Fujimoto sucked in air through his teeth again. "*Saaa . . .* I wish to God that I did. There is no telling what kind of trouble she is in. She was always a mischievous girl. A problem child. Reckless and wild. I hope that the police will locate her soon. I am very worried about her."

"I'd like to find her, too," Bond said. "I want to ask her a few things. After all, she's the sole inheritor of the family's shares in CureLab, isn't she?"

Fujimoto nodded. "Yes, but I am sure she had nothing to do with this. My niece had not spoken to Mayumi in four years. This has caused my niece much pain. Peter too."

"What kind of relationship did they have when Mayumi was younger?"

"It seemed to be always bad. Mayumi is a very smart girl but she was not a good student in school, she rebelled at an early age. She always fought with her parents and sisters. As long as I can remember. I hate to say this now, but when she ran away from home four years ago, I told my niece that she was better off without her."

"How did your niece react to that?"

"She was very upset. She made me apologise."

Bond shifted on the cushion. "What will happen to the company now?"

"The shareholders will decide the company's fate," Fujimoto said with conviction. "If and when Mayumi is found, she will have to deal with selling her share of the stock, I suppose. She knows nothing about the company itself. I can't imagine that she would want to remain involved. Peter and Junko owned sixty per cent of the stock. I own twenty per cent, so CureLab has always been controlled by the family. The other twenty per cent is owned privately."

"Who owns the other twenty per cent?" Bond asked.

Fujimoto shrugged. "Different private individuals. I suppose I can find out and get you the names?"

Tanaka asked, "Did not Yonai attempt to buy CureLab?"

"Yes, they are our biggest rival. Yonai Enterprises has made several bids for a takeover, but Peter always refused to sell. Yonai will want to buy Mayumi's shares, and that concerns me. I would hate to see CureLab under their thumb."

"Why is that?" Bond asked.

"They use . . . questionable business practices."

"And if Mayumi can't be found? What will happen?"

Fujimoto shrugged. "As I am the only other relative and I hold a letter from Mayumi's parents giving me power of attorney to act in the event of their deaths, I suppose I will continue to run the company. The board has already voted that I will be acting president for now."

"And would you sell your stock?"

Fujimoto reached for his glass of liquor, took a sip, and began to cough violently.

"Did it go down the wrong pipe?" Tanaka asked.

Fujimoto nodded as he set down the glass and made an attempt to control his cough. He wiped his damp forehead with a handkerchief and stammered, "Excuse me. Now, what were you asking?"

"I asked if you would sell your stock," Bond repeated.

"My brother built the company from the ground, and I would not want to see it leave the family. Assuming she reappears what Mayumi decides to do with her sixty per cent will have a major impact on what happens to us in the future. If she cannot be found, then I will use the power of attorney to hold on to her stock in the family name. I do not understand why you are asking me all these questions. My niece's family is dead due to a tragic accident. Why does all this about the company concern you?"

"Fujimoto-san, we are simply trying to cover all angles," Tanaka said.

Bond thought it was time to ask the man the crucial question. "Tell me, why did your brother not leave the company to you? You were with him at the start-up. Why did he leave it to his only daughter?"

Fujimoto frowned. He didn't like that inquiry. "As my brother is no longer with us, I cannot speak for him."

Tiger's mobile rang. He answered it, spoke some quick words, and then rang off.

"That was Miss Tamura," he said. "She is in Shinjuku. It's Mayumi's old boyfriend, Umeki. He's dead. Looks like a homicide. We should go."

Fujimoto gasped. "How did it happen?"

"I do not know yet," Tiger said. He turned to Bond and said, "What did I tell you about that boy?"

Bond stood and thanked Fujimoto for his time.

"Please feel free to contact me at any time, day or night," Fujimoto said. "I would like to help with your investigation as much as possible."

Bond thanked him and said, "We'll be in touch. In the meantime if Mayumi contacts you or you are successful in reaching her, please let us know."

"I will."

They said their goodbyes, bowed, and left the house. As they got back into the Majesta, Tiger remarked, "I think I know why Hideo Fujimoto left the company to his daughter and not to his brother."

"Why is that?" Bond asked.

"Because Shinji Fujimoto is not a leader. You can see that. He was

EIGHT

YAKUZA TERRITORY

SHINJUKU IS A MASSIVE COMMERCIAL AND ENTERTAINMENT CENTRE THAT surpasses Times Square, Piccadilly, the Sunset Strip and Las Vegas. One would not have to go much further than here to find nearly everything that makes Tokyo tick. With the highest concentration of skyscrapers in Japan, the country's busiest rail station, government offices, high-class department stores, discount shopping arcades, theatres, pachinko parlours, restaurants, stand-up noodle bars, hostess clubs, strip clubs, hidden shrines and crowds upon crowds of people, Shinjuku is the place to see and be seen.

It was late afternoon when the Majesta got stuck in traffic right near the famous Studio Alta video screen. Fashion clips, information and commercials were broadcast non-stop from the large video billboard on the side of a building.

"Let's walk," Tiger said.

They got out after Tiger issued some instructions to the driver. Then he led Bond to the pavement and began to push through the mass of humanity.

"We're going to Kabuki-cho," he said. "It's still daylight now, but watch your step. This is yakuza territory."

They walked north, passing all sorts of colourful and noisy characters. Bond knew about Kabuki-cho. It was a notorious red light district, containing strip clubs, peep shows and pornography shops as well as bars, restaurants and the uniquely Japanese "love hotels." These were places where an amorous couple could rent a room for a few hours during the day to get away from the relative non-privacy they might have at home. Since families usually lived together in houses made with thin walls, couples often found it difficult to make love there. Love hotels did a booming business and were designed around themes: a fairy tale castle, a pirate lair, 1970s disco, 1950s Americana and other fantasy dreamlands. They were also completely discreet; a couple checking in never saw the staff. The exchange of money and keys was done through little windows the size of a hand. Obviously, the love hotels were popular among couples having illicit affairs.

"This place *really* comes alive at night," Tiger said.

"It's not exactly sleeping now," Bond replied, his senses overloaded.

There were signs advertising all kinds of sex for sale; one didn't need a translation to get the gist. High-pitched female voices called out invitations through distorted sound systems to enter their establishments. Rough-looking young men and women stood on the street handing out flyers. Some hawkers were aggressive, following the men for a half-block until Tanaka turned abruptly and shouted at them. One hawker wouldn't take no for an answer and kept on their heels. Finally, Tiger pulled out a badge and shoved it into the man's face. His eyes widened; he apologised profusely and bowed rapidly.

"It is not much further, Bondo-san," Tiger said. "There, I see Miss Tamura now."

A police car and motorcycle with lights flashing were parked in the middle of a small side street. Reiko, still dressed in a suit, was speaking to several uniformed officers. She saw them out of the corner of her eye and waved.

As they approached, she bowed to them. "Tanaka-san, James-san, please come this way."

She led them into an empty noodle shop. The chef, a skinny old man, was sitting at a table smoking a cigarette. He looked shaken. A woman, presumably his wife, sat with him.

"The owners of this restaurant found him in the back. Come and look," Reiko said.

She took them into the back alley where the rubbish was piled in bags and boxes. Police tape had been strung around it. Several plain clothed and uniformed officers stood taking notes and photographs.

Falling out of the heap of rubbish was the body of a young man in his twenties. He was covered in dried blood and bent at a grotesque angle. The corpse was dressed in black leather and his long mop-top haircut was dyed red.

"Kenji Umeki," Reiko said. "The detectives are still examining the crime scene, but it looks like he was killed last night. Stabbed to death and dumped here. Look—"

She bent under the tape and pointed to the dead man's hand. Bond saw that all of the fingers had been chopped off, leaving bloody stubs.

"*So desu ka,*" Tiger muttered. "He was killed by yakuza," he said to Bond. "The removal of all the fingers on the hand is a signature of the Ryujin-kai."

"Don't some of them cut their own fingers off?" Bond asked.

"Yes, but that is a penance to an *oyabun*. Something they do to make amends for a wrong that they might have committed."

"But didn't he work for the Ryujin-kai?"

"The relationship between *bosozoku* and parent yakuza are not always harmonious, Bondo-san," Reiko said.

"When did you say he contacted you for our meeting today?"

"Yesterday," Tiger replied.

"Is it just a coincidence that he was killed a few hours later?"

"You are thinking the same thing as I am, Bondo-san. Was he murdered for the information he was going to give us?"

"Perhaps his cousin, Abo, maybe he knows something," Reiko said.

"Let's talk to him," Bond said.

One of the detectives said something to Reiko and showed her a bag full of small gold-coloured, metal plates. She nodded and turned back to Bond and Tiger.

"Pachinko winnings," she said. "They give you those metal plates in exchange for the balls when you win. Then, you exchange those plates for money at an exchange shop in a different location. He had a bag with him, not worth a lot, but he might have just come from one of the parlours around here when he was killed."

"Perhaps we should visit a few of them and ask if our friend was seen," Bond suggested.

"That is police work, Bondo-san," Tiger said. "You would not enjoy it."

"What are you talking about, Tiger?" Bond said. "I'm here in your country to do police work. What else would you call it? Come on, let's take a look around. Besides, this area fascinates me. It's alive with electricity."

Tanaka's mobile rang. He answered it, *"Moshi moshi."* He listened, then spoke a few words.

"I must go to headquarters," he said. "Miss Tamura, if our British friend really wants to tour Kabuki-cho and stick his *gaijin* nose into the business of the yakuza, by all means, we should allow him to do so. But would you please accompany him and make sure that he gets into no trouble?"

"It would be my pleasure, Tanaka-san," Reiko said, bowing.

Tiger shook Bond's hand. "You will be in good company. I will speak to you later."

"Absolutely," Bond said. Tiger turned and walked back the way they had come.

"Come on, James-san," Reiko said. "Our tour of Sin City begins here."

They walked away from the crime scene and turned the corner. A placard that displayed the word "SOAP" and featured the faces of four lovely young Japanese girls stood on the middle of the pavement.

"Soaplands," Reiko said. "You know about them?"

"Only a little. Massage parlours, aren't they?"

"Much more than that," she explained. "Soaplands are the highest level of prostitution in this country. Technically, prostitution is illegal, but it's been an accepted part of our society since the beginning of time. When the Occupation outlawed the 'water trade,' as it's called, the yakuza took it over and it still thrives today. It's a wink-wink enterprise now. No one talks about it but everyone knows it's there. Supposedly you are going in to have a bath and massage, but you have sex, too."

"Why are they called soaplands?"

"I was afraid that you would ask me that. It's because they rub you down with soap. The girl uses her body to lather you up. It is very elaborate, from what I understand. Of course, I have no experience in these things!"

"Of course not!"

She laughed, perhaps to conceal her embarrassment at discussing these matters with an attractive man. Or perhaps not. Bond couldn't tell. Reiko continued, "Actually they used to be called Turkish baths, but the Turkish embassy complained about it some years ago. So the name was changed. Soaplands are very expensive. Sometimes soapland girls become very rich and marry someone of importance. Just the other day there was an article in the newspaper. One of the Diet members announced his marriage to a former soaplands girl and no one thought anything of it. The girls often marry celebrities or politicians. On one hand the girls are considered prostitutes and lower-class citizens; on the other hand they are admired and respected because to be a soapland girl you have to be the best. And usually soaplands do not take foreigners. Japanese only. There are some exceptions, if you are interested."

"No thanks."

"Oh," she said, "you don't find Japanese women attractive?"

"I didn't say that." Bond glanced at her and she smiled flirtatiously.

They passed a stand-up food stall and she asked, "Are you hungry?"

"Quite."

"Let's have some noodles."

They both ordered bowls of fresh *udon*, thick white noodles made from kneaded wheat flour. They were served in a hot broth mixed with fried soybean curd and spices such as red pepper that they could shake into the bowl according to taste. Bond found it delicious and ordered two cans of cold Kirin beer to go with the meal.

Bond noticed that the chef and another man at the stall were staring at her.

"Don't pay any attention to them," Reiko said as she slurped her soup. "Most young women are probably afraid to go to a stand-up noodle stall. It's usually for elderly salarymen. But you know what? I don't care. About four years ago I made up my mind that I wanted to eat at one of these stalls and so I did. I have ever since."

"Reiko-san," Bond began, "if the soaplands are at the top of the water trade, what is below them?"

Reiko sucked a noodle into her mouth like spaghetti. "Mmm, *gomennasai*. Well, then you have the regular massage parlours, the so-called health clubs, the strip clubs, the image clubs, hostess bars, and everything else you can imagine. The lower you go, the worse the conditions. That's where you'll find imported Thai or Korean girls, or Filipinos, brought into this country illegally and forced to work for the yakuza. They believe they are going to Japan to work in a nice job as a hostess somewhere, but they end up being enslaved."

"That happens a lot in other countries as well," Bond said.

"Yes. But never mind about all of that. How are your noodles?"

"Delicious." He pulled out a wallet but she stopped him.

"No, no, you are our guest," she said. "I will pay."

Bond thought that her formality was appealing. *"Arigato,"* he said.

"You're welcome. Come on."

They headed towards the nearest pachinko parlour, just down the street. A big business in Japan and mostly yakuza controlled, pachinko was the equivalent of Western slot machines and the parlours were similar to game arcades. The establishments were hugely popular and they were almost always crowded.

They went inside and were greeted by two thugs wearing money belts. One of them asked Reiko if she needed change but she shook her head.

The noise was worse than in the casinos of Las Vegas. A pachinko machine resembles a vertical pinball table that uses dozens of tiny metal balls. Colourful designs adorn the front, behind the glass, where the balls fall through pins. This particular parlour charged a

2,000 yen minimum to play. Coins were dropped into the slot and a mass of balls emptied into a tray at the bottom of the machine. They were then fed automatically into the machine when the player depressed a handle. The balls shot up to the top and fell down through the pins, dropping into slots that were worth points. The player could control the speed and force of the balls with a throttle knob. The skill apparently came from knowing how much speed and force to use. If the balls fell into a specific catcher, then three wheels containing numbers and pictures would spin, like on a slot machine. The goal was to finish with more balls than one started with. They could then be exchanged for prizes.

"It's gambling," Reiko said, "but not really. You can't exchange the balls for money. Gambling is illegal. You exchange them for things like cigarettes, biscuits and other prizes. But as I said earlier, you can exchange those gold plates at other places for money. More yakuza controlled business."

"Do you have Umeki's photograph?" Bond asked.

"Yes, I have it here." She pulled it out. It showed two arrest shots, full front and profile. "This was taken a year ago when he was picked up for gang fighting. Let's ask these boys if they saw him last night."

She showed one of them the photograph and spoke to him rapidly. The kid barely looked at it and shook his head. He called over his friend, who also gave it a cursory glance and shrugged.

"I don't think we will get anywhere here," she said.

"Shall we try another place?"

They left the building and walked across the street to another parlour that was multi-level. Bright neon described it as "Pachinko Heaven."

Once again, they were regarded with suspicion by the staff. One boy who had a scar on his face and three gold teeth took the photo for a closer look. Bond noticed that the first joint on the little finger of his left hand was missing. The fellow smiled and said something to Reiko. She asked him more questions but he shook his head.

After he walked away, she said to Bond, "He knew Umeki. Said that he used to come in here a lot. I asked if Umeki was in here last night and he said that he didn't know. But he said something odd."

"What's that?"

"That Umeki finally got what was coming to him. I asked him how did he know that, and he replied that the word on the street travels fast."

"Did you see his little finger?" Bond asked.

"Yes. He is definitely yakuza. Or *bosozoku,* more likely. He is young."

"Tiger said that he must have made a mistake or something for him to do that."

"That's right. The ritual cutting off of the fingers is called *yubitsume.* When one of them does something wrong, they have to do the cutting themselves. They start with the first joint of the little finger, cut it off with a sharp knife, and they give the piece of finger to the *kaicho* as an apology. If they make more mistakes, the next joint goes and so on. Sometimes we see yakuza who are missing several fingers!"

"And what we saw on Umeki? What did that signify?"

"That he had done something *very* bad. His fingers were removed by his killer or killers to make a statement."

"Come on, let's try another place."

As they left the building, the thug who had identified Umeki pulled out a mobile phone and made a quick call.

It was growing darker. Now the Kabuki-cho neon was blinding. The buildings were solid walls of illuminated *kanji, kana* and masses of bright colours that flashed and demanded attention.

A Mercedes with dark windows drove past them on the street.

"Yakuza," Reiko said. "A Mercedes is one of their status symbols."

The atmosphere in the area had changed markedly. Nightfall had brought out even more touts, hoods and riffraff. Mixed in with these picturesque characters were members of Japan's working force: the salarymen. They were still dressed in the suits they had worn all day at the office, walking in groups of three or four, and they were already beginning the evening's debauchery. By 9:00 p.m. they would be completely drunk.

"One of the products of our fierce Japanese work ethic," Reiko explained when one salaryman accidentally bumped into Bond. He apologised, slurring his speech, bowed, and walked on. "We are encouraged to work ten hours a day or more. The men especially. Then they are pressured to go out drinking with their colleagues after the day is over. They don't get home to their families until late at night. The pressures of playing the corporate game are tremendous. No wonder they all drink so much."

"And the women?"

"Women in the work force are called 'office ladies,' and they can't hope to progress in a corporation like the men do. Housewives have to put up with never seeing their husbands except on the weekends. That's family time. I only saw my father on Sundays, never during the week. It is the wife who holds the purse strings. The husband brings home the pay cheque and immediately hands it over to his wife. She then gives him an allowance and manages the household herself. I am lucky. I have a man's job. That's a different situation."

The explosive sound of a motorcycle interrupted their conversation. A black Kawasaki ZRX blasted down the street, zipping around cars until it nearly sideswiped Bond and Reiko.

"Look out!" Bond shouted, pulling Reiko out of the way just in time. They fell on the pavement but were unharmed.

The rider turned back to them and raised his middle finger. He was dressed in black leather and wore a yellow scarf to mask his face.

Bond stood and helped her up. Reiko said, "Creep. He was a Route 66—*bosozoku*—and that was no accident. They sometimes do things like that to intimidate someone. I would bet that one of the punks we have spoken to in the last couple of hours has put the word out that we are asking questions."

"I hear more bikes."

Bond was right. They could hear motorcycles revving their engines not far away.

"James-san, I think we have outstayed our welcome in Kabuki-cho. Let's go."

They started to walk fast against the flow of pedestrian traffic, back past the touts who had solicited them once already. The noise of the bikes drew closer, so Reiko grabbed Bond's hand and picked up her pace. She navigated through the crowd quickly but as soon as they got to the corner, three bikes zoomed around to face them.

The ZRX was back, and a Suzuki Inazuma and a Kawasaki Zephyr had joined it. They had four-stroke, four-cylinder engines and no fairings; what were generally called "naked" bikes. The mufflers had been cut off so that they were outrageously loud.

All three riders wore black leather. Unlike most yakuza, their black hair was long and it blew in the breeze. Their eyes bore down on them from above the yellow scarves.

"Route 66," she whispered.

She did an about face and pulled Bond with her. As they ran back the way they came, the cycles revved and two of them shot forward. Pedestrians jumped out of the way and some screamed. The Zephyr rode onto the pavement behind Bond and Reiko and increased its speed. The couple was forced to break hands as the bike sliced between them. Reiko fell against a soaplands placard and grunted. Bond reached for her hand and helped her up.

The Zephyr and the ZRX met again in front of them and this time they were obstructing traffic. A Honda Beat attempted to go around them but the biker nearest to it shouted obscenities at the driver.

Bond looked back. The Inazuma was still there, blocking that way. They were trapped.

The three bikers revved their engines and sat there menacingly.

"Reiko-san, I believe we have encountered an extreme emergency." He reached for his gun but she grabbed his arm.

"No, James-san, do not draw your weapon. They are teenagers. They are probably unarmed. Maybe they have knives, but I doubt they have guns. Let's walk calmly back the other way."

They turned and walked towards the Inazuma but the bikers continued to blast their engines. Then the ZRX burst forward violently, curved around a taxi and pulled up beside them. The rider shouted something at Reiko. Bond picked up the words "do not come back." Before the biker sped away, he noted that the kid had blue eyes and blond eyebrows.

"Come on," Reiko said, walking ahead.

"What did he say?"

"That we should get our asses out of here and never come back."

The three cycles followed them onto the street and began to ride up and down the block, back and forth.

"Good of them to take the trouble of escorting us out," Bond remarked.

They crossed at the intersection and walked into the next block. The other pedestrians seemed oblivious to what was going on, although some stopped to stare at the noisy motorcycles.

The ZRX pulled to the side of the curb behind them, then it leapt forward to sideswipe the couple. Bond quickly grabbed a soaplands placard and swung it at the biker. The wooden sign smashed into the kid, causing the bike to skid on the road several metres ahead of them until it crashed into the back of a van. The biker rolled off and then got up fairly easily. The loose scarf hung around his neck and the blue eyes and blond eyebrows seemed to glow in the neon. He strode towards Bond and unwrapped a chain from around his waist. He was ready for a fight.

Bond took a defensive stance and was prepared when the boy swung. Bond ducked as the chain cut the air a few inches above his head. By the time the thug had control of his weapon again, Bond had parleyed back. He stepped forward once again, this time swinging the chain above his head like a lasso.

"*Ki o tsukete!*" Reiko shouted as she pulled a Glock M26 out of her handbag and pointed it at the hoodlum.

The biker stopped swinging the chain.

Reiko barked more words at him and he slowly backed away. Finally, he went to his fallen bike, picked it up, mounted, and kicked the starter. The engine roared. Again, he pointed his third finger at them, then sped away.

"I take it that the situation evolved into an emergency," Bond said.

"*Shippai shita wa,*" she said, holstering her gun. "I was mistaken earlier. Besides he looked much older than a teenager, don't you think?"

"More like twenty-one, perhaps."

"I know him," she said, pulling Bond onward and putting her handgun back in her bag. "His name escapes me, but he is a well-known hoodlum. One of the *bosozoku* leaders. I can look it up at headquarters."

As the couple crossed the last intersection and walked out of Kabuki-cho the other bikers took off after their boss, making as much noise as possible.

NINE

MORNING MAYHEM

THE EFFECTS OF JET LAG NOTWITHSTANDING, BOND COULD HAVE LANGUISHED in bed as his suite in the Imperial Hotel was among the most luxurious he had experienced. Bond had the perk of staying at first-class hotels because his cover sometimes necessitated it. On occasion he had to play the part of a rich playboy businessman who was accustomed to nothing less than the best. Miss Moneypenny had booked him into the Imperial without discussion.

Bond liked hotels with unique histories. Not only was the Imperial originally built at the behest of Japan's imperial family in 1890, but it was also one of the first hotels in the country to serve pork and beef dishes in its restaurant. The first building was designed to impress powerful international guests with the level of Japan's modernisation after three centuries of isolation and it boasted the newest in western luxury. Frank Lloyd Wright designed a second incarnation of the hotel, and when it opened in 1923, it became Tokyo's social centre for both foreign residents and tourists. There was a well-known story of how, one evening in the thirties, the ultra-nationalist Black Dragon Society invaded a posh dinner dance at the hotel and with drawn, razor-sharp samurai swords began harassing the well-heeled collection of frightened foreigners. The guests were held hostage for four days until the rebels finally surrendered to the military forces outside.

The current building replaced Wright's fanciful hotel in 1970, and in 1983 the handsome thirty-one-storey Imperial Tower was added. Bond's corner suite was on the thirtieth floor of the tower and it had a spectacular view of the city on two sides.

Bond finally swung his legs out of the comfortable king-sized bed, stood and stretched. He opened the curtains and gazed out of the window.

Tokyo lay before him, a sprawling, metropolitan machine.

He and Reiko had agreed to meet early for breakfast and then she would take him to Tsukiji Fish Market for a chat with Kenji Umeki's cousin. "Dress casually," she had told him.

Bond did his morning callisthenics, showered with first hot and then cold water, shaved, and dressed in a navy blue short-sleeved polo shirt, pale khaki trousers and a linen jacket. When he was ready, he went downstairs to find Reiko Tamura waiting for him in the lobby, right on time.

She was dressed more casually than before, in a short-sleeved white blouse and vest, black Capri pants and a baseball cap. She looked years younger and the glasses made her look even more like a student.

"*Ohayo gozaimasu,* James-san," she said.

"Good morning to you, too, Reiko-san."

"Come on, let's go. It's a twenty-minute walk to the fish market. We can have breakfast there."

"All right."

They walked out of the hotel, turned toward the Ginza and headed south-east towards the water. It was a beautiful day.

"I have some news," she said. "I identified that character on the motorbike. Remember I said that I knew his face? His name is Noburo Ichihara. He is *socho* of the *bosozoku* that Kenji Umeki was in. *Socho* means leader, the same as *kaicho* or *oyabun* in the yakuza. Ichihara has been arrested three times, served some time for assault. Wears contact lenses, that's why his eyes are blue. And guess what?"

"What?"

"His *bosozoku* gang works for the Ryujin-kai branch here in Tokyo."

"Tiger told me about them. What does Ichihara do for them?"

"Well, we have evidence that links him and several of his gang to a drug bust that occurred in Kabuki-cho a few months ago. It was the Ryujin-kai that was behind the operation, importing drugs into Tokyo and shipping them north to Sapporo and then points beyond. They use the *bosozoku* as carriers sometimes."

"Interesting. And what about our dead friend Kenji Umeki?"

"Word on the street is that he was killed over some grievance between him and his gang bosses."

"Could this Ichihara character be Umeki's killer?"

"Possibly, although the finger cutting indicates that it was yakuza who did the killing. Sometimes members of a *bosozoku* have to commit a murder like that as an initiation to get into the parent yakuza. It's usually not done to one of their own members unless he had done something really bad. It is a mystery. Hopefully the cousin, Abo, will know something."

They crossed Chuo Ichiba and entered the Tsukiji Fish Market, a huge wholesale market. Most of it was laid out under a roof that ran along the dock, where fishermen delivered the early morning catch to wholesalers, who then sold the product to fish shop owners and restaurant cooks who gathered there at the crack of dawn. The big tuna auction usually occurred at around five o'clock in the morning, but there was still a lot of action going on as Bond and Reiko arrived.

The concrete floor was soaked in water and muck. Workers wore big rubber boots, some wore slickers over their torsos and they all had tools called *tekagi* that looked like gaffers' hooks—a wooden handle about a foot long, with a nasty two-pronged hook on the end for picking up fish carcasses. Rows of tables lined the interior and all manner of sea creatures from exotic corners of the Far East were displayed, raw and, in some cases, still alive. Octopus, tuna, shellfish, salmon, shrimp and the more exotic catches such as eel, squid, fugu and shark were all available. The pathways between the rows were extremely narrow, just large enough for *ta-ray*, mini-motorised trucks with steering wheels in the centre, much like forklifts, to move through.

Bond and Reiko dodged a *ta-ray* that shot past them, forcing them to squeeze against a table, front to front. Their eyes met in a moment of intimacy, but the couple pulled away from each other without saying a word.

The market was a beehive of activity. The place was utter chaos but in that uniquely Japanese way there was an efficient order to the madness. Workers shouted back and forth to their colleagues, the *ta-ray* and forklifts zipped around carrying cartons of goods, men loaded delivery vehicles with produce, areas were sprayed down with hoses to wash away the offal and vendors hawked their stuff to anyone who walked by their stalls.

The smell was particularly memorable.

Bond dodged a forklift as Reiko led him through the thicket of workers into the inner bowels of the market. They walked past a group of men using their *tekagi* hooks on the biggest tuna carcasses Bond had ever seen. The heads and tails had already been removed and the white, barrel-shaped cadavers were being tossed from man to man as if they weighed as little as a rugby ball instead of hundreds of pounds each.

Reiko led him through a maze of vendors to an area where several *ta-rays* were carrying cartons from a vendor to a delivery truck parked on the dock. She pointed at a rough-looking man in his thirties who was driving one of them.

"That's Takuya Abo," she said.

"Does he know you?"

"Yes, I've talked with him before. Sometimes we use him as an informant."

The man glanced at them as they walked towards him. She waved and he glared for a moment, then pulled the *ta-ray* over to where they were standing.

"What are you doing here?" he demanded. He wasn't happy.

"We need to speak with you," she said. "This is Commander Bondo-san from England."

"I can't talk now! Are you crazy? This is the busiest time of the day for me!" he said, irritated.

"When can we talk? It's important!"

Abo looked pained. Then, with a sullen look, he asked softly, "Is it about Kenji?"

She nodded. "I'm sorry about your cousin."

Abo inhaled loudly then nodded his head. Only then did he turn to Bond and bow slightly. He said in English, "Pleased to meet you. I am Takuya Abo."

Bond bowed and then shook his hand, which was rough and coarse. He couldn't help but notice that Abo was missing his entire little finger.

"Pleased to meet you."

Abo turned to Reiko and said, "Look, come back in a couple of hours. Go get something to eat. I can talk then."

"All right," she said. "We'll be back."

She led Bond back through the busy market until they came to an outlying area that featured a few fresh sushi restaurants in rows of one-storey barrack-like buildings.

"Let's have a sushi breakfast," she suggested.

They went into the narrow place, which was about ten feet wide, and sat at the counter with several workers, still clad in rubber boots. Reiko ordered several pieces of tuna, salmon, and fish roe for them to share, along with a *tekka-maki,* a tuna roll wrapped in seaweed cut into six portions, and a *kappa-maki,* a roll stuffed with cucumber. Bond ordered extra *wasabi* to mix with the soy sauce, as he was not fond of raw fish. But he was willing to give it a go.

"That's a very Western thing to do," Reiko said.

"I know," Bond admitted. "But I like the feeling of the *wasabi* going up the back of my nose. Opens the sinuses." He quickly changed the subject. "I noticed Abo's missing finger."

"That's how he was able to leave the gangs," she replied. "After he had been in prison for three years, he asked the leader of Route 66 to let him go straight. He was told that if he offered his finger then they would let him walk away. Abo performed *yubitsume* and gave his whole finger to the leader. He gained great face doing that. Now Abo is *katagi,* the yakuza word for a straight citizen. It means 'a person who walks in the sun,' as opposed to the yakuza, who are men of the dark."

"Is this Ichihara fellow the leader who had Abo's finger?"

"Possibly. I am not sure how long Ichihara has been leader, but that is a good assumption."

They killed a little time after breakfast strolling through the market. Bond watched her as she examined and commented on the colourful varieties of seafood. Her intelligence combined with her vitality and good looks made her extremely attractive.

When they walked out of the market and along the dock, she asked him, "Do you have a girlfriend, James-san?"

He shook his head. "No. It makes life too complicated," he said, surprising himself with the truth.

"I know what you mean," she said. "I can never keep a boyfriend longer than a couple of months. They get tired of my having to work all the time."

"Do you work out of the country?"

"Most of the time. I am here now because of the upcoming G8 conference. Otherwise, I'd probably be in Korea, China, Thailand or somewhere. Lovers won't wait. I found that out the hard way."

Bond shrugged and said, "Tangential encounters are more practical for people in our profession than they are for the rest of the population."

She glanced at him sideways and smiled seductively. "You think so?"

He wanted to kiss her but the Japanese frowned upon public displays of affection. She read his mind though.

"Go ahead, if you want," she said.

He leaned in and pressed his mouth lightly against hers. Her lips were soft and tasted a bit salty from the breakfast. She was delicious.

When their mouths separated, he continued to stare into her almond eyes.

"*Sugoi!*" she whispered. It was the Japanese equivalent of saying, "Wow." Then she smiled and said, "We had better get back to Abo."

They walked back through the market, which by noon had calmed down considerably. The vendors were still selling their wares furiously, but the loading, the unloading and the truck traffic had diminished.

Abo was sitting on his truck eating a sandwich and drinking cola, looking out over the dock and the waterway that snaked out of Tokyo to the ocean.

"Abo-san," Reiko said, "we are back. Now is a good time?"

"As good as any," he said.

"My condolences for the loss of your cousin," Bond said.

"Thank you. But Kenji was asking for trouble. It wasn't going to be long before something bad happened. I had tried to get him out of that business, but he never listened to me."

"Abo-san," Bond said, "your cousin told us that he had information pertaining to Mayumi McMahon's whereabouts. Do you know anything about this?"

The man sucked air through his teeth and said, "All that Kenji told me was that she was in Sapporo, working in the water trade."

"She's a prostitute?" Bond asked.

"Soaplands girl," Abo corrected. There was a difference, apparently.

"Do you know why the Ryujin-kai would have Umeki-san killed?"

Abo stuffed the sandwich wrapper into a paper bag and wiped his mouth with the outside of the bag. "The Ryujin-kai didn't kill my cousin."

"Oh? Who did?"

"A kappa killed him."

Reiko said, "You are not serious."

Abo shrugged.

Reiko explained. "A kappa is a mythical creature that appears in Japanese folklore. It's a type of vampire, I guess. It lives in ponds or rivers and is said to resemble a cross between a human and a turtle or a frog. They can be remorseless killers. Their heads are misshapen— their skulls have a depression in the top that holds a little water. They say that if that water spills, then the kappa will lose its powers. They supposedly have a strong sense of loyalty to anyone who does them a good turn. Spare the life of a kappa and he'll be your friend forever. And they like to eat cucumbers. One of the rolls we had for breakfast is called a *kappa-maki* because it has cucumber in it."

Bond narrowed his eyes. This was nonsense, of course, but an instinct warned him not to ignore Abo. He turned back to the man and asked, "What makes you think that a kappa killed Kenji?"

"Because Kenji told me that a kappa was stalking him. Apparently he saw him a couple of times. Listen, I could get in very big trouble if I am seen talking to you."

"This is important, Abo-san," Reiko said.

"So is my life," Abo said. "When I got out of the *bosozoku*, I made a vow not to talk to the authorities about anything! I have already acted as informant on two occasions for you people. Route 66 are becoming suspicious. I was sent a warning the last time. Why don't you go away now?"

"Please, just a couple more questions, Abo-san, and we'll leave you alone," Bond said. "Have you heard anything about the Ryujin-kai being involved with the deaths of the McMahons? You know about that, right?"

"Yes, I read the newspapers. It is no secret that McMahon-san was an enemy of the Ryujin-kai. I do not know any more about that, but I do know that the Ryujin-kai is working on something big."

"What do you mean?" Reiko asked.

"Something top secret. I have my sources. I don't know what it is, but they are preparing something with that nationalist, Goro Yoshida."

At last! An important piece of the puzzle. "Yoshida? Are you sure?"

"Yoshida is the *Yami Shogun* of the Ryujin-kai. The dark master."

"Do you know where Yoshida is located?"

"No, not exactly. No one does," Abo said. "He is somewhere in the—"

But before he could finish his sentence, there was the sound of a gunshot and Abo's head jerked back violently. Blood splattered against a post behind him.

Bond and Reiko instinctively ducked and turned to see Noburo Ichihara fifteen feet away, holding what appeared to be a Heckler & Koch VP70. He fired again and the bullets sliced the air over Bond's head.

Years of training prevented both Bond and Reiko from being killed. Reiko rolled to the side and took hold of the single front tyre on Abo's truck. Using that for leverage, she performed a neat flip over to the other side of the vehicle. Bond spun the opposite way and positioned himself behind a thick concrete post. But by that time, Ichihara had run.

Bond drew the Walther and shot in the assailant's direction. The bullet missed, ricocheting off the back fender on a forklift. Ichihara ran straight into the vendor area of the fish market.

Bond leapt to his feet and chased him, shouting for civilians to get out of the way. Reiko had to take a moment to catch her breath before she could get up. She thought that she might have twisted her body badly when she had performed that manoeuvre, for there was a burning pain in her side.

There were too many people about for Bond to shoot again. It was just too risky. He managed to holster the gun as he ran, jumping over a dolly full of tuna.

Ichihara turned and fired in Bond's direction. A woman screamed from behind a food stall. Workers jumped back and tried to avoid the hoodlum, but he ran right into a big stallholder. The men collided with a crash and fell. Ichihara's pistol slid across the concrete and under a table laden with shellfish. Bond ran and leaped to tackle Ichihara before he could get up. The two men crashed into the table, knocking the slippery raw fish to the floor. Ichihara grabbed a handful of sea scallops and thrust them into Bond's face as they wrestled in front of stunned onlookers. Reiko caught up to the scene just as Ichihara kicked Bond off of him and got to his feet. The killer seized a hook from a frightened worker. He turned to Bond and swung it quickly, back and forth. The hook whistled as it cut through the space in front of him. Bond dodged it repeatedly in the confined space between rows of tables. Ichihara advanced, coming closer to Bond until Reiko picked up a ten-pound octopus and flung it at the attacker. The wet, slippery invertebrate slapped Ichihara in the face and chest, taking him by surprise. He ripped it off his body, threw it at Bond, and turned to run again.

"Are you all right?" Reiko asked Bond, helping him pull off the slimy creature.

"Yes!" Bond spat. He started to take off in pursuit again when he noticed the blood on Reiko's blouse. She followed his eyes, looked down and saw that her side and stomach were soaked in blood.

"Oh!" she gasped, completely unaware that she was injured. She panicked as she pulled up her blouse. Bond's hands went to her abdomen, assessing the damage.

"You're not hit badly," he said. "The bullet grazed your side."

"I didn't feel it when it happened, James-san! Now it hurts like hell," she gasped.

"Stay here. You have your mobile?"

"Yes."

"Call Tiger and he'll get an ambulance faster than anyone. Do it now! I'm going to catch a fish."

Bond kissed her on the forehead, then gave chase.

Outside the fish market, Ichihara ran onto busy Chuo Ichiba. Horns blared as several cars screeched to a halt to avoid hitting the thug. A taxicab barely stopped in time but still collided with him. Ichihara fell over the car's bonnet and rolled over to the other side. He landed on his feet and continued running towards the Ginza with Bond not far behind.

Ichihara sped onto Showa Dori Street, a boulevard full of high-priced shops and restaurants. The killer ran past a huge crowd of waiting theatregoers queuing in front of the Kabukiza Theatre and then disappeared around the corner of the building.

Bond had no choice but to follow him.

TEN

KABUKI MATINEE

BOND SPRINTED DOWN THE SIDE STREET AND SAW THAT ICHIHARA HAD ducked into the theatre's employee entrance. He acknowledged this smart move with a muttered oath. No *gaijin* could simply walk into the stage door of Japan's most famous kabuki theatre.

He peered in the open doorway and saw a foyer lined with pigeon-holes for storing shoes. Slots were designated for every theatre employee and most of them were full. An elderly man who sat on a chair beside the shoe shelves appeared agitated. Apparently his job was to help employees with their shoes as they came in, but it was obvious that the last person who had come through had upset him. The corridor went past the man through double doors and into the backstage areas of the building.

Bond acted quickly. He walked in, kicked off his shoes and stepped up to the caretaker. The old man looked up at him, confused.

"*Konnichi wa,*" Bond said as he put his feet in a pair of slippers that were sitting on the platform. Then he walked purposefully through the double doors before the aide could stop him.

The corridor was empty. Bond moved forward into an area full of bulletin boards that displayed call sheets and other information for the employees. The administrative offices were here, apparently, so Bond walked quickly past them. The last thing he needed was someone authoritative to confront him.

He went around a corner and found a door with a half curtain hanging over it. Bond carefully inched an edge of the curtain to the side and looked in.

It was a costume room. Men sitting on *tatami* mats were working with the fabrics. Traditional kabuki costumes hung on racks behind them.

Bond went on and into a corridor that contained the actors' dressing rooms. Each of the star actors had his own room, with his name written on the curtain over the doorway. Bond peered into each one, finding some actors meditating in costume or in the act of dressing; some of the rooms were empty. No sign of Ichihara.

Bond wasn't very familiar with kabuki. He did know that it was a traditional form of Japanese theatre, like Noh and Kyogen. It was noted for its stylised acting, gorgeous period costumes, beautiful scenery and stories on an epic scale. He knew that the actors were all male, even the ones playing female roles, and that the famous ones were descendants of the original kabuki acting families. Best not to bother any of them.

He left the dressing room area and moved along the main corridor until he came to a stairwell. He took the steps two at a time to the second floor, where he saw Ichihara creeping along and looking for a place to hide. Their eyes met. The killer froze in shock but after a second, he darted down the hall, which opened on to a metal fire escape. Bond dashed after him, kicking off the slippers as he went.

Ichihara clambered up the fire escape and into the third-floor entrance. Bond looked down briefly and saw that the metal stairs hung over the stage door by which he had first come in at street level. He climbed the stairs and entered the building again.

The hallway on the third floor was full of people—actors, stage-hands and other staff. The dressing rooms for the supporting actors and musicians were up here, as well as other technical offices. One man shouted at Bond, commanding him to halt. Bond drew his Walther and ran past, ignoring him. His presence must have been imposing enough to quiet the man.

Bond looked into a room and found more technicians sitting on *tatami* and making wigs. Ichihara was standing inside the archway and surprised Bond with a series of lightning-fast *tsuki* blows, which made Bond drop his weapon and retreat as Ichihara jumped into the hall, swinging and kicking with great speed. Bond fell back into a wheeled rack of costumes. Ichihara turned and ran.

Bond looked frantically for his Walther, didn't see it, and decided to continue the chase rather than waste time searching for it. He got up and pursued his prey down two flights of stairs back to the first floor. This stairway emptied into a quiet corridor with a swinging door. Bond pushed through and found himself in the stage wings.

The sound of a strange recitation flooded his ears. A *shamisen's* strings were being plucked and the voice continued the eerie chanting that was typical of a kabuki performance.

My God, the matinee had begun!

Bond ignored the stagehands looking at him in confusion.

Where had Ichihara gone?

Bond swept around the black curtains at the side of the stage and sprinted behind the cyclorama that spread across the back of the scenery. He got a glimpse of the audience as he passed beside a small slit in the curtains. It was a full house. There were two actors on stage. One was the *aragoto*, the type of character known for the style of acting that expressed anger in a highly stylised manner. This character was usually tragically sent to the next world to become a supernatural being and returned to this world for revenge. His makeup was fierce and demonic.

The other man was the *oyama*, the actor who played a woman. His appearance was totally convincing; his costume and makeup were elaborate and breathtakingly beautiful, which added to the illusion that he was a female.

Both actors were seated on the stage and speaking in a slow, flowing language that Bond couldn't understand at all.

He saw a movement out of the corner of his eye. Someone moved between the curtains on the other side of the stage. Bond looked across the scenery from stage left to stage right and saw Ichihara. Bond turned to scan the area around him and found a prop table upon which sat a large *odachi*, a samurai broadsword more than two metres long. Bond took it and began to move behind the cyclorama again to the other side of the stage.

Ichihara met him halfway. He was holding another type of samurai sword called a *katana*.

Bond wondered if the stage props would be sharpened. Even if they weren't, the tips could certainly pierce a body.

Ichihara swung the sword in a long arc, slicing the air in front of Bond. Bond dodged, drew his own sword and dropped the sheath. The two men engaged in quiet, but deadly, combat while the kabuki play continued, the performers oblivious to what was happening behind the scenery.

The *bosozoku* adopted a traditional and common *Chudan no kamae* stance, holding the sword at middle height, pointed forward, while all Bond cared about was simply defending himself. The weapons clashed, this time making some noise. The sound of scraping metal carried through the house, but neither the audience nor the actors knew what it was. The two men continued to spar and parry, inching their way back through a large opening that led to the scene shop. Carpenters and painters stopped what they were doing and stared in disbelief.

The fight continued, now noisier than before. Ichihara shouted a *kiai* when he struck at Bond, a tactic used to frighten opponents and focus energy. The metal clanged. Several of the spectators implored them to stop. One said that he was calling the police.

Bond went on the offensive, moved forward, and swung his sword back and forth. The blade was heavier than it looked, and Bond was merely adequate at the skill. He had taken two kendo classes and one basic training session in *kenjutsu*, but lacked the years of practice of a professional.

Luckily, Ichihara was not much better. He, too, was an amateur who knew only a few moves. He was reckless and didn't have the discipline or stamina to be effective. Instead, he swung the sword with abandon, hitting whatever objects were in his way.

Bond backed him to a staircase that descended to the basement level. Ichihara lost his balance and fell, rolling down the steps as he went. Bond followed him down, but Ichihara got up and ran beneath the stage. Before Bond could stop him, the killer had jumped onto the *seri*, a platform that could be raised and lowered from below the stage to make actors appear and disappear. Ichihara flipped the switch and the platform began to rise. A trap door on the stage floor opened as the killer rose up into the unfolding drama on display in front of the audience.

People gasped and shouted at Ichihara. The actors froze, not sure what they should do. Stagehands immediately ran out onto the stage to apprehend the intruder, but Ichihara jumped away and ran down the *hanamichi*, the ramp extending through the audience along the aisle from the stage to the rear of the theatre. Actors often used this area of the stage for intimate rapport with the spectators. Several women screamed as the killer hurried to the back of the house and theatre staff pursued him. Ichihara turned and swung the sword, holding them at bay. Then he burst through the auditorium doors and into the lobby.

Police sirens were wailing in the distance. Bond was about to run to the stage as well, but several stagehands blocked his way. They were understandably angry and were shouting at him to drop the sword. He realised that there was no eloquent way out of this one, so he dropped the sword and tried to explain that he was a law enforcement officer.

Ichihara, on the other hand, escaped out of the front doors of the theatre and disappeared into the throng of pedestrians.

Reiko had alerted Tanaka when Bond left her. Tanaka had traced Bond to the theatre with the homing device in Bond's mobile and was able to get through to the police and issue instructions before Bond was put through the humiliation of a ride to the police station. A police sergeant found Bond's Walther PPK amidst the spilled costumes in one of the hallways, grilled him for three hours in the theatre administrative offices and finally released him as the sun was on its way down.

Bond used his phone after he got to the street.

Tiger's voice came through loud and clear. "Bondo-san? Are you all right?"

"Fine, but it's been a bloody wasteful day," Bond said. "How's Reiko-san?"

"She will be all right," Tiger replied. "She had to have a few stitches. She has been released and ordered to rest for a day or two. She will be back on the job in no time."

"Well, that's good to hear. What's the score with Noburo Ichihara?"

"We are looking for him. We have tried all of his usual haunts but he seems to have disappeared. It's not surprising. I suggest you go back to your hotel and call it a night. There is one other bit of news. The CureLab board of directors was in an emergency meeting all day today. Many of them left at the end of the day in disgust. I predict that some kind of announcement about the company will appear in the papers very soon."

"Have you tried calling Shinji Fujimoto and asking him what went on?"

"Yes, but there was no answer."

"Then I will sign off, grab a bite to eat, and go back to the Imperial. Good night, Tiger."

"Good night, Bondo-san. I will contact you first thing in the morning."

Bond rang off and started walking through the Ginza towards the Imperial. The neon had already fired up and the area was a gridlock of traffic and pedestrians. Not surprising, since this was one of the more fashionable and expensive areas of the city. There were couples dressed up for the evening, walking quickly to make their dinner appointments; salarymen and office ladies on their way home or to the local bar; and at least a handful of ad hoc product give-away booths set up where pretty young girls dressed in short skirts handed out samples of the latest perfume, soap or deodorant. These were always accompanied by banners or placards displaying the company's logo and mascot that was almost invariably a much-too-cute cartoon animal with large eyes.

Bond stopped at a noodle shop and had a quick bowl of *udon*, then continued walking to the hotel.

"Mister Bond?" a voice said in English.

Speak of the devil . . . ! Bond turned to see Shinji Fujimoto sitting in the passenger side of a Toyota Celsior that had pulled over to the curb. A young man was in the driver's seat.

"*Konban wa,*" Bond said, bowing slightly.

"Good evening to you, too. I thought I recognised you walking down the street. May I offer you a lift?"

Bond's internal radar flashed a warning. "Thank you, but it's not much further. I prefer to walk."

"Actually, I'm glad I saw you. I have something I would like you to see. It concerns my great niece, Mayumi."

Bond was wary, but he decided to hear what the man had to say. "What is it?"

"It is at my office. It's not far. Won't you get in? You haven't seen the CureLab headquarters yet, have you?"

Why not? Bond thought. Now was as good a time as any. He opened the door to the back seat and got in.

"I am hoping you can interpret the message I received. It is from Mayumi but I am not sure I understand what she says," Fujimoto said.

"Why would I?" Bond asked.

"It's written in English!"

The car drove a few blocks into the Ginza as Fujimoto spoke rapidly into his mobile phone, then the driver stopped in front of a twenty-four-storey building. Fujimoto got out and issued some instructions to the driver.

"This is it, Mister Bond," Fujimoto said, opening the back door. Bond got out and stood on the pavement with him.

"Our offices are on floors eighteen and nineteen. Come with me. I imagine the building is fairly quiet this time of night."

Bond followed him through the front door and into a lobby where a security guard acknowledged Fujimoto and greeted him.

"He's with me," Fujimoto said, indicating Bond. The guard bowed.

They got into a lift and Fujimoto pressed the button for floor 19.

"I might as well see Peter McMahon's office while I'm here," Bond suggested.

"Good idea," Fujimoto replied.

The lift arrived and Fujimoto gestured for Bond to exit. "Please, after you."

It was an ultra-modern building, very high tech and designed in a pseudo-futuristic decor that seemed to be popular with sophisticated Japanese corporations. The walls lining the corridor were a shiny stainless steel and the carpet was plush. There was an antiseptic quality to the place that reminded Bond of the infirmary at MI6.

Closed steel double doors stood at the end of the hallway. An engraved sign read "CureLab Inc." in both English and *katakana*. Fujimoto took a key card out of his pocket and swiped it through the slot in the wall. The doors slid open with a soft hum. They stepped into a thoroughly modern reception area with a space-age design scheme. Fujimoto swiped his card again and another set of doors slid open.

"This way," he said.

Bond followed him past several offices and a conference room, and finally to a closed door marked with Fujimoto's name and title. The card was swiped once more and the door opened. Fujimoto stepped aside and again gestured for Bond to enter first. Bond stepped through the door and a heavy object came crashing down on his head.

A slap in the face roused him.

His head was pounding and his eyes were blurry, but eventually he focused on Fujimoto's face.

Another slap.

"I think he's awake now," Fujimoto said to someone else.

Bond took in his surroundings. He was in Fujimoto's spacious office, complete with a stylish glass-top desk, computer, filing cabinets and bookshelves. There was a portable fan standing next to the desk. A large picture window looked out onto the bright lights of Ginza. There were three other men in the room, all teenagers or very young adults, dressed like yakuza. One of them was Noburo Ichihara.

"Close the curtains," Fujimoto ordered, and one of them pulled the cord that shut the drapes.

Bond saw his Walther lying on the desk, along with the Palm Pilot and DoCoMo phone, but they had left the antacid blister pack and the cigar holder in his jacket pocket. They had placed a plastic painting sheet on the carpet underneath Bond's chair.

"Hold him," Fujimoto commanded. One of the gang went behind Bond, bent down and grabbed their captive's forearms. He pulled them back tightly and held them in a vicelike grip. Fujimoto nodded at Ichihara.

The killer slowly slipped on black leather gloves as he grinned, revealing a large gold tooth. Then he stepped in front of Bond and punched him hard in the face. Bond felt a shockwave from his jaw to the top of his skull. His mouth began to bleed.

"Again," Fujimoto ordered.

The angry fist smashed into Bond's lips a second time.

"Again."

This went on repeatedly for several minutes. When Fujimoto decided that his captive had had enough, Bond's face was a bloody mess.

"What do you want, Mister Bond? Why are you in Japan?" Fujimoto asked.

Bond groaned, barely able to keep his head up. "You . . . know . . . why . . ."

"Well, officially you are here to investigate the deaths of Peter McMahon, my niece, and their daughters. You are to try to find the wayward girl, Mayumi. We know all that. But what else are you after? Talk, Mister Bond, or this will become very unpleasant."

"I don't know what the hell you're talking about, Fujimoto," Bond said, his words slurring. He had difficulty enunciating.

"You are in Japan for another reason, Mister Bond. What is it?"

Bond had to think. The summit conference? Was that what the bastard was on about?

Wait . . . ! How classified was that information? It was a secret G8 meeting, wasn't it?

"Nothing," Bond said. "I just want to find your great niece and get the hell out of this country."

"My great niece's whereabouts is none of your business and it is none of your country's business. Her father may have been a British citizen, but she is not. This is family business and I shall take care of it myself."

"You have taken care of it, haven't you?" Bond whispered.

"What did you say, Mister Bond?"

"You killed them. You were responsible for their deaths. You murdered your own niece and her family."

"And why would I do that?"

"So you could control the company. You were always jealous of your older brother's success and resented him for not leaving CureLab to you. I would bet that you're going to sell out completely. You're going to sell your shares to Yonai Enterprises. Aren't you?"

"You are in no position to ask questions, Mister Bond," Fujimoto said. "Peter McMahon outlived his usefulness. He was just a barbarian foreigner who had seduced the daughter of the company's chairman. He took over a Japanese company—what should have been *my* company—and he finally met his karmic destiny."

"So you admit killing them?"

"I admit nothing. Tomorrow is a new day, Mister Bond. Things will be different. Tomorrow, under the eyes of the *Daibutsu*, CureLab Incorporated will rise to a new level of existence and be entirely controlled by Japanese. CureLab will be under new management. And you, Mister Bond, will be dead."

"What is the yakuza paying you, Fujimoto?" Bond spat. "What kind of deal did you make with them?" Fujimoto shook his head and started to walk out of the room. He stood beside a rather large rubbish bin on wheels that janitors used to wheel around the building when they cleaned offices.

"Ichihara, you know what to do. Try not to make a mess of my office. Put the body in here when you're done and you can wheel it to the van. Take him somewhere where he won't be found."

"*Hai!*" Ichihara barked, and then he turned to Bond and smiled. The gold tooth sparkled in his mouth.

ELEVEN

SMOKE SCREENS

Bond was alone with the three hoods. Blood covered his face and clothes and he was dazed from the beating, but he knew that he had to snap out of it and defend himself. Bond willed himself to concentrate, commanding his senses to be alert. Timing would be everything, and if he couldn't use the element of surprise then all could be lost.

Ichihara moved towards him, fists ready. Bond clumsily attempted to leap out of the chair and attack the thug but Ichihara easily punched him hard in the face. Bond fell on top of the plastic sheet and lay still.

"What did you do?" one of the others asked.

"He's out," the other one ventured.

Ichihara laughed. "Some tough guy. Come on, let's pick him up and get him out of here."

"Shouldn't we kill him first?"

"We can have more fun doing that where we're going."

Bond's body was limp. The three men hoisted him off the floor and carried him to the rubbish bin. One man managed to open the lid and then they dumped Bond inside. He crumpled like a rag doll. They shut the lid and began to wheel their cargo out of the office.

Inside the container, Bond reached into his pocket and grabbed the antacid blister pack that Major Boothroyd had given him. He extracted two pink tablets and then knocked on the lid.

"He's awake," one man said. "Let's take him out and kill him!"

"I told you we should have done that in the first place," the third man said.

"All right," Ichihara replied.

They closed the office door again and moved the bin back to the middle of the room. Ichihara stood away and reached to open it, just in case the *gaijin* tried something funny.

As soon as he saw the fluorescent strip lights on the office ceiling above him, Bond shut his eyes and threw one of the tablets as hard as he could. It struck the ceiling and burst and a dark cloud of smoke quickly enveloped the area. Water immediately shot out of sprinklers built into the ceiling.

The three men shouted in surprise and moved back, temporarily blinded by the flash. Under the cover of the smoke, Bond climbed out of the bin. He couldn't see through the smoke, but at least he could discern shapes. One of the thugs was three feet away from him, waving at the smoke in an attempt to clear it. Bond slugged him hard in the stomach. The man went "Ooompf!" and doubled over. Bond clasped his hands together and brought them down hard on the back of the man's neck. He heard the bones crack.

One down, two to go.

"What was that?" Ichihara shouted.

"He's escaped!"

"Get him!"

Bond moved quickly to the desk and picked up the Walther and his other items. Then he moved around the room in a circle, carefully avoiding the two men.

The building's fire alarms went off. Bond knew that they would have company very soon.

Ichihara, still unable to see, drew a Browning 9mm and pointed it into the smoke. He fired twice, aiming nowhere near Bond.

"Are you crazy?" the other man shouted. "What are you doing?"

Ichihara didn't listen. He started turning around, firing a bullet every couple of feet. Bond moved to the portable fan that was beside the desk, pointed it towards the centre of the room, and flicked it on. The blades began to whirr, blowing the smoke away.

The black billows immediately dissipated, leaving the two men standing and rubbing their eyes. Ichihara was pointing his gun in the opposite direction from where Bond was now.

"I'm over here," Bond said. It was one of those rare moments when he received utter and complete satisfaction.

Ichihara turned and the Walther recoiled. Bond performed what was known as a Mozambique shot: "Three shots—two to the chest and one to the head, knocks him down and makes him dead." Ichihara slammed backwards into a filing cabinet and slid to the floor.

The other man saw what had happened. His eyes wide with fright, he thrust up his hands. "Don't shoot!" he cried.

Bond levelled the pistol at him. "Get inside," he said, gesturing to the rubbish bin. The man didn't have to be asked twice. He quickly climbed over the side and got in. Bond put the lid on and snapped it shut. He then pulled the plastic sheet out from underneath the chair and wrapped it around the bin so that the man would be unable to open it from the inside.

Now he was ready. Bond listened at the door; satisfied that no one was nearby, he opened it. Then two security guards appeared at the other end of the hallway, running towards him. Bond counted to four, then stepped outside the office.

He threw another pink antacid tablet into the hallway, where it struck the metal wall hard and exploded. Another cloud of black smoke filled the corridor, blocking the security guards' vision. Bond then inched along the wall as the two men blindly walked right past him.

As he approached the main reception area he heard the lift bell chime and the doors open. There were several voices.

Bond ducked into a conference room and shut the door. He heard the rushing footsteps down the hallway, started to open the door but stopped when he saw what was in the room.

Large anatomical colour illustrations of mosquitoes had been posted on three walls of the room. It was also furnished with a round conference table and chairs, a podium and a computer. The monitor was on and there appeared to be some kind of Power Point slide presentation in progress. Someone had been in the room working on something and had left very recently. A pad of paper and a pen, a mug of coffee and an ashtray full of cigarette ends were next to the computer and a sports jacket was draped around a chair.

Bond decided to risk taking a look. First he examined the posters. All of the text was written in *kanji* except for the words "Hokkaido Mosquito and Vector Control Centre" in the bottom corner of each illustration. The posters had been stamped with an address in a town called Noboribetsu. The mosquitoes were of different species, slightly different in shape and colouring. Bond turned his attention to the computer. A Palm Pilot was sitting in a cradle that was hooked up to the CPU; it was downloading the files. The slideshow in operation also featured mosquitoes. There were shots of a female mosquito laying eggs, shots of eggs hatching into larvae, the larvae shedding skins to become pupae and then finally adult mosquitoes emerging from the pupal skins. Some *kanji* text appeared on the screens, then more pictures of mosquitoes—biting a human arm, mating and alighting on water.

Finally a slide appeared that featured a miniature bonsai waterfall like the one he had seen at the McMahon home. Bond knew that he had found something important.

Bond removed the Palm Pilot on the table and replaced it with his own. He quickly pressed some buttons and began to download the entire slideshow onto his device. While he waited, he took the sports jacket that was hung over the chair and used it to wipe off blood from his face, hands and clothes.

He heard shouts and more people running through the hallway.

Hurry up! he silently commanded the device. He dropped the now-bloody jacket onto the chair, then took his DoCoMo phone out of his pocket. He punched the speed dial button for Tiger, who answered it after one ring.

"Bondo-san?"

"Tiger, I've made a slight detour."

"Where are you?"

"CureLab office in Ginza."

"Ah, yes, I see the indicator on the map. Your homing device is still working. Do you need help?"

"Affirmative. I need an escape route quickly."

"Can you make it to the front of the building?"

"I can try."

"Give me ten minutes."

There was a voice directly outside the conference room door. Bond shut off the phone, quickly moved to the wall beside the door and drew the Walther. He levelled it so that whoever came in would get a face full of lead.

The door opened and a man started to walk in, but someone called him from down the hall. Bond only got a glimpse of him. He was a Japanese man of about thirty, slight of build, with glasses and a crewcut. Whatever he was, Bond knew that he was no killer: a scientist, perhaps, or a doctor. He looked very familiar.

"What?" the man shouted back.

The voice called him again.

"Hmpf," the man said, then closed the door without coming in.

Of course! It was Fujio Aida, the missing molecular biologist! What the hell was he doing at the CureLab office? Hadn't he been fired for being a spy and traitor? What was the big mystery with him being "missing"? Here he was, alive and well, and apparently working on a project involving mosquitoes.

How long before he'd be back? Bond wondered. He ran back to the computer and saw that the download was eighty per cent done. Bond glanced at the pad of paper on the table but couldn't understand a word of what was written on it. He tore the page off, folded it and put it in his pocket.

Finally the download ended. Bond retrieved his Palm Pilot and then moved back to the door. He listened but wasn't able to discern how many men were in the hallway. There was no way that he was going to be able to walk out of the room without being seen.

Time for another antacid.

Bond palmed a pink tablet in his left hand and kept the pistol in his right. He pushed the button and the door slid open. He looked out and saw several men at the end of the hall near Fujimoto's office. The other way, in the direction of the lifts, was clear. Bond stepped out and walked swiftly towards reception but someone saw him and shouted.

"You! Stop!"

Bond turned and threw the tablet, bursting it against the wall. The dark smoke filled the corridor once again and Bond ran for it. He reached the lift as bullets flew in his direction. He punched the button and pounded on the door. There were shouts in the hallway as the sound of running boots grew louder.

"Come on, damn you!" Bond said aloud.

The lift chimed and the doors split open just as the men began to swarm through the smoke. Bond jumped inside, turned and fired the Walther once at a guard who had made it to the lift. The guard jerked back, dropped his weapon and fell back into the arms of another man. The doors closed and Bond was on his way down.

When he got to the ground floor, he was surprised to see that no one was there. The security guard who had let him and Fujimoto into the building was not at his post. Probably upstairs on the nineteenth floor, Bond thought.

Bond casually went through the front doors and out to the street. A fire engine was already there, and he could hear more sirens approaching.

"Bondo-san!"

Tiger was in the Majesta, which was parked by the kerb nearby. Bond ran and got into the back, then the driver sped away just as another fire engine and police cars swerved around the block and pulled up to the building.

"Do you need to go to hospital?" Tiger asked, his brow wrinkled with concern.

"I'm all right," Bond said as he held a cloth filled with ice to his face. "I'll probably just look like Frankenstein's monster for a few days. Nothing's broken. I can still talk."

"At least you didn't let him live to tell the tale." Tiger handed him a glass of whisky from the mini-bar in the back of the Majesta. Bond took a long, burning drink and gasped with pleasure. "God, that felt good," he said. *"Arigato."*

Tiger laughed. "Bondo-san, you have the highest tolerance for pain of anyone I know."

"I'll take that as a compliment."

"Bondo-san, you must realise that all of these murders involving Abo and Umeki could have absolutely nothing to do with the McMahons. It could very well be yakuza and *bosozoku* business."

Bond pulled out the Palm Pilot and gave it to Tiger. "We have to take a look at what's on here. CureLab has something going on with mosquitoes, that's for certain." He related everything that he had seen in the conference room, including his identification of Fujio Aida.

"So what is Aida doing back at CureLab?" Tanaka asked.

"Obviously working on mosquitoes. Tiger, that bonsai contraption was just like the one we found at the McMahons'."

"I believe you. I will ask our lab to rush the analysis of it." Tiger took the Palm Pilot and flipped a switch on the armrest. The back of the driver's seat pulled down to reveal a laptop computer. Tiger booted it up and placed the Palm Pilot in the cradle.

"This should only take a few moments."

"I also got this," Bond said, pulling out the piece of paper from the notepad. Tiger took it and gave it a cursory look.

"It says, 'Life cycle from eggs hatching to adult mosquito has been reduced to one week. Still need to work on transom-varial transmission.' What does that mean, Bondo-san?"

"I'm not sure. Something to do with the female's eggs. Did Reiko-san tell you what Abo told us?"

"About Yoshida?"

"Yes."

Tiger nodded. "Very worrisome. My superiors are beginning to take all of this a bit more seriously."

The car pulled up in front of the Imperial Hotel and parked. They waited until the computer had finished uploading the files from the Palm Pilot. Tiger typed on the keyboard and the slideshow began. It was just as Bond had seen in the office: photos of mosquitoes going through their natural life cycles accompanied by *kanji*.

"This is all about mosquito biology," Tiger said. "CureLab does work with disease-carrying insects."

"But Fujimoto told us that they didn't work with mosquitoes, remember?"

"Ah, you are right, Bondo-san. We will turn this material over to someone who understands it and obtain a proper evaluation."

"I'm convinced that bastard was in on the McMahons' deaths. He practically admitted it." Bond told Tiger what Fujimoto had said about Peter McMahon. "And he said that 'tomorrow, under the eyes of the *Daibutsu,* CureLab will rise to a new level of existence and be entirely controlled by Japanese.' "

"The *Daibutsu?* That's in Kamakura."

"What's a *Daibutsu?*" Bond asked.

"The Great Buddha. It's the largest bronze Buddha in the world. He's been sitting in Kamakura for over seven centuries."

"How far away is that?"

"Not far. About an hour's train ride."

"Why Kamakura?"

"Because Fujimoto has a home there, as I understand it. He keeps a flat in Tokyo but goes to Kamakura on the weekends. I've always wanted to see the *Daibutsu* again. It has been a long time. Get some rest, Bondo-san. Put some antiseptic on those cuts and we will pick you up in the morning at seven o'clock."

Bond left his friend and walked into the Imperial lobby. Ignoring the stares from the concierge and other staff, he went straight to the lift and took it to his floor in the tower. Once he got into his room, Bond finally looked at himself in the mirror. The damage looked worse than it was, but it was bad enough. He cleaned and doctored his face, took a scalding hot shower, crawled into bed and was asleep in less than a minute.

TWELVE

THE DISTANT PAIN OF DEATH

YASUTAKE TSUKAMOTO AWOKE ABRUPTLY TO THE SOUND OF HIS PRIVATE phone ringing. He glanced at the digital clock beside his bed and was horrified to see that it read 4:15. His wife stirred and grumbled sleepily.

"*Moshi moshi,*" Tsukamoto said into the phone, not too pleasantly.

"Tsukamoto."

He shuddered. It was the *Yami Shogun.*

"*Hai!*"

"Did I wake you?" Goro Yoshida asked.

"It is all right. Please, let me change phones." He pushed the Hold button and hung up.

"Who is it?" his wife asked.

"Business problem. Go back to sleep."

Tsukamoto got out of bed, went out of the room and walked into his study. While most of the house was traditional Japanese, this room looked like it would be more at home in a British law firm's office. Besides a traditional desk and filing cabinets made from Hakone polished wood, the walls were covered with books. Over half of them were law books. Tsukamoto had long ago decided that he should know a thing or two about the law.

His home in Sapporo was a large one, very luxurious and very well guarded. His men kept vigil around the compound twenty-four hours a day, for being the *kaicho* of the Ryujin-kai not only afforded him great opulence but also brought danger. There were plenty of other yakuza that hated him.

He sat at the desk, picked up the phone and pushed the button to get back on the line.

"I am here," he said.

"Good. Is everything ready for the transfer of CureLab?" Yoshida asked.

"Yes. Kano is going to Kamakura today to meet with Fujimoto."

"What's this I hear about some trouble at the CureLab office in Tokyo?"

Tsukamoto drew in a breath and said, "*Saaaa* . . . Fujimoto took matters into his own hands. Very bad situation. There is an Englishman in Japan. He is here to investigate the deaths of the McMahon family. Fujimoto tried to have him killed last night."

"And the Englishman got away?"

"Yes."

"What does he know?"

"We are not sure. He may have seen things. We have no way of knowing."

There was silence at the other end. Finally, Yoshida said, "We can't afford to have undue attention on CureLab at the moment. Fujimoto has outlived his usefulness."

"I agree. Shinji Fujimoto is a bumbling fool."

"Then see to it that he experiences great pleasure today," Yoshida said. "He will go to Kamakura and make the deal he has been preparing for all these many months, and for a short while he will be a very wealthy man. But as my mentor, Mishima-san, once wrote: 'The distant pain of death refines the awareness of pleasure.' We must ensure that Fujimoto knows both of these sensations."

"It has already been arranged," Tsukamoto said.

"Good. Now what about the Englishman?"

"I will take care of it. Do not worry."

"I won't. Tell me, how did yesterday's tests go?"

"Splendidly. We cut the incubation time down to exactly six days. The life span of the insects is still very short, but it's long enough for them to do the damage we seek. The best news is that with the latest delivery from CureLab we have been able to further mutate the virus so that the onset of symptoms is much faster. Laboratory animals became sick within an hour."

"That is good news. Keep the engineers working on it. After this phase is completed, we must be ready to unleash a new and improved version of our product."

"Yes, I understand."

"What about the McMahon girl? Has she been eliminated?"

"Not yet."

"Why not?"

"With all due respect, I have been asked by the *so-honbucho*, Kubo, that I speak to you about this. The girl is a big earner. She is one of the most popular girls in the establishment. And he wanted to have her around for the send-off of the carriers. You yourself instructed us to give the carriers a night on the town that they wouldn't forget."

"I did indeed, but that was two days ago. You can find other girls. There are always other girls. Get rid of her. She is dangerous to have alive."

"Very well. She will not live to see the weekend."

After a short pause, Yoshida said, "Good night, Tsukamoto."

"Good night, Yoshida."

Tsukamoto hung up the phone and contemplated the original painting by Ogata Korin that hung on the wall between sets of bookshelves. He knew now that he would not be able to get back to sleep. He lit a cigarette and rang the servant whose duty was to stay up all night in case the master of the house needed anything. Tsukamoto ordered some coffee and yoghurt, then settled back in his chair to meditate.

It was going to be an interesting week.

Bond and Tiger arrived in Kamakura around 9:00 the next morning. One of Tiger's men had been posted at the *Daibutsu* since the grounds opened at 7:00, but he reported by mobile phone that he had not yet seen Shinji Fujimoto. Tiger instructed the driver to take them directly to the Great Buddha and to park the car somewhere. Tiger and Bond got out in front of the main gates.

Bond was stiff and sore from the beating he had taken the night before and his face was a mess. There were contusions around his mouth, an abrasion on his left cheek and swelling around the left side of his jaw. He had noticed the hotel staff grimacing at him behind his back when he had strolled through the Imperial lobby to meet the Toyota out in front before the hour-long drive.

"Have you been to Kamakura before, Bondo-san?" Tiger asked.

"If I have, I don't remember it."

"It's a beautiful place. It was an early capital of Japan and there is an abundance of Buddhist temples and some shrines here. The *Daibutsu* has been here since 1252. It used to be housed in a huge hall, but the building was washed away by a *tsunami* in the late 1400s."

They walked up the path to the entrance, which was guarded by two statues on either side that portrayed the Buddha at two different stages—at the beginning of life and at the end.

Tiger stopped at the pavilion to purify his hands. Bond did the same; the cold water felt good on his wounds as he swished it around in his mouth and spat it out. They continued into the courtyard where the impressive bronze Buddha sat, all-knowing and all-seeing. The metal was discoloured but the statue was in remarkably good shape considering its age. The figure towered a little over eleven metres tall.

"Look at the curly hair, Bondo-san," Tiger pointed out. "There are 656 curls altogether and it has a white hair curl on the forehead. This symbolises wisdom."

Abbreviated tea ceremonies were performed at regular intervals on one side of the courtyard. A group of tourists had already begun to gather there and some were looking at the souvenir kiosks on the opposite side.

"Do you see our man?" Bond asked.

"No. We should sit down over there and wait. And we should keep you out of sight." He pointed to some benches at the back of the courtyard.

"I look that bad, do I?"

Tiger laughed. "I meant in case our friend shows up soon. We don't want him to see either of us. Don't worry, Bondo-san, you will be a handsome man again. Those cuts and bruises will heal in no time."

They sat under the shade of a large cherry tree. Bond inhaled deeply, enjoying the fresh air. The weather was pleasant and not too hot. The tranquillity of the place was infectious.

"Quite a peaceful place for a business deal," Bond said.

"Yes, I'm not surprised by the choice. So many people come here and since Fujimoto lives in town, no one would think twice about him coming to pay his respects to the Buddha. The question is, where is the actual meeting going to take place?"

"I think we'll know in a few minutes," Bond said, gesturing with his head. "There he is now." They held open newspapers to cover their faces.

Shinji Fujimoto entered the courtyard alone. He looked around nervously, then continued walking towards the Buddha. He pretended to show great interest in the statue, then walked over to the tea ceremony area and sat down. Obviously his contact was not there yet. Bond and Tiger watched from across the courtyard as Fujimoto was served green tea by the women wearing kimonos.

"He appears ill at ease," Bond noted.

It wasn't long before two men entered the courtyard and Tiger perked up. "Here we go," he said. "That's Masuzo Kano, the president of Yonai Enterprises." He was referring to a tall grey-haired man who walked as if he owned the world. With him was what appeared to be a dwarf. The small man was the strangest looking human being Bond had ever seen. From this distance, Bond thought that the dwarfs head must be deformed, for it was oddly shaped. The top of his head was bald except for a few long strands of hair that had been greased and combed over the scalp. His skull had an unusual bowl-like depression in the top. They were too far away to study his facial features but it wasn't difficult to see that he had the face of a monster.

"Who's the other fellow?" Bond asked.

"I don't know. He looks like a frog."

The dwarf was carrying a large metal briefcase. Like Kano he was dressed in a suit, which made him seem all the more out of place. The man reminded Bond of something. He was short, frog-like . . . *of course!* The "kappa." Takuya Abo had mentioned a kappa, something out of Japanese supernatural fairy tales.

"Tiger, do you know what a kappa is?" Bond asked.

"Of course I do, Bondo-san." Tiger paused a moment as he considered what Bond was getting at. "You are right, Bondo-san! That man does look like a kappa! I will have to call in his description and see if the police have anything on him. I have a feeling that one should not be deceived by his size. That little fellow is probably quite formidable or else he would not be accompanying Kano."

They watched as the two men approached the souvenir stand and made a show of looking at the trinkets which included charms like the ones sold at the Meiji shrine in Tokyo, miniature replicas of the Buddha, postcards and other items. Fujimoto finished his tea and bowed to the women, left the tented area and walked to the Buddha. Without acknowledging the other men, he paid the admission fee to go inside the statue, then went around the back of the monument to the entrance.

The dwarf bought something from the kiosk then he and Masuzo Kano nonchalantly walked to the Buddha, paid the fee and disappeared behind the statue.

Tiger punched a number and put his mobile to his ear. "My man is posted on the other side of courtyard," he explained. He spoke quietly into the phone, listened, then rang off. "He says that they are inside the Buddha. Now we wait until they come out."

Ten minutes later, Masuzo Kano came out alone. He purposefully strode away from the Buddha and out of the courtyard. A few minutes later, Shinji Fujimoto emerged, carrying the metal briefcase. He, too, walked towards the exit but took his time in doing so. He stopped at a souvenir kiosk and pretended to study the trinkets, then finally left the grounds.

"What happened to the kappa?" Bond asked.

"He must still be inside the Buddha," Tiger replied. Bond got up and walked around the courtyard, then paid the twenty yen required to go inside the statue. He ducked his head in the short doorway, then stood in the centre of the metal figure. The interior looked nothing like the Buddha. It was just discoloured bronze. The idol's head was but a cavity in the metal. There was scaffolding set up inside where some repair work was in progress, but no workmen were there and there was no sign of the kappa.

Bond emerged and met Tiger at the front gate. "I don't know what the hell happened to the little fellow," Bond said. "No one was in there."

Tiger asked his colleague on the phone about it. The man replied that he never saw the dwarf leave the statue.

"Come on, let's follow Fujimoto," Tiger said.

They left the *Daibutsu* grounds and saw Fujimoto walking up the hill toward Hase-dera, one of Kamakura's more popular Buddhist temples. Bond and Tanaka followed him from a distance.

"I suspect there is money in the briefcase. What is he going to do, make a donation to the temple?" Tiger asked sarcastically.

They entered the temple grounds, which contains several build-ings that date from the 1300s, a beautiful garden and a fascinating collection of statues of Jizo, who, as Tiger quietly explained, is the guardian of the souls of departed children. The two men made their way around the garden over a wooden bridge and then shadowed Fujimoto to the front of Kannon Hall, where the image of Kannon, the Bodhisattva of the goddess of mercy, is represented by a statue with eleven faces.

Fujimoto appeared to be praying. He rang a bell and placed sev-eral wads of bills in the collection box.

"That man has a guilty conscience," Bond remarked.

Fujimoto turned suddenly and almost saw them. Bond and Tiger ducked behind a post and waited until the man moved away. They started to follow him over the bridge and into the garden when they saw the dwarf again. The kappa had appeared from nowhere and was trailing behind Fujimoto by a few metres.

"Where did he come from?" Bond asked.

"I don't know!"

Fujimoto went around a group of cherry trees and was soon out of sight. The dwarf walked in the same direction.

"Let's go," Tiger said. They continued their surveillance, moving over the bridge and stopping behind the trees. They saw Fujimoto, but the dwarf was gone.

"He's disappeared again!" Tiger exclaimed. "That thing really *is* a kappa!"

"Don't be ridiculous, Tiger," Bond said. "He's obviously skilled in stealth."

"I have a very bad feeling about this, Bondo-san."

Fujimoto left the temple and walked down the hill towards the street. Bond and Tiger carefully scanned the area but saw no sign of the dwarf. They got down to the street and surveyed the line of cars parked along the kerb. Fujimoto was on his way towards the main thoroughfare, where several side streets intersected. He turned a corner and was gone.

"Come on," Tiger urged.

They moved swiftly towards the first cross street and there it was—Fujimoto's Toyota Celsior. Other than that, the street was deserted.

Bond and Tiger stepped up to the car and looked inside. The driver was slumped forward over the wheel. Fujimoto was in the back seat, lying at an awkward angle. Tiger opened the door and they saw that the vice president of CureLab had been stabbed numerous times. Blood covered the seat and dripped onto the floor. The driver's throat had been cut.

"We're too late," Tiger said. He got out his mobile and immediately called for the police and an ambulance.

Bond examined the car as best as he could. "That briefcase is gone," he said. "And look here."

He pointed to Fujimoto's hand. All of the fingers had been sliced off. Next to it was a miniature replica of the Great Buddha—the trinket that the kappa-man had bought from the souvenir stand.

THIRTEEN

LOOSE ENDS

THEY WERE IN A SATELLITE KOAN-CHOSA-CHO OFFICE LOCATED IN THE elaborate Takanawa Prince Hotel complex in the Shinagawa district of the city. The room was on the top floor of one of the newer hotels, Sakura Tower. Bond could look out of the window and gaze at the famous city landmark, Tokyo Tower, Japan's larger equivalent of the Eiffel Tower. The service owned the small private workspace and Tiger liked to use it since his pseudo-retirement. There was a complete link-up to the main headquarters so Tiger didn't have to deal with any bureaucracy when he wanted to access electronic files. He also had full use of the hotel's room service, which wasn't a bad deal.

Tiger and Bond had spent the remainder of the previous day in Kamakura, working with the local police investigating the murder of Shinji Fujimoto. Frustrating as it was, they both remained on the scene as the police worked and later gave statements at the police station. The police were unsuccessful in unearthing anything useful. Other than the miniature Buddha, no other clue was found at the crime scene that might indicate who the killer was.

But Bond and Tanaka had a pretty good idea.

Now they sat in the small office that overlooked the busy commercial district and worked on tying up loose ends. Tiger typed on a PC in an effort to identify the strange dwarf they had seen and Bond watched the news on television, waiting for the expected story on CureLab.

"My agents have confirmed what I suspected all along," Tiger said, punching up a report on his computer. "The so-called private individuals who own the twenty per cent of CureLab stock are all on the board of directors of Yonai Enterprises."

"What a surprise," Bond said. "That fits with the news we got last night. Shinji Fujimoto sold his shares the day before he was killed. That makes Yonai a significant shareholder of CureLab. Pieces of the jigsaw are falling into place. I wonder if our little killer in Kamakura is one of the shareholders."

"I'm telling you, he was a kappa," Tiger said facetiously, hoping to get a rise out of Bond.

"Would you shut up with that kappa nonsense? Look, I think it's coming on."

The first thing that appeared on the screen was the logo and name, "Yonai Enterprises." The reporter said, "Big news in the business sector today. Yonai Enterprises, a Sapporo-based conglomerate, has announced a merger with CureLab Inc., a Tokyo-based corporation. The move was not a surprise to analysts, as Yonai had made several public bids for acquisition of the company that had been run in recent years by Englishman Peter McMahon. Peter McMahon and his family died of an unknown illness eight days ago."

Peter McMahon's portrait flashed on the television.

"The deal was further complicated by the murder of CureLab vice president and acting chairman Fujimoto Shinji yesterday in Kamakura. He had stunned his board of directors the day before at an emergency meeting by announcing that he had sold his own twenty per cent of CureLab stock to Yonai Enterprises."

They watched as a familiar scene appeared. It was Shinji Fujimoto's Toyota Celsior, parked on that side street in Kamakura. Police tape was stretched around it and several uniformed men could be seen hovering around.

The programme cut to a clip of Yonai's president, Masuzo Kano, speaking into a microphone and saying that together the staff of

Yonai Enterprises and CureLab would work to reach even greater heights than either of their two companies had done thus far.

The reporter continued, "Police are not saying if Fujimoto's murder is related to organised crime. Yonai Enterprises has long had to fight the accusations by some that it is allegedly involved in yakuza business."

A new clip: Yasutake Tsukamoto, walking with bodyguards in front of his office in Sapporo. Several reporters hounded him. Bond recognised him from the file that Tanaka had given him.

"No comment. Go away," Tsukamoto said into the camera.

The *kaicho* got into a Mercedes as the picture cut back to the reporter. "CureLab Inc. is known for its work in pharmaceuticals and cures for diseases. Kano-san says that the company will fit in nicely within the chemical engineering areas of Yonai Enterprises. Now on to sports . . ."

"There you have the motive," Bond said. "Fujimoto was killed once he'd sold his shares and agreed to the merger with Yonai. The yakuza is behind it all. They orchestrated the McMahons' deaths all right."

"I agree with you, but all we have to go on is speculation," Tiger replied. "No proof. Ah, wait, here we may have it." He punched up a new e-mail. "The report on the bonsai waterfall came in. You were right, Bondo-san, there were traces of mosquito eggs and shed pupal skins in the reservoir where the water sits. Mosquitoes need water to hatch, right? Since the motor had malfunctioned, the water had been still for a week. That was enough time to hatch those eggs, apparently. The question is, did someone put those eggs inside it? And did Fujimoto know about it?"

"Tiger, it has to be the answer. It was part of his grand plan to sell his stock to the yakuza. I wonder what they promised him besides a great deal of money."

"He did not even receive that in the end," Tiger observed. He read some more of the report. "The egg remains and other organic material have been sent to toxicology to see if they can determine if the virus came from there."

"I think we have to go on the assumption that it did. Someone has invented a deadly biological weapon with an ingenious delivery system—those mosquitoes. It takes a molecular biologist to do something like that, doesn't it? Someone like Fujio Aida? With everything I saw at CureLab about mosquitoes, can you have any doubts?"

"Aida's probably capable of creating the virus. It took the merging of Yonai and CureLab—their separate technologies—to make this weapon."

"But there had to have been insiders at CureLab for some time. The McMahons were killed last week so if Yonai or the yakuza were responsible for this, they would have had to possess the virus technology before yesterday."

"I think we know who the insiders were, Bondo-san," Tiger said, his eyebrows raised.

Bond nodded and said, "Shinji Fujimoto and Fujio Aida. Tiger, this weapon—we have to stop whatever these people might want to do with it next and destroy it. You don't want another incident like the sarin gas subway attacks a few years ago. I suggest that you set up a meeting with a mosquito expert as soon as possible. We need a crash course in insect biology."

"I agree. I must consult with my colleagues at headquarters and inform them of our hypothesis. If this is true, then the yakuza has become even more dangerous than ever."

He picked up his mobile and made a call.

Headquarters was located in Kasumigaseki, the district adjacent to Nagata-cho, where the Japanese Diet Building sits. It was an unusually nondescript government building on the exterior; however the interior possessed an energy that Bond thought was reminiscent of the Tsukiji Fish Market. The only difference was that the personnel wore business attire. The level of beehive-like activity was just as chaotic at the Koan-Chosa-Cho as it had been at the market; but once again, when Bond looked closer he could see the order and mechanical efficiency of the Japanese people at work.

Reiko Tamura had quickly arranged to bring in an entomologist to give them an overview of mosquitoes. She had been discharged from the hospital when Bond was in Kamakura and had reported for duty, even though she had been given a few days' leave.

"This is Dr. Okumura," Reiko said, introducing an unusually tall, slender woman in her thirties. Tiger and Bond bowed to her and exchanged business cards, then the four of them went into a conference room.

"I have been studying the samples that Tamura-san provided to me," the doctor began, "and I have come to the conclusion that the mosquitoes involved here are *Aedes aegypti*. This is a species that lays eggs above water and can breed in small containers. The eggs can remain dry and survive for a considerable amount of time and they hatch when they come into contact with water."

"Instant mosquitoes, just add water," Bond said.

"Something like that," she said. She showed them pictures of mosquito eggs. They resembled black caraway seeds. "It normally takes a week to ten days for them to go through the cycle from eggs to adult mosquitoes; some species take a week or more longer. Eggs hatch into larvae that live in water for several days. Stagnant, standing water is the best environment for these things."

"So it was fairly easy for mosquitoes to breed inside that bonsai waterfall contraption," Bond said.

"Yes, as long as they had food. Larvae eat just about anything with protein, usually microscopic organisms that live in the water. The larvae eventually become pupae and then after a few days, the adult mosquitoes emerge. The females are the only ones that bite. They immediately need to find a blood host, which gives them the protein needed to lay eggs. The male mosquitoes feed off things that provide sugar and are basically harmless to humans. The males and females can mate at any time after they emerge from the pupal state. Females live longer than the males, so some entomologists call them 'red widows.'"

"I've known a couple of those in my time," Bond muttered.

"How long do the adult mosquitoes live?" Tiger asked.

"Males live less than a week. Females can live longer if they're not killed by the elements, slapped by a human hand or eaten by other creatures, which is what usually happens. Very rarely do we see mosquitoes live to be a ripe old age which conceivably could be three or four weeks."

Bond asked, "If someone were to have the ability to change the genetic structure of a mosquito, what advantages could be gained?"

Dr. Okumura shrugged. "I understand that many companies in the pesticide business are working on that type of technology. If you could genetically engineer a mosquito not to bite, I suppose that would be good, yes?"

Bond frowned. "But if that is possible, then is it also possible to genetically engineer a mosquito's behaviour in other ways? Say, to bite even more zealously?"

"Yes, that is possible."

Bond and Tiger shared a look.

"Is this *Aedes aegypti* able to transmit diseases?" Bond asked.

"Oh, yes," the doctor said. "They are one of the main species that is a vector, or carrier, for yellow fever, encephalitis and West Nile disease. There are others, but this one is known for that."

"How does that work?" Reiko asked.

"The female mosquito bites an infected host, becomes infected herself, then goes and bites a human. Simply a transference of blood."

"Wait a second," Bond said. "So the mosquito isn't born with the disease? It has to pick it up somewhere else?"

"That's right."

"Is it possible for mosquitoes to pass the disease on to their young, via the eggs?"

The doctor made a face and said, "Some species can do that, but not this one. Thank goodness."

"Then is it possible for them to be genetically engineered to do so?"

"Perhaps. Although I don't know why anyone would want to do that," the doctor replied.

"Is there a name for that?" Reiko asked.

"Yes, it's called 'transovarial transmission.' "

Again, Bond and Tiger shared a look. This time Reiko joined them.

The meeting with the entomologist went on for a few more minutes; Dr. Okumura left after offering her help for any other inquiries they might have. Bond had a look at some of the literature she had given them, found a picture of the *Aedes aegypti,* and studied it.

"From the notes you found at CureLab the other night, Bondo-san, it seems that they are working on producing a strain of mosquitoes that can transfer the disease to their eggs," Tanaka suggested.

"Red widows," Bond added.

"We've had a look at that slideshow that James-san brought from CureLab," Reiko said. "There's nothing suspicious in it. It's basically a crash course on the biology of a mosquito. Toward the end it talks about how the company should genetically engineer the mosquitoes for the good of mankind. Knock out their reproductive instincts, or make them so they don't bite. That kind of thing."

Tiger's mobile rang. He answered it and listened, then he rang off and said, "We have found our kappa. I'll be right back." He got up and left the room.

"Poor James-san," Reiko said. "You must be in terrible pain. Those are nasty cuts on your face."

"It only hurts when I kiss someone," Bond said. It was true that he still looked battered.

"I would still kiss you, James-san, but I am afraid that you would find it painful," she said.

"Perhaps we should experiment?" Bond asked. "How's the wound?"

"Much better. Still hurts a little."

"Reiko?"

"Yes, James-san?"

"How about when I'm finished with this assignment, we go somewhere on a holiday, just the two of us?"

Reiko's eyes widened. "Oh my, James-san. I don't know what to say. Where do you suggest we go?"

"Is there somewhere you've always wanted to see?"

She thought a moment. "I have always dreamed of going to the Hawaiian Islands."

"What a coincidence. I have too. Hawaii it is. Will you think about it?"

She nodded quietly and looked down as Tiger came back into the room.

"Look what I have," Tiger said as he went to the computer and inserted a floppy disk into the drive. He used the mouse and brought up an image of the kappa killer. "This is him."

"It certainly is," Bond said.

"His name is Junji Kon. Nickname: 'Kappa!' He has a police record, all right. Kon was an orphan; his parents probably got rid of him because of his deformities. Historically in Japan children who were born deformed were either killed or left to die somewhere. It was a sad fact of life. Junji Kon managed to survive, working in a circus until he was in his teens. That's when the arrests began. Shoplifting, burglary, assault and a number of more serious charges. He was arrested once for murder but was released for lack of evidence. He was known to be a *shatei,* or younger brother, of the yakuza by the time he was twenty. Sometimes the yakuza will accept misfits from society because they're the only family that will have them. It makes sense."

"Indeed."

"It says here that Kappa is very good with a knife and always carries a Balisong, what we call a butterfly knife."

"I'm familiar with it," Bond said. It was a nasty weapon used by many gangs in the Far East. It consisted of two hinged handles that fitted around the blade, which could be exposed by spinning one handle around in an arc with a flick of the wrist. Bond had seen men who could manipulate the Balisong with blinding-fast manoeuvres.

Tiger continued, "Because of his size, he is adept at stealth skills. In the circus he performed as a freak in a sideshow but also as a magician's assistant."

"That explains why he seemed to appear and disappear at will in Kamakura," Bond said. "He walked out of that Buddha under our noses and we didn't notice."

"It also says that Kappa is suspected of being a hit-man for the

Ryujin-kai. Very interesting. I will file a report stating that we suspect him of being Shinji Fujimoto's killer. He will be wanted for questioning."

"If anyone can find him," Reiko said. "Where does he live?"

"It does not say. He is known to be in Tokyo but has been seen in Sapporo as well."

Tiger's phone rang again. He rolled his eyes and answered it. He listened and said, *"Hai!"* He hung up and said, "There is news about the summit conference. They've finally picked a site."

"It's about time," Reiko said. "It's only six days away."

"It is to take place where I suggested. It is a remote location in the Inland Sea, on Naoshima Island. It is just off the shore south of Okayama, just east of the Seto-Ohashi Bridge. It is perfect for a G8 meeting. Benesse Corporation bought a portion of the island and turned it into 'Benesse Island' and they built a beautiful art museum and hotel there called Benesse House. It is one of Japan's little treasures that not too many people know about. The conference will be held at the art museum and the guests will stay in the lodgings there."

"When do we have to be there?" Bond asked.

"The day before. My people will already be on the island days earlier, of course, to make sure that security is well placed. This location is top secret, so I cannot imagine that the threats we have received can be credible. Still, one cannot be too careful. I have been put in charge of the security. And as this is an international gathering, I have made you my second in command, Bondo-san."

"Thanks, Tiger. I'm honoured," Bond said dryly.

"You are welcome!" Tiger said, enjoying the moment.

Bond looked back at the mosquito documents that were on the table. "You have people in Sapporo, don't you?"

"Of course. I have a very good man in Sapporo. He's Ainu, a very interesting fellow."

Tiger was referring to the race of people who are believed to be the original inhabitants of Japan. The Ainu live mostly in the northern parts of the country and in the Kuril Islands.

"I think it's time for me to go north and try to find Mayumi

McMahon," Bond said. "Put a word in to your man that I'm looking for her and see what he can dig up. I'd also like to put in a visit to this Hokkaido Mosquito and Vector Control Centre. Those posters I saw at the CureLab office came from there. Where is Noboribetsu, exactly?"

"That's a resort town south of Sapporo with a lot of hot springs and spas," Reiko replied. "Hotels. Tourists. The Hokkaido Mosquito and Vector Control Centre is a public health facility located just outside the town."

Tiger said, "Very well. We shall send you to Hokkaido, Bondo-san. I think you should have Miss Tamura accompany you, what do you think?"

"I'd be delighted," Bond said. "It helps to have a native speaker along for the ride."

Reiko blushed again and looked away. "I will have my assistant check on flights," she said as she fiddled with her Palm Pilot. "When do you want to leave?"

"Today if possible," Bond said. "But no flights. I have a feeling that our friends in the Ryujin-kai might be watching the airports. Let's take a train. We can do that, can't we?"

Reiko shrugged. "Sure. There's an overnight train from Ueno Station. We could have sleeper compartments. It's not as fast but it gets us there."

"I adore train travel," Bond said. "Book two sleepers. For tonight."

FOURTEEN

NIGHT TRAIN

REIKO WAS SUCCESSFUL IN SECURING TWO SLEEPER SUITES ON THE TWO-storey *Cassiopeia*, touted as Japan's most luxurious train. It travelled between Tokyo's Ueno Station and Sapporo three times a week on a journey lasting seventeen hours. All carriages were first-class sleeper cars. The train also offered shower rooms, an observation lounge and an excellent restaurant car that provided French or Japanese dinners.

Bond checked out of the Imperial, had a quick dinner with Tiger, then met Reiko at the station half an hour before departure time. Bond had the "Cassiopeia Suite," the only one of its type on the train. It was located at the very front of the lower floor and had all the amenities of a hotel room: two double beds, a private bathroom and a small sitting area by the front windows that could be used for work or dining. The suite took up the entire width of the train. Reiko got the slightly less luxurious "Deluxe Suite" just down the corridor from Bond. It contained two single beds, a private bathroom and fold-up tables. The beds could be turned into day-seats and the room was on one side of the train.

"Why did you get me the most expensive compartment on the train?" Bond asked her.

"Because you are our special guest in Japan," she said. "You said that you adored trains, so I provided you with the best."

"You know, we could have shared one room and saved the Koan-Chosa-Cho some money."

She wagged her finger and gave him one of those looks that suggested that he was a naughty boy. "James-san, you know that if we did that, the people who process our expense reports would spread rumours about us!"

Bond shrugged and smiled.

The train departed precisely on time, something that Japan Rail advertised proudly. Bond had to admit that the country's rail service was indeed the best in the world.

Bond spent a half-hour in his suite enjoying the view of the landscape rushing at him. It was after dark, so there wasn't much to see in terms of scenery but there was something hypnotic and soothing about watching the parallel lines of train tracks, illuminated by the engine's headlamps, whipping towards him. The train was steadily shooting toward its destination, northward to the upper tip of Honshu, where it would go through the Seikan Tunnel to the island of Hokkaido. The tunnel would be interesting, Bond thought, as it was the longest rail tunnel in the world at over fifty kilometres between the two ends and had taken twenty-four years to build. Bond had always been interested in architecture and structural engineering but more from a practical point of view than an artistic one. He appreciated the thought that went into the way buildings, bridges and tunnels were designed and constructed and admired the men who could do it.

He opened one of the small bottles of sake that Tiger had given to him as a parting gift and poured a glass. He thought that perhaps he should ask Reiko to join him but at this point he wasn't sure how she really felt about him. It was true that she had allowed him to kiss her but it was sometimes difficult to discern whether a Japanese girl was serious in her flirting or not. Reiko was a professional and she would probably behave like one until the assignment was over. But they were all alone on an overnight train! How much more romantic could life get? Bond wondered if she might be willing to entertain such notions. Should he get up, go and rap on her door?

A knock at his compartment answered his query.

Reiko stood in the corridor, having changed into a *yukata*. She, too, held a bottle of sake.

"I thought you might be lonely," she said. "I know I was."

"Come in!"

She went past him into the suite, walked straight to the sitting area and placed the bottle next to Bond's.

"I see you started without me," she said. "I have some catching up to do. *Sugoi,* what a view!"

"Isn't it?"

"I have an idea. How about we order room service and stay here?" She swallowed and batted her eyelashes at him. He could see that she was a little nervous. He walked to her and stroked her smooth black hair.

"I think that's a lovely idea," he whispered. He leaned in to kiss her and she hungrily embraced him.

It was nearly midnight.

Reiko's skin felt warm and smooth as she wrapped a slender leg around him and snuggled into his chest. She playfully rubbed at the hair there.

"I like this stuff," she said, almost giggling. "We Japanese women don't see that very often."

"Are we so different from Japanese men?"

"Yes and no. I mean, you have hair in places that Japanese men don't, and you obviously look different. You're very tall, so you're a bit of a giant compared to most Japanese men. What about us?"

"You mean Japanese women? Possibly the most beautiful in the world."

She hit him lightly on the shoulder. "You know how to flatter. Will we really go to Hawaii?"

"If you'd like."

"We could lie on the beach all day and make love all night."

"We could pick a different beach each day."

Reiko laughed. She was ready for him. The gentle rocking of the train added to their pleasure. Reiko wrapped her legs around his waist and locked him against her, allowing the motion of the train to do all the work.

Bond was sleeping soundly when Reiko awoke a couple of hours later. The wound on her side hurt; she must have rubbed it accidentally during the lovemaking, which at one point had become rather turbulent.

Damn, she thought. The painkillers were in her suite. She didn't really want to have to get dressed and leave, but she was afraid that she would be unable to go back to sleep if she didn't. She quietly got out of the bed, put on her *yukata* and slippers and trod softly toward the door.

"Reiko?" Bond mumbled as he stirred.

"It's all right," she whispered. "I'm going back to my room for a minute. I'll be back."

"Take my key," he said. "There on the counter."

She found it, blew him a kiss and went out of the room.

The train corridor was quiet and dark. As it was probably two o'clock in the morning, everyone with any sense was asleep. She walked down to her room, unlocked the door and went inside. Once there, she found her pills and looked for something to take them with.

Oh no, she thought. Nothing to drink. The restaurant car was closed at this hour but the lounge had a vending machine. Come to think of it, there were snacks in the machines there, too. She was a little hungry. The room service box dinner had been tasty but not very filling. Bond had complained that he had still felt hungry after they had eaten, too. Reiko decided that she'd make a quick trip to the lounge and bring back some sweets and drinks to share with him and then perhaps they would be energised for another round of passion.

She put on a pair of blue jeans and a T-shirt and went back into the corridor. The lounge car was on the top floor of the train, all the way at the back. She made her way out of their car and into the second one, then up the steps to the next level. A conductor was walking her way and greeted her. She asked him if there was any food left in the vending machines and the man replied that there was. Reiko thanked him and went on.

She went through several cars, past the many regular twin suites that filled the train, until she came to car eleven. She was about to open the sliding metal door to car twelve, the lounge car, when she saw something that sent a chill up her spine.

Through the window, she could see a small man in the lounge car putting money into a vending machine. He was a dwarf with a bald, misshapen head.

It was Kappa.

What was he doing on the train? Did he know they were on it? She had to go and inform James immediately!

But wait, she thought, perhaps she should find out what sleeper he was in.

Kappa retrieved a can of juice from the machine and began to walk towards her. Reiko ducked and squeezed herself into a cranny that held a pay telephone. Thinking quickly, she turned her back to the corridor, picked up the receiver, and began to talk to a non-existent party. The door opened behind her and she heard the man leave the lounge car and walk past her. Reiko waited a few seconds, then hung up the phone. She peered into the corridor and saw Kappa opening the opposite door and going into the next car.

She ran to follow him, waited a moment, and then opened the door. She went into the car and watched him unlock one of the compartments and step inside. Once she was certain that he had closed and locked the door, she crept down to see what number it was. Car 10, compartment 22.

All thoughts of hunger had vanished and her heart was pounding with excitement. Without returning to the lounge car, Reiko went back to Bond's suite and let herself in with his key. He was still in bed, breathing deeply. She took some of the unfinished sake and swallowed her pill, then sat on the bed beside him. She ran her fingers through his hair until he stirred.

"Hey wake up, mister," she said.

"Hey." He turned and smiled at her. "You're dressed."

"I have some news. Guess who is aboard the train."

"The Emperor."

"No. Kappa. Junji Kon himself."

Bond sat up. "Are you sure? How do you know?"

"I just saw him. And . . . I know what compartment he is in."

"Good girl." Bond thought a moment and said, "So, is he on this train because we're on it, or is he simply travelling to Sapporo with no idea that we're here? Did he see you?"

"I don't think so."

"I would love to get into his compartment and take a look around. What time is it?"

"I don't know. It's the middle of the night."

"He'll have to come out in the morning. Do you think he'll go to the restaurant car for breakfast?"

"Hard to say," she said. "Since he looks the way he does, he may try to avoid people. He might order room service, like we did last night."

"We have to think of something."

"Let's go talk to the conductor. I saw him walking through the train earlier."

Bond quickly put on some clothes and the two of them went out into the corridor. They made their way through the car to the stair-well, then up to the second floor. They caught up with the conductor in car 7.

Reiko showed him her identification card. "Excuse me, we are with the Public Security Investigation Agency. We have learned that there is a dangerous criminal aboard the train."

The conductor looked alarmed.

"Don't be frightened. We could use your help. He's a dwarf and he's in compartment twenty-two, car ten. Have you seen him?"

"Yes," the conductor said. "Strange fellow. Gives me the creeps."

"Will you be up the rest of the night?" she asked.

"Yes, I'm on night duty until we reach Hokkaido."

"Could you possibly keep an eye on his compartment? We would like to have a look around his room should he happen to leave. Would you do that for us?"

"That's not exactly legal, madam."

"Please? It might mean the safety of your passengers." She batted her eyelashes at him and gently placed a hand on his upper arm.

The conductor blushed and bowed. "Yes. I will try."

She gave him hers and Bond's compartment numbers, bowed, and left with Bond to go back to his suite.

The conductor smiled as he walked through the train to his own compartment, which happened to be in the same car that contained Bond and Reiko's suites. What a pretty girl! he thought. Sometimes it really paid to work for Japan Rail.

He unlocked the door to his little room. Inside there was a place to sit down and not much more. An emergency pull-cord was located in every conductor's compartment, and this could be used to stop the train if he had to do it. There were also communication phones to the other posts on the train and to the engineer and control panels for the lights and doors. The conductor opened a cabinet and pulled out his carry-on bag. He dug inside for the sandwich his wife had packed for him.

There was a knock on the door.

He put down the bag and opened the door. At first he didn't see anyone. It was only when he looked down that he gasped.

The butterfly knife in Kappa's hand whipped viciously back and forth without making a sound.

FIFTEEN

THE DESIRE FOR DEATH

IT HAD HAPPENED AGAIN.

Goro Yoshida awoke in his bunker and had to shake off the remnants of another nightmare. It was a recurring one, something that normally wouldn't have disturbed him if it hadn't been for Yukio Mishima's role in it.

In the dream, Yoshida was kneeling on the floor, naked to the waist, and was prepared to commit ritual *seppuku*. Mishima, his mentor, stood over him with a sword, ready to cut off Yoshida's head. The problem was that when Yoshida attempted to plunge the dagger into his belly, the skin wouldn't budge. The blade just wouldn't penetrate. Mishima would get angry and yell that Yoshida was a coward. And just as Mishima raised the sword to lop off Yoshida's head, Goro would wake up.

There was no morning sun in the bunker. That had been the most difficult thing about going into exile and having to live underground. Yoshida used to enjoy rising with the sun. It was said that dawn was the ideal time to commit *seppuku*. At the end of one of Yoshida's favourite books by Mishima, the hero gallantly commits ritual *seppuku* on a mountaintop, plunging the dagger into his belly just as the "bright disk of the sun soared up and exploded behind his eyelids."

The digital clock indicated that it was indeed morning. It was time to get up. There was much work to be done, but instead Yoshida lay there wallowing in memories of the man he admired so much.

Yoshida had been a part of Mishima's Shield Society, the private army that the poet and novelist had formed in the late 1960s as a token of his dedication to the emperor and to the traditional values of Japan. Yoshida had looked up to Mishima-san and revered the *sensei*'s every word. He volunteered to be a cadet in the Shield Society and trained along with Mishima and the rest of the students. He worked to improve his body and mind with kendo and other martial arts. He read the doctrines prescribed by his mentor. He was prepared to follow Mishima in whatever the *sensei* chose to do.

Then Mishima learned that Yoshida was involved with the yakuza. Even though he was an intelligent and freethinking individual, Mishima did not approve. It was true that Mishima had right-wing tendencies and believed in many of the same principles as the yakuza did, such as the purification of Japan, but he drew the line at organised crime. Mishima told Yoshida that he must leave the Shield Society.

Yoshida had never felt so disgraced in his life. The man he looked up to had dismissed him. Yoshida had wanted to commit *seppuku* then and there, but his friends in the yakuza convinced him not to. He was persuaded to use his knowledge and skills for the good of the Ryujin-kai, where he could someday become a *kaicho*.

And so Yoshida turned his back on the Shield Society and tried to forget about Yukio Mishima until that fateful day in November of 1970, when Mishima and his four most trusted cadets boldly walked into the army's command headquarters and held General Kanetoshi Mashita hostage. Then, as twelve hundred soldiers gathered on the parade ground, Mishima stepped onto the balcony and delivered a rousing, impassioned speech that most of the men heckled. He questioned the troops' motivation for guarding the constitution that, he claimed, denied them the true essence of what was once Imperial Japan. He pleaded with the men to "stand up and fight" or "die together" for the sake of nationalism.

But his words fell on cynical ears. Finally giving up the cause,

Mishima shouted, *"Tenno Heika Banzai!"*—"Long live the Emperor!"
He stepped back from the balcony and proceeded to perform in precise detail the traditional *seppuku* ceremony. He went into the office
where the general was being held, stripped to the waist and knelt on
the floor. He probed the left side of his abdomen and put the cere-
monial dagger in place. Then he thrust it deep into his flesh.
Standing behind him, Morita, his most trusted cadet, raised his
sword to cut off Mishima's head. He missed the first time, gravely
wounding Mishima. It took two more tries and the help of another
cadet before Mishima's head rolled onto the floor. To complete the
ceremony, Morita plunged a dagger into his own stomach and yet
another cadet lopped off Morita's head. Shedding tears, the three sur-
viving cadets saluted the two dead men and surrendered to the general's aides. It was reported later that Mishima's seventeen-centimetre
incision displayed a "degree of mastery over physical reflex, and over
pain itself, unparalleled in modern records of this ritual."

Goro Yoshida's admiration of Mishima increased ten-fold after the
incident. What a brave and noble thing to do! Mishima had been serious
about his convictions all along. He had made the ritual act of *seppuku* a
part of his art. While many critics might have thought that what
Mishima did was insane, Yoshida felt that he was a man who never
forgot his wartime catechism: the doctrine of Japan as a ritually ordered
state, the samurai way of life characterised by manly courage and feminine grace and the vision of imminent death as the catalyst of life.

Yoshida finally got up off of the futon and walked away, leaving his
woman sleeping. Naked, he walked across the *tatami* and took the cer-
emonial dagger from a drawer in his desk. He knelt on the floor in the
correct position and placed the point of the dagger against his skin,
touching the bright red tail of a tattooed dragon that wrapped around
his waist. He pressed the blade, ever so slightly, feeling the sharp tip's
desire to penetrate his body and wondered if his blood would be dis-
tinguishable from the crimson artwork adorning his belly.

When the time came, would *he* be able to do what Mishima had
done? If everything that he and his followers had worked for ended
up failing completely, then he would have no other choice.

"What are you doing?"

The woman had awoken and looked at him in horror.

Yoshida answered, "Nothing. Go back to sleep."

She frowned but after a moment finally turned over and put her head down.

Yoshida could see her bare shoulders and back. For many men, such beauty would be enough, but he was reminded of Mishima's words: "A man's determination to become a beautiful person is very different from the same desire in a woman; in a man it is always the desire for death."

How true, Yoshida thought. How true.

Bond finished the *natto* Reiko had insisted on his trying. The bloody stuff was awful. This putrid concoction created from fermented soy-beans nearly made him gag. It had an atrocious nutty flavour, a disturbing aroma and stickiness, all held together like a spider web by gooey strands.

"I can see you enjoyed that!" Reiko said brightly. "I told you it was good."

"Mmm," Bond said with a smile.

She finished the last bit of her own bowl of *natto* and looked past Bond, across the dining car towards the entrance. Her eyes gave her away.

"James-san, another guest for breakfast," she whispered.

Bond knew whom she meant without looking.

The dwarf known as Kappa waddled into the dining car, was greeted by the hostess, and then shown to an empty table for two. He was dressed in a suit and tie, as if he were ready for a day at the bank. He wore no hat, so his glistening misshapen head was in full view. Virtually everyone in the dining car was staring at him, for he was an extraordinarily bizarre sight. Behind Kappa's back, the hostess gave a wide-eyed look to the waiter, who bowed to the dwarf before taking his order. After the waiter walked away, Kappa unfolded a newspaper and began to read.

"Does he know we're here?" Bond asked.

"He hasn't looked at us," she said. "He hasn't looked at anyone but people are sure looking at *him*."

"He's ordering breakfast?"

"That's what it looks like."

"You have your mobile with you?"

"Of course."

She patted the pocket of her business suit. They were both dressed a bit more formally since they would be arriving in Sapporo later in the morning.

"You stay here. Have some coffee or something. Watch him and if he gets up to leave, call me."

"You're going to his room now?"

"Hush."

Bond got up from the table, turned, and casually walked across the compartment. He passed the dwarf and bowed slightly to the hostess. Kappa did not look up from his newspaper.

Bond went into the corridor of the next car and continued through the train until he came to car 10. He found compartment 22, looked both ways to make sure the hallway was clear, then lifted his left foot so that he could access the heel of his shoe. He used his index finger to find the slight impression next to a seam and press it. A thin metal wire released itself into his hand.

Bond gently inserted the lockpick into the keyhole. He twisted the wire carefully until he heard a snap. The door opened. He stepped inside, closed the door and replaced the lockpick in his shoe.

The room was a standard twin with two bunks at a ninety-degree angle to each other. On one of the fold-down trays sat a bottle of orange juice, an empty paper cup and a plate with three slices of cucumber.

Bond went straight for the luggage and began to rummage through it. He found mostly clothes, personal effects, nothing of interest.

Under one of the bunks was a square box. It was like a hatbox but much smaller. Bond pulled it out and lifted the lid. Inside was a glass jar with a strange seal on the top. There appeared to be a hinge attached to the rim of the seal and the top surface contained several mesh-covered holes. The seal couldn't be unscrewed or popped open. Bond looked for a keyhole that might release the hinged top but didn't see one. He held the jar up to the light and peered into it.

It contained live mosquitoes and an inch of water. The insects were crawling on the inside of the jar and lid, perpetually trying to find a way out. Bond counted ten.

His mobile rang, startling him. He pulled it out of his jacket pocket and answered the call.

"James-san, he's getting ready to leave," Reiko said.

"Thanks." Bond rang off and put the mobile back in the pocket, then replaced the square box under the bunk. The glass jar he stuck in his other pocket.

Bond took a quick look around the room to make sure that nothing appeared out of place, then he quickly opened the door and scanned the hallway. All clear. He stepped out, closed the door and made sure that it was locked. Then he began to walk back to the dining car.

As he went through one set of doors between cars, Bond saw Kappa coming from the opposite end toward him. They would pass each other in the centre of the car.

Since it was too late to turn back, Bond kept going. He expected to make eye contact, but Kappa never looked at him. Bond had to stop and allow the little man to squeeze past him. Bond said, *"Sumi-masen,"* but Kappa didn't acknowledge him. The dwarf kept walking and was soon going through the automatic door at the end of the car. Only after he had cleared the door did Kappa look back and grin to himself, but Bond didn't see this. He had gone on to the dining car and found Reiko still at the table.

"Did you see him?" she asked.

"Uh huh, and he ignored me," Bond said. "I have a funny feeling about it. It's like he's making a show out of not noticing us."

"Did you find anything?"

"Yes, but I had better let you see it back in the suite. Let's go."

She held the jar close to her face as she examined the movements of one mosquito crawling up the side of the jar.

"So those holes are in the top so they can breathe?" Reiko asked.

"That's right."

"I bet that one's pregnant," Reiko said. "She's dragging a big belly."

The insects were a dull red colour but otherwise were not unusually large or out of the ordinary in appearance. Reiko pondered the significance of a small cube with a tiny tube extending from it that was attached to the side of the glass.

"You know what?" she said. "I think that little thing on the side had food in it for the larvae. This is a mosquito incubator, James-san! There were eggs in here, then they hatched into larvae, grew into pupae and became mosquitoes. I'm not sure how it opens."

"It has some kind of locking mechanism. See the hinge? The top flips up but I can't determine how it's done. Not that I'd want to. I think we're just fine with those things safely trapped in the jar."

"I agree with you. What do we do now?"

"I guess we wait and see," Bond said. "Either he'll discover it's missing and do something about it or he'll get off the train in Sapporo and we'll follow him."

She continued to peer at the insects. "Do you think these bugs might have the virus?"

"What do *you* think?"

"We'd better hide it."

"Give it to me," Bond said. He took the jar and squatted beside the bed. He reached under the frame and balanced the container on top of a metal support that was a part of the structure.

"That will do for now. I suggest we remain in the room until we reach Sapporo."

Reiko smiled. "Sounds good to *me*."

Junji Kon smiled to himself. Perfect timing. The mosquitoes had shed their pupal skins thirty hours ago. The insects' shells would be hard now and they could fly. The fool had taken the container back to his compartment. The mission would be a success. Everything was going as planned. He would bring great honour to his name. The world would look at him with respect, something he had never experienced except from other members of the yakuza. Junji Kon was no longer an outcast. He had integrated into a new society and found acceptance. He made good money and he enjoyed what he did.

Kappa looked at his wristwatch just as the train entered the long Seikan Tunnel. All light from the outside was extinguished as the locomotive sped under the sea on its way to Hokkaido. It was time to act.

He put on his jacket, took his luggage and walked through the door. He made his way to the lower floor and walked to the first car. He listened at the conductor's compartment. It appeared that no one had discovered his handiwork yet.

Then he stood outside Bond's suite. First making sure that no one was looking, Kappa removed a small radio transmitter from his pocket. He pulled out the two-inch antenna and turned on the power. There was only one other button and Kappa pushed it to transmit a signal.

He could see it happening in his mind's eye. Inside the suite, where the *gaijin* lay with the secret service woman, the signal was received by the ingenious device housed in the top of the jar of mosquitoes. The hinged lid silently opened. The mosquitoes, suddenly discovering that they were free, crawled out of the jar and began to fly around the room. All females, especially hungry for a blood host.

The next thing Kappa did was move to Bond's door and insert one of the keys on the ring he had taken from the conductor. It went into the lock easily. Kappa turned it once, then clasped both hands and slammed them down on it as hard as he could. The key broke in the lock.

Kappa went back to the conductor's compartment, unlocked it and stepped inside. It was difficult avoiding the mess of the bloody, crumpled conductor's body, folded into a corner of the cubicle like origami.

The dwarf examined the control panel on the wall and found the switch to turn off the lights in the car. Nearby was the mechanism that opened the outside car doors.

He looked at his watch and reached for the emergency brake cord that hung in a little recess on the wall. He grasped the handle and waited.

A few more seconds, he thought, as he looked at his watch.

This was going to be *fun*.

Reiko snuggled against Bond's neck as they relaxed into the gentle rumbling motion of the train. They were enjoying the last few solitary moments on the train in each other's arms, their clothing discarded about the room.

"I hear that Maui is the best island," she said as she tightened the hold around his chest.

"Well, the big one, Hawaii, and Oahu are supposed to be charming."

"We'll have to hit them all. Go to a luau or two."

"There are other people at luaus. Don't you want to be alone together?"

"At least ninety-five per cent of the time. We could go there and, hey—!" She interrupted herself with a slap on her arm. She lifted her palm and revealed a smashed mosquito.

"James-san!"

Bond leaped out of bed and looked under the bed.

"The damned thing is open!" he said in horror. He pulled out the jar. The hinged top was indeed at a right angle to the container. Bond went to the door and tried to open it. He struggled with it and said, "We're locked in."

"Oh, God, look, I see another one!" she cried, pointing at the air. Bond attempted to see where she was pointing but the light and movement of the train inhibited his ability to spot the wretched insects. Then he saw one and batted at it.

"Get dressed, cover your arms," Bond shouted.

They both leaped around the room grabbing their respective articles of clothing and raced to put them on. Reiko then picked up one of the train brochures to use as a weapon.

"There's one!" she said, swatting the insect on the mirror. It left a wet, stringy smudge.

Suddenly, the train lurched violently, screeching with a horrible noise. Bond and Reiko were tossed forward. Reiko slammed into the table and cried out as Bond fell on the floor. The train quickly lost its forward momentum, audibly kicking and screaming as it went. Finally, it slowed to a crawl and eventually stopped. The exhaling sound of compressed air that followed was loud and jarring.

"Are you all right?" Bond asked, standing and helping her up.

"I think so. Oww, I hurt my side again," she said. "What just happened?"

Before he could answer, the lights in the compartment went out and they were plunged into darkness.

SIXTEEN

IN THE TUNNEL

TO STOP UNEXPECTEDLY INSIDE THE SEIKAN TUNNEL WAS CAUSE FOR ALARM for the passengers who were aware of what it might mean. Trains didn't just stop in a tunnel two hundred metres underground, especially when the tunnel was beneath the tons of water in Tsugaru Straits. Japan Rail staff immediately attempted to determine who stopped the train and why. Many passengers came out into the corridor to inquire what was going on and the staff did their best to keep things calm. As the scene was reasonably chaotic, none of the employees noticed that they were missing a conductor.

Inside the dark suite, Bond and Reiko attempted to keep their cool but knew that they were in a predicament. They had no idea where the mosquitoes were but as a precaution they both continuously rubbed their arms and necks—any patch of bare skin that was exposed to the air. Bond had tried banging on the door to no avail. Even the phone was dead.

"Reiko, where are you?" Bond asked.

"Over here, by the bed," she said in the blackness.

"Okay, stay there and sit down. I'm going to try something."

Bond reached into his pocket and found the cigar holder that Major Boothroyd had given him, then he felt his way to the door. Using his sense of touch, Bond popped the lid off the container, removed the cigar and squeezed out a small amount of the tooth-paste-like explosive and lined the lock with it. Satisfied that he hadn't applied too much, Bond dropped what was left of the cigar and set the timer. He thrust the canister into the paste and moved back to where Reiko was sitting.

"You might want to hold your ears," Bond whispered as he mentally counted backwards from ten and pulled Reiko to the floor.

The entire door blew off in a loud, trembling blast that rocked the train. Pieces of wood and plaster flew about the room and a thick cloud of smoke obliterated any sight line to the corridor.

"*Sugoi,*" Reiko said after it had settled.

"Okay, so I used a little too much," Bond said. He pulled her up and they waved the smoke away. They could see the corridor now, and were surprised to find it just as dark as the room.

"So much for containing the mosquitoes. If they survived that blast, they're in the rest of the train now," Bond said.

"Let's go find out what has happened," Reiko said.

They came out into the corridor and felt their way along the wall to the exit alcove. The doors were wide open. At least the tunnel lights were on so they could see something at last.

"I'll bet he got off the train," Bond said. "I should go after him."

"All right. I will stay and look for the mosquitoes, James-san," Reiko said. "I will crush them when I see them."

"At this point they could be anywhere. Are you sure?"

"Yes! Go!"

Bond looked into the tunnel. "They could have flown out. Let's just hope they die soon." He turned to her and said, "If we get separated, you know the rendezvous location."

She nodded.

Bond kissed her on the cheek and then bolted out to the narrow platform. Unsure which way to go, he looked back and forth and finally gambled on what appeared to be the closest of the passages that ran at right angles to the main rail tunnel and went that way.

Two conductors carrying torches burst into the car. They were extremely agitated and began to shout at Reiko, demanding to know what had been going on. Reiko flashed her official identification and did her best to explain that they had been locked in the suite by whoever it was that stopped the train. One of the men banged on the door to the conductor's compartment. When there was no answer, he unlocked it with his own key and opened it. He cried out in alarm.

The torches illuminated the little room so that everyone could see the horrid display of butchery.

"Who did this terrible thing?" one man whispered.

Reiko replied, "A very bad man."

The torch revealed the damaged panel that controlled the lights in the car.

"Call the police," a conductor told another man. "And apprise Control Centre of the situation."

Reiko inched away from the men who were now preoccupied with the scene in car 1. She turned and went through the doors into the next car, which was, thankfully, well lit. Passengers were standing in the corridor; some of them asked what was happening.

Reiko played dumb and said that she didn't know. One man wanted to go past her into the first car but Reiko stopped him. "I don't think that is a good idea," she told him. "The rail people are in there trying to figure out what happened. They said not to bother them and that they would make an announcement in a moment."

"I want to find out what's going on!" the belligerent man shouted.

Reiko's eyes went wide. A mosquito was flying lightly near the man's face. Reiko watched it intently as the man babbled about how Japan Rail trains never break down and this was the first time it had happened to him. The insect circled the man's head, as if trying to find a good landing site. The man continued to rant as the mosquito finally lit on his neck. Reiko lifted the train brochure that she still had in her hand and slapped the man, squashing the insect. The man shut up and looked at Reiko in horror.

"Hush up and calm down," she said. "They are doing the best they can!" Then she pushed past him and continued down the corridor, leaving the man dumbstruck.

—·◆·—

The Seikan Tunnel is actually made up of a grid-like series of inter-connecting tunnels. Besides the main tunnel that is wide enough for two sets of train tracks and a track for maintenance vehicles in the middle, there is also a service tunnel running parallel and attached to it by "connecting galleries"—short tunnels spaced at intervals along the main passage. Shafts run from the surface on Honshu and Hokkaido to the tunnel—vertical ones for hauling machinery and materials in lifts and inclined ones for cable cars and for walking. In case of emergency, passengers can be evacuated out of the main tunnel, through the nearest connecting gallery and into the service tunnel. From there they can walk to the closest end and then go up the inclined shaft by foot or cable car to the outside world. There are two undersea train stations on either side of the strait as well in case trains need to stop in the tunnel. At the moment, the *Cassiopeia* was stopped a mile past the Tappi undersea station on the Honshu side.

Bond hurried through a connecting gallery and found himself in the service tunnel. There was enough illumination from the work lights to allow him to get a good look around. The tunnel stretched as far as he could see. Bond noted the many connecting galleries that lined the way and also the cameras that appeared to be set every forty metres. No doubt the Japan Rail people in the Control Centre could switch on any of the cameras to see what was going on in the tunnels.

Bond ran down to the next connecting gallery, then shot through it, across to the main tunnel once again.

It was a world of concrete, steel and plaster. Service pipes and cables were neatly painted and attached to the sides of the tunnels, giving the appearance of one solid surface. There was a musty smell to the place, but the air was cool. Bond knew that care had been taken to ensure that the tunnel had adequate ventilation as well as an efficient drainage system to pump out water in case any leaked in. The tunnels were remarkably clean, if a bit damp, cold and lifeless.

He ran towards the Tappi station, hoping that he could catch up with the dwarf. After witnessing Kappa's tricks in Kamakura, Bond wondered if pursuing the killer might have been folly on his part. The runt could hide anywhere and eventually make his way out of the tunnel unseen, even under the gaze of the cameras. Perhaps he should go back to the train and get on it before it left.

The attack startled Bond, who normally took great pride in his ability to avoid being surprised. Junji Kon dropped onto Bond's head like a sandbag. He had been hanging on to one of the large pipes that ran along the tunnel ceiling several feet overhead. The two men fell to the pavement and rolled. Before Bond could react, Kappa had bounced to his feet and twisted like a top until he had positioned himself to deliver what was a stunning aerial kick at Bond's face. The dwarf then dropped to the ground and used his arm to springboard back into the auto kick with the other leg, this time into Bond's chest, which was being propelled backwards from the force of the first kick. Bond fell, the pain searing through his sternum. It had been a strong blow but not one meant to kill. Bond knew that if this man had wanted to, he could have shattered his breastbone.

The dwarf known as Kappa stood casually on the pavement like a pixie, watching to see what his victim would do next. Bond turned and got to his hands and knees, which was always a bad position to be in but he had no choice. Before he could get up, he saw the glint of steel in Kappa's right hand.

The Balisong came swishing at him with the speed of a snake. Luckily, Bond had recovered just enough to summon his lifesaving skills of self-defence. He, too, had trained many years to be lightning fast. When an opponent attacked with a knife, you had to be.

Bond's left hand, the one that Kappa hadn't expected Bond to use, shot out and grabbed Kappa's wrist like a lizard's tongue catches a fly. The impact of his palm on Kappa's arm sent the Balisong flying across the pavement and onto the tracks.

The dwarf didn't let that subdue him. He jumped, allowing Bond's grasp to hold him in the air. Then he swung out and kicked Bond again in the face. Bond reflexively let go of Kappa's wrist and fell back. Bond rolled on the pavement, shook his head and looked up.

Kappa was gone.

The staff in the Hakodate Control Centre were monitoring the situation in the tunnel very closely. Their job was to get the train moving again as quickly as possible after determining that there was no danger to passengers. They had visual links to all of the cameras in the tunnel but they could turn on only selected cameras at a time. Communications equipment was still working properly and they had established a dialogue with the train staff.

The Operations Manager on duty that morning, Hiroki Yamanote, considered what had been reported. A passenger had stopped the train and jumped off after first murdering a conductor and locking another passenger in his suite. The second passenger was a government law enforcement agent and had taken off on foot through the tunnel in search of the killer.

Fine, he thought. As long as the rest of the passengers were safe, what did he care if killers butchered each other? He got on the phone to the train's engineer.

"Close the doors and leave," he ordered. "We have already delayed some trains behind you."

The engineer on the *Cassiopeia* announced to the staff that they were going on and an announcement was made over the train's intercom. Passengers were told that the staff were sorry for the interruption of service and that they would try to make up for lost time on their way to Sapporo.

In the meantime, Yamanote arranged for the train to be met by police at Hakodate, where it would make a short stop before continuing its journey.

One of the technicians alerted Yamanote that he had a visual on one of the camera view screens. The Operations Manager stepped behind the display and saw the figure of James Bond walking through the tunnel. The *gaijin* looked dishevelled and appeared confused. He had a pistol in his hand and was obviously searching for someone.

"Better send police down the shaft," he told an assistant.

Meanwhile, on the train, Reiko was continuing her reconnaissance mission through the cars looking for near-invisible flying insects. As the announcement that the train was leaving came on the intercom,

Reiko muttered a Western swear word under her breath. She wished that she had talked James-san out of chasing that killer.

A mosquito! She saw it out of the corner of her eye, flying alone near one of the windows. The train's engines fired up and the locomotive began to move as Reiko followed the insect down the corridor. Wait, she lost it! Where did it go? Reiko looked around frantically. It was like searching for a speck in the sand.

A passenger came out of a room and looked at her. "Are we finally leaving?" he asked.

"Yes!" Reiko snapped. She continued creeping along the wall, not caring how she might have looked to the passenger. The man gave her a funny stare and went back into his room.

There it was! The little thing was gliding along the perimeter of a window, instinctively looking for a way out. Reiko raised the train brochure and swatted the window. She removed the brochure and saw that she had squashed the insect.

Oh no, she thought. The smear on the window and brochure was red with blood—human blood.

Bond rubbed his chest with one hand as he moved silently along the tunnel wall. The Walther was in his other hand, safety off, ready to shoot the first thing that moved. The little attacker had enraged him. It was one thing to be beaten by an opponent; it was another thing to be beaten by someone so small. Bond wanted to pick the runt up by the neck and shake him, then give him a taste of his own medicine. The killer probably got away with a lot because his opponents probably held back their punches.

But that wasn't going to stop Bond at this point. He was ready to wring the bastard's little neck.

He heard a rumble and the blast of a train's horn. The *Cassiopeia* was leaving. Bond stood on the platform and watched it pass by. He waited there for a minute, watching its red taillights disappear into the endless tunnel.

Then he was alone with the silence. He moved on, looking for any telltale clue that Kappa might have left behind. But he knew that was probably futile; Junji Kon was a master of stealth. He could hide in any nook or cranny and his speed was freakish. He could be in any of the dozens of interconnecting tunnels. Perhaps Tiger had been right—the man *was* a supernatural being!

There was a sound in the distance that resembled a can being kicked. It was difficult to discern where it had come from. Bond peered down a connecting gallery to the service tunnel. Yes, it definitely came from there. He turned and moved in that direction, his gun steady. He inched to the edge of the wall and looked around. Nothing there. He rounded the corner and continued on, his ears attuned to the slightest sounds. All that he heard were occasional drips and the faint blowing of air, what they called "tunnel effect."

There! Something moved! Bond fired the Walther and it reverberated in the tunnel, the shot repeating itself down the length of the shaft until it faded away.

Bond moved carefully to the next connecting gallery, searching intently for his prey.

In the Control Centre, Operations Manager Yamanote could see Bond's back on the view screen as he moved away from the camera that was pointed at him. Then he saw the second figure creeping up behind Bond. At first he thought it was a child until he saw the way the man was moving. It was a little person, or a dwarf, some kind of strange person. Was he the criminal who had killed the conductor on the *Cassiopeia?*

The little man was nearly upon the *gaijin*. Yamanote had to warn Bond somehow. He reached over the shoulder of the technician and flipped a switch.

Suddenly, the tunnel's sprinkler system shot on above Bond and Kappa's heads. The water surprised them both and they reacted by jumping back. Bond saw Kappa just as the little man leaped at him. Bond fired but missed as the dwarf slammed into him. Bond dropped the PPK but managed to take hold of the dwarfs shoulders and, using the killer's own momentum, hurled Kappa over his head and into the wall. The plaster crumbled slightly as the small but solid body struck it. Bond let him fall to the pavement as he scrambled to retrieve the

Walther. But Kappa bounced off the concrete and sprung at Bond, fists clenched. The two bodies collided and fell to the cement. They rolled twice, the little man punching Bond hard wherever he could land a blow. Bond did his best to push Kappa away and connect a punch too, but the dwarf was just too fast. He moved like a whirling dervish and was impossible to pin down.

The men separated and got to their feet. The evil pixie stood facing Bond with hatred in his eyes. The image was surreal: water filled the depression in the dwarfs head as if it were a bowl. Then, before Bond could plan a strategy, Kappa leaped into the air like something from the netherworld. His right foot connected with his opponent's jaw with such force that Bond went reeling backwards. Bond stepped into a puddle of water and slipped. Kappa landed but kept up the offensive, kicking and punching until Bond was on the ground. Bond tried to grab the killer's foot but this time it didn't work. Bond was too stunned to react with the speed that was required.

Kappa delivered two, three, four hard kicks to the head. Bond attempted to raise himself to ward off another blow, but the fifth kick sent him into the black hole of unconsciousness.

SEVENTEEN

OLD GHOSTS

REIKO REACHED THE LAST CAR ON THE LOWER LEVEL OF THE TRAIN. OTHER than the two she had already killed, she hadn't seen any more mosquitoes.

Looking for the things was worse than threading a needle, she thought as she stopped for a moment, removed her glasses and rubbed her eyes. She had a splitting headache that had come on suddenly a few minutes ago.

How long had it been since the train left? Five minutes? Ten? And what about James-san? Was he all right? She wondered if Tanaka-san had been contacted and—

Oh no! she thought to herself. *She* should be calling Tanaka-san! What was wrong with her? Why hadn't she done that immediately! Her head was so cloudy it was difficult to think. She *had* been a bit preoccupied. That was it. She chalked it up to the urgency of finding the deadly mosquitoes. If they *were* deadly.

Reiko leaned against the wall and looked at the stairwell in front of her. Could there be mosquitoes on the top floor? Reiko didn't want to think about it. At the moment she had no energy and felt drained. Why was she so disoriented? She should get going, climb the stairs, look for invisible insects and talk to Tanaka-san on her mobile as she searched.

The effort that was required to take that first step up surprised her, but she took a deep breath and willed herself to go on. It felt as if each step took a lifetime.

As she climbed, she reached around behind her neck without thinking and scratched an itch.

At first Bond thought it was thunder.

The roar of a train reverberated in his ears. He opened his eyes and saw a blur. There were some pinpoints of light in an otherwise dark mass of nothing. But the noise was growing louder.

What the hell? Bond thought. What happened?

Then he remembered. He was fighting with Kappa and must have been knocked unconscious. He was still in the Seikan Tunnel.

Bond instinctively attempted to reach up and rub his face but found that his wrists were bound in front of him. He could move his arms up and down freely; it was just that they were tied together.

The volume of the approaching storm intensified. He tried to move his body and discovered that he was secured to something.

Wait a minute . . . ! Bond couldn't feel the floor. There was a strong tugging sensation on his upper torso.

My God? he thought. He was suspended from the tunnel's ceiling! A rope had been harnessed around his chest under his arms and then looped up and around a pipe running along the top of the tunnel. He was dangling four or five feet above the tracks.

That's when the adrenaline kicked in. Bond's senses became fully alert as he forcibly cleared the haze. He pushed the pain in his head away and focused sharply on his surroundings.

The sound that was growing louder and louder had to be a train headed his way. In fact, those pinpoints of light were its headlamps. How far away was it?

Think! If there was a time that he had to move fast, it was now.

Bond momentarily flashed on the absurd notion that the service had never trained the Double-Os what to do in case they were tied up over a bloody railway track and a bloody train was coming.

But they had trained him to use the tools at his disposal. Painfully,

Bond raised his bound wrists to his shirt collar. He felt underneath for the slit and pulled out the special collar stay that Q Branch made available to field agents. He removed the thin plastic sheath that covered it, and then made sure that the sharpened edge was facing the right way. Bond then held the thin blade down to the rope that was around his chest. He began to saw, pressing the knife into the rope with his thumbs.

The train's headlamps were getting bigger. The entire tunnel was shaking with a deafening roar.

Cut through, damn you! he willed. He moved the blade back and forth, pushing it into the hemp as hard as he could. It was awkward and uncomfortable and the muscles in his hand began to hurt.

One strand split! He was halfway through!

Bond immediately moved the blade to another loop in the rope, one that, if cut, would assure his freedom. He began to saw again when the collar stiffener slipped out of his hand and fell to the tracks below.

No!

Bond reached up to his neck and pulled out the other collar stay. If he dropped this one he was done for.

Now he could see the outline of the train. It was no longer merely two dots of light.

He sawed while pushing with his thumbs and fighting the cramp that inched up his thumbs and into his wrists. Every second counted now. The locomotive's fierce bullet-shaped nose was growing larger and larger. There was the blast of a horn. Could they see him? It was doubtful. The light was too dim in the tunnel. Only when it was too late would the engineer be able to see that something was hanging in the middle of the tunnel. It would not register that what he saw was a man. It would be the last thing the engineer would think of.

The blade was almost through. Just a little harder . . .

The tunnel vibrated with intensity. The train was now clearly visible. Bond could see that it was red. He figured that if he could tell what colour it was, then it was too damned close.

Finally, the blade was through! The bindings loosened around his chest. Before he dropped, Bond grabbed the strands and began to swing on the rope. The clamour of the approaching hulk of power drowned out all other thoughts. One more arc and he would have enough momentum to swing over to the edge.

Now! Bond let go of the rope, landed and rolled to the side of the tunnel just as the train roared past him.

He lay there a moment and caught his breath. His heart was pounding. His head hurt like hell. Ever since Bond had received a particularly bad head injury during an assignment a few years ago, he had been more susceptible to the effects of blows to the skull.

Time to get up.

Bond sat on the pavement. He took stock of the damage and found that aside from the minor cuts that had re-opened on his face, the lump on his head was the only thing that needed immediate attention.

He stood and began to walk toward the Tappi station. Five minutes later, he heard voices. The police and rail authorities had finally arrived.

The *shatei-gashira* watched as one of the men from the north fed bills into the pachinko machine. Many of them had played non-stop since they got to Tokyo the night before. It was as if they suspected that they would never be able to play pachinko again.

"Phone call, boss," his right-hand man called from the other side of the parlour. It was a busy morning. The kids were out of school and had filled the place, so it was difficult to hear what his man was saying. His colleague raised a mobile phone and pointed to it.

The *shatei* walked across the busy arcade and took the mobile. "I'll take it in the back," he said as he went behind the door marked "Private" and into a small office.

It was Yasutake Tsukamoto, calling from Sapporo. The *shatei* had been expecting him.

"*Hai!*" he answered.

"Is everything satisfactory?" Tsukamoto asked.

"Yes, *kaicho,*" the man said. "The twenty men arrived last night. The equipment just arrived this morning. Everything is in order."

"That's very good, the *Yami Shogun* will be pleased."

The *shatei* said goodbye to his *kaicho* and hung up. He walked through another door in the office and into a large storeroom and lounge area. Some of the "carriers" were relaxing there, three of them asleep on cots. The two trunks marked "CureLab Inc." sat on the floor unopened. That event wouldn't occur until this afternoon, at CureLab headquarters.

One of the men approached him and asked when lunch would be served.

"Very soon, my friend. How did you sleep last night?" the *shatei* asked.

"Good. I was very tired. We have been on the go for several days."

"I hear you had a nice night out on the town in Sapporo?"

"Oh, yes! Tsukamoto-san was our host. We had a wonderful expensive dinner and then spent several hours at a soaplands! It was the best I have ever had!"

"I envy you!" The *shatei* gestured to the cases. "So what's in those things?"

The man shook his head. "I am sorry, but I cannot reveal that. It's part of our mission."

The *shatei* bowed. "Forgive me. I understand." He looked at his watch. "Another hour before lunch, and then this afternoon the cars will come to pick you up and take you all to CureLab for your meeting."

The man laughed. "More meetings. I wish we'd just get on with it. We are all well trained and we know what to do. I don't see why we have to wait five days."

"It's because the materials are not quite ready," another carrier said. He was the leader, a man named Ukita. "And stop talking about our mission."

The other carrier bowed rapidly, "I apologise, *sempai*." He walked away quickly. Ukita looked at the *shatei* and said, "I am sorry. We are under orders not to talk about it."

"I understand," the *shatei* said. When Ukita walked away, the *shatei* shrugged, left the lounge and strode back through the building to the public pachinko parlour.

—·—

Yasutake Tsukamoto picked up the phone in his Sapporo office and dialled the number that only three people in the world knew. The other two were the *Yami Shogun* himself, and the Ryujin-kai's *waka-gashira,* or number two man.

Goro Yoshida answered.

"*Ohayo gozaimasu,*" Tsukamoto said.

"*Ohayo* to you, too, Tsukamoto," Yoshida said.

"I am calling to report that everything is in order. The carriers arrived at the distribution centre in Tokyo on schedule and the equipment was delivered this morning. It will go to CureLab this afternoon."

"That's good news. I trust that the new version will be completed within five days?"

"If it needs to be completed in five days, then it will be completed in five days."

"Ah, but will it work? What do you think, Tsukamoto?"

"You have always known my feelings about this project, Yoshida. Our chief engineer tells me that it will work but I am not a man of science."

"Tsukamoto, you surprise me. You still have doubts about our motives, don't you?"

If they had been with each other in person, Tsukamoto would have bowed to his master. The *Yami Shogun* was displeased.

"Forgive me, Yoshida. I have complete faith in you and in the project. I never meant to question it."

"Very well. And what of our British friend who has been sticking his nose into our business?"

"Kappa arrived this morning, master. According to him, our British friend is now the front ornament on the *shinkansen.*"

Tsukamoto heard Yoshida chuckle, and he wished that he could see it. Goro Yoshida rarely laughed. He hardly ever smiled, for that matter.

"And the McMahon girl?" Yoshida asked. Tsukamoto had been anticipating the question.

"Kubo at the soaplands tells me that she has been eliminated."

"Good. We couldn't afford to have her around."

"Yes, you are right, as always."

After they rang off, Tsukamoto sat back in his leather swivel chair. He looked out the window at a patch of azalea in the park across the street. The lavender colour was a staple of Hokkaido. In the country, especially, it spread over the landscape like spilled paint.

Why did he feel so wretched? Tsukamoto wondered. Why didn't he feel comfortable with the project? Because it was wrong? Because he *knew* it was wrong? That was ridiculous. He had done many things that were wrong. He had killed men. He had stolen money. He had committed crimes that could put him away for life, but the wall of the yakuza organisation protected him from that fate. He was untouchable.

So why did this particular project disturb him? Was it because it involved a deadly biological weapon? Was it because they would be delivering a strike against several countries, including Japan herself? Why should he feel bad about that? After all, it was the established Japanese government that still catered to the West. The project was meant to be a blow at the enemies of traditional Japan, and that included those within the boundaries of the country itself.

Tsukamoto stood and walked to the window. He stared into the park, fourteen storeys below, and watched a pair of birds fly over the purple blot of azalea. A mother was wheeling her baby in a stroller. It was a beautiful day.

It was no use pretending that he didn't know. What bothered him about the project was the fact that it was completely mad. It was a symbolic strike, to be sure, but one that could possibly bring the wrath of foreign nations and the Japanese government down upon their heads. It had no further purpose but to make a statement. There was no profit to be made from it, it was extremely dangerous and the yakuza had no business waging a war of terrorism on the rest of the world. It was total, utter madness.

But it's what the man with the red tattoo wanted and that was what he was going to get.

———•———

Bond had been picked up by the authorities and put onto the next train at Tappi station. He disembarked at Goryo-kaku station in Hokkaido and made phone contact with Tanaka, who had helped clear his activities with the police. Unfortunately, Tanaka had not heard from Reiko. The *Cassiopeia* had stopped at Goryo-kaku as well because "some passengers were ill." That was all that he knew.

Now that the train had arrived, perhaps he could find out something. Two officials who introduced themselves as Eto and Akira met him on the platform. Eto explained that they worked for the Public Security Investigation Agency and that they needed to debrief him.

"What about agent Tamura?" Bond asked. "Has anyone heard from her?"

The two men exchanged glances. Eto inhaled through his teeth and frowned.

Bad news.

"Tamura-san was one of the ill passengers," Eto said. "She was taken to the hospital."

"Take me there now," Bond commanded. "We can talk in the car."

They walked through the small station and got into a Suzuki Wagon-R. As they drove the short distance to the medical centre, Eto revealed more.

"Three passengers and Tamura-san came down with a serious illness on the train," he said.

"What were the symptoms?"

"High fever, bad headaches and finally, loss of consciousness. We will find out more when we talk to the doctors."

It took them only a few minutes to get to the busy Hakodate Municipal Hospital, which was located very close to the rail station. It was a large, six-storey building that was the principal medical facility in southern Hokkaido.

Eto and Akira led Bond inside the brown and grey structure and took the lift to the fifth floor, where they found the doctor in charge of the passengers who had been brought in. He was a man in his thirties who appeared to be overworked and under a great deal of stress. When Eto asked about Reiko, the doctor looked grave.

"Come with me," he said. He led them into a small office and shut the door. "We are trying to figure out what happened to these people. One man has died, just minutes ago. He had a temperature of a hundred and six. He was in his seventies, so it's not surprising that he didn't survive. The other passengers are younger and healthier, so it is difficult to say whether or not they will pull through. From the small amount of information we have, it appears that these people were stricken with some powerful virus, an encephalitis of some sort."

"West Nile disease?" Bond asked.

"Very similar," the doctor said, nodding. "Only much stronger. I understand it came upon them suddenly and reached a peak very quickly."

"Do you happen to know if any of them have mosquito bites?"

The doctor squinted at Bond. "Do you know more about this? What is it that you are not telling me?"

"Doctor, I don't know a lot, but I believe that there were some genetically engineered mosquitoes aboard that train. They escaped and might have bitten these people. I can't tell you what that virus is, but it's probably man-made."

"Then we will examine the patients and see what we can find. Why don't you gentlemen wait here and I'll be back in a few moments after I give instructions to the nurses. They are afraid of touching the patients for fear of catching whatever it is."

"So far we have no reason to believe that the disease is contagious," Bond said. "But I suppose you can't be too careful."

"We don't touch them without wearing gloves and masks. Pardon me."

He left the room and Bond got back on the phone to Tanaka. Tiger listened as Bond explained the situation and then said, "She is strong, Bondo-san. If anyone can pull through this, Miss Tamura can. Try not to worry."

"I'm going to stay here until we know for certain."

"Thank you, Bondo-san. I am sure Miss Tamura will appreciate that. Now, have you had your head looked at?"

"Not yet."

"Do it. I don't want you walking around with a concussion."

"What about Sapporo?" Bond asked, changing the subject. "Is my contact expecting me?"

"Yes. His name is Ikuo Yamamaru. He's the Ainu gentleman I told you about. Very good man. He will meet you at the Sapporo Beer Garden tomorrow for lunch."

"How will I know him?"

"He will know you. Now go and have a doctor take a look at you. Since you are working under my authority I can say 'that's an order,' Bondo-san. But it's also for your own good."

"All right, Tiger."

When the doctor came back, he said, "You were right. Tamura-san has a mosquito bite on the back of her neck. The elderly gentleman who died has two bites on his arm. The other two patients both have bites on their arms as well. They look like fresh mosquito bites."

"So what do we do now?"

The doctor shrugged. "I have done all I can for now. We have to pray and wait." He looked at his clipboard and noted something. "It says here that you received a head injury, Mr. Bond."

Bond nodded reluctantly. "Really, I'm fine."

"Let's go in an examination room and let me take a look."

The doctor performed the necessary tests to make sure that there was nothing seriously wrong with Bond. There was indeed a small lump above his right temple where the dwarfs shoe tip had struck. The doctor gave him some painkillers and said in English, "You have very hard head. You lucky man."

"May I see Tamura-san now?" Bond asked.

"I suppose it would not hurt." He led Bond into the critical ward and to a bed where Reiko lay. An IV was in her arm and she was wearing an oxygen mask. Her skin was pale but she was breathing slowly and deeply. She looked so helpless and fragile that Bond wanted to take her into his arms, hold her close, and protect her from whatever was in store for her.

He placed his palm on her forehead. The skin was hot but dry. She was burning up. Bond leaned over and kissed her above her eyebrows.

He whispered in her ear, "I'm here, Reiko-san. I will wait for you. Be strong. You have to pull through, you know. We have that date in Maui."

Reiko remained still and quiet. Could she hear him? Bond didn't know.

Then the doctor asked him to wait in the lounge.

Bond spent the next half-hour talking to Eto and Akira about the dwarf and the incidents on the train. They took copious notes, Bond signed a statement, and then the two men left him alone.

The day turned into night as Bond sat in the lobby staring out of the window first at the matchbox-like cars on the streets, then at the lights in the various buildings that could be seen from the hospital. He was dead tired.

So this was the score, he thought. The ghosts had struck again. Just when he began to invest a little of himself into someone, something happened to wreck it. Was he forever going to be bad luck to anyone he came close to? All the women whom he had loved had come to a bad end. Vesper, Tracy, Kissy . . . Was this the price he had to pay for the lives he had taken throughout his career? Was this his fate, to be forever alone because whatever he touched turned to dust?

Stop it, he commanded himself. Don't be morose. Reiko will pull through. As Tiger said, she was strong.

As he looked at his reflection in the window, Bond remembered the doubts and fears he had experienced before coming to Japan. Those old ghosts that he didn't want to see were certainly nearby.

"It is not your fault, Taro-san," Kissy said. She sat next to him, gazing out the window, dressed in the *yukata* she had always worn before bedtime.

"Yes it is," Bond replied. "I bring death wherever I go. It's a curse."

"No, Taro-san," she said, softly. "It is merely the hand of fate. You travel in a dark and dangerous world but you do so because it is your destiny. You could not exist in any other world, Taro-san."

"I should never have left you," Bond said. "Life was simpler on that island."

"It may have been, but you must not feel bad," she said. "You would not be complete if you had changed your path. Trust me, Taro-san."

In that illogical way that things happened in a dreamworld, Kissy became Reiko. Bond could feel her gazing at him longingly. Then, she slowly smiled and put on her glasses. He thought that she whispered *"Arigato,"* but he wasn't sure.

Bond felt his heart being squeezed. He turned to look at the person beside him but there was no one there.

The doctor woke him just after midnight. Bond had fallen asleep in the lobby in front of the large window.

"I have bad news," the doctor said.

Bond sat up and prepared himself for what he knew was coming.

"Tamura-san died ten minutes ago. I am sorry."

EIGHTEEN

THE SEARCH FOR MAYUMI

"DID EVERYTHING GO WELL REGARDING THE GIRL?" TSUKAMOTO ASKED Kubo, the *shatei* who ran the Casanova Club, the most exclusive and expensive soaplands in Sapporo. He was calling from his office, having put off the inevitable for long enough.

"Yes, *kaicho*," Kubo said. "Everything has been taken care of."

"Good. I assume that any traces of her existence have been destroyed?"

"Yes."

"Do I need to send some men there tonight to have a look around?"

Kubo was quiet for a brief moment and then said, "That is not necessary *kaicho*. I will personally see to it that there is no evidence."

"Very well."

Tsukamoto hung up and drummed his fingers on his desk. Should he trust Kubo to do a proper job? Perhaps he should go ahead and send some men anyway. If it were known that the McMahon girl had been at the soaplands, there could be a lot of trouble that even the Ryujin-kai might not be able to clear away.

He picked up the phone again and made the call.

James Bond was subdued when he arrived at the Sapporo Beer

Garden and Museum grounds, which were located in the northeastern corner of Sapporo, Hokkaido's largest city. He still felt pun-
ished by the previous night's events. He had been unable to sleep in
the brief time available to him. The sun had risen when he left for the
train station and he had only managed to nod off for a short time on
the morning express train to the city.

Now, having arrived in Sapporo, he fully understood how hard
Reiko's death had hit him. He had gone to Japan with the misplaced
notion that the assignment would be a holiday. Instead, they had
made it personal and Bond was grimly determined to avenge Reiko's
death. She had been an ally, a professional colleague, they had shared
wounds and danger and briefly something more. He vowed not to
leave the country that had brought him so much personal pain
without smashing Yoshida's plans and—if possible—liquidating the
evil man himself.

It was time to leave the pain behind and move on.

Bond got out of the car in front of the beer garden entrance and
surveyed the area. There were several red-brick buildings that made
up the museum, the complex of restaurants and the refineries. Bond
was well aware of Sapporo beer and preferred it when he did drink
beer in Japan. He therefore recognised the company's emblem, a red
star, painted on a tall brick smokestack that rose above everything
else. The beer garden was a popular tourist haunt that had been
around for a hundred years; visitors could tour the refineries, taste
beer, learn about the history of the beverage in the museum and have
their choice of a few kinds of Japanese barbecue for lunch.

Bond walked into the information centre and gift shop, where one
could purchase various souvenirs and tickets for the museum and
make reservations for lunch. He was greeted with an enthusiastic,
"Irrashaimase!" from every employee in the place, a greeting spoken
in businesses throughout Japan, welcoming the customer.

Bond smiled and bowed slightly, then approached the reservations
desk. He confirmed that there was a table for two under the name,
"Yamamaru," and was led to a table in the Classic Hall on the ground
floor.

It was done up like a German beer garden and, in fact, the words *"Sapporo Bier Garten"* were painted above the bar. An elaborately painted wooden street organ was prominently displayed on the floor of the restaurant and wooden tables and benches surrounded it. The kitchen's smoky grills were visible on one side of the room, staffed by a number of chefs dressed in white.

He was led to a table near the organ where a man was sitting. He rose when he saw Bond and said, *"Hajime mashite,* I am Ikuo Yamamaru. Welcome to Sapporo." He offered his business card and bowed.

Bond repeated the ritual, and then they shook hands and sat down.

He was immediately taken with Yamamaru. Bond usually had good instincts about people and he knew that this man was made of the same stuff as he.

The Ainu are believed to be indigenous to Japan but very little of the original lineage remains. They are often compared to the Native American Indians and possess some striking cultural similarities.

Yamamaru had bushy eyebrows over large blue eyes and his round full cheeks gave his face a lot of character. His long hair, tied into a ponytail, was black and streaked with grey. Bond guessed him to be about fifty years old. Yamamaru wore a *ruunpe*, a traditional garment elaborately embroidered with delicate appliqué in Ainu patterns, which were similar in style to those of Native Americans.

"I understand you lost your partner from Tokyo," he said in English. "I am very sorry."

"I am too."

The waitress came with a tray of drinks.

"I took the liberty of ordering beer for us," Yamamaru said. "I hope you don't mind."

"No, not at all."

They were each served a three-beer sampler consisting of large glasses of types of Sapporo beer, displayed in a Lazy Susan carrier that neatly held all three glasses. The Classic Draft Hokkaido Limited and Yebisu Draft were light beers; Bond particularly liked the third, Black Draft, a dark beer that had a strong caramel taste.

Yamamaru insisted on ordering for them and asked for the grilled platter for two.

After the waitress left, he pushed a package across the table to Bond. "From Tanaka-san," he said. "It is a replacement firearm. A Walther PPK, correct?"

"Yes, thank you," Bond said as he took the parcel and put it in his pocket.

"Now, Bond-san, how can I help you?"

"I need to find Mayumi McMahon. She is supposed to be in Sapporo, probably the girlfriend of a high-ranking yakuza. One source suggested that she might be working for the yakuza in the water trade."

Yamamaru nodded. "I have a contact in the yakuza. When Tanaka-san first asked me to try and find this girl, I contacted this man. He is usually able to find out some things and will talk for a price. We've worked together before. I imagine that the yakuza would keep her whereabouts a secret these days."

"If she's still alive," Bond said.

"Yes. At any rate you are just in time. I have a meeting with my contact this afternoon. He has already indicated that he has some news for me. I would ask you to accompany me, but I am afraid that he would feel more comfortable seeing me alone."

"I understand."

The food came and was served on a flat heated grill that was placed on the table. The food was fresh off the kitchen's barbecue grill and consisted of beef, lamb, shrimp, king crab, scallops and sausage, all complemented with sauerkraut and German style potatoes. Once it was in front of him, Bond realised how ravenous he was. He began to eat with fervour.

"Have you been to Sapporo before, Bond-san?"

"No. I'm not familiar with Hokkaido at all."

"You must try to visit our Ainu village while you are here. Have dinner, stay the night. We'll let you feed the bears."

Tiger had told Bond that the Ainu were animists, that is, they deified certain animals, especially bears. Most Ainu villages had at least one bear kept in captivity to serve as their god, mascot and sight-seeing attraction for tourists. Some villages had several.

"Where is your village?"

"South. Noboribetsu. Very near Bear Park, which my people operate. I'm originally from Shiraoi. I have an apartment here in Sapporo, but my family is in Noboribetsu."

"Do you know where the Hokkaido Mosquito and Vector Control Centre is in Noboribetsu?"

"Sure. It is outside of town. Tucked away in the woods, out of sight. It is interesting that you mention it. In the past several months, unusual things have been going on there."

"What do you mean?"

Yamamaru shifted his eyes around to make certain that no one was near enough to hear him. "It is a public health facility, isn't it? It used to be that anyone could go there and walk in. Now they have a high fence around it. Locked gate. Employees need a key card to get inside. Very strange."

"Can you get me in?"

"Very difficult. Security is very tight there. It is almost as if it is run by a completely different organisation." Then the Ainu grinned broadly. "But I enjoy a challenge! I will see what I can do."

Bond was silent for a moment as he relished the taste of a king crab leg on his palate, then said, "Just tell me how to get there and I'll worry about getting inside."

"I'll draw you a map."

The food was delicious and the beer took the edge off Bond's emotional fatigue.

"How did you get involved with the Koan-Chosa-Cho?" he asked the Ainu.

"When I did my military service back in the dark ages, when I was a young man, I was posted in an intelligence unit. I met Tanaka-san there and we became friends. He invited me to join later. The fact that I am Ainu is actually very good cover. There are not many Ainu who work in the Japanese government. Most of us operate replicas of traditional Ainu villages for tourists. We are a race that is slowly dying out, or rather, we are integrating more and more into modern society and are losing the Ainu ways."

"Is there much intelligence work for you to do up here?"

"Oh yes," Yamamaru said. "Mostly watching the Russians. They are always smuggling stuff in or out. We keep track of what their mafia is doing. There are some Korean criminal elements operating in Hokkaido. We keep an eye on them too."

"What about Goro Yoshida? Any idea where he is?"

"Hiding somewhere in the Northern Territories. He's another one who has been causing some trouble. Reportedly he has a small private army with him, and yet our intelligence forces have still been unable to exactly locate him. The Russians don't make it any easier for us. They don't like it when we do reconnaissance flights over the islands. Perhaps that's why I enjoy them! Some of my colleagues tell me that I am reckless. Anyway, I have my suspicions about where he is, mainly from what I hear through the Ainu grapevine. I believe he is holed up on the island of Etorofu. It's large enough and it's covered with natural camouflage. Lots of forest. Many Ainu live there."

After the meal, they left the restaurant, strolled through the beer garden grounds and had a smoke. Yamamaru offered Bond one of his cigarettes, made from tobacco grown by the Ainu. Bond found the taste pleasant but not strong enough.

"What dealings have you had with the Ryujin-kai?" Bond asked.

"Not much. I know Yasutake Tsukamoto. Well, a little. We met at a trade show for chemical engineering suppliers."

"What do you think of him?"

The Ainu shrugged. "He is a very powerful *oyabun*. Very rich. Getting old. When we met, he barely looked at me. I have heard from many sources that he can be a very honourable man. For a criminal."

Yamamaru eventually looked at his watch and said that he had to leave for his appointment. They agreed to meet that night at Bond's hotel. If all went well with his contact that afternoon, the Ainu would have some information for him.

Bond's next target was the Yonai Enterprises office in Sapporo. It was located in the city centre in an office building not far from Odori Park, the dividing line between the north and south sides of the city. Unlike other Japanese cities, Sapporo was conveniently divided into a grid, named and numbered according to the points of the compass. The street names reflected how many blocks and the direction they lay from the city's centre. Yonai Enterprises was on South 1.

It was a shiny twenty-four-storey building that took up half a block. To Bond it looked like any other ordinary office building in Japan: there was no indication that the occupants might be in bed with organised crime. He circled the block and made his way to a loading dock area behind the building. There he found men loading boxes and crates into a lorry.

Two security guards eyed him suspiciously as he approached. Bond smiled at them but they remained expressionless. He came closer to the lorry and stopped to make a show of lighting a cigarette. As he did so, he studied the address labels on the boxes and crates and saw that along with the Japanese characters a legend in English read: "Hokkaido Mosquito and Vector Control Centre."

That explained why the public health facility had recently added a fence and tight security. This confirmed his suspicions that it was now being run by Yonai Enterprises.

"May I help you, sir?"

It was a woman with a clipboard, standing on the loading dock. She had spoken in English.

"Oh, hello," Bond said, assuming the role of the stupid *gaijin*. He introduced himself as a tourist from Britain who was lost.

"Please go around the building that way," the woman said. "There is a tourist information office one block to the west."

"Right, I'll do that. Pardon me, I didn't mean to intrude."

"That's all right."

Bond caught a cab that took him straight to the Sapporo Prince Hotel, where Tanaka had arranged for him to stay.

After he had left the loading dock area, the woman with the clipboard made a phone call to her superior. As she had been instructed, the woman reported that a *gaijin* had been seen snooping around.

Her boss thanked her for her diligence and hung up. This message was then passed on to his boss, who, in turn, passed it on to Yasu-take Tsukamoto.

Kubo was extremely nervous. He had disobeyed a direct order from the *kaicho*. He had deceived the yakuza. He would surely lose a finger or two. Maybe even his life.

As he sat in the small office of the Casanova Club and nursed a flask of Japanese whisky, he went over the various options he had available to him. Unfortunately, there weren't many.

Why had he fallen for the girl? She was no different from any other soaplands girl in the business. Well, that wasn't entirely true, he thought. In fact, it wasn't true at all. Mayumi McMahon was *very* different. She was an angel, a goddess sent from heaven! Kubo had never mixed business with pleasure before she had arrived at the soaplands but he had been completely bewitched by Mayumi. Per-haps it was her independent streak that had attracted him, some-thing that was uncommon among most soaplands girls. She had come to the Casanova Club declaring with a determined swagger that she was going to be the best soaplands girl in the business. Too bad it hadn't worked out that way for her. Now the yakuza wouldn't let her leave. Kubo knew that she was unhappy and was desperate to break away, even though she was making lots of money for the club.

Why did they want to kill her? It was unfathomable! Such an exotic creature and such a good earner too! When Kubo received the order to have her done away with, he couldn't bring himself to follow it. One day he would pay for his disobedience.

Now he had to hide her somewhere else. She could no longer stay in the upstairs room he had provided for her. She had believed him when he had told her that it wasn't safe for her to go home to her apartment, but now she was restless. She had been complaining about having to stay there.

Kubo had a lead on another apartment outside of Sapporo. He had just enough time to go out and talk to the landlord and arrange it.

Then, later that night after the guards were asleep and the soaplands was closed, he would move Mayumi out.

Her freedom, as well as his peace of mind, was worth a finger or two.

Tanaka had put Bond in the corner suite on the top floor of the Sapporo Prince Hotel Annex, which was newer than the main building across the road and its rooms were the hotel's best. As Bond waited for his appointment with Yamamaru, he sat and looked out of the window, watching the sunset and the Sapporo lights as they began to dominate the skyline. Mayumi McMahon was somewhere out there.

The phone rang. Bond answered it, acknowledged Yamamaru, and told him to come up.

"*Konban wa,* Yamamaru-san," Bond said.

"Please," he said, "You may call me Ikuo. I like dispensing with formalities every now and then."

Bond offered him some of the sake that was in the refrigerator, compliments of Tiger, and then they sat around the low glass table and clinked glasses.

"I have some good news," Yamamaru said. "I found Mayumi McMahon."

"I was hoping that you would say that. Go on."

"She is a soaplands girl. In one of the biggest and most expensive establishments in Sapporo run by the Ryujin-kai. Apparently, Ms. McMahon came to Sapporo and changed her name to Tomoko. She was put up in a very nice apartment. She can come and go as she pleases."

"Then how come she hasn't been found up until now?"

"Because even though she has freedom of movement, she is guarded. And she has a new identity. The yakuza have men watch her. It took my friend several days to locate her. There is another problem. The girl has not been seen for several days."

"Does that mean . . . ?"

Yamamaru put up a hand. "No, Bond-san. She is alive. My friend put me in touch with another girl who works there. She goes by the name of Norika. I was able to speak to her today before she went to work.

Norika says that Mayumi is being kept in a room on one of the upper floors and has not been allowed to work for a few days. For 10,000 yen, Norika said she would try to arrange for you to meet Mayumi."

"Then I had better go to the soaplands to see her."

"I suspected you would say that. Usually this place does not let *gaijin* in except for VIPs. Take this card."

He handed Bond a business card with *kanji* on it.

"This will get you in. Show that to the man at the front. You have to pay 20,000 yen to get in."

"What does the card say?"

"It says that you are an important *gaijin* doing business with Yasu-take Tsukamoto. Ask for Norika. Do you know Susukino? It's easy to navigate. It's the entertainment district." He pulled out a map and pointed to the location. Bond could walk there easily. "What do you plan to do with Ms. McMahon once you have found her?"

"If I can get her out, I'm taking her back to Tokyo," Bond said.

Yamamaru looked sceptical. "She may not want to go. Have you thought of that?"

"Yes, but she may not know that her parents have been killed."

Yamamaru was silent for a moment, as if considering how much of an impossible task it might be.

"Good luck, Bond-san," was all that he said.

Susukino was Sapporo's equivalent of Tokyo's Kabuki-cho. At night it was yet another spectacular display of neon and noise, and Bond felt that it was a little more "wild west" than Tokyo's red light district. Here, things seemed looser, more in the open. Billboards and side-walk placards on major streets prominently advertised the variety of sexual entertainment one could sample, from soaplands to strip clubs to hostess bars. The area was also full of restaurants, bars and pachinko parlours, exhibiting the same level of energy and deca-dence that Bond had found in Tokyo. Touts were just as aggressive, perhaps more so because Susukino catered to foreigners, especially Russians. A *gaijin* would probably have an easier time gaining access to some of the establishments here than in Tokyo.

Bond found the soaplands in question, the Casanova Club, and approached the doorman, a bulky strong-arm with a punch perm. Before Bond could utter a complete sentence, the man held up his hand and said, "No *gaijin*." Bond showed him the card that Yama-maru had given him. The bouncer studied it, rubbed his chin, and said, "Just a minute." He went inside and left Bond standing on the pavement. A pretty girl walked by and tried to hand him a flyer. He smiled and refused, but she insisted. When the bouncer returned, she quickly walked away.

"All right, come in," the doorman said. "You are welcome."

Bond climbed a set of stairs to the first floor, where he was met by a couple of sleazy-looking yakuza who were all smiles. By now, Bond had learned to recognise the trademark punch perms, the gaudy suits and the swaggering manner. Neither of them spoke English. Bond told them that he had heard about a girl named Norika who worked there.

One of them said, "There is a house charge of 20,000 yen."

Bond paid it and was led to a lounge area with a velvet-lined sofa, a coffee table with some skin magazines and an ashtray on it and a couple of comfortable chairs. They asked Bond what he wanted to drink. He asked for vodka on the rocks and then lit a cigarette.

"Would you like to see the selection of girls available?" one of the punch perms asked.

"No," Bond said. "Just Norika, please."

The man shrugged, handed Bond his drink, and left the room. Five minutes later, a young woman walked in and sat down in front of him. The punch perm was right behind her.

"This is Norika," the man said.

She was attractive and dressed in the type of outfit that might be worn by a bareback rider in a circus; the topcoat and tails of a tuxedo, very tight shorts, fishnet stockings and high heels.

Bond realised that he was supposed to indicate that she was indeed his choice.

"She'll do," he said to the man.

The punch perm nodded to the girl, who rose and gestured for Bond to follow her. She led him to a small room that contained a number of items: a double bed, a Japanese shower area on a tile floor, a bathtub, a vinyl inflatable mat, a cabinet and a locker.

Norika closed the door and looked at him expectantly.

"I'm here to see Tomoko," Bond said. He reached into his jacket pocket and pulled out 10,000 yen. "I believe that was the arrangement?"

Norika nodded, counted the money quickly, stuffed it into her shorts, and left the room after taking a look out into the hallway.

Bond sat on the bed and waited. A few minutes later the door opened and a young woman he recognised as Mayumi McMahon came in.

She was stunningly beautiful. Her photo did not do her justice. Bond had seen many lovely women in Japan, but none possessed a face as elegant as Mayumi McMahon's. The blend of Japanese and European features created an exotic portrait; she certainly looked more Asian than not, but Bond could see hints of Western influence in her genes. For one thing, her almond-shaped eyes were blue, not brown. She had a wide, sensual mouth and a complexion that was as pure and creamy as buttermilk. Her long black hair was shiny and silky and full of body.

She was short, probably about five feet two inches, with a compact, hourglass figure. She wore a *yukata* over loose silk pants and was barefoot.

"Norika says you want to see me," she said. "Who are you? What's this about?"

"I just want to talk," Bond replied.

She grimaced and nodded. "Oh, you're one of those. Listen, I'm not working now. The boss—he hasn't let me work for the past few days. I don't know why." There was very little Asian accent to her speech. She could have passed for someone raised in Britain.

"I just need a few minutes of your time. I'll pay you."

She considered this a moment, looked back into the hallway, then shut the door. "What's your name?" she asked.

Bond didn't mind telling her the truth. "James."

She sat beside him and crossed her legs. Bond could see why a girl like her could make a fortune. She was practically perfect in every way.

"So what do you want to talk about, James?"

NINETEEN

SECRETS

"Listen to me, Mayumi," Bond said. "I have something to tell you."

The girl's eyes widened. "Who are you? How did you know my name?"

"My name is Bond. James Bond. I work for the British government. I've come to take you home."

At first she almost burst out laughing. "Are you crazy?" she asked. Then her demeanour changed and her eyes flashed with anger. "Did my father send you?" she spat. She stood and put her hands on her hips.

"In a way," Bond replied. "Calm down and listen to me."

"No. Who the hell do you think you are? You think you can just waltz in here and take me home? Do you know who runs this place? Do you have any idea what they would do to you if they knew you were talking to me like this?"

"Please, Mayumi, just listen to me for a minute."

She looked appraisingly at him for a moment, and said, "All right. I'm listening. I'll give you a minute but talk fast. You should know that all I have to do is push the button on the intercom over there if you cause any trouble."

"Can they hear us?" Bond asked.

"No."

"You had better sit down."

"I'm fine right here."

"Very well, then I shall tell you straight out. Your parents are dead."

Mayumi looked as if she had been slapped. "What?"

"Your parents and both of your sisters are dead. I'm sorry. I was hoping I would be able to break the news to you gently, but you didn't give me much choice."

She moved to the bed and sat beside him.

"How did it happen?" she whispered, obviously shocked.

"We're pretty sure that the Ryujin-kai killed them."

She looked at him with disbelief in her eyes.

"Yes, the people who run this place, the men who employ you. They did it. The yakuza you work for. They wanted to take over your father's company. Your great uncle was a part of it. He's dead now, too."

Mayumi trembled a little. She swallowed and asked, "When . . . when did all this happen?"

"About a week ago."

"A week ago?" She stood again and began to pace around the room. "Why didn't anyone tell me? How come I didn't know?"

"Mayumi, it was in all the papers and on the news."

"I don't look at any of that stuff," she said.

Bond considered whether or not he should risk blasting his way out of there and taking her with him. What were the odds? There were the two men at the front. There could be others. Did he want to cause a disturbance at this point? Was there another way? It would certainly be better to get her out discreetly and quietly.

"Why don't you sit down?" he urged.

"I don't *want* to sit down!"

She was obviously very upset about the news, but was struggling to master her emotions. The girl obviously had a fiery resolve; she was used to being in control in this room and was fiercely resisting Bond taking it from her.

"Mayumi," he said, "can we leave and talk somewhere else?"

"No," she said. "They've been keeping me here for the past two days. They won't let me leave the building. I've been staying in a room upstairs. I don't know what's going on."

"Did they give you a reason why you couldn't leave or work?"

"They said my life was in danger. I was told that it was some business-related thing between a jealous client and Kubo, the manager here. Apparently this client threatened to have me killed because I'm the Casanova Club's most valuable asset. Kubo said that I had to stay here for a few days and not go home because my apartment was being watched."

"Mayumi, your life is just as much in danger if you stay here."

Her eyes narrowed as she studied him. He could see the thoughts passing through her head. Could he be trusted? Was he telling the truth? What was this *really* about?

She sat down again on the bed. "Tell me what is going on."

Bond took her hand. "My government sent me to Japan to investigate your parents' deaths. They died of a deadly man-made virus manufactured by Yonai Enterprises. They needed your father's company for its technology—specifically, the virus itself—and they use genetically engineered mosquitoes to transmit it."

"But why . . . why my mother and sisters, too?"

"So no one but Fujimoto would control the family's stock. The board of directors was free to agree to a merger with Yonai. Your great uncle masterminded the plan, then he was killed by the Ryujin-kai, after he had outlived his usefulness."

"This is too incredible . . ." she whispered. His words were beginning to sink in.

"I've been asked to bring you back to Tokyo," he continued. "With you back in the picture, the merger could be made void. To tell you the truth, I find it amazing that you're still alive."

"But I don't want to go back to Tokyo. Especially now. Besides, from what you're telling me, the Ryujin-kai is not going to let me go even if I wanted to."

"Mayumi, don't you see that you're a slave?" Bond said.

Those words seemed to hit a nerve. "I never wanted to look at it that way," she said. "I was brought here by one of the *oyabun* of the Ryujin-kai. For a while I was treated in style as the girlfriend of a powerful yakuza. Then he was killed in a gun battle with a rival gang.

I wanted to go back to Tokyo, but they put me to work here. They 'provided' for me, because the man I was with was well respected. At first I thought I couldn't work here, but to tell you the truth, I became determined to become the best soaplands girl in the business. And I am. Then . . . I don't know . . . things changed."

Bond waited a moment for her to continue.

She shrugged, unwilling to admit the truth. "Let's just say that it's not as glamorous as I thought it would be."

Bond sensed that there was pain behind her pride. He elected not to press her on it. "What can you tell me about the Ryujin-kai? Have you heard anything about something they might be planning?"

"Listen, Mister Bond, is it? This is crazy. Why would the yakuza suddenly turn against me? I have remained loyal to them."

Bond felt exasperated by her delusion. He said, rather brutally, "Mayumi, many people will die if you don't talk to me about it. This has become bigger than you or your family."

Suddenly she put her hand to her mouth and clenched her face, fighting the urge to cry. She clearly didn't want to do so in front of Bond. He waited patiently, giving her a few moments.

Finally, she took a deep breath, composed herself and said, "A lot of high-ranking men come here. A few nights ago there were men from the Northern Territories here and I had to help entertain them. Kubo made a big deal out of that. Yasutake Tsukamoto, the *oyabun*, was here with them. He was giving them a send-off. They were on their way to Tokyo on some kind of secret mission for the Ryujin-kai."

"This is very important," Bond said. "What else do you remember?"

But Mayumi couldn't concentrate. She rose once again and walked over to the sink. She gazed at her reflection in the mirror and said, "I hated my parents for so long. But now that they're gone, I . . . I just don't know how I feel . . . ."

"I understand."

"And my sisters. I didn't get to say goodbye." Her voice cracked but she still refused to cry. Bond could see that this girl had an iron will. She was tough, unpredictable and very attractive. She was also very young, vulnerable and in terrible danger.

She took a tissue and wiped her nose. "About a month ago, they took me to some place outside of Noboribetsu," she said.

"Go on."

"It was a place that had a lot of tanks full of insects. A laboratory of some kind. I had a peek into a big room where I probably wasn't supposed to be. Anyway, there was some kind of high-level meeting there with Ryujin-kai top-ranking officials. I was hired, along with four other girls, to service them there. I heard a bit of their conversation but I didn't think anything of it then."

"What did they say?"

"They were talking about infectious diseases. In a very general way. But I remember Tsukamoto asking someone about *their* disease. I distinctly recall being struck by his choice of words, like it was something they were in possession of. The other man replied that it was ready."

Mayumi came back to the bed and sat down beside him.

"Don't you feel used, Mayumi?" he asked gently. "You can't want to stay here. It's not the life for you."

"How do you know that?" she asked him casually, with no anger. "You are not in London any more. You do not understand Japan. The conditions are not as bad as one might think. Some of my clients are celebrities. All of them are rich. I already have a reputation for being the best girl in the place. My apartment is very nice; I can come and go as I please. Some people might say that I'm a bad girl, but I like to think of myself as a party girl, Mister Bond. I prefer it that way. My family never understood that. I didn't want their lifestyle. I have everything I want here."

Bond allowed his eyes to travel around the characterless yet faintly sordid room. She saw this and her face tightened. "I'm paid very well." As she spoke, Mayumi's eyes betrayed her. She didn't believe what she was saying. These words were meant to convince her as well as him.

"You know that's a delusion," Bond said gently. "You don't have your freedom. Mayumi, they're going to kill you."

There was a moment's pause and she whispered "Then what should I do?"

"Is there any way that you can get out of here?"

She thought a minute and shrugged. "There's a fire escape in the room upstairs. The window is locked but I can always break it." She got up again. "What am I talking about? I *can't* leave! I have nowhere to go."

"I'll see that you get back to Tokyo safely."

"I don't want to go to Tokyo! Anywhere but there. Look, I can't believe they're going to kill me. James? That's your name?"

"Yes."

"I'm too valuable a commodity. I look Japanese but I speak English. I have blue eyes. I'm exotic. I have a lot of important clients. From Russia, from Korea, from America. From *Britain*."

"You're mistaken, Mayumi," Bond said. "You are a trophy. You are the daughter of a rival and your presence here makes them feel superior. You are the spoils of war and a prisoner."

She was quiet after that.

"I'm not leaving until you tell me that you're going to come back with me to Tokyo," he said.

She sighed and said, "I need to think about all of this. I can't promise anything. If I try to leave, I had better do it very early tomorrow morning. Where shall I meet you?"

"I'll come back here and wait for you."

"No," she said. "I want to get away from here. Let's meet somewhere in the city centre."

"All right. Let's meet at the Tokei-dai clock tower," Bond said.

"You've been reading too many guide books. All right. *If* I decide to believe your story and *if* I make it out of here, I'll be there at four o'clock. Now go away. Maybe I'll see you later."

He nodded. "Trust me. If you can get that far, I'll get us out of Sapporo safely."

They stood and went to the door. Bond reached for his wallet but she put a hand on his arm. "No," she said. "You have to pay Norika."

Norika met them outside the door. Mayumi went past her and up the stairs, not looking back. Norika then quietly said, "Thirty thousand yen please."

Bond didn't flinch. He pulled the bills out of his wallet and gave them to her. She took the money and put it in a small purse. Then she led Bond back to the reception area, where, in front of the men, she kissed him demurely on the cheek. She said goodbye and for him to "come back again soon." The two punch perms glared at Bond as he bowed to them and left the premises.

Mayumi went up to her room, shut the door, and considered everything that she had just been told. Was she really in danger? Did the Ryujin-kai really kill her family?

Her family . . . mum . . . dad . . . her sisters . . . Oh God, what had she done . . . ?

She finally broke down and cried.

TWENTY

ESCAPE FROM SAPPORO

AT THREE O'CLOCK IN THE MORNING, MAYUMI MCMAHON, DRESSED IN jeans and a T-shirt, opened the door to her room on the top floor of the Casanova Club and peered into the hallway. Everything was quiet and still. Kubo had been gone since the afternoon, leaving only the two men downstairs to watch over the place . . . and her. They had been there every night since she was told that she couldn't go home.

She crept down the stairs and inched around the corner to take a look. Both men were asleep in their chairs, mouths open, snoring away.

Some guards, she thought.

Mayumi went back upstairs to her room and shut the door. For the fifth time she examined the locked window that gave access to the fire escape.

What did they think would happen if there really was a fire? she wondered.

The last few hours had been tough. The full impact of what the Englishman had revealed to her had not hit her until a few hours later. Then she stayed in her room and cried herself to sleep. She woke up disoriented.

She felt shell-shocked and numb. It was very confusing.

Mayumi had spent the last five or six years absolutely hating her parents. Her teenage years had been miserable and she blamed them.

They had been so controlling and strict, much more so with her than they had been with her older sisters. Of course, Kyoko and Shizuka were model daughters. They never complained, were always dutiful and well behaved.

As an adolescent, Mayumi had done as she pleased. Although her IQ was high, she was a poor student in school because she simply didn't care. She often skipped classes. More often than not, she was hanging out with other young troublemakers in pachinko parlours. When she was fifteen, she posed nude for a photographer who specialised in pornography. She got in with a rough crowd.

Things really started happening when she met Kenji Umeki through her association with the photographer. Umeki was part of a *bosozoku* and Mayumi had found that exciting. He worked as a bouncer at a soaplands in Kabuki-cho and she got to know how those places operated.

By the time she was sixteen, she was enjoying the lifestyle of a gangster's girlfriend. She got into all the best clubs, dabbled with drugs and had a great time living on the dark side of life.

Mayumi McMahon had thought that she had it all under control until that one night. The night that opened her eyes to the truth about her father.

But now that he was dead, Mayumi wasn't sure how she felt about him. She grieved for her mother and sisters, as they weren't so bad. But her father? After the years of his being "disappointed" with her and the hundreds of times he had shouted at her that she was "no damned good?"

God, how she hated him. What a hypocrite.

Still undecided about what to do, Mayumi paced the floor. She still couldn't believe that the gang would want to kill her. Kubo liked her. He wouldn't let any harm come to her. Kubo wouldn't—

There was a knock at the door.

"Who is it?" she asked.

"Kubo."

Wary, Mayumi unlocked and opened the door a crack. He was standing alone in the corridor.

"What do you want?"

"Get your things," Kubo said. "I'm moving you out. We have to be quiet. The guards are asleep."

"What are you talking about?"

"I was gone most of the day trying to find you a new place to live."

"But I like my apartment. Why can't I go back there?"

"It's too dangerous!" he hissed. "Hurry! Get your things, now!"

She was confused but she also picked up on Kubo's nervousness. Something was wrong.

"All right. Wait a second." She shut the door and quickly piled some clothes into a small bag that she had brought from her apartment a few days before.

Then she heard a door slam downstairs, followed by shouting. Mayumi recognised Kubo's voice and then heard some scuffling. She set down her bag and opened the door. As she lightly stepped down the stairs, she could hear Kubo talking to other men. When she got near enough to hear what they were saying, Mayumi stopped on the stairs, unseen by the men.

"No, you can't go upstairs!" Kubo was saying.

"Get out of our way, Kubo-san. The *kaicho* gave us orders."

"But she is already dead, I tell you! I killed her myself!"

"Then why won't you let us go upstairs?"

"You can't! She—"

Then there was the sound of a struggle that went on for several seconds until a gunshot made Mayumi jump out of her skin. She heard Kubo groan. Another shot silenced the fighting.

Now trembling with fear, Mayumi strained to listen to the newcomers downstairs. They were talking with the two guards. When she heard a guard say, "She's upstairs," she quickly backed up the stairs and ran to the sanctuary of her room, prison cell that it was. She locked the door and turned her attention to the fire escape window. It was her only hope.

Mayumi picked up a wooden chair and threw it at the window. The glass shattered, leaving shards within the frame.

It had made much more noise than she had thought was possible. They must have heard it.

As she climbed through the window she cut her calf and cried out. She fell onto the fire escape platform, clutching her leg. It was dark but she could see that her jeans were torn and that she had a pretty bad cut. It was bleeding profusely.

She swore softly and got up. She limped down the stairs—one floor, two floors—and then she heard voices at the broken window above her.

The men were shouting for her to come back up.

Mayumi practically fell down the final flight of stairs, but she made it to the ground and took off, only to slam right into one of the thugs who was waiting for her. He tried to grab her, but she instinctively jumped and delivered an expert *ushiro-geri* back kick into the man's jaw. He fell backwards, dropping something. He hit his head hard on the pavement and stopped moving. Mayumi paused to check if he was still alive but couldn't tell.

Then she saw what he had dropped. It was a pistol, a semiautomatic. Kenji had once shown her how to fire a gun and he had also taught her a few karate moves such as the one she had just delivered. Mayumi picked up the gun and ran, leaving a trail of blood spots behind her.

Bond arrived at the Tokei-dai clock tower at 3:45. He stood across the street in front of the tourist information office and watched for Mayumi. Sapporo was asleep. An occasional car appeared on the street but otherwise the city was quiet and dark.

The clock tower was quite an anomaly. Built in the style of a New England colonial hall, the structure was now a museum and library. It looked very strange set against the rest of Sapporo's more modern and quintessentially Japanese architecture. Stranger still was the fact that it was the meeting place for a British secret agent and a soaplands girl on the run at 4:00 in the morning.

At five minutes to four, Bond saw Mayumi come around the corner and walk towards the clock tower. She was limping! He could see blood seeping from a rag wrapped around her right leg.

Bond ran across the street to meet her. "Mayumi!"

She was panting and looked scared. "I cut myself on the window when I climbed out of there. You were right, James-san, they were going to kill me. I overheard them talking about it. They're not far behind."

Whatever else, the girl had pluck. Bond had to admit that she intrigued him.

"I hope you have a way out of here and fast," she said.

Bond looked at his Rolex. Another thirty seconds.

"Here, lean against me." She did and he felt a lump concealed in the waist of her jeans. "What the hell is that?"

"Oh, I took it from one of the guards. Don't worry, I know how to use it. Listen, I'm about to start running again if you don't get us out of here."

Bond looked at his Rolex again. Where *was* he?

Suddenly, a Honda Today, to Bond's eyes a ridiculously small commuter car, screamed around the corner and pulled up in front of the clock tower. Ikuo Yamamaru was at the wheel. He threw open the door.

"Get in!" he called.

A black Mercedes swerved around the corner. Bond could see that the man in the passenger seat had a punch perm.

"How are all three of us supposed to fit in there?" Mayumi asked.

"Move, Mayumi! Quick!" Bond shouted.

Bond shoved her into the back seat and he jumped into the front. A gunshot echoed through the street and they heard the bullet ricochet off the road. Ikuo accelerated and the little car's wheels shrieked. The Mercedes skidded noisily as it torpedoed past the clock tower in pursuit.

Ikuo jumped a red light, almost hitting a lone city bus on its way to begin its early morning route. He slammed on the brakes and turned the wheel sharply. Mayumi screamed and covered her eyes as the car screeched, narrowly avoiding a broadside with the vehicle.

"Sorry!" he said. He turned the wheel violently and floored the accelerator. The car bolted out of the intersection and onto a north-south street containing light traffic. Luckily, the Honda was so small that it could easily run up onto the pavement, which was precisely what Ikuo did.

"Try not to kill anyone," Bond said.

"Especially us," Mayumi said. "Who is this guy, anyway?"

"I am Ikuo Yamamaru, *hajime mashite*," the driver said quickly.

"Did you borrow this car from your mother?" Bond asked him.

Ikuo said, "Laugh if you want, Bond-san, but I have outfitted this little car with an engine that makes your English sports cars seem like golf carts."

The Ainu put the car into fourth and they sped along the street, heading towards the huge NHK television tower that dominated the skyline in the centre of town. It was in the middle of a paved square with a few park benches. Dozens of pigeons had arrived for sunrise and were feasting on crumbs. The little Honda jumped the kerb, scattering the birds in a rush of flapping wings.

The Mercedes was not far behind. They had also driven onto the pavement to bypass the traffic, but the car could not match the Honda's souped-up engine. The man in the passenger seat leaned out of the car and fired a pistol, knocking out a brakelight.

"Get down!" Bond shouted to Mayumi. He didn't have to tell her twice. She was very frightened. "Ikuo, get us out of here!"

But more bullets tore into the front and rear tyres. Ikuo lost control of the car as it skidded toward one of the tower's steel legs. Bond saw it coming through the windscreen and shielded his head just as the car crashed into a girder. The impact threw Mayumi into the front seat on top of Bond.

Ikuo had an ugly gash on his forehead. The window on the driver's side was cracked where he had struck it.

The sound of nearby gunfire jolted them out of the temporary haze. Bond drew the Walther and said, "When I say so, jump out of the car and take cover."

He peered through the shattered back windscreen and saw that there were three of them. The yakuza had stopped the Mercedes about thirty feet away and had taken cover behind the vehicle.

"Now!"

Bond jumped first and crouched behind the engine block, followed by Ikuo. Mayumi rolled out of the car and got behind the steel girder that was a part of the tower's leg. Both men fired at the Mercedes as soon as they were in position. Bond knocked out a headlamp, but otherwise their shots were wildly inaccurate because both men had been shaken by the collision. Bond heard a third gun resound, turned, and was surprised to see Mayumi firing her Browning at the yakuza. She managed to blast a hole through the Mercedes' windscreen.

"We're trapped," Ikuo said. "There is no place to run."

He was right. Bond surveyed the square and realised that they were wide open. The only possibility would be to run beneath the tower, but then they would be moving targets without cover. Bond had to find a way to take them out.

Police sirens were growing louder. They would be on the scene any minute. At this point, Bond didn't want them involved. He had to get Mayumi out of Sapporo without interference or delays.

He loaded a new magazine and ducked low, beneath the Honda's chassis. He could just get a bead on the feet of one of the yakuza thugs, which could be seen below the bottom edge of the Mercedes' door. Bond fired the gun laterally, two inches above the level pavement. The bullet shattered the man's ankle. He screamed and fell from behind the cover of the car door. Ikuo got a clear shot and hit him in the chest.

"One down, two to go," Bond said.

Realising that they needed to get out before the police arrived, the remaining yakuza got back into the Mercedes. The driver gunned the engine and drove towards them. The other man leaned out of the passenger window, ready to shoot whomever he could see as the car shot past them.

"Both of you, go for the gunman," Bond commanded. "I'll take the driver."

He positioned himself on one knee and aimed carefully at the shape behind the wheel. Ikuo and Mayumi concentrated their firepower on the passenger, spraying him with a barrage of bullets. Bond squeezed the trigger once. He saw a spider web appear on the windscreen and then the Mercedes suddenly veered to the left. The shooter jerked violently and dropped his weapon as several rounds hit his upper body. The Mercedes kept going until it rammed into one of the tower's opposite legs. The front end was smashed pretty badly.

Keeping his gun trained on the car, Bond got up and ran to it. He opened the passenger door and the gunman fell out onto the pavement. He ran around to the other side and pulled the dead driver out of the car. Ikuo and Mayumi were right behind him.

"Nice of them to let us borrow their car," Bond said, nodding at Ikuo, who immediately got into the driver's seat.

The police sirens were very near, perhaps a block away.

Ikuo threw the car into reverse, backed off of the girder, and then drove into the street. He turned the corner and sped away from the scene just as the police cars began to arrive.

Bond looked over and saw that Ikuo had blood all over his shirt.

"Ikuo, you've been hit," he said.

"I know," Yamamaru replied. "I'll be fine."

Bond reached over and felt Ikuo's chest. The wound was on the right, just beneath the collarbone.

"We have to get you to a doctor," he said. He turned back to Mayumi. "How's your leg?"

"What leg?" she asked.

Bond looked pointedly at her blood soaked jeans.

"I'm all right," she said. "Really. It looks worse than it is."

Ikuo drove like a whirlwind to the southern outskirts of Sapporo and got on the main highway, but after ten minutes Bond insisted that he pull the car over to the side of the road. Ikuo looked quite pale and was sweating freely.

"I'll drive, Ikuo. Change places with me," Bond said.

Once they were buckled in, Bond guided the car back into the traffic flow.

"There is an emergency medical centre just up the road," Ikuo muttered. "I am afraid we had better stop there. You can drop me off and go on."

"I think Miss McMahon needs some attention too, despite her protests," Bond said. "Perhaps they'll give us a bulk discount."

It was a small clinic that was used primarily for road accidents. The staff were accustomed to those but they had never seen a gunshot wound before. Ikuo showed them an official ID so that he wouldn't have to answer questions. The Ainu was placed on a trolley and wheeled into a room marked "Treatment." Bond stayed with Mayumi, who was looked at by a young female doctor.

"This is a bad cut, how did it happen?" she asked, examining Mayumi's leg.

"Broken glass."

The doctor cleaned the wound, put in several stitches, and gave Mayumi a tetanus shot. After a sterile bandage was wrapped around her calf, the doctor said that she could leave.

"Can we see our friend?" Bond asked.

The doctor told him to wait a minute and then disappeared into the treatment room.

She soon returned with a note from Ikuo, which said: "Go to hotel in Noboribetsu. Will contact you tomorrow morning."

Bond turned to Mayumi and said, "Come on, let's go. We can't do any more here."

Ten minutes later they were in the back of a taxi on their way to Noboribetsu.

Mayumi asked, "Won't they be looking for us?"

"Undoubtedly," Bond said. "But let's worry about that if they find us."

The taxi pulled onto the expressway and headed south, leaving Sapporo and the main hub of the Ryujin-kai behind.

TWENTY-ONE

DEMONS FROM HELL

TSUKAMOTO PICKED UP THE PHONE AND KNEW INSTANTLY THAT THE *YAMI Shogun* was on the other end. There was something about the sound of the *air* in the earpiece that was distinctive. He rubbed his hand over his stomach and realised that there was indeed a correlation between the sudden attacks of anxiety he had been experiencing over the last few weeks and talking with the *Yami Shogun*.

"Good morning, Tsukamoto," Yoshida said.

Tsukamoto swallowed hard. "Good morning to you, too, Yoshida. How are you?"

"Fine. And you?"

"Very well, thank you," Tsukamoto lied. "I shall leave for Nobori-betsu in an hour. The results of the tests are encouraging."

"I am happy to hear that. I have thought of an appropriate name for our plan. Red Widow Dawn. In honour of our insect assassins."

"Very good, Yoshida. I shall inspect the product today and if it meets our criteria, then Red Widow Dawn will commence as planned."

"The product must meet our criteria."

"The product works as it is now. You could go ahead with today's version."

"Our mission requires the best. The more reliable the weapon, the more foolproof the plan. Tsukamoto, I am waiting for your confirmation that *everything* is prepared."

"Yes, I understand. You need not worry."

There was silence at the other end of the line. Tsukamoto felt his stomach churn. What was the master thinking? Did he know about what had happened in Sapporo?

Finally, Yoshida said, "I sense that something is wrong. What is it, Tsukamoto? You are not hiding something from me, are you?"

Tsukamoto shuddered. "We had a problem," he said. "Kubo was a traitor and disobeyed my orders to have the girl killed. He had kept her alive without any of us knowing. She escaped early this morning, killing one of our men. Now she is with that British agent. Kubo has been taken care of. But more of our men were killed in Sapporo."

There was an ominous silence. Tsukamoto broke it, saying, "I will gladly cut off one of my fingers, Yoshida." He hung his head in shame.

"Tsukamoto, I want them killed and I want it done now. You have failed in a very simple task. Find them and do the job *right*."

The simplicity of this remark sent a chill down Tsukamoto's spine. He found himself talking too much and too quickly in an effort to dispel his fear. "Our best men are on it. We sent the word out to all of the *honbu* around the country. They have received descriptions of both the Englishman and the McMahon girl. There was a third man with them, an Ainu, someone whom we believe is an employee of the Public Security Investigation Agency. We will kill him, too. We believe they are probably on their way back to Tokyo so we—"

"Stop babbling, Tsukamoto," Yoshida snapped. "It does not become you. Just . . . find them. We cannot afford interference at this juncture. You know what happens in four days."

"I understand, Yoshida."

Yoshida raised his voice—something he rarely did. "*I do not think you do!* This is our time of glory! The master Mishima-san is watching over us from heaven. He is proud of our intentions to rid Japan of the barbarians who desecrate and pollute our culture and our land. We must not let him down! The only consequence of failure is *death!*"

Tsukamoto clenched his eyes. His boyhood friend was truly mad. Mishima-san would never have approved of what they were about to do. Yukio Mishima was no terrorist. Yoshida had taken his tenets and twisted them. How was this going to end?

"Yes, *sensei*," was all that Tsukamoto could say.

"Call me from Noboribetsu."

"*Hai!*"

Tsukamoto hung up the phone. He had slipped again and called Yoshida *sensei*. This time Yoshida had not reproached him.

He looked at the clock. He dreaded going to Noboribetsu and taking charge of the operation. He had to follow the *Yami Shogun's* orders and stand behind them. Supporting Goro Yoshida to victory was going to be a very honourable action, but Tsukamoto felt nothing but dread. Something terrible was going to happen and he was going to be caught in the middle of it.

Yasutake Tsukamoto, the head of one of the most powerful yakuza crime syndicates in the world, was afraid. He was aware that a day of reckoning would come, sooner rather than later. And that was when he would have to answer for his life of crime.

The taxi ride to Noboribetsu from the medical clinic had taken a little over an hour. Bond and Mayumi were let off in front of the Dai-ichi Takimotokan, the largest and most luxurious hotel and spa in a town famous for its abundant hot springs. It was a complex made up of four buildings, 399 rooms, two restaurants and a souvenir shop. Tanaka had booked them into the hotel with the reasoning that it was an unlikely place for them to be found. Bond had insisted on investigating the Hokkaido Mosquito Vector and Control Centre outside town before heading back to Tokyo, but he and Mayumi both needed a few hours' rest. Mayumi's face was grey with pain, but she was too stubborn to complain.

The area around the town was volcanic and Bond had to admit that the scenery was extraordinary. A patch of land just behind the Dai-ichi, called *Jigokudani*, or "Hell Valley," was a national park full of steaming, sulphurous vents and streams of hot water bubbling out of vividly coloured rocks. This was the source of the hot springs that fed the hotel's thirty different baths.

The predominant mascot of Noboribetsu was an *oni*, a demon known as the King of Hell. He was a fierce-looking, red, horned ogre who carried a club and he was everywhere. A huge statue of him guarded the town, sculptures adorned hotel lobbies and miniature figures of the demon could be purchased in the souvenir shops.

When they entered the hotel, they were greeted in the lobby by a line of chambermaids and bellboys who called out in unison, *"Irrashaimase!"* Tanaka had taken care of the reservations; Bond and Mayumi had separate Japanese-style rooms with futons on *tatami* mats.

"The first thing I'm going to do is get into one of those hot sulphur baths," Mayumi said as they walked away from the lobby.

"Not on your life," Bond replied. "We're going to stay in our rooms. We can't afford to be seen. By anyone."

"What? Come on, the baths are what makes this place great. And what about food?"

"We'll have room service delivered. Which I will organise. I mean it, Mayumi. We're not out of danger yet."

"You're absolutely no fun at all," she pouted.

They walked past one of the hotel's main attractions; a uniquely Japanese two-storey-tall mechanical clock shaped like the ogre's club. At various times during the day, the clock would "strike," and it did so now. Several doors on it opened and mechanical fairy-tale figures emerged and danced to an elaborately orchestrated soundtrack that resounded throughout the lobby.

This distraction kept Bond from noticing the two men sitting with drinks in the lounge, which was set apart from the lobby but in plain view of it. Both men had crew cuts and were wearing *yukata* and *tanzen* provided by the hotel. They did not need to exchange a glance when Bond and Mayumi walked through. One man took the mobile out of his pocket and made a call.

It was just before sunset when Bond had a brief conversation with Tanaka over the phone.

"Yamamaru-san is all right and was discharged from the clinic," Tanaka said. "He will rendezvous with you later. Get some rest. However, I must warn you that his Ainu contacts in Noboribetsu have reported that there is a lot of yakuza activity there. Keep a low profile. They are looking for you."

They discussed what must be done with Mayumi McMahon and agreed that Bond should get her back to Tokyo as soon as possible. But both men decided that having a look at the mosquito control facility in Noboribetsu was a good idea, provided that Bond could get inside it without causing a major disturbance. Bond didn't particularly want to wait until nightfall, but he resigned himself to sitting out the next few hours with Mayumi. He hated waiting, and he had done a lot of it in his line of work. Normally he couldn't bear to sit in a hotel room or an airport lobby waiting for instructions or a message from superiors. Now even in these luxurious surroundings, he felt restless and anxious for something to happen.

Bond decided to check on Mayumi. He called her room, but the phone rang and rang. Angrily, he hung up, threw on a *yukata* and glanced at his shoulder holster hanging over a chair. Not practical. Instead, Bond took the small plastic dagger from his field-issue shoe heel and hid it inside the *yukata*. He quickly left his room, walked down two doors to Mayumi's, and knocked loudly. There was no answer.

Bond swore under his breath. He looked down the corridor and saw a chambermaid about to enter one of the rooms. Bond sprinted to her and asked if she had seen a young girl come out of room 223. The woman replied that yes, she had. The girl had asked her how to get to the baths.

Bond took the lift down to the *onsen* complex in the hotel. While in some Japanese *onsen* men and women shared one bathhouse, here it was not so. To hell with it, he thought. He was going in the women's side.

The sight of two dressed men entering the women's baths ahead of him hardened his resolve. They had crew cuts and looked like bodybuilders. Bond smelled yakuza.

Bond hurried into the locker room. Several women in states of undress were upset and calling for help. The two men must have gone on through to the baths. Bond heard screams coming from that direction. He kicked off his slippers and ran through the locker room and into the baths complex. The baths occupied more than one level of the hotel and guests were allowed to wander from floor to floor trying out the hot mineral pools, waterfalls, walking pools, freezing cold pools, steam room and swimming pool.

Bond found himself in a hot and steamy room. Naked and frightened women were huddled together, clutching their towels. Bond ran across the wet tiled floor searching frantically for his prey in the various pools, but a scream that sounded like Mayumi directed him towards the outdoor terrace, where guests could sit in a gigantic hot tub under the stars.

More wet, naked women ran shrieking past Bond as he ran through the door to the terrace. The two yakuza had pulled Mayumi out of the water and were struggling with her. One of them had a cord around the girl's neck and was attempting to choke her to death.

The man who was trying to hold Mayumi down saw Bond rushing towards them. He let go of Mayumi so that he could counter-attack but he wasn't fast enough. Bond pulled back his right fist and put his full weight into a power punch to the man's chin. The yakuza's head jerked back with a snap and he fell to the ground.

The other man was still trying to choke Mayumi but he was having a very difficult time holding her alone. Bond leaped onto him and locked his arm around the man's throat.

"Let her go," Bond said through his teeth.

But the yakuza ignored him. Allowing his anger to get the better of him, Bond grabbed a tight hold of the man's head and then jerked it to the right sharply and forcefully. The sound of the man's neck snapping was extremely satisfying. The cord loosened and Mayumi fell to her knees, coughing and sputtering. Bond let the man's body crumple to the ground and pushed it into the hot tub with his foot.

But before he could see to Mayumi, someone slammed into Bond's back, knocking him into the water. The heat was intense. He immediately broke the surface to gasp for air and caught sight of three men jumping into the tub after him. Obviously a second team of killers had targeted Bond and followed him into the baths.

Bond placed his hands behind him on the edge of the tub so that he could raise himself out of the water, but the two men on either side of him grabbed his arms. Bond broke one man's grip, the one on his right, and lashed out with a forceful blow to the yakuza's nose. The other man, however, threw himself into Bond and shoved him into the hot water. The third man moved across the tub to join the mêlée. Bond found himself being held below the surface by all three men as they gripped his arms, head and shoulders. Bond struggled but it was no use. If he hadn't been submerged he might have been able to break their hold, but the weight of the water slowed his defensive manoeuvres. Fighting in the water was difficult. No matter how hard he pushed, the speed was always the same. Strength was about the only tool he had, and Bond was outnumbered three to one.

Although he was able to hold his breath for an extraordinary amount of time, he could not resist the laws of physics. His lungs burned as they screamed for air. He tried clawing and pinching, but the men just tightened their vicelike grips.

Do something! Bond commanded himself. Wait! The knife! He had felt it come loose from his *yukata* and watched it float to the bottom of the tub. Bond felt the tub floor with his bare foot and finally found it. Grasping it with his toes, he managed to pull it up far enough so that he could take it with his hands. He pulled out the blade, held it firmly, and then slashed the man on his right across the stomach. From underwater, Bond heard the man scream. He loosened his grip, allowing Bond to wriggle out from under the other two through water now thickened with blood.

He surfaced and gasped for air. The two remaining yakuza lunged at him, knocking him back against the side of the tub. Bond thrust out his arm and couldn't help making a wild, reckless arc with the knife. It connected with something and one of the men yelped, clutching his face.

The uninjured attacker backed off, giving Bond time to scramble out of the tub. Once he was standing, he kicked the man with the stomach wound in the face and knocked him into the water. The second injured man was already blinded, shouting for help. Bond ignored him and focused his attention on the one man who was still standing in the water.

"Here, catch!" Bond said.

He flung the knife at the man. It spun in the air and skewered the yakuza's eye. The man's mouth opened wide in horror as he fell back into the water, which was now foaming with blood.

Bond then knelt beside Mayumi. She put her arms around him, still gasping and sobbing. Her neck bore a livid red welt where the cord had burned her skin.

"How—how did they find us?" she stuttered.

"Determination and the Japanese work ethic," Bond said.

He noticed that she was clutching something in her hand.

"What's that?" he asked.

Mayumi coughed again and tried to breathe deeply. She exhaled loudly and said, "One of them had this in his jacket pocket. I was grabbing at anything and everything and happened to pull it out."

It was an employee identification card. Bond took it from her and examined it. The card read "Hokkaido Mosquito and Vector Control Centre" and there was a photo of the man and a magnetic strip on it.

"Mayumi, this is a key card. These men were from that facility I need to see."

"I never knew that the Hokkaido government employed yakuza hit-men," she said.

"Employees of Yonai Enterprises, more likely. Or soldiers with the Ryujin-kai who act as security guards at the place."

The doors to the spa burst open and four hotel security guards shouted at them.

Bond stood and held up his hands. The guards were unarmed, as was the policy in Japan—the police never carried firearms either—but the guards exhibited enough malevolence to convince Bond that he shouldn't try to escape. Besides, Tiger would fix everything.

"Come on, Mayumi," Bond said. "I think it's time to check out."

TWENTY-TWO

CAUGHT!

"I'M COMING WITH YOU!" MAYUMI SAID, GRITTING HER TEETH AND FOLDING her arms in front of her. The angry red welt on her neck seemed to intensify when she asserted herself. She had changed into the T-shirt and designer jeans that Bond had bought her along with a hat and sunglasses in the hotel boutique. She looked like a student.

"It's too dangerous," Bond insisted.

The sun had set and the lights of Noboribetsu were bright and flashy but the small resort town was nothing like the bigger cities. The shops and restaurants on the main street were alive and open for business but the areas beyond that were dark and foreboding. The mountains in the distance and the woods surrounding them created the illusion that the little town was in the middle of a deep, dark forest, miles away from civilisation.

"I want you to check into another hotel and wait until I come back," Bond said as he unfolded a map that Ikuo had given him. The mosquito control centre was clearly marked, located on a side road not very far from the Dai-ichi Takimotokan.

"No," she said stubbornly. "I'm staying with you. I owe it to my mother and my sisters to see this through."

"Why not your father?" Bond asked.

She grew silent.

"Him too, I guess," she muttered finally.

"Why do you hate him so much?"

"Because he's a liar and a hypocrite."

"How so?"

"Never mind. I don't want to talk about it."

"Mayumi, if you know something that might help us, then—"

"Shut up!" she spat. "I said I don't want to talk about it!"

"Mayumi, it's simply not safe for you to come with me," he said with a sigh.

"Look, if I don't come with you, I'm leaving," she said, digging in her heels. "And you won't be able to stop me."

Bond shook his head and looked at the heavens. She was an impossible girl. It was no wonder that she had been in constant conflict with her parents. She was perhaps the most wilful girl he'd ever known.

Finally, Bond said through clenched teeth, "Well, if you're coming with me, then I insist that you do everything I say. You're to be quiet and follow my orders, do you understand?"

"Yes, master."

Bond scowled at her but she simply smiled wickedly at him.

"You can be pretty sexy when you're a bully, James-san," she said.

He ignored her and said, "It's close enough to walk there. It will be safer."

They walked up the hill away from the Dai-ichi and towards the Valley of Hell. A narrow two-lane road jutted off into the woods on the other side of the main street. The couple turned and began to walk in that direction, where there were no street lamps or any other lamps. It was almost pitch black.

An animal ran across the road in front of them and Mayumi shrieked.

"Did you see that? A fox!" she whispered.

"Quiet!" Bond silently cursed the girl. Women could not be relied upon to keep their mouths shut.

They continued until, twenty minutes later, they came to a fork. The larger road continued on, curving to the right, while an unpaved road split off to the left. A sign was marked in Japanese and English: "Private Property, Keep Out."

"Do you recall any of this from when you were here?" Bond asked.

"I remember this road. I was pretty stoned that night so I don't remember much else."

They walked quietly down the dirt path and eventually came to a high steel fence. Bond examined the gate and found that there was an electronic lock and numeric keypad attached to it. The key card she had taken from the thug at the hotel was not compatible with it.

"I don't suppose you know the code," Bond said.

"Afraid not, master."

"I'm not in the mood for your nonsense," he said. Bond reached into his pocket and removed the Palm Pilot. Major Boothroyd had said that the electro-magnetic device was weak but that it might disable small electric appliances. Would it work on an electronic keypad?

"What's that?" she asked.

"Shhh."

Bond opened the Palm and held it next to the lock.

"I'm guessing that there is a failsafe mechanism on the system," he whispered. "In the event that power is knocked out to the compound, say, because of a fire, they wouldn't want everyone locked in, would they?"

"What are you talking about?" she asked.

"Never mind." He pressed the appropriate buttons and held the contraption steady. It hummed softly and slightly vibrated, the illuminated LED on the gate's keypad flickered once, twice, and then went out.

Bond tried the gate and it opened with a click. He had guessed correctly: the mechanism unlocked when the power was interrupted.

"Hey, it worked!" Mayumi said. "That was pretty cool! How did you do that?"

"Magic. Now be quiet."

The dirt road curved through a group of trees some fifty metres ahead until it stopped at a squat one-storey building made of concrete and stone. The design was typically Japanese and very modern, with diagonal lines and a slanting roof; it looked more like an art museum than a scientific laboratory. The windows were frosted but light shone through them. There were people inside.

"A late night at the office," murmured Bond. "Let's go round the back."

They circled the building and found a gravelled car park containing nine cars. A door marked as an employee entrance opened suddenly. Bond pulled Mayumi against the wall, unwittingly knocking the breath out of her. She gasped and Bond put his hand over her mouth.

Two men came out of the building, laughing about something. They didn't see the couple in the shadows. Instead, they walked past them to a 4 [x] 4, got in it, and drove away.

Mayumi breathed deeply for a moment. "You could be a bit more gentle," she said.

"You insisted on coming. You play by my rules. Now, wait for me here while I go inside."

"Screw that, I'm coming with you. Lead on."

Bond thought for a moment. She would be more of a liability outside and restless.

Christ! This girl was a millstone around his neck. "Okay," he said. "Follow me. But keep your mouth shut."

Bond took her key card and swiped it through the slot next to the employee entrance. The catch clicked.

Bond carefully opened the door and peered inside. It was a shiny and sterile steel-lined corridor. The coast was clear.

"Let's go."

They crept through the corridor and heard voices in other parts of the building. When they reached the end of the hallway, the corridor branched in a T. It appeared that offices were to the right. To the left was a set of double steel doors with small, yellow-tinted windows in the centres. Bond looked through them to see one end of a fairly large laboratory. Men were busy at workstations, all wearing full-body protective suits, much like the kind worn against exposure to radiation.

The laboratory consisted of a variety of metal tables, computers, machines, and what appeared to be glass cubicles built into the walls. The sterility and stainless steel furnishings reminded Bond of a surgical theatre.

Two workers began to walk towards the doors.

"Against the wall!" Bond hissed. He pushed her behind the door and he took the position on the opposite side. Bond drew the Walther and held it by the barrel. The doors swung open and the two men wearing protective suits came through. As soon as the doors closed, Bond swung out and struck one man on the back of the head with the butt of the gun. Without waiting to see if his blow was successful, he immediately raised his arm to hit the other man but his target turned to ward off the attack. He was fast: he grabbed Bond's wrist in mid-air and pushed him against the wall. The first man collapsed onto the floor, out cold. Bond attempted to knee the second man in the groin but the protective suit was too bulky for the strike to be effective. Mayumi, who was standing behind Bond's attacker, drew the Browning from her waist and slammed the butt down on the man's head. He jerked and Bond could see the man's eyes roll up into his head behind the tinted faceplate.

"Good work," Bond said as the man fell to the floor.

"See? Aren't you glad I came along?" she said, winking at him.

"No. But as you're here, take that man. I'll get this one." Bond grabbed the other man by the shoulders and dragged him down the corridor the way they had come. Mayumi copied him. Bond listened at the first door they came to and after satisfying himself that the room was empty, he opened it.

It was a small office. Bond pulled his man inside and Mayumi followed. They closed the door and began to strip their victims of the protective suits.

One of the men looked familiar to Bond. He was slight, with spectacles and a crew cut. Where had he seen this man before? In Tokyo? Yes, that was it! This was the man from the CureLab office, the one who had been working on the mosquito sideshow presentation. Bond looked at his ID card and verified that his name was Fujio Aida.

Five minutes later, Bond and Mayumi, dressed in the protective suits, walked out of the office and purposefully headed toward the lab as if they knew exactly what they were doing. They opened the doors and walked inside, turned the corner and beheld the full extent of the complex.

It was huge. The size of the building's exterior had been deceptive. The lab was easily the size of two cricket pitches side by side. Machines and computers dominated the room, but of particular interest were the glass chambers along one side of the lab that appeared to contain flying insects. Terraria lined another wall and some of these were half-filled with water and appeared to be insect breeding incubators. At least ten other men were in the room, busy at the terminals or working with test tubes and beakers.

Bond and Mayumi nonchalantly made their way to the chambers to get a closer look. In fact, the cubicles were man-sized terraria. Water covered the floors of each chamber, supplemented by plant life and rocks to make the habitat seem more natural. One of the rooms contained a live goat, presumably a host for the mosquitoes inside. Another chamber held mice. Some were running around frantically; others were huddled and trembling in the corner. A couple of them looked dead. Each chamber had an air lock.

As he examined the chambers, Bond put together what he was looking at. Each chamber housed mosquitoes that were in different stages of their life cycle. The first one was empty except for the pond. Bond presumed that there were eggs in the water or attached to some of the plants. The second one was also seemingly empty, probably containing larvae in the water. Indeed, there was an enlarged photograph of mosquito larvae posted on the exterior of the chamber. They were long, transparent, tube-like creatures that hung down in the water with their "mouths" attached to the surface to bring in air. The third chamber held pupae, and through a magnifier built in to the glass, Bond could see that some of the pupal skins had already been shed. Young mosquitoes were gliding in the air within the cubicle, looking for a way out. The fourth chamber was full of live mosquitoes. They were crawling on the inside of the glass, covering the surface of the pond, and flying listlessly.

An extensive workspace separated these chambers from another large room that contained several cages holding various live animals; rats, guinea pigs and goats.

A technician looked at Bond and Mayumi and barked an order at them. Mayumi bowed to the man and gestured for Bond to follow her.

"What did he say?" Bond whispered. "I didn't catch it."

"He wants us to go into the chamber and check on the mice," she said. "What do we do?"

They walked towards the fourth chamber, the one that was full of flying mosquitoes. Inside, some of the mice were still running back and forth but it seemed that a few more had died since they had last looked. A technician punched a button on his computer and the outer doors opened.

"I'm not going in there," Mayumi whispered.

"We're wearing suits, it should be all right," Bond said. He stepped into the air lock and Mayumi reluctantly followed him. The technician closed the outer door and then opened the inner door to the chamber.

Immediately dozens of mosquitoes landed on Bond's face-mask. They crawled over the surface, hungrily searching for a way in to the warm flesh. The insects did the same to Mayumi and she couldn't stifle a scream.

Some of the other technicians heard her and looked up. They weren't used to hearing a woman's voice in the lab.

"Mayumi, we're blown," Bond whispered.

One of the men stepped forward to get a closer look at them through the glass. Bond and Mayumi turned away so that he couldn't see inside the faceplates, but the man shouted at his colleagues. Two men grabbed phones and alerted security, while the others ran to the chamber.

"Let's get out of here before they bring in the heavy artillery," Bond said. He went for the inner door but found that he couldn't open it. The bastards had locked it by remote control. They were caught.

Bond banged on the glass. "Let us out or I'll break the glass and release the mosquitoes."

"I am afraid you cannot break the glass," said a man as he entered the room through a sliding steel door, followed by two armed guards. "As it is most certainly bullet-proof, I can assure you that it is fist-proof."

Bond recognised him at once. He had white hair, smiling eyes, and a commanding presence.

"We have not been properly introduced," the man continued. "I know who you are, Bond-san, but you do not know me. I am Yasu-take Tsukamoto."

He bowed, but not very low.

"Pardon me for not presenting you my *meishi*," Bond said, not returning the bow.

Tsukamoto's demeanour changed rapidly. The smiling eyes vanished as he frowned, obviously insulted.

"Get them out of there," Tsukamoto said to one of the technicians. "The *Yami Shogun* wants to see them helpless before him."

TWENTY-THREE

BITTER GLORY

THE FIRST THING THEY DID WAS TO MAKE BOND AND MAYUMI REMOVE THE protective suits, revealing their street clothes underneath. Then a guard thoroughly searched the couple and their guns were taken from them. When he found the Palm Pilot, the guard studied it, attempting to decide whether or not it constituted a weapon. Bond grabbed the device out of his hand and the two men struggled for possession of it until another guard raised his rifle and butted Bond on the right side of the face. Bond fell and the Palm Pilot was taken from him.

"Put it over there with the rest," Tsukamoto ordered. The guard placed the Palm Pilot on a table, alongside the two guns and Bond's mobile.

Mayumi knelt beside Bond. He was clutching his cheek in agony.

"James-san?" she asked.

Bond clenched his teeth and forced the pain to dissipate, hoping that his cheekbone was merely bruised and not broken. It felt like hell.

"I'm all right," he muttered, then allowed her to help him stand.

Tsukamoto stood and addressed them. The two guards, Aida and several lab technicians flanked him. Bond considered the odds. Not great, but it appeared that only the two guards were armed. One of them had an Uzi. If he could just get to his weapon in time, or perhaps wrestle the Uzi away . . .

"The Yonai Enterprises office in Sapporo warned us that you might be coming this way," Tsukamoto said. "I am happy that you have decided to pay us a visit. There is someone who would like to speak with you. This is a teleconference. He can see and hear you just as you can see and hear him. Please focus your attention on the screen beside you."

A technician brought up an image on a large screen built into one of the walls. A Japanese man came into focus. He appeared to be in his fifties and was dressed in full samurai regalia. A long sword, a *tachi,* hung at his side. The upper edges of a bright red tattoo could be seen on his neck. The man was sitting cross-legged on a pillow.

"Good evening, Mister Bond," he said. "I am Goro Yoshida." And then he bowed.

Yoshida! At last, Bond was able to gaze upon the man he had been studying for over a year. This was the man who had built an army of terrorists, who had instigated the bombing attack in France and countless other incidents around the globe. This was the most dangerous man alive, and yet he was not what Bond had expected. Bond thought the man would be wearing army fatigues, but Yoshida was dressed in a medieval costume. It was a ghastly sight; it confirmed that the man was a deluded psychopath.

Bond stood his ground and refused to bow to Yoshida. The terrorist sat straight and said, "If I had known who you were, Mister Bond, I would have had you killed within the first twenty-four hours of your stepping foot in Japan. You interfered with a business arrangement of mine in France a while ago."

The man's English was surprisingly refined. "I don't know very much about you, Mister Bond, but I understand that you have a certain . . . *reputation* that precedes you so therefore I will show you respect." He bowed again.

Bond said, "I think you know what you can do with your respect, Yoshida."

Tsukamoto gasped at the insult. "Do not speak to the *Yami Shogun* that way!" he spat. He gestured for the guard to do something to Bond but Yoshida sat upright, waved his hand, and said, "Stop." The guard held his stance. "Mister Bond, you choose to waste your last moments with insults."

"Let the girl go," Bond said. "This has nothing to do with her."

"You are mistaken, Mister Bond," Yoshida said. "This has *every-thing* to do with her. Her father's company was instrumental in the construction of our project."

"She is no threat to you. Let her go."

"Mister Bond, are you forgetting that she *owns* the majority of shares in the company?"

"Where are you planning to unleash the mosquitoes, Yoshida, in the subway system? Is this another mission from God like the sarin gas attacks?"

"I respect your thirst for knowledge, Mister Bond. You are a soldier, just like me. I will explain. I don't want you to die ignorant of how we have beaten you, *gaijin*."

Tsukamoto and the others present grinned at that.

"Aida and Tsukamoto, perhaps you would like to tell our distinguished uninformed guest about our new technology," Yoshida said.

Fujio Aida, still rubbing his head and glaring at Bond, said, "Certainly, *sensei*." He looked at Tsukamoto for approval. The *kaicho* nodded subtly.

Aida stepped forward and went to a computer workstation. He used the mouse and keyboard and the screen's image changed. A magnified, red mosquito replaced Yoshida.

"Until a few months ago, I was Head of Research and Development at CureLab Inc. My task there was to work with known viruses in attempts to create cures for them. One particular virus interested me greatly—West Nile. Unfortunately, I was unable to find a cure for it, but I found that I was able to alter it—mutate it—so that it would do what I wanted it to do. In studying the disease, I began to learn more about the biology of mosquitoes, since they are the primary carrier of the disease."

The movies on the screen began to illustrate Aida's words. Images showing the life cycle of the mosquito flashed before them; from egg laying and hatching to clips of adult mosquitoes mating.

"As I worked on the genetic possibilities of altering the mosquito's physiology, I discovered that I could inject their eggs with certain proteins and chemicals which would affect the mosquitoes that hatched out of them and eventually grew into adulthood. But what I needed was better access to mosquitoes and a laboratory where I could work with them."

Tsukamoto took over the narration. "Yonai Enterprises *owns* this facility. The government contracts its use as a public health organisation. Its purpose is to study mosquitoes and transmittable viruses in an effort to control the spread of those diseases. Since Yonai has a special relationship with the Ryujin-kai, it was no great difficulty for us to take over the management and running of the place. When the *Yami Shogun* learned of the disease research, he instructed Aida to create a mutation of West Nile disease, one with far more powerful and faster effects than the original. At the same time, the Ryujin-kai made Aida an offer."

"I defected," Aida said. "I went to Yonai from CureLab. And I took my research with me."

"We made it possible for him to 'disappear,'" Tsukamoto said. "Tell him about our little assassin."

Aida bowed slightly and said, "What we ended up doing was to breed a mosquito with special characteristics. Using genetic splicing and a great deal of experimentation, we eventually took a normal female *Aedes aegypti* mosquito and genetically altered her so that she would bite furiously. Unfortunately, our mosquitoes have an extremely short lifespan. The adults, after emerging from the pupal state, live only a few hours. We're still working on solving that problem. Nevertheless, we began to refer to these red widows as 'kamikaze' mosquitoes. They are willing to risk their lives just to bite something living. Well, with power like that, we realised that we should find a way to infuse the mutated virus into the genetic formula. So now we have kamikaze mosquitoes that can deliver a deadly disease to any target, providing the target is contained in an enclosed space."

"A flying death squad," Bond said.

"Something like that," Tsukamoto said.

"The trick is to then set a perfectly timed trap," Aida continued. "You want to deliver the mosquito eggs to the target destination at the right moment, cleverly disguised but able to rest in or near standing water so that at the desired time the mosquitoes will emerge from the pupae and attack. The males, of course, do nothing but fly around and look for food from plants, as they normally do, and mate. The females, however, are full of the virus and crave blood for nourishment. Normal female mosquitoes will bite convenient hosts when they are about to mate or are already pregnant, which in our case, occurs rather quickly."

"The bonsai waterfall in the McMahon house," Bond said. "You planted the eggs inside the porous rocks, which were filled with water. The fountain's motor was disabled when we found it. The water was standing still . . ."

Tsukamoto nodded. "You are correct, Mister Bond. The fountain was delivered to their home as a gift, one week before the McMahon family reunion. The motor was fixed to fail so the water became stagnant. As I understand it, Shinji Fujimoto brought the fountain to the house. When the family informed him the next day that it didn't work, he promised his niece that he would collect it in a few days and return it to the store where he had bought it."

Aida continued. "So the device sat there in the house as the mosquito eggs hatched into larvae which lived in the water inside the fountain. The larvae fed on food that we provided from a timed-release feeder. They formed into pupae and then became adult mosquitoes—all in seven days. It took another twenty-four to forty-eight hours for the adult mosquitoes' shells to harden, and by then they were, of course, very hungry for a blood meal. They flew out of the granite rocks and found their victims—the McMahons." Bond could hear the sound of a sob escape from Mayumi.

"So Shinji Fujimoto was working with you all along," Bond said. "Why did you kill him?"

"Because he was a fool but a briefly useful one. Fujimoto always felt that his brother Hideo short-changed him with regard to the company. When Hideo Fujimoto died and left CureLab to his daughter, Shinji felt betrayed. The Ryujin-kai recognised a potential ally in him, so he was easily bought."

Mayumi spoke up for the first time. "My great uncle was really responsible for killing my family? I don't believe it."

Yoshida's image reappeared on the screen as Tsukamoto explained, "He didn't know that the bonsai waterfall contained the mosquitoes. He was ordered to deliver the device to the family as a gift. It appears that after they had died, Fujimoto realised what he had done to his niece and her family. He attempted to cover his tracks and obliterate evidence, the fool. He only succeeded in throwing more suspicion on our organisation. Shinji Fujimoto was a nuisance. He was eliminated after he sold his CureLab stock to Yonai."

Now it was clear to Bond. He said, "So the yakuza hoodlums in London—the ones who tried to take Kyoko McMahon's body from the mortuary—they were hired by Shinji Fujimoto. And the arsonists in Tokyo were paid to destroy the bodies of Peter McMahon, his wife and eldest daughter."

Tsukamoto said, "That was all Fujimoto's doing and had nothing to do with us. He was an idiot. We only needed him in the short term. There was another person from CureLab who was co-operating with us, someone who was providing us with everything we needed to instigate our plan."

"Then why was the merger necessary?" Bond asked. "It sounds as if you already had the technology you needed."

"The merger simply solidified our possession of the technology. We did not want to rely on the continuing co-operation or trust the discretion of the insider."

"And are you going to tell us who that was?"

"I don't think so." Tsukamoto grinned.

"Why was Kenji Umeki killed?" Bond asked. Mayumi gasped. Another shock.

Tsukamoto answered, "That was entirely unrelated to our business here. Umeki-san was about to reveal the girl's whereabouts to the authorities. He could not be trusted."

"What difference did it make if they knew where I was?" Mayumi asked. "I wasn't going anywhere. You wouldn't let me leave. After all I was working for you," she said bitterly.

"Once all of this began, we realised that you were a valuable pawn—and a dangerous one. We couldn't afford to let the authorities find you before the project was finished. You were supposed to have been killed."

"And just what is the project?" Bond asked. "You have your killer mosquitoes, what do you intend to do with them?"

Yoshida was relishing every minute of this game he was playing. He asked, "What is it, Mister Bond, that is classified about your assignment in Japan? Why are you here?"

"Why don't *you* tell *me*? You seem to know more about my movements than I know myself." But Bond knew what he was going to say.

"Come, come, Mister Bond. The G8 summit conference. It's in three days. I don't think I'll go into any detail at this juncture, but you can assume that several world leaders are about to issue their last press statements."

"You're mad, Yoshida," Bond said. "You're going to kill your own people! Japan is a G8 country."

"The Japanese who are co-operating with Western countries deserve to die. Japan needs to remain pure. To retain the former glory that she once enjoyed, we must hold our noses and swallow our medicine. As the great poet and novelist Yukio Mishima wrote, 'Glory, as anyone knows, is bitter stuff.'"

"It will accomplish nothing, Yoshida," Bond said.

"On the contrary," Yoshida said. "The G8 conference is only the beginning. My message will be delivered far beyond the boundaries of Japan. And this morning we have had a technological breakthrough. Aida, please tell Mister Bond what we are now able to do."

Aida smiled smugly and said, "Transovarial transmission. We have successfully engineered the mosquitoes to pass on the virus to their eggs. This version of our kamikaze insects will mate with zeal upon maturing. Before the adults die, the females will lay eggs, out of which will emerge more infected mosquitoes."

"That's crazy!" Bond spat.

Yoshida chuckled. "A little payback for the Great War in the Pacific, wouldn't you say? Tsukamoto!"

"*Hai!*"

Yoshida's eyes betrayed the madness behind them. His evil stare travelled through the hundreds of miles of the telecommunication system's fibre optics and clutched Bond and Mayumi's souls. They both felt a shiver run down their spines as he said, "Place them in the mosquito tank. Let them experience first hand the fruits of our work."

TWENTY-FOUR

EARTH'S HEARTBEAT

WHEN BOND HAD STRUGGLED WITH THE GUARD FOR POSSESSION OF THE Palm Pilot, he had deftly managed to activate the timer for the built-in explosive. The problem was that he didn't know exactly how long he had set it for. He had manipulated the device with his fingers, feeling for the correct buttons while at the same time pulling on the Palm to keep it out of the guard's hands.

Tsukamoto walked away from the centre of the room and stood by the door. He pressed a button and the door slid open. Aida had remained close to the two guards, while the technicians who had elected to remain in the lab to watch the goings-on stayed at their workstations. The teleconference link was maintained so that Yoshida could view the festivities. Both guards pointed their guns at the captives and gestured towards the air lock attached to the chamber full of mosquitoes. Bond eyed the Uzi and calculated the odds of jumping the man, but ultimately decided that it wouldn't work. Before Bond could wrestle the Uzi away from the guard, the other man would have shot him and probably Mayumi as well.

"Open the outer door," Aida ordered.

A technician flipped a switch and the door to the air lock opened with a *swish*. One of the guards jabbed the barrel of his rifle into Bond's back.

"James-san?" Mayumi asked. Her eyes were full of fear.

"It will be all right," he whispered. "We'll go together."

She finally went into the cubicle with Bond right behind her.

"Close the outer door," Aida commanded.

The technician obeyed the order—the door shut and locked. Bond and Mayumi were standing in the no man's land of the air lock. For the moment, they were safe.

"I have yet to see how my mosquitoes will feed upon human beings," Aida said. "So far we have used only laboratory animals for testing purposes. This will be a treat." As a smile played upon his lips, Aida commanded, "Open the inner door."

The technician reached for the control but at that moment the Palm Pilot exploded with such force that he was knocked off his chair. Three other technicians were thrown across the floor and one of the guards was engulfed by the blast. Tsukamoto ducked out of the room and shut the laboratory door.

Bond and Mayumi were unharmed. The reinforced door had protected them from the explosion, but the glass had cracked. In fact, the lock mechanism was disabled. When Bond kicked it the door opened and he ran to the guard who had dropped the Uzi. He was blinded, screaming in pain. Bond picked up the Uzi and used the butt to put the man out of his misery.

Bond felt a bullet fly past him, frighteningly close to his face. He turned and saw Aida crouching behind a workstation, pointing a handgun at him. Bond directed the Uzi at that end of the room and let loose with a barrage of firepower. The bullets hit the computers, creating bright eruptions of electrical discharges all over the machines. Aida, his body riddled with holes, screamed and fell to the floor. The technicians who were left alive crouched behind what cover they could find and raised their hands in terror. Bond swept the room with the gun and determined that there was no longer a serious threat.

Bond held out his hand for Mayumi. "Come on," he said. Wide eyed, she stepped out of the chamber and clasped his hand tightly.

They went to the destroyed table that had held their weapons. It was such a mess that Bond couldn't find any trace of their guns.

"Well, that's two Walthers I've lost on this trip," he said.

He did find the smashed DoCoMo phone in the rubble and picked it up. "It's probably useless but you never know," he said, putting it in his pocket.

The alarms in the building rang out.

"Let's get the hell out of here!"

Bond ran to the door and slapped a button. The door slid open and he stepped into the corridor. Two more guards were rushing at him with handguns drawn. Bond dispatched them with the Uzi and then gestured for Mayumi.

"Coast clear, let's go!"

They ran down the hall towards the offices and the employee entrance at the back of the building. Another guard appeared at the T intersection and Bond blasted him before the man could raise his gun.

They made it to the back door with no further hindrance. Bond punched the button on the wall and the door unlocked.

"James!"

Bullets exploded around their heads. Bond grabbed Mayumi and pulled her to the floor. Then, on his side, he fired the Uzi at the guards who had just appeared at the opposite end of the hall. They jumped, taking cover around the corner. Bond reached up and opened the door.

"Stay down!" he cried.

They both rolled out of the door. Bond slammed it shut and helped Mayumi stand. "Are you hit?"

"No." She was panting.

"We have to run. Can you make it?"

"Yes."

They ran across the dark car park and onto the dirt road, but more men had come out of the front of the building, circled around to the road and blocked their escape. Bond attempted to fire at them and found that the Uzi was out of ammunition. He tossed it behind him.

"Into the woods!" Bond led her through the trees, off the main path and into the pitch-black forest. They couldn't see a thing. Gunfire erupted around them, but they had the satisfaction of knowing that the guards couldn't see them either.

Then Mayumi tripped over an exposed tree root and cried as she fell hard. Bond stopped to help her up. "Hold my hand. We have to keep going," he said.

"I . . . I can't!" she gasped.

"You have to!"

More gunfire. Bark flew off of the trees around them. Mayumi struggled to her feet and began to run again at Bond's side.

They bolted through the forest, not knowing in what direction they were headed. They cared only about losing their pursuers and, after a while, it seemed that they had done so. Bond stopped and told Mayumi to be quiet so that he could listen to the sounds around them. In the distance, they heard shouts and some gunfire, but the noise seemed so far away that they might actually be safe.

They continued on, now treading carefully and quietly. The shouts of the guards seemed to fade further in the distance.

"Where are we?" she whispered.

"I have no idea," Bond said. "Let's just keep going. We'll come out of these woods eventually. We are still in Noboribetsu, or certainly on the outskirts."

He led her through the forest but they couldn't help getting scraped and cut by branches and bushes that were too dark to notice. Every now and then Mayumi made a sharp exclamation of pain.

"I think there's a clearing ahead," Bond said. There were some lights glinting through the mass of foliage ahead of them. When they emerged, they found themselves on the main road that led back to the Dai-ichi Takimotokan.

"You are a genius, James-san!" Mayumi said.

"Animal instinct," he said, wryly. "The wounded fox always finds its way home. Come on, let's hope our friends have given up." They started down the road just as the sound of engines could be heard coming towards them. Bond could see headlamps coming from the direction of the laboratory.

"Damn," he muttered. He took her hand and ran toward the hotel, but a Jeep that pulled out of nowhere blocked their way, some fifty feet ahead of them. Three men got out and gestured at them. One of them began shooting at them.

"Run!"

Bond and Mayumi bolted across the road and found themselves at the edge of the *Jigokudani*, the Valley of Hell. A sign made it perfectly clear that it was very dangerous to go further. Large spotlights illuminated the area, accentuating the multitude of colours in the rocks and soil. Smoke billowed out of holes in the ground and small bubbling pools of sulphurous water dotted the landscape. Bond estimated that the entire valley was almost half a kilometre across.

"We haven't any choice. Come on!" Bond said, then climbed over the wooden fence that kept people out of the property.

"I'm not going in there!" Mayumi cried.

The continuing gunfire convinced her otherwise. She climbed over the fence and took Bond's hand.

"Tread carefully!" he warned. They stepped gingerly onto the ashen rock. A piece of it gave way under Mayumi's foot.

"Oww, that's hot!" she cried.

"Try to stay off the white rocks. They're fragile," Bond said.

As they zigzagged their way across the alien landscape, the stench of the sulphur made breathing ragged and difficult. They could also hear a faint, deep beating coming from the ground, as if someone were hitting a drum. Bond realised after a few minutes that it was the sound of water squirting out of the holes.

"It's the earth's heartbeat," Mayumi said. She had read his mind.

They heard shouts behind them. Two guards had jumped the fence and were now running recklessly in their direction.

"Don't look back, just keep going!" Bond said.

The heat was intense and almost unbearable. Every now and then Bond stepped on a blazing hot rock. He would curse, quickly spring off it, and keep going, directing Mayumi away from the worst places. They eventually came to a wooden wishing well. A planked bridge led from it up to the pedestrian walkway that encircled the valley. Unfortunately, the guards had taken that route and were headed their way.

Bond pulled Mayumi down behind the well. The smoke issuing from the rocks around them was fierce and they found it difficult to breathe. He held his finger to his lips to quiet her and waited until he heard the guard's boots on the walkway near the well.

Wait for it . . . A bit closer . . .

Bond leapt up and grabbed the man. The guard shouted, but Bond managed to hit him hard, knocking him over the rail and into the well. His body fell into the bubbling, green boiling water. He screamed horribly as Bond grabbed Mayumi's hand and led her further out into the valley. They were halfway across.

The remaining two guards stumbled along the rocks in pursuit, every now and then firing blindly at the dark figures who were at least fifty metres away. The floodlights illuminated the valley well enough to expose the spectacular colours and geysers, but they weren't sufficient to adequately light their targets. Bond used this to his advantage by moving in diagonal patterns and staying low.

They reached the top of a hill and she slowed, completely out of breath. "I must rest a second, please."

"We can't stop, Mayumi."

But she turned her ankle on a rock and stumbled, striking her bare forearm on the ground. She cried out in pain and immediately jumped to her feet, holding her arm. Even in the dim light, they could see that her skin was seared.

"Right," she said, "let's keep moving."

They rounded the hill just as they heard a guard scream. Bond turned to see that the man had stepped onto one of the fragile ashen rocks. It had collapsed and he had fallen into a pit of blazing hot stones.

They moved on, finally out of Hell Valley and on to a steep hill. He couldn't hear any gunshots or shouts behind him, so when they got to the top of the hill he stopped to scan the landscape.

"Do you think we lost them?" she asked.

"Let's hope so," Bond said. "Come on, let's keep going this way. I want to put as much distance as possible between us and them before we stop to rest."

She sighed and followed him without complaining. She limped a little, not only because of the twisted ankle she had experienced a few minutes ago, but also because the gash in her calf was throbbing. Mayumi wondered if her stitches had loosened.

As they came over the hill, they saw a paved road at the bottom. Beyond that was an empty car park next to a small lake surrounded by a fence. The unusual thing about the lake was that it was emitting smoke.

"That's *Oyunuma*," Mayumi said. "It's always boiling. Another tourist attraction, like *Jigokudani*."

"Remind me to buy a postcard," was all that Bond could say.

They made their way down to the edge of it. Even though it was very dark, Bond could see that the pond's sickly, greenish surface was bubbling violently and producing an immense amount of steam. They could feel its heat from where they were standing.

"I can't go on," Mayumi said as she walked to a bench that was situated on a platform built near the pond. This time, Bond could see that she had no choice but to rest.

"At least we know the road goes back to Noboribetsu," she panted. "We're not lost."

Bond removed the mobile from his pocket and shook it. It rattled, useless. "So much for calling a taxi," Bond observed.

"You may have spoken too soon, James-san. Look."

She pointed to the end of the road. Headlamps came around the bend and headed towards the car park.

"Quick, hide!" he said as he pulled her behind the bench. He peered around to watch the vehicle approaching. Was there an available escape route? The only way out was back up the hill, but that was in full view of the car park. The boiling lake was behind them. They were trapped.

Once it was close enough, Bond saw that it was a Mazda Bongo Friendy, a conventional mini-van with a camper popup roof. Not a typical yakuza mode of transportation.

Bond watched as it pulled to the edge of the car park and stopped. The driver got out and shone a torch over the area. There was something familiar about the figure.

It was Ikuo Yamamaru, his arm in a sling.

Bond jumped up and called to him. The Ainu jerked his head around.

"Bond-san!" he called. "I have been searching for you!"

"I should have guessed from that tin can of a car that it was you," Bond said. "We're very glad to see you."

"The homing device in your mobile led me to you," Ikuo said. "It works like a charm."

"I thought the damned thing was demolished."

Ikuo chuckled. "The police band has been going crazy. I heard someone ran across *Jigokudani!* Was that you?"

"I'm afraid so."

"Are you mad? You could have been killed!"

"We had no choice. Don't worry, we're all right. Just lightly char-grilled."

"Quick, get in the car," Ikuo said. "Ryujin-kai are all over the place. They have every road covered that the police don't. This is going to be tricky."

They piled into the van and Ikuo got behind the wheel.

"How's the bullet wound?" Bond asked.

"They took some metal out of me," the Ainu said. "I was very lucky. It just damaged some muscle. It didn't hit my collarbone or anything else important. I have to wear this sling for a few days, though."

Ikuo pulled out of the car park and got on the main road.

"Do you see the mobile mounted on the side there?" Ikuo asked Bond.

"Yes."

"Take it and punch Memory Zero."

Bond did as he was told and held it to Ikuo's ear. When the other party answered, Ikuo spoke a language into the phone that was unfamiliar to Bond but it was similar to Japanese. When Ikuo was finished he listened and then replied affirmatively. The Ainu nodded at Bond, who lowered the mobile and shut it off.

"My friends are expecting us," the Ainu said, smiling broadly.

"Now if we can just make it through town without being seen. All day long I think I have been watched. They may know my affiliation with you, Bond-san, so before nightfall I changed cars with a friend. I hope they're not looking for a van like this one."

He turned the van onto the main street through Noboribetsu and said, "Perhaps you should keep down."

Bond and Mayumi got on the floor of the van as they drove past the Dai-ichi Takimotokan. A black Mercedes and a motorcycle were idling on the other side of the street.

"Enemy spotted," Ikuo reported. "One Mercedes and a Kawasaki . . . uhm . . . what *is* that . . . ? Oh, it's a Z400FX! Huh. I haven't seen one of those in a long time. Looks like two men in the car."

When the van passed them, the yakuza reacted and pointed. The man on the Kawasaki burst away from the kerb and rode close behind the van.

"I was afraid of that," Ikuo said. "We have been seen, Bond-san."

The tyres screeched and the van lurched forward. Ikuo looked in the rear-view mirror and saw the Mercedes pull out and join the chase. The biker was gaining on them easily.

Hoping to divert them, Ikuo swerved off the road toward the statues of *oni* that guarded the edge of town. The King of Hell, angry and demonic, loomed over them as they circled the display. The Mercedes and biker were right behind, but Ikuo made a sudden swerve and doubled back with a screech. When the Mercedes attempted to do the same, it collided with the statue. The *oni* toppled, landing on the bonnet of the car. The biker pulled around the wreckage and stayed on the Mazda's tail, not easily shaken off.

"I'm sure those fellows in the Mercedes are radioing for back-up," Bond said. "And we still have company behind us."

"See if you can get rid of him," Ikuo suggested.

"I've lost my gun," Bond said, looking back at the rider.

"Ah. Look under the seat."

Bond reached beneath and felt a cloth bag containing something very hard. He pulled the bag out, opened it, and removed a shiny new Walther PPK.

"Don't tell me," he said. "It's from Tiger."

Ikuo grinned and concentrated on driving. Meanwhile Bond checked the firearm, loaded a magazine and then leaned out of the window. The Walther recoiled with a familiar jolt and the rider was knocked off the motorcycle as if he had been kicked in the chest. The bike ran on and crashed into the trees on the side of the road.

"Nice work, Bond-san!" Ikuo said. "You got him on the first shot."

Bond sat and holstered the gun. "Many thanks, Ikuo. I felt naked without one."

"No problem. Look, here we are."

The van drove into a car park and stopped in front of a skylift station. The signs indicated that visitors were at Bear Park. The place was closed, but Ikuo got out and told the others to follow him. The three of them ran to the building, where Ikuo unlocked the door with a set of keys he had in his pocket. Then they made their way to the skylift port area. A gondola hung in front of them, inert. Ikuo unlocked a control panel on the wall and flipped a few switches. The skylift powered up and the gondolas began to move.

Ikuo ran to the next gondola and said, "Hurry! Get in!" The three of them jumped inside and sat just as the automatic doors closed. The gondola lifted and began to glide along the cable across a deep ravine. The vista was a vast forest of darkness. In the distance they could see the glittering surface of Lake Kuttara as a black but starry sky enveloped them.

When the gondola reached the other side, a trip that took five minutes, the automatic door opened and they stepped out. Three of Ikuo's Ainu friends were there to greet them. They chatted in their language for a moment and then Ikuo turned to Bond.

"Another Mercedes followed us here. They just got in the skylift. My friends saw them on television monitors." He pointed to small black and white screens on the wall that displayed a view of the lower station.

"Shut it off when they're over the ravine," Bond said.

"I have a better idea," Ikuo said. "Come on."

They followed Ikuo and the other men into Bear Park, a theme park run by and featuring the culture of the Ainu people. It consisted primarily of a zoo filled with Hokkaido brown bears, a small museum and a quaint reproduction of a *kotan*, an ancient Ainu village.

Ikuo explained as they rushed into the dark and quiet preserve, "The Ainu believe that the bear is a god from heaven, come to bring us fur and meat." He pointed to the centre of his forehead. "The god lives in between the bear's eyes, right here."

Mayumi looked over a rail into a deep pit and saw dozens of dark shapes.

"Are those bears?" she asked a little too loudly. One of the animals growled at her ferociously, breaking the silence of the night air. This caused her to cry out, which woke up most of the other bears.

"Mayumi!" Bond urged.

"Sorry!" She followed him into a building, where a few other men were waiting. Ikuo greeted them and issued some instructions, opened the shades on the window, and shut off the lights. From there they had a good view of the main path through the park. It was just as they had left it—silent and still. But after a moment, two figures came walking up the path from the skylift port.

"They look like yakuza, all right," Bond said.

The two men nervously crept forward, looking all around as they walked.

"The Ainu keep the bears, raise them and take care of them," Ikuo whispered. "We perform sacred rituals with them and we use them to attract tourists. We also *train* some of them. Watch."

The two yakuza had their pistols out, ready to fire at anything that moved.

The roars came suddenly and were tremendously loud. Everyone in the control room jumped except for Ikuo.

The two adult Hokkaido brown bears stood upright, six feet away from them, and began to bellow at the two men. Paralysed with fear, they both dropped their guns. Then the bears lunged forward on all fours. The men turned and fled, screaming for their lives.

The bears followed them to the gondola port and finally could no longer be seen; only the roars could be heard in the distance.

"Maybe they'll get away, maybe they won't," Ikuo said. He switched to a different camera so that the port station was on the monitor. The men jumped into the frame and scrambled into a gondola. The bears could be seen at the edge of the screen, frustrated that they couldn't catch their prey. As the skylift pulled away from the station, the animals meekly turned and ambled back to the village.

TWENTY-FIVE

G8 EVE

NAOSHIMA ISLAND IS LOCATED IN THE INLAND SEA, SOUTH OF OSAKA AND Kobe, about halfway to Hiroshima. Most people reach the island from Okayama by taking a train to Uno and then hopping aboard a ferry that spirits visitors to the island on a twenty-minute ride. In full view is the extraordinary Seto-Ohashi Bridge, which links Honshu with Shikoku, the smallest of Japan's four major landmasses. Benesse House, a luxury hotel on the southern tip of the island, adjoins the Naoshima Contemporary Art Museum. Works collected and exhibited by the museum are not confined to the inside of the building but are also dispersed through its grounds, creating a superb contrast between nature and man-made art. Designed by world-renowned Japanese architect Tadao Ando, Benesse House is a symbiosis of nature, architecture and art striving to devise a space where people can reflect upon humanity. A perfect spot to hold a G8 summit conference.

James Bond arrived on the island the day after the escape from Noboribetsu. After a long and healing night's sleep at Ikuo's home in the Ainu village near Bear Park Bond and Mayumi had flown back to Tokyo. By that time, Japan's National Police Agency, in a rare collaboration with the Koan-Chosa-Cho, had raided the Hokkaido Mosquito and Vector Control Centre and taken possession of the building and its contents. Everyone connected with the company was held for questioning.

Simultaneously, the offices of CureLab Inc. in Tokyo were raided. By the end of the day, seventy-two people were under arrest. The merger with Yonai Enterprises was voided and the authorities had launched an investigation into all of Yonai's business dealings.

Mayumi was ensconced at the Imperial Hotel with Bond in adjoining rooms until the morning of his departure. The plan was that she would stay there until after the summit conference and then she would face up to the legal wrangling over CureLab and the McMahon estate. Before he had left the hotel, Mayumi made Bond promise that he would return in one piece and come back to see her.

"I hate to admit it, James-san," she had said, "but I like you. Just a little."

"Well, I like you, too," Bond replied. He thought for a moment before adding, "You should try not to be so angry at the world. You're a lovely, clever girl and you don't need to be mixed up with deadbeats. You have a marvellous future ahead of you," he smiled, "if you use your pretty little head."

"Don't patronise me."

"I'm serious. Look, I'll be away for two days, three at the most. When I come back I will help you as much as I can with all of this family business. I'm not an expert but I believe the lawyers are going to try to prove that the merger was illegal as it was done without your consent as the major shareholder and the power of attorney was a forgery. You will be meeting with lawyers over the next two days. Pay attention and consider everything they have to say."

Before he had left, she put her arms around him and kissed him, then abruptly turned and went back to her room.

Bond's flight out of Tokyo flew south-west over magnificent Mount Fuji to Okayama, where a company car met him and took him to the small port town of Uno. There, he caught the ferry to the island, where Tanaka greeted him at the dock.

"Bondo-san, I am so happy to see you," Tiger said, giving him a warm embrace. "I see that you have survived your adventures in Hokkaido and are no wear for worse."

"Tiger, you're picking up too many Western colloquialisms," Bond said. "It's 'worse for wear.'"

"Whatever. Come, let's go to the site."

They got into a chauffeur-driven Toyota Celsior that had been provided by Benesse House's president for Tanaka's exclusive use. It was well equipped, complete with a bar, telephone and a television in the back seat.

To get from the ferry port to Benesse House, the car had to pass through Naoshima Cultural Village. Tiger pointed out items of interest along the way, including the recently built Town Hall and several traditional Japanese "homes" that were in fact works of art. Tanaka explained that the interiors of the homes contained multimedia artwork designed by Tadao Ando in collaboration with artists from other countries. In essence, the houses themselves became the art.

"Naoshima means 'honesty island.' The inhabitants of the island still live simply," Tiger said as they drove out of the village. "Much of the island is owned by Mitsubishi Material and they run copper and gold factories that employ practically everyone."

The car soon entered the section of the island that had been purchased by Benesse Corporation and had been renamed Benesse Island. They went through the gates and drove up a steep hill to a magnificent modern building made of marble, concrete and steel. Benesse House was designed to incorporate the three basic geometric shapes—a square, a circle and a triangle—in an impressive, imposing structure that faced the Inland Sea. Further up the hill was the Annex, connected to the main house by monorail. The Annex contained more luxury hotel rooms surrounding a unique, continuously flowing "flat" fountain. Bond was immediately taken with the place, not only because of his appreciation for inventive architecture, but for its serene and peaceful ambience that was palpable as soon as they got out of the car.

Tanaka accompanied Bond as he checked in and then proceeded to show him around the building. There was already a flurry of activity. Amongst the caterers, Tanaka's staff of twenty men from the Koan-Chosa-Cho was busy making sure that the building was secure.

They walked through the first large gallery in the museum, which was cylindrical in shape and three storeys tall. An inclined ramp circled the outer edge of the room, allowing visitors to walk up to the other floors and still view the artwork in the gallery. The main piece exhibited there was a unique multimedia sculpture designed by Bruce Nauman called "100 Live and Die." It consisted of 100 idiomatic expressions written in neon light that combined common human states or moods (sick, well, fear, black, red) and activities (eat, touch, play, cry, love) each combined with the phrases "and live" and "and die." Phrases—"speak and live," "smile and die," "think and live," "love and die"—flashed randomly on and off, creating a collage of contemplative ideas.

They continued into the large gallery on the basement floor that extended upwards by staircase into the ground floor. The staff were setting up tables for the conference alongside the pieces of art that adorned the walls and occupied space on the floor.

"The opening breakfast reception will be held in here," Tanaka explained. "It's the largest room in the building, so there is enough space to sit and eat or walk around and mingle. The more intense meetings will take place in the conference rooms upstairs on the first floor."

Tanaka got everyone's attention. "For those of you who have not met him, this is James Bond, a member of British Intelligence. He is to be my deputy in command during the conference. He is also my very good friend. Should he ask for anything, I expect you to oblige him to the best of your ability."

They all shouted, *"Hai!"* and bowed deeply to Bond.

A young man approached them and Tanaka said, "Bondo-san, I am pleased to introduce my personal assistant, Yoshi Nakayama. If ever you need something and cannot find me, please ask Nakayama."

Nakayama bowed and then shook Bond's hand.

The men returned to work and Bond stood back to survey the

gallery. It was a long rectangular room with a staircase on one side that allowed visitors to go from the basement level to the ground floor. Sculptures and artwork adorned the walls. The far end of the room was made of plate-glass windows that opened to the outside, where two marble sculptures were displayed in a concrete pit that could be viewed from the ground above or from below within the museum. The pieces in the pit were flat, smooth blobs of polished marble that gave the impression that they had been dropped from the sky. The entire display was designed by Kan Yasuda and was called "The Secret of the Sky." Other artists represented in the gallery included Jackson Pollock, Andy Warhol, David Hockney, Frank Stella, Yukinori Yanagi and Alberto Giacometti.

A large anatomically correct plaster heart, complete with aortas and ventricles, dominated the centre of the room. It was exquisitely painted and sat on a pedestal that was electrically powered so that the object could rotate when it was turned on. What was particularly unusual was that a large stake pierced it at an angle. The heart was about six feet in diameter. Entitled "Love Hurts," it was created by an artist named William Kanas and was part of a new temporary exhibit of sensational, controversial works by young British artists. Bond recognised the styles of some of them, like the one with six pieces of a llama suspended in formaldehyde solution in six separate tanks.

"Some of this stuff was brought in specially for the conference," Tanaka explained. "All of the flowers, the plants . . . The hotel management told me that the decorations were delivered a week ago by a florist and interior design firm that they always use. We have potted them up and checked the earth. We also made sure that the florist and design firm checks out."

Bond indicated the bonsai waterfall devices that had been lined up in a crate at the side of the room. "Well, I don't like those things," he said. "We know about those."

"You are right. We are getting rid of them. We will smash them to pieces and burn the remains. We don't want anything in here to contain mosquito eggs."

Tanaka issued some orders to his men, who immediately began removing the crates from the gallery.

"What about all these pieces of art?" Bond asked. "Granted that might be too generous a description for some of it."

Tanaka sucked air through his teeth. "Much of it is part of a new exhibition that was brought in three days ago. That big heart, those weird things over there, they're all part of a touring private collection. The curators will not allow us to touch them or remove them. We've checked them out against insurance documents and catalogue details."

Bond frowned. "I'm not happy about that."

"Nor I. But there's nothing we can do about it. The insurance costs for the pieces are astronomical."

"Who owns the collection?"

"A wealthy Japanese patron of the arts who has a long association with Benesse, who insist he's OK."

Bond nodded and moved on. "What about pesticides? Do we have mosquito repellent?"

Again, Tiger inhaled through his teeth and replied, "Management of the museum would not allow us to use it. I did not want to alarm them by going into too much detail about what we were looking for and they have forbidden the use of pesticides in here. But we have some other tricks up our sleeves."

Bond began to walk slowly around the room, inspecting the flowerpots and planters. They were filled with rich soil and contained all manner of exotic Japanese plants and flowers. He wasn't familiar with some of the species, but he recognised blue, plum and white-coloured irises that originated in the Far East, as well as a variety of red and white lotus flowers.

Bond continued walking and took a look at the tables and settings. He examined the entrances and exits. A large object covered with a tablecloth was set to the side of the room.

"What's under here?" he asked.

"Ah, Bondo-san, that is our secret weapon. I will tell you about it later."

"In that case, Tiger, I'm afraid that I'm going to be superfluous and will be bored to death at this conference. You have everything under control," he said.

Tiger laughed. "Come, let's go see your room."

By late afternoon, delegates from the G8 countries began to arrive by helicopter from Osaka. Helicopters landed on the temporary wood and brick helipad that had been built on a clearing near the beach.

James Bond was assigned to watch over the arrivals, greet the delegates and send them on their way to Benesse House in specially hired cars. Bond met each of the representatives from the eight members of G8: the United States (the President himself had decided to attend), Britain (the Prime Minister, whom Bond already knew), Japan, Canada, France, Italy, Germany and the newest member, Russia. As was always the case with G8 summit conferences, one additional representative from the European Community joined the meeting: in this instance the delegate was from Spain. Each representative brought along an entourage of aides and bodyguards so the hotel was at complete capacity.

The conference was to begin in the morning with a breakfast reception and an address by Benesse Corporation's president. The meetings were to proceed following that and would continue for two days. Bond wasn't privy to what was being discussed at the conference and he frankly didn't care. His only concern was to make sure that everyone remained safe and healthy. As M had put it, this was a babysitting job, and such as it was, Bond was resolved to do it right.

That evening, he and Tanaka ate with some of the delegates in the restaurant. They were served a traditional *kaiseki* meal, but they both refrained from having sake since they were on duty. Bond was on the alert, so he ate very little. He was watching everyone in the room, looking for the slightest hint of something out of the ordinary. It was all going too smoothly. From what he had seen in Noboribetsu, he knew that the Ryujin-kai were clever. If they wanted to infiltrate this thing, then they would find a way to do so. But the hotel and restaurant staff had been thoroughly vetted, all vendors who had come and

gone had been checked out, and the respective governments had verified the backgrounds of every man and woman on the guest list.
Everything really did seem to be in order.

Bond noticed that Tanaka was breathing heavily and had a pained
look on his face.

"Are you all right, Tiger?" he asked.

Tanaka nodded and held a hand to his chest. "Heartburn. It will
pass in a little while."

"When's the last time you saw your doctor?"

"Just before you arrived in Japan. Do not worry, Bondo-san. I
know the difference between heartburn and a heart attack. What is
the saying? I am a shell of my former self. But as long as the brain
still functions properly, I don't mind."

Tanaka held up his glass of water and waited for Bond to do the
same. He then clinked the glasses together and said, *"Kampai."*

At three o'clock in the morning, the delegates were asleep, the
building was completely silent and the night guard made his rounds
throughout Benesse House for the fifth time that night. He started in
the basement's main gallery, where the reception would be held in
just a few hours.

Walking up and down the aisles formed by the cloth-covered
tables and planters, he focused the beam of his torch over every
object and surface. Nothing appeared to be amiss. He made a nota-
tion in his logbook, then climbed the stairs to the first floor. He
would return in one hour to repeat the process.

The first indication that the gallery was not completely vacant was
the slight scraping noise that came from the plaster heart in the
centre of the gallery. An astute listener might have recognised the
sound as the unscrewing of a panel from the inside of the hollow
object, but no one was around to hear it.

The heart appeared seamless but in fact it was made of several
panels that had been fitted and fastened together from the inside.
Very slowly and quietly, one panel was removed and placed inside the
object. After a moment, two small legs popped out of the opening,

followed by the trunk, arms and head of Junji Kon, the killer dwarf known as Kappa.

He had spent the last four days inside the heart, but he was used to confined quarters. He was equipped with everything he could possibly need: food, water, a portable toilet, even reading material and a light and the all-important clock. The inwardly curved bottom of the sphere was lined with cushions that a normal-sized man might find uncomfortable to sleep on, but it was perfect for one the size of Kappa.

The Koan-Chosa-Cho knew that the heart was owned by a wealthy patron of the arts. What they and the staff at Benesse House didn't know was that the collector was Yasutake Tsukamoto's *Saiko-komon*, or advisor, the equivalent of the Italian Mafia's *consigliere*. The *Saiko-komon* had used his influence to dictate how the heart was built and delivered to Naoshima Island. Kappa was installed in the finished work of art and it was brought to the island in one piece. It only had to be fitted on its pedestal once it was inside the museum.

Kappa emerged from his lair, reached back inside and removed a case that he placed on the floor. He opened it and revealed a number of glass mosquito canisters exactly like the one he had used on the *Cassiopeia*. Each container had a timed hinge and was filled with water and recently hatched mosquitoes. The insects had been developing for a week, had become adults and would have dry shells within a few hours.

Diligently and meticulously, Kappa went around the room and, using his trowel, dug holes in the flowerpots and planters. He then buried one canister in the soil of each stationary pot and planter so that the containers were spread out over the entire room. When he was finished, he went back over his handiwork to make sure that the soil was flattened and did not appear to have been disturbed.

Glancing at his clock, Kappa saw that he had a little more time before the guard returned. It felt good to be out of that heart for a while! He reached inside, pulled a raw cucumber out of a plastic bag and began to munch it. After he had eaten half of it, Kappa set the remains on the heart's pedestal and then proceeded to stretch his short legs, perform lifts on his toes and reach for the ceiling to exercise his back. He was about to repeat the regimen when he heard a door creak somewhere nearby, alerting him to the guard's imminent return. Carefully picking up his tools, Kappa crawled back inside the heart and replaced the panel. When it was screwed on tightly, he settled onto his cushions and went to sleep.

TWENTY-SIX

RED WIDOW DAWN

THE DAWN BROUGHT A BEAUTIFUL CLEAR DAY, ALTHOUGH THE FORECAST predicted that the temperature would rise considerably. Alone in his room, Bond was already feeling the heat and it was not yet seven o'clock.

The outfit that Tiger had provided him with was not exactly summer wear, either. Beneath his three-piece Ozwald Boateng suit Bond wore something that had been made exclusively for the situation at hand. Patterned after the full-bodied *ninja* suits, the garment was worn underneath the outer clothes like a complete body stocking and had extensions that could be rolled out to cover hands and head. In case of a mosquito attack, Bond could quickly protect his exposed skin. It wasn't foolproof but it was better than nothing.

He took a moment in front of the mirror, examining his hard face. The scars and scabs from the beating were still present but looked much better. Nevertheless, Bond noticed that many of the people he had met the day before were nervous in his presence. Perhaps that was a bonus.

Zero hour!

Bond made sure that his headset was working and then he left his room. He took the monorail down the hill to the main building, made his way down the stairs and into the main gallery, where

Tanaka, Nakayama and the other men were already busy with last minute preparations.

"Bondo-san, *ohayo gozaimasu!*" Tanaka said warmly. "Are you ready for another day of international espionage and combating terrorism?"

Bond laughed. "*Ohayo gozaimasu* to you, too."

"This line of work beats going to an office every day, does it not?"

"Office or not, I've clocked on," Bond replied. "Are we on time?"

"Everything begins in an hour. So far everything is on schedule."

Bond squinted at his friend and said, "Tiger, you still look a little pale."

Tanaka frowned, rubbed his chest, and said, "Do not worry, Bondo-san, I am all right. It's probably just nerves."

Bond nodded and then turned to inspect the room. He walked along the perimeter, paying special attention to the plants and flowers. He noted that the plaster heart was rotating on its pedestal, the motor emitting a low hum. The tables looked immaculate, as they were now dressed with fine china, chopsticks and silverware for those guests who were unaccustomed to using them. Satisfied that Tanaka's men knew what they were doing, Bond stood out of the way beside three standing figures that were a part of the museum's permanent art collection. They were painted, flat silhouettes of men with mechanised jaws that moved up and down. The piece was appropriately named "Three Chattering Men." Bond surveyed the entire room one more time from this vantagepoint and then went to check on the British contingent to the conference.

By 8:15 the room was packed with people. The main delegates sat at the head table with Benesse Corporation's president, Soichiro Fukutake. Bodyguards stood behind the table looking particularly conspicuous while attempting to be the opposite. The aides and other conference attendees filled the other tables. Breakfast was part-Japanese, part-Western to accommodate everyone's tastes. Glasses of orange juice and champagne were served for toasting purposes and that duty was handled graciously by Mr. Fukutake, who welcomed the delegates to his museum and hotel. While people ate, conversation was lively and animated throughout the room. None of the guests had been informed of the possible terrorist threat. It had been decided early on that it was unnecessary to alarm anyone unless the Koan-Chosa-Cho had evidence of something concrete. Tanaka had made the decision to keep a low profile for the time being.

Bond, Tanaka and the other secret service men patrolled the perimeter of the room, keeping an eye out for anything unusual. Tanaka positioned himself near the plate-glass window looking out at the pit containing the marble "Secret of the Sky" sculptures. He happened to glance at the planter full of lovely white irises that was sitting beside him.

Was the soil *moving?*

Tanaka leaned over to examine the dirt more closely. It *was* moving! Something was buried beneath the soil and was attempting to dig out, like a mole might do. It was some kind of trap door—no, the lid of a jar, Tanaka thought.

Then, the hinged top of the glass container opened fully, knocking aside the soil that was on top of it. Tanaka was horrified to see a swarm of mosquitoes fly out of the container and into the air.

He spoke into his headset, "Alert! Alert! There is—" but he found it difficult to continue speaking. He was seized with a sudden, sharp and excruciating pain in his left arm and chest.

No! he thought. *Not again!*

The iron crab clutched at his heart, paralysing him, squeezing the breath out of his lungs. He broke out in a sweat and the lights dimmed to black. He stumbled backwards and tried to catch something to hold on to, but it was useless.

He didn't feel the floor when he crashed headlong onto it.

Bond saw Tanaka fall and spoke rapidly into his headset. "May Day, May Day, Tanaka is down!" He and three other agents rushed to the end of the room and knelt beside the unconscious man.

"Call for medical help," Bond ordered Nakayama. "Quickly!"

The delegates and other personnel stopped chattering and craned their heads to see what was happening. Bond stood and addressed them.

"No cause for alarm," he said. "It appears we have a man with a heart condition. We have sent for help. Please, there is no cause for alarm."

Fukutake approached Bond and said that the helicopter was on its way. It would take Tanaka to Okayama immediately. After a moment, four members from the emergency medical team that was stationed outside the building entered with a stretcher. They spent a few minutes on the floor with Tanaka, trying to revive him but they quickly realised that they would do better in the ambulance. They capably loaded him onto the stretcher and carried it outside. Bond watched from the front door as his friend was loaded into the vehicle. Before long it sped away towards the beach and the helipad.

"You are in charge now, Bond-san," said Nakayama, who was standing behind him. "This was Tanaka-san's order." Distracted, Bond nodded and turned to rejoin the breakfast meeting in the main gallery.

The commotion had served to distract everyone in the room from what was happening around them. Operation Red Widow Dawn had commenced, silently and with meticulous timing. The rest of the mosquito containers had opened inside their respective planters and flowerpots, releasing the deadly insects into the air. No one noticed them at all; the insects were practically invisible, especially in the bright light of the morning sun that streamed in through the plate glass windows and the skylight.

Bond wiped his brow as he re-entered the room. He was concerned for his friend, but it was out of his hands; he had to hope and pray that the doctors could do enough.

Slap!

Bond whirled around to see one of the women from Italy with her hand on her bare arm. She then looked at her palm and made a face.

Bond's heart skipped a beat. He snapped his head up, turning his gaze to the space above the guests' heads.

Another slap on skin, this time from the British Prime Minister's aide.

"Someone let in a mosquito," the man said casually.

"*Get everyone out, now!*" Bond called into the headset.

His eyes darted back and forth as he felt a rush of adrenaline. Were they in the room? Was it happening?

And then he saw them. Sure enough, dozens of mosquitoes were flying above the guests' heads, gliding lightly and delicately and looking for targets on which to land.

The bodyguards and aides leaped into action. "Ladies and gentlemen, please come this way. Do not panic!" Nakayama called out. An evacuation had been rehearsed among Tanaka's staff and therefore was initiated smoothly and efficiently. The delegates, not at all sure what was going on, rose from their seats and began to file out of the room in an orderly fashion.

The Prime Minister addressed Bond, saying, "Double-O Seven, would you mind telling me what is happening?"

"Please, sir, just get out of the room," Bond said, his eyes still searching the space above their heads. "Nakayama-san, please make sure that door doesn't stay open for too long," he ordered. The men at the door acknowledged him by closing it after three people went through, then opening it again for three more.

As the evacuation progressed, Bond unrolled the extra pieces of his undersuit, put on gloves and unfolded the mask and hood that neatly covered his head. He reached into his pocket and pulled out goggles to wear. They were specially tinted to highlight objects that were in front of a light background. Once the goggles were in place, he could see the insects much more clearly. They were coming out of the planters!

Bond ran to the covered object in the corner of the room. He pulled off the cloth, exposing the strange contraption.

It was a Mosquito Magnet, a device originally created in America but adapted by the Japanese. It resembled the type of professional hairdryer that was found in a salon, only there was no chair. The device is commonly used by vector control organisations to attract and blow mosquitoes into a collection container so that their population density can be tested for viruses. Its operation is simple enough—a warm, moist carbon dioxide plume is produced from propane gas to attract the bloodsucking insects. Mosquitoes are naturally attracted to carbon dioxide, as well as to body heat and other chemicals present in the breath of warm-blooded hosts. As they approach the source, they are vacuumed into a net where they dehydrate and die. It is powerful enough to be effective outdoors in an area the size of nearly an acre.

As soon as Bond flipped the switch on, he could see many of the insects change their flight plan and head towards it. He watched in amazement as the mosquitoes flew straight into the container; they were trapped and had no escape route.

Another item sat on the floor next to the Mosquito Magnet—a large metal bucket full of machine oil, something that would come into play shortly.

Bond checked on the progress of the evacuation and was relieved to see that nearly everyone was out of the gallery. "Nakayama-san, after you have the conference attendees safely outside, get all of your men out. I don't want to take the chance of anyone getting bitten."

"Bond-san, some of us should stay and help you," Nakayama replied through the headset.

"That's an order, Nakayama-san."

"*Hai!*"

Bond immediately began to move from planter to planter, removing the glass containers from the soil. After he gathered an armful of them, he then went back to the table and dropped them into the bucket of oil, thereby immediately killing any remaining pupae and eggs. He continued this procedure until he had gone completely around the gallery.

Next he went back to the Mosquito Magnet to check on its progress. There were dozens of mosquitoes trapped in the can. He scanned the air around him and noted that there were a few insects still flying. He rotated the machine so that it faced toward the centre of the room and waited until he could see that more of the mosquitoes were gravitating towards the fan. Bond tapped his headset and said, "Nakayama-san, I think I've done all that I can do in here. I'm coming out. Let's seal the room and wait a while. These bugs will either be caught in the trap or they'll die in a few hours. I just hope that none got out of the gallery."

"Me too, Bond-san."

"How are things out there?"

"Fine. Some of the delegates are demanding to know what has happened and why they weren't told about it beforehand."

"I'll let your government handle that one."

"I believe that three people were bitten," Nakayama said. "A bodyguard for the German diplomat, an Italian woman and an aide to the British Prime Minister."

"Bad luck. Perhaps if we get them to the hospital before symptoms occur, they might have a chance."

"They're on their way."

Bond moved away from the table and walked past the plaster heart in the centre of the room. He reached down to switch off the rotation motor and noticed something peculiar.

Half a raw cucumber was lying on the edge of the pedestal.

Bond picked it up and studied it. Why were alarms bells going off in his head?

Then he remembered.

He turned his attention to the plaster heart and tapped it. Hearing the hollow sound was the catalyst that he needed. Bond picked up a chair and swung it as hard as he could at the heart, shattering its shell. He struck the object again, this time enlarging the hole he had made. He kept at it, striking the heart as if it were a Mexican *piñata*. But no sweets or prizes fell out of the object when he was done—there was just a big hole.

Could his hunch have been wrong?

He carefully moved closer to the heart so that he could peer inside. Nothing.

Kappa leaped out of the object, grabbed hold of Bond's upper body and wrestled him to the floor. Bond grappled with the dwarf and felt a sharp pain on his left shoulder. Kappa held a Balisong and had managed to slash through Bond's suit and cut him. Bond put all of his energy into blocking the dwarfs jabs but the assassin was fast and

stronger than he looked. Bond didn't want a repeat of what had happened in the Seikan Tunnel, so he locked both of his hands on
Kappa's wrist. He dug his thumbs *hard* into the soft spot, causing the
dwarf to yelp in pain and drop the butterfly knife. Bond let go of the
wrist and backhanded the killer with a sharp, surprising blow that
knocked Kappa completely off him and onto the floor.

The dwarf used his uncanny ability to bounce back to his feet, but
instead of attacking Bond, he ran towards the exit. By the time Bond
had got up, the dwarf was already at the door that led into the circular gallery at the front of the museum. Bond chased him into it but
when he got there, the dwarf was nowhere to be seen.

Damn! The trickster had used his freakish skill to hide.

"Nakayama-san," he said into his headset. "Be on the lookout for
a dwarf."

"A dwarf?" Nakayama asked.

The "100 Live and Die" sculpture blinked randomly at Bond . . .
*Speak and Die . . . Kill and Live . . . Stand and Die . . . Sick and Live . . .
Yellow and Die . . . Smell and Live . . .*

The stone staircase curved around the room to the top floor. The
dwarf couldn't have made it up that far. Nakayama and his men were
beyond the front entrance and reception area, so the killer couldn't
have gone that way either. There was only one place he could be.

Bond stepped around the sculpture and pulled his enemy up by
the neck. He slammed Kappa against the stone wall and clutched his
throat, holding him several feet off the ground.

"Please!" Kappa choked, his voice a high-pitched whine. "Spare
my life . . . and I will tell you . . . our secrets!"

"Shut up," Bond spat. "You're going to answer for Reiko Tamura."

The dwarf could hardly breathe. "Wait!" he gasped. "There is a
major . . . attack . . . in progress . . . on . . . the West . . ."

Bond loosened his grip—a little.

"This had better not be a trick."

"Spare me . . . please! I know where . . . Yoshida is . . . ! You . . .
can . . . stop . . . Red . . . Widow . . . Dawn . . . !"

Bond was suddenly reminded of the folklore legend about the

supernatural kappa. The creature supposedly had an honourable nature and would bargain for his life.

"Then talk." Bond relaxed his grip enough to allow the dwarf to speak clearly.

Kappa looked at him with surprise. "You are an honourable man, Bond-san. I will tell you what I know. Twenty men, carrying deadly mosquito eggs, are on their way to America. Some are travelling to the West Coast, some to the central states, and some to the East Coast. They will distribute the eggs in major cities. I can provide you with their exact destinations."

"How do you know this?"

"I am part of the Ryujin-kai's inner circle. There is one other thing that you should know."

"Go on."

"The mosquito eggs that they carry . . . they are different from these. The ones they have are samples of the new version—the mosquitoes that can pass the virus on to their own eggs."

Bond felt a flicker of fear.

Nakayama and several men ran into the room, guns drawn. Bond let the dwarf down and turned him over to them.

"Nakayama-san," he said. "Take him into a conference room, and fast. He has some things to tell us." Bond looked at Kappa and added, "And they had better not be folk tales."

TWENTY-SEVEN

QUICK RESPONSE

AFTER THE DISCOVERIES AT THE HOKKAIDO MOSQUITO AND VECTOR Control Centre were presented along with Junji Kon's statement to the Japanese government, the Koan-Chosa-Cho and the National Police Agency's report was taken seriously. A quick response was ordered against what was unanimously agreed to be a threat to Japan's national security, not to mention the rest of the world.

Kappa's statement claimed that Goro Yoshida's private army, with the help of the Ryujin-kai, was about to attack the United States with a biological weapon, namely the mutated, fast-acting West Nile virus, using genetically engineered mosquitoes capable of transferring the disease to their eggs. Twenty carriers had taken off from Tokyo that very morning on various flights that would arrive in the US several hours later. Eight men were to arrive in Los Angeles, six men would be in Chicago shortly after that and the remaining six would land in New York. Each courier held dried mosquito eggs attached to ordinary laboratory filter paper hidden in a modest envelope inside a jacket pocket. Neither the eggs nor the filter paper were detectable by airport X-ray. Since dried mosquito eggs could still hatch once they were soaked, they were the ideal conduits for smuggling a biological weapon into the country. Each carrier had a specific assignment that directed him to a public place with standing water present: a pond, a lake, or a pool. The eggs would be released into the water where, during the course of about seven days, the deadly mosquitoes would hatch, bite hosts, lay eggs and die. The new eggs would hatch a week later and another swarm of mosquitoes would repeat the deadly cycle. In another week, a fullblown epidemic would be sweeping the country.

The Japanese decided to contact the American government immediately and at the same time turned the case over to the Japan Ground Self Defence Force. Launching an air strike on what was essentially Russian territory was obviously a diplomatic challenge but clearly necessary. Goro Yoshida had shown that he had committed treason against Japan, had taken steps to attack the country and was an enemy to world peace. The Russian government that may or may not have known that Yoshida had resided on the island of Etorofu for years reluctantly gave Japan permission to bomb the terrorist camp provided that the air force did not travel beyond the coordinates that Junji Kon had provided.

James Bond and Nakayama insisted on flying in one of the six combat helicopters that was to take part in the raid on the Kuril Islands. They sat in a Boeing CH-47J Chinook, a large chopper that transports personnel and vehicles. Accompanying them were three Bell AH-1S Huey Cobras, helicopters that were capable of anti-tank combat, and two Bell UH-1J Hueys, medium-sized choppers that carried personnel or equipment. Bond and Nakayama had flown to Osaka, where they caught a shuttle flight to Hokkaido. They arrived just in time to join the attack force. M, alert to international protocol, had warned Bond that his official capacity was as an observer, and that he was not to use any weapons. Of course, they both knew that in self-defence he could cancel that particular directive.

About the time that the task force was leaving Hokkaido, the first wave of carriers arrived in California. FBI and Customs officials immediately arrested the incoming passengers at the gate, confiscated their luggage and took them into custody.

The JGSDF force flew over Etorofu and reached the target site not long after the events in California. They were expected. Yoshida's ground forces met the helicopters with heavy resistance. His army was in possession of a Stinger and a 30mm automatic cannon with a radar fire-control system in a revolving turret that was mounted on an AMX 13 type tracked chassis. Yoshida had purchased the weapons from the Russian mafia.

The AA gun, perched in a well-protected dugout, was successful in knocking down one of the Cobras within the first two minutes of the attack. The aircraft exploded and hurtled to the ground, where it burst into a gigantic ball of black smoke.

"Take out that cannon!" the commander in charge ordered.

The remaining five choppers were armed with SNIA BPD HL-12-70 rocket launchers, Bofors Bantam anti-tank missiles, AS.12 attack missiles and other weapons capable of obliterating an entire village. The teams directed this immense firepower at the AA gun, blowing it to pieces in the space of ten seconds. When the smoke cleared, there was nothing left of the dugout.

Before the five choppers could reposition themselves for a full strike on the entire complex, a stinger missile shot out of nowhere and sliced through the Huey that was flying only sixty metres away from Bond's. As that chopper went down in a heartbreaking trail of fire and smoke Bond spotted the soldier with the stinger and pointed him out to Nakayama. The man was perched behind sandbags covered in camouflage netting. Nakayama passed the news on to the door gunner, who walked his fire onto the stinger's position. The rounds kicked up dirt and dust, taking out the enemy just before two Hellfire rockets from one of the Cobras completely obliterated the area.

The remaining four helicopters unleashed an inferno on the terrorist camp. Bond felt a surge of adrenaline as he watched the landscape torn apart by the bombardment. The entire operation took thirteen minutes and forty-two seconds before the officer in charge made the "cease fire" call.

A blow-by-blow replay of the events that had occurred a few hours earlier in Los Angeles interrupted normal service at Chicago's O'Hare airport. Two hours later, FBI and Customs agents met the arrivals into JFK airport in New York.

The confiscated mosquito eggs were sent to the Center for Disease

Control in Atlanta, Georgia, for analysis. All of the agencies concerned agreed that if it hadn't been for the British Intelligence agent who had delivered the information to the Japanese government so quickly, America would have had a disaster on her hands. No one wanted to think about what might have occurred had the carriers dispersed after arriving in the country.

Back in Etorofu, more than thirty of Yoshida's soldiers were waiting to surrender when the helicopters set down on the camp's airstrip. Bond was forced to take a secondary position as the troops went on to search through the remains of the bunkers for survivors. The Japanese government, still embarrassed by the prominent role a British Intelligence *gaijin* had played in bringing Yoshida's plans to light, were at least able to save face by claiming sole responsibility for the success of the raid.

The only disconcerting thing was that Goro Yoshida, dead or alive, was never found.

Shortly before sunset on the day after the successful raid on Goro Yoshida's camp, Yoshi Nakayama delivered a package to the suite in the Imperial Hotel.

"I hope I am not interrupting anything?" he asked politely.

Bond was dressed in a *yukata* but held the door open for him. "Not at all. Come on in."

"Thank you." Nakayama entered, carrying a large elongated package wrapped in brown paper.

"What is the latest news on Tanaka-san?" Bond asked.

"As you know, the bypass repair was successful," Nakayama said. "Even Tanaka-san will need to rest now. But he is fine. I spoke to him an hour ago. He sounded weak and tired, but in good spirits. He said to give you his best wishes and to thank you for everything you have done."

Bond waved away the words and said, "I'm just happy that he's going to be all right. Now what's that you're carrying?"

Nakayama handed the package to Bond and said, "This is for you, in gratitude from the Koan-Chosa-Cho." He bowed.

Bond returned the bow and said, "Nakayama-san, this was not necessary."

Nakayama held up a hand and said, "Please. You have done a wonderful service for Japan. That is for you, and you are cleared to take it through Customs back to England."

"I'm intrigued," Bond said as he began to open it. Mayumi came in from the bedroom, also wearing a *yukata*. Nakayama's eyes widened at the sight.

"What's going on?" she asked. "Is it your birthday?"

"No, but I feel like it is," Bond said. He tore the wrapper off and opened the box. Inside was a beautiful black and gold *katana*. The *saya*, or scabbard, was inlaid with an intricate red and yellow floral design. The *kashira* was black with a firm leather grip.

"It's beautiful," Bond said with reverence in his voice.

"James-san!" Mayumi said. "That's a rare antique!"

"It is from the twelfth century, Bond-san," Nakayama said. "It was originally owned by a samurai who had been in service to the emperor."

Bond unsheathed the blade and noted the temper line pattern on the border of the cutting edge.

"It was made by Masamune, the greatest Japanese swordsmith," Nakayama said, interpreting the symbols etched on the *tang*, which was hidden inside the grip.

"I am deeply honoured," Bond said. *"Domo arigato."* He bowed again.

"You are welcome."

Bond placed the sword on the table near the large picture window that looked out on the city of Tokyo. The sun had become a blazing red sliver that was quickly dipping behind the cityscape.

"So tell me, Yoshi, what has happened? I've been looking at spreadsheets with Mayumi today, as promised, and I haven't been able to watch the news." Mayumi put her hand to her lips to stifle a giggle.

"There has been a flurry of activity with regard to CureLab and Yonai Enterprises. The whole plot has been exposed. Masuzo Kano, the chairman and president of Yonai Enterprises, committed suicide by jumping out of a twenty-seventh floor window. The merger is declared void."

"As we had guessed." Bond looked at Mayumi. "This means that you're a very wealthy lady, Mayumi."

She shook her head in disbelief.

Nakayama handed Bond a packet of papers. "These are copies of documents that we found in a hidden safe in McMahon-san's office at CureLab. Not too much that is very interesting, I'm afraid, but we also found an envelope addressed to Mayumi-san, to be delivered in case of her father's death. I give it to you now." He handed it to her and she held it in her hands as if it were something dreadful. Her name was written in her father's script in both English and Japanese.

"Do you want to open it?" Bond asked.

"Not yet," she said, a little shaken.

Bond turned back to Nakayama. "What about the Ryujin-kai? Their boss, the *oyabun*—Tsukamoto. What of him?"

"He has disappeared. No one knows where he is, but there is a warrant out for his arrest. A team is also still going through the destroyed bunkers on Etorofu in an attempt to locate Goro Yoshida's body. We are afraid that he may have left the island before the raid."

"So he's probably still out there somewhere," Bond said. "That's not a very comforting thought."

"It's one of the reasons why I am here. We need to provide you with twenty-four hour protection until you leave the country."

"Thank you, Nakayama-san," Bond said, "but I have never needed 'protection.' I can take care of myself."

"Famous last words," Mayumi said.

"Nevertheless, Bond-san," Nakayama said, "we will have a man posted outside your room." On his way out, Nakayama introduced Bond to the guard that sat in a chair in the corridor, then he shook hands, bowed, and said goodbye.

When Bond came back to the room, he found Mayumi lost in thought with the envelope in her hand.

"This has been a very strange few days," she said. Her eyes welled up. "The only good thing about them was meeting you."

"You've left one line of business and must now run another. That's much more important," Bond replied.

She shook her head sadly. "How do you know I won't go back to a life on the dark side? I can't see myself running the company. I never asked for this. I keep thinking about my poor sisters. Kyoko had spent her whole short life preparing to take over the business. All I can do is wish I was not my father's daughter." A few tears ran down her smooth, beautiful face.

"What is it that happened between you and your father that caused you to hate him so?"

"He deceived the family. He was one of them, James-san, he was part of the Ryujin-kai."

Bond blinked. "What are you talking about?"

"It's true. He did business with Yasutake Tsukamoto. When Tsukamoto-san said that there was someone besides my great uncle who provided the Ryujin-kai with what they wanted, he was talking about my father. I saw him once . . . at the soaplands where my boyfriend worked in Tokyo. I was hanging round there with my friends."

"Are you serious?"

"He was Tsukamoto's guest. The two of them came one night. Tsukamoto apparently didn't know that I was there. He brought my father and we saw each other. Needless to say, we were both shocked beyond words. From that moment on, he could never look me in the eye. He knew that I saw through him. So I ran away from home."

"Then what happened?"

"I went to Sapporo, got in deeper with the yakuza. I heard through various sources that he continued to work with the Ryujin-kai. He did things for them."

"Provided them with trade secrets?"

"Yes. Now . . . now I think I was doing all that to spite him. To throw it all back into his face."

"Mayumi, you should have told me this earlier."

She held her hand over her face. Bond pitied her, knowing full well how much pain she was in. But perhaps this pain was necessary.

"Why don't you open the envelope?" he suggested quietly.

Mayumi sniffed and nodded. She tore it open and pulled out a single page covered in her father's handwriting. Mayumi read it silently, and then handed it to Bond. The letterhead bore the name "Peter McMahon" and the handwriting was neat and legible.

Darling Mayumi

I know that you believe I let you down. I want you to know that my involvement with the yakuza was an inheritance from your grandfather, who had been doing business with them ever since Fujimoto Lab Inc. was founded. I was in the process of trying to break relations with them when the disastrous incident at the soaplands occurred. For that I am truly sorry. It is the greatest regret of my life. After you left home, the only way I could keep track of you and make sure that you were safe was by continuing to co-operate with them. They told me that you were working for the Ryujin-kai in Sapporo and that you would remain safe and would be taken care of as long as I helped them with what they wanted. I didn't feel I had a choice. Please understand that your parents both love you very much. I only wish I could have held you in my arms, my darling daughter, and told you all of this myself. Your poor mother knows nothing of this.

It was signed, simply, "Dad."

Mayumi looked lost and bewildered.

Bond handed the note back to her. "Your father provided those trade secrets because it was the only way he could receive news of your well being. Don't you see? That's exactly the way the yakuza works. They gave assurances to your father that you were safe, working in Sapporo, and as long as he helped them, then you would continue to be safe. Mayumi, he did it to protect you."

Mayumi's lip quivered a moment, and then the tears flowed freely. "I'm sorry," she managed to say.

Bond sighed and then held her close. She clung to his chest. "I don't know what to do, James-san. I don't know whether to grieve or to be happy."

"Hush," he said. "You are free to do anything you want. You can sell your shares for billions of yen."

She sniffed and was quiet for a while.

"You have a way of making me feel better," she said. "Are you sure that you have to leave tomorrow?"

"I'm afraid so. How shall we spend the time?"

"In bed. Come on."

TWENTY-EIGHT

THE FINAL ACTION

THEY HAD MADE LOVE INTO THE NIGHT. MAYUMI FINALLY DECLARED THAT she wanted to relax with a bath, and invited Bond to join her. He thought it sounded like a terrific idea but suggested that he fetch a bottle of sake to enjoy while they soaked. She began to sing the traditional Japanese folk song *Sakura* as she went off to the bathroom to fill the tub and light a few scented candles in order to create a more romantic atmosphere while Bond put on a *yukata*.

He could still hear her singing and the sound of the water running as he went into the other room, opened the fridge and removed the bottle of Ginjo sake that they had opened earlier in the day. He grabbed two glasses, turned and started to head back towards the bathroom when he noticed that the door to the suite was ajar.

Bond's senses became alive, activated to full alert.

The front room of the suite was empty. The cupboards were closed. How and when did the door get opened?

He set the bottle and glasses on the counter and crept to the door. When he peered into the corridor, he saw that the guard that had been posted outside was lying on the carpet in a pool of blood. From the severity of the wound on the man's neck, Bond could see that whoever had done this had attempted to behead his victim.

Bond shut the door, locked it, whirled around, and scanned the room again. Mayumi was still singing in the bathroom. Should he use the telephone on the desk? His mobile was in the bedroom.

He had moved four steps into the room when the voice halted him.

"Forget the telephone, Mister Bond. It cannot save you."

Goro Yoshida was standing in the open doorway of the large walk-in wardrobe, the door of which had been closed earlier when Bond passed through the room. Yoshida was dressed in a kimono that included the *montsuki hakama* half-coat emblazoned with the wearer's family crest of a dragon and a *hakama*, a culotte-like garment worn over the kimono. The edges of the hot red tattoo on his skin threatened to leap out of his clothing. He wore a magnificent *katana* sword at his side, along with the shorter, dagger-like *wakizashi*.

Yoshida stepped into the room, followed by Yasutake Tsukamoto, who had been standing behind his friend and master. Tsukamoto was wearing ordinary clothes, which created a skewed contrast to the *Yami Shogun*, and he was pointing a Glock at Bond.

Bond said, "Yoshida-san, I was wondering if you would turn up. *Konban wa*, Tsukamoto-san, it's good to see you again." Bond bowed, keeping his eyes glued to Yoshida's.

"Shall I get the girl?" Tsukamoto asked Yoshida.

"Not yet," Yoshida said. "By the time she is aware of our presence it will be too late. You can deal with her next." He stepped forward and addressed Bond. "We are both men of action, Mister Bond. The great writer Yukio Mishima once said that 'a man of action is destined to endure a long period of strain and concentration until the last moment when he completes his life by his final action: death.' That moment has come for you, Mister Bond. I have risked my safety coming into the country like this and had it not been for the efforts of the Ryujin-kai I would not be here to personally see you destroyed."

He drew the sword and assumed a *Gedan no kamae*, the stance of holding the *katana* at middle height but with the tip dipped down, inviting the opponent to attack.

"I'm afraid you have me at a disadvantage, Yoshida, I don't have my sword with me," Bond said. He started to walk casually to the desk on the other side of the room, where he had left the gift Nakayama had given him.

Keep calm! he willed himself. He concentrated on keeping levity in the situation to throw them off guard. "I was just about to pour some sake," he said. "Would you like some?"

"Stop where you are!" Yoshida lunged with a perfectly executed *Morote uchi,* a two-handed cut intended to slice deeply into a man's trunk, but Bond's agility saved him. He leaped forward and performed a forward roll on the floor. The sword nearly struck the carpet. As a trained swordsman, Yoshida did not allow the blade to swing past the intended point.

Once he was on his feet, Bond's momentum catapulted him to the desk. He grasped the scabbard and pulled it toward him as he fell to the floor.

The sword came at him again with a *swish!* Bond rolled to the side and pushed himself to a standing position. Bond unsheathed his *katana* and tossed the scabbard behind him. He, too, smoothly adopted the more traditional stance, the *Chudan no kamae.*

Yoshida pulled back and froze in a *Haso no kamae,* a stance in which the sword was held vertically, with the hands by the right shoulder. At first his face revealed surprise that Bond could arm himself so quickly but he slowly smiled and projected a powerful self-confidence.

"Very well," Yoshida said with a glint in his eye. "You have shown your resourcefulness. Tsukamoto, put away the gun. Mister Bond and I shall fight honourably."

"No, Yoshida," Tsukamoto said, lowering the gun but keeping it in his hand. "I will shoot him if I have to."

"You will not have to," Yoshida said.

What had he got himself into? Bond suddenly thought. Just as he had thought when he had faced Ichihara backstage at the kabuki theatre, Bond was not sure if he could best his opponent. He had gone through a short, inadequate course in *kenjutsu* during his general training. He knew a few basic moves but he was no match for Goro

Yoshida, an experienced *kenjutsu* disciple. Bond feared that he didn't stand a chance.

The two men silently faced each other for an eternity. Yoshida stood like a statue, the smile never wavering. He exuded a calmness that was frightening. Bond could easily see how the man's charisma had seduced an entire yakuza gang.

Behind him, Tsukamoto sweated heavily.

Yoshida was waiting. Bond remembered a maxim of Japanese swordfighting: that whoever attacked first, lost. The better swordsman almost never attacked first. Frantically, Bond attempted to recall everything his instructor had taught him, but there wasn't much to draw upon. Bond did remember a technique called *enzen no metsuke,* or "gaze at the far mountains." This was a way to watch an opponent so that you saw all of him simultaneously. It was not wise to concentrate on one part to the exclusion of another. This helped to avoid falling for a feint or move meant to distract or mislead.

Bond reminded himself about breath control. That was one thing the instructor had drilled into them. One's *kokyu,* the ability to manage one's breath, was vital to maintaining control. By breathing deeply and slowly, a good swordsman fought against the body's natural tendency to become agitated under the stress of combat.

And then there was the most important concept of swordsmanship: *zanshin.* Awareness. Watchfulness. A "lingering heart." Without *zanshin,* a swordsman could never hope to vanquish an opponent.

It was Bond's *zanshin* that saved his life. Keeping his eyes locked with Yoshida's, Bond foresaw the attack. Yoshida's eyes betrayed him: his pupils dilated the split second before he acted.

Yoshida jumped forward and attempted a *kesa giri,* a diagonal cut that could open the victim from his upper left to lower right. It was called this because it followed the same line of a Buddhist monk's *kesa,* the sash hanging from the left shoulder to the right hip. Bond, however, flashed the *katana* in front of him just in time, warding off the strike. The metal blades clashed with a harshness that reverberated throughout the suite. Once the swords were swinging, they didn't stop. Yoshida and Bond slashed at each other repeatedly.

Yoshida was toying with him, Bond thought. He had reached his limit and Yoshida was blocking his blows effortlessly.

When the terrorist went on the offensive, all Bond could do was back away and keep his sword in front of him, warding off the powerful swipes. He collided with the sofa and fell back onto it; the worst thing that could possibly happen. Yoshida raised the sword above his head and brought it down hard, hoping for a *kiri kudashi,* the finishing cut. But Bond rolled and crashed onto the table, shattering the glass top. The sword stopped short of chopping through the sofa cushions, giving Bond time to get up. His own sword had never left his hand, so he took the opportunity to swing it backhanded at Yoshida. The blade struck the terrorist's left arm, embedding into his flesh.

Yoshida cried out and recoiled. He let go of his sword and fell on the floor. Tsukamoto pointed his pistol at Bond but Yoshida shouted, "No!" Clutching his bleeding arm, Yoshida got to his feet, retrieved his sword and assumed the *Gedan no kamae* stance. Bond, much of his body cut and scraped by the broken glass, stepped back and resumed his own position.

The staring contest resumed. No one noticed that the sounds coming from the bathroom in the back of the suite had ceased. The only thing that could be heard was the breathing of the two men.

Then, the blades flashed once again, striking each other in a firestorm of metal and sparks.

Bond concentrated on the basic moves. Give and take. Receive and deflect. The two men executed these manoeuvres repeatedly as they danced around the room, smashing into furniture, stamping on glass and creating a shambles.

Blood gushed out of Yoshida's arm. Bond had severely damaged a major artery and part of a muscle, but the madman kept attacking as if it had been a mere flesh wound. He swung the sword with the speed of a demon, keeping Bond on the edge of disaster. Bond parlayed the blows, creating a *clish-clash, clish-clash* clamour that made Tsukamoto flinch.

When Bond saw the glint of metal spark off of his own sword and felt a sting on his neck, he knew that he'd been hit but not badly. Yoshida's blade had touched his skin but Bond had deflected the cut just in time to prevent serious damage. The conflict halted momentarily as Bond stepped back and resumed his stance. He slowly put his hand to his neck and felt the blood.

The staring recommenced. Again, the lunge of metal and the ferocious colliding of blades. Again, they waltzed around the room in a macabre ballet, each man intent on ending the life of his opponent.

Bond shouted a *kiai* then lunged with a *gyaku kesa giri,* a diagonal upward cut. Unfortunately, Yoshida had somehow anticipated the manoeuvre and blocked Bond's *katana* hard with a downward strike. Bond's sword flew out of his hand and slid across the room. He was defenceless.

Yoshida stopped, held the sword pointed forward in *Chudan no kamae,* and prepared to pierce Bond's chest. He lunged quickly, forcing Bond to propel himself backward onto the floor to avoid being stabbed. The *Yami Shogun* stepped over Bond and raised the sword high above his head, ready to bring it down on his victim.

A shot rang out. Yoshida froze with the sword in the air. Everyone in the room turned their heads to see Mayumi, standing in the doorway to the bedroom. She was wearing a *yukata* and she was holding her Browning. She had fired it at Yoshida and now swung it toward Tsukamoto.

"Drop it," she commanded. "Next time I won't miss."

Tsukamoto tossed the Glock away. Mayumi then trained the gun on Yoshida.

"I called the Koan-Chosa-Cho and they have alerted the police," she said. "Drop the sword and give up."

Sirens could be heard on the streets below, but it would take the authorities several minutes before they could make it up the tower to the thirtieth floor.

Yoshida smiled, then slowly lowered the *katana.* He dropped it on the floor and turned to Bond. "Mister Bond, I could have killed you just now, but I suppose she would have shot me."

"I certainly would have," Mayumi said. "One of the things I've learned in the last few days is to keep a gun in the bedroom." She moved next to Bond.

Yoshida looked at Tsukamoto and said, "Did I not tell you that our actions tonight might result in our deaths? This is not the way I want to die. It would not be honourable." From the inner folds of his kimono, he produced a jar that looked frighteningly familiar to Bond.

It was a container full of mosquitoes just like the one Kappa had on the train.

The madman said, "All I have to do is release the top and dozens of hungry, infected mosquitoes will fly out into this room, into the ventilation ducts, and all over the hotel."

Bond took the gun from Mayumi and pointed it at Yoshida. "Come on, Yoshida, you don't want to do that."

"Why not? It would vanquish you, my enemy, and I would die like the kamikaze, honourably, and with courage."

"Your death would be futile."

"Futile? No death can be called futile," he said. "Mishima-san said, 'If we value so highly the dignity of life, how can we not also value the dignity of death?' " He turned to his compatriot and said, "Tsukamoto, prepare for the ritual. It is time." He handed the *katana* to the head of the Ryujin-kai, who had a look of abject terror on his face.

"Yoshida, please, do not do this," he whispered.

"Do you want to go to prison?" Yoshida asked. "You know as well as I that in a few minutes there will be no escape from this hotel except through death. You should follow me after you have performed your duty as my second." He looked at Bond and Mayumi. "You two, stand back," he said. "Or I will unleash the insects. Mister Bond, you can put away your gun. If you stand back and do not interfere, I will give you the jar unopened. I am no longer a threat to you."

Bond suddenly realised what Yoshida intended to do. He felt himself to be in a situation that defied the normal laws of sense and self-preservation, a world where rules of conduct and a notion of honour had been laid down centuries before. Slowly, Bond lowered the gun.

Yoshida knelt on the floor. He reached up to the collar of his *montsuki hakama* and tore it off his shoulders. He then pulled it down so that he was bare to the waist. His entire chest, arms and back were covered in the blinding crimson tattoos and the deep wound Bond had inflicted upon his left arm was bleeding heavily.

While holding the insect jar in one hand, Yoshida pulled the *wakizashi* from his belt. He put the scabbard between his teeth and unsheathed the blade, then dropped the scabbard.

The sound of voices and running feet outside the suite grew louder. The authorities had arrived.

"Are you ready, Tsukamoto?" Yoshida asked as he turned the point of the dagger toward himself, resting the tip gently against his exposed abdomen.

Tsukamoto was shaking. "Goro. *Sensei*. Can I at last call you *sensei*? You have always been a *sensei* to me. Please, do not do this."

Yoshida replied, "Yasutake, you have always been my friend. I thank you for your loyalty. Now perform your duty."

Tsukamoto paused a moment and quietly said, "Yes, *sensei*." He took a position behind Yoshida and raised the sword high.

Yoshida whispered a brief, silent prayer, then he carefully placed the insect container on the floor beside him.

The police banged on the door and called out. In a few seconds they would bash it down.

The man with the red tattoo glared at Bond and then thrust the *wakazashi* deeply into his flesh. Yoshida's eyes bulged and watered, but he was determined to go through with the *seppuku*. He tugged on the blade until it moved along his trunk horizontally, splitting his gut. As the entrails began to gush out of the open red crevasse, Tsukamoto brought the sword down quickly and cleanly.

Goro Yoshida's head flew off his torso, hit the floor, and rolled to where Bond was standing. Mayumi screamed and hid her face in Bond's arms.

The door burst open and in seconds the place was swarming with armed officers. Yoshi Nakayama entered, took one look at the room and then ordered that Tsukamoto be arrested. The officers immediately relieved the Ryujin-kai's *oyabun* of his sword and handcuffed him.

Bond reached for the mosquito container and carefully picked it up. He gingerly handed it to one of the men, who promptly placed it in a reinforced container made for transporting bombs.

As they started to take him out of the room, Tsukamoto said, "Wait." The escorts stopped, allowing Tsukamoto to turn to Bond and say, "The *Yami Shogun* died the way he wanted, as Mishima did. He sacrificed his life in an honourable way rather than go through the humiliation of the courts. As for me, well, we shall see what my lawyers can do. If they are unsuccessful in freeing me, then my destiny is sealed. I have been aware of this for some time now and I am ready. I did not always approve of what the *Yami Shogun* wanted to do but I must take responsibility for my part in it. Instead of shame, I feel pride. As for you, Bond-san: your victory is empty. Goro Yoshida robbed you of the finishing blow, the *kiri kudashi*. This was *his* victory."

Bond stared at the man coldly and said, "You know something, Tsukamoto? I don't give a damn. He's bloody *dead*, and that's all I care about."

Tsukamoto's eyes flared but the men pushed him out of the room before he could say anything else.

It seemed like hours later, but in fact Nakayama and his men finished with them in forty-five minutes. Bond and Mayumi were moved to a different suite. The minor cuts Bond had suffered were treated. The couple answered questions and signed statements and then they were alone again.

For a while, they sat together in silence. Neither of them could forget what they had witnessed. Mayumi knew that it was something that would haunt her forever.

"I'm going to sell my shares," she said, breaking the stillness. "And I am going to start something new. Something I like. I don't know what that is yet, but it will be something with a future."

Bond squeezed her arm in encouragement. "You have strength, ingenuity and courage. You should be all right. Beauty helps, of course."

"James-san, I think that's the first nice thing you've said to me. But I suppose it is safe to say such things when you are flying back to London tomorrow."

"Have you heard my flight has been delayed? I have some unfinished business here. Rather more than I thought."

She broke into a smile. "James-san, you really are most diligent."

Bond allowed himself a slight bow. Mayumi laughed, then stretched out sensuously on the bed. Bond marvelled again at her beauty. He moved down beside her and gazed admiringly along the length of her body at her soft translucent skin. He murmured softly into her neck, "My researches into some of the—finer—details of this case are incomplete. Perhaps you might be able to help."

"Co-operate with your inquiries?" she suggested with a wicked smile.

"I hoped you might understand," he whispered as he began to lay the ghosts of the past to rest once more.

SOURCES

For readers who are interested in the works of Yukio Mishima, the following were used as sources for this book:

CHAPTER 12: *Patriotism*, published by New Directions Books, 1995

CHAPTER 15: *Runaway Horses*, Alfred Knopf, 1973

CHAPTER 15: "Kyoko's House," 1959 quoted in *Mishima* by John Nathan, Little Brown & Co., 1974

CHAPTER 23: *The Sailor who fell from Grace with the Sea*, Alfred Knopf, 1965

CHAPTER 28: *The Hagakure: A Code to the Way of Samurai*, Hokuseido Press (Tokyo), 1980

MIDSUMMER NIGHT'S DOOM

FIVE MINUTES INTO THE BRIEFING, M TURNED HER CHAIR TO FACE HIM AND asked, "What do you know about *Playboy*, 007?"

James Bond blinked. "Ma'am?"

"The magazine, 007, what do you know about it?"

Bond shrugged and said, "Only that some people actually have been known to read the articles, and that I need to renew my subscription."

M was not amused. Although she was often opinionated and could speak freely about most anything, for some reason Barbara Mawdsley found herself irritated and oddly embarrassed at the notion of a "men's magazine."

"I don't suppose you know Hugh Hefner, do you?" she asked, drolly. "You seem to have a lot in common with him."

Bond ignored the inference and said, "As a matter of fact, I met him once, in Jamaica. It was a long time ago. I doubt if he would remember me. He was on a yacht with an entourage and a beautiful woman. Playboy were scouting locations for a club and casino. I happened to be fishing with my Jamaican friend, 'Old Man' Ramsey, when Hefner's yacht pulled up alongside our boat. Hefner invited us aboard for cocktails. He asked my opinion of choice spots on the northern side of Jamacia. I'll never forget the girl, she was one of his centerfolds . . ."

"Hmpf," M grunted, sounding much like her predecessor, Sir Miles Messervy. "It looks as if—"

". . . I think her name was Donna Michelle . . ." Bond continued, lost for a moment in a private reverie. After a brief pause, he snapped out of it and asked the inevitable, "Why?"

"I was about to say it's the bloody leak in the Ministry of Defence again," she said. "There's a river of information flowing out of there and it's changing hands at parties being held at the Playboy Mansion, Mr. Hefner's home in Los Angeles."

"Why would Hugh Hefner be involved in something like that?" Bond asked.

"He's not. One of his frequent guests is. Hefner is completely unaware. Now, we've had yet a third report that sensitive material has shown up for sale on the black market. The latest is a set of designs for a new class of infrared focal plane arrays, or FPAs, as they're called. These new ones will be known as 'smart' FPAs because they imitate human-eye capabilities, such as focusing, visualization and processing."

"I've heard about them," Bond said. "The smart FPAs can pre-process data at the sensor itself in image-processing applications such as . . . oh, say, target detection, and then they would pass some-what refined information to dedicated signal-processors. Smart FPAs would make advanced military applications affordable because of the significant reductions in size, weight and power consumption. I hadn't realized the designs had been completed."

"Thank heaven you understand them, because I don't," she said, glancing upward. "Anyway, MI5 have handed over the investigation to us because they believe that the designs were copied on to minia-ture microfilm and smuggled out of the UK to America."

"Do we know who was responsible?"

"Yes. Martin Tuttle."

"Martin Tuttle?" He had to think a moment. "You mean the rock musician?"

"That's right. It seems that Mr. Tuttle's former wife works at the Ministry. Or rather, she used to, before she was arrested yesterday. You remember how public their divorce was a couple of years ago?"

"I don't read the tabloids, ma'am," Bond said. He knew that the famous rock star from Clapham had married a girl from Glasgow in an equally public wedding, but the honeymoon had been spoiled by messy accusations of drunken orgies on the road. Bond couldn't care less. He wasn't a fan of rock music and he particularly disliked the rock star lifestyle.

"Tuttle's wife was under suspicion for some time. Although the Tuttles had publicly denounced each other, constant surveillance proved otherwise. They were seen meeting on numerous occasions—having lunch together, that sort of thing—and appeared to be perfectly happy. More evidence was gathered that proved they had a pretty good swindle going, so she was arrested just as Martin Tuttle flew from England to Los Angeles, where he currently lives. She confessed to supplying him with all of the documents that went missing over the last year, which he apparently took with him to California. She said all of the exchanges took place at the Playboy Mansion every few months, whenever they held elaborate parties. She doesn't know who his contact is and MI5 believe her. So far Tuttle doesn't know that she has been arrested."

M leaned forward in her chair. "We think Tuttle is selling the material to the Russian mafia," M said. "Our Afghanistan station intercepted coded messages from a syndicate in Moscow indicating that they would soon have smart FPAs for sale."

"Where do I come in, ma'am?" Bond asked.

"SIS is arranging for you to be invited to a forthcoming party, 007. You're to observe Mr. Tuttle and retrieve the microfilm, if possible. But we're most interested in finding out who his contact is, so try to catch him in the act."

After the briefing, Bond left the office and found Miss Moneypenny with a mischievous twinkle in her eyes as she prepared the envelope containing his paperwork.

"I know that look, Penny, and it usually means you'd like to say something naughty but won't," he said.

"Only that they're turning you loose at the Playboy Mansion. I think you had better have a chaperone," she said, looking at her calendar. "Oh dear, I'm not doing anything that night . . ."

Bond smiled. "Penny, if I could take you, I'd love to, but it will probably be a bore. I expect that it's nothing like what one imagines a Playboy party to be."

"The invitation says that it's 'a place where fantasy becomes reality.'"

"I have no fantasies. What is it, black tie?"

"You have to wear pajamas."

"You must be joking."

"It's true. It's the annual 'Midsummer Night's Dream' party, and everyone is required to wear nightshirts, pajamas or lingerie."

Bond groaned. "I take back what I said, then. It all sounds terribly decadent and hedonistic."

"It sounds just your cup of tea," she gibed.

Bond snatched the envelope out of her hand, leaned over, and kissed her on the forehead.

Hugh Hefner's magnificent Playboy Mansion West is located in the exclusive Holmby Hills area of Los Angeles, adjacent to Bel Air, Beverly Hills, U.C.L.A. and the Los Angeles Country Club. Bond drove his Jaguar XK8 coupe to the imposing wrought iron gate at the bottom of a tree-lined drive off of Sunset Boulevard, and was greeted by a voice in a large rock on the driver's side. Bond provided his credentials, and the gate opened slowly. He drove through and was treated to a spectacular view of a marble frieze, a replica of a painting by Guido Reni displayed in the Rospigiosi Palace in Rome. The car made its way up the steep, curving drive that was lined with redwood trees and juniper hedges, ending at a circular drive with an ornate, flower-ringed marble fountain in the centre. Busy valets signaled for Bond to stop. Even though he had arrived unfashionably early, there was already a queue of cars waiting to be parked.

Bond entrusted the Jaguar to the boy and took a moment to gaze at the mansion's front, a marvelous stone edifice in a 16th Century Perpendicular Gothic style. Bond thought there might be some Scottish influence as well.

"Mr. Bond?" A radiant blonde in her late twenties appeared

through the open, massive oaken door. She was dressed in a white baby-doll slip dress, high heels and a smile. Bond thought she might as well have been an angel from heaven.

"I'm Lisa Dergan. If you read the magazine, I'm Miss July 1998. I've been asked to greet you, give you a brief tour, and take you to Mr. Hefner."

"I'm delighted," Bond said, taking her hand. Her bright green eyes disclosed an air of self-confidence and intelligence. He could easily get lost in them.

She led him into the Great Hall, a splendid foyer with a Botticini marble floor and hand carved oak paneling. A beautiful antique chandelier hung over the room, and two sets of curved stairs guarded by hand-carved, eighteenth century greeting monkeys led to the second floor and balcony overlooking the hall. Bond noticed Dali and Matisse originals out of the corner of his eye and asked, "How old is the mansion?"

"It was completed in 1927. Hef is the third owner, not counting a brief period when it was a place where heads of state came to stay— people like the King and Queen of Siam, the King of Sweden and loads of others. I've been a visitor here several times, so I learned all kinds of stuff about it."

She took him into a living room, where clusters of people stood with hors d'oeuvres and drinks. The men were dressed in silk pajamas and robes, and the women were draped in lacy lingerie and other forms of transparent sleeping attire. The room was furnished with 17th century antiques, a Steinway grand piano and more hand-carved oak paneling.

"What did Mr. Hefner add to the existing property?" Bond asked.

"It was re-designed to his specifications. The tennis courts and pool were put in then, as well as the sauna, bathhouse and the one-of-a-kind 'grotto' and jaccuzi. You've got to see it to believe it."

"Will you show it to me?" Bond asked.

"Later, perhaps," she said, blushing.

She took him through the rest of the ground floor, including the exquisite dining room where De Kooning's *Woman* hung over a marble fireplace and three 15th Century French tapestries of lions hung above the sideboard. Bond was impressed and enchanted by the manor. It was a palace fit for any king, and there was a warm, friendly atmosphere that pervaded every room.

As they came back into the Great Hall, Bond noticed Hugh Hefner himself, talking with guests and holding a glass of Jack Daniels on the rocks. He was wearing purple, tailor-made silk pajamas and a smoking jacket. Two gorgeous young women, a blonde and a brunette, were on either side of him. They were wearing next to nothing.

Bond loved pajamas, so he felt some kinship with his host in that respect. He had decided to wear a set of navy satin ones, also tailor-made, covered by his beloved Hong Kong housecoat decorated in Chinese characters, which comfortably concealed his shoulder-holstered Walther PPK.

"Excuse me, Mr. Hefner," Lisa said, stepping up to the group.

He turned to her and beamed. "Lisa!" he said, interrupting his conversation to give her a hug. "You look lovely."

"Thank you. May I introduce Mr. Bond?"

He held out his hand to Bond and said, "Hugh Hefner."

"Bond. James Bond." The handshake was firm and dry.

The founder and publisher of *Playboy* magazine looked fit and energetic, and seemed to be taller than Bond remembered. He carried himself with authority and dignity, yet he also exhibited characteristics of playfulness and good humour.

"Welcome to the mansion." He indicated the others standing near him. "This is my personal physician, Dr. Mark Saginor, and this is one of our great American singers, Mel Torme." He introduced the two young women as "Tracy" and "Sandy." Apparently Hefner had not one, but two dates for the party.

"It's a pleasure to be here," Bond said, shaking hands with the others.

Hefner said, "Excuse me, I need to speak with Mr. Bond alone. Thank you, Lisa."

She smiled at Bond and said, "If you need anything else, just look for me. There's a lot more you haven't seen."

"Especially that grotto," Bond said. Lisa wagged her finger at him, as Hefner and Bond withdrew. They went into the library, where they were alone. The library boasted a Leroy Neiman original and a backgammon table designed and built especially for Hefner. An elegant bookcase was built into the wall next to the fireplace. It held leather bound volumes of all the *Playboy* magazines dating back to 1953.

"The CIA came to see me today to tell me what you're here to do," Hefner said.

Bond nodded. He knew that Hefner would have been briefed. After all, if there was any threat of violence at a social event attended by five hundred celebrities and centerfolds, he should know about it.

"If there's anything I can do, just ask," he said.

"Just try to relax and enjoy your party, sir," Bond said. "No one else knows of my real purpose here?"

"No one. Not even the security guards."

"Do you know if Martin Tuttle has arrived?"

"I haven't seen him. You know, there was always something I didn't like about the guy. I'm not sure why I kept letting him visit the mansion. I suppose some of our younger guests enjoyed having him around. I always found him to be obnoxious."

"Do you have any idea who his contact might be?" Bond asked.

Hefner thought a minute. "It could be a lot of people. He has several friends here tonight. Show business people."

"Such as?"

"Another musician, Chocky Day. A couple of film stars are in his circle."

"Is there anyone out of the ordinary coming tonight?"

"I would hope so or it wouldn't be a party at the Playboy Mansion!" Hefner grinned broadly. "But I know what you mean. We have some foreigners coming tonight. I'll have to ask Mary O'Connor, my personal assistant, to point them out. They're all in the film industry. I'm sure there will be dozens of people here tonight whom I've never met before. I suppose it could be anyone. Sorry."

"That's quite all right, you've been very helpful," Bond said.

Bond was fairly sure that Hefner had not recognized him. Their encounter in Jamaica had been a long time ago.

He turned to go, saying, "I'd like to walk around the grounds and get a feel for the place before the big crowds arrive."

"By all means," Hefner said. "Wait, I have something I want to give you. You might find it useful."

He opened a cabinet next to the backgammon table and took out three objects. One was a Sheaffer-Levenger exclusive "Mediterranean" fountain pen. It was made of beautiful blue translucent polymer with a jewel-like appearance, further enhanced by gold-plated rings and pocket clips. The other objects were a black device the size and shape of a cassette tape case and a small waxy thing that looked like an ear plug.

"This is an ordinary fountain pen with a fourteen carat gold tip," Hefner said, handing it to Bond. "What's unusual about it is that it's also a CSS 600 UHF transmitter with a range of a thousand meters. The receiver will fit neatly in the pocket of your housecoat, and you can listen discreetly with this tiny ear piece. No wires are needed. It has two channels, but you'll only need one. If you can get the pen attached to Tuttle somehow, you'll be able to listen to everything he says."

Bond was amused and impressed. "Where did you get this?" he asked, taking the receiver and ear plug.

"People give me thing-a-ma-jigs all the time," Hefner said with a smile. "My two greatest interests are gadgets and girls."

"I can relate to that."

Bond surveyed the grounds, which were decorated with an Arabian Nights theme and entirely covered by connecting tents extending to the swimming pool, the grotto, and beyond. Bright coloured flowers and fairy lights covered the hillside, bushes and trees, and by nightfall the effect was magical. There were bars at the pool and in the main tent area. Staff circulated with plates of Rumaki, skewered Nile River shrimps, cold mussels stuffed with pine nuts and rice, Egyptian meatballs, grape leaves stuffed with lamb, and Phyllo dough puffs with spinach and feta cheese.

Bond had heard the place described as a "Shangri-la where time stands still," and it was true.

An endless parade of California's elite began to arrive, and within an hour, the party was in full swing. A disc jockey provided music while guests danced to everything from big band and disco to fifties doo-wop and modern rap. The sight of scantily-clad women of all ages gyrating on the dance floor attracted a large group of spectators. Celebrities from all fields—entertainment, sports, politics—were among the guests. Bond recognized actor Tony Curtis with two lovely young girls. He was introducing them to another actor, Robert Culp, as "Monday" and "Tuesday." ("The rest of the week couldn't make it," he explained.) Bond noticed famed attorney Vincent Bugliosi in a heated discussion with writer Larry Gelbart. American actor and former football star Jim Brown was dancing with his date. Hefner and his two girlfriends seemed to know everyone and he was always greeted with enthusiasm and affection.

Bond noticed that the party was not without security. There were several well-built men standing about, not so inconspicuously, armed with unconcealed Beretta Model 92F 9mm handguns.

He was scanning the crowd near the main buffet line when he noticed Lisa Dergan talking to another striking blonde who had just entered with a tall, handsome man in his fifties. Behind him was an even taller man, a beefed-up bodyguard. The blonde was in her mid-twenties and had a wide face, clear blue eyes, a fabulous figure, and not much covering it. She was wearing a black, skintight, leather catsuit with a low neckline and open-laced sides from her arms down to her ankles. An impressive pearl necklace competently accented her cleavage. Her companion had short, curly hair, brown eyes and a swarthy complexion. He looked as if he had eastern European gypsy ancestry.

"Oh, there you are," Lisa said, beckoning to him. "Mr. Bond, this is my friend Victoria Zdrok, she was Miss October in 1994."

Victoria beamed and shook his hand. "How do you do?" She had a distinct accent that Bond placed immediately.

"What's a nice Ukranian girl like you doing in a place like this?" he asked.

She smiled with a sexy smirk. "Maybe I'm not so nice," she purred. "How did you know where I came from?"

"Oh, let's just say that Russia and her neighbors were one of my hobbies, once."

"Victoria was one of the first students from the Soviet Union to come to America for high school and college. She finished college before she was eighteen and now has a law degree and a Masters in clinical psychology, is that right?" Lisa said.

"That's correct," Victoria said.

"Be careful," the man warned with a much thicker Russian accent, "she will prosecute you before you can say *na'zdrovya*." Bond placed him nearer to Moscow.

Lisa continued, "And this is Anton Redenius, the movie producer."

"James Bond," 007 said, shaking the man's hand. Redenius had a vice-like grip.

"What brings you here, Mr. Bond?"

"I work for Playboy, I'm a lawyer in their UK office."

Redenius pulled away his hand as if he had burned it. "Aaiieee, a lawyer! God help us!" He laughed, and the girls laughed with him. When the bodyguard didn't laugh, Redenius scowled at him. The thug forced a guffaw, satisfying his boss.

"You must forgive Estragon, he has no sense of humour," Redenius said to Bond.

The man was boorish, Bond thought. He was the type of person who used his power and charisma to bully people and get what we wanted from them.

"Redenius . . . that sounds German," Bond said.

"My father was German, my mother was Russian. I was born in what became East Germany, but I was raised in the Soviet Union," the man said. "I live in Hollywood now, make movies and play golf!"

"I want to dance," Victoria said. "Anton, will you dance with me?"

"No, no, my dear," the man said. "I must have something to eat. Please join me for some of this incredible food first."

"I'm not hungry. Mr. Bond, will you dance with me?" she purred.

Unable to refuse, he said, "Certainly," then allowed Miss October 1994 to pull him towards the dance floor

It was a song with a heavy beat, something Bond had never heard. He normally disliked disco dancing. He preferred the more traditional ballroom and big band swing. But he had learned very early on, when he was a young man in the sixth form, that being able to dance went a long way toward impressing the opposite sex.

Victoria began to bump and grind in front of him, then took his arms and pulled him to her. He followed along, gazing into her eyes. The sleepwear made the body contact extremely sensual. She pressed her breasts into his chest. The pearl necklace glinted in the mirror ball lights, serving as a road map to her magnificent cleavage.

"That's quite a necklace," Bond said.

"Thank you!" Victoria replied. "It was a present from Anton."

"Really?"

"Can you believe it? He's asked me to star in his next movie! We're going to film it in Russia. We leave in two days. I'm so excited! I try to go back once a year anyway."

"I thought Miss Dergan said you had a law degree."

"I do. I'll continue that, of course, but acting might be fun. I still model, so it's really the same thing, isn't it? It's only for two months. I wouldn't want to make a career out of it because I need more intellectual stimulation. He needed a blonde Russian girl who speaks English, so he asked me. I suppose it didn't hurt that we've been dating."

"Ah ha," Bond said, "the old casting couch trick . . ."

She shoved him playfully. "Stop, it's not like that. Besides, I still date other men, too. I'm terribly unfaithful." With that, she moved closer to him. "You like the pearls? Anton gave them to me for my birthday and wants me to wear them all the time we're in Russia. It's part of the character. I'll be nervous wearing something worth as much as he said. But I think pearls are sexy, don't you?"

As they continued to dance silently, Victoria slowly removed the pearl necklace and used it as a prop to tantalize Bond. She pulled it up along his face, over his head and down the other side. She rolled the pearls on his skin, allowing him to feel the smooth texture. Then she placed the string against his mouth. He opened his lips and sucked three pearls into his mouth. He gently ground them in his teeth, noting the slimy, smooth feel.

Bond reached up and took the necklace out of her hands and replaced it around her neck. The song ended, and before she could start another dance, he glanced up and saw Martin Tuttle enter the tent.

"Thank you," he said to the girl. "That was thoroughly enjoyable. However, you must excuse me. There's someone I must speak to."

"That's okay," she said. "I enjoyed that, too. I hope I'll see you later!"

Bond hated to leave such a beautiful woman on the dance floor, but Victoria quickly snared renowned band leader Ray Anthony from the sidelines as the music picked up with a 70s disco hit.

Martin Tuttle was dressed in a white terry cloth robe with big pockets, much like one provided by a hotel. His date was a young woman with a pierced nose and crimson hair. Behind them were two more couples of the same ilk.

Lisa Dergan stepped up to Bond and hooked his arm, saying, "Who's this handsome guy standing over here by himself? You want to get someting to eat?—Oh, look, there's Martin Tuttle and Chocky Day!" She squeezed his arm. "Sorry, I'm just not used to being star struck, this is all pretty new to me!" she said. "I knew being a Playmate would put me in contact with a lot of famous people, but I had no *idea* . . . ! Come on, Mr. Bond, let's go talk to him."

"All right. But you have to call me James."

They walked across the floor and caught Tuttle and his entourage heading for the buffet line. Bond and Lisa joined the queue behind them. Tuttle was telling Day how his manager had swindled him.

"You're going to have to sue," Day said.

"Well, that's certainly possible, but I just might not have to now," Tuttle replied.

"Oh? Got something up your sleeve?"

"Definitely."

"Excuse me, Mr. Tuttle?" Lisa interrupted. "I'm Lisa Dergan, Miss July 1998. I just wanted to meet you. I love your music."

Tuttle's eyes widened when he saw the lovely girl. "Well, hello." He held out his hand. "Nice to meet you."

"This is embarrassing, I swear, but can I have your autograph?" Lisa gushed. She picked up a napkin with "Midsummer Night's Dream" printed on it. "I don't usually do this, but I just had to ask." She was so good-natured about it that Tuttle laughed.

"Of course," he said. "You have a pen?"

"I do," Bond said. He handed the Sheaffer-Levenger to Tuttle. The rock star took a second to admire it, then wrote his name with a flourish. He handed the napkin to Lisa and said, "Here you are."

"Thank you!"

Tuttle offered the pen back to Bond and said, "Thanks."

"Keep it."

"Huh?"

"Go ahead, you can have it," Bond said. "You might be accosted by more fans tonight."

"Why, thank you, this is a nice pen." Tuttle stuck the pen in his robe pocket, as Bond hoped he would. "Say, you're from my side of the pond, aren't you?"

"That's right," Bond said without elaborating.

The buffet spread was the *piece de resistance* of the party. Cubes of fruit varieties formed a three foot tall pyramid, cascading down mirrored blocks into a river of colours on the table. There were five special salads of Middle Eastern cuisine. Dinner consisted of roasted crown of lamb; grilled skewered swordfish marinated in lemon juice, olive oil and bay leaves; grilled kebabs of tomato wedges and three-colour bell peppers; Musakka'a made traditionally with extra-lean ground beef and lamb, eggplant, tomato and cheese; and a saffron-scented pilav.

Bond and Lisa sat on cushions on the floor and ate at a low table. The place was packed now, and the scene reminded Bond of a sultan's harem. One woman in a bra and panties removed her top and began feeding grapes to a man lying on his back with his head in her lap. As the party had progressed into the night, the amount of semi-nudity had increased. The atmosphere became erotically charged as disrobed couples went swimming or disappeared into some of the more private areas such as the grotto, the bathhouse, or the more intimate rooms in the Game House. The older guests were more modest, but they seemed to be reveling in the spirit of the event as much as the younger crowd.

"Isn't Hef a nice man?" Lisa asked. "For his birthday I baked him a chocolate chip cookie in the shape of a rabbit. It was big, too, it filled a pizza box! Hey, do you golf?"

"A little," Bond replied with a shrug.

Bond found her charming. Her dazzling girl-next-door wholesomeness was a contrast to Victoria's more worldly bad-girl image. When Lisa wasn't looking, though, Bond slipped the earphone in his ear and adjusted the volume on the receiver in his housecoat pocket. He immediately heard Martin Tuttle talking to his date.

"We'll go back to England as soon as I finish the job," he was saying.

"But you *promised*, Martin!" she said.

They continued the conversation for a few minutes, then Tuttle said to his friends, "I'll be right back. Watch my food, will you?" He slipped through the crowd and left the main tent. Bond concentrated on listening to Tuttle but Lisa was attempting to make conversation. He did his best to pay attention to her, but when he heard Tuttle's voice whisper, "There you are, I've been looking for you," Bond held up his hand to shut her up.

"What?" she asked, confused.

"Shhh," he said.

Another man's voice, one with a thick accent, replied, "What are you worried about? We were bound to run into each other, Martin." It was the Russian filmmaker, Anton Redenius.

"Look, I delivered your stuff yesterday. You promised me my money tonight. A deal is a deal," Tuttle said.

"Quite so. Haven't you made plenty of money on our little deals? Fine, we are prepared to give you your payment for this one," Redenius said. "Estragon?"

Tuttle gasped and made a choking sound.

Bond jumped up from the pillows, cat-like, without saying a word to his bewildered Playmate companion and ran past the pool and out of the tent. Outside he heard the gurgling and wheezing sounds intensify.

"I'm sorry, Martin. This is your midsummer night's doom," Redenius said. "Keep him quiet, Estragon, we don't want anyone to hear us."

Tuttle continued to choke and gag. Bond ran past one of the security guards, who was dressed in a lightweight suit.

"Sir, you need to stay within the—hey!" he shouted as Bond jumped across a rope barrier and ran into the darkness. The guard followed, but Bond was already way ahead of him.

He ran past the squirrel monkey cage, causing an outburst of chattering, and into a grove of redwood trees. Then he saw them. Anton Redenius and his henchman, Estragon, were standing over the body of Martin Tuttle. Estragon was holding a wire garrote extended from his wristwatch. He looked up and saw Bond, then released the wire, which snapped back into his watch.

Bond drew his gun and said, "Freeze!"

"No, *you* freeze!" came a voice behind him. It was the security guard, training his Beretta on Bond.

Bond didn't move, but said, "These men are criminals. The tall one just murdered the man on the ground. I work for the British government."

"Don't be a fool!" Redenius said to the guard. "We found this man here. I think it was this Brit who killed him!"

"All three of you!" the guard said. "Hands up. You, drop the gun. Now!"

Bond reluctantly did as he was told. All three men raised their hands. The guard kicked the Walther away and gestured with the Beretta. "All right, walk back toward the tents, slowly."

The guard reached for a walkie-talkie with his free hand and spoke into it. "John, I've got a dead man in the woods and three suspects. We're walking toward the tents from the redwoods. Send backup immedi—"

His words were cut short as Estragon surprised him. The brute grabbed the guard's gun-arm with a well-practiced manoeuvre and brought it down hard on his knee, snapping it in two. The Beretta flew into the air. Estragon deftly caught it, then kicked the guard in the chest. The man went down, crying in agony. Estragon swung the gun around to Bond and prepared to fire, but 007 was a second ahead of him. He lunged for the big man's waist, tackling him. The gun went off in the air. They struggled for control of the weapon as the guard writhed helplessly. Anton Redenius, meanwhile, slipped away and disappeared into the darkness.

Estragon punched Bond several times in the face in rapid succession. The blows stunned him, giving the bodyguard time to get to his feet and run. Dazed, Bond stood up, got his bearings and chased after the man.

Estragon was big and agile, but he wasn't fast on his feet. Bond caught up to him inside the tent at the pool, just as other guards arrived on the scene. Bond leaped for the man and they both went into the water with a splash. Naked revelers screamed, jumped out of the way, and climbed onto the sides to grab their towels.

Two guards drew their guns and aimed at the two men, but they were stopped by Hugh Hefner, who appeared behind them with his head of security. "Hold your fire!" he shouted.

The fight continued in the pool, where Bond was in his element. An expert swimmer and one of the three Double-O agents who had taken a first in SIS's Underwater Combat course, Bond quickly gained an advantage by using Estragon's weight and size against him. Bond got the man's neck in the crook of his arm and squeezed, pulling him down below the surface. Able to hold his breath for an extraordinary amount of time, Bond had no problem keeping his opponent submerged until he began to panic. Bond had saved an ounce of strength for this very moment. He applied more pressure, locking Estragon's neck in a vice-like grip, forcing him to swallow water. The struggling continued for another minute, and then the bodyguard went limp.

Bond pulled him out of the water and rolled him onto the side of the pool. Completely beaten, Estragon began to cough and gasp as two guards expertly handcuffed him. Two more guards approached Bond with cuffs, but Hefner said, "Wait. Not him."

By now, a large semi-dressed crowd had gathered by the pool. They had heard the commotion and the gunshot. Lisa Dergan was there, as was Victoria Zdrok and her companion, Anton Redenius.

Bond pointed at him. "He's the one you need to arrest," he said, fighting for breath. "He's a killer and a spy."

"How dare you!" Redenius said. "I shall sue you for slander! No one lies about me that way!"

Bond stood up and faced him. "You are involved in organized crime in Russia. Martin Tuttle stole classified strategic information from my country and gave it to you. You're planning to smuggle it into Russia when you go there to make your movie, then sell it to your mafia friends. Martin Tuttle has been supplying you with data for some time now, but instead of paying him off, you had him killed."

"Lies!" Redenius shouted. He turned to the shocked crowd. "He tells lies!" Victoria was looking at him oddly. "Is this true, Anton?" she asked.

"Of course not! He can't prove anything he says!"

Bond calmly approached Victoria and said, "I can prove it. May I borrow your necklace, please?"

"What?"

"Your valuable pearl necklace. May I?" He held out his hand.

She hesitated for a second, then unclasped the necklace and gave it to him.

Bond asked one of the guards to shine his flashlight on the ground. Then, surprising everyone, Bond dropped the necklace into a pool of light. He squatted down, picked up a stone, and crushed the pearls with one blow. Victoria screamed.

Bond sifted through the pearls' debris and picked up three tiny black objects.

"Miniature microfilm cartridges," Bond said, holding them in his palm. "I'm sorry, Victoria, I didn't have the heart to tell you before, but those pearls were fake. This man was using you as an unwitting courier for stolen state secrets. If you had been caught, you could have gone to jail for the rest of your life."

"How—how did you know?" she asked.

"When you put the necklace in my mouth, I tested the pearls with my teeth. That's how you can tell if they're real or not. If they feel slimy and smooth, then they're fake. Cultured pearls are gritty, like sandpaper. I knew immediately that they were hollow. I had to be sure that Redenius was Tuttle's man before I told you."

Victoria gasped aloud and looked at Redenius.

"You bastard," she said through her teeth, then slapped him hard on the face, almost knocking him down. Redenius was dumbfounded and humiliated.

Victoria turned, saw Dr. Saginor watching with amazement, and said, "Come on, doctor, let's dance." She took him by the hand and led him out of the crowd.

"Wait, my dear!" Redenius called after her, but the guards roughly descended upon him. He was cuffed and taken away as he shouted obscenities and protests.

Hefner addressed the rest of the crowd. "Please, go on with the party. I apologize for this disturbance. The party *will* go on!"

The guards helped disperse the spectators and the swimmers dropped their towels and jumped back into the pool. Lisa remained behind with Hefner and Bond. The head of security returned Bond's Walther PPK to him, saying that the crime scene in the woods had been sealed off for the police.

"You got what you came for?" Hefner asked.

"Yes," Bond said, pocketing the microfilm and holstering his gun. He gave the receiver and earphone back to Hefner. "You'll find your fountain pen in the pocket of Martin Tuttle's robe."

"I don't care about that, I have three or four of them," Hefner said. "You know, that was good advice you gave me in Jamaica. We had a nice club in Ocho Rios."

Bond was amazed. "I'm surprised you remember that day, Mr. Hefner," he said.

"We've always kept up with you, James," Hefner said with a wink. "We're a lot alike, you and I. And please, call me Hef."

Lisa said, "James, you'll probably have to make a statement to the police when they get here."

Bond nodded. "That will kill the rest of the evening. We don't have much time."

Hef cleared his throat, shook Bond's hand and politely withdrew.

"Come on, let's continue that tour," she said, taking Bond's arm and leading him toward the grotto.

It was a dimly lit and misty facsimile of a small cavern with a warm spring running through it. There were at least two other couples snuggled in the nooks and crannies. Lisa chose a small alcove that was lined with cushions.

They got comfortable, lying together arm in arm.

"This is wonderful," he said. She kissed him lightly on the cheek. Then, she raised a bit and slipped the straps of her slip dress off her shoulders, letting it drop down to reveal firm, round breasts.

She put her arms around his neck, reclined next to him, and whispered, "I don't normally do this sort of thing, you know. But they say the Playboy Mansion is a place where fantasy becomes reality."

Bond ran a hand through her hair and said, "I've heard that before. Whoever 'they' are, they have my vote of complete confidence."

Then he brought his mouth ruthlessly down on hers.

ACKNOWLEDGMENTS

ZERO MINUS TEN

The author wishes to thank the following individuals and organizations for their assistance:

IN THE U.S. AND CANADA:

Kevin Chin, Paul F. Dantuono, Sandra Groark, Alexandra Harris, Dan Harvey, Daisy Koh, Joseph Lau, Hen Chen Lee, Charles Plante, Doug Redenius, David A. Reinhardt, Moana Re Robertson, Kathy Tootelian (for the *mahjong* illustrations), Mike VanBlaricum, Amanda Wu, Kenneth Yung, and everyone at Viacom New Media.

IN THE U.K.:

Peter Janson-Smith, Carolyn Caughey, Man Wei Tam, Pradip Patel and Rina Gokani of the Chiswick Pharmacy, Corinne B. Turner, the staff of Glidrose Publications Ltd., and the heirs of the late Ian Lancaster Fleming.

IN HONG KONG AND AUSTRALIA:

Sarah Cairns and Henry Ho of the Mandarin Oriental; Terry Foo of the Hongkong and Shanghai Bank; Eric Lockeyear, Mark Bowles, and Peter IP Pau-juk of the Royal Hong Kong Police; Marg Mason of the

Kalgoorlie-Boulder Tourist Centre; Jacqueline L.S. Ng; James Pickard; and Jeanie Wong and Stephen Wong of the Hong Kong Tourist Association. Special acknowledgement is made to the Royal Hong Kong Police for permission to use material from the Government Press book *Triad Societies in Hong Kong* by W.P. Morgan (Crown Copyright Reserved, 1960).

THE FACTS OF DEATH

The author wishes to thank the following individuals and organizations for their help in the writing of this book.

IN THE U.S. AND CANADA

Robert Coats; Susan Elder and Invacare; Dr. Ed Fugger and Fairfax CryoBank; James Goodner; Kathleen Hamilton and Jaguar Cars; Dan Harvey; Ambassador Namik Korhan; Stephen McKelvain and Interarms; James McMahon; Page Nordstrom and Chuy's Restaurant; Charles Plante; Doug Redenius; David A. Reinhardt; Moana Re Robertson; Gary Rosenfeld; Thomas J. Savvides and National Travel Service, Inc.; Dan Workman; and my wonderful wife, Randi

IN THE U.K.:

Carolyn Caughey; Peter Janson-Smith; Lucy Oliver; Fergus Pollock (for the Jaguar design); Corinne B. Turner; Elaine Wiltshire; and the heirs of the late Ian Lancaster Fleming

IN GREECE:

Casino Au Mont Parnes; C. Dino Vondjidis and the Hotel Grande Bretagne

IN CYPRUS:

Zehra Basaran; Ambassador Kenneth Brill; Louis Travel Service; Valerie Mawdsley; Christina Mita; Ashley Spencer, Captain Sean Tully and the Sovereign Base Areas Administration.

A very special thanks to Panos Sambrakos, my guide in Greece, for the initial Inspiration.

THE MAN WITH THE RED TATTOO

The author and publishers would like to thank the following individuals and organisations for their help in the preparation of this book:

IN THE U.S. AND CANADA:

Paul Baack; Claude Berman; Tom Colgan; Contra Costa Mosquito and Vector Control District (Concord, CA): Steve Schutz; John Heaton; Imperial Hotel Tokyo (Chicago): Walter Hladko; Japan Airlines (Chicago): Yasuharu Noda, Toshinara Akita and Otoya Yurugi; Japan National Tourist Organisation (Chicago): Yasutake Tsukamoto, Masahiro Iwatsuki, Risa Sekiguchi and John Ventrella; Lawrence Keller; Prince Hotels Japan (Chicago): Yasuko Machida-Chang; Doug Redenius; David Reinhardt; My wife Randi and my son Max

IN JAPAN:

The Ainu Museum (Shiraoi): Ikuo Yamamaru, Miyuki Muraki and Shigeru Funahashi; Tadao Ando; Aomori JR Rail Station: Meiji Araya, Yoshio Kuroda and Yoshiki Tamura; Aomori Prefectural Government: Takashi Okawara, Yutaka Ogasawara, Yoshiko Abo and Keri-anne Panos; Bear Park (Noboribetsu): Genzo Kawakami and Naoko Maeda; Christopher Belton; Benesse House and Benesse Corporation: Soichiro Fukutake, Reiko Fukutake, Yuji Akimoto, Ryoji Kasahara, Kayo Tokuda and Yukiko Tanaka; Dai-ichi Takimotokan (Noboribetsu): Tomoko Okumura; Don Juan Men's Club (Tokyo): Keita Ono and "Rei"; Imperial Hotel Tokyo: Mari Miyazaki, Hideya Sadayasu and Yohkoh Sato; Japan National Tourist Organisation (Tokyo): Hideaki Mukaiyama, Mariko Tatsumi, Masaki Hirata, Yoshitaka Hara and Isao Yoshiike; Kabuki-za Theater: Munehiro Matsumoto and Simon Yoshizumi; Yoshiko Kitanishi and family; Mie Hama; Glen A. Hill; Hokkaido Prefectural Government: Masaaki Hirano, Rie Toyama and Seiji Miura; Reiko Ishizaki; Yoshihisa Nakayama; Randy Rice; Sapporo Prince Hotel: Taniguchi Akihiko and Murakami Yoshiki; Seikan Tunnel Museum and Seikan Tunnel: Hiromitsu Hamaya, Kazuhiro Horiba, Masahiro Ichijo, Mitsugu Tamai and

Hiroshi Inayama; Takanawa Prince Hotel/Sakura Tower (Tokyo): Yusuke Watanabe, Kajiwara Satoshi and Hiroshi Moriyama; Tokyo Convention and Visitors Bureau: Naotaka Odake, Yasuyuki Yabuki, Yuka Takahashi and Koichi Hagiwara; Yayoi Torikai; Akiko Wakabayasni

IN THE U.K.:
Carolyn Caughey; Hillingdon and Uxbridge Coroner's Office: Bob Greenwell; Ian Fleming (Glidrose) Publications Ltd; and, as always, the Heirs of Ian Lancaster Fleming

A special thank-you to the Japan National Tourist Organisation for their generous contributions to the making of this book, and to James McMahon for being my "Richard Hughes" while in Japan.